Fiddle Game

Books by Richard Thompson

Fiddle Game
Frag Box

Fiddle Game

Richard A. Thompson

Poisoned Pen Press

Library of Congress Catalog Card Number: 2007935666

ISBN: 978-1-59058-680-8 Trade Paperback

Poisoned Pen Press
6962 E. First Ave., Ste. 103
Scottsdale, AZ 85251
www.poisonedpenpress.com
info@poisonedpenpress.com

Printed in the United States of America

For Bud George, who introduced me to the mystery

Acknowledgments

In real life as much as in fiction, the hero's journey is never accomplished without a host of seen and unseen helping hands. In my own journey from construction engineer to author, I have been helped enormously by the following fine people:

Ginny Hansen, who gave me the first encouragement;
Blaine Cross, who gave me the first validation;
Ellen Hart, who gave me the tool kit;
The members, past and present, of the brave little writers' group known as Murder Ink, who gave invaluable feedback and priceless ongoing fanfare—Peter Farley, Phil Finklestein, Margaret Milne, Elizabeth Ravden, Virginia Scheff, and Ingrid Trausch;
My wonderful Canadian friends, Lyn Hamilton and Mary Jane Maffini, who first made me feel welcome in the broader community of professional authors;
My untiring fellow traveler, Margaret Yang,
the Bard of Ann Arbor;
And finally, Roger Baldwin, wherever he may be, who gave me a love of the lore of stringed musical instruments that has lasted over 45 years.

Thanks doesn't begin to cover it.

Author's Note

Residents of the city of Saint Paul will be quick to point out that I have taken enormous liberties with its geography. Some of the sites and images I have used are real, or were in 1996, but are not quite in their proper location or time frame. Others, such as Lefty's Poolhall and the Happy Dragon, are purely from the back side of my mind and have never existed in the real world at all. Still others are composites of the real and the fanciful. For this, I make no apology. The story has its needs and so do I. The flavor and aura of Saint Paul, I believe, are occasionally correct, but for all other purposes, it would be best to regard the Saint Paul of this story as completely fictitious.

With the characters and events of the story, there is no such ambiguity. They are entirely the products of my imagination, and any resemblance to anyone or anything in the real world is purely coincidental.

Chapter One

Waiting for the Dough

On the day of the first killing, it rained. Not an easy rain, but the kind of endless, pounding deluge that makes people wonder if they really did throw out that old boat catalog, and if not, whether it listed any arks. Personally, I gave up looking for arks a long time ago, the wooden ones or any other kind. I like the rain. Agnes, my secretary, says that's just perversity, liking anything that puts other people in a bad mood, but she isn't always right. Not always. On that particular wet day in 1996, nobody was right.

I looked out the streaked glass of my single storefront window, past the neon sign that says "24-Hour Service" backwards, and assessed the prospects of a flash flood.

You can tell a lot about a city by what's in its old, core downtown. Across the street from me is an old time resident hotel, long ago gone to seed. There used to be a nightclub on the ground floor under it, but that's been boarded up and closed for longer than anybody remembers. Farther down is a place called Pawn USA, a hole-in-the wall deli, and a pornographic book store. They've all been around long enough to be landmarks. The pawn shop, run by a sometime friend of mine named Nickel Pete Carchetti, just expanded and got its trendy new name, which I suspect came from the title of a textbook on modern economics. Farther down the street lie a Dunn Brothers coffee shop, an upscale tattoo parlor, and a manicure emporium called Big City Nails. Kitty-corner across from me stands the newly renovated Courthouse, taking up a whole square block, and behind it, connected to it by tunnel, is the County Jail. The long fingernails, tribal markings, and chi-chi coffee are current hot-ticket items, but I don't expect them to last. The trendy shops come and go. Here in St. Paul, Minnesota, the capitol of Midwest niceness, the only really solid growth industries we have are government and crime.

Strangely enough, the cops don't have a building in downtown proper, merely one on the fringe of it, though they definitely have a street presence. Maybe that's the way it should be, since they are really just the gatekeepers to the criminal justice system. And if that's the case, then I'm the man in the tollbooth. My name is Herman Jackson, and I'm a bail bondsman.

Behind me, Agnes sat at her PC clattering keys sporadically. I could tell by the rhythm that it wasn't work-related, but since she is my chief office organizer, accountant, PR expert, and generally indispensable confidant, as well as my secretary, she's entitled to spend her time as she sees fit. The computer was making funny noises, like tinny fanfare or electronic oohs and aahs, and occasionally she would make an "ooh" of her own.

"Video games, pornography, or the stock market?" I asked, without turning around.

"Stocks. I don't do games." She said nothing about porn, I noticed. "You should look at this, Herman. Amtech-dot-com is down to sixteen and a half today. It's a fluke, has to be."

"The market is reacting to news of an outbreak of moldy sowbellies in Katmandu." Which made exactly as much sense as most of what I hear out of market analysts.

"Seriously, at that price, you could make a killing. Double your money in a couple months, tops. You could afford to take a little flier like that now and then, you know. On your latest profit-and-loss sheet, you showed…"

"I don't gamble, Aggie."

"You gamble on pool."

"That's not gambling, that's social intercourse. I never bet more than a hundred on a game, and I never try a double-back off the side rail if I've had more than two drinks." And if that isn't prudence and self-discipline, I don't know the stuff. And I do. I paid full price for it, and now it's my biggest asset.

"The market's not really gambling, either," she said. "It's more like reversible bidding at a garage sale. After all the hype blows away, there's always a real piece of merchandise of some kind there."

"Except when there isn't. How much did you lose on Enron? Isn't that why you're still driving to work in your beat-up Toyota instead of your new Lexus?"

"That's not fair, Herman. People a lot smarter than me got burned in that scam."

"And people smarter yet didn't play."

"Like you? Like that time you got arrested for somebody else's homicide and had to liquidate your business in Detroit and run off to the boonies?"

It was her ultimate weapon in any argument, and I had no defense for it. The incident she referred to was back in my high-roller days, when my ship really had come in, but I was dumb enough to torpedo it at the dock. Sometimes I let myself think those days might come back, but I don't really believe it. There aren't any big scores in the bonding business. Not usually, anyway. What you see up front is what you get, and sometimes you don't even get that. And in any case, the great god Odz doesn't forgive that kind of stupidity. St. Paul is my Elba, and if a delegation of leaderless Frenchmen came one day to rescue me from it, I would run from them in terror.

"Low blow, Aggie. I wasn't as smart then, in a lot of ways, and I admit it."

"You want a cookie for 'fessing up like a good boy?"

"You want to answer that ringing thing? It might be the phone."

She picked up the phone, and the pulse of the day's real business began.

Most of my business comes to me by phone, or at least the first contact does. I get a call from a defense lawyer or a PD, with the daily list of souls in bondage who want to buy a ticket to freedom. The logistics of paper and money flow are worked out, and the wheels begin to turn. I'm not allowed to start the process by approaching them, in the courtroom or the jail. It's sort of like ambulance chasing for a lawyer; not actually illegal, but sudden death to a professional reputation. Instead, I imitate Mohammed and wait for the accused mountains to come to me.

For most customers, it's a standard proposition: ten percent non-refundable fee and some kind of negotiable security for the rest. If you think about it, it's a crummy deal for the client. He's paying a hell of a wad of cash for a short burst of liberty that he's probably going to lose anyhow, and if he jumps bail, or even appears to, he loses the security, to boot. But of course, they're all going to be acquitted, so they don't worry about that. Meanwhile, they wait for the authorities or the gods or the odds to come around, and the prospect of a short time in jail is horrifying. The prospect of a much longer time in prison doesn't seem to bother them so much. People have no grasp of time. All they can deal with is never and forever. They don't handle cause and effect real well, either.

If the first call is from a lawyer I know, sometimes we work out some other terms. It's a quid pro quo thing. I give up a little quid, in the form of reduced or eliminated security for a trustworthy customer, and the lawyer gives me some quo in the form of telling me what his clients are really like, including which ones are going to run like rabbits the minute the cuffs are off. I could do away with this little part of the whole game, treat everybody the same, but I like the action. And that's not gambling, either.

Most of the time, I never see the actual client. But I do see a regular parade of siblings, parents, friends, lovers, business partners, and significant-whatevers, come to do the dirty job of bargaining for somebody else's freedom. They range from sensible to pathetic, and they bring me enough stories to make an endless soap opera script and put scar tissue on my soul.

While Agnes talked on the phone, doing what I always think of as making book, I watched the little wisp of a blonde cross the street in the rain and head for my door. She had a dark raincoat that hung like a crumpled trash bag, shoes that were too low for the wet streets, and one of those clear plastic rain-bonnet things on her head. She carried a violin case as if it were her first born child, pressed against her bosom, and she walked with a limp. *Nice touch*, I thought. In a business that's full of Oscar-quality performances, the limp was a perfect bit of understatement. I made a mental note not to ask her how she got it. Under the bonnet, she had high cheekbones, big doe eyes, and a prominent, sharpish nose and chin, bracketing a thin-lipped mouth. It was very dramatic and oddly attractive. Sondra Locke clutching her bundle of secret hurt and rage.

Even hunched up against the rain, she didn't have much in the way of shoulders, but she damn sure had a chip on at least one of them. I made a move to push the door open for her, but she snatched it angrily away from me, stomped in as well as one can stomp with a game leg, and shook off her bonnet at me. I was surprised. Usually, people get to know me a bit better before they're that hostile.

"Can we help you, Miss...?"

Aggie rolled her eyes. The orphan of the storm glared with hers.

"*Ms.* Amy Cox," she said, drenching the title in acid. I don't know how I could have been so politically incorrect. I must have still been thinking about *Ms.* Locke.

"What can we do for you, Ms. Cox?"

"I'm here to let you suck my blood. Probably all of it."

"I beg your pardon?"

"I think you have him confused with your lawyer, sweetheart," said Agnes. I've never figured out how she can get away with "sweetheart," when I can't even drop an occasional "Miss," but she can.

"I don't have anybody or anything confused." She tried out another glare. When nobody took the bait, she relaxed a little and did a half-hearted shrug. "But I suppose you didn't invent the system, did you? I take it nobody called? About my brother?"

I gave her my best David Carradine look. The grasshopper, waiting to be enlightened.

"I have to get a bail bond for my brother, Jimmy."

Agnes turned back to her PC and began scrolling through the list of the day's happy candidates. "Got him," she said, after a few seconds. "James W. Cox, right? Double GTA, five counts of MPD, handful of moving traffic violations. Bail is eighteen K."

GTA is grand theft auto, and MPD is malicious property damage, better known as vandalism. Two counts of GTA told me he had gotten away at least once, since it's unusual that a suspect has time to steal a second car while he's in the middle of a high speed chase with the first one. Even so, and even with the vandalism rolled in, the bail seemed high. Had he pissed off the judge? I pictured some dopey kid, hauled in for a crash-and-burn spree, maybe still lit up a bit, and stupid enough to mouth off to hizzoner. Not that I cared about any of that, except as a way of guessing how big a flight risk this guy was. So far, he sounded high-to-certain.

"Is your brother a young person?" I said. "A little on the wild side, maybe? Sometimes does a little booze, a little drugs, a joyride with some bad…"

"He's not like that."

Of course he's not. Your own brother never is. "What is he like, exactly?"

"He's a neo-Luddite."

That even stopped Agnes. I shifted to something easier.

"Is your brother underage?"

"I wish." She plopped down into my best neo-1955 motel chair, not bothering to take her coat off. "If he were still a kid, I could hope he might grow out of it. But he's pushing thirty-two now, and he's, well…"

"Crazy," said Agnes, ever eager to help out.

"Fanatical is more like it, I think. He's not really violent, at least not towards people. He thinks modern society is insane, and he imagines he's making some kind of big, heroic statement. It's his own term, neo-Luddite. The first Luddites were a bunch of people in the early eighteen hundreds who thought the Industrial Revolution was ruining the world, so they went around smashing power looms, burning mills, that sort of thing. Jimmy goes out and steals fifty-thousand-dollar SUVs and crashes them through the windows of Starbucks."

I looked out the window to see if perhaps little Jimmy had been to visit my neighborhood while my attention was turned elsewhere. Nope. The brown and green storefront seemed to have all its glass intact.

"What he imagines he's accomplishing is beyond me. Other than bankrupting the entire family. Mom and Dad disowned him years ago. I'm all he's got now. And the judge wasn't just being mean with the bond amount, Mr. Jackson."

Wow, a "Mister." Did that mean I was no longer the vile bloodsucker or the chauvinist pig? Was I about to get the inside dope? "I take it he's done this before?"

"Five times, in three other states."

Bingo.

"What you will need, Ms. Cox, is..."

"I know what I need. I can give you a check for the eighteen hundred. It wipes out the last of my savings, but if my stupid little brother doesn't care, why should you? Our lawyer explained that in a flight-risk case, I'll have to post something for security for the full eighteen thousand, as well."

If she was hoping I would disagree with her, she was about to be disappointed.

"All I have is my violin," she said.

I wanted to say, "Must be one hell of a fiddle," but it didn't seem to fit. My expression must have said it for me.

"It's an Amati," she said. "It's over four hundred years old."

Silly me, I thought the Amati was a car that Studebaker quit making in 1965. I didn't want one of them, and I didn't want a fancy antique fiddle, either.

"It's probably priceless," she said, "but it's been appraised at sixty thousand dollars. And that was almost twenty years ago."

On the other hand, old violins spill very little oil on the floor and never, ever rust out. Maybe I'd been a bit hasty.

She produced a much-folded paper from her purse and handed it to me. It appeared to be a professional appraisal, and as I scanned it, I began to assess the situation. And all the possible combinations and permutations. There was still the question of possession. "Is there a title document of some kind?"

"None. Never was. My grandfather brought it home after the Second World War. We never knew how he got it, and probably wouldn't want to. When I took up playing the violin seriously in high school, he put me in his will to receive it. After he died, it was something of a family joke at first, then the source of a lot of bad feelings. It turned out the whole rest of his estate wasn't worth that much. But I kept it. It was the first really fine instrument I ever got to play, and I swore I'd never give it up."

"Until now," I said.

"For your stupid little brother," said Agnes.

"Yes." It was a word, but it sounded more like a sob. She stood up, put the case on my desk, and opened it for my inspection.

I leaned over and took a look, not touching the instrument, in case it was ready to crumble into dust. It looked a lot like a violin. Not very shiny, I thought, but after four hundred years, what is? I tried to remember something about a secret varnish formula. Maybe that was Stradivarius.

"You understand that for something like this, with no title, I can't just attach a lien against it? I'll have to actually take possession, or have some mutually acceptable third person do it."

She nodded. "The problem is, I have to have something to play. It's what I do. I play for the Opera, and sometimes for the Chamber Orchestra, and I teach a little. I have to have an instrument."

I glanced over at Agnes, and she shot me a look that said "Don't you dare even think about it." But I was thinking about a different angle than waiving possession.

"What's a run-of-the-mill, professional-quality instrument cost?"

"Two, maybe three thousand. I already told you, the eighteen hundred is all…"

I held up my hand. "I'll have to get somebody else to take a look at the Amati anyway, to tell me if your certificate is really talking about this exact instrument. That's as good a place as any to do it." I gestured at the window and the street beyond, towards Nickel Pete's. "Maybe we can work out something with a loaner, while we're there."

She looked, and her face fell. "A pawn shop? My God, have I come to this?"

Trust me, sweetie, there's lots worse places to come to. I put on my trenchcoat, grabbed an umbrella, and we headed out into the rain.

‹›‹›‹›

The streets were empty except for a dark Ford LTD parked at the curb a half block down, so we crossed against the light and hurried down to the emporium of discarded dreams. Pete's shop was a mixture of traditional and new, with a modern, open sales floor up front, to display all the bulky stuff like exercise machines and huge TVs, and the old-style teller's cage in the back, guarding the cases of the smaller and more precious goods, as well as the firearms. Pete greeted us the way he greets everybody, sitting owl-faced at his cage with both hands under the counter. I knew that he had one hand poised to push an alarm button, while the other gripped a sawed-off shotgun. When he saw it was me, he folded his hands on top of the counter.

"Herman, old friend." His ancient troll's face morphed into what passed for a smile. "How's business? Mine's great. You ever get ready to expand, take on a new partner, I got the capital and the disposition for it. All's I need is the referrals."

"You've got the disposition of an undertaker."

"Then we'll get along fine, won't we?" He laughed, went into a coughing spasm, and finally treated himself to a pink antacid tablet from a bottle that he kept next to the cash register. It was a regular ritual of his. The ball was back in my court.

"This lady," I said, "needs a professional violin. You got anything of any quality?"

"One or two, I think. The good ones are in the back."

"Let's see them. And while she's checking them out, I want you to take a look at the one she's carrying, give me your opinion."

"Is this a professional consultation? Do I get a fee?"

"Yes, it is, and no, you don't."

"You always were a cheap sonofabitch, Herman." It wasn't true, but I let him get away with it, and he went into the back room and emerged with one violin whose case said it was a Yamaha and another, older-looking one that had no label. He passed them over to Amy Cox, and then proceeded to have a look at the maybe-Amati and the appraisal document. Then he took out his jeweler's loupe and had a real look, and an attitude of reverence spread across his face.

"I don't usually deal in goods of this quality, you know. I have no market, no contacts. The best I could do on it…"

"I'm not asking you to do anything on it, Pete. Just tell me if it's the Amati the paper talks about."

"Oh, it's the violin in the appraisal, all right. As to whether it's a real Amati, that's not such a simple question."

"Is it worth twenty-one grand?"

"The paper says sixty, plus inflation."

"It doesn't have to be worth sixty. The bond she needs is for eighteen, plus she needs enough to get one of those fiddles you just showed her. Is it worth that much or not?"

"Absolutely. You want I should advance it?"

"No. We'll do it a little different."

Amy Cox picked out the Yamaha. Pete said it was worth twenty-seven hundred, Amy said twelve, tops, and we all knew we were eventually going to settle on eighteen, if only for the beautiful irony of the number. Pete put the Amati away somewhere in the back and wrote a pawn ticket for eighteen hundred, made out to me. The deal was that I would issue the bail bond for the wayward, neo-Luddite Jimmy. If he showed up at his trial like a good little boy, and the bond got released, then his sister could come and get the ticket from me and redeem her own violin by bringing back the Yamaha and paying the interest. If little Jimmy reverted to type and took a hike, then I was out eighteen grand to the Sheriff's office, but the Amati was mine for the eighteen hundred, plus interest. In that case, Amy could keep her substitute, so she wouldn't have to go to her job at the Chamber Orchestra with a kazoo, but she lost first rights to her heirloom. It was the deal of the century. For somebody, anyway. She took it. We went back to my office to have Agnes draw up the formal papers.

The length of time it takes to mortgage all your past dreams to pay for tomorrow's reduced hopes is heartbreakingly short. Before Amy Cox had time to feel the cold lump in the pit of her stomach spread to the rest of her soul, or to look at her new violin and cry a bit, she was signed, notarized, wished the best of luck, and sent back out into the rain. I stood in the same spot where I had been when I first saw her, looking through the neon letters, watching her go. Once again, she had her shoulders hunched against the rain, but now she held her violin case under one arm, at her side.

"Cute, wasn't she? In a prickly sort of way."

I turned around to see Agnes looking disgustingly smug. "Was she?" I said.

"Oh, listen to him. The ice man. This is me you're talking to, okay? If she'd put her hooks into you any deeper, you'd need sutures."

Had she? "You are obviously mistaking my professional manner of…"

I was interrupted by the sound of a loud thump, out in the street, and I looked back that way in time to see Amy Cox flying through the air like a rag doll. She hit the wet pavement with a sickening second thud and lay motionless. Behind her, the dark LTD I had noticed earlier was braking to a stop.

"Call 9-1-1!" I screamed over my shoulder. I ran out the door and into the street, where the rain hit me in the face like a slap with a wet towel. The LTD was at the scene ahead of me, and the driver's door opened to disgorge a large man in a dark overcoat. He bent over the victim briefly, then ran back to the car and got in. He immediately floored it, spinning the tires on the wet pavement, running over the crumpled body, and fleeing into the mist. I couldn't believe I had seen him do that. I think I screamed again, something obscene, but I'm not sure.

I tried my damnedest, but with the rain spitting in my eyes, I couldn't read the departing license plate. I kept running until I got to where Amy Cox lay like a pile of broken sticks, one leg bent the wrong way, an arm thrown over her head, blood trailing from her mouth and ears, wide eyes staring at nothing. I bent down and felt for a pulse in her throat, but I was already pretty sure I wasn't going to find one. She looked as dead as anybody I've ever seen. I hunkered down beside her, not sure what to do.

Down the street, Sheriff's deputies and cops were running out of the courthouse, and I could already hear an ambulance siren. I was surprised to also hear myself moaning. I rocked back on my heels and let somebody pull me up and guide me off to one side. I looked around, dazed. Twenty yards down the road were the shoes that were too low for the wet streets. The speeding car had knocked her right out of them. Closer to me was her small purse, from which she had produced the certificate of appraisal. Here and there were a few scattered papers and what may have been some gouts of blood. I looked all around, scanning the area in progressively widening sweeps, zoning it off, making sure I missed nothing. That seemed important, for some reason.

There was nothing, anywhere, remotely resembling a violin case.

Chapter Two

Picking Up Sticks

Someplace far away, a boom box was playing an odd, slow version of white rap. Or maybe it was a call-in radio show.

"Anybody see the accident?"

"That guy might have. He was the first one on the scene, far as I could tell."

"The dopey-looking one, standing around with no raincoat? What's his name?"

"We didn't talk to him. He was bent over the body when we got there. Groaning, sort of."

"Is he okay?"

"I don't think he got hit or anything. He's just shook up. But if anybody saw the vehicle, it'd be him."

"Excuse me? Sir?"

There was a hand on my upper arm, I realized, not pressing hard, but insistent. I guessed the dopey-looking guy they were talking about must have gone someplace else.

"Sir?" Blue and brass, the square bulk of an armored vest showing, even through the uniform jacket. Lots of black leather pouches and snaps, like a bunch of fanny packs from the Harley store. A cop, not a Sheriff's deputy. Right. That was the way it should be. We weren't in front of his courthouse, but it was still his street, his case. Only, if it turned into a real case, they would take it away from him and give it to a couple of plainclothes detectives. That made me sad, for some reason. Maybe I just wanted to be sad.

"Are you all right, sir?"

The paramedics had zipped Amy Cox up in a body bag and were taking their time loading her into the meat wagon. I don't know how long I had been standing there or what I thought I was doing.

"Hey, fella, I asked if you're all right?"

"I'm not injured, officer."

"Did you see the accident?"

Was it an accident? What little I saw looked awfully damned cold-blooded and deliberate to me. "I didn't see the actual impact," I said. "I saw her flying through the air, and I saw her hit the pavement. Then I saw the bastards run over her a second time. They stole her violin."

"They?"

I thought for a minute and blinked. "I only saw one, come to think about it. But it was a big car, with blackout glass all around. There could have been a small mob in there."

A notebook came out of his upper pocket, and he hunched over, trying to keep the rain off it. When he tipped his head down to write, a stream came off the brim of his hat, onto the pages.

"They make waterproof notebooks, you know, officer. Nickel Pete, down the street there, showed me one once. They make them for surveyors. He gets all kinds of strange merchandise, but never the same kind twice. It was his violin, too, come to think of it. He traded it for…"

"I'll need your name, sir."

It was as polite a way as anybody had ever told me that I was babbling, and I shifted down a gear or two, and told him my name and what little I knew. I could see his disappointment grow at every key point, like no description of the driver, no license number, and inexact year on the car.

"Did you know the victim, Mr. Jackson?"

"Just met her. She was a customer, came to me to get a bond for her brother." I told him the gist of the situation, including the name of the yuppie-hating brother. The pencil scribbled on the wet pages, and the cop made a face when it didn't work right.

"Maybe you should try circling the drops first, so you don't run into them and get the lead wet," I said. He didn't.

"You say she had a violin?"

I nodded. "Carrying it under her right arm. The guy who got out of the car must have taken it." I noticed that the pencil had stopped moving altogether. Fair enough. Why struggle with wet paper, trying to write a statement that didn't make any sense? And it didn't. If somebody's going to mug you for a lousy violin, they don't hit you with two tons of metal first. Even if they don't give a damn about you, they could smash the instrument that way. And if the accident really is just an accident, then they don't get out and steal the violin, just to have a nice souvenir of the event. And finally, if it was purely a case of opportunistic theft, why hadn't they also taken her purse, which was right out there in front of God and everybody? I wouldn't write it down, either.

"Why would this guy stop to steal her violin?" said the cop.

My intellectual peer, obviously. Went right to the key question without even being led. A perceptive fellow, this beat-pounder.

"Because he thought it was valuable. Very valuable. It wasn't, really, because it wasn't the right one, but somebody thought it was supposed to be." Somebody who wasn't paying attention when Amy Cox and I went in and out of Nickel Pete's, or who couldn't see well enough in the rain, or was confused because there were two of us, or was busy taking a leak in a plastic bottle or using his fantastic cell phone technology to argue with his mother or his girlfriend. But by the time Ms. Cox left my office the second time, that somebody was back on the job, with a vengeance. But what was the job, exactly? Killing her?

"That still doesn't make any sense," said the cop.

I hate it when people steal my own arguments. But he was right, it didn't, and I had pushed my thinking as far as I could. I suddenly became aware of being very wet. There was a hissing sound in the back of my head that I gradually realized was a passing car, tires spraying road water. In the front of my head, my mouth was sticky-dry.

"Maybe you should get out of the rain, Mr. Jackson, sit down and collect your thoughts a bit."

Too damn right I should. But not with him. If I needed a ventriloquist's dummy, I'd go see what Pete had on hand. I pulled a soggy card from my pocket and gave it to the cop. "You can get me there most of the time if you have any more questions," I said. I pointed at my office. He looked at the card and nodded, and that was the end of the interview.

<> <> <>

I have a room in the back of the office with a cot and a kitchenette and a closet with some spare clothes, for times when I'm sweating a round-the-clock skip-recovery case. I went straight there, without talking to Agnes on my way through the front.

I took off my tie and looked at it briefly, holding it out at arm's length. It used to be maroon, I think. I thanked it for long, if undistinguished, service, and threw it in the trash. I hung my suit coat on a hanger to dry, dumped my wet shirt on the floor, and toweled off my hair. Buttoning up a fresh shirt, I went back out into the reception room and poured myself the last of the toxic waste from the Mr. Coffee in the corner. I think it was a blend called Refried Dreams. After steeping half the day, it tasted the way corroded batteries look, but I barely noticed.

"Is the bond ready yet for Jimmy Cox?"

"All set," said Agnes. "You want me to take it over? You look like you could use a little down time."

I shook my head. "I'd rather be moving around a bit, while I'm trying to sort things out. Besides, delivering the bond is the closest thing to a dying request that I've ever had laid on me. Seems like I ought to do it myself."

"I saw the body bag. Did she suffer much?"

That was a very nice way of asking me if I had botched up giving first aid. Suddenly everybody was being nice to me. Did they think that blunt trauma was contagious and I might have caught some? I shook my head again. "Bastards smashed her all to hell, squashed her like a nasty bug. Even a doctor couldn't have done anything for her."

"I wasn't accusing you of anything."

"You didn't have to. I'll probably do enough accusing for both of us. Just give me the bond."

I put the document in a zippered vinyl pouch with several others, put on my trenchcoat, grabbed the umbrella, and headed for the door.

"Maybe you ought to comb your hair."

"What for? The cops think I'm dopey-looking, anyway, and Amy Cox and her brother damn sure won't care."

Most arrests in the metro area are made by city cops, but the City, as such, has no courts. So the cases are charged and tried in the Ramsey County court system, and bail bonds are delivered to the County Sheriff's office. It's in one corner of the County Jail, which is a multi-story affair hung on the face of the stone river bluff. You can enter via a little pill box at street level or through a tunnel from the basement of the courthouse. I usually do pill box. I'm a regular customer there, and a tall, cute brunette deputy named Janice Whitney smiled at me when I came in. She used to be even cuter, before body armor became part of the regular uniform. Now she has no waist, and not much in the way of a bosom, either. Hazards of war, I guess. She logs in the bonds the same, either way, but it's not as much fun as it used to be. Nothing ever is.

"Hey, it's the ticket master," she said. "Neither rain nor sleet, and all that other bullshit."

"Hey, yourself, Jan. How's business?"

"Business is good. Maybe we should quit advertising."

"Maybe you should. Take that budget and use it for an office golf outing or something."

If I'd suggested a prayer meeting, I'd have gotten the same look. "I've been known to do a little swinging with my fellow workers," she said, "but not with any stupid golf club. What have you got for me?"

I opened the vinyl case, pulled out the stack of bonds, and dropped them on the counter. She took each one in turn, shoved it in a machine that stamped the date and time, then manually logged it into a green, hardcover day book. The Cox bond was the last one in the stack.

"You might be sticking your neck out a bit on this one," she said. "He only got arraigned this morning, and already I've heard about him. If he was any nuttier, they'd chop him up and make Snickers bars."

"Just a high-spirited kid, Jan. Misunderstood. Doesn't like Luds. Or maybe he does like them, I forget which way it works."

"Like Timothy McVeigh didn't like concrete?"

"McVeigh was a flat-earther, as I recall. Didn't like anything vertical. But he did like really big bangs. The two guys are nothing alike."

"You're right about that. McVeigh knew enough to keep his mouth shut in court. Not Cox."

"Well, it doesn't matter now, anyway. The bond is paid for, and I can't refund it, so you might as well go ahead and log it in."

"Your funeral. I'm just saying, watch this one. You want me to have him mustered out through here, so you can meet him, maybe give him a little pep talk?"

Her eyes flashed wickedly. What she really meant was that she would give me a chance to slip a tracer bug into the guy's pocket. It was something she never officially knew about and I never officially did. Afterwards, I sometimes took her out to a fancy candlelight dinner, just to keep her feeling unofficially rewarded. It pays to have friends in the working end of the power structure. Better than in high places, any day.

"Thanks anyway, Jan, but they've probably already pulled him out of the lockup. His sister just got run over by a Ford tank, and they'll be looking for somebody to ID the body."

"Are you serious?"

"Happened right out there, less than an hour ago." I pointed at the now-deserted street.

"Oh, wow, that one? I was outside having a smoke, and I saw the paramedics come. That was the Monkey-boy's sister, huh? What a funny world. Makes you think, doesn't it?"

"It made Amy Cox stop thinking."

It didn't have that effect on me. The Sheriff's office was not the place for heavy meditation, though, and neither was my own place. I mumbled some kind of farewell to Deputy Janice and wandered back out into the rain. Five blocks and three corners later, I found myself at the entrance to Lefty's Billiard Parlor.

Lefty's is a real, old-fashioned pool hall, where you buy time on the tables from a teller, rather than constantly stuffing coins in a slot. That means you can still play straight pool, and you can abide by the classical rules for scratch shots, whatever game you play. The place is also one long flight of rickety, dark stairs up from street level, a tradition in pool halls that I've never understood. A regulation table weighs over a ton, so why put it on the second story, where you have to reinforce the floor and hoist the table in through a skylight, with a crane? Maybe it makes it harder to break the lease, is all I can think. And it damn sure discourages anybody from stealing a table.

Anyhow, Lefty's is a walkup joint, in strict violation of the federal handicap access laws, and it's as good a place as I know to go practice on a quiet corner table and let the click of the balls knit your unraveled thoughts back together. Unlike Ames' in *The Hustler*, it also has a bar and a decent grill, though Lefty will watch you like a hawk and charge you if you spill grease or ketchup on his precious green felt. Beer he doesn't seem to mind. There's also a sign by the upper entry that says, "This is a Smoke-Free Establishment. Any Smoke You Find Here is Absolutely Free." Lefty isn't real big on regulations, other than his own.

It was late afternoon by the time I walked in, and some guy I didn't know was tending bar and keeping time on the tables, all by himself. I ordered a shot of vodka and a Guinness. I downed the shot and took just a sip of the stout, to give it a bit of after-flavor. Dark brews, I have always thought, are for sipping and contemplation. If your pint doesn't get up to room temperature before you finish it, you're drinking it too fast. White liquor, by contrast, is for impact, to start the negotiating process with the back of your mind. It has no other qualities, and there's no point in savoring it.

I got a rack of balls for an empty table by the windows and another shot to take with me. I told the bartender to take his time getting me a California burger with extra onions and some lattice fries. Then I laid out the balls on the table, planted my drinks on the window sill, and picked out a house cue from a rack on the wall. It was a bit heavier than I usually like, but it was only warped in one direction and looked like somebody had actually chalked the tip now and then.

Two tables over, Wide Track Wilkie was shooting a game of nine ball with some Asian kid, while the kid's girlfriend watched. He looked like he was doing some serious hustling and didn't need any interference, which was fine with me. Wilkie is a three-hundred-plus pound movable barrier of African and Puerto Rican descent, with more in the mix. I was just as glad he was in St. Paul, because I occasionally like to hire him as a bounty hunter. Besides that and hustling pool, I have no idea what he does for a living.

In another part of the room, some teenagers were doing a bad imitation of playing snooker, and clowning around about their own ineptitude. Otherwise, the place was empty. There was no jukebox or piped-in Muzak, just the click of the balls and the whir of overhead fans and whatever the players had to say. In that respect, Lefty's is just like Ames'. You want to be surrounded by sound, go to a rave.

I put the belly of the warped cue stick downward and stroked a nice, clean break. Not a money break. I almost never sink anything on the break, and I've given up trying. That's why I like the longer games—rotation or straight pool—where there's time for a few wild cards to emerge and enough pauses to work the opposition's head a little. I studied the spread after the break for a while and decided I was shooting eight ball. Ten shots later, my burger came, in a cute little basket that looked like it was made for holding a fancy wine bottle. The no-name bartender put it down on the window sill, next to my drinks, along with another basket that had napkins, salt and pepper in heavy glass shakers, and ketchup in a wide-mouthed jar instead of one of those plastic squeeze bottles. Lefty's is a classy place.

I ate about half of the burger, punctuating the last chew of each mouthful with a little bit of alcohol and foam. It was good stuff, and my body was grateful for it, but my eyes kept wandering back to the table. I didn't consciously decide to put the food down, but pretty soon I was back to staring down the cue stick, sizing up a long, single-cushion shot on the ten ball. Going into my spatial meditation mode.

Shots with a lot of open green are a kind of Zen thing for me. At first, I can't see the angle and can't compute my way to it, either. Might as well shoot with my eyes closed. But if I wait, take my time, and sort of *identify* with the space of the setup, suddenly the line will reveal itself to me and I absolutely can't miss. When I drop the ball, it will look like a lucky fluke, but luck has nothing to do with it. I did a few practice strokes and waited for the line to appear. Did luck have anything to do with Amy Cox? A lot of long green on that table. Much less on Jimmy Cox's bond. Eighteen K is little people's dreams, not the stuff of conspiracy or murder. Sixty gets a bit more interesting, but whoever killed Amy wouldn't actually get their hands on even the eighteen, much less the big money. *Did I use enough chalk? You have to put it on before you go out in the rain. Otherwise it won't stick, and you'll wind up like…*Jesus, where did that come from? And why couldn't I see the line yet?

The felt turned a slightly darker shade of green, and I looked up to see two guys blocking the light from the window. Closest to me, looking as if he expected something, was a big, shapeless, forty-something guy with an oversized head and puffy, babylike features. The kind of guy that will still look like Baby Huey when he's eighty. Scowl marks by the mouth and eyes told me that he worked a bit too hard at overcoming that image. The other guy was smaller in every dimension, with dark, stringy hair and a gaunt face that looked like a poster for European famine relief. As if he had read my mind, he made a show of eating the rest of my burger.

Both guys had brimmed hats pulled low and semi-respect-able topcoats that were bulky enough to hide all kinds of hardware. And they were both working very hard at looking mean and serious. Was I about to be leaned on? What the hell for? I looked over to where Wide Track was still shooting with the Asian kids. If he had picked up on the situation, he made no sign, but then, he wouldn't. Hollow Cheeks spoke first, while Babyface continued to stare me down.

"Good burger. Get me another one, will you?"

"You think so?" I said. "I put it down after I thought I saw something moving in the onions, but maybe that was just my imagination."

"Bullshit." Obviously, not the captain of his high school debating team. I continued to bend over and sight down the pool cue, only now I was visually measuring its length against the distance between me and the big guy.

"You Herman Jackson?" Babyface, this time.

"Who's asking, exactly?" Too far. I needed to get about two feet closer, for a really effective swing.

"Detective Evans, Homicide. My partner over there, with the tape worm, is Stroud. We gotta show you our badges?"

"If we're talking business here, that would be the professional way to proceed, wouldn't it?" I stood partway up, but I didn't let go of the cue stick.

Evans made a show of looking put out, but he pulled a gold badge out of an inner pocket and gave me all of a three-second look at it. His partner gave me an even shorter look at his. I tried to think of a recent homicide case that I had carried a bond on, but I was coming up empty. "Did one of my customers show up missing?"

"Not as far as I know. We're here about the woman who got killed in front of your office today."

I finally let go of the cue and stood up. "Amy Cox," I said. "You've decided to call it a murder?"

"Yeah, we call it murder. But we don't call her Amy Cox. And we're very interested to know why you do."

"How about because that's who she is? Get a clue here, detectives. Haven't you talked to her brother yet?"

"We talked to a James Cox, recently released on a bond provided by you."

"And?"

"He says he doesn't have a sister."

"What?" Now it was my turn to say "bullshit," but I didn't want to sound just as lame as Detective Stroud. "Did you make him go look at the body anyway?"

"You're not too bright, are you, Jackson?" Stroud was shifting away from the window, towards me. I think he was trying to be menacing, but he didn't have the stature or the presence for it. "If he doesn't have a sister, he can't exactly tell us if that's her, can he?"

"We made him look," said Evans, ignoring his partner.

"And?"

"Says he never saw her before."

"Then why would she hock her heirloom violin to bail him out?"

"Well, we don't really know that she did, do we?"

"No," said Stroud, now moving around so he and his partner flanked me at the table. "Alls we know is what Jackson here told the officer at the scene."

"Officer Krupke?" I said. That wasn't the officer's name, of course, but it seemed like a clever thing to say.

"Yeah, Krupke," said Stroud. "Good cop, but he don't always know to ask the right questions."

Oops. If that didn't clinch it for me, it should have.

"So we're thinking," said Evans, "that you maybe ought to just show us the contract you had the woman sign."

"And maybe the violin you say she gave you for security, too," said Stroud.

"And maybe you'd like to show me a warrant," I said.

"Maybe we could get one."

"Maybe you couldn't, too. What do you think you have probable cause to suspect, anyway, issuing a bond to the wrong client?" I bent back down and took the shot on the ten ball, missing it badly. *Wait for the Zen moment, Jackson?* But the new lie of the balls gave me an excuse to move out from between my new friends and take a stance by the opposite rail. As I moved around the table, I looked over at the ongoing nine ball game. Wide Track Wilkie was nowhere to be seen. I began to get a very bad feeling in my gut that had nothing to do with Lefty's onions.

"Murder," said Evans.

"We agree about that," I said, bending down to sight the new shot, again measuring the geometry of space and bodies. "So why aren't you guys out checking body shops and outstanding traffic warrants?"

"Because the car didn't kill her," said Stroud.

"Excuse me all to hell," I said, mentally adding *you dumb shits.* "I was there, remember? I saw them put her in a body bag."

"Oh, she was dead, all right. Wasn't she, Detective Stroud?"

"Dead, Detective Evans. Broken neck. But it wasn't broken by any car. According to the M.E., somebody did it to her with his hands, real up-close and personal, like."

"We think maybe it was you," said Evans. "So, like we were saying, we think maybe you better show us that contract."

"And that violin," said Stroud.

The room was starting to feel very small. "I think you're both so full of shit your eyeballs are brown," I said. "I don't believe the M.E. has even looked at her yet. I want to see the medical report."

"Oh, we'll do better than that," said Evans. "We'll take you down to the Morgue, and you can see for yourself. We'll go there on our way to the precinct, to talk it all out."

"After he gives…" began Stroud.

"Shows," corrected Evans.

"…yeah, shows us the violin."

They were single-minded goons, I had to give them that. "Am I under arrest?" I said.

"You want to be?"

I thought about it for a minute. Forcing them into one more formality might slow them down a bit, but I didn't need the extra handicap of wearing cuffs. And I now had no doubt that I was going to have to go with them, whether I insisted on formalities or not. "No," I said, "but I want to call my lawyer."

"Be our guest."

They would say that, wouldn't they? Especially since we all knew we weren't going anywhere near any cop station. I went over to the bar and asked non-Lefty for a phone. He produced one from somewhere in or near the sink and plonked it down on the polished top with his dishwater-wrinkled hand, saying, "No long-distance."

"The least of my needs," I said.

I figured they'd notice and cut me off if I dialed 9-1-1, so I called my own office instead, and mentally cursed when I got my voice mail. After the piercing little beep, I said, "Listen, Agnes, get ahold of the cops as fast as you can. I'm about to be abducted from Lefty's Poolhall by a couple of thugs posing as police detectives." I gave her a quick description of my companions, including the names they were using. "After the cops, call Nickel Pete and tell him not to give the Amati to anybody, including me, unless I'm alone. Then call every damn bounty hunter we ever use and tell them…"

"Done yet?" Evans loomed over me like a glacier about to calve.

"Not quite."

"I think you are." He pushed the button on the receiver cradle, and the phone went dead. I hung up and shrugged into my trenchcoat, which he had thoughtfully brought from the back of the hall, and we proceeded to the door. There wasn't a lot else I could do. I began to wonder if I had any of my electronic tracer gizmos in my pocket. They wouldn't help my present situation much, but I thought it might be nice if somebody found my corpse.

Chapter Three

The Zen Moment

The stairway to Lefty's is too narrow for three people to go abreast, so the skinny guy went ahead of us while Babyface Evans stayed tight to me, on my left and slightly behind. He didn't poke a gun in my ribs, but I figured he had one handy, if not already out. Stroud didn't use the handrail, and I thought about how easy it would be to reach my foot out, tap the back of one of his knees, and send him crashing down the rest of the flight. Then I would only have the big guy to take out.

Tempting. A lot of people assume that since bonding is a non-violent, even sedentary profession, all of us are flabby little wimps who haven't been in a fight since the age of seven and would faint dead away at the sight of a gun. In a lot of cases, it's true. "Nothing but Milquetoast, on the gravy train," is the saying.

I grew up in a neighborhood where people thought *The Godfather* was a sitcom. Becoming a bondsman was a way of graduating, not running away, from my own violent past. If these two thugs didn't know that, it could give me a significant edge. But only once. Not yet, I decided, since I couldn't see what Evans was doing until I was already committed to a move. But soon. It had to be soon, or it wouldn't work at all.

We clumped down the sloped shaft and out onto the street, where both the daylight and the rain were running out of juice. Somewhere in the distance, some noisy pigeons were announcing the end of the deluge. I don't know if any of them had an olive branch in his beak. Parked at the curb was a massive Chevy of the kind the cops use a lot, a Caprice or some such model, but without the extra bells and whistles. What it did have was a right rear tire that was flatter than my Aunt Hannah's bra. When Evans and I came out the door, Stroud was already looking at it, fists on his hips, as if he had never seen such a calamity before. Evans acted more like he had seen a lot of them and took them all as personal insults.

"Look at that, man. Is that all we need, or what? I mean, my God."

"I see it, Stroud. I'm sharp on that kind of shit, you know? Picked right up on it."

"So, what do we do?"

"We? What I do, is I babysit our friend here. What you do is, you change the tire. That's what *we* do."

"Why's it always me that's got to do the hard stuff?"

"Yeah, why does he?" I asked. Not that I gave a damn who changed the stupid tire. I just liked the way the partnership was coming unglued, and I thought I'd help it along a bit.

Evans ignored me and glared at Stroud. "Why?" he said. "Because you're a sneaky, lazy, stupid Rom who isn't worth the powder to blow you to hell or the match to touch it off with, that's why. Because you've screwed up this operation from day one, and you probably drove over something to blow that tire, too. And because if you don't, I'm going to kick your skinny little ass around the block a few times, just to keep my foot from going to sleep. Is that enough 'whys' for you?"

I wondered what a Rom was, but I figured it wasn't a good time to ask.

"Your time's gonna come," said Stroud. But his voice had no conviction, and he was already putting the key in the trunk lock.

"And when it gets here, I'll kick your ass, then, too," said Evans.

He had taken a step away from me, to intimidate his partner better, and I was considering what to do about that when Stroud popped open the trunk on the Chevy and got instantly sucked into it like a dust bunny into a vacuum cleaner pipe.

"What in hell…" said Evans.

I didn't care what in hell. I clipped him in the back of the knee, the way I had wanted to do to Stroud on the stairs, and as he was dropping to the pavement, I pretended his head was a soccer ball and the car was a goal net. I didn't know how hard I kicked him, and I didn't care. Three seconds later, I was around the corner and running like a scared rabbit.

I turned into an alley a couple of blocks away and chanced a look back. Nobody was following me. I slowed down to a trot and then a walk, looking for a place to hide among the trash bins, piles of junk, and service doors. I liked what I saw. Lots of back doors in that alley, and lots of fire escape ladders. Too many places for a pair of pursuers to check by themselves, unless they already had a glimpse of their quarry.

The smell of fresh rain mixed with that of old garbage, plus something else that took me a minute to identify, something sweet and vaguely oily. Glycol, I decided. Antifreeze.

Parked tight to a brick wall a half block away was an ancient ton-and-a-half truck with the back of the cab cut off and a square, homemade, windowless van body crudely grafted to the frame. The sides were badly warped plywood, covered with faded-out slogans and biblical quotations, done in an amateur sign-painting hand. Or maybe they weren't exactly biblical. One said, "He that bloweth not his own horn, Neither shall it be Blown." Another was something, mostly unreadable, about strumpets sounding at "the crank of dawn" and the "Horn of Babylon" having something to do with the "Car Lot of Jerusalem." Across the back was one that had been renewed several times, in several colors. It simply said, "Yah! Is My God!" The plywood looked grateful for any paint it could get. Near the front of the vehicle, green fluid trickled down onto the pavement and formed a small stream that meandered towards the center of the alley, producing the smell I had noticed. If the truck wasn't already a goner, it was definitely bleeding to death. Yah, with or without exclamation mark, was clearly not the god of radiators. I decided the truck looked like a good blind, and I followed the slimy green path.

Sitting on what was left of the rear bumper was a black man who could have been any age except young, reading a battered paperback that had no cover, and absent-mindedly stirring a pot of something on a Coleman camp stove. He looked up at my approach, huge, fierce eyes peering through a tangle of dark locks.

"Praise Yah!" he said, putting plenty of breath into it.

"Yeah?"

"You pronounce it wrong, pilgrim." His voice had a rich, melodic quality. It wasn't strident enough for a preacher, but it definitely got your attention.

"There's a lot of that going around."

"You making fun of me, asshole?"

"No."

"Lucky for you." He grinned, the whitest teeth I've ever seen accenting his dense beard. Then he chuckled. "But you're right, too. There is a lot of that going around. A lot of damn heathens in this valley of sorrows." He took the pot off the fire and stood up, offering his hand. "I'm the Prophet," he said. "No doubt, you've read my work."

"No doubt." His hand was frail, almost bird-like, but his grip was firm. "Listen," I said, "I need…"

"I knew you were coming here."

"Of course you did." I turned to watch the alley behind me. I was still clear, but I absolutely did not have time for this kind of crap.

"Yah! told me."

"Well he would, wouldn't he? Listen…"

"A man in a shitload of trouble, said Yah! A man in need of sanctuary. A man with a riddle."

"Right. I don't suppose Yah told you what to do about him?" I didn't bother to ask if Yah had told him all that before or after he saw me out of breath and looking over my shoulder.

"Yah! does not meddle in the affairs of Caesar."

"What the hell does that mean?"

"Twenty bucks to hide in the truck for an hour."

"Seems like sanctuary is a pretty good business."

"It has a trap door in the floor and spy holes in all four sides."

"Deal."

While he unhooked the padlock on the flimsy door, I reached in my wallet and pulled out two twenties. "If trouble is still following me," I said, "it's going to be here a lot sooner than an hour. When that happens, I could use a bit of diverting bullshit, okay?"

"I am a prophet and a holy man, brother." He straightened up and solemnly laid a palm against his breast. "Bullshit, I got." He took the twenties and ushered me inside.

I stepped into a cluttered space lit by a tiny plastic skylight that doubled as a vent. When the Prophet closed the door again, I could see that each wall had not one, but two spy holes, one with a wide-angle lens, like a hotel or apartment door, and one that was just a plain hole. There was a four-legged stool on the floor, and I put it by the back door, planted myself on it, and looked out. The Prophet went back to reading his book and cooking his potion. When I didn't see any other action for ten minutes or so, I looked around the interior a bit. The trap door was easy enough to spot, if you were looking for it. It was off to one side, presumably to miss the drive shaft. That's if the truck still had a drive shaft. It looked like it hadn't moved for several decades and if it did, about half a ton of junk would immediately wind up on the floor, along with the flimsy roof. It smelled like dust and brake fluid and old, damp paper. Somehow, that seemed right for an ersatz holy man's cave.

I looked again at the spy holes. The plain ones were about an inch in diameter and just down and to the right of those with the fish-eye lenses. Just the right size and location for a gun muzzle, I thought. Did my man the Prophet go in for holy wars? I was about to turn away from the hole and have a closer look at the cabinets on the walls, when I saw something move outside.

The big Chevy nosed into the alley, bouncing heavily on its springs, stalking, sniffing. It straightened out and cruised straight at us, taking its time.

"Tally ho," I said through the hole.

"Trust in Yah!" said the Prophet. "And keep your ass down."

When the car got within twenty feet of my hidey hole, it stopped. The driver's door opened and a shape emerged. And emerged some more. A bigger shape than the phony cop, by at least a hundred pounds. Apparently, Wide Track Wilkie hadn't abandoned me, after all.

"Praise Yah!" said the prophet.

"What's he done for me lately?" Wilkie wasn't big on chit chat, as a rule.

"He has led you to me."

"Yeah? Well, you better hope he doesn't tell me to stay. I'm looking for a guy might have run by here fifteen minutes ago."

"Might have. You can build a universe on 'might have,' pilgrim. Perhaps you've read my theological work on islands of alternate consciousness in the bicameral…"

"Look into my eyes, asshole." He came close enough for the man to do exactly that. "Do I look like a philosopher, to you? Do I look patient?"

"Up," said the Prophet, backing against the truck.

"Up what?"

"A hunted man always goes up. It's a primal instinct." He stretched out a bony arm to point at the fire escapes on the other side of the alley, and Wilkie backed off a half a step.

"Which one?" said Wilkie.

"On the back of the locksmith shop."

"That's more like it." He turned on his heel and strode away, his tent-like coat billowing out behind him like the wake of a garbage scow.

I decided the show was over, so I opened the door and stepped out. "Nice to see you, Wide," I said.

"Hey, Herman." He spun around and smiled. "I thought you looked like you didn't like your blind date much, up there in Lefty's, so I stowed away in the limo. Was that okay?"

"Much more than okay."

"Glad you think so, because that was a really horseshit little space. I don't know why they can't make a vehicle with a bigger trunk."

"Like a Euclid truck?"

"Just like that." He came back over to the truck and gave me a bear hug that fractured a rib or two. "You all right, man?"

"I was, until you did that. Where's my two new friends?"

"The big guy is having a little nap in the trunk. I took his gun and the other stuff out of his pockets, just so he wouldn't be too uncomfortable."

"Very considerate. What about his partner?"

"He took off, after I made him change the tire. Never saw a man so scared of a little bit of work."

"You think that was smart?"

"Making him change the tire?"

"Letting him go."

"Well, I thought if I bopped him one, he might just get chickenshit later on, and finger me for assault. He looked like that kind of wuss. And he isn't going anywhere very far, right away. Seems to have lost all his clothes, poor bastard. Also his money and ID."

"Shoes, too?"

"Hey, am I a thorough professional, or what?"

I laughed out loud at the image of Stroud padding down the sidewalk in his bare feet and skivvies.

The Prophet seemed to like it, too, and he added, "The wolves shall devour each other, and the loin shall lie down with the limb."

"I got my twenty bucks' worth of bullshit already, " I said.

"Me, too," said Wilkie. "Go preach to a stone, or something." Turning to me, he said, "So, what's the story, Herman? I could see you needed some cavalry back there, but that wasn't your usual kind of action, to say the least."

"Tell me about it," I said. I filled him in on the high points of the day's events. The Prophet also leaned into the conversation, as if he were an old conspirator. Wilkie gave him a dirty look now and then, but otherwise left him alone. I decided it couldn't hurt to have a possibly crazy person listening in on a definitely crazy story, and I left him alone, too.

"What the hell is going on?" said Wilkie, when I had finished.

"Well put," I said. "I haven't a clue."

"What's in the trunk?" said the Proph.

"An unhappy camper," said Wilkie. "The other stuff, I put in the back seat."

"And it is…?" I said.

"Interesting," said Wilkie. He led us over to the car and opened the back door.

"The little guy…"

"You mean Stroud," I said.

"Stroud, my ass. The guy had a briefcase full of phony ID, some of it pretty good, and his own little printing press and art supplies for making some more." He pointed to a pile of papers and cards in an open case. "He's got more damn names than a downtown law firm. Look at this: James Stroud, Strom Jameson, Tom Wade, Wade Thomas—you see a bit of a pattern here?—James Cox…"

"James Cox? Are you sure?"

"Sure, I'm sure. That's one of his better sets, even has a real-looking driver's license. Is that important?"

"Son of a bitch," I said.

"Which one?" said the Proph.

"That's the name of the guy I wrote the bond for."

"I take it, you don't believe in coincidence," said Wilkie.

"Do you?"

"Never," said Wilkie.

"Always," said the Proph.

"There's more," said Wilkie. "The little guy was carrying, a great big nine-millie Browning High Power, looks like it weighs more than he does. Only it's a phony."

"It's not a real Browning?"

"Hell, it's not even a real gun. All plastic, shoots gumball pellets or some damn thing. His badge is also phony, but it's an awfully good one. A casting, probably. An exact replica of the one the big guy had."

"I don't think I like where this is going," I said.

"You're right. You don't like it at all. As far as I can tell, your other guy, Evans, is a real cop. Real badge, real gun, and probably real mad when he wakes up."

"Oh, shit."

"That's about it, all right."

◇◇◇

"How's your workload these days, Wide?"

"You owe me two hundred."

"How's that, exactly?"

"That's what I figure the Korean kid was good for, if I hadn't had to leave the nine ball game early."

Wilkie was a lot better pool player when he was figuring than when he was shooting, but I let it pass. Two hundred for an impromptu deliverance was a good deal, any day. We were sitting in the Chevy, me and Wilkie in the back seat and the Proph behind the wheel, pretending he was Yah's road warrior, making motor noises in his throat. Nobody seemed to know what to do next. Is it the Navy, where they teach people, "Do something, even if it's wrong?" One of those fanatical outfits, anyway. I was starting to feel that way. Somebody had sucked me into a game without telling me the rules, and it was pissing me off. I wanted to be the shooter, for a change, even if I couldn't see the Zen line.

"I'll tell Agnes to cut you a check," I said.

"I like the other stuff better, if it's all the same to you. The green stuff that the government doesn't know about."

"No problem," I said. "You need it right away? If so, I've got to go run an errand."

"Tomorrow's good enough. Leave it with Agnes, if you're not around."

"Fair enough. Besides that, do you need a job?"

"Like checking up on a real cop who travels with a phony one?"

"Maybe."

"I can't do that."

"You've worked for me plenty of times before."

"Yeah, but only bounty hunting. Any fool can do that. But to do investigating, you need a PI license. A carry permit is nice to have, too. You get caught with an unregistered gun when you're chasing a bail-jumping scumbag, they might not even take it away from you. But you get caught carrying heat while you're investigating somebody, you're in deep shit, dig?"

"For somebody who just stuffed a cop in a trunk, you're awfully scrupulous, all of a sudden."

"Hey, you're the one who kicked him. Anyway, I've been officially warned, okay?"

"Ah. But only warned about doing PI work?"

"That's it."

"I'm hip."

"Vroooom," said the Proph.

"Shut up," said Wilkie.

"So, how's your workload?" I said.

"I could use some."

"I've got some for you. You don't know anything about the fiddle or the phony-cop-real-cop affair, okay?"

"What affair is that?"

"Exactly. This is a bounty hunting job."

"That's what I do, all right. Who am I hunting?"

"Amy Cox."

"Not her brother?"

"We seem to be able to find him, easily enough. Whether we want to or not."

"Her, too. Isn't she in the morgue?"

"You don't know that, and you're going to forget to look there. Assume that's somebody else. I want the real Amy Cox. Find her and bring her in, and I'll give you five thousand."

"And if she can't be found?"

"Then give me some progress reports, and I'll give you a partial payment."

"What kind of progress reports?"

"Detailed ones. What you found out along the way."

"Written?"

"Absolutely not."

"Herman, my man, you are definitely on."

"Are you going to be wanting this car anymore?" said the Proph.

We thought about it for a minute.

"I got my own wheels," said Wilkie. "Three blocks back. What about you, Herm?"

"I never did like Chevrolets." I looked at the gleeful figure behind the wheel. "What are you going to do with it?" I asked him.

"There are some truths that even a pilgrim should not seek. Vroom!"

"I don't think he trusts us," said Wilkie.

"Look, Mr. Prophet..."

"The Prophet is only the Prophet," said the prophet.

"Fine," I said. "Listen, Prophet, I couldn't care less what happens to the car, but I'm not going to be party to a murder here, of a cop or anybody else."

"Trust in Yah!"

"I'd prefer a statement of intent."

"The karma of the man in the trunk is mystically linked with the sidewalk in front of the emergency entrance at United Hospital."

"Will his karma get him there?"

"If not, his car will. But it will not wait around to rejoice in his enlightenment."

"That, I can accept."

"He will learn much from it." He quit making motor noises and nodded solemnly.

"What do you want to do with all this other junk?" said Wilkie.

The proph looked at me hopefully.

"Leave Evans his badge and gun," I said.

"That works," said Wilkie. "Cops get vicious as hell, you take that stuff away. Better leave him his wallet, too."

"I am not leaving him any bullets," said the proph.

I was impressed. Pearls of wisdom come out of the oddest shells, sometimes.

"Throw the rest of the stuff back in the briefcase," I said. "I'll hang onto it for now. Maybe there's a clue in there somewhere."

"So that's it?" said Wilkie. "Are we done for now?" He hoisted his bulk up from the back seat and started making departure motions.

"One other thing," I said. "Ever hear of a Rom?"

"You mean, like a computer thing?"

"I don't think so. I think it's some kind of a person."

"Never heard of the bum. I'm out of here, okay?"

"Later," I said. I watched him walk down the alley, then looked back over at my new Chevrolet owner, who seemed to be pondering some deep truth.

"It's not a person," he said, "it's a scourge."

"You mean Wilkie? He's okay, when you get to know him."

"Not him. The Rom. If they are here, then truly, the barbarians have breached the gate."

"Would you care to elaborate on that?"

"I'm in the elaboration business, Pilgrim."

"Call me Herman."

"Then, let me tell you how the world will end, Herman."

"Is this going to take long?"

"Absolutely."

"How about a short version?"

"Okay. If you meet a Rom on the road, kill him."

Chapter Four

High Road to Chinatown

I wanted to hear what the Proph had to say about the Rom, but I really didn't have the time. I suddenly remembered the phone message I had left with Agnes, and I could think of a hundred good reasons why I wanted to stop her before she acted on it.

"Listen," I said to the Proph, who was still behind the wheel, "I need a quick lift back to my office. You think you can come down from the mountain long enough to handle that?"

"Chauffeuring is not a path to spiritual enlightenment. It'll cost you."

"In a Buddha's eye, it will. I already gave you forty bucks and a car. You can afford to spot me a freebie."

"Your karma must be high. You are profound."

"I'm also right."

"That, too. Pull in your feet, shut the door, and navigate."

He was off before I had time to do any of those things. He drove like a kid playing a video game of the kind where you get three free crashes before you're really dead. But I noticed that he also checked his mirrors a lot and kept his hands on the two-and ten-o'clock positions on the wheel. In some ways, at least, he was not the lunatic he seemed. I gave him directions and advice which he mostly ignored, and three minutes later, we were in front of my office. I was ready to leap out, commando-style, in case he forgot to stop, but he came to a normal halt and even waited around for a minute and talked to me through the window.

"Do you really want to know about the Rom?" he asked.

"You tell me. Do I?"

"A good answer. The true pilgrim does not know the name of his own quest. Yes, you do want to know. But you don't want to mess with them, no, no, no."

"Exactly how would I go about learning without messing?"

"You would need a guide,"

"And I'll just bet I know where I'm going to get one, too, don't I?"

"It's possible I know somebody. Only possible. Give me a day to see if I can set up a meeting."

"All right. Do I check back with you in the alley, or what?"

"I will find you."

I thought about the undead body in the trunk and what it might do when it became reanimated. "In a day, I may have to be making myself hard to find."

"Yah! will tell me where you are."

"Silly me. How could I have forgotten?"

"Keep the faith, Herman." And he was gone in a cloud of very nonspiritual exhaust. I think he was aiming for a lightpost in the middle of the next block. I wondered what faith it was he wanted me to keep.

I turned back to the office and saw Agnes standing in the doorway, her face the image of sisterly concern and possible disapproval. It's not always her most attractive expression, but this time, it looked terrific. Or maybe I was just glad to be alive to see it.

"Is everything all right, Herman? There were two detectives here looking for you earlier. Pushy, nasty types. I told them I thought you were gone for the day."

"I thought I was gone for good, for a while there. I take it you haven't listened to your voice mail?"

"Not lately. Should I? I always check the email first. It's so much easier to sort."

"I left you a message, telling you I was in a lot of trouble."

"You should have left me an email. You can highlight the urgent messages with a little picture of a red envelope, you know."

"I'll remember that next time I'm stranded in the jungle. Erase the voice mail, okay?"

"Should I listen to it first?"

"Probably not. It would just upset you."

"Then I'll erase it tomorrow, if it's all the same to you. I was just going to lock up for the day. I'm late as it is."

I gave her a raised eyebrow that said, "You have a date?" and she gave me one raised even higher that said, "None of your damn business." Did I mention that I don't cope all that well with the fairer sex?

"You go on, Aggie. I'll close up shop. Wide Track Wilkie will be in sometime tomorrow, by the way, and..."

"You mean Wendell?"

"He's a Wendell? Wow. All these years, I never suspected him of anything of the sort."

"I really am late, Herman."

"So you said. Okay, Wendell, if you insist, will be by tomorrow. If I'm not around, give him two hundred dollars, cash, and copies of all the stuff we got from Amy Cox."

"Including the ID?"

"Especially the ID."

"What's going on, Herman?"

"That's what he's going to try to find out. Go keep your appointment, why don't you? We'll talk tomorrow."

We said good night and she headed down the street towards the Garrick Ramp, where her Toyota waited to thank her properly for keeping it out of the rain. I went inside the office, locking the door behind me and throwing Stroud's briefcase on the desk. Suddenly, it was feeling like an awfully long day, and I killed the main lights, closed the safe, and headed for the cot in the back room. I think I got my whole body on it before I fell asleep. If not, it was close enough.

<>◇<>

It was more like falling into a bottomless hole than sleep. When I woke up, it was full-blown night, and the room was lit only by a bit of spilled light from the neon sign in the front office. It took me a while to remember where I was, even longer to remember why. As the pieces of the day came back, first grudgingly and then with greater ease, I went to the sink and washed my face, then changed out of my rumpled clothes and thought about what to do next. Going home seemed like more trouble than it was worth, and there wasn't anybody waiting for me there, in any case. I went into the front office to see if Agnes had shut down her computer for the night. Stroud's briefcase was where I had left it, and I flipped it open and rifled idly through the contents, looking for some inspiration. Not finding any, I put the phony badge in my pocket, to look it over later, and went over to the computer.

The screen on the monitor was dark, but when I fooled with a few keys, it came to life, showing the in-box on the email. It reminded me of what Agnes had said, and I wondered if we might be on the brink of an age when an arrested criminal will demand a laptop, rather than a phone. Brave new squirrels.

There were several unopened new messages. As far as I was concerned, they could stay that way until morning. Except for one, that caught my eye because it had the little red envelope-picture that Agnes had told me about. It also had a return address that included COX in the middle of a lot of other jumbled letters. I sat down in front of the monitor, grabbed the mouse, and did a double click on that line. I don't know how to do much on Agnes' machine, but what I do know, I know all to hell. The incoming message, what little there was of it, filled a new window.

mr. jackson,

i believe you are in possession of a certain valuable musical instrument that is the rightful property of my family.

i understand that you acquired it in good faith, and i am prepared to reward you handsomely for its return.

can we talk?

That was it. No name, no phone number, no particulars at all. It didn't even come right out and say the word "Amati." From whom were we keeping secrets, I wondered? I stared at the message for a while, not sure how to react. My first instinct was that it had "Phony" stamped all over it. But my instincts have been wrong before, so I decided not to erase it just yet. I might decide later that I wanted to reply to it, after all, so I left it where it was and shut down the machine. I forget why. Agnes must have told me once that it was a good thing to do.

By now, my stomach was waking up also, reminding me that I hadn't had anything to eat since the half hamburger at Lefty's, about two years ago. It was pushing eleven-thirty. Joe Bock's hot dog cart, which he fondly referred to as "Bock's Car," would have been rolled away for the night a long time ago, and Lew's Half-Deli and C-store down the street and The Downtowner Café would likewise be closed. There were a few bars downtown, besides Lefty's, where you could get a sandwich or a microwave pizza, but I didn't feel like bar food. And I definitely didn't feel like Lefty's. I decided to take a walk. This isn't a big enough city to have a Chinatown, but we do have an area of mixed Asian, Italian, Irish, and Unaligned Redneck, where some of the joints are open late, and I thought a stroll in the night air might clear my head. I put on a light windbreaker and left, locking the door behind me.

I headed west, past the Courthouse and the County Jail, past high-rise offices with selective blocks of floors lit up for the night cleaning crews, past the Central Library that looks like the Bank of England and the Catholic soup kitchen that looks like nothing at all, towards the oldest part of the city. The semaphores got farther apart after a while, the street lights were replaced by antique replicas that worked just as badly as the originals, and the canopy of dark sky got closer to street level, trying to take over completely. Past Seven Corners, it had almost succeeded. But then an island of light appeared in the distance, a jumble of color and glitter, like a beacon across a dark sea. West Seventh, calling to all the wandering barks of the night, all the lost vessels laden with the pilgrims of the square world. Jesus, I was starting to sound like the Proph. So much for the night air clearing my head.

The jumble of lights resolved itself into a strip of shops and restaurants, and my stomach urged me to up my pace a bit. I didn't have a favorite place here, but I wasn't feeling all that fussy. One that was open for business and served food would be good. If the food was good, that would be even better. The nearest one had a red-painted storefront with curtained windows and a neon sign that proclaimed it to be Shanghai. And it had seemed like such a short walk. Across the street was a place with only incandescent lights and a no-color front. It was called the Happy Dragon, and it had several hand-lettered signs in the windows:

Cantonese, Viet Namese, and American
Breakfast All times, bacons and eggs
No Sushi, Thank You Please

No wonder the dragon was happy. I was about to follow the wonderful smells of hot oil, soy, and ginger across the street, when two cars, one a regular police prowl car and the other an unmarked sedan, came tooling up from behind me and did an assault-landing at the very curb I was headed for. Doors flew open and bodies piled out, some with and some without uniforms, all very full of their own importance. They left the car doors hanging open and pushed each other into the restaurant, like a bunch of frat boys who heard a rumor of free beer. One of the without-uniforms was a big figure in a baggy topcoat and a wide-brimmed hat. I couldn't tell for sure if it was Evans, but it definitely could have been.

Since I didn't see any jackets with INS written on them, the most likely explanation was a raid on an illegal gambling operation in some bean-curd cellar. Our current mayor was very big on cracking down on crimes that the people who elected him never indulged in, like cheating at mah-jong. But I didn't feel like finding out. Even if the Proph was right about my karma being high, the stuff could have worn itself out by now. I did a one-eighty without breaking my stride. At the first cross street, I headed away from West Seventh, as fast as I could walk without looking like a fugitive.

Two blocks later, I started changing direction at every corner. Half an hour after that, I decided I was alone, and I slowed to a more casual pace and tried to figure out where I was. Somewhere in an area of mixed blue-collar housing and assorted old industrial buildings. The neighborhood hadn't been "discovered" and gentrified yet, so it didn't have a name, but I vaguely recognized it. There were streetlights only at the intersections, and the dark sidewalks and streets in between were deserted, except for me. This was good.

With my adrenalin back to maintenance levels, I could again afford to think about my stomach, which was becoming vocal in its complaints. Somewhere nearby, a commercial bakery was saturating the night air with the smell of fresh bread, making me giddy with longing. Maybe they had an outlet shop. If not, I might have to catch an alley cat and roast it over my cigarette lighter soon.

The street dead-ended into a five or six-story brick building that could have been built as a factory or an office. Now it was occupied by a lot of small businesses, each with its own logo or lighted sign. A lot of them had their lights on, and a tattoo parlor on the second floor had a neon sign that actually said, "OPEN." If it was, the building had to be, too. I decided to go in and look for the Keebler elves or the Tastee bakers, whichever came first. Before I got to the front door, though, something caught my eye down at one end of the building.

Under a harsh, sodium floodlight, a truck was backed up to a loading dock, and some guy with a gray uniform was wheeling pallets of flat, openwork, plastic crates into it. Crates of fresh bread that smelled like heaven. As I got closer, I could read "Cottage Bakers," on the side of the truck. The guy with the pallet jack stopped and gave me a pained look.

"We don't sell out of the truck," he said.

"That's too bad." I reached for the phony badge in my inside pocket. I was debating whether to impersonate a health inspector or a cop when the doughboy made up my mind for me.

"Oh, a cop, huh?"

"Well, see..."

"Yeah, I see. Undercover. You should've said something."

"We don't like to draw attention to ourselves."

"Got you." He gave me an exaggerated conspiratorial wink that made me want to smack him one, just for being so insufferably cute. But I managed to keep my mouth shut and my hands to myself, and he pointed to a stack of blue crates in the corner of the truck box.

"Frosted cinnamon rolls and filled Danish," he said. "Help yourself."

"Right." I stopped myself short of saying, "thanks." If I had, I figured he'd know for sure I wasn't a real cop. I was finding this impersonating business a lot easier than I had ever imagined. I took a plastic-wrapped package of something warm out of one crate. Then at the urging gestures of Mr. Wink, I took two more out of another crate. Maybe the Proph had been right about my karma, after all. I headed into the building to look for a coffee machine.

Over my shoulder I heard, "You part of the stakeout, then?"

"I guess you figured us out, all right." *What stakeout?*

"Share some with the guys in blue, hey?"

"You got it." I hoped the man was hallucinating.

The main lobby was half a flight above the loading dock, and almost a full flight above street level. It had no reception desk, just a tenant directory, a pair of elevators, and signs directing people to the restrooms and phones. I decided the vending machines, if any, would be near an easy source of water piping, and I followed the signs. A wide corridor had storefront windows looking into some of the tenant spaces, and as I passed one of them, I did a double-take, backed up a half step, and stopped altogether.

The sign said "G. B. Feinstein, Luthier: Fine Musical Instruments." Did I know that name from somewhere? Inside, a man was carving a large piece of wood that was attached somehow to a pedestal. He was peeling off long, curly shavings as if he had a plane, but he used only a large chisel or gouge, pushed with one hand and guided artfully with the other. Must have been one hell of a sharp chisel, I thought. The piece he was working on was the face or back of a bass fiddle, and he bent over it with total intensity and focus, a dead cigarette hanging from his mouth and drops of sweat clinging to his forehead and eyebrows. He would be tall if he stood up, I thought. He had bony elbows and shoulder blades poking out in every direction, a nose that may have extended further than his cigarette, and wire spectacles perched on top of it. Ichabod Crane with a leather apron. And quite possibly, just the man I wanted to talk to.

I knocked on the door, but he didn't look up from his work. A louder knock worked no better. I tried the knob, found it unlocked, and let myself in. I walked past formal glass display cases and walls lined with dark, gleaming violins. Toward the back, the space got more shop-like, with heavy wood benches cluttered with tools and strange-looking parts. I went up to the chisel-master, who still had not acknowledged my presence. As I got closer, he spoke without looking up.

"I don't sell out of the shop," he said. He must have belonged to the same union as the bakery-truck driver.

"You'll have to go to a dealer, one of the better ones." When that didn't get rid of me, he added, "I do some commissions, but right now, I'm booked three years in advance."

"I'm not looking for an instrument," I said.

Finally, he put down the chisel and looked up. "Then why are you here? Feinstein is the master. Everybody who comes here is looking for an instrument." He spoke with a slight accent that might have been German. It made him sound dignified and maybe important.

I held out a package of warm cinnamon rolls in their steamed-up plastic wrap.

"Got any coffee?" I said.

"I can make some *macht schnell.*" German, it was. "You are proposing an exchange?"

"More like share and share alike."

"Sharing is good." If his eyes had been heat lamps, the plastic wrap would have melted. "What is, as they say, the catcher?"

"I'm also looking for some information."

"I got out of the spy business years ago. What kind of information?"

"Information about old violins," I said.

"Ah, yes. Well. Now, that would be quite another matter. What I do know about old violins could fill books. How much time do you have?"

I thought about the alleged police stakeout, and the fact that wherever it was, it did not appear to be in this workshop.

"For once in my life," I said, "time is not a problem."

Chapter Five
Cinnamon Rolls and Other Weighty Topics

I followed Feinstein to the back of the shop, where he cleared glue pots and strange-looking tools off a counter and fired up an industrial gas ring burner. He brewed his coffee in a way I had heard of but never seen before, boiling the grounds, all unfiltered, in an enameled metal pot and then throwing in a raw egg to collect the grits. He measured the grounds with his hand, and the water not at all. Four fistfuls to a splash or two. I didn't want to know what he did with the egg afterwards.

"For the instruments, I have precision, instinct, and soul," he said. "But first and always, precision. For coffee, however, one needs only instinct."

"Was I complaining?"

"You looked skeptical."

"Sorry. Sometimes, that's the only look I've got. Probably comes from the Scottish side of my family."

"Poor fellow. I'll ignore it, then. Now, let us see if those rolls are still hot enough to melt butter."

He opened a drawer in a wooden parts cabinet and took out a dish with a slab of pale yellow stuff and a small spatula. My heart threatened to rat me out to my doctor later, and I told it to shut up and enjoy itself. I can always give up doctors, but real butter, on hot rolls, is a biological imperative. The rich smell of the boiling coffee began to overcome the atmosphere of hide glue, varnish, and musty-sweet wood dust, as we ripped open a package of rolls and performed the definitive melt-test. The butter didn't go all the way to drizzly-flowy, but it slumped down agreeably, mixing with the white frosting, and we pronounced it a success. I inhaled the first roll, I think. Never even put a tooth mark in it. Then I slowed down and savored the next one a bit. The instrument man looked me over between bites and talked around a mouthful of dough and topping.

"You will forgive the possible presumption, *mein Herr*, but I don't see you as quite seedy enough to be a musician or wealthy enough to be a serious collector. What is your interest in old violins, exactly?"

"No apology needed. I should have introduced myself before." I wiped off my hand on my pocket lining, gave him a business card, and told him my name. "I'm a bail bondsman, and I seem to have acquired an old violin as a security forfeit. I don't know what it's worth on the open market, but one person may have literally died for it, and at least two others are willing to break the law to get their hands on it. I'd like to figure out why."

"A good story."

"You don't believe it?"

"Oh, I didn't mean it was a lie. Fine violins often have an air of intrigue about them. The great ones, tragedy and perhaps even death. So a good, preferably dark, story is appropriate. It's no guarantee of quality, mind you, but it's a start."

He took a rag from the bench top and used it to protect his hand while he poured boiling coffee into two battered mugs. I was surprised at how gritty it did not look, though it was certainly dark. He left about an inch of space at the top of each mug, and I was about to tell him that I didn't take cream, when he produced a bottle of cognac from another cabinet and held it out inquiringly. I gave him my best "why not?" expression, and he topped off both mugs, adding a spoonful of sugar from a bag in another cubbyhole. Now we had all the major food groups: alcohol, sugar, caffeine, and fat. I blew on the hot liquid, took a sip, and remembered what it used to be like to believe in heaven. He bit into another roll and went on.

"You say this violin is very old?"

"All I said was 'old,' but it's supposed to be four hundred years and counting."

"Supposed to be."

"It has an appraisal document"

"Does it also have a label?"

I shook my head. "I'm told it's an Amati. I don't know where to look for a label."

"Ah," he said. He wiped his hands on a wet rag and passed it to me to do the same. "Come over here. I show you some things."

He selected a smallish, light-colored violin from his wall display and took it over to a bench, where he turned on an intense fluorescent drafting lamp.

"This is a Roger Baldwin," he said. "Not a great instrument, but certainly a very good one."

"So you're a collector, as well as a maker?"

"All makers are also collectors and repairers. That's how one learns the possibilities of the art. That's also why one locates in a city like this, with a famous chamber orchestra and a symphony nearby. It means there are lots of available examples. Now look at this one."

"Is this the same Baldwin as the pianos?"

"It is not. This violin is from a one-man shop of some obscurity. It's about a hundred and fifty years old."

"It's sort of small." That was as close as I could come to perceptive observation.

"Very good. It is what was once called a knapsack fiddle. For wandering musicians, you see. Quite possibly, it was carried by some soldier in your Civil War. This one is better than most of the type, though. Look here." He pointed out the little stripe around the edge of the top, which he called the "purfling," and told me what kind of wood it ought to be made of, which it was. Then he talked about the arch of the top and back. "It's like the curve of a beautiful woman's buttock," he said. "Every one is slightly different, a subtle variation on a timeless theme. But even so, there is good and there is not so good. A true connoisseur learns to feel the quality of the line, even though he cannot define it. This one has a fine, if somewhat flamboyant character. Now take a look inside." He handed me a tiny flashlight and a little mirror on a stick, like dentists use.

"What am I looking for?"

"Just tell me what you see."

I slipped the mirror down through one of the f-shaped holes and panned it around. I really needed another set of tools and at least one more hand. If I used the mirror to direct the light, then I couldn't get my eye anyplace where I could see what it was reflecting. I decided I was not on the threshold of a new vocation here.

"What do you see?"

"I see the dark, dusty inside of a very complicated-looking box."

"That's a start. What else?"

"Some kind of stick going between the top and the bottom."

"That's the sound post, to keep the tension on the strings from collapsing the top. Ignore that. It's most unlikely to be the original."

"They wear out and have to be replaced?"

"The sound box changes shape slightly, with seasoning, and it needs a different size post."

"Good thing, since I can't get a good look at it, anyway."

"Tell me what you *can* get a look at."

"There's a piece of paper that could be a label, but I can't make out any of the printing on it. It isn't under the hole."

"It shouldn't be, it should be in the center. Symmetry is important in a thing that is made to resonate. It would have been put on before the box was assembled. But it could be a fake, anyway, or a later addition. The real maker's mark would be a brand, literally, scorched into the wood, under the label. Paper eventually crumbles, and nothing is easier than to add a new piece. Sometimes there are several layers, just accumulated. You wouldn't believe the inscriptions I find on some of them."

"Like, 'If you can read this, you're very, very small'?"

"More often a blessing, or a curse to scare off thieves. Sometimes something about the owner. This particular one identifies the maker as one R. Baldwin, and it's actually written backwards, meant to be read with a mirror."

I moved my eye to the hole that didn't have the mirror in it, shined the light in the other one, and made out the faint capitals R and B in the reflection.

"I'll be damned."

"It dates it, you see, but only forward. It means that we're well into the industrial age, when specialized mirrors would have been widely available. What else do you see?"

I felt like quitting while I was ahead, but he seemed most insistent.

"There's a lot of little ridges and grooves in the back," I said. I wondered if the rolls were getting cold yet.

"Tool marks, from gouges and scrapers. You see? You are more observant than you think. The marks also date it, this time the right way. It means that the production predates the invention of sandpaper. You can tell that from the outside of the instrument, too, but it takes a more practiced eye. You have to learn to look for something called 'truing lines.'"

"And those are good?"

"Not necessarily, but like your story, they are a start."

This whole conversation was starting to drive me crazy, and I turned away to have some more laced coffee and break open another package of rolls. The last one seemed to have evaporated. Feinstein topped off our cups and started another pot brewing. For a while, we ate and drank in silence. I looked at the walls covered with violins and decided I was no closer than I had been to knowing why one was worth three grand and another one twenty times that, much less why one would be worth killing over. Feinstein might have read my mind, or at least my face.

"It's a funny market, the market in old instruments," he said. "It's like the art market, only it isn't."

I must have been feeling the alcohol, because that made perfect sense to me. "Of course," I said.

"A certain Van Gogh, say, or a Michelangelo is worth such and such many million because there is only one of it and there are never going to be any more and the world has been taking care of it for a very long time now."

"And because somebody is willing to pay that much for it."

"Just so. It has nothing whatever to do with anybody getting a million dollars' worth of uplifting inspiration from looking at it."

"I personally think the same argument can be applied to a Mercedes Benz."

"That's not as stupid as it sounds."

That sounded stupid? How strong was that cognac, anyway?

"They are both a matter of assigned value." he said. "But with a violin, there is such a thing as intrinsic value, as well. It is, after all, made to play music. Sadly, the people best able to judge the real quality are those least likely to be able to afford it."

"Musicians."

He nodded and took more coffee. "Scum of the earth. Steal from their own mothers to buy a set of strings. Cash in advance for them, always."

It was hard for me to see Amy Cox in that light, but I nodded anyway, to encourage him. Or maybe the evening had just started to turn mellow.

"So musicians get hired to evaluate instruments they can't afford to buy?"

"Mostly, they do not. Nobody wants to take the chance that the Stradivarius they just paid half a million dollars for sounds like a cigar-box fiddle. And it can happen. So the serious buyer settles for pedigrees and proofs of age. Nobody argues with age."

"They just don't make them like they used to," I said.

"Utter rubbish," he said, spilling coffee with a dismissive gesture. "We make them as well or better than they ever did. And there's no secret varnish, either. No secrets of any kind, just the finest workmanship you can get out." He calmed down, refilled his mug from the new pot, and took another sip. "But a new instrument is a new instrument, and there's no arguing with that. It won't find its true voice for at least twenty years, sometimes twice that long. And its soul? Well, if it's going to have one at all, it won't acquire that for at least a hundred."

"Or four?"

"Four hundred years is better, sometimes."

"Why only sometimes?"

"Sometimes it destroys itself before then. You know anything about engines, Mr. Jackson?"

"Engines? You mean like in cars?"

"Exactly like that."

"I turn the key, and mine goes. If it doesn't go, I call a garage."

"How nice for you. When I was a young man in the Army, before I had a vocation, I worked on engines. I learned that diesel engines, specifically, have a peculiar trait. They are the easiest to start, smoothest, and most powerful when they are at the end of their natural life span, ready for a complete overhaul or a trip to the junkyard. The same thing is true of violins.

"It is said that the sweetest sound ever heard from a set of strings was once when Jascha Heifetz played the Tchaikovsky concerto—there is only one, you know—on his Stradivarius, at Carnegie Hall. People who don't even like Tchaikovsky wept and cheered and gave him a fifteen-minute standing ovation." He took a bite of Danish and a gulp of coffee and got a far-away look in his eyes, picturing the scene. "After the concert, he put the instrument in its case, the same as always, and it immediately fractured into a thousand splinters, impossible to repair. The timing of its life, you see, was exquisite."

"This is true?"

"True? Probably not. I have heard the story many times. Sometimes it is Heifetz and the Tchaikovsky and sometimes it is Isaac Stern playing a Bach partita or Itzhak Perlman and a Paganini caprice. It is most likely a professional myth. But the heart of it is true enough. The instrument, any stringed instrument, is at its sweetest just before it dies."

"And they all die?"

"Just like you and me, my friend." He leaned over to clink his mug against mine in a toast to the essential sadness of the universe. It seemed like the right thing to do.

"But not just yet," I said.

He nodded solemnly, then smiled. "But not just yet."

"Of course," he added, "some come to an earlier end than others. Getting put in a museum or a private collector's case is a kind of early death, rather like being embalmed while you're still walking around. Then there are accidents and weather and just general lack of care. And of course, there are always the Gypsies."

"Gypsies kill violins?" I tried to picture some swarthy, mustachioed type, like Omar Sharif, with a bandana on his head and a billowing peasant shirt, plunging his dagger into the f-hole of an old fiddle, but it just didn't work.

"They don't kill them, exactly. Not right away, at least. A Gypsy could take that Baldwin, scrape down the inside to sweeten the tap tone, loosen the purfling, and make it sound like an Amati, for a while. But it wouldn't last long after that."

"A mere hundred years or so?"

"If it did, then it would be truly a fine violin, a real collector's item, but that is most unlikely. Who knows? I, myself, do not know the exact life of the violins I build. But I know that a Gypsy would take one, make it sound like an instant masterpiece, and shorten its life dramatically. You never heard of a Gypsy violin?"

"I thought that was just an expression, like Dutch courage or a Chinese fire drill. I didn't know Gypsies actually made violins."

"Make? No. They do not make, they fake. The point of all effort with them is fraud. And they are very good at it. Throughout history, they have complicated the lives of both serious luthiers and their customers. And they have destroyed many fine instruments and many lives. The Nazis should have left the Jews alone and concentrated on the damned Rom, and the world would have thanked them for it."

I almost choked on my coffee. "What did you call them?" I asked.

"Is something wrong, *Herr* Jackson?"

"Just tell me what you called them."

"Damned Rom? What of it?"

"What does that mean?"

"It means I don't think much of them."

"Not the 'damned,' the other."

"Oh, you mean Rom? It's what they call themselves. Also their language. Rom, Gypsy, all the same thing. Horrible people. Worse than musicians, which many of them are, as well. If you meet one, grab your wallet and run for your life."

"Or kill him?"

"That would be better, yes."

"*Déja vu.*"

"I don't understand."

"I don't either, but I'm starting to."

I took my mug and strolled over to the outside window, deep in thought. A wind had come up while we were talking, and the thrashing branches of an elm tree made monochrome kaleidoscope patterns with the corner street light. Now and then, they illuminated a squat, dark shape in the middle of the block.

"Is this a tough neighborhood, Mr. Feinstein?"

"We are old drinking friends now. Call me G.B. And no, I don't think this is an especially bad area."

"Is there always a squad car parked across the street, G.B.?"

"No. It has been there since late this afternoon."

"Do you know why?"

"I think they are waiting for you, *Herr* Herman."

So much for karma.

Chapter Six

Flight to Avoid

I suppose most people would have made a mad dash for the rear exit then and there, but I had used up my panic reflex for the day. I moved away from the window, had another sip of coffee, and looked at the man who had been my host for the past couple of hours.

"Why do you say they're looking for me, G.B.?" But even as I said it, I suddenly knew the answer. *The name on the shop door, that I hadn't quite recognized, was also on the certificate of authenticity for the Amati.* It was an automatic connection, and I had walked right into it.

"I'm not positive, mind you. They didn't tell me a name, only that I should be watching for a man who was looking for a very old violin."

"Looking for one? Are you sure they didn't say he would be bringing one for you to look at?"

He shook his head. "They said what I just told you. But then, they didn't strike me as the sharpest tools on the bench, either. They could have got it wrong. They fooled around with my instruments, like a bunch of obnoxious little children, and then they tried to act serious and important. I didn't like them very much."

"Are they still here, in the building?"

"Only the uniformed officer out in the car, I think. Maybe another one out in front. I haven't looked there for a while."

"So what do you intend to do?"

"Do? Why would I do anything? I already told you, I didn't like them."

"And that's it?" I said. "That's all you need to be willing to harbor a possible fugitive?"

"I have lived in places where the police know how to intimidate people, Herr Herman. Intimidate and hurt. I assure you, these fellows are amateurs, and not very talented ones at that. I don't like them, and I do rather like you. Yes, that is all I need. What do you need?"

I thought about it for a while and then told him.

When I went over to the squad car at the curb, the officer inside was busy tapping something into the keyboard of his big onboard computer, which left him looking away from me and the building I had just come from. That explained a lot. He seemed to have a computer instead of a partner, and I had to wonder how much comfort that was when the shooting started. It was the coming trend, though. Robo Friday, virtual partner.

"Are things as dull out here as they are inside?" I said.

He whirled around to face me and began to reach for his pistol. Then his eyes registered the phony badge that I had carefully placed just peeking out from behind the lapel of Feinstein's raincoat, and he relaxed and gave me a more leisurely look.

"I didn't know we had a man inside," he said.

"It figures, doesn't it? It wasn't enough of a bullshit operation to start with, so they threw some more manpower at it."

"You got the 'bullshit' part right, anyway."

"Yeah, well, it all pays the same, they say." I stuffed my hands deep in my pockets, the way I hoped a bored detective would.

"That's what they say, all right," said the cop. "And it all counts for thirty." What a stimulating conversation. It even made me feel like a cop. So far, so good, but sooner or later, he would...

"I don't think I know you, detective."

That, right there, is what he would do. And with his hand alarmingly close to his weapon again, too. Well, there was nothing for it now but to pick a name and try it out.

"Hanes," I said, offering my hand. "I work with Evans." *And in my off-duty time, I manufacture underwear.*

"Bunco, huh? I don't get over there much. Been on the strawberry wagon a lot lately. Lots of action, but no weight, if you know what I mean. I'm Benson." He took my hand and, to my astonishment and joy, shook it, rather than cuffing the wrist it was attached to.

"Yeah," I said, "I know exactly what you mean. Pleased to meet you." I had no clue what he meant. But the information about Evans being on the Bunco Squad was certainly interesting. Not Homicide at all, but the division that dealt with con games and grifts. My, my, my. I would also have liked to find out what case Evans was officially working at that exact moment, but I figured I had pushed my luck far enough. Time to wrap up this little bit of street theater, before the set fell apart on me.

"How long you been out here?" I said.

"Three and a half hours, but who's counting?"

"Nobody relieved you?"

"Do I look relieved?"

"That really sucks, man."

"Tell me about it."

"Tell you what, Benson," I said. "I'm on my way out, but if you want, I'll stay with the unit for fifteen, while you take a code seven." I may not know what a "strawberry wagon" is, but I do know that a car is a "unit," and a "code seven" is a rest break. In this case, it was also the magic phrase.

"You sure about that?"

"Absolutely." If he only knew how sure.

"You're on." He hoisted himself out of the car, dropped his flashlight in its holster, and motioned to me to take his place.

"Use the computer, if you want," he said. "But don't forget, CIS can tell every site you went to, even if you erase it, okay?"

Still more unsolicited information. I was starting to like this guy a lot. Maybe I wouldn't steal his squad car, after all. I nodded and climbed in the driver's seat, and he went off toward the building, walking like a man who has just remembered he has a bladder he's been neglecting. I figured he wouldn't be gone long, though. After all, I never did find a coffee machine in the building, and Feinstein damn sure wasn't going to give him anything.

I decided to leave the car, and the sooner the better, but first I wanted a look at that computer. I'm not even slightly proficient with these things, but it was an opportunity I couldn't resist. The screen was full of dialogue between Benson's unit and at least two others, mostly in some language known only to cops. Not what I wanted, even if I could decipher it. I looked around for a mouse and found none, but I did find a cute little black pad that made the cursor move when I fingered it, and I figured the bar at the bottom of the pad was the equivalent of the mouse-clicker. Or whatever the hell it's called. I sent the chit-chat display off into some electronic Never Never Land and looked at a screen full of icons. I didn't see any that might be a gateway to homicide or bunco files. I tried opening something that called itself Day Book, but found that I needed a password. Seeing none written on the windshield or dashboard in magic marker, I gave up on that. I looked instead at the little bars at the bottom of the screen that showed what files were already open. One of them was labeled APBs, and I clicked it into a new window.

There were about twenty listings of outstanding warrants, a couple of which had added notes about recent apprehensions. When I scrolled down, I could see the lists from previous days, too. A lot of familiar names there. Some good, long-time customers and some I wished I had never heard of. Hector Ruiz, a regular of mine, was wanted for smacking his grandmother around again, and Henderson the Pain King was wanted for smacking anybody he could find. Willie Martin, better known as Whisper, was wanted for murder one. That would make the fourth time, if memory served. No bond there, and that didn't break my heart in the slightest. That guy gave me the creeps.

I went on down the list of candidates for County housing, smiling at the predictable repeaters. Actual and potential scenes of confrontation or flight, fight, arrest, and even death, were all laid out in a crisp shorthand that was positively chilling. One officer had been shot that day, though not fatally, and one drug dealer named Slick Cicero had gone down, rather than go in. My man Benson hadn't made a high-profile arrest in days, poor soul. But then, as we had both just said, it all pays the same.

My own name was about halfway down the list. *Shit.*

I was only "wanted for questioning in connection with…," which wasn't too bad, except that I was listed as "armed and extremely dangerous." Get *real* here, folks. Maybe Evans just didn't want to admit he'd been taken out of the play by an unarmed amateur, but the other cops reading the list wouldn't know that. Or maybe he just wanted me to get shot. Too many maybes to contemplate, and I had already tarried too long behind enemy lines. The simple fact was that I was wanted. It was a different game now.

I closed the APB window, left the real window on the real cop car open, and got my wanted body out of there. A glance back at the building told me that Officer Benson was still making the most of his break, while at one of the windows, G. B. Feinstein was giving me a thumbs up. I gave him a quick wave back and melted into the shadows between the nearest two apartment buildings. I trotted for a while, putting several blocks and a freeway ramp between me and the abandoned "unit." Then I slowed to a more leisurely pace, switching to alleys and backyards. The Stealth Bondsman vanishes again. What a guy. I could hardly wait to see what he would do next.

A man on the run needs three things: money, transportation, and a destination, which is not the same as merely a place to lay low. All three of those needs are possible traps.

A lot of wanted felons don't make it past need number one. They get picked up waiting around for their bank to open, or going into a traceable cache, or just talking to somebody who owes them money or might conceivably loan it to them. Or if they're really dumb, which most criminals definitely are, they get nailed adding an armed robbery or two to the list of performances they're already wanted for.

Those who manage to get some operating cash without blowing the whistle on themselves may still get caught by driving their own car too long or traveling on plastic. And of the ones who avoid all those pitfalls, a large percentage are picked up at their homes, their girlfriends' pads, their favorite bars, or Mom's place. Especially that last one. It is a wonderful bit of trade irony that the more dangerous and desperate a fugitive is, the more likely he is to go to Mom. I've never even tried to figure that one out, but I've seen it enough to believe it absolutely. Jackson's Theorem Number Six: If a man goes to hide with his mother, apprehend him with extreme prejudice and a lot of firepower.

I have also observed that if a man commits none of the above acts of criminal stupidity, travels without using plastic, and goes to a place he has never been and has no reason to ever go, he is virtually impossible to catch. Until he comes back, and there's the rub. That's why a place to lay low is not the same as a destination. If your ultimate plan involves getting your old life back, then any hiding place that doesn't let you work on that problem is just a dead end. Most fugitives do come back, and so would I, but not until I had arranged a better script for my reception party. Meanwhile, it was definitely time to go to ground.

The stakeout with Patrolman Benson was most likely an informal operation, set up on Evans' personal authority. If he was only Bunco, he wouldn't have enough clout to set it up for multiple sites. So I could probably risk one trip back there, if I didn't linger. Also on the plus side, the computer listing for me had not included any mention of my car, so it should be safe for me to drive it around for a few hours at least. After that, I had better be financed and gone.

I headed back towards downtown, keeping to alleys and poorly-lit streets. Walking past the back of a block of tenements,

I was surprised at how many lights were still on in the shabby apartments, despite the late hour. Jumbled black and gray background, with dim little windows of yellow light, floating in space, showing film clips of other people's lives.

My instinct was to stare, and I felt a bit dirty about it, like an intruder, even though there was nothing very interesting to see. In one dingy kitchen, some men sat around a table, playing cards and drinking beer. In another, a frail white-haired woman was feeding a scrawny cat on top of a similar table. Several windows were filled with the flickering blue light of TV sets. The TVs were animated, but the black silhouettes in front of them were not. In yet another kitchen, a man and a woman were standing in the middle of the room, holding each other. Not hugging and kissing and fondling, just holding. Each one claiming the other as a sole ally against the night. The reason could be deliverance or tragedy, joy or unbearable sorrow: the phone call from the hospital, the telegram from the Army, the layoff slip or the bonus in the pay packet, the good or bad numbers in the lottery, the check that was or wasn't in the mail. All with the same result. That's what couples do, I thought, if they're real. They hold.

Watching them, I suddenly knew. I didn't have a mom to get me trapped, or a woman to hold, or any other family that anybody knew about, but I knew where I needed to go.

I got back to my office, cased it front and back from a block away first, and then went in, leaving the lights off. The floor safe under Agnes' desk had a little less than a thousand dollars in it. I left the two hundred I had promised to Wilkie, plus another two for operating capital for Aggie, and took the rest. I threw it and some clothes into the briefcase I had gotten with Stroud's stuff, locked up again, and left without a backwards glance. No phone calls, no notes, no computer nonsense, just in and out in less than five minutes. The streets were still empty, the night quiet, and I held back premature thoughts about being home free. Two blocks away, I cased the parking ramp as carefully as I had my office. The place was deserted, and I quickly found my old BMW on the third level and took it out, driving neither fast nor slow.

I drove straight to the Amtrak depot on Cleveland Avenue, where I parked in the long-term part of the lot and locked the car up. Inside, I bought a ticket on the morning train to Chicago, with a connection to Seattle on the Empire Builder, complete with observation car and diner. But I didn't get a sleeping compartment. People with sleepers get catered to and remembered. Coach-class passengers might as well be cattle, for all the notice that's taken of them. I paid for the ticket with a credit card. The train didn't board for another three hours, and I made a point of asking the ticket agent if there was a good coffee shop nearby. I have no idea what he told me, but we had a nice chat about it. This was good. I also went to the lobby ATM and drew another $500 out of two separate accounts.

Outside, I found a vacant cab to take me to the Hertz agency at the main Twin Cities airport, where I rented a Pontiac sedan. I used the Cox credit card and driver's license from the briefcase, the ones Wilkie had said were really good fakes. They had better be.

"You don't look much like your photo, Mr. Stroud," said the agent at the counter.

"It's old," I told her. "I've put on a lot of weight since then. The disease, I'm afraid. Probably terminal."

"Oh, my God, I'm so sorry." She began doing busy, important things with papers. Nice kid, but a bit on the ditzy side.

"My problem. Don't trouble yourself about it."

"Geez, that's so brave." Then she paused and got a thoughtful look, which may have been a bit of a strain for her. "I thought most diseases made you thin, not fat."

"You think I'm fat?"

"No, I didn't mean that, at all. I think you're actually, kind of, um. Well, I just meant…"

"When I get depressed, I eat a lot."

"Oh, yeah. Sure. I can see doing that. Me, too." She did some more important things with papers, working even harder at being helpful now. "Great, then. Just sign here, and initial here, here, and here. I don't suppose you want the supplemental insurance? I mean, I'm sorry, but I have to ask, you know?"

"How much is it?"

She told me, and I said, "Sure."

"Really?"

"You can't have too much insurance."

"I guess. But I mean, well…wow."

Two minutes later, I was headed out of the lot, having kicked the tires, inspected all the existing scratches in the paint, and assured the agent that she really didn't have to worry about me. It almost seemed a pity to go. I think she wanted to take me home with her. Probably not the holding type, but she did a good "wow."

The Pontiac had kind of a rubbery ride, I thought, and it smelled of air freshener, but it had pretty good sight lines and plenty of power, and it looked like a million other cars on the road. It would do. The clock on the dash read 3:22, which was just fine. It was about six hours, plus rest stops, to where I was going, and there was no point in getting there before mid-morning. Upstate, they call it, and every state has one. Way upstate. So far, in fact, that it was in a different state altogether. There, the only real family I ever had, my Uncle Fred, was doing his third stretch in a prison called the Bomb Factory.

Chapter Seven

Upstate

It wasn't called the Bomb Factory because it was full of anarchists, but because that's what it had originally been. It was built in World War II to make bombs and artillery shells. Maybe napalm, too, though only the people who worked there knew for sure. They were very big on secrecy back then. A slip of the lip could sink a ship, even a thousand miles from any ocean. They were also very paranoid about saboteurs. The high concrete walls that ringed the complex were built to keep people out, not in. The machine gun towers at the corners were also original, and a mile of open marshland in every direction gave them a free field of fire. Against whom, your guess is as good as mine. Neo-Luddites, maybe.

Its first name was the Redrock Munitions Facility. Now it's called the Redrock State Penitentiary, and it's a medium-security prison for nonviolent repeat offenders, like my Uncle Fred. The old smokestacks are still there, and the open lowland, the cost of wrecking and reclaiming being astronomical. The stacks lean a bit now, and the walls that surround them are cracked and crooked in places. Someday, the whole complex may simply sink into the surrounding marsh, which would leave nobody either surprised or sad. Meanwhile, it's actually not the worst place in the world to do time, I'm told. In any case, nobody has ever escaped from it. Maybe nobody has ever tried. Least of all, Uncle Fred.

I think Redrock is where he always wanted to be, though I can't tell him that to his face. If it isn't, I'll never figure out how somebody so street-smart couldn't manage to stay on the outside. "Some things just aren't worth worrying about, Hermie, my boy," he used to say. Like keeping two sets of books for his front business and washable numbers sheets for his real operation. Uncle Fred was a bookie, a numbers man, and a loan shark, and he was very successful, except for when he got caught. I always thought he just couldn't take the rarefied air of freedom for too long. But with respect to other people and the pitfalls and traps of the cruel old world, he is absolutely the wisest man I have ever known. He could figure out everybody and everything except himself. And if you think about it, that's really not such bad odds to be playing with. He's also the closest thing I ever had to a real father.

I grew up in a Rust Belt slum of blue-collar Detroit. If I knew my father, I don't remember him anymore. Uncle Fred would, of course, being his brother and all, but he never spoke of him. My mother, I would just as soon forget, though I can't always manage that. I don't know what it was she wanted out of life, but a son definitely wasn't it. I spent my childhood running away from foster homes and orphanages, and working small street scams, always trying to build up enough of a stash so I could run so far I would never have to come back. Uncle Fred took me under his wing and made it more or less moot. He didn't actually let me live with him, but he gave me a job and made me sort of an unofficial apprentice. Everything I know about money, numbers, and odds, plus a lot of what I know about human frailty, I learned from him. He gave me an identity. I became a numbers man. In any way that really counts, I still am.

And he was proud of his student. He wasn't big on the whole idea of family, but I often felt that he saw me as the son he never had. When he went away to prison the first time, he let me run the business for him in his absence. I rewarded this amazing display of trust by liquidating the whole operation and using the capital to start my first bonding agency. He didn't like the idea much at first, his favorite nephew going legit, but as the money started to flow in, with no penal risk attached, he grudgingly approved and eventually even admired. Before he got out from his first stretch, I had salted away enough cash to repay him, and I was off and running on my own. Playing with the house money, they call it.

The business worked, but my life didn't. I got involved in the wrong way with one of my own clients and wound up having to flee Detroit permanently, walking away from a lot of money and a nominal wife who in any case was not the holding type. Also from my Uncle Fred. That's the short version. I'm not especially fond of telling the longer one, though I have no bitterness about it. If there's anything I learned from my apprenticeship, it's that you play the hand you're dealt and don't whine about it, even to yourself.

I'm 43 going on ancient now, reestablished and in some ways reborn. New business, new part of the country, new life. I might as well be in the Witness Relocation Program, except that I was never a witness to anything that I admitted. I seldom risk contacting Uncle Fred, though I think of him often. I've never been to Redrock to visit him before. It just wasn't worth the worry. My friend Nickel Pete sometimes takes vacations in exotic places like Mexico, Hawaii, and Italy, and while he's there, he mails cards and letters to Redrock for me. I like to imagine that my uncle knows perfectly well what kind of fraud is going on and laughs his ass off about it. It's as much as I can do for him. And without any help from me, he himself had also managed to build up a new business and lose it again by going back to the slammer, not once but twice. So how much help could he stand? Maybe I'll ask him someday.

I stopped twice for gas and coffee on the road, and once for ham and eggs with some of those terrific fried potatoes that only small town diners know how to make. I also bought half a dozen candy bars and a carton of cigarettes at a truck stop, a standard visitor's gift. I was feeling tired but eager as the blacktop road broke out of the autumn landscape of scrubby farms and small groves and into the last mile of low, blighted land that still surrounds Redrock. It loomed black and ugly on the horizon, and its leaning chimneys made it look like a set from a bad horror movie. The big archway through the outer wall had a rolling steel gate that was open, and the courtyard inside had a visitor parking lot where a big sign told me to lock my car, take my keys, and leave no valuables in plain sight. I guess they don't get a very classy clientele there. Mostly lawyers, probably.

Another sign told me that all visitors had to register at the front office, but it didn't say I had to have a photo ID. I rummaged through the phony credentials in the briefcase and decided I would be Samuel Hill, Attorney at Law. A lame joke, maybe, but who was going to complain? I locked the Pontiac, leaving no valuables in plain sight, and went in. Five minutes later, a uniformed guard had searched me for lethal substances or devices and was escorting me into the compound. When I heard the massive steel gates clang shut behind me, even though I was just a visitor, I knew what doom sounded like. I decided to avoid it a while longer.

The visitor area was just a big gym-sized room with a lot of tables and chairs. The tables were bolted to the floor in neat rows, and guards strolled the aisles between them. The fluorescent lighting was just a little brighter than the sun, and the place smelled of Lysol and cigarette smoke. It also had several video cameras, up high in the corners, but none of the glass separators with phones that you see in the high-security joints. Visitors and cons could actually touch here, as long as they didn't get carried away about it.

It took them about half an hour to find my Uncle Fred and get him there. I suppose he didn't believe them at first, telling him he had a lawyer for a visitor. When they led him in, he looked confused and crabby, but when he saw me, he smiled slyly and gave me a wink, and the years since we had last seen each other dropped away. That was my uncle, all right. We shook hands just like a real lawyer and client would, then sat down to talk.

"So, what's up, Mr. Shyster?"

"Hey, Mr. Con. Good to see you, too. Yes, I've been well thank you. How about yourself? Bernice and the kids send their love. We're all praying for your appeal."

We sat down and leaned together, and he lowered his voice a notch.

"Who the hell is Bernice?"

"I just made her up."

He chuckled. "Cute. You just playing to the cameras, or are you trying to make me think you care about me?"

"You trying to pretend that I don't?"

"You don't visit me here, ever."

"If I did, I could wind up joining you."

"A smart guy like you? Never happen."

"Yeah, well, some days I'm smarter than others."

"Ain't we all, though?" He laughed, then, and visibly relaxed. "God*damn*, it's good to see you, Hermie."

"You, too, Unc. You look pretty good, for a geezer and a lifer." Actually, I thought he looked like nine miles of bad road. His salt and pepper hair had gone to full white, his moustache had no shape to it anymore, and he seemed about two inches shorter than I remembered him. If he still had a jaw, it was lost now in the folds of his shapeless neck. The glint was still in the eyes, though, the hard intelligence and spirit of a game player who would die playing.

"I'm only a borderline geezer," he said, "and I get one more shot before I'm a lifer."

"Really? I thought three times down and you were out."

"Nah, that's all political bullshit. Us nonviolent types get a little more slack. It's not like they got a big shortage of inmates, you know? I'm figuring on parole in a couple years. Meanwhile, I keep my manly physique ready for all those eager women out there, by eating only organic foods and pumping iron every day, which I'm sure you can tell. What do you do?"

"I pump wood at a place called Lefty's Pool Hall."

"That's better. We had a pool table here, I'd be a rich man by now. You bring any smokes?"

I pulled the paper bag from under my chair and plopped it on the table. He opened the top and peered in. "What the hell are these?" he demanded.

"They're called cigarettes. Old Golds, your usual brand. Remember?"

"Yeah, but they're regulars. I can't take that kind no more. I got to have the sissy ultra lights, or I go all asthmatic, have to give up my daily marathon training and everything."

"I'm sorry."

"You wouldn't know, I guess. Well, they're good for capital, anyway. Thanks, kid."

"Do I need to ask what you need capital for?"

"If you do, I didn't teach you much. Book is a good business here. Cons will bet on any damn thing, and they got no clue what the odds ought to be. You gotta stay away from craps, though. Guys get crazy over craps, make me forsake all the nonviolent training I got from Hot Mama Gandhi. What about you? You still writing GET OUT OF JAIL FREE cards for exorbitant fees?"

"That and pool are the only games I know anymore."

"And I'm up for sainthood next year. So what's the problem?"

"Did I say there was a problem?"

"Don't try to con an old con, Hermie. You didn't come here just to listen to me lie about my health."

"Well, since you mentioned it…"

"I mentioned, already. Give."

So I gave. I told Uncle Fred everything that had happened, from the time Amy Cox had first walked into my office until I had walked into the visitor lobby at Redrock. Shortly after I got started, he lit a cigarette from the carton he had said was the wrong kind, then offered me one. I figured he was letting me know that the video cameras were high-resolution. I took the offered smoke, and whenever I came to the parts about running afoul of the law, I made sure I had the cigarette and my hand in front of my mouth, to stymie any lip-readers. He sat back in his chair, crossed his legs, and listened. Once in a while, he would make a note on a little lined pad he had in his shirt pocket. He looked comfortable, and so was I. Focused. Talking business was more natural to either of us than talking sentiment.

After I finished, he looked at his notes for a while, scowled a few times, and massaged his chin with his scrawny hand.

"It's a con," he said.

"Hey, no kidding? What gave you the first clue?" Sometimes Uncle Fred talks to me as if I were still a little kid, and since real fathers everywhere do that, too, I don't even try to break him of it. Sooner or later, he would get to the paydirt.

"But it's not so simple," he said.

"Oh, I see. Did it look simple at some point? Somehow, I missed that part."

"You ever hear of the 'old fiddle game?'"

"Sure," I said. "Of course. Everybody has, but it doesn't apply here."

He was referring to a classic, two-man short con, the kind that doesn't give the victim enough time to think things over before it's already sprung.

It works this way: Grifter Number One eats a meal in a fancy restaurant, then tells the manager he can't pay because he just realized he left his wallet in his hotel room. But if the manager will wait for him to go get it, he will leave his violin for security. He opens an old-looking violin case, flashes the violin around a bit, and leaves, acting hurried and embarrassed. After he goes, another customer, Grifter Number Two, comes up to pay his own bill and asks to have a closer look at the instrument. He's a collector, he says, and would like to buy it. He offers a huge chunk of money, at least ten times what the restaurant is likely to have for cash on-hand. The manager, of course, says it's not his to sell, but if Number Two will wait a bit, the owner will be back shortly. Number Two says sorry, but he has to catch a hot flight to Timbuktu, and he splits. But he leaves the manager his business card and asks him to have the owner of the fiddle call.

When Number One comes back, the manager, if he's as greedy as the grifters hope and trust, negotiates a quick purchase of the violin. Grifter Number One doesn't want to sell, he says, but he finally agrees to do so for all the money in the place, cash only. Then he, also, suddenly remembers a hot date somewhere very far away, and he takes the money and runs. The "collector's" business card, of course, is as phony as the two grifters, and the violin turns out to be worth maybe fifty bucks, tops. But by the time the manager knows he's been had, both players are long gone. There are lots of variations, but that's the purest version.

"I thought of it right away," I said, "but the only thing I can see that it has in common with my situation is an old violin and a security arrangement. What are you seeing that I'm not?"

"I'm seeing two completely different operations, Hermie."

"You want to lay that out for me?"

"Look, when you wipe away all the byplay, like the limp that the cute broad had, and…"

"Did I say she was cute?"

"You didn't have to. You wipe away that, and the business with the kneeled tights…"

"Neo-Luddites, Uncle Fred."

"Will you cut that shit out and listen for a minute?"

"Yes."

He glared at me for a bit, daring me to interrupt him again. When I didn't, he lit another cigarette and continued. "You sift through all the byplay, I'm saying, and if the scam still looks too complicated, then there's something else going on."

I waited. He made a gesture with his hand that said, *Your turn.*

"Like murder?" I said.

"Just like that. The killing wasn't part of the grift. Con men aren't hit men. If they were, they'd give up conning and go to armed robbery or extortion or murder for hire. Something with a lot more loot and a faster payoff."

"Excuse me for being a little slow," I said, "but I don't see where there's any payoff in this scheme, fast or slow. If I have to give eighteen grand to the court, that doesn't help anybody else."

"You won't have to. You got a bent cop in on the scam…"

"Evans."

"Yeah, Evans. You watch. When the time comes for the Cox kid's trial, something will show up in the police records, makes the whole thing go away, null and void. The arrest was just to get your attention, get you to look at the violin."

"Why me?"

"Because bondsmen have more money than restaurant managers."

"Fair enough. But I still don't see where the payoff comes in."

"That's because we haven't seen the hook yet, only the bait."

"But I don't have to buy the violin from any phony musician. I already have it."

"Do you?"

"Well, Pete does."

"Does he?"

"Sure, he does."

"If you say so."

"What are you saying, Unc? That Pete's in on the con?"

"He wouldn't have to be. You trust him, that's good enough for me. I'm just saying I'd look, that's all. Maybe there's a little pigeon drop going on here, too."

The "pigeon drop" is another classic short con, in which the victim literally winds up holding the bag. The bag is supposed to be full of money, but it turns out to be stuffed with worthless paper. I sighed.

"Couldn't just one thing be what it looks like?" I said.

"In this sorry old world, probably not much."

"What about the killing? You figure Evans for it?"

"Could be, but I don't think so. If he did it, it was a mistake, and he's trying to pin it on you. But if he's clean, then he might really think you did it. Either way, you've got some running time."

"How's that?"

"I figure Evans is in on the con, no matter what. He'll let you be a wanted man for a while, just to keep you off balance, but he isn't going to let you go down until the game plays itself out and some money changes hands. If Plan A didn't work, he'll go to Plan B or Z, but he won't give up on it. There's too much invested at this point, and the gang has its little hearts set on the payoff."

"Which I'm not going to give them."

"Are you sure? People who do this for a living are awfully good at it, you know. You might not see the hook until it's too late. At this point, you probably haven't even seen all the players."

"So what do you suggest?"

"Well, you can't turn State's evidence, because you don't have any evidence."

"This is true."

"So the only thing to do is see another card. Then turn the hook back on the grifters, if you can. If you can't, at least you might find out who killed the girl, get clear of it yourself."

"Play the hand I'm dealt? Where have I heard that before?"

"Play the hand out, damn straight. But keep a gun under the table, you hear? This thing is going to get ugly before it's done."

"You think so?"

"I know so. Murder by automobile is not the professional's method of choice. It's a caper with a lot more rage than thought. Believe me, there's still plenty of it left floating around for you."

"Okay, so I need a gun."

"An untraceable gun."

"Absolutely. Who do I shoot with it?"

"Well, that's the art of it, you know? If it's not clear by the time the last card's turned, you could be in deep shit."

"You're just full of good advice today, aren't you?"

"You remember the story I used to tell about the horse trader in Constantinople?"

A guard was going around the tables, telling people their time was up.

"You mean the one with the little kid who saw..." I began. Uncle Fred motioned to me to cut it off.

"Yeah, that one," he said. "You keep that one in mind, and you'll be fine."

"I don't see how it applies here."

"Then you'll just have to find a way to make it apply, won't you?"

The guard was about to come up and poke one or both of us, so we preempted him by standing up and shaking hands again.

"Twenty miles south of here," said Uncle Fred, "there's a little dump of a town, has a diner on Main Street. The house specialty is pecan pie. You ought to stop and try it."

I didn't for a minute take that to be a casual suggestion.

"Pecan, you say?"

"That's the stuff. You got to ask about it. Rosie, the waitress will know." He gave me another wink and a final squeeze of my hand.

"You take care of yourself." I stopped myself short of calling him "Unc" in front of the guard.

"Count on it." He thought for a moment. "Count on it, Mister Sam Hill. And you watch your back."

Chapter Eight

Pecan Pie at the Last Chance Café

The rush of being on the run and the pleasure of seeing my uncle were long gone by the time I headed the Pontiac back through the blighted lowland, and the road back seemed longer than it was on the way out. But I was in no hurry. I needed a solid block of sleep and then a solid plan before I went anywhere. First, though, I needed to check out the locally famous pecan pie.

The town didn't look much different from the one where I had stopped for breakfast: tiny, tired, and nearly deserted. Norman Rockwell might have painted it once, but even he wouldn't look at it now. Thomas Hart Benton, never. The sign at the city limits said NEW SALEM, pop. 312, and I suspected the number included cats and dogs. Even counting pets, it was probably an exaggeration. But there was, as promised, a diner on Main Street, between a grain elevator and a boarded-up creamery. The sign over the door simply said CAFE. I guessed they didn't have to worry about being confused with the competition.

Down by the grain elevator stood a couple of dirty pickups and one ton-and-a-half stakebed parked nose-in to the curb. By the café, there was only a rusted and battered old Trans Am that looked as if it had been painted with a brush, bright blue with crooked white racing stripes. The rear lid was popped up, and a hay bale took up all of the trunk space, and then some. I thought it looked hilarious. The rest of the street was deserted. I parked ten yards away from the Trans Am and went into the café.

The door's old-fashioned jingle-bell ringer woke up the two or three resident flies and sent them spiraling up to do battle with a lazy ceiling fan. There were high-backed booths along one wall and tables in the rest of the place, with a counter up at the end. In one of the booths, a couple of well-fed rural types in Big Smith overalls and DeKalb baseball caps were hunched over heavy china plates, mopping up gravy with small loaves of bread. When I walked in, they gave me a look that openly asked if I came from another planet. I gave them one back that said I certainly hoped so. They didn't look away and I didn't waste my time trying to stare them down.

The rest of the place was empty, so I went to the back and sat on a stool, hoping a Munchkin named Rosie might be lurking behind the counter. She wasn't, so I grabbed a menu from behind a paper napkin holder. The regular house special was something called the Whole Cow Steakburger, while the special of the day was a hot turkey sandwich with mashed potatoes and sage dressing and savory cranberry sauce. Both of them came with gravy. Apple, cherry, and blueberry pie were also listed, but no pecan. If I were really feeling daring, I could try something called Aunt Mary's Chocolate Bombe. A misspelling, no doubt.

After I had read both sides of the plastic-coated menu and put it back down, a double-action door with a porthole in it swung toward me. A coffee pot emerged from the secret room behind, followed by a shapely arm and a thirty-something blonde. She was maybe five foot six, not really heavy, but with a solid look, like a somewhat softer version of one of those Amazons from the cover of a body building magazine. She had watery blue eyes, flat cheek planes and the strong jaw and mobile mouth of a Norwegian or Finn.

Fifteen years earlier or so, she must have driven the local 4-H boys wild. Now she still bulged and receded in all the right places, but she was on the threshold of losing it. In another ten years, she could go to either purely voluptuous or just plain fat, depending. Her expression told me she didn't really care. But like my uncle Fred, she had a glint in her eyes that implied too much energy for a place like this.

"Coffee?" she said, flipping a mug from under the counter.

"Sure."

"Hey, Laurie," came a noise from the booth, "you got other people want coffee, too, you know. Real customers, not some half-assed tourists." The voice was gravelly and lazy, like that of a long-term drunk, and there was no humor in it.

"Any that ever tip?" she said, without looking over.

"We decide to tip you, babe, you'll walk funny for a week." The other hayseed had a younger voice, but no friendlier. He guffawed at his own crude joke. The waitress ignored them and calmly filled my cup.

"If you want to hit one of them upside the head with the coffee pot," I said, "I'll swear it was self-defense."

She gave me a funny, crooked smile. "You won't have to swear to anything. The law around here is like everything else: mostly homemade. But if I need any help burying the bodies, I'll let you know."

"My doctor says I should avoid heavy lifting."

"Yeah, I bet." Her look said she knew all about me, them, and just about everybody else, and had had just about enough of all of us. I've seen that look in some of my clients. It's not exactly the thousand-yard stare, but it's at least five hundred of it. It's not a good sign. "Be right back," she said.

She took her time strolling over to the booth, where she plopped down two green paper checks and splashed coffee into two mugs. The younger cornball got a sly grin on his face and started to reach around to grab her ass, but she moved quickly out of range, put a hand on one hip, and gave him a look that would kill jimson weed to the root. That's a weed they have in the crops around there. I learned about it from a radio commercial, on the way out. A lifelong student, that's me. The guy dropped the grin and stared into his coffee, muttering, and the waitress came back over to me.

"What takes your fancy?" she said, pulling a pencil from behind one ear.

"You want to be careful who you give that line to."

"I am. You want anything on the menu, or not?"

"I was hoping to talk to Rosie."

"I'm not rosy enough for you?" She gave me about a half-second flash of a phony stage smile, all teeth and dimples, and instantly reverted to her expression of studied indifference. I laughed in spite of myself.

"You're probably enough of anything for any man, but I was told Rosie could get me some pecan pie."

"Who told you that?"

"A guy named Numbers Jackson."

She raised both eyebrows. "He's in Redrock."

"That's him."

"Yeah, huh?" She tapped her pencil rhythmically on the order pad and looked at me as if for the first time, sizing me up, deciding something. She suddenly looked tougher than before, and it looked good on her, like a piece of animation that had been missing. "What's your name?" she said.

"Herman." I can't imagine why I didn't tell her "Sam Hill," but I didn't.

"You're kidding, right?"

"Afraid not." More afraid than she could imagine.

"We all have our problems, I guess." She shook her head. "I'm Laura. Rosie left years ago."

"Maybe she got tired of riveter jokes."

"That and a lot of other things. Wait until the others leave, okay? We'll talk. Meanwhile, pick something off the menu, look like you belong here."

"That could be tough."

It was her turn to laugh. "Picking something, or looking like you belong?"

"Either one."

She gave me the crooked smile again, this time with bit of warmth in it. It looked better than the stare. "I know that tune better than you do," she said.

"It shows."

"It ought to. Tell you what: have a fried egg sandwich. It's the cheapest thing on the menu, and even the dumb kid we've got out in the kitchen can't mess it up."

"I had eggs this morning. How about a plain burger?"

"Your funeral. Onions?"

"Absolutely."

"A man after my own heart." Why did I know she would say that? "That comes with French fries or hash browns."

"How about a salad?"

"How about sprouts and hollandaise sauce? Where do you think you are, civilization? The fries aren't too bad."

"Okay, fries, then. If they're no good, you can eat them."

Again the smile. "I can be had, Herman, but I'm not that cheap." I never thought for a minute that she was.

She went up to the pass window, impaled an order slip on a spike, and slapped a little bell. Then she went back through the kitchen door. While she was gone, Homer and Jethro came up to the counter to pay their bill. They glared at the dark porthole for a while, then at me. They were good at glaring. Finally, they left some money on the counter and turned to go. I concentrated on slurping some coffee, which wasn't as good as G. B. Feinstein's, but wasn't bad, either. The older one, with the cheap-booze voice and beer belly, looked like he wanted to start something but couldn't remember how. The younger one did it for him.

"We don't get a whole lot of strangers around here."

"Sounds right to me," I said, without looking up.

"Sounds right to us, too. Better, we don't get any."

"Somehow, I don't think you have to worry about that."

"I gotta spell it out for you? You ain't wanted here. I'm telling you to get out whilst you can still do it under your own power."

"I see." And I looked and did see, all the while thinking, *I absolutely do not need this shit.* The guy fronting me had a lot of muscle under the fat, but he didn't look either quick or smart. His buddy looked as if his chief contribution to any fight would be sitting on people, plus nasty little chores like gouging eyes and spitting on them. Neither one of them was worth messing up my plans over.

"Well, since you're so nice about it," I said, "I'll tell you something, too. You have no idea what you're fucking with here." Of course, neither did I, but this was not the time for that kind of timid thoughts. I slipped half off the stool, planted my feet in an easy intro to a half-stride fighter's stance, and pushed my right hand deep into my pocket. "I'm going to have a hamburger and then I'm going to go. If you want to make that a problem, that's up to you. But I'm never coming back here, and that means I don't care what kind of mess I leave behind for the cops or the ambulance. Think about it for a minute." And I gave them what I hoped was a cold smile.

I closed the hand inside my pocket, as if I had grasped something, and slowly began to bring it back out. Hayseed Junior stuck his finger at me as if he were going to poke it in my chest, but the older guy pulled his arm away. Too bad, in a way. That finger was practically begging to be broken.

"Leave it alone, Ditto," he said. "Come away."

"Aah..."

"It ain't the time. And I ain't backin' you up against some big city street fighter."

"We don't know that he is."

"And we don't know he ain't, neither. Come on, now."

"Oh, fuck it all, anahow." The belligerent one snatched his arm indignantly away and let himself be herded to the door, making a show of refusing to be hurried.

At the door, he turned and said, "She ain't going with you, no ways. She ain't never going with nobody but me."

So that's what it was all about. "That's right," I said. "She isn't." I began to think about how many hours of roaring tractors, bellowing cows, fertilizer commercials, and whining, hard-lard music it took to induce permanent brain damage. However many it was, he'd had a lot more than that.

He glowered at me for a while longer, then got bored with it and stomped out with his pal. I took my hand back out of my pocket, glad that I hadn't been forced to show that it had nothing in it but a pack of smokes, a Zippo lighter, and a lot of lint.

The waitress came back in a few minutes with my food and some utensils. "I made a call," she said.

"I'm happy for you."

"You carry a lot of weight with this Numbers guy."

"We go back a long ways." I salted the burger, put some anemic-looking pickle slices on it, and closed the bun. *How did they manage to make the bun greasy?*

"You must. The word is, don't charge you."

"For the burger?"

"For the pie."

"Oh, that." How could I have forgotten?

"Yeah, that. You like it heavy or light?"

I began to seriously wonder what we were talking about here. "What have you got?" I said.

"I've got a .380 semi-auto, a .357 revolver, and a couple flavors of nine millimeter. Anything else, we have to go someplace to get. It's a ways from here."

Oh, that, indeed. "Give me the three-eighty," I said. "Something that's easy to conceal. If I'm far enough away to need the heavy artillery, I'll run instead of shoot, every time."

"I like that in a man."

"Cowardice?"

"Sense. There's not much of that around these days."

"Seems to me Plato noticed that, too."

"You read a lot of Plato, do you?"

"No, but I thought it sounded more impressive than saying I picked it up from Rocky and Bullwinkle."

"Uh, huh." She did not sound impressed, and when I thought about it, that was just fine with me.

"You want a holster?" she said.

"With a belt clip, if you've got one."

"I've got." She went in the back again and returned with something that really did look like a pie box, heavy white cardboard with tricky fastener tabs.

"You've got a box of shells in there, too," she said, "but only one extra magazine. Also a velcro strap, in case you want to carry it on your ankle. Have fun."

I spared her my standard lecture on guns and fun. She pushed the box across the counter to me, then scribbled on one of her green slips and put that on top. She had charged me $12.85 for pie. With the burger and coffee and taxes, the whole tab came to $20.32. And people think it's cheap to live in small towns. I put a twenty and a five on the counter. She rang it all up on a genuine non-electronic cash register, along with the slips from the two hayseeds. She started to hand me change, but I waved it away, so she shrugged and dropped it into the pocket on her faded pink uniform. Then she poured herself a cup of coffee, came around the counter, and sat down next to me. She helped herself to one of my fries. I concentrated on chewing my burger.

"Take me with you."

I'd been half expecting that, but not this soon and definitely not this straightforward. It served me right, for flirting with her. "No," I said.

"Just like that? Just 'no'?"

"Just like that."

"I'll make it worth your while."

Was she really talking about what it sounded like? If she was from my uncle's world, it was a distinct possibility. His people made and dissolved relationships on just that whimsical a moment, and some of them turned out to be tight and durable. Uncle Fred himself lived for over twenty years with a woman he claimed to have won in a card game. She had never seemed cheap to me, but she never disputed the assertion, either. Whether or not they held each other against the night, I'll never know. In any case, I could hardly judge them. I personally went the route of conventional marriage, and that turned out to be the biggest catastrophe of my then-young life.

I thought about how long it had been since I had touched a woman. Agnes is really like a sister to me, or maybe a buddy, and Deputy Janice is business. And business is business, another irrefutable little lesson from my long apprenticeship. Having a real woman again could be a fine thing. But it was a luxury I couldn't afford right then. It was already too much that she knew my real first name and that I had been to Redrock to see Uncle Fred. If she also saw where I lived, it would be a disaster.

"You're a big girl," I said. "You can leave any time you want, find a man any place you go. What do you need me for?"

"That's easy for you to say. It's not so easy for a woman, you know?"

"No, I don't."

"There are places you can't go unless you at least look like you're with a man. Being alone is like having a sign on your forehead that says 'Victim.'"

"And what makes you think I'm going any of those places?"

"Hey, I give up. Where are you going, anyway?"

"If I'm honest about it, I don't know."

"That's a good place. I can help you find it."

"No." I tried to make it sound more final this time, but it didn't come out that way, so I tried something else.

"You don't know anything about me," I said.

"I know enough."

"Oh, really? For all you know, I have a body in the trunk of my car."

"Better than a bale of hay." She had a point.

"I could be a psycho-sadist, with half the cops in the country looking for me, and a compulsive gambler and woman-hater and a closet vegetarian, to boot."

"You could be, but you're not. You're on the run from something, but you're not an asshole or a loser."

"Is that what you found out from your phone call?"

"No, I figured it out, all by my lonesome. I'm not stupid, Herman."

"I didn't think you were. So what are you doing in a dump like this? You from here, originally?"

"For a while. I ran away when I was sixteen, to the big city. You know, to get the things you can only get in a real city?"

"Including an abortion?"

"You're not stupid, either, are you, Herman? See? I was right about you, from the get-go. Anyway, I kept moving for fifteen years. Good times or bad, I never even thought about coming back here. My asshole of a father died, and I sent a THANK YOU card to the funeral parlor. Then my mom died, too. I came home to bury her, and I got suckered in by the prospect of inheriting this joint, free and clear. It seemed safe, you know? Easy, for a change. Like safe and easy is something you should give a rat's ass about. Now I can't even spit in the owner's eye and walk out. I'm losing my edge, big time. If I don't get out soon, I never will."

"I can see that," I said. "But it's not my problem, and I can't let it be."

"Sure you can. It's simple: when you get your own little problem solved, you're going back to where you come from. You can leave me wherever we happen to be when that happens, no complaints. Meanwhile, we help each other down the road."

"Really? And how are you going to help me, exactly?"

"Can you travel on plastic?"

"Don't have any."

"Bullshit. You have it, but you don't dare use it. That's why Numbers said not to charge you for the heat."

Well, I did say she wasn't stupid, didn't I?

"We can travel on mine," she said. "I've got a lot of it, and the bills all come here, where I'm never coming back, where I want a reason why I can't come back. It'll work, Herman. I don't exactly have a Sunday-school past, but I'm not wanted anywhere."

"Except by the doofus with the bad haircut and the Trans Am."

"Put your finger right on it, didn't you? That should be his problem, entirely. But he's trying hard to make it mine, and sooner or later, he'll do it. When that happens, I'm going to have to kill him, no choice." She turned and studied my face. "You believe that?' she said.

I looked in her eyes and saw about eight hundred yards of stare now, the threshold of the place where consequences don't matter any more. "Yes," I said.

"Much better all around if I'm just not here, wouldn't you say? Come on, Herman, what have you got to lose? Don't you ever need somebody to hold, just to keep away the night?"

I had to admit, she knew which buttons to push. But that didn't make the whole proposition any more sensible. "It's not a good time," I said.

"It's never a good time, unless you make it one."

"I'm sorry. I really am."

"You'll be sorrier when you're a hundred miles down the road, in a world of trouble, and all by yourself."

"Could be, but that's the hand I was dealt."

"You trying to break my heart?"

"See you, Laura."

"You could, but you won't. And that is definitely your loss."

"I'm prepared to believe that."

"And?"

"Goodbye."

"I was wrong; you are a loser." She flung the plate of fries away with an angry flick of dark-enameled nails. They crashed against the kitchen door just before she went back through it for the last time.

I didn't call after her.

Chapter Nine

Travels With Rosie

I chewed on the gristly burger for a while and argued with myself. I had definitely done the right thing, but why did I feel so shitty about it? *Herman, my man, what you feel and what you've got to do are two completely unrelated topics. You learned that a long time ago, remember?* I remembered. *So, why are you still here? Do you really like that burger?* No, I didn't, much. *Then get your sentimental ass out of here.* I picked up my pie box and got.

I hadn't noticed that the café was especially dark, but when I stepped outside, the sunlight hit me like an industrial strength flashbulb. I stopped on the sidewalk and fished in my jacket pocket for my shades. Over by my rented car, I heard the unmistakable noise of the gravel-voiced hick, telling me I wasn't going to get away completely clean, after all.

"There he is, Pud."

"I see him, Ditto."

Well. Not Homer and Jethro, after all, but Pud and Ditto. Very original, these rustic folk.

"Hey, Slick," the fat one again this time, "You're pretty good at sniffing around old Laurie in there. You any good at anything out here?"

I swear, the little one, Ditto, said, "Hee, hee, hee." Gomer Pyle, psychopath. Just what I needed.

"I'm good at leaving," I said. "And that's what I'm going to do, okay?"

"Not with her, you ain't."

With the shades on, I could see that they both had knives, ugly, curved things, too big to have been in their pockets. I wondered if they were called "corn knives." It would be a shame if they weren't. They had gone out to the car to arm themselves, apparently. And along the way, they had run into the waitress. The young goon had her pushed up against my car now, a meaty hand folded around her throat and an ugly knife held against one cheek. The knife didn't worry me so much, but a cop once told me that going for the throat was a very bad sign. On the ground nearby was a small suitcase that I assumed was hers. Not such an easy woman to brush off, after all. Her eyes were wide, but she looked more outraged than afraid. Outraged and determined. And that, I have to admit, made all the difference.

I composed myself and gave them the same smile I had used in the café. Then I turned and walked away from them.

"Hey, where the fuck you think you're going?"

I reached in my pocket again and grabbed my lighter.

"We're talking to you, asshole."

I didn't turn around or pause, refusing to let them show me what they wanted to do to the woman. Instead, I went straight over to the blue Trans Am.

"What in hell does he think he's playing at?"

"Oh, dear, sweet Jesus, no. Not my car!"

There were some grunts and squeals then, and some scuffling noises, but I still didn't turn around. The hay bale was nicely dried out, and it lit like fine kindling. I had been going to start on one end and work my way across, but one spot turned out to be enough. The whole thing went from wisps of white-blue smoke to a full inferno faster than you could say, "Gaw-lee gee, Pud."

When I turned back, the fat man was running towards the Trans Am, eyes bulging and belly bouncing, gravelly voice shouting something incoherent. The younger guy was still back by my car, only now he was lying on the ground in a fetal position. He had blood on his face, which matched a blotch on the waitress' elbow. She stood over and behind him now, fire in her eye, methodically kicking his kidneys and spine. Enough of anything for any man, yes, indeed. Quick and possibly lethal, too. And God help me, I was about to go down the road with her.

I unlocked the rental car and got in. "You coming?" I said. "Or have you got better things to do now?"

"Just one little spot I missed," she said. No need to ask where that might be. I heard a meaty "thunk" and a prolonged, "Aaagh," and then she and her bag were in the car with me and we were gone.

<><><>

Three minutes later, I slowed at a blacktop crossroads and asked her which way the nearest big town was.

"South," she said, "the way we're going, but I don't want…"

I hooked a hard left and put the pedal down.

"This is east," she said.

I nodded. "If the gas tank on that wreck was going to blow, it would have done it by now, and we would have heard it. If it didn't, your two fine friends might come after us for a bit of instant replay. We'll go a direction they won't expect you to pick."

"Nice," she said. "Always a pleasure, dealing with a professional."

"I'm a bondsman."

"Are you, really?"

"For years."

"What a trip. We've only just met, and already you never cease to amaze me."

"There's a lot of that going around."

We drove in silence for a while, and finally I said, "Your name isn't really Laura, is it?"

"That's what they know me as, back there. Your friends at Redrock know me as Rosie. I've had a lot of names over the years. Changing them seems to come naturally to me. Maybe I'm part Gypsy."

"Good Lord, not you, too."

"Not me too, what?"

"Everybody I meet lately seems to have something to do with Gypsies. All my problems keep pointing me back to them, and until a couple days ago, I didn't even know there were any left in the modern world." Or was it a couple of years?

"You want to learn all about them?"

"No, but I'd damn well better."

"Well, then, there's only one place to go: Skokie."

"Is that a place or an adjective?"

"Three fourths of the Gypsies in the country live within ten miles of Skokie, Illinois."

My turn to be amazed. "Why on earth?" I said.

"Beats me, but they do. I learned that from a bartender at a strip jo…um, a place in Chicago where I worked for a while. He wasn't exactly my type"—she made an exaggerated limp-wrist gesture—"but we were friends, and he knew a lot of things, and nobody else ever talked to him. He was sort of a disinherited Gypsy. Or excommunicated, or something like that."

I couldn't think of a thing to say to any of that.

"Didn't I tell you I'd help you find your way?"

"Oh you told me, all right. You have any idea where this Skokie place is?"

"More or less. North of Chicago."

"Then you can more or less drive."

I pulled over onto the gravel shoulder and changed places with her. She adjusted the driver's seat, fastened her harness, and checked the mirrors. Then she peeled off like a stock car driver. All around, a formidable woman, this former prairie flower, gun moll, stripper, café owner, martial arts expert, and God knew what else. "So, what do I call you?" I said.

"Call me Rosie. That's the one I always liked the best."

"Good night, Rosie." I tilted the seat back as far as it would go, pulled my jacket up over my chest and chin, and closed my eyes. Except for the nap in my office after the Proph brought me back, I hadn't had any sleep in the last thirty hours or more, and it was starting to weigh on me. "If you decide to drive into Lake Michigan, wake me up first, will you?"

"Herman?"

I opened my left eye and looked over at her. She had the crooked smile again, this time with wrinkles in the corners of her eyes to match. She was having a good time. *A lunatic fleeing the asylum. Wonderful.*

"I'm unconscious," I said.

"I did good back there, didn't I?" The way she said it, it was a gleeful boast, not a question. I didn't know if she was talking about kicking the hick in the nuts or about getting me to take her along, and I decided not to ask.

"You did good, Rosie." *Do better: let me sleep.*

"You're going to be glad you took me along. I know it."

That made one of us.

"Where do you want to stop for the night?"

"Someplace near an outside phone booth and a terminal where I can get on the Internet," I said. "Other than that, I couldn't care less."

"Sounds like you have a plan."

"It does sound like that, doesn't it?" Sometimes these things just sneak up on you.

The subdued hum of the machine, the road noise, and the gentle breeze from Rosie driving with her window down were better than a hot toddy and a massage. Magic. I felt my consciousness drop like a submarine on a crash dive, and I made no attempt to slow its descent. Somewhere on the way to the bottom, it passed some whales that looked a lot like violins with flippers and tails, and a mermaid that looked a lot like Rosie, but we plunged on past, to the depths that even the light can't penetrate. Somewhere down there, answers were waiting for me. Answers and a real plan. And oblivion. And even if I was wrong about the rest, the oblivion was enough for now.

We stopped at least once for gas and whatever, I think, but it didn't seem worth waking up for. Later I cracked an eye open briefly to see the light dying on a landscape of featureless prairie that probably looked better in the dark anyway. *Land that only a farmer could love,* I thought. *A place where he's got lots of room to park his two-acre, all-in-one rolling factory that Cyrus McCormick would never recognize.* It made me miss the city more than a little kid at summer camp. I had never been to summer camp myself, but I figured I knew the feeling. St. Paul wasn't exactly Detroit or Chicago, but at least it wasn't open flatlands. I drifted back off. After a second stop, I woke slowly to the smell of coffee and garlic, with maybe a touch of tomato paste for counterpoint. I put the seat back up, threw my jacket in the back, and lit a cigarette.

"Do you have to do that?" she said.

"No, but I'm going to." If she had an aversion to smoke, I could find a way to accommodate that. But if she turned out to be a closet do-gooder and health nut, this was going to be a very short-lived partnership. I rolled my window partway down and tasted a bit more of my newfound waking state.

"You have any other nasty habits that I ought to know about?"

"Now's a hell of a time to ask."

"Well, we had other things on our minds, back in New Salem."

"Which you, of course, did nothing to cause."

"Why Herman, whatever are you accusing me of?"

"You seemed to have had a bag packed awfully conveniently."

"Oh, is that all that's bothering you? 'Packed' is the word, all right."

"What does that mean?"

"Have a look, if you want to. It's on the back seat."

I unscrewed two or three of my vertebrae from their sockets, twisting around in the seat, and popped the latches on the old fashioned overnight case. Inside was a leather purse, a lot of loose money, and the three other guns she had described to me back at the café. The revolver looked like a cannon with a handle.

There was also something dark that could have been a ski mask. I didn't even want to think about that.

"Good grief," I said.

"I only took the important stuff," she said. "You can see, it really was a spur-of-the-moment thing. Well, mostly. A marriage of convenience, you could say."

"If that was convenience, I'll pass on the harder parts. And don't even think about using that other word."

"Have it your way. Anyway, I need to do some shopping."

That was one of the things she needed, all right. A good therapist also came to mind. "What's the smell?" I said.

"Dark coffee and pepperoni pizza-flavored egg rolls."

"Classy."

"BP Roadside Gourmet, the sign said. Not the chef's choice, though. He tried to sell me Ding Dongs. Says they don't mess up the steering wheel so much."

"Clean steering wheels are highly overrated. Especially if somebody else is driving." I threw the cigarette out the window and tried an egg roll. It actually wasn't bad. The coffee tasted more like Dow-Corning than Colombian, but it wasn't bad, either. I must have been ready to come back to life. Outside, the prairie was giving way to sodium floodlights and buildings. Better. The outskirts of Chicago, I decided, though it looked less like the threshold of a great metropolis than a compacted bunch of 1950s suburbs. One and two story businesses of no architectural style were jammed together with modest houses just as nondescript. The only way you could tell you were getting close to a major city was that the spaces between them kept getting smaller and the traffic denser and less polite. The chief industries seemed to be auto parts stores and unclaimed freight marts, with an occasional bowling alley or laundromat. If there were any libraries, parks, or public buildings, they were underground. Civilization, like prosperity, never really trickles down very far from its citadels. But there was an undeniable pulse to the streets that quickened as we got closer to the unseen lake and the famous skyline, and it was infectious.

We passed a small strip mall with a row of hotels across from it, and Rosie looked over at me and arched an eyebrow. I pointed at a Kinko's in the middle of the strip. We stopped, and I bought a couple hours on one of their PC terminals.

"Do you need any help with it?" The clerk was decked out in pimples and improbable studs.

"I just need to send and receive some email."

"Email or e-messaging?"

"Is that a trick question?"

"If you have a registered handle, you can do e-messaging, get an instant reply back."

"If I had a handle, I'd be using a CB."

"Gee, I don't know that technology. Sorry."

Sometimes I get very sick of being a dinosaur.

Rosie interrupted us to ask if she could go do some shopping and book us a room for the night.

"Sure," I said. "Where shall I find you?"

"I'll check back here once. If that doesn't work, look for me in the bar of that hotel." She pointed to the fanciest one of the row across the street, one that looked like it had maybe started its life as an Embassy Suites. I took her elbow and moved her aside, out of earshot of the gawking techie, and told her that if they asked her to write down the license number of the car, she should reverse the last two digits.

Her eyebrows tried to merge into a face-wide frown, but they didn't quite meet at the center. "Whatever for?"

"If somebody is checking to see if the car belongs in their parking lot, they'll just assume it was a mistake in writing it down. But if somebody is doing a computer search for the car, they'll come up empty."

The frown changed to a look of open admiration. "In the bar," she said. "Two hours, tops. You can pretend you're picking me up."

"I did that once. I think it was a mistake."

"I'll see what I can do about that." She gave me a kiss on the cheek which I had to admit was rather nice. The techie-type stared in obvious envy and possible astonishment.

"Show me about this e-mess business," I said.

He showed me, and also set me up with a "handle" for the chat sites, in case I felt chatty. I decided to be "Gypsy," but that turned out to be taken already. So was "Hermes," with or without an apostrophe. After several other tries, I settled for being "Numbersman." As if that weren't enough of an ordeal, I also needed an eight-digit or longer password. I picked MI5KGBCIA. If you're going to play at cloak-and-dagger, you might as well go all the way. Besides, I thought I could remember it.

"Can I get messages here after I leave?"

The techie gave me a funny look. "How can you get anything here after you leave, man? That's like spooky. And you said *I* asked trick questions?"

"What I mean is, if I come back here tomorrow and buy some more time, will I be able to get any messages that came in the meantime?"

"Oh, like that. Well, of course. That's the whole point, isn't it? Anything else?"

"Show me where there's an outside public phone."

"What do you want a phone for, if you've got e-messaging?"

"I'm a renaissance man."

"Wow, I don't know that one, either. Is that a Microsoft program?"

<> <> <>

I took the number off a pay phone at the end of the parking lot, in front of a bagel store, and then came back and sat down at the computer. I emailed Agnes first, remembering to add the cute little red envelope that seemed to be the key to all things urgent in her world. My return address, of course, was out of my control, but I could type in a subject title that she would see before she opened the message. I used "Detroit refugee calls home," and typed in the following message:

How's the heat there?

Forward the message to me, here, from the something-Cox

address, the one about the valuable instrument. Then get hold of WTW and give him the number at the bottom of this message. Tell him to call me there every hour on the hour, starting at 9:00 tomorrow morning, until he gets me.

If the bond collateral is no good, tell me so at this address tomorrow at 8:00, when you come in for the day. I will check this site then and again around the middle of the day.

All best

Wandering Boy

I added the number from the pay phone and clicked the mouse on the phony picture of a SEND button. The "collateral" business, of course, referred to the possibility that somebody was looking over Agnes' shoulder when she opened my message, and the pay phone number was therefore compromised. If that happened, I was giving myself a couple hours to set up an alternate one and/or get the hell out of there, since we both knew that Agnes really got into the office at 6:00, not 8:00. Pretty clever, us spooks.

I thought about what to say in the reply to the message about the violin, but I really needed to see it again first. Like Agnes, I don't do video games or surf the web, and I was wondering what to do with the rest of my time on the terminal, when to my wondering eyes a message from Agnes appeared, complete with cute little red envelope. She was working late, apparently. I wondered why.

Hey, Wandering Boy, I've been worried about you.

Lots of heat earlier today, but it's cool and quiet now.

Collateral is good. WTW says he has news to report. I'll give him the phone # as soon as I finish this, plus forward the message you wanted.

Be careful out there. Strange things going on.

Stay away from dark alleys and loose women, ha ha.

I won't ask where you are,

Ag

I decided not to tell her that her advice about loose women was a bit late. I typed in a quick thank you and attaboy note and no sooner had it sent than the forwarded message popped up on my screen, again with the red envelope. Agnes really liked those red envelopes.

mr. jackson

i believe you are in possession of a certain valuable musical instrument that is the rightful property of my family.

i understand that you acquired it in good faith, and i am prepared to reward you handsomely for its return.

can we talk?

Can we talk, indeed. I decided to cut right to the chase.

Re: "certain valuable musical instrument:"

Just how handsomely, exactly?

I presume we're talking about the Amati violin. It is in my possession, but its legal ownership is somewhat unclear at the moment.

That was putting it mildly. If Jimmy Cox skipped out on his next court appearance, it was mine, no question about it. But if he showed up and my bond was released, I was legally obliged to return the violin to a person who was no longer alive. And there was no use asking if she had a will, because she might not have been the real Amy Cox, if there even was a real Amy Cox. Jimmy Cox was supposed to have said he had no sister, but I only knew this from a phony cop who might also sometimes be a phony Jimmy Cox and who might or might not be the person who was arrested for careless Ludding. So whom did it revert to? The guy writing the email? The kid in jail, as I was sure he would be? I decided not to make any promises I might regret.

I might consider selling a Quit-claim deed for my interest in the Amati. Anything else would be premature at this time.

Then, astonished that I hadn't thought of it earlier, I added:

Who the hell are you, anyway?

H. Jackson

Once again, I had nothing to do but wait for a reply that I wasn't likely to get very soon. I thought about what I had just sent to the mysterious person with the instrument-owning family and also about something my Uncle Fred had said to me back at Redrock. Suddenly, I felt an irresistible urge to get to a phone. I called over to my friendly clerk-technician.

"I have to go make a call, okay?"

"You've got time left on the machine."

"That's why I'm telling you. I want it back."

"Oh, I get it. I won't let anybody else use it until you come back. Is that what you mean?"

"That's it." Maybe it has nothing to do with being a dinosaur.

I walked down the strip to a Snyder drug store and bought a phone card, then headed over to the booth by the bagel shop. Agnes tells me at least once a day that I ought to get a cell phone, of course. Since I don't want to hurt her feelings, I mostly pretend I don't hear her. The truth is, I would rather die than have one of those damned electronic leashes stuck on my ear like an alien parasite. That probably makes me some kind of techno-curmudgeon, and if I think about it, I might even like that title. In any case, I headed for the booth.

We must not have been very far into the Chicago metro area yet, because the phone was intact and working. I punched in a number I knew by heart.

Nickel Pete closes his pawn shop for the day anywhere from five to eleven, as the spirit moves him and depending on whether he's made any money yet. But he lives in an apartment above the place, and that's where I called him, letting the phone ring a dozen times before he finally picked up. I said hello, and he recognized my voice, which I found touching.

"You're a lot of damn trouble for the amount of business you bring me, Herman."

"It's nice to talk to you, too, Pete."

"Of course it's nice. That's because I'm not dragging you out of bed in the middle of the night."

"It's not exactly the middle of the night, for most people. Were you really in bed?"

"Would you believe with a hot little redhead who's trying to persuade me to give back her heirloom wedding rings?"

"No."

"No. Well, it was worth a try. With a bowl of popcorn and a dirty video, then. What the hell do you want?"

"You know the Amati violin I left with you?"

"Is this a memory test? Of course I know it. What do you want me to do with it?"

"I don't want you to do anything with it. Just go see if it's still there."

"Believe me, it's there. Fort Knox would kill for the alarm systems I got. If I was broke into, I'd know it."

"Would you take a look, as a favor? And take a flashlight with you. Shine it in the f-holes, see if there's a label."

"Now he not only wants a favor, he wants to tell me my business."

"Indulge me, will you? I'll owe you one."

"Damn right you will. You want to hold on, or should I call you back?"

"I'll hold." A lot of my profession consists of nothing more than waiting for a phone to ring, but I didn't seem to be wired for it just then. I waited through dim background noises of grunts and coughs, doors opening and slamming, and a soundtrack that really might have been from a dirty movie, at that. That, or Pete had a very large cat with serious hairball problems.

He was gone a long time, and I spent it looking around at the parking lot, memorizing the ways in and out and the possible places from which the booth could be watched. It wasn't a bad setup, for a random pick. Easy to spot somebody in the booth, but not so easy to trap him there. I wondered if the bagel shop had a back door. I would find out before I left. I also wondered if they had filet mignon with mushroom caps and bordelaise sauce. The pizza rolls were starting to feel a bit inadequate for the demands of the night.

Finally I heard the clunking sounds of the receiver being bounced off the floor and picked up again, and Pete's wheezing breath.

"I can't figure it out, Herman."

I felt a knot begin to form in my stomach. "What?"

"I swear, nobody's ever pulled anything like this on me before. And mind you, they've tried."

"Will you please just spit it out? Is the violin there or isn't it?"

"Sort of."

"Well, that certainly clears it all up. Sort of. Are you having a senility attack, or are you capable of explaining that to me?" The knot in my stomach somehow got tighter and turned to ice, all at the same time.

"The case is there. The same case we both saw. I'm sure of it. And there's an old violin in it."

"But."

"But when I looked in the f-hole, like you told me?"

"You have to be coaxed for every damn word, don't you? What did you see, termites?"

"I saw a label that says Yamaha."

Pigeon drop.

Chapter Ten

You've Got Mail

I checked out the rear exit of the bagel shop, pretending to be looking for the restroom. I bought half a dozen bagels first, on the theory that regular customers are less likely to be remembered clearly than sneaky-looking idiots who just wander in and look for the back door. Behind the place was a wide gravel service drive and then a steep berm covered with untended weeds and brush. A chain link fence about halfway up would be climbable, but a car couldn't get through it without major damage to itself.

I hiked up as far as the fence and looked over the ridge. Beyond it were several train tracks and then a clutter of warehouses and freight yards. There was an opening in the fence, opposite the end of the mall buildings, overgrown and hard to see from below. I went through it and up to the top, for a better look. In the black sky above, a big airliner suddenly switched on its landing lights and came screaming straight at me, like a fighter jet on a strafing run, only nose-high and with all its flaps and wheels hanging out. It passed over my head in a metallic storm of noise and flashing lights and then was suddenly gone, eager to flatten its tires on the tarmac at Midway or O'Hare.

A thousand yards farther ahead of me, a freeway passed by on elevated pylons, the lights of the cars giving an eerie internal illumination to a linear cloud of exhaust and aerated road grime. Service ladders went up some of the pylons, and twisted paths went away into dark places. All around, a thoroughly nasty landscape. It had complexity, distraction, and chaos. If I had to run, this would be the place to go.

I went back down the hill and walked around the outside of the bagel shop and back towards the main shopping center. The strip was laid out like a big horseshoe, with the bagels on one prong, a store selling dumpy shirts with the label sewn on the outside on the other, and the Kinko's down at the cleat in the middle. I imagined Rosie went someplace else altogether to do her shopping.

Rosie. I thought about what I had told her about the license number on the rented car. Did I really believe all that clandestine crap? If not, why did I make it up? *Because you wanted to impress her.* I did not. Where the hell was that coming from? *Denial is the surest indicator of a lie.* Sometimes I hate being so damn smart.

At least two thirds of the stores were closed for the night, and the parking lot was mostly deserted. A couple of semis were pulled up in the middle of it, the drivers taking a sleep break, and a squad car lazily cruising the perimeter didn't seem to care. I suppose the world always has a lot of cops in the background in public places. Somehow, I never noticed before. Now, I seemed to run into them constantly.

Maybe it was another example of what Uncle Fred used to call "The Green Volvo Syndrome." There isn't a single green Volvo in your neighborhood, the theory goes, until you go out and buy one. Then the whole world is instantly full of the stupid things. It's a morphing thing. Chevrolets and Fords morph into Volvos and ordinary citizens morph into cops. There's an automatic Nobel Prize in physics there, if I could just figure out where to publish my findings.

The short odds were that neither the morphed nor the regular cops would be looking for me here in Almost-Chicago, but I didn't want to count on that assumption. I decided a bold diagonal across the lot was a bit conspicuous, and I walked across the gap between the prongs of the horseshoe instead, where I could stay on the fringe of the light island. I wondered who I would be, if I got asked, and I realized I should have worked that out with Rosie before she went off. "Rosie's husband" didn't sound like a very convincing alias. James Stroud was probably even worse. Herman Jackson was still what most of the stuff in my wallet said, and I decided I had better do something about that. That was as far as my thinking went just then.

The squad car moved even more slowly than I walked, and I made it back to the Kinko's before he managed to get interested in me. But he did seem to be interested in the phone booth I had so recently occupied. He cruised over to it, then got out and had a look at the "instrument," as the former Ma Bell employees insist on calling it. That bothered the hell out of me.

"You got a message," said my friendly techie. He didn't know the half of it. I could hardly wait to see the one that he knew about.

"What's it say?" I said. I wanted to watch the cop a while longer before I went back to the terminal.

"Hey, I wouldn't open your mail. But it makes a little 'ding!' noise for 'Incoming.'"

"Better than a whoosh and then a big boom."

"Huh?"

Talking with young people is so refreshing.

The email message was longer than the first one. Apparently, my mystery man had found my reply stimulating.

mr. jackson

you talk like a lawyer or a confidence man. for your sake i hope you are neither. i do not take well to being toyed with. please do not waste my time with any talk about titles. i know that you have the amati. produce it and i will pay you $50,000, no questions asked. how you account for its disappearance is your problem. i can have cash ready in two business days.

where can we meet to make the exchange?

i am gerald cox.

Well. Not exactly a threatening letter, but close enough. And on the surface, at least, not part of the original scam. If this guy was the equivalent of the bogus "collector" in the classic hustle, he should have offered me more money, for one thing. Enough to be irresistible, but not enough to sound phony. Twenty years worth of inflation on a starting value of sixty thou was about a hundred and sixty or so, by my fast and dirty mental arithmetic. So someplace within about fifteen or twenty of that figure would be the right…

"Ding!" More incoming. Get your head down, soldier. This was from a different address, one I hadn't seen before:

> *The writer calling himself Gerald Cox is a fraud. Do not meet with him, if he suggests it. It could be dangerous.*
>
> *For a price, I can tell you how to get the real Amati back.*
>
> *A friend.*

A friend, was it? Sounded awfully hostile to me. Also awfully convenient. Could the timing of the second message have been a coincidence? I didn't know anybody except the Proph who would think so. I looked out the glass storefront again and saw the cop still over by the pay phone. Then I went back to my newfound technical advisor.

"You seem to know a lot about computers, um"—I snuck a quick look at his employee name tag—"Brian." I lied. He didn't really seem to know what time of day it was, but I wanted some advice, and I figured it couldn't hurt to stroke him a little.

"It's like totally what I do, is all. My parents don't understand that, you know? They actually think I should go to college. They can't see that all the, you know, knowledge and stuff in the world is just right there on your keyboard, waiting to be downloaded."

"Maybe they want you to get some kind of knowledge that doesn't download." Parents get silly ideas like that sometimes.

"They want me to study law. Can you believe that?"

"No way." *You bet I can. They want you in a profession where being brain damaged is not a handicap.*

"I mean, the law is just so totally stupid," he said.

"I think Dickens said something like that, too."

"Is he a hacker?"

"Depends on who you ask." I wasn't going to go down that road.

"Listen," I said, "this stuff I've been getting and sending here is completely secure, right? I mean, nobody can trace it back to this site?"

"Well, yeah. I mean, duh-uuh. That's the whole point, you know?"

"They can trace it back to this place?"

"You said this site, not this place."

"Oh." Isn't semantics fun? "So what about this place?"

"No way."

"And nobody else can read it, either? I mean, without having access to the computer on one end of the message or the other?"

He shook his head. "Not unless they've got a sniffer."

I was afraid he was going to say something like that. I looked out the window and saw the cop leaving the phone booth and going back to his car.

"What's a sniffer?"

"It's like a wiretap, only for computers. But it has to have a dedicated phone line. Too many signals to sort out, otherwise."

"How comforting. And who would have one of these sniffers?"

"Them."

"Them."

"Yeah, you know. Men in Black, the Forces of Evil, aliens, the government, all like that. *Them.*"

"Oh, Them."

"You're making fun of me, aren't you?"

"Perish the thought, Brian. Who else could have a sniffer?"

"Rich people, I guess. And industrial spies. It's illegal for anybody, of course. Even the cops are supposed to get a court order first. But if you've got enough money, you can get any kind of hardware you want."

"And somebody like you to make it work."

He stood a little straighter and smiled around a stud.

"Sure, I could do that."

And if *he* could, the world was full of people who could. And one of them could have definitely asked the local fuzz to check out a phone number. I looked out the store window and saw the squad car leave the phone booth and head straight for us, though still in no hurry. Ahead of him, though, a brownish-red Pontiac stopped at the curb in front of the door.

At first I didn't recognize the blonde at the steering wheel. Rosie was wearing a low-cut white dress and lipstick, and she had her hair pulled back into some kind of roll. She looked five years younger than when we had last talked and a lot cuter, and her crooked smile told me she knew as much. She leaned over to look in the plate glass window, searching. I caught her eye and held up a hand that I hoped said, "Wait right there." Three seconds later, I was getting in the passenger door, ignoring the comments from young Brian that followed me out.

"Kiss me," I said.

"Why, Herman, I thought you'd never…"

"Kiss me like I'm your loving spouse, finally done copying the work he always takes home with him."

"Like this?"

"Mmph." I had been going to say, "Too passionate," but her tongue got in the way. She had a very talented tongue. Quite possibly electric, also, since it definitely activated things far removed from my mouth. I wasn't giving it the attention it deserved, though. Above her shoulder, I could see the squad car slow and hesitate, having to rethink the scenario he had just worked out. This was good. We held the kiss for a while longer, and then I got the rest of the way into the car and buckled my seat belt.

"Now cruise on out of here, nice and smooth and respectable. If that cop stares at you, give him a pretty smile and a wave."

But he didn't. He kept heading for the print shop. "Go out around the end of the mall by the shirt store, and watch your mirror."

"Hey, it was a great kiss for me, too, but you don't have to get all gushy about it."

"Is he following us?"

"No." She watched the mirror for a couple seconds. "Oops, yes, now he is. But not fast. Aren't you going to tell me I look stunning?"

"Actually, you do. How far back?"

"All the way to my irresistible round ass, what do you think?"

"How far back is the cop?"

"Oh, him. Half the length of the parking lot. Thanks for the compliment."

"My pleasure."

She turned by the trendy rag store, and by the time we got to the service drive entrance, the cop still hadn't made the corner behind us. "Turn in here," I said, pointing. "Put on a little speed, but don't spin your wheels. We don't want to leave a lot of dust."

We turned down the service road and accelerated, and we were almost to the next corner, where we could turn again and be out of sight behind the main mall, when the cop swung in behind us and turned on his flashers.

"So much for finesse."

"You want me to lose him?"

"Are you serious?" I asked. "You know what you're doing?"

"Watch me."

"All right, I will."

"Really?"

"Punch it."

She stood on the brakes first, and when the I'm-smarter-than-you-are system wouldn't lock up the wheels, she hit the hand brake.

"Lots of dust," she said, by way of explanation.

"I noticed."

As soon as the brown cloud started to roll around us, she killed the lights and hit the gas, hard, taking the corner around the mall in a power slide and continuing to accelerate out of it. Halfway down the back service drive, the speedometer was passing sixty.

"I don't want to tell you your business," I said, "but for what it's worth, there's a break in that fence up there that a car could get through."

"Where?"

"Right by the back door of the bagel joint."

"Perfect. Hold tight. I think you'll like this."

We flew past the fence opening at seventy-plus. She spotted it and hit the hand brake again, throwing the car into a one-eighty half spin on the gravel.

"More dust," she said. I just nodded and hung on. We came out of our own cloud, slowly and smoothly now, turned up the berm, and went through the fence. Down at the far end of the mall, the way we had just come from, the cop's lights were just starting to emerge from the first dust cloud, slowly, tentatively. Before he was clear of it, we were gone, over the crest. In another world. Literally vanished in a cloud of dust. I was impressed.

The back side of the berm was less impressive. You wouldn't exactly call it a drivable surface, but the fact that it was downhill made it easier to jolt over the rocks and leap the chasms. The fact that it wasn't my own car whose undercarriage we were destroying didn't hurt my feelings any, either. I just hoped we didn't trip any air bags.

At the bottom was another service road, this one paved with cinders, that paralleled the railroad tracks. Rosie followed it for a quarter mile or so, until we came to a sort of crossing, and then we went over a bunch of tracks and down into the industrial backwaters. We were well out of sight of the mall now, even from the top of the berm, and she put the headlights back on and settled into an easy twenty-five. I toggled down my window and listened for sirens. Nothing. Just distant freeway noise and an occasional airplane.

"Slick," I said.

"Wow, an unsolicited compliment. Thank you. I had a lot of practice as a kid, chasing jackrabbits over plowed fields in a pickup."

"Ever catch any?"

"Of course not. Why would I want to catch a jackrabbit?"

Ask a silly question.

"If we want to get clear of this area in a hurry," she said, "we could go like a bat between two sets of train tracks." She obviously liked the idea a lot.

"Until we come to a bridge or a switch block."

"Fuss, fuss. What's a chase without risks?"

"A successful escape."

"You know, you really ought to learn to lighten up once in a while, Herman." Her shoulders slumped and she gave an exaggerated sigh. "Okay. So what's our plan?"

"Hide someplace in this area for a few hours, until our cop and all the friends he's calling right now get some other things to think about besides us."

"Pretty daring. You see a place you like?"

"Not yet. Cruise a bit." Another jetliner popped out of the sky with a full array of lights, and a block or so away, I saw a flash of what I wanted. "That way," I said, and she turned into the wake of the jet.

"Who are we, by the way?"

"I said I'd be your guide, not your shrink. If you're going to do identity crisis, you're on your own."

"I mean who are we if we get asked, like by a cop or a desk clerk, okay?"

"We don't talk to cops. Shoot the bastards on sight." She took both hands off the wheel and pantomimed mowing down the blue hordes with a machine gun.

"Will you please sober up?"

"Oh, all right. I don't know what to tell the cops, okay? As far as the hotel is concerned, I'm Ms. Rosemary Wapczech, and you're none of their damn business."

"Gee, for some reason, I thought it would be O'Grady."

"Nope, Rosie the Polack. Sorry. You want it to be O'Grady?"

"For the hotel, I want it to be whatever is on your plastic. But the none-of-their-damned business is no good. They might decide you're a hooker and toss you out for the sake of their fine reputation."

"Oh come on, Herman. Do I look like a hooker?"

"The classier ones are hard to tell from real women, you know."

"Based on your vast experience."

"Some of my best customers." Actually, my experience was that the high-tone prostitutes—the society women who got their thrills with a little role-playing and a little walk on the wild side, or the spoiled college girls who didn't want to wait to cash in on the good life, or even the expensive call girls with their remarkable beauty and penthouse condos and silk-suited lawyers—were among my worst customers. They would stiff me, any chance they got. The real, hard-working street walkers, on the other hand, the ones with too much makeup and too little of everything else, including looks and brains, tended to be rock-solid reliable. I think it has something to do with honor and dignity being more valuable to the people who don't normally get any of the stuff. I don't have it all worked out yet. And I didn't try to tell Rosie about it.

"For the hotel staff, I'll be Herman—what is it, again?"

"Wapczech. It's easy to remember: just think, 'Italian bank draft.' But you don't have any ID."

"They won't ask, as long as we're using your credit cards. For the cops, though, we'll need something else. I have a sort of printing press in my briefcase. Maybe we'll cook something up when we get to settle down for a bit."

"Maybe, huh? Meanwhile, maybe we can just be who we are, and you can be taking me back home for jumping bail."

I thought about it for a minute. "You know, that's actually not bad. If they have a bulletin on me, we would have to reverse the roles, but it might still work. It would be even better if we had some handcuffs."

"I have some in my purse."

"You're kidding. Why would you…"

"Is that where you want to park?"

"That's it." *Handcuffs?*

We picked a spot in a steel recycling yard, where a lot of old cars were massed together, waiting to be crushed into bales and then fed into a blast furnace. I picked the padlock on the fence with a paper clip from Kinko's. After we were inside and re-locked, I took off our wheel covers and license plates and put them in the trunk, stuck a cardboard placard from another car on the windshield, and kicked a little extra dirt on the front end. Then we backed in between two other cars, so close on each side that our doors couldn't be opened. More to the point, it was also too close for anybody looking us over to walk up to the side of the car. It would do, if anything would.

"Snug," said Rosie.

"Inconspicuous, anyway. Tilt your seat back, so our heads don't stick up above the dash."

"Comfy. Can we call room service now?"

"I have to admit, that sounds good. I have some bagels, if you're starving."

"Hey, yeah? I have a bottle of champagne and some fancy chocolate-covered black cherries."

By now, I knew better than to ask if she was kidding, and I laughed instead. "You're just a bundle of surprises, Rosie."

"I am, aren't I? I want you to realize, by the way, that I booked us a deluxe suite at the Crown Regal Inn, with a Jacuzzi and a kitchenette."

"You want me to feel guilty?"

"Very, very guilty. Or disappointed, at the least."

"I can handle both of those."

"Anyway, I could see you were going to be a hard sell, so I picked up some goodies. I figured if I can't get laid, at least I can get high."

If I'd been eating a bagel, I'd have choked on it. Finally I managed to say, "You're going to get high on chocolate cherries?"

"You take your pleasure where you find it, Herman."

You do indeed, don't you? "Have a bagel, Rosie." I passed the bag over to her.

"Delighted, Herman. Have a swig of champagne. You have to open it, though. I'm terrible with those things. Also, I don't want to stain my new dress. That's okay, isn't it?"

"Why would you need my permission not to stain your dress?"

"Just thought I'd ask." With that, she leaned forward to undo her zipper, then slipped the dress over her head and placed it neatly in the back seat. "I didn't have time to shop for any underwear," she said.

I found myself recalling G. B. Feinstein's line about fine curves: *A subtle variation on a timeless theme.* Hers weren't all that subtle, maybe, but they were definitely fine.

"You are…"

"'Irrepressible' is the word that I always liked."

"'Sneaky,' is what I was going to say."

"That, too." She insinuated an arm around the back of my neck, and I didn't seem to do anything to stop her.

"You know, I never…" I began.

"No, you didn't. And you don't have to."

I was talking about promises. I hoped she was, too, since…

"You know why I never ran down any jackrabbits?"

"Um. Because you're too kindhearted?"

"Because I prefer the ambush."

She did good ambush. I have to say, though, handcuffs are not as much fun as people generally suppose. By the time we got around to the champagne, it was warm, and it exploded all over hell. But we didn't get any on our clothes.

Chapter Eleven

Love Among the Ruins

"Are you awake, Herman?"

"I am, but I'm in the middle of an intense intellectual exercise." I pulled my coat back up over her shoulder, where she had shaken it off in her sleep, and she snuggled a bit closer, making my left arm, if possible, even more numb. I did not look forward to the time when it quit being numb.

"Trying to figure out how you wound up sleeping in the middle of a junkyard with a strange woman?"

"No, I'm trying to decide which is more boring, the ceiling in a dentist's office or the head liner in this car."

"I thought a headliner was an overpaid performer."

"It's also the upholstery they put on the bottom of a car roof."

She rolled partway over and looked up. "You're right; that's pretty boring. Does it win?"

"It's a tough call. My dentist has artsy pictures on his ceiling, but the hygienist doesn't wrap her leg around my waist."

"That's why they need the pictures." She flexed the aforementioned limb a bit for emphasis and added an arm to the gesture, and the phrase *holding against the night* flashed into my mind. Maybe the holding thing is like the green Volvo: it only shows up when you're not looking for it. But my mind jumped just as quickly to a vision of a murderous black LTD, and the moment was suddenly gone.

"Do you have a watch, Rosie?"

"Don't you?"

"I do, but I no longer have the arm it was attached to."

She sat up, picked up my dead arm, squinted at the wrist, and let it flop back down. The arm woke up just enough to promise me a lifetime of agony.

"Three-thirty," she said. "You want to leave?"

"Give it another half hour. In a lot of towns, cops change their shifts at four. We'll slip out in the transition time."

She stretched and grimaced. "I'd suggest something very nifty to do with that half hour, but I think my back is broken."

"That's because you've been sleeping on top of a hand brake and a shifting lever."

"Tell me about it. Your arm helped some, though."

"I'm glad you feel that way. I'm thinking of having it amputated. Do we have any champagne left?"

She rolled back over to the driver's seat with a few appropriate groans, grabbed the bottle from under the brake pedal, and shook it.

"A little," she said. She took a swig and passed it over to me. "Also one bagel. You want?"

"Breakfast of champions," I said. "But I'll share."

She broke the bagel in two and handed me half, and we listened to our jaws work for a while.

"So, why are you on the run, Herman?"

"I bopped a cop."

"That doesn't sound so bad."

"Put that way, it doesn't, does it? I bopped a cop who was trying to abduct me. He's also trying to pin a murder on me."

"That sounds worse. So you gave him some more ammunition, by running."

"That I did. Seemed like the thing to do at the time. Still does, for that matter. Are there any more cherries?"

"If there are, they're all in the cracks between the seats." She made a "gimme" gesture, and I passed the bottle back to her.

"I thought I was the impulsive one here," she said. "Why didn't you just stay where you were and rat this guy out?" She tipped back her head to drain the bottle, making a lovely line that started at her chin and swooped down, graceful and unbroken, all the way to the punctuation of her nipples. I made a heroic effort to return to my other train of thought.

"I can't do that, exactly."

"Then do it not exactly. Use a go-between. You want me to do it for you? While I'm at it, I'll accuse him of rape. You're staring, by the way."

"You don't have any evidence. And of course I'm staring. Don't you want me to?"

"Sure I do. I have plenty of evidence of sex. Beat me up some, and then I'll have a rape case, too."

"I wouldn't do that, Rosie."

"You're not supposed to enjoy it."

"Staring?"

"No, beating me up. It's okay to enjoy staring."

"You're crazy, you know that?" I gave her a very brotherly kiss on the end of her nose.

"That's me, all right."

"What happened to admiring good sense?"

"I admire that in you, not in me. Any time I completely quit being crazy, I feel dead."

"You definitely don't look dead."

"Well, I was. Very dead. People like you can be sane and logical and practical without being dead, but I'm not wired that way. That's why we're a natural pair."

"Oh, now we're a natural pair, no less. Where are you going with that?"

"Not where you think. Tell me why you can't rat out this cop, directly or indirectly."

"Because I can't have people looking into my business too deeply."

"Too many connections?"

"Too much history."

"That damn stuff." She tried to throw the empty bottle out the window, but it bounced off the junker next to us and came back. It bounced around the steering wheel for a while, until she caught it by the neck. "We all get that, don't we? But I thought a bail bondsman had to have a clean record."

"They do. And I do. But if you look back enough years, you'll come to a blank page. I can't have people trying to fill that page. Sooner or later they'll find an open arrest warrant. It doesn't have my name on it, but the file attached to it has my prints. That's why I can't ever go back to Detroit."

"Maybe the statute of limitations has run out."

"There is no statute of limitations on murder."

"Wow." She threw the bottle again, this time reaching an arm out the window to toss it backwards over the roof. It landed someplace behind us with a hollow "plonk" sound and stayed put. "You're wanted for a lot of murders, for such a sensible type. Some people would say you hang with the wrong crowd."

"Be careful whom you malign."

She laughed. I was starting to like that laugh. "Got me," she said. "I want you to know, though, that you were wrong about the abortion."

"What are you talking about?"

"Back at the café, you said I went away to Chicago for an abortion."

I had forgotten it almost as soon as I said it. It's a common enough reason for a young girl to go running off to the big city, especially if she's not otherwise stupid.

"It was a guess, that's all. But I didn't attach any..."

"You were wrong." The laugh and the smile were gone now, and she stared intently into my eyes.

"Okay," I said

"Don't humor me, Herman. I'm serious."

"I said, 'okay.'" I didn't back away from the stare.

She turned away first, and in the glow from the yard lights, I thought her cheek looked wet. "Tell me about the Gypsies," she said.

It seemed like a good idea to change the subject, so I told her the salient points, and I hardly lied about any of them. By the time I had finished, it was after four.

"You need to see my friendly bartender," she said.

"This time of night?"

"Trust me."

I did. We put our clothes on, put the car back together, and headed into the city.

Someplace south of the Loop, we parked at the curb on a narrow street where you wouldn't want to walk after dark alone and unarmed. Maybe not in the daylight, either. Rosie confirmed that impression by putting a nine-millimeter in her purse before we got out of the car, and I took the hint and pocketed my new three-eighty. We locked the car and headed out, and I felt like John Paul Jones, telling the Congress, "Give me a fast ship, for I intend to take her in harm's way." So of course, they gave him an under-gunned, worn out tub that steered like a lumber barge with the anchor dragging. He made history with it. I wasn't feeling that lucky.

"The street looks deserted," I said. "Are you sure this is going to work?"

"They shut off the lights and pretend they're closed at two," she said, "but the show goes on all day and all night. After hours, you just have to go in the back way and don't act like a cop or a social worker. It's actually the safest time. No rough crowds, just hardcore drunken oglers and the occasional pimp who's trying to recruit."

"Sounds wonderful."

"Nothing around here is wonderful. But if my Gypsy friend still works here, this would be his usual shift."

With the neon signs off, the street barely had enough light to navigate by. Marquees with names like *The Bronze Beaver*, *Sex City*, and *Hooter Heaven* were all totally dark, as were the smaller banner-panels with their understated headlines like,

"Real, Nude, Naked, Live Girls, On Stage!!!" That about covered all the possibilities, I guessed. A few glassed-in stage pictures on the walls were still lit, like windows in the night. The photos looked ancient and yellowed, the girls in them, underaged and prematurely tough. They had names like Crystal Bryte, Ginger Snatch, and Betty Boobs. We walked past the front of a place called the New Lost City and turned into a narrow alley, by a picture of a blonde. It was a three-quarter rear shot, fully nude, with the poser looking over her shoulder at the camera. She had a splayed handprint painted on her ass in red. The name scrolled across the photo was "Third Hand Rose." I started to do a double take, but Rosie pulled me away, saying, "You'll never know."

Halfway down the alley, there was a door with a single light-bulb above it and a sign that said SERVICE. I bet.

"What now? Do we peek in a little door and say, 'Joe sent me'?"

"Nothing that fancy. We just walk in, and if we look like trouble, somebody throws us out again. If not, they collect a cover charge. Funny you should say that, though. Joe is the guy we're going to see."

The door was one of those metal-clad bombproof jobs that weighed about half a ton, but it swung away easily enough. We went into a blue-lit corridor, passed some restrooms and empty booze cases, and emerged into a large club room. If it had a decor, it was too dark to tell. Dark enough for the patrons to play with themselves or each other, I guessed, while somebody like Crystal Bryte did her best to inspire them. Mostly, what it had was space. It had a long, glossy bar on one wall that was lit, and a large stage with a runway and a couple of brass fire poles that were bathed in hot red and orange floods.

Some kind of grinding R&B tune was blaring on the PA system, while a young woman on the runway was doing some grinding of her own, getting a lot of mileage out of her ample hips. She was peeling off pieces of wispy costume and tossing them to three middle-aged business types at a front table. Even in the colored light, she looked ghostly pale, and I decided she used a lot of white body powder, accented by very dark eye makeup and lipstick, for a sort of vampire look. Her customers looked more like real vampires. Not pale, but definitely hungry, though a few of them looked barely conscious. Now and then, she would do a gyrating squat by a ringside table, and some of them would get up and stuff money into her g-string.

"She's running out of places to stick that stuff," I said.

"She'll make a pass around the far end of the runway and hand it off to somebody behind the curtain pretty soon," said Rosie. "Then she'll come back and give them a little reward. She'll toss the g-string and hump up to the brass pole a bit. If she likes them, she might even let one of them cop a pinch or a feel."

"Whaddaya, tourists? Out slumming?" The voice was sand-paper basso, and I turned around to see a figure that would have blotted out the sky, if there had been any sky. I thought of asking if his name was Joe, but I wasn't sure I wanted it to be.

Rosie took the lead. "My husband's bored, thinks I should learn some new moves."

"Yeah? Well, you wanna watch, you gotta sit down and pay, like everybody else. You gotta buy a drink, too."

"Okay," I said. "Anyplace? How about at the bar?"

"You too cheap to tip the waitress? Don't matter. You still gotta pay the cover. Twenty bucks."

I reached for my wallet.

"Apiece," said the monster. Rosie gave me a frown, but I couldn't tell if it meant the bouncer was lying or that I shouldn't make trouble.

"That's crap," I said, "and we both know it. Tell you what, though: how about if I give you fifty and I don't see you any more?"

"That'll work." It was hard to tell in that light and with his face so high up, but I think he smiled. "Don't be makin' no trouble for the artistes, though, or I'll be on you like holy on the Pope."

"Hey, you said it first—we're just out slumming."

"Yeah, whatever. Just don't say you wasn't told." He moved off into a dark cave somewhere, pausing on his way to whisper in my ear. Up on the stage, the writhing vampiress had ditched her wad of bills, just as Rosie had predicted, and she was working herself up to a finale. I pried my eyes away long enough to look over at the bar, which was being tended by a short, dark guy with a white shirt, black bow tie, and sleeve garters. He had a wedge-shaped face, sort of like Stroud, the phony detective, with a pencil moustache and slicked-back hair. His eyes seemed too big for the rest of his head, and he looked sort of fidgety, as if he were wired too tight for the job. Kevin Kline, trying to do a low-key role.

"Is that our man?"

"That's Joe, all right. I caught his eye when we came in. If we sit down, he'll come over. What did the bouncer say to you?"

"Tell you later." I fondled a chair in the dark to make sure it didn't already have anybody on it, then motioned to her to sit.

"Tell me now," she said.

I patted down another chair for myself and sat down opposite her. "Here comes our waitress."

The waitress looked young and out of place, not sexy enough to be up on the stage or tough enough to be down on the floor, and definitely not comfortable with the skimpy uniform of tight, shiny short-shorts and an abbreviated leather vest with no blouse under it. Susie Sorority, trying to work her way through Sociology 101 at some community college. She took our orders and fled.

"She didn't seem to recognize you," I said.

"She's not an old-timer."

"Doesn't look like she's about to become one, either."

"That's for sure. What did the bouncer say to you?"

"You won't like it."

"Tell me, already."

"He was warning me. He thinks you're a cop. Or a decoy."

"Why would he think that?"

"Because you accessorize your sexy cocktail dress with shoes that have rubber soles and arch supports."

"That asshole! I'll kill him."

"Hey, he's just giving a tip to another *guy*."

"If he'd shut up, you might not have noticed."

"You're right, I wouldn't have." And wouldn't have cared, if I had.

"I'll kill him, that's all." She drummed her fingers on the table and glowered.

I'll never understand what some people take seriously. While Rosie fumed, the bartender at the far wall put a couple of drinks on a tray, waved the nervous waitress away, and headed over to our table with them himself. When he got close, he started talking to Rosie's back.

"Looks like some people just don't know when they're well off. That *is* you, isn't it, Lisa?"

Lisa? Rosie turned in her chair and said, "Hey, Joe. How've you been?" Well, she did tell me she had used a lot of names.

"I've been here," he said. "What else do you have to know? Been down so long, it looks like up to me. Who's your friend?"

"He's good people, Joe. He rescued me from a fate worse than death. Joe Patello, this is Howard Jacobson."

God, it was a compulsion with her. I held out my hand and said I was happy to meet him.

"No offense, Mr. Jacobson, but I don't shake hands. It's a hygiene thing. It's also not a good idea if I look like I'm getting too friendly with the customers. Believe me, you do not want to get thrown out of here."

"I heard that," I said, and took my hand back. Joe put the drinks down in front of us, collected another wad of money from me, and sat down next to Rosie. He did not exactly have the attitude of an old friend.

"What brings you back to the No Lost Titties, Lisa? I assume you're not here to audition."

"Howard here needs some information about Gypsies, and you're the only one I know."

"Does he now? Why? Is he a cop?"

"No," I said.

"A victim, then. Looking for some payback?"

"Why do you say that?"

"Because only cops and victims have any interest in Gypsies. And they have no interest at all in you."

"Are you sure?" I said. "Maybe I'm a writer. Maybe I'm about to make you rich and famous."

"If I believed that, which I do not for a minute, it would move you from uninteresting to unwelcome. We may be the only people left in America who don't want that."

"Getting rich?"

"Getting famous. Having our culture strip-mined for some half-assed book or movie."

"I'm not a writer. That was just a 'maybe.'"

"Maybe you should tell me what you really do for a living, before I get totally pissed."

"I'm a bail bondsman."

He sat back for a moment, looking stunned, as if I had just changed the rules and he needed to think up a new game plan.

"I haven't needed a bondsman for a long time," he said, "but that could make you very interesting to the *familya* or the *kumpania*. Maybe even the *rom baro*. But I don't have their ear anymore, so I can't help you."

"Ro...I mean Lisa, said you were excommunicated, or something."

He smiled for the first time, showing a row of teeth that would make my dentist, the one with the ceiling-pictures, proud. "Is that what she called it? It should be so easy. I'm *marime*, is what I am. For your *Gadje* ears, that means unclean."

"*Gadje* just means us," said Rosie. "It's not an insult."

"Depends on your point of view," said Joe.

"Maybe I can help you." I had no idea how, but it seemed like a good thing to say.

"You?" He gave what could have been a laugh or a snort. "That would be like a coal miner offering to clean your linens. Nobody can help me. Our court, the *kris*, has found me *marime*, and there's no getting rid of that, ever. Are you from a farm background?"

"No," I said.

"Yes," said Rosie. "As far from it as I can get."

"I'll tell you a little rural humor. It's not the sort of thing a good Gypsy would tell, but since I'm unclean anyway, it can't matter much. You can stick a few bricks together with some mortar, the saying goes, but that doesn't make you a mason. And you can pound a few nails, but that doesn't make you a carpenter. But get caught in the barnyard with your pants down just once, and you're a pig fucker for the rest of your life."

"That's very colorful," I said. "I hadn't heard that before. Is that what happened to you?"

"Worse than that. The pig I got caught with—and all *Gadje* are pigs—was a man."

"Am I supposed to blush now? This is almost the end of the twentieth century, already."

"Not in the *familya*, it isn't. Probably never will be. Gypsy society has the most traditional, absolute moral code in the world."

I thought about it for a minute. Rosie was playing with her swizzle stick, looking bored. She had apparently heard it all before, but it was news to me.

"Nothing personal," I said, "but everybody I talk to says Gypsies are a bunch of…"

"Thieves, liars, con artists and cheats," he said. "All true. And we're very good at it. But that's all."

"Excuse me?" *Isn't that enough?*

"In all other things, we are the most moral people who ever lived." I must have looked skeptical, because he went on. "I'll tell you a story, Mr. non-writer. It goes back to the year zero."

"As in the Garden of Eden?"

"Not such a nice place, and not that far back. Think 'Roman calendar.' Originally, the Gypsies were blacksmiths. One day some Roman soldiers came to a Gypsy blacksmith and ordered him to make four nails, for the crucifixion of Christ the next day. He didn't know who Christ was, but you can bet he made the nails. You didn't argue with the Romans back then." He leaned forward.

"But one of the nails kept glowing, long after it was out of the hot forge. That night, an angel came to the blacksmith and told him that the glowing nail was meant to be driven into the heart of Jesus. That was just too damn much of an atrocity, even for what was supposed to be an atrocity. So she told him to steal the nail and run away, which he did. Later, he was on the road, wondering what to do next, when the angel came to him again. From then on, the angel said, his people would always be nomads, without a land to call their own. But because of his service, they would always be free to steal whatever they wanted. And they would always be lucky at stealing."

"But in everything else, they were super-moral."

"Well, sure. I mean, what would you be like if one of your ancestors had worked for an angel?"

I'd probably be shopping for an asylum. "That's quite a story."

"It's our touchstone: who we are and what we do."

"Do you also do murder?"

"Never. Weren't you paying attention to what I just said?"

"One of your people was murdered outside my place of business the day before yesterday. I'm trying to find out why."

"How do you know he was one of us?"

"She. Because she was working the 'old fiddle' scam."

"Anybody could do that. It's probably been around for longer than fiddles. Used to be the 'old lyre' scam. Greeks did it to Persians."

"She was using a phony identity. She also had a brother who has a dozen identities that he carries around in a briefcase, and a cop called him a Rom. Now he claims he never heard of her. And she switched the violins, smoother than I can believe."

He pulled at his chin and took a deep breath, pondering. "The identity shuffle would fit. The CIA doesn't have any secrets as well kept as the true, birth name of a Gypsy. But switching the fiddle is all wrong. The whole point of the con is to leave the pigeon with the object he thought he wanted. Otherwise, it's an egg without salt, if you get my meaning."

"It was a variation," I said. "She had to get the original back, because it really was very valuable. It was an old Amati."

Rosie still looked bored and restless, but Joe, if that was really his name here in the House of Aliases, was suddenly looking intensely alert.

"The Wolf Amati?" he said.

I'd never heard that name before, but candor didn't seem to be the order of the night.

"Yes," I said.

"Holy Mother of God. Could it really be?" He sat back on his chair and looked at the ceiling. "You wouldn't be trying to run a scam on me now, would you, Mr. J.?"

"Hey, I'm not the one whose ancestor stole a nail." As far as I knew.

He looked at the black ceiling for another moment, then jerked back forward, stood, and walked briskly away. "Wait here," he said over his shoulder.

"Sure," I said to his empty chair. To Rosie, I said, "Nice fellow."

"Believe it or not, he was being nice. His people take great pride in being rude." But she wasn't looking at me as she said it. She was now paying attention to the stage, where a new dancer had replaced Miss Blood Loss. This one was taller as well as curvier than the first, and she had short, thick black hair that she wore like a helmet. Prince Valiant's sister, maybe.

She did a slow, sinuous routine, and she shed her upper costume almost immediately, showing off the fact that her ample breasts did not need any external support. She kept her cavalier boots, g-string, and pasties, but they didn't matter much. She had one of those bodies that implies even more nudity than it shows. My Uncle Fred would have said, "She's got a lot of features, is the thing. And not all of them are shaped quite the way you expected, so you got to stare a lot."

So I did. And to my surprise, she stared back, completely ignoring the rest of the audience, which was now hooting and grunting for her attention. She did a series of torso thrusts that started at the ankles and rippled up through her whole body like a wave, all the while holding eye contact, then pulled off the pasties, one at a time. I thought I could hear a tearing sound, like a bandage being ripped off, and I wondered if that was a way of staging a nipple erection. I was going to ask Rosie, but when I looked over at her, she was positively radiating disapproval. Before I could ask her why, the dancer got our attention again by throwing the pasties on our table.

A drunk at another table yelled, "She wants your bod, guy."

"Wrong," shouted another one. "What she wants is his bankroll."

"With her, same thing," said the first. "Trush me, I know."

"Why me?" I said to Rosie. "Why doesn't she play to the guy who yelled? Or somebody else who doesn't have a woman with him?"

The dancer was down on the edge of the apron now, nearly doing the splits on her knees, and thrusting her breasts at me as if I were a gravity well. Rosie picked up a pastie from the table and threw it on the floor, glaring at the stage.

"She thinks you're safe, figures I won't let you attack her. But that's just the cover reason. What she really wants…"

Joe was back suddenly, with a piece of paper that he stuck into my shirt pocket without waiting for me to reach for it.

"Go to that address tomorrow after ten," he said. "That's the *vista officia*, the check-in place for all the Yugoslav Rom. If you say you know where the Wolf Amati is—and don't tell me if you really do know or not—the *rom baro* might see you. He'll know I sent you, but don't say it. Don't say my name to him at all. And don't ask for him, either, just wait for him to appear. Pretend you're a customer."

"Do I tell him about the woman who was killed?"

"If he gives you coffee, look to see if the cup is chipped. If it isn't, then he likes you and he'll talk to you for a while without any profit. You can tell him about the woman if you want to. If the cup is chipped, you're wasting your time, no matter what you say. If Lisa goes along, she should wear a long skirt. And she should keep absolutely quiet. If she doesn't, all you'll accomplish is dropping some money, which you should figure on doing in any case."

"I have to pay for information?"

"No, you have to pay for being a *Gadje*. No matter what, you do that. But if you act right, you might get beyond that."

"Sounds like a sucker game."

"It is what it is. And that's as much as I can do for you. I shouldn't be saying this to a *Gadje*, but Lisa's an old friend: Good luck to both of you." I stifled the impulse to shake his hand, and he left as abruptly as he had come.

Up on the stage, the curvaceous Dane was again writhing in our direction, making come-hither gestures at me. Rosie picked up the second pastie and threw it at her, which prompted a look of mock indignation and amusement.

"Let's get out of here," she said.

"Okay, but what were…"

"Now."

The dancer threw a pout at Rosie and a kiss at me. I mouthed a silent "ciao" at her, waved, and followed Rosie back out into the night.

<>‹›‹›

Walking back to the car, I said, "You were about to tell me something else about the dancer, when Joe interrupted."

"Was I? I forget."

"No, you don't."

"I was mad. You don't want to hear it."

"Yes, I do."

"I was going to say she was trying to take you away from me."

"Are you serious?"

"Believe it. She wanted it bad. As bad as she wanted to spite me."

"Why would she want that?"

"Because she's a mean, hateful little bitch."

"Nuh-uh. Not good enough."

She slowed her pace, finally, and looked down at her ratted-on, rubber-soled shoes.

"She was telling me I'm not the star anymore, okay? And as lousy as that life was, it still hurts to be told I'm a has-been. But you wouldn't know about that, would you?"

As a matter of fact, I would.

Chapter Twelve

A Death in the Familyia

"This location is compromised. I can't take a call here after this one." I didn't say hello or my name. I figured Wide Track Wilkie would know nobody else would be answering a pay phone at six in the morning. And by now, he would have taken the trouble to find out that it was a pay phone

"You want I should hang up now?"

"No," I said. "I don't know that we're being tapped, but a cop came by the booth last night and looked at the phone."

"Checking the number against the listed location?"

"That's the way I figure it. Checking on behalf of a fellow officer in another state, maybe. So I can't be seen here again. If he doesn't come back, somebody else will."

"Got you. Can you take down a number?"

"Shoot."

He gave me a number, and I wrote it on the piece of paper that Joe the Gypsy had stuffed in my pocket. "If you wind up ending this call in a hell of a hurry," he said, "I'll wait for you to call me there in ten minutes."

"Good." I tried to remember my underworld protocol for talk on open phone lines. "Ten minutes" either meant one hour, since it had a one and a zero, or it meant ten o'clock, for the same reason, or it meant the same time, one day from then. Maybe it meant all three. Hell, maybe it even meant ten minutes. Shit.

I was out of practice at this fugitive stuff. And I had already violated the first rule: Never make contact with your old life.

I looked over the parking lot. The two semis were still parked where they had been the night before, their windshields glistening with heavy dew in the predawn light. Down by the other end of the mall, an old junker Toyota had the same covering, marking it for somebody's humble go-to-work vehicle that decided it had gone enough, thank you. In the center of the shopping strip, a step van was unloading something into the Kinko's, where the computer had found no new email for me that day. If my phone booth really was blown, Agnes didn't know it yet. At least, the receiver didn't have a bug in it, though. I checked, as well as I knew how. And the parking lot looked serene enough.

"What have you got for me?" I said.

"First off, I know you told me to strictly work on the woman, but you ought to know we could shift to her little brother now."

"You said you couldn't do PI work." Openly, anyway.

"Don't have to. He's a skip now."

"How can he be? His case won't come up for weeks yet."

"Yeah, and he won't be there for it. He's busy being dead. At least, if he's the same guy who was impersonating the detective, he is. Has a nice stainless steel drawer, right next to the sister he claims he never heard of."

"You saw him?"

"In the flesh. Which was not in very good shape, I might add. He's a John Doe at the moment. I didn't offer to identify him, figured the CIC will match his prints pretty soon."

"How the hell did you get into the morgue?"

"I pretended to be dead, okay?"

"Must have been a hell of an act."

"Hey, I don't ask about your trade secrets. You want to hear about the guy or not?"

"Yes." Did I ever.

"He's a hit-and-run victim, just like the woman. And just like her, he had his neck broken by somebody who was definitely not a motor vehicle. Your real cop/phony cop pair were telling you the truth about that, it turns out."

"That's what the ME's people say?"

"Official and final. It's two homicides now."

"Holy shit. I don't suppose you found out what time they came to that conclusion about her?"

"Why do we care?"

"Because Evans told me about the broken neck when he 'fronted me in Lefty's. If that was before the examiners knew, that would mean he saw it happen."

"Aha. Or did it himself."

"There's that distinct possibility," I said.

"That's too bad."

"Why is that too bad?"

"Because I didn't find that out."

"Can't you do it now?"

"Hey, how many times you think I can play dead? People get suspicious, you do it twice."

"You're right: that's too bad."

The semi closest to me suddenly fired up its huge diesel, its twin stacks sending up black flumes that could probably be seen from the Sears Tower. The ground shook, and the plastic glazing in my phone booth rattled.

"So, what did you find out about the woman?" I said.

"What?"

I said it again, shouting this time, and Wilkie started to recite a list of aliases as long as that of little Jimmy-cum-Stroud. I couldn't hear them well enough to write them down, and I didn't see that it would help me any if I had. Eventually, he moved from aliases to a list of possible former addresses, none of which rang any bells for me.

As Wilkie talked, the semi driver decided he had played to an empty house for long enough, and he proceeded to put his show on the road. Either the engine was still pretty cold, or he had a hell of a load, because he pulled out really slowly, keeping it in super-low gear. I watched the pattern of the wheels with fascination. Four sets of four and one set of two, for a total of eighteen wheels, five of them facing towards me, all turning in perfect unison. I looked under the trailer frame and watched the outboard wheels, in deepest shadow, turning to the same rhythm, and beyond them, the dawn-lit wheels of the second truck, not turning at all. It all had a certain mechanical poetry to it. Until my eyes stopped on the farther wheels. There were too damn many wheels behind the moving truck. And four of them belonged to a low-slung, heavy car.

"...really did teach violin, in a little hole-in-the-wall studio over in the Macalister Groveland neighborhood, but she never played in the Chamber Orchestra, under any name, or..."

Wide Track went on with his recitation, but I wasn't listening. Why the hell does a car park between two semis, when there's four hundred open spaces in the rest of the lot? Sleeping off an all-nighter, maybe, someplace where he wouldn't be too conspicuous? Or getting set to stake out a phone booth, where there wasn't supposed to be anybody for another two hours? As inconspicuous a place as you could get, for that.

The front bumper of the car jerked upward slightly, from the torque of the motor starting up, and that decided it for me. A hung over party animal would not immediately move his car when the cover moved or got noisy. He'd just roll over and give God and the universe a piece of his blurry mind. I dropped the receiver without hanging up and headed for the bagel shop, before my cover, also, was gone.

The front door wasn't open yet, so I ran around the side, to the back service drive. The rented Pontiac was back at the hotel with Rosie, so I had exactly two options: go in the back door of the bagel shop, cover my face with flour and pretend to be the Pillsbury Doughboy, or go over the hill and into the area where Rosie and I had driven the night before. The big semi was rolling pretty good now, shifting up a gear, and I had no idea if he had screened the view of me for long enough. It occurred to me that I shouldn't have left the phone receiver dangling, but it was too late to go back and take care of it now. Over the roar of the diesel, I thought I could hear the chirp of smaller tires peeling off on the blacktop. I ran through the opening in the brush and didn't look back. Over the hill, as they say.

It had seemed smaller from behind the windshield, just a nice little berm that would make a good visual screen. It had grown since then, into one of the foothills of the Himalayas, and I scrambled frantically for the ridge, frequently stumbling on large rocks. A lot of rocks on that damn hill. I decided I would not look at the undercarriage of the rented Pontiac, assuming I ever got to see it again at all.

I finally made it over the crest, gasping for air and vowing to think again about that exercise program that I used to think about, I forget when. Or maybe not. The hill was probably just steeper and longer than I had remembered. What the hell, the Pontiac had needed 200 horsepower to get over it, and even with that, it wasn't happy about it. I stopped just over the crest, dove into a mass of low, tangly brush, and chanced a look back.

Below me, a big, dark gray Chevy was cruising around the corner of the strip mall, slowly. I couldn't see the driver's face, but the car damn sure looked familiar. I had almost taken the last ride of my life in a car just like that, and unlike the Proph, I did not believe in coincidence. The car stopped just around the corner, and I hunkered down lower, hoping the driver hadn't seen me. The sun was rising almost behind me now, so the odds were in my favor. I felt like Josey Wales with the rising sun behind me, about to waste the *Comancheros*, single-handed. *"Yup, it's always nice to have an edge."* I needed some tobacco juice to spit.

Behind the strip mall, one of the jolly bagel bakers, a young man of about my build, had just tossed a big plastic trash bag into a dented green dumpster and stopped to have a smoke, looking around furtively first, taking no apparent notice of the Chevy. He turned his back to the wind, to shelter his lighter, also turning away from the corner of the mall. Behind him, the car spun its wheels on the gravel, and its heavily muffled engine made a noise like a turbine winding up. Good God, he was going to run the kid down! *Déja vu*, all over again.

I stood up and yelled. The kid didn't seem to hear me, so I cupped my hands and did it again, as loud as I could.

"Get the hell out of there! *Anywhere!* Run!"

He wasn't back by the door to the bagel factory anymore, but he looked up in time to see the speeding car and to jump into the recess at a back door from some other shop. The car tore past him, sideswiping the wall and leaving paint on the concrete block. Then it swerved back away from the building, did a clumsy high speed U-turn, and stopped again. The driver's window wound slowly down.

Nice work, Jackson. You're still standing up, idiot.

"Oh, shit," I said aloud. The face in the car window, even from that distance and with a hand up to screen his eyes from the sun, was unmistakable: Evans. And there was no doubt that he had seen me.

I turned and ran down the back side of the berm, going straight across the road at the bottom, down through a small ditch, and up again, onto the black rock ballast of a railroad embankment. Behind me, I heard the blurbling turbine-like noise again and then the sound of the engine screaming, revving out of control. Off to my right, a freight train was highballing toward me, maybe a quarter of a mile away, and the engineer blew his horn. Maybe he saw me, or maybe he just liked to blow his horn. In any case, I relieved him of the awesome responsibility of running me down.

I crossed the tracks, went down another narrow ditch and up another embankment to more tracks. There was a train coming here, too, from my left, but not as fast and not as close. I could beat it, easily. Its engines were laboring hard, belching diesel smoke, hauling their load up a long grade. If the engineer saw me, he didn't bother to say so by blowing his horn. Behind me, the uncontrolled revving of the Chevy engine got louder, and I wondered if the car had rolled over.

I went back the way I had come, to where I could just see over the first tracks. Evans' car was hung up on the ridge of the berm, both wheels on the driver's side completely off the ground.

He spun his wheels wildly for a bit longer, then threw open the door and piled out, breaking into a jerky, half-stumbling run, his loose coat flapping behind him. At the bottom of the slope, he stopped, looked around, then pulled out his sidearm. Good grief, was he seriously planning on shooting me? Hell, I was only "wanted for questioning in connection with." And we hadn't finished playing out the fiddle scam yet. And even if he was having a moment of pure lunacy, could he hit anything at this range and with the sun in his eyes? I hardly thought so.

Wrong. All wrong. He spotted me watching him, took a one-handed target stance, so he could use the other hand to shade his eyes, and methodically emptied his magazine. He walked the shots up the embankment like a machine-gunner finding his range, and just before the fast freight flashed in front of me, some rounds hit the rocks behind me and the rails off to either side. This guy was an obscenely good shot. I hunched down to look between the passing train wheels and saw him calmly eject the magazine and insert another, as he walked forward, closing the range. Time to move.

The second freight had caught up with me by then, and I was stuck in the space between the two trains. I tried to remember what I had heard about jumping a freight, from an old time hobo who had needed a bond for a breaking and entering charge once. "Take a ladder at the front of a car, not the back, so if you miss your handhold and fall off, the next set of wheels ain't so close to you." Maybe. Or maybe it was, "Take the one at the back end of a car, so…"

Oh, to hell with it. I picked a flatcar full of packaged lumber on the slower train, ran alongside until I was almost up to his speed, found a rung and a handhold, and pulled myself up, even as more bullets ricocheted off steel wheels and machinery. My grip held, and I became one with the rattling freight. The distance to the other train closed down rapidly, the space between them getting noisy and claustrophobic.

At some level, my mind knew that the two trains wouldn't actually hit each other, but my instincts didn't believe it. I worked my way across a machinery platform, to the opposite side of the car. Then I swung myself around to the side of a lumber cube and looked back. By the time the fast freight had quit blocking my view, the shopping center, Evans, and his bullets were long gone. Once again, I had fled into another world. I wondered how many times I could keep doing that.

The train snaked its way through the industrial backyard of greater Chicago, passing new and abandoned factories, slums, switchyards, and grown-over land that looked as if the city had simply forgotten it. Far off to my right, in the east, I could see glimpses of the famous skyline, but it didn't seem to have anything to do with the back-alley world I was moving through. We never picked up very much speed, but sometimes we passed other trains that were going even slower. At one of them, I decided to make a change. I read a newspaper article once about a young man who wanted to try his luck at being a hobo and wound up getting crushed to death by a shifting load of lumber, on the first freight he ever hopped. So the next time we slowed for a long grade with another train alongside us, I jumped down and changed to an empty flatcar. It was just behind a boxcar with the five-pointed star of anarchy spray-painted on it, along with "RACINE IS A MEAN CHICKENSHIT JERKWATER TOWN," in big, three-colored shadow letters. Wow. A lot of paint in that statement. It must have carried some heavy passion. Since that was pretty much what I thought of Racine, too, I took it as an invitation. The flatcar was fairly clean and had a big center frame for securing some kind of freight. I leaned up against it, made a pillow out of my rolled-up jacket, and settled down for a long haul to I knew not where.

We seemed to be going north, which was as good as anything else I could think of. I didn't know where I was going, but I damn sure knew what I was going from. Evans was a complicated character, I thought, and his actions up to now could be interpreted

in a lot of ways. But there was only one way to interpret the
bullets by the railroad tracks: He wanted to kill me.

Why? That wouldn't get him a violin or a wad of money, or
even a big fat promotion with the cops. It was simply irrational.
I thought back to what my Uncle Fred had said about murder
by motor vehicle being a crime of rage. Was Evans full of rage?
And if so, how in hell did it get directed towards me? I didn't
think the answers were anywhere ahead of me on the tracks, but
I didn't know where else to go at the moment.

I faced forward and amused myself by waving at people in
tenement yards and reading the black and white signs that occasionally passed by, written in railroad gibberish. I had almost
stopped trying to make sense of them when I passed the one
that said SKOKIE.

I mentally took back all the sarcastic things I had thought
about the Proph and his ideas. This absolutely had to be karma.
The train was going faster now, but there were patches of tall
grass along the tracks that looked fairly soft. I picked one and
jumped. It may have been soft, but my body didn't think so. It
promised to remind me of this silly stunt for a good long time.
But I didn't break or seriously wrench anything, so I got up to
look for something that might be the center of town.

I found a C-store not far from the tracks, and I bought a throw-
away shaving kit, some moist towelettes, cigarettes, a cup of
coffee, and a couple of stale doughnuts.

"Restroom's back in that corner," said the clerk, a dumpling-
shaped, frizzy redhead who looked as if she probably drove a
Harley to work.

"Thanks," I said. I didn't ask how she knew I needed one.

"You don't look like a regular 'bo," she said. I think she may
have been trying to give me a come-hither look, but it was hard
to tell on her.

"Thanks again, I think."

"Yeah, you do that," she said. "You think."

I beat a hasty retreat to the room she had pointed to, where I shaved, cleaned my clothes up a bit, and generally tried to make myself look like a candidate for humanity. I tried some coffee, which wasn't bad, and a doughnut, which was awful. I would have thrown it in the toilet, but I didn't want to plug the poor thing up. On the way out, I asked the clerk if there was a good restaurant anywhere close.

"Them doughnuts ain't much, are they?" she said.

"Oh, I wouldn't say that." They were much, all right.

"I make a lot better ones myself, but they don't let me sell 'em here. The company says we gotta sell the ones off the big truck, which ain't here on time, mostly."

"Well, that's a big company for you. No respect for individual talent."

"Ain't that the truth?" I think she batted an eyelash at me. When I appeared to be immune to it, she gave me directions to a 24-hour pancake house. "Comb your hair," she said.

Then I showed her the paper with the address that Joe the Gypsy had given me. "Where would that be?" I said.

Her expression couldn't have changed faster if I'd tried to rifle the cash drawer. "Aw, shit," she said. "You one of them?"

"Not exactly."

"What's that supposed to mean?"

"It's a long story."

"I just bet. Get out of here and tell it to somebody else."

I didn't wait for her to add an "or else." Fifteen minutes later, I found the pancake house. It was pushing nine o'clock by then. Instead of showing the waitress the address in my pocket, I asked her where I could find a city map, which turned out to be a much better strategy. She gave me more coffee than I asked for, heated up my apple pie, and let me look at a map in the front of a phone book, though she didn't let me tear it out. Then she told me about the local city bus schedule and where to catch one. So much for not looking like a regular 'bo.

A little after ten, I was getting off a bus and walking up to a heavily curtained storefront. The sign said "Spiritual

Consultations," and in smaller print, "Madam Vadoma, Seeress." There was also a picture of a hand with a lot of numbers and lines and an eyeball in the middle of the palm. If that was a sign I should have recognized, I flunked out. I might as well have been playing Scrabble in a foreign language. But in the time-honored phrase, it was the only game in town. A bell just like the one at Rosie's café announced my arrival, and I stepped into a world of dark drapes and dim candlelight.

"*Droboy tume Romale*," said a voice in the shadows.

"I'm sorry, I don't understand."

"Of course, you do not. You are *Gadje*, then."

"Yes."

"Shut the door." The voice was soft and feminine and a touch breathless, but it carried authority. It also carried some kind of eastern European accent, but I couldn't identify it any more exactly than that. I stepped the rest of the way into the tiny shop and closed the door behind me. This time, it didn't jingle.

"Sit." Again, the velvet-covered command. I sat.

The woman who sat behind the small table was neither young nor old. She had high cheeks, a hawk-like nose, and eyes too wild for the rest of her manner and too big for the rest of her face. She also had silky black hair that seemed to flow everywhere. And while I wouldn't have said she was either sexy or beautiful, she had a definite *presence*. If I were the sort of person who goes to a spiritual consultant, I would have said she had a strong aura. Of course, that could have been the lighting. With the sunlight streaming in through the open door, the place had been merely a tired old office, with threadbare carpet, a lot of dark drapery on the walls, and a round table covered with dark red felt. With the door shut, it was a place of mystery, even possible magic. Exotic incense hung in the air, the corners disappeared, and the woman's dramatic features were highlighted by candlelight and carefully placed pin spots. And the crystal ball.

I have to admit, I was impressed by the crystal ball. I had always thought they were a mere cartoon cliché, and I never expected to actually see one. This one was maybe six inches across, lit from within or below with a blue-white glow, and it seemed to have tiny wisps of smoke slowly curling around inside it. The woman cupped her hands over the ball without touching the glass, then opened them, slowly, sinuously, like an exotic flower unfolding dark petals. She may have been as phony as a politician's promises, but she definitely had style. In spite of myself, I decided I was going to like this game. She looked up.

"The crystal is clouded," she said. "You see?"

"It's not always like that?"

"It reacts to your troubles."

"Oh. Well it would, wouldn't it?"

"You mock me? That would be a great mistake. I have the gift of the evil eye. I can make you wish for the rest of your life that you had never walked into this place."

I didn't know which eye was evil, but I looked at both of them, and I believed her. "I'm not mocking you," I said.

"Then you are wise, to that extent. Now you make a gesture of good faith."

I didn't have to be told what that might be. Fifty seemed to be the minimal unit of trade here in greater Chi-town, and I laid my last one on the table. She didn't lay either eye on me, so I guessed I picked the right amount. She passed her hand over the table without touching it, and the bill vanished. A simple enough trick for a practiced conjurer, but still impressive. Then she asked for my hand.

She held my hand in hers, palm up, and studied it. Her touch felt hot and slightly electric.

"I see you have much strength of character."

"How nice for me."

"Not always. You are a man with a troubled past."

Well, who the hell wasn't?

"You acquire fine things, then you lose them."

"I don't know what you mean." *The keys to my safe deposit box? My life back in Detroit? My wife? Or merely the Amati?*

"Yes," she said. "All of those." Cute. I began to see how the fortune-telling game worked.

"But there is one object, in particular, that troubles you. A recent one. You must get it and bring it to me."

"It troubles me less than the people who died over it."

She looked up abruptly. Her eyes got even bigger, and her mouth made a round "o". Then she peered intently at my hand again. "Death?" she said. "I see no blood here."

"No. Not on my hands."

"Then it is the object that is the evil. To be free of it, you must get it and…"

"Understand something very clearly, Madam Vadoma: I can bear to part with the violin, maybe even be cheated out of it, but not without finding out who did the killing. If you can't help me with that, then I've come a long way for nothing."

"It is a violin, then?" she said.

"Of course, it's a violin. Weren't you told?"

"I was only told that a *Gadje* would come, a man in a great deal of trouble, who…"

I was thinking that she must use the same prompt book as the Proph, when she was interrupted by another voice, a deep bass belonging to a man who had come up behind her without either of us noticing.

"I will talk to this gentleman now."

"But I was…"

"It is all right, Vadoma. Go and bring us some coffee."

She looked as if she were suppressing a passionate desire to either punch him out or stomp on his instep, but she gathered herself up in a flurry of skirts and hair and rushed out, taking her crystal ball with her. I was surprised to see that there was not a hole in the table with a light coming through it. The crystal must have had its own illumination. But then, I was supposed to think that, wasn't I?

"I am Stefan Yonkos," he said. "I am the *Rom Baro*. And you are Howard Jacobson."

Good thing he told me. I wasn't sure I could remember the name Rosie had used for me in the strip joint.

When he came farther into the light, I could see why he would be accustomed to moving around in the dark without bumping into anything. His eyes had no pupils at all, just rolled up whites, making him look like a fugitive from a zombie movie. And though he had to be as blind as a mob lawyer, I felt as though he were staring at me, right into my soul.

Unlike the other Gypsies I had met up to then, he was square and solid, with features that looked as if they were carved out of ancient oak with a chain saw, then left unfinished. He had thick, wavy hair and a Stalin moustache, both of them salt-and-pepper now gone almost entirely to white. And though his neck had shrunk a bit and his jowls sagged, they, too, looked solid. Only his posture looked like that of a younger man. He carried himself like ex-military, and when he sat at the table, there was no doubt that he took charge of it. If the seeress had a strong aura, his was thermonuclear.

"I apologize for the woman," he said, spreading his hands.

"Why? I thought she was very good."

"She rushed you. That cannot be allowed, ever. The game has a rhythm that must be respected. But she has not so much experience yet. She will learn."

"And if I didn't come here to play a game?"

"No? Why then, you would be a fool. And an easy mark. But I do not think you are a fool. I do not think a fool would have a priceless violin, for one thing."

"Even a blind squirrel finds a nut once in a while. No offense."

He chuckled at that, and pointed at me in a gesture that said I had scored the first point in our strange game. But not the last. "Very good, Mr. Jacobson. You talk like me. We shall have a fine time lying to each other. No offense. Vadoma! Where is that coffee?"

The woman came back in as if she had been waiting for her cue, just offstage. She put a tray on the table, took a cup from it for Stefan, and poured steaming liquid from an ornate, antique pot. As she was reaching for a second cup, he said, "Make sure you take a good cup for Mr. Jacobson. We would not want to offend him."

And just like that, I was in. An audience with the big kahuna, an unchipped cup, and everything. Or I was the biggest pigeon on the north side of Chicago, neatly set up by a bartender who chose his words just as carefully as the man in front of me. And the only way to find out was to play out the hand. I waited until the woman left, then took a sip of coffee and made appreciative noises.

"You know about the violin?" I said.

"I am told you have the Wolf Amati."

"Possibly, maybe not." *What the hell is the "Wolf" part, anyway?*

"Explain this to me."

"I wish I could," I said. "A woman calling herself Amy Cox gave me an old violin as security on a bond for her brother. Then she was killed in front of my place of business. Now the brother has been killed, too, and another man calling himself Cox wants me to give him the violin, for a lot of money. I have reason to think they are, or were, all Gypsies. I came here hoping to find out enough about them to help me figure it all out, but all anybody wants to talk about is the damn fiddle. If the thing you call the Wolf Amati has something to do with a family called Cox, and if the family is one of yours, then maybe we can help each other. If not, we may both be wasting our time."

"You come straight to the point, don't you? Very artless, but it moves me to believe you, I must say."

"Well, we're here to move each other, aren't we?"

"So we are," he said, nodding solemnly. "But I am supposed to be better at it than you."

"Then I'll do my best to let you think you are."

He laughed heartily this time, slapping the table and making it bounce. Something about the laugh seemed hollow, though, a stage laugh for an audience of one.

"By God, I like you more and more!" he said. "Will you take some brandy in your coffee?"

"Will you?"

"Alas, I cannot. A stomach condition." He patted his midsection, which looked about as fragile as a boiler plate.

"What a coincidence. Me, too."

He smiled out of one side of his mouth. "Perhaps it is some-thing contagious."

"Quite possibly."

"What about some pastry, then?"

"That would be fine."

This time Vadoma came in without being called, bringing a carved wooden tray of little date and nut-filled tarts that tasted like pecan pie without the Southern accent. I was tempted to put a few in my pockets. After all, who knew what kind of transport I would be taking out of here, or in what direction?

"So you are a bondsman, Mr. Jacobson?"

"Yes, but not in Illinois, I'm afraid."

"A pity. We might have done some business. It is good to have a bondsman in one's, um…"

"Pocket?" *And an occasional policeman, too, I suspect.*

"How very original. I was going to say 'acquaintance.'"

"Of course. But we might yet do some business, Mr. Yonkos. Tell me about the Coxs."

"Again, you come straight to the point, and so shall I. Amy Cox and her brother, or the people who were using those names, were my people, yes. And their deaths leave a great hollow place in my heart that can never be filled."

This time, I believed him completely. As craggy as his face was, it was capable of registering deep pain.

"But this is my burden," he went on. "For your part, do you truly not care about the collateral?"

"I never said I didn't care about it. I said I care about the dead people more."

He chewed on a tart, and I was positive he was staring into my eyes again.

"We have a saying," he said. "With one rump, you cannot ride two horses. Which horse do you ride, Mr. Unkempt Bondsman?"

"The one that takes me to a killer."

"Why? So the dead can get what street people nowadays call 'their propers?' Their propers are a hole in the ground and a place in heaven, both far from here. It is a very bad business, involving oneself with the dead. And in any case, it would be my business, not yours."

"You have no desire to set things right at all?"

"Now you speak of revenge."

"Maybe just simple justice," I said.

"There are things that can never be forgiven, Mr. Jacobson, debts that can only be repaid in kind. But not blood. The blood feud can never be our way. It would be the death of the *familyia*, and that is unthinkable. There are many luxuries one can have in this world, but vengeance is too expensive for anyone. For us, anyway. The grief will be with us forever, but there will be no payback."

"But the violin is another matter."

"Not exactly. It is the one member of the *familyia* that may actually come back home." He smiled. "And you have it, you say?"

"I didn't actually say that."

"Not quite, but close enough, I think. This violin is very bad for you. If you don't know that already, you will find it out soon enough. The woman, Vadoma, was not deceiving you when she said it is evil. You would be better off rid of it."

"And I just bet I know somebody who will help me in that regard, don't I?"

His smile could have charmed birds out of an empty sky, and again I had the feeling that the blank eyes were watching me. "I think perhaps we both know such a person," he said.

"If it's really so evil, why do you want it? Why not let it work its ways on a worthless *Gadje* and let it go at that?"

"Neither money nor the devil, they say, can ever stay at peace. But a Gypsy can keep a devil in a bottle, because he knows how and when to let it out to play. A *Gadje* can only get hurt by it. Especially a demon as powerful as the one in the Wolf."

"You still haven't told me why you think I have that exact one. Why is that, I wonder? It makes me wonder what else you aren't telling me."

"Again, you go straight to the heart of the matter, don't you? But first things first, I think. You claim to have come all the way here to find a killer. You are not the police. Why would you do such a thing, go to so much trouble?"

"Well, there is also the small matter of clearing my name."

"Aha." He paused to pour himself more coffee, never spilling a drop, then gestured to me to do the same. I assumed we were respecting the rhythm of the game again, and I obliged him.

"Now I see," he said. "Names are so important to you who have only one of them. Yes. And I think Howard Jacobson is not quite the one you are concerned about, yes?"

"Maybe not."

"Well, maybe mine is not quite Stefan Yonkos, either. Fair enough. And for the sake of your fine name, which you do not care to tell to me, you would be willing to part with this violin?"

"In principle, yes."

"Again, the two horses. One cannot do business 'in principle.'"

"No, one can only have an understanding."

"Just so. In the interest of understanding, then, I will tell you a story."

"Does it begin in the year zero? I heard that one already."

"It does not. It begins a little over fifty years ago, in what my father and grandfathers liked to call 'the old country.' I think you will like it."

Chapter Thirteen

The Fox in the Forest

March 15, 1945
The Ardenne Forest

Mist rose silently from the forest floor and filled the ravines that ran through the dense black-green stands of fir and spruce. It could have been snow evaporating in the warmth of the coming dawn, or new fog, or just lingering smoke. Against the lightening sky, the silhouettes of the trees were fractured and bent at frequent intervals, and the mist smelled faintly of cordite and high explosive. There had been heavy fighting here, with armor and artillery, but it had all moved south now, as the invading armies closed in on Berlin, faster and faster, smelling its blood, thirsting for the kill shot.

It would all be over soon enough, but the man who threaded his way through the trees couldn't wait. He had escaped from a death camp, with no money and no papers and a damning tattoo on his arm, and he knew he would be hunted. People were not allowed to escape, ever, and the fact of it had to be eradicated. He had to be eradicated. Better to give up the last bridge over the Rhine than to admit that a single, wretched Rom had escaped from the world's most adept jailers, history's most airtight prisons.

It was hard navigating in the dense woods, especially with no stars and the frequent stumbles over hazards of corpses and abandoned hardware, hidden by the indifferent snow. But it was a traditional skill among his people, an inherited instinct, and he was confident that he was still headed north, into the low country. There would be a lot of confusion there, and a careful man, a resourceful one, could make his way to a neutral country, or even a liberated one. Maybe even one where his skills and his people's reputation were unknown.

He pushed on, ignoring his wet feet and chilled body, wanting to get as far as possible before the daylight forced him to hide and creep. The floor of the forest pitched up uniformly, coming to a roadbed, and he quickened his pace, driving himself up the embankment. His foot broke a fallen tree branch, making a sharp crack in the cold air, and he cursed silently and slowed a bit, straining to see into the mist.

"Halt!"

The word was the same in German and English, he knew, but the accent made it unmistakably a Hun. One of Little Adolph's rear echelons, pretending the world wasn't crumbling around him. The Rom stopped in his tracks and scanned the dim landscape intently. It was too dark to see colors yet, but the silhouette showed the unmistakable coattails of a winter greatcoat. This was good. It meant Wermacht, not SS or Gestapo. The fact that the figure was hunched over was also good. It meant that he had a rifle, not a Schmeisser machine gun. If the Rom ran, the man would have to aim, not merely spray. It also meant that he was probably rearguard, a reservist, too young or too old or just too unfit to be a regular combat soldier. And that was best of all. It meant that he could probably be bribed. And if he could be bribed, he could also be cheated.

"*Don't shoot,*" *he said in German.* "*I'm only a civilian.*"

"*Come out where I can see you. Now!*"

"*Ya, ya, I come. Only, don't shoot.*" *He reached in his improvised backpack and took out the violin case, holding it aloft as he advanced, now making plenty of noise on the forest floor.*

"*What is that in your hand?*"

"*It is not a weapon, sir, I swear. Only my violin that I don't want to damage. It is very old, you see.*" *He stopped again.* "*I will put it down, if you want me to. See, here I am, putting it down.*"

"*Bring it here.*"

Bribable, yes, indeed. A man who takes himself very seriously, though. He would probably prefer to think that he had stolen something. Well, the Rom knew how to arrange that. Or rather, he didn't know it yet, but it would come to him. It always did. He walked up the roadway embankment and stopped when the German told him to.

"*Let me see it.*"

"*Of course, your honor.*" *He bent down on one knee, took off the work cap he had stolen at a farmhouse the day before, and placed it on the ground. Then he put the violin on top of it, enhancing the image of value without being too blatant about it, and opened it towards the soldier. Inside its case, the instrument gleamed dully in the dim light.*

"*This is a good fiddle?*"

"*The best, your excellency. It is 350 years old, made by a famous luthier named Amati.*"

"*You stole it.*" *Not a question. By this time of the war, anybody who had anything valuable must have stolen it.*

Unless, of course, he were a Nazi, in which case he had confiscated it from some subhuman scum. This was not stealing, merely restoring the natural order of things.

"It is mine. A family heirloom. I play it in the Berlin Symphony. Or I did, before they told us all to leave."

Never tell a lie that doesn't have at least a crumb of truth, he told himself for the thousandth time. Complete fabrications are hard to remember, and they will come back to trip you up. He truly had played in an orchestra for a while, but it wasn't the Berlin, it was the forced ensemble of the Treblinka death camp. And the instrument really was a family heirloom. It had been used by his family in scams of one kind or another for more generations than they could easily count. It was not truly his yet, though. Not because he had not inherited it, nor even because his hand had not modified it, but because he had not yet used it to cheat anybody. With any kind of luck, that was about to change.

"The Symphony has gone? Why would they do such a thing?"

"I hesitate to tell a brave man like yourself, it's so..."

"You had better tell me, and be quick about it, too."

"Everyone is fleeing Berlin, sir. The end is near, and nobody wants to be captured by the Russians. But we did our duty, all the same, playing every Sunday, until some officers came and told us to leave. They told us to go north or west, to look for the Americans or the British."

This was also essentially true, if only by coincidence. The Rom had surmised it from bits of rumors that came in with the trainloads of the doomed, adding a heavy dose of his own wishful thinking. He didn't really have any facts, but his account made sense, and he told it haltingly, for the fullest possible effect on the soldier in front of him.

"I don't believe you. I think you are a thief and a liar, and probably a Jew, to boot. I don't even believe you are a musician. You look like a peasant." He raised his rifle again, menacing, working himself up to do the unthinkable.

"If I were a peasant, I would be wearing the feldgrau now, just like you. I was deferred to play in the great symphony, which is now, alas, scattered to the winds. As for being a Jew, do you want me to drop my trousers and show you the proof?"

"What do you take me for, a pervert?"

"Perhaps you would prefer that I play something, then, to prove that I am a musician."

"Now you think you can bluff me. Play, peasant. And it had better sound good. Don't think for a moment that I don't know real music, just because I'm only a foot soldier. Make a fool of me, and you will not live to gloat about it."

We'll see about that, thought the Rom. He put a bit of rosin on his bow, took the instrument from the case, and began to play, a popularized version of Tales From the Vienna Woods. It was complicated enough to sound like a serious work, but simple enough for the Rom to play it well, even exceptionally. He had no formal training, but he was good, a natural talent with a perfect ear and instinctive phrasing. He let the instrument run the gamut, from sweet to coarse, subtle to insistent, but always returning to mellow, heart-rending richness. And it was, indeed, a fine instrument.

As he played, he watched the soldier relax, then slump, until he looked as if he were about to cry. The Rom wished the soldier would interrupt him, since he couldn't remember how the piece was supposed to end, but the man gestured him to play on. He improvised an ending, based on the dominant theme of the opening stanzas, and before he could be challenged on it, he slipped into a lively Strauss waltz.

At least, he thought it was Strauss. It seemed to suffice, whatever it was.

The German sat down on a fallen tree trunk, his rifle upright between his knees and a faraway look in his eyes. Putty.

"I heard the Symphony once," he said. "Before the war. We went to Berlin, my parents and I, to see the city and to take my father to a famous hospital there. He had been in the Great War, you see, had his lungs burned out. They were going to try some new treatment, we were told. I think they lied, just to get him off the pension rolls. My mother and I left him at the hospital and never saw him alive again."

"I thought only we Germans had the poison gas in the last war."

"That's what they tell you, isn't it? But you know what? The wind doesn't give a pfennig who released the terrible stuff. Unlike my poor father, it doesn't always go where it's told."

"A great tragedy for you." He touched the strings lightly again, slipping into a slow, high version of Lilli Marlene. He spoke while he played, watching the soldier with great care. "They don't care about the little people, do they? About the ones who just follow orders?"

"Ya, ya," he said, now rocking back and forth slightly. "This is so true."

"They left the orchestra to fend for itself and now they leave you to be captured by Russians. They hate us, you know." He didn't say if he meant the Russians or the high German leaders.

"That's what you say. I think this is a safe enough place. I think I will be here when the war is over. Then I will just put on some woodsman's clothes and melt into the landscape. Maybe I will have a violin to keep me company, hey?" His eyes lost their faraway look and began to turn menacing again.

"Or the Russians will."

"They will not come here. My lieutenant told me so."

"And where is he now? Eating hot soup in some prisoner camp, fifty kilometers west of here, out of harm's way? I passed an advance Russian patrol the day before yesterday. Wild, crazy men with submachine guns, looking for anything to shoot or burn. I hid from them, but there will be more. And they will come this way, soon enough."

"You lie."

"Kill me and take my violin, and you can only find out the hard way." He shifted to playing Deutschland Über Alles, slowly and transposed into a minor key, as if it were a dirge.

"Where were they, exactly?"

"Why should I tell you?"

"So I don't shoot you?"

"Much good it would do you."

"Then what do you propose, herr musician-peasant?"

"You wish to survive the war?" Suddenly the plan that he had been looking for became crystal clear, laid out before him like a multicolor battle map. All his best schemes came to him that way, quite unbidden and unforeseen.

"Ya, I wish to survive the war. Who does not?"

"Then follow me. I will take you past the patrols, to a safe place. Along the way, we will look for a dead American with a uniform that will fit me, and I will coach you in a most wonderful charade that we are going to play."

"Why do we need to play at anything?"

"Because when we run into another Russian patrol, then I

*am an American GI, and you are my prisoner. They won't
like it, but they won't interfere with us."*

"I hope you know what you are doing."

*That made two of them. The Rom repacked the violin,
crossed over the road, and continued to walk north, the
rising sun on his right now illuminating the forest floor,
displaying the litter of battle. There was a tense moment
or two when he thought he could feel the German aiming
his rifle at the center of his back, but finally he heard the
man shoulder his gear and trudge after him. The man made
more noise than a Tiger tank, which was what the Rom
had really hidden from two days earlier. Then, after dark,
he had garroted the watch stander on the turret and stolen
the man's field rations. He could have killed the private
who now followed him, too, any of several times in the
last few minutes, but he had faith in his own ruse, and he
needed the man for a shill. And he was tired of both the
killing and the hiding. Killing is not the Gypsy way. He
was ready for a more honorable and interesting game, one
more suited to his talents. He was ready to perpetrate the
biggest fraud of his career.*

*Six days later, a gaunt and disheveled U.S. Army corporal
wearing the insignia of the 101st Airborne walked into
an advance camp of a combined U.S.-British task force in
Belgium. The man had lost his weapon, but he carried a
Mauser rifle and a violin case. He had also apparently lost
his memory and was suffering from what was then called
"battle fatigue." He was sent to England for treatment and
evaluation, and then home to an early discharge, a modest
pension, and a family who didn't seem to know him. His
dog tags said his name was Gerald Cox.*

Chapter Fourteen

...and the Fox in the Town

The coffee had cooled to tepid by the time he had finished, but the woman, Vadoma, brought in a new tray, with fresh coffee and different pastries, and we again attended to the rhythm of the game. Or maybe we were doing something else. This time, Vadoma didn't leave. She stood off in a corner of the room, behind me, with her arms folded, as if she were waiting for orders of some kind. Or acting as a guard. I began to think I was being deliberately detained.

"You're right," I said. "I like your story. How much of it is true?"

"Truth, you want, also? Sometimes truth is more eel than fish, my friend. It is a story. I was not there when it happened, nor was the man who told it to me, nor, I'm sure, the man who told it to him. But for us, it is always a question of how much needs to be true, to be useful."

"And how much of this needs to be true?"

"Only the bones. It accounts for many things. There was a violin, famous among our people, that disappeared about that time. There is no doubt about that. And it was valuable, so it should have turned up in a market somewhere, sooner or later, but it did not. Believe me, we would have known.

"There was also a young Gypsy man who vanished, but that is less in need of explanation. Many, many were lost in that terrible time. The Jews like to think the Holocaust is their own personal horror, but there were many other groups targeted, as well. The only difference is that some of the others were better at running away. We Rom have been running for a long time. Our instinct for it is well developed. Still, many were killed."

"But some were not."

"Just so. And those who were not, but were scattered across the earth, told their stories to anybody who would listen. That's important to us, always. Stories travel, just like people. And if a man's story makes its way back to the *Natsia*, they will know to look for him."

"And put a light in the window?" I said.

"Something like that, yes."

"But nobody came to the light."

"Many came, after the war, but not a young man with a violin. There has been no epilogue to the story until you came here." He spread his hands out on the table, as if it were my turn to speak. While I debated what to say, the woman stepped forward and whispered something short and urgent into Yonkos' ear. He nodded and gestured to her to be calm.

"If I'm supposed to come to a conclusion from all that," I said, "I don't know what it is."

"Then, maybe it's your turn to tell a story, to match mine. I have already heard one other, you see, about a man named Jackson who killed a poor Gypsy woman and stole her violin."

And as suddenly as it had begun, the party was over.

"From a bent cop named Evans? It's a lie," I said.

"Of course it is." He spread his hands again, smiling. "All stories are lies, at some level. The question, Mr. Jackson, is whose story is more useful, yours or his? And which one will get the famous violin back where it belongs? If I were you, I would be making this simple Gypsy an offer right now."

"The violin for Amy Cox's murderer?"

"That would be fair, wouldn't it? But I do not have that to offer, I'm afraid. You will have to settle for the violin for your freedom. You see, I've already been offered the violin for your head. Or some part of your anatomy, anyway. But I don't think the man, Evans, has the object to offer yet. In fact, I'm not even sure he knows where it is. He may have the foolish notion that if he hurts, maims, and threatens to kill you, you will then take him to it."

"And then he will kill me, anyway."

"He does seem to want that very badly, yes. And it is a sad fact that policemen don't seem to be capable of a small amount of innocent corruption. Once they step over the line, they lose their way completely, and there is nothing they won't stoop to. A delicate thing, dealing with them."

And with you, I thought, and I casually let my right hand settle onto my lap, to reassure myself that the .380 was still in my pocket.

"But you are a different animal, aren't you?" said Stefan.

Now where the hell is he going? "I don't think I've heard it put quite that way before. I take it that's a compliment?"

"In a way, yes. As I said, I like you. And fool that I am, I'm sentimental about who I do business with."

It was my turn to laugh, but I wasn't sure if he had really been joking. "And if you indulge your foolishness and deal with me," I said, "how would you be sure of delivery?"

"That is a problem," he said. "Yes. With you or him. It comes down to trust. I think I do not trust Evans. Can I trust you?"

"Trust me to deliver the violin in return for no more than a dash out into Main Street at high noon, with a trigger-happy posse in hot pursuit? No. Hell, no. Without my name, I have no freedom."

"And what if I can resolve that little problem for you?"

I thought about it for a minute, and about the many ways the game could play from there, and Uncle Fred's advice that it could get bloody before it was done. For the moment, at least, Stefan seemed like the best option I had.

"Do that," I said, "and you have yourself a deal."

"A deal, you say. And a violin?"

"That's the deal."

"This I like. It is more difficult, but it will work." His hands went palms-down on the table, and he nodded with his whole upper body. "I will make a call to our people in St. Paul, set something in motion. Mind you, we may not be able to find your killer…"

"It could be Evans himself, you know."

"Or it could not. No matter. We can get you clear of the whole business without resolving that. We are good at getting clear, Mr. Jackson. Will this do?"

"Yes," I said.

"Yes. Then it shall be so. But I have one last problem. I cannot look into your eyes to judge your sincerity." Funny, but I'd have sworn he was doing exactly that.

"What am I supposed to do about that?"

"Shake my hand, Mr. Jackson."

"Really? I thought Gypsies didn't do that."

"It is only a hand. It can be cleansed. Do it now. We do not have much time."

We stood up and shook hands, and I wondered if he crushed croquet balls for idle amusement, or merely walnuts. I gave him what I hoped was a reassuringly firm grip in return, thinking I could find a physical therapist for my hand later. From her spot near the wall, Vadoma said, "*Ove yilo isi?*" Or something like it.

"Yes," said Stefan.

"I think so, too," she said.

"Then it's unanimous," I said. At least, I hoped that's what it was.

"Push your chair away," said Stefan.

"I don't understand."

"You understand 'chair?'"

"Yes, but…"

"Then put it behind you, as the saying goes."

I pushed my chair back with my heel, keeping my eyes on the man and woman. As I did so, he added, "It has been a pleasure, Mr. Jackson, I assure you. Now, prepare to have your horizons expanded."

Then the lights went out.

I felt the breath go out of me with a violent whoosh and my knees buckle, and I was suddenly sitting down on something not quite soft. Sand, I decided, when I felt it with my hands. I had been dropped through a trap door, just like a stage magician, and I was sitting under the Rom office, on a dirt floor. Above me, I could hear muffled shouts and some frantic steps on the floor. I think the woman shouted, "No, don't go that way! The police are out in front!" Then there were quick steps in that direction and the sound of a door being slammed, complete with the jingle bells.

The rest was not so clear. A heavier set of steps entered from the back, and there was a lot of angry shouting that I couldn't quite make out. Evans' voice was clear enough, though, screaming "Bullshit!" several times. Whether he was refusing to believe that I had fled through the front door or that the two Gypsies had tried to stop me, I couldn't tell. The volume increased, but the clarity didn't get any better. There was some scuffling, and the woman shrieked a couple times and somebody fell to the floor once, hard. If my newfound allies were doing a bit of street theater, they were very good at it. It was also possible that Evans was part of the show, as well, the three of them doing an elaborate shadow play for an audience that couldn't peek through the curtain.

I sat tight and waited for my eyes to become accustomed to the darkness. It didn't help. There wasn't one candle's worth of light in the whole damn place. The trap door above me was defined by a thin, faint yellow outline of light, but that was all, and it wasn't much. Then the bullets punched some holes in the floor, and light came through them like tiny spotlight beams sprinkled with dust motes. In another life, I would have said they were pretty.

There were two shots at first, in rapid succession, then more shouting and then a third. The argument still continued after that, though, so I assumed Evans was just trying to intimidate people. By shooting through the floor, where he couldn't hurt anybody, that is. Right. Swell. I hoped he had made his point.

Without really knowing what I was going to do with it, I reached in my pocket and pulled out the .380. It was a good thing I hadn't had to draw it in a hurry, because after all the bouncing around of my recent travels, it came out pointing backwards, at me. I carefully corrected the error of its ways and held it in one of the light beams, to check whether there was a shell in the chamber. There wasn't, but I couldn't think of a silent way to put one there, so I left it for the moment. I didn't check to see how many rounds I had in the magazine, either. Whatever the number was, it would have to be enough. I had no spares. I reached in another pocket and took out my lighter.

I could make out a pull chain in the gloom now, hanging from a bare light bulb, but I didn't yank it. If Evans was restaging the Saint Valentine's Day Massacre upstairs, it probably wouldn't be too good for him to see his bullet holes suddenly lighting up. But I figured I could risk the flame of the lighter.

I moved away from the sparkly light beams, to an outside wall of rough stone, and used my lighter and my considerable groping skills to work my way around to a doorway and into a narrow passageway beyond it. I wasn't sure if I owed Stefan Yonkos anything else for that handshake, or even if he needed any help, but there was little enough I could do for him and Vadoma, in any case. I had a loaded gun, but the Marines don't attack from the low ground, and neither would I. I stumbled through the moldy-smelling tunnel until I came to a dead end with a crude wooden ladder fastened to the wall, and I went up. The rungs were irregular and rotten, and it was slow going.

Behind me, the sounds were more muffled than before, but I clearly heard another shot and another thud on the floor. After that, the arguing voices were all male. Oh, shit. That stupid bastard, Evans, had shot the woman. *Shit, shit, shit. Goddamn him to hell!* I stopped on the ladder for a moment, then felt my feet going back down. Then they were on the floor and going back down the tunnel, the way I had come. I still had no idea what I was going to do, but somehow, now I couldn't leave. I had done nothing but run and hide since this whole, sorry business started, and I just couldn't do it any more. And at some level, I knew that just sticking around to be a through-the-floor witness wasn't going to work, either. Maybe it was time to die, I wasn't sure. *What the hell, everybody's got to die of something.* It was damn sure somebody's time.

My stomach was a solid knot when I got back to the area under the trap door, and I had to work hard at breathing. I was sweating heavily, too, and I did not imagine that it had anything to do with the temperature in the cellar. I swallowed the taste of tarnished pennies, decided that was just too damn bad, and looked up.

Above me, there were now only two holes letting light through the floor. I thought I could dimly see the third hole dripping some kind of liquid, but that was probably just my hyped-up imagination. The next two shots were real enough, though. The first was followed by a low, guttural cry, which could have been a Gypsy curse or just an involuntary grunt. After the second one, there was nothing. I jacked a shell into the magazine of the .380 and tried to find a place with enough light to let me see the sights. I think I heard myself snarl.

Evans must have heard me, too. I heard some confused muttering above, then a distinct shout.

"Jackson, you asshole, is that you? Are you hiding under this floor like the fucking rat you are? Answer me, or I'll ventilate this place!"

One of the last two light-bearing holes went dark, and I assumed Evans was bending down to get a look or a better shouting spot.

This is it, kid. He's a better shot than you are, he has the high ground, and he probably has more ammunition than you do. This is as good a chance as you get.

I pointed the gun up, held it in both hands, and emptied it into the floor around the darkened hole. Splinters of wood flew back in my face and the world was full of noise and fire. I found it strangely fascinating that I could hear the empty shells being ejected and clinking against each other on the floor, but

I didn't seem to hear the shots. Four of the rounds made new light-holes. The rest did not. Evans let out something that could have been either a scream or a shout or both. There were some more rapid shots, but this time, none of them came through the floor. Then everything fell deathly silent.

I found the pull chain again and jerked it, squinting at the sudden glare. I didn't know what Evans' state was, but there was no more point in being secretive. There was also no point in sticking around. Another ladder stood by the hinge side of the trap door, but I couldn't see any way to trip the hatch from down here, so I headed back to the tunnel I had found before.

I was still drenched in sweat, but my breathing was easier now, and I took my time. Time went back to normal, and relief flooded through me like a cool tide. I seemed to be preoccupied with the monumental question of which I wanted more, a hot shower, a stiff drink, or a long, long nap.

Do it in the right order, and you can have it all.

True enough, but first, I had to…

Behind me, I heard the sound of the trap door opening again, and I turned around to see Evans hit the dirt in a heap. He rolled over, groaned loudly, looked around, and propped himself up on one elbow. With his other hand, he slowly extended his huge semiauto in my direction. His shirtfront and one side of his face were covered with blood, drool was coming out of his mouth, and one of his legs was twitching oddly. But there was no doubt that he had me squarely in his sights. And at this range, he couldn't miss. Hell, in that narrow little passage, he could have bounced the bullets off the walls and still been sure of hitting me. From the shop above, I thought there was the sound of the jingle bells again, but it was hard to imagine them doing me any good.

"Out of bullets, are we?" he said. "What a fucking shame."

We both looked at my right hand, where I still held the .380, the open chamber clearly advertising that it was empty.

"Why don't you hop a freight train again, asshole?"

"That's a good idea," I said. "Know where I can find one?"

"I just happen to have one, pointed straight at you. And you are standing on the tracks, right where I want you. I'd rather run you down with a car, of course, but we don't…"

"Why, for crying out loud?"

"Huh? The hell you mean, 'why?'"

"Why means why, is all. Why a car, why me, why Amy Cox, why any of it? If you're going to waste me anyway, you could at least tell me."

"You trying to confuse me now?"

Do I have that option? Damn right. "What do you mean?"

"What do you mean, what do I mean? You think I'm half gone, you can play with my mind? I ain't that far gone. Tell you what, though: you tell me where the violin is, and I'll let you off with a nice, clean, painless head shot. Or better yet, don't tell me, and I'll just shoot both your kneecaps off and let you bleed out. I'd like that a lot."

"Or maybe you ought to just drop the gun now, while you still can." The voice came from above, through the still-open trap door. Rosie, bless her rabbit-hunting, free-spirited little heart. I could only see her in backlit silhouette, but she had never looked so good to me.

"Who the fuck are you?" said Evans, and without waiting for an answer, he rolled over, pointed his gun up, and started to squeeze the trigger. Or at least, he looked like he was going to squeeze it, and that was enough. Rosie let fly with three shots that pounded him into the dirt floor as if a building had dropped on him. His gun arm flopped to the dirt beside him, and he didn't move after that.

"Herman?" Rosie came partway down the ladder and squinted into the cellar. "Are you down there, Herman? God, I hope you are, because otherwise, I just killed a man for some complete stranger."

"Relax, Rosie."

"Are you all right, Herman?"

"I am now." I laughed, first a giggle and then a roar. I couldn't help it. After what seemed like ages, I sobered up, kicked the gun away from Evans' inert hand, just to be safe, and climbed the ladder by the trap door. "Let's get out of here, my love," I said.

"What did you call me?"

People say the damnedest things under stress.

Chapter Fifteen

Aftershock

"Praise Yah!" said the voice on the phone.

"I absolutely do not believe this. Prophet?"

"Himself. The disembodied voice in the wilderness, the unobserved of all observers. How goes the sojourn, Pilgrim?"

"I've had better trips. What the hell are you doing on Wilkie's phone?"

"As usual, the pilgrim sees but does not comprehend. It is the big man who is at my phone, not the other way around. Except that at the moment, he's at my laptop, probing the dark secrets of the cosmos. You wish me to interrupt him?"

"I wish." *Your laptop? Dark secrets of the cosmos?*

I waited and listened to some predictable background noises, while outside the plastic half-egg canopy of the public phone I was using, a thousand seagulls kept up a running argument with the waves that exploded against the breakwaters in front of Chicago's old Navy Pier. The place had been converted since I was last there into a sort of combination upscale flea market and fast food emporium. It was a good place to get lost in a crowd. Lots of young families there, with loud, badly-behaved little kids. People like that only pay attention to themselves and their own little broods. It was better, Rosie said, than Grant Park, which had a lot of old people on benches, people who watched and remembered everything and everybody.

Rosie was out by the rocks, throwing popcorn at the gulls and looking fresh and smart in some new slacks and a pullover and jacket from Marshall Fields. She had been shopping again, while I took a tourists' boat ride up the Chicago river, complete with running commentary by an architecture student from the University of Illinois. Along the way, I dropped the disassembled pieces from my .380 and Rosie's nine-millimeter over the stern, in six different places. I dropped one of the receiver assemblies within sight of the old Jewelers Building, which, according to our guide, used to be one of the operations centers for Al Capone. It seemed like a fitting thing to do. Not a tribute so much as an addition. The last two pieces, the actual gun barrels, Rosie now tossed into Lake Michigan, along with more popcorn. If anybody noticed the large, dark lumps flying off among the smaller white ones, they damn sure were not going to jump into that kind of surf to check things out. The gulls didn't seem to care, one way or the other.

Rosie's sharp new outfit also included a pair of stylish unlined driving gloves. Neither of us knew if latent fingerprints could survive being underwater, so we had wiped down all the metal and handled it literally with kid gloves after that. If somebody else's prints were on the shells left in the magazine, that was their problem. All in all, the events of the late morning were already starting to seem like another lifetime.

I pretended not to have survivor's euphoria, mainly because I didn't want Rosie to think I was celebrating the fact that she had been forced to kill a man. The fact that I would have gleefully killed him myself if I hadn't been out of bullets was beside the point. Killing is never a trivial event, and I wasn't sure how it would hit her when it finally soaked in. Hell, I wasn't sure how it would hit me. The only thing that will affect your psyche more profoundly than killing is being killed yourself, and we're not even sure about that. So Rosie romped with the gulls, and I took that as a good thing, while I privately drifted between elation at still being alive and sorrow over what we had left.

Stefan Yonkos had still been alive when we left him, though his odds for staying that way did not look good at all. We made some crude but effective compress bandages for him from the fotune-telling table cloth, then put his feet up a bit and covered him with a drape to help with the shock. That was as much as we knew how to do. Vadoma was beyond help. Evans had shot her in the head, and she was probably dead before she hit the floor. The sight of her had made me want to kill him all over again. *Easy, there, Herman. You're just a minor referee in the big league justice game, remember?* Like hell. I calmed myself with a major force of will and remembered to wipe down the coffee cup that had been the token of my acceptance, way back when. Then we split.

When we left, there were still no sounds of sirens. Apparently Gypsies only call the cops if they are *their* cops. And if there was a doctor on the way, he must have been riding one of those horses that Yonkos said requires a whole rump. Rosie and I casually slipped into the rented Pontiac and cruised away without meeting a single emergency vehicle. We stopped at the first gas station, used a pay phone to call 911, and left again without giving the operator any unnecessary chitchat, like who we were. A clean exit, but a sorry business to leave behind.

Not that I expected anybody to be sorry about Evans. If there was a Mrs. Evans, we could probably have hit her up for a service fee. But there I go, taking people at face value again, which is exactly what bondsmen, cops and judges do, and exactly what human beings should not. Shaky Bill said it best: one man in his time plays many parts, and the people who sometimes act like assholes are not always evil from the ground up.

We have an entire industry devoted to judging people for specific acts, not basic worth, and for better or worse, I'm part of it. Most of the time, I play the part with professional detachment. I think of myself as being like the croupier at a craps table. It's none of my business that most of the people who bet too much shouldn't even be playing, or that I can see when they're going to lose even before the dice start to turn on them, or that I can spot the cheats from across the room. I just collect the fees and make sure everybody plays by the rules and gets the same, pathetic chances. As much as anybody, I have a right to be cynical about it. But it's hard to see things that way when it's personal.

Personal or not, I thought I had learned as much as I could here on the sparkling shores of Lake Michigan. True or false, Evans and Yonkos had told me all they were going to. And one thing Evans had told me, whether he meant to or not, was that, rotten as he might have been, he did not kill Amy Cox. I still hadn't figured out why he wanted to kill me, but I did not think his confusion, when I had asked him about Amy, had been faked. So the truth, whatever it was, lay somewhere along the road that had brought me here. Time to go back. If I could.

"Herman, my man! You remembered the code."

I did? I looked at my watch and saw that it was just after one o'clock. God, was that possible? Three hours since I had first stepped into the world of the crystal ball? A lifetime and a blink. *How time flies when you're halving guns.* I chuckled at my own horrible joke, realizing that I had been strung much too tight for much too long.

"Good to hear your voice, Wide. What are you doing with the Proph?"

"Would you believe it's his cell phone you're calling?"

"No. What would he be doing with a cell phone?" *Not to mention a laptop.*

"Just because you're a holy man doesn't mean you have to be a techno-dumbshit, he says. That's not how he said it, but..."

"I'm hip."

"Yeah, that's what he says, too. You're hip. Personally, I never know what the hell he's talking about. Anyway, I'm out doing a little poking around here and there yesterday, earning your money and all, and he keeps popping up in my shadow. Says he has a holy mission to find you again, and some kind of Carmen bullshit, and I should give you his cell phone number, in case you need an untraceable contact point."

"Oh, really? You think he actually knows if it's untraceable or not?"

"Beats me, but he knows a whole shitload more stuff than I would have guessed. He's got a laptop that's wired into more damn secure databases than you can shake holy water at, and he knows how to massage them all. Would you believe I checked out the Amy Cox ME report that way? It doesn't give a time of discovery, by the way, only a time of death and the time of the autopsy. I flunked out there. I suppose I could try to schmooze one of the lab staff. There's a really ugly broad there who thinks I'm kind of..."

"Forget it. It's not an issue anymore."

"It's not? Why's that?"

"Tell you later. I don't suppose the Proph does all this high-powered computer searching just for the good of his and your souls?"

"No damn way. He may be goofier than a clock going backwards, but he's not stupid. I'm into him for a yard and a half already, and more getting added up right now. You did say it was all right to run up some expenses, didn't you?"

"I didn't say, but it is. In fact, it might be more than all right. With all those high-powered illegal entry portals, can he get into military records?"

"You mean like where the Pentagon hides the ICBMs and the good booze?"

"No, I mean like Army personnel records. Discharges, duty stations, stuff like that."

"Hell, is that all? He can probably get *Cuban* army personnel records, with CIA footnotes on them. You want I should ask?"

"Ask." There was some more background noise while I waited again and watched Rosie frolic around the waterfront like a little kid. I found myself staring at her shoes. This time around, she had managed to include shoes in her shopping, and the ones she was wearing now were white, with a sort of squashed, compromise high heel that gave her foot a very nice line. *And so what?* So what, indeed? Since when did I become a fancier of shoes? They must have reminded me of something else, something back at the scene I didn't much want to remember, back in the cellar and the dark, when...

"The Proph says if you've got the bread, he's definitely got the meat."

"What the hell does that mean?" I said.

"It means tell me what kind of records you want to see, and he can get them, but the meter is running."

"Remind him that I gave him a Chevy and a holy mission, will you? You got something to write on there?"

"Fire away."

"Okay, I want the service record of one Gerald Cox, Gerald with a 'G,' who served with the 101st Airborne in World War Two."

"Jesus, Herman, why don't you give me a toughie? The Army never heard of computers back then."

"The Proph says he can get it, so let's give it a try. I'm especially interested in his mustering-out physical exam. Get a print of that if you can. If there's anything on what happened to him after the war, that would be good, too. In fact, that would be better."

"I can see the dollar signs rolling up in his big, spaced-out eyes now."

"If he comes through, it'll be worth it. Tell him if he doesn't, you won't pay him at all."

"No starter's purse, huh?"

"None. My money, my rules."

"That ought to do it. Anything else?"

"Two things. Go see Agnes and find out if the check we got from Amy Cox was any good. If it was, find out where the funds came from. I want to know a person, if possible, not just an account number."

"That ought to be an easy one. What's the other?"

"Have Agnes show you a couple of emails I got from somebody claiming to be Gerald Cox. He wanted to set up a meeting, to buy the Amati violin. Send him a reply telling him you accept, or I do. Have Aggie draft it. She knows how I write. But don't send a final confirmation until you and I get a chance to talk about the place for the meet. I want someplace where you can cover my back."

"Hey, I know how to do that. Does this mean you're on your way back? Is the heat off?"

"Good question. You really believe this is a secure phone?"

"No."

"Me neither. Look into it a little, okay? I'll call you tomorrow, same time."

"I'll be here. The Proph says to keep the faith, by the way. Am I supposed to know what that means?"

"If you figure it out, let me know."

"Not likely. Tomorrow, my man."

"Talk at you, Wide."

I hung up just in time to turn and get an open-mouthed kiss from Rosie, who was apparently out of popcorn but not energy. And either I felt the same way or it was infectious.

"You were staring at me again," she said.

"Again?" She couldn't possibly have seen me looking at her shoes.

"The last time, I didn't have any clothes on, remember?"

"Oh, that time. Well, that'll do it."

"Maybe it's time to do it again, see what happens when there's no brake lever to get in the way."

"I do seem to remember something about a hotel room," I said.

"You figure it's safe now?"

"Since when do you use words like 'safe?'"

"Since I started hanging around with this guy who needs an armed escort."

"You ought to dump him. He's going to get you seriously killed one of these days."

"Uh huh. Well, in the meantime, he better be ready to make it all worth my while. What temperature do you like the Jacuzzi?"

So much for the question of how the events of the morning were going to hit us.

Much later, we sat at a table by the window of a Hungarian restaurant Rosie knew called Csardas, back on the near-north side, in the middle of a Hispanic-looking neighborhood. The streets there had more people on them than cars, all in a high state of animation and noise, and it was another good place to get lost.

It had turned out to be quite a day. A little pursuit, a little intrigue, a little adrenaline, a lot of blood, a bit of prudent track-covering, and finally some celebratory sex and coma-like sleep. All that activity tends to make one hungry. We had gorged ourselves on food with unpronounceable names like *halászlé* and *gulyás*, which was about half paprika and totally delicious. Now we were drinking a sparkling wine called *Törley* and seriously working at the business of doing nothing. It was dark outside by then, and the waiters were going around lighting the candles on the tables, while the yellowish overhead lights bumped up a notch, accenting the stamped metal ceiling panels. Fans lazily turned below them, rustling the plastic leaves on some phony grape arbors. In the back of the place, a troupe of Gypsy musicians were getting their gear out and warming up.

"You didn't tell me this place had live music," I said.

"I didn't remember that. You want to leave?"

"When they start, maybe. Somehow, I don't feel like hearing a Gypsy violin just now."

"Gee, I can't imagine why you'd feel that way. Did you at least find out what you needed to, back in Skokie?"

"Is that where we were? I thought it was Tombstone. Or Dodge City. How did you find the place, by the way?"

"Well, I heard Joe tell you the time, back at the club, but not the place. When you didn't come back from your phone call, I figured either you had walked out on me or something had gone very wrong."

"That would be a fair description of it, yes."

"Either way, I thought you'd try to make the appointment if you could. So I went to downtown Skokie and looked for a fortune-teller's sign that was different from all the others."

"Different, how?"

"I didn't know how, at first. But finally I found the one with that gross picture of the eyeball on the hand. The others didn't have that. I figured that made it either the secret inner sanctum or a Gypsy optometrist. It took me a while to find it, though. And even after I found it, I wasn't sure if I should go in. For all I knew, you were about to wrap up the deal of a lifetime. Then I heard the shots, and I decided I not only better go in, I better go in ready to shoot."

"That's the way a gangster or a cop thinks," I said. "Why didn't you just drive away?"

"Hey, if I did that, I'd never know if you really meant to dump me, would I?"

"Are you serious?"

"What do you think?"

"Tell you what, Rosie: if I decide to sneak out on you, I'll tell you about it first, okay?"

"I'll hold you to that, Herman."

In the rear, the musicians were starting to stroll and perform. I beckoned the waiter over to our table, ordered another bottle of bubbly, and gave him a twenty to give to the band, with the request that they leave us alone.

"You are sure?" he said. "Is very nice music, make the lady feel very romantic."

"We need some quiet time to talk," I said. "We're working out the terms of the divorce."

"Aw," he said. "So sad. And she is so beautiful. I will tell them." After he turned his back, I think he said, "Bullshit" under his breath. Rosie was obviously having a hard time keeping a straight face.

"So, ratface," she said, in a voice louder than necessary, "how did it go with the lawyers today?"

I pretended to slam my fist on the table and said, "You'll never get a damn penny!" Then I lowered my voice and talked about what was really on my mind. The adrenaline and the glee were long gone by then, the wine was starting to do its work, and I badly needed to unload. I told her everything I could remember from my meeting with Stefan and Vadoma, elaborating when she asked questions, trying to set it all firmly in my own mind. I didn't know what points would be important later on, so I worked hard at being able to recite them all. Somewhere in there was more information than I knew I had, of that much I was sure.

"So this Evans guy was the same cop you bopped, back home?" said Rosie.

"That's the one," I said. "He also had a phony partner named Stroud, who turned out to be the maybe-brother of the also maybe-phony Amy Cox, the woman who was killed in front of my place. Before I had to run this morning, I found out that Stroud has been killed, too. Should I draw you a score card for all this?"

"It probably wouldn't help. With or without it, though, aren't your problems over now? If Evans killed the Cox woman and tried to pin it on you…"

"He didn't kill her."

"Excuse me? Are you hanging that on the fact that he was a little confused when you asked him about it? He was a mess, Herman. He'd have had trouble if you'd asked him how high was up."

"That's what gave me the first suspicion, but you're right: it's hardly state's evidence. But then I remembered the violin. Evans wanted me to tell him where the violin is. It's the only reason he didn't shoot me when he had the chance."

"So? It's worth a lot of money, you said."

"Yes it is, and whoever broke Amy Cox's neck has it."

"Oh."

"Oh, it is."

The waiter interrupted us then with our new bottle of wine and wouldn't leave until I had admired the cork, sipped the wine, and praised it all lavishly. As he was leaving, he said very quietly but firmly, "Is very good music." I still didn't want the musicians hanging around our table, but he had managed to make me feel guilty about it.

"Where were we?" I said.

"Talking about what Evans didn't know. Mostly, it seems to me that he got here awfully fast."

I nodded and sipped some more wine. "I thought about that, too. No way I believe my car has a bug in it. I figure he must have tapped my email or my phone back in St. Paul, and he hit the road as soon as he got the location of the phone booth by the Kinko's. That probably also means he was traveling when the maybe-brother got hit."

"Let's put that aside for a minute. It seems to me he had already done a lot of wheeling and dealing with Yonkos before you ever got there."

"Dead on." God, I love a smart woman. "I think they knew each other long before Amy Cox ever walked into my office. I think Yonkos was a bigger boss than I thought, had his fingers in Gypsy doings and their dealings with crooked cops as far away as my humble little town."

"Or if he didn't play an active part, he at least knew about them."

"That's more likely, I agree. Either way, when Evans lost me at the shopping center, he probably went to see his old buddy Stefan for some advice. He must have been blown away by his own good luck when he found out I was on my way there, too."

"Or horrified at it," she said.

"How's that?"

"Well, Evans was a cop. If he was trying to keep his ties to the Gypsies a secret, he had to know that game was going to come apart when you came here. Maybe that's why he wanted to kill you."

"That would fit, all right, but that wasn't his reason."

"How do you know?"

And suddenly, I did know. "Because of his shoes," I said.

"Huh?" She made a cradle out of her folded fingers and dropped her chin into it with a look of wide-eyed bewilderment. "Maybe I need that score card, after all. I thought I was doing great, up to then."

"Think back on the scene in the basement, Rosie."

"Must I?"

"Well, maybe not all of it. But try to picture Evans' shoes."

She closed her eyes for a moment.

"Sorry," she said. "It's a pretty ordinary pair of shoes."

"Expensive?"

"Are you kidding? Discount store. Plastic soles. Not even a good big-brand knockoff. His suit, the same thing."

"That's what I think, too. It's not just a matter of taste. This was a guy who never bought anything that wasn't cheap to start with, and on sale besides."

"What I said. So?"

"So how do you get to be a plainclothes cop?"

"Is this a test? Do I get a prize if I guess right?"

"You already got your prize."

"Oh, dreadful macho vanity there. What's your point, slick?"

"My point is that you get to be a detective by putting in your time in a uniform first. And uniformed cops, just like you when you were waiting tables, get to appreciate good shoes. So this detective goes on the take to a bunch of con artists, risks his badge and his pension, even. I'm saying that even if he is too smart to make a big splash with his ill-gotten extra money anyplace else, he at least buys himself a really good pair of shoes."

She thought it over for a minute. "Okay," she said. "So he wasn't on the take, had to scrape by on a mere fifty-five thou a year, or whatever cops make, poor baby."

"But he was definitely in cahoots with the Rom on the fiddle scam, all the way. He even accused the young guy, Jimmy, of screwing it up."

"You're arguing with yourself, Herman. People pay therapists a lot of money to deal with that, you know."

"No, I'm not. I'm saying Evans was in on the con, and probably others as well, up to his badge, okay? But not for the money."

"What else is there?"

"I'm surprised at you, Rosie. You of all people, to ask such a question."

"Are you telling me that he was Amy Cox's lover?"

"Bingo. It makes everything else fit, doesn't it?"

"I guess. And he wanted to kill you because…"

"Because he really did think I had murdered her. That was where all the rage came from."

"Good grief," she said. "So he wound up almost killing you and getting killed himself, all because he wasn't a very smart detective."

"That's about the size of it."

"And we're right back at square one."

"No, we're not," I said. "But that's where we're going."

Chapter Sixteen

Looking Backwards

Even in a real war, they don't campaign every day. Sometimes they have to wait for the Lost Patrol to find itself or the supply lines to catch up with the advance columns, and sometimes they just have to stop and figure out what the hell is going on. I needed a day for Wide Track to sniff around and find out if I could come back to St. Paul without a lawyer at my side. And to be honest, I still didn't know where I would go when I got there.

We went to a different hotel that night, a huge new highrise down by the Chicago River, either because I don't like leaving an easy trail or because Rosie just liked the looks of it. Maybe both reasons, plus the fact that she was still working at running up such a huge tab on her plastic that she wouldn't ever be tempted to go back to the diner in New Salem.

She had noticed the place from down on the lakefront, and she wondered if the rooms right under the massive lit-up sign would be bathed in flashing red light, just like in an old cheap-detective movie. They weren't, as it turned out, and the desk clerk said he got really tired of people asking him about it. But we booked a top-floor room anyway, with another Jacuzzi and a view of the lake and the city skyline. In the morning, we had eggs benedict and fresh fruit brought up by room service and watched the morning sun burn off picture-postcard layers of orange and magenta clouds over a lake that looked like lead glass.

"Is this how it feels to be rich?" said Rosie.

"No, this is how rich people thought it was going to feel. By the time they get there, they can't remember the feeling or the reason anymore. Then they get a little deranged."

"That's pretty cynical," she said. "Are you speaking from experience again? You have millions stashed away that you haven't told me about?"

I smiled and poured myself some more coffee. The thin, crisp-edged porcelain cups with the hotel logo on them reminded me of the ones Yonkos and I had used, and I thought of the way his sightless eyes had seemed to light up when we talked about the Amati. It was his only display of weakness.

"There was a time," I said, "when I chased the big bucks as hard as any other idiot. But I've made and lost enough money since then to say that of all the phony dreams they sell you in this country, the joy of being rich is the phoniest."

"Yeah, huh? Well let me tell you, being poor isn't so hot, either."

I smiled again. I've been there, too. Bought the tee shirt, rode the tour bus, did the whole scene. She was right: It sucked.

"Too true," I said. "Either poverty or wealth can own you. The trick is to stay in the middle, where you might actually find out what's important."

"And that is…?"

"Did I say I knew?"

"You know more than you think, Herman."

I certainly hope so.

To kill some time until I could call Wilkie again, we went out and acted like typical tourists for a while, strolling through the downtown parks and shopping in the Loop for things we didn't need. Rosie bought me a watch, with more fancy dials than anybody could read and a lot of extra buttons. I've owned cars that cost less.

"I don't need that," I said.

"Your old one looks like a dime store Timex."

182 Richard A. Thompson

"It is a dime store Timex. What's wrong with that?"

"You're a successful businessman," she said. "You should look like it."

"Back in the real world, what I am is an officer of the court. A coat and tie are my work clothes, but it's actually better if they're not too flashy. Successful businessmen these days dress like wannabe bums, except that they have designer labels sewn on the wrong side of their rags and cell phones grafted to the sides of their heads. I wouldn't look like that if you threatened me. I was proud, the first time I could afford a real suit."

"Be proud again. Wear a nice watch."

What do you say to something like that? I decided to be proud. I should have also drawn a conclusion, but I didn't.

We went to a yuppie coffee bar downtown, and I used one of their public PCs to check in with Agnes again. The coffee there was three to five dollars a pop, even in a paper cup, and their pastries were so expensive they kept them in a locked case, like fine jewelry. But the Internet time was free. I'm not sure how it all balanced out.

I sent Agnes a short message, telling her I was all right and would be talking to Wilkie later in the day. She gave me a cheery little acknowledgment and added that nobody had been around looking for me recently, except for Wilkie with the chores I'd given him, plus a deranged, babbling street preacher, whom she had thrown out. Served him right. Holy mission or not, the Proph shouldn't be bothering my secretary. There wasn't any other incoming traffic right then, which made me wonder if Evans had been the author of some or all of my earlier e-mails, and hence there would be no more of them. I had Agnes forward me a copy of the sales offer I had told Wilkie to send under my name.

Re: Amati violin

Your offer is accepted in principle, but the minimum price is $75k.

*If this is acceptable, where and when do we meet to conduct
the sale?*

H J

I had been right: Agnes knew exactly how to write it. I
wouldn't have changed a word. There was no printer in the coffee
shop, but I also had her forward me the earlier messages again,
and I reread them, making a few notes. The one that was signed
"a friend" did not offer to sell me back the Amati, I noticed,
merely to sell me some information on how to get it. So the
writer didn't have it but claimed to know where it was. He or
she also told me Gerald Cox was very bad news and much to be
avoided. Interesting. A falling out among thieves, maybe?

The writer claiming to be Gerald Cox, on the other hand,
flatly stated that he *knew* I had the violin, which suggested
to me that whoever he was, he was not Amy Cox's killer. Or
did it? Maybe he was just upping the ante for the anonymous
"friend."

I tried to think of another scenario, one in which the same
person had sent both messages, to see which one I would bite
at, but I couldn't quite make it all hold together. While I was
busy knitting my brows over it, the reply came back to Wilkie's
message, and Agnes dutifully forwarded it to me at once.

mr. jackson again

*you should have accepted my offer when i made it. now there
is blood involved, and what you have to offer is worth much
less on the open market. i suggest that i would be doing you
a favor by simply taking it off your hands, but i will be
magnanimous and give you the fitting sum of $18,000.*

time and place to follow.

how do you like beautiful downtown skokie, by the way?

g c

Oh shit flashed into my mind, but that didn't begin to cover
it. Somebody—probably somebody very bad—not only knew

how to reach out and touch me here on the road, he also knew just way too damn much about my affairs. I wondered if it was even safe to go back to the hotel. The cold feeling in the pit of my stomach was starting to feel like a familiar but unwanted guest. I grabbed a notepad off the counter and copied down the message verbatim. Then I looked at my fancy new watch. Still almost two hours until it was time for my call, and not a single useful thing I could do before then. I collected Rosie from where she was ogling the pastry case, and we went off for another casual stroll. If we talked, I have no idea about what.

We had a junk food lunch, Chicago-style hot dogs and fries from a street vendor. The hot dogs had about a pound of veggies and onions on them and dripped with sauce, and I wondered if they sold the same kind at the baseball games there. If so, they must hose down the bleachers after every game. After we ate, we washed our hands in a public drinking fountain, while a couple of monumental bronze statues frowned down on us in disapproval. Then we went back to the hotel to pick up the car and drove until we found another pay phone.

"Praise Yah, okay?" Wilkie's voice carried a distinct lack of enthusiasm.

"He's got you saying it, too?" I said.

"He wouldn't let me answer the phone unless I promised to. You believe that?"

"I don't believe you actually did it. You got anything for me?"

"I got a lot, but not all of it exactly in my hot little hand. The military records you wanted are all paper. We could get some PFC clerk to fax them, if we had a fax number that would stand up to a hard look, but that's as high tech as they can go. We can't use the Internet for it."

I thought for a moment and got one of my rare inspirations. "Go over to the County Sheriff's office, across from the Courthouse," I said. "See a deputy named Janice Whitney and tell her I need a favor. She'll probably give you their fax number and even pick up the stuff for you, if you ask her nice. She owes me one."

"Is she cute?"

"What difference does that make?"

"I seem to make out better with broads who aren't cute."

"You're not supposed to make out, you're just supposed to get a fax number. And yes, she's cute."

"That's too bad."

"Would I hire you for something easy? What else have you got?"

"Well, the big news is, our good buddy the shady detective has got himself dead, no less, in some 'burb outside Chicago. Shot."

"I'm shocked."

"I figured."

"How'd you find out?" I said.

"Hey, I called his work number. Thought I'd say I got a post-card from you from Ixtapa or some such shit, ask him did he want the address or wasn't he interested anymore? And somebody told me he checked out."

"They tell you if they're looking for anybody special for it?"

"They're not looking for you, at least not yet. Not much being given out, but it sounds like a hell of a complicated mess. I took one of the lower-downs in the department there out to lunch, a very much not-cute gal named..."

"Spare me."

"Okay then, this *person* I know says we got three people dead, all with some kind of bad history or other. Some major turf war going on between cops, too. The locals think our boy was bent, so how can his own people be trusted to investigate his killing? But our people think *all* the cops over there in Illinois are bent, so how can they be trusted to investigate the price of free doughnuts? They'll probably never get it all straightened out. You don't know a thing about any of it, right?"

"A check of my credit card records will show that I was on a train to Seattle," I said. "And the ticket clerk should remember me, too."

"Good deal. How is it in Seattle these days?"

"Windy. I'm thinking of coming back."

"I would say that's not a problem. According to the Prophet's computer, you're not on any wanted lists."

"I was," I said, "but maybe they were all put out on the personal authority of our one guy. When he died, so did they."

"Yeah, could be. And as far as the thing in Chicago goes, there's not enough of you to make a good suspect."

"Excuse me?"

"Well, it's just the guy was shot by at least three different people. I guess I didn't mention that before. I mean, he really knew how to piss off a lot of very bad actors."

"Are you sure about that, Wide? You're absolutely sure it was three, not two?"

"Hey, that's one of the few things everybody agrees on in this case. Three shooters: one with a three-eighty, one with a nine, and one with a seven millimeter. The seven is why everybody remembers it. You don't see a lot of them."

"No, you don't," I said. I had that strange feeling again, as if that should tell me something really important. I think I hung up without saying goodbye.

I went back to where Rosie was sitting behind the wheel of the Pontiac, ready to do another fast getaway should the phone suddenly turn into a monster or a cop. I slid into the passenger seat and tried to make some sense of what I had just heard.

"Rosie," I said, "back when you found me at the fortune-telling parlor…"

"Rescued, Herman. The operative word is definitely 'rescued.'"

"Okay. Back when you were the cavalry and I was up to my ass in bloodthirsty Indians…"

"Oh, much better. Yes, back then, what?"

"How did you open the trap door?"

"Huh?"

"That's not the reassuring reply I had been hoping for."

"What are you talking about?" she said. "It was already open. It was a hole in the floor, with your voice coming out of it and

some goon all covered with blood at the bottom of it. I didn't
open anything. How would I?"

"Good question. So who did, I wonder?"

"What difference does it make? It was open, okay? I mean,
it had to be..." She stopped and turned to look at my face.

"No, Herman. Damn it all to hell, no."

"No what?" I gave her what I hoped was an innocent look.

"You've got that look, like a doctor about to give out one of
those awful good-news-bad-news things. Don't tell me what I
can see you're about to tell me." I switched to faking a reassuring
smile, but that obviously didn't work, either.

"It's crazy and it won't accomplish anything," she said.

"Then just drop me off, okay?"

"You know about how likely I am to do that?"

"Yes," I said. "So let's go."

"We are talking about the same thing here, right? For some
utterly insane and self-destructive reason, you want to go back
to the Gypsy *officia?*"

"That's the plan, yes."

"The plan sucks."

"It does, doesn't it? Hit it."

"Shit." She peeled away from the curb without looking, and
a cabbie she had cut off blew his horn. She did as elegant a job
as I have ever seen of flipping him the bird.

"You know, I'm supposed to be the crazy one," she said.

"Isn't it interesting, how roles sometimes reverse?"

"No."

<> <> <>

The storefront had yellow crime scene tape over it, but all the
action had long since gone elsewhere. There were no cars and
no activity anywhere on the block.

"Cruise on past it," I said. "Keep your head pointed forward,
just watching the road like any other slightly lost driver." While
she did, I tried to scan the windows and roof parapets across the
street without making a show of craning my neck.

"Anything?" said Rosie.

I nodded. "Second floor, two thirds of the way down the block. Either somebody with the biggest eyeglasses ever made likes to sit in the dark, or there's a goon in there with a pair of binoculars."

"A cop, you think?"

"That would be my guess, yes. They deliberately cleared the street to keep from scaring anybody off. Now they're waiting to see who shows up, if anybody. They must not have any real leads to follow at all."

"So that's it, right? As in, 'We're out of here?'"

"Wrong. It's just harder now. But there's still something I've got to find out here. Go straight until we're out of sight of him, then look for a big drugstore."

"You need some antidepressants? I do."

"Tools," I said.

We found a Walgreens half a mile away, and I went in and got disposable latex gloves, a pair of needle-nosed pliers, some paper clips and hairpins, a spray can of penetrating oil, and two good, big flashlights. Wonderful places, these modern pharmacies. Just on principle, I added a roll of duct tape, too. Remembering the unpredictability of some of my recent meals, I also stocked up on mixed nuts, beef jerky, potato chips and pop. And some chocolate-covered cherries for Rosie. Never let it be said that I'm an inconsiderate date.

I got back in the car and we headed back the general way we had come, but on a parallel street a block over from the one with the Gypsy building. While Rosie drove, I set about converting the paper clips and hairpins into a set of lock picks. If the Gypsy community had gone all electronic, then the picks wouldn't help me, but I was betting that people whose ancestors talked to angels were even lower-tech than I. We passed a second hand clothing store along the way, and while I hadn't given any thought to trying to disguise ourselves, it seemed like a good idea to at least get something that would make our features hard to make out. We went in and got some nondescript, oversized shirts and jackets, plus hats with big, floppy brims.

"You go to a costume party?" said the withered woman at the cash register.

"Something like that."

"*Ashlen Devlese, Romale.*"

"*Ashlen Devlese,*" I said, nodding solemnly. I must have said it right, because she smiled through about a thousand wrinkles and gave me a wink.

"What was all that?" said Rosie after we got back outside.

"Beats the hell out of me, but I have a good ear for accents, don't you think?"

She giggled. "And you said we weren't a natural pair."

We parked three blocks away from the *officia*, put on our make-shift disguises, and walked through the alleys to the back of the row of connected stores. If there was another watcher in the shadows somewhere, I couldn't spot him.

"You think the back door won't be flagged off, too?"

"I'm sure it is," I said. "But we're not going in the back door. That cellar I was in had a tunnel going out of it, maybe thirty feet long. We're looking for the building where it comes out."

"It's the middle of the day, Herman. Don't you think anybody will notice?"

"It's also an official crime scene in the middle of Gypsy home turf. I figure the locals are all off on urgent, unexpected visits to their relatives in Pago Pago."

"And if they're not?"

"Hey, I'm a homeboy. I speak Rom. Didn't you notice?"

"God help us."

Two stores down from the fortune-telling parlor was a carpet store that looked as if its last customer had been Aladdin. I strode up the steps of the loading dock as if I had every right in the world to do so, went up to the small door at one side, slipped on a pair of latex gloves, and proceeded to work the lock. Rosie stood behind me with her hands on her hips, so her elbows stuck out and gave me some visual screening. If I ever decided to turn to a life of crime, she would definitely be my first choice for an accomplice.

"Yes?" she said.

"Ka-lunk," said the lock. We were in.

We went through the door casually, making little gestures with our hands, as if we were in the middle of an animated conversation. Once inside, we relocked the door and got away from the glass as fast as possible. Then we pulled out the flashlights and looked the place over. The interior held several rolls of carpet, piled in no observable order, an old desk with scattered papers on it, some trash cans, and the kind of serious dust and cobwebs that only come with long neglect. But the dust on the floor had tracks in it, so the place wasn't completely abandoned. We traced the paths of the tracks with our beams. Most of them went to a door that must have led to the front of the store, where I was hoping I wouldn't have to go. Some wandered around aimlessly, and a few led to a crudely framed closet that poked out from a side wall. We followed that set.

The closet was also locked, with a heavy-duty Schlage cylinder that looked even more ancient than the one outside the dock. I gave it a shot of spray oil first, then went to work on it with the picks. For something that looked like late pre-Industrial Revolution, it slipped open with amazing ease and smoothness. And the door opened without a sound. A perfectly built fallback exit, if I had ever seen one.

Inside, the tiny room was lined with electrical panels and telephone switch gear that looked as ancient as the lock. A lot of it had no wires left, just empty metal fuse boxes and knobby terminals. I looked for one that had signs of being handled recently, and found a main disconnect with a tattered decal remnant that now said "DANG...HI....AGE." I rather liked that. So did somebody else. When I threw the big switch arm on the side of the box, a piece of the floor sprang up to greet me. A sigh of clammy air came with it, laced with the scent of damp limestone and old secrets, and the familiar chill settled into my lower guts again. If somebody else had tried to make me go down there, I'd have told them to take a hike. Inside and below was the shaky ladder that I had last seen from the bottom end only. I tested the top rung to see if it would hold me and, unable to think of any excuse not to, descended. The floor below was soft and gritty, just as I had remembered it.

"Are you going to leave me here, Herman?"

"Only if you don't come along."

"I was afraid you'd say something like that."

I stepped to one side of the ladder and shone my flashlight on the floor below it while Rosie came after me.

"Did you close the door after yourself?" I said.

"What are you, my mom?"

"No, I'm your paranoid partner." I went back up the ladder. At the top, I looked through the closet door and back to the one where we had first come in, the one with the small window in it that I hadn't paid any attention to. Something was definitely obscuring the light in the dirty glass panel. I tried to remember if there was a big dirt smear on the glass. If not, then there was a person trying to peer in. Swell. And I had to make a joke about being paranoid. But if it was a person, it wasn't doing anything but looking. No door rattling, no flashlight, no automatic weapons, no concussion grenade. Whatever was out there, we could deal with it later. I closed the closet door quietly and ever so slowly, relocked it, and went back down the ladder. At the bottom of the shaft, the blackness closed around us like Methodist gloom.

Chapter Seventeen

Flashbacks

"Whoever was here last was either very fastidious or really cheap," I said. "When you and I left the place, there was a light on."

"I just hope there aren't any tiger traps or land mines. Are these the biggest flashlights you could get?"

"The biggest ones you could hope to hide under a jacket, anyway." I had to admit, they seemed like a couple of candles in a coal mine. When I played the beam of mine across the ceiling, I heard a soft rustling sound, which I took to be the resident cockroaches, running away from the light. A lot of them. I decided not to mention that to Rosie, nor the rather evil smells that had been added to the general decay and must since I was last here. I switched to sweeping the light over the dirt floor ahead of us.

"Lots of footprints," I said. "The forensic crew had a real party down here. That should mean we don't have to worry about wiping out our own tracks when we leave. There are already so many, they'd never sort them out."

"How nice. It probably also means there's nothing left for us to find. What did you see at the top of the ladder, by the way?"

"Did I say I saw anything?"

"Stop it, Herman, okay? I saw how careful you were when you closed the closet door."

"If you absolutely must know, I think there may be somebody outside, on the loading dock."

"You *think* there *may* be."

"Yup, that's about the size of it. See? You should have let me lie about it. Keep your voice down, by the way."

"You think they might add disturbing the peace to the charges of breaking and entering and murder?" But she was whispering now.

"Only if they catch us," I said.

"Well if they do, don't blame it on me. Did you bring a gun?"

"I didn't have to. I travel with this woman who always has a bagful of the things."

"You take a lot for granted, you know that?" She shoved a semiautomatic nine into my free hand. "How are you fixed for socks and underwear?" she said.

"You should know."

"Yeah, huh? I guess my focus was somewhere else when I could have checked."

I led the way through the narrow tunnel and into the cellar where Evans body had been, being careful not to step in any of the stains. The trap door was shut again, preserving the total blackness. This time, I did not pull the chain to turn on the overhead light.

"So what is it that we're looking for, again?"

"This." I went over to the free standing ladder by the door and shone my beam up. On the bottom side of the lid, there was a lot of odd looking hardware that all connected to some device by the hinge. And coming out of the nameless gizmo were several skinny wires. Some of them went to a switch box by the top of the ladder and the others led to a small hole in the floor, further back, by the far wall. I went up the ladder a bit and touched the box, which turned out to have not one, but two toggle switches. I picked one at random, took a deep breath, and put my finger on it.

"Lights out," I said, switching off my own beam.

"You're going to open that thing? Seriously?"

"As seriously as I know how."

"Wait one sec." She took a half-stride stance and extended both arms up, towards the trap door, one holding her pistol and the other the flashlight. She shut off the light with her thumb, and we were in blackout again. "Okay, do it," she said.

I threw the toggle and the trap door snapped open with incredible speed, then immediately slammed shut again. It was a good thing I wasn't directly in its path, or it would have knocked me into next week. I mean, that thing *moved.* I returned the toggle to its original position, flipped it again, and the door repeated its performance. Open, shut. Wham, bam, thank you ma'am. A guillotine should be so fast. The brief strobe view of the room above was poorly lit, except compared to where we were. It looked as if the place was abandoned. I flipped the switch once more to be sure, then returned it to the neutral position. Then I tried the other switch. This time the door flew open and stayed that way.

"Is this a good thing?" Rosie's body said otherwise. She still had her gun pointed up, and she was doing a good impression of a big bomb with a very short fuse.

"Tell you in a bit, when I see where the other wires go." I climbed up the ladder and into the fortune-telling, shootout room, keeping low and checking sight lines to the outside world as I went. The heavy floor-length drapes in the front were barely cracked open, too little for our silent watcher across the street to see anything. The back door out of the room opened into a short hallway that ended at a high window with frilly, once-white curtains over it. It gave the place enough light to move around by, but not much more than that. So far, so good. I called quietly for Rosie to come up.

"Can I use my flashlight?"

I nodded. "Just be careful not to point it outside. And don't put the gun away just yet."

"I heard that." She came up quicker than necessary, and it occurred to me that she knew perfectly well what the rustling sounds had been.

"What am I trying to find?"

"The upstairs duplicates of the switches I just used on the trap door. They have to be in this room somewhere."

The round, velvet-covered table was still in the middle of the room, though it looked as if it had been knocked around a bit. We checked there first, looking and feeling all around the edge and bottom for something that somebody seated at the table could have reached. Nothing. I chanced using my flashlight a bit then, exploring first the floor and then the walls, unintentionally lingering on the area where we had last left Stefan Yonkos. More nothing. Bullet holes all over the damn place, though. Also a lot more bloodstains than I had remembered. Hadn't we done the compress bandage right? Or had Yonkos been shot yet again, after we left?

Finally, I peeled back a drape on the back wall and hit pay dirt. A pair of toggles just like the ones in the cellar were mounted into the plaster, just under a regular light switch. Painted the same dirty yellow-cream as the walls, they would be almost unnoticeable if you weren't looking for them.

"Are you clear of the trap door?" I said.

"If there's only one of them, then I'm clear of it."

I worked the wall switches and got the same result as with the first set. One switch had an open and a closed position, and the other one triggered a quick open-shut action. So back when I had been unceremoniously dropped into the cellar, the switch had not been tripped by Yonkos, who was still seated at the table, hands clearly visible. It had to have been done by the woman, Vadoma. That was why she had been standing back by the wall, looking like a sentinel or a bodyguard. But later, when the trap door opened again and stayed open, dumping the wounded Evans down into my world, it couldn't have been tripped by her. She was already dead. Nor was it tripped by Yonkos, who would have been slumped against the adjacent wall by then, oozing his essential fluids, nor by Evans himself. There was no way the same person could stand on the trap door and also reach the switch.

Rosie continued to use her flashlight to look at bullet holes and bloodstains, not paying much attention to what I was doing or to the expression on my face. "What do we know now that we didn't?" she said.

"We know there was another person in this room, just before you came in."

"What? You mean like another shooter?"

"Just like that."

"Then why are you and I still alive?"

"When you started to open the front door, he couldn't have known who it was. He must have assumed it was the cops and split by the back exit."

She knitted her brows a bit and shook her head. "No way. I'd have heard the door."

"Maybe he didn't go all the way out."

"Oh, that's a cheery thought."

"Isn't it, though? Let's see what's back there."

"Must we?"

"In for a penny, and all that." I led the way into the back corridor, gun ahead of me, flashlight ready to use as a light or a club.

Directly behind the parlor was a small kitchen and pantry, and a toilet beyond that. At the back, the short hallway split into a T, with a back door to the alley on one end and a narrow stairway going up on the other. Neither the little window nor the glass in the back door showed us anybody lurking outside, but we didn't linger there anyway. I went up the stairs quickly, leading Rosie by the hand behind me.

Upstairs were two tiny bedrooms, furnished in garage sale decor with the occasional genuine antique thrown in. The floors were all covered with ornate throw rugs, rather than carpet. *The mark of a perpetually transient people?* There was also another bathroom, several closets, and a steep staircase leading up to the roof. The whole place, and the kitchen below as well, hadn't exactly been trashed, but it had been searched more crudely than the crime lab team would have done it. Pillows and mattresses were cut open but not disemboweled, and most of the furniture was still upright, though all the drawers and doors were open, all the contents dumped. The lid of the tank on the toilet was off, also.

"They didn't rip the backer paper off the pictures," said Rosie, "or smash the glass in the mirrors."

"No," I said. "They wouldn't."

"Oh?"

"They weren't looking for anything that you could hide in the back of a picture or a mirror. They were looking for the violin."

"That fits what we're seeing," she said. "But you said Yonkos made a deal with you, for you to go get it. Why would it already be here?"

"It wouldn't. But somebody didn't know that, or they thought I might have brought it to him." *Somebody. Somebody didn't know it wasn't here. Evans didn't know where the hell it was and Yonkos didn't know either, but he had faith in me finding it. One emailer says he knows I have it, but Nickel Pete says it's been swapped. So Amy Cox had to have it with her when she was killed, but if her killer was also the secret gunman here in Skokie, why didn't he already know where it was? In fact, why didn't he already have it? Another emailer says he can tell me where to find it. As if it were lost. So who lost it? Amy's killer, maybe? Or somebody from the Ardennes Forest, with an old, old score to settle? Was that possible, after all these years?*

"A man I know named G. B. Feinstein says great violins have dark stories attached to them," I said. "He also thinks they have souls, and I guess the souls could be dark, too. Stefan Yonkos said this one is evil, a demon, something that destroys people."

"You believe that?"

"I don't know if I really believe in evil, but I definitely believe in luck. And that stupid fiddle is bad luck, if I've ever seen the stuff. Everybody wants the damn thing, everybody who has anything to do with it seems to wind up dead, and everybody, I mean absolutely everybody, thinks I have it."

Rosie shrugged. "Maybe you do."

I gave that a moment's thought. "Maybe I do at that," I said. "If that were true, it could be the real reason why we are still alive."

"I'm not sure I like that reason," she said. "It sounds to me like one that could be canceled at any moment."

"There is that," I said. "But somehow, I don't think this is the moment."

I went over to the side of a window that faced the street and risked a peek out the edge of a tattered curtain. The window down the block where I had seen the watcher with the binoculars was still dark, unreadable. A quick look out the back window into the alley was just as inconclusive at first, but then something made me do a double take. I didn't have a good enough view of the loading dock, where we had come in, to see if anybody was hanging around down there. But on the other side of the alley, further down, in deep shadow between two buildings, was something that definitely didn't belong with the rest of the general clutter. Dark, massive, and almost out of view was the unmistakable front end of a shiny black LTD.

"Time for us to get the hell out of here," I said.

"A man after my own heart," said Rosie.

"Quiet and smooth."

"You forgot 'quick.'"

"No, I didn't." But I took two steps down the stairs and froze. This time there was no question about it. There was somebody standing outside the back door, possibly also working on the lock.

Rosie bumped into me from behind, nearly knocking us both down the rest of the steps. "What happened to the quick part?" she said.

"It got a little more complicated. Go check out the door to the roof."

She left and I backed slowly up, the way I had come.

"It's locked," she said from behind me.

"Does it open onto the alley side or the street side?"

"Damfino. Let's see, north is where the little dipper points to the big hand on your watch, if there's any moss on it, and..."

"Will you please cut that out?"

"I'm nervous, okay? Street side, I think. What are you going to do, pick the lock, pop out and drop a water balloon?"

"No, I'm going to go enlist the aid of our spy across the street," I said. "Stay where you are a minute."

I went to the front of the flat and deliberately shone my flashlight out the window, ruffling the curtains a bit for good measure. Then I thought, *what the hell, why fool around being subtle?* and I cracked one of the panes with my elbow, adding a little noise to the bait. Down the street, on the dark second floor, the shiny twin discs of the binoculars flashed as they swung around towards me, then disappeared into the shadows again. The guy was alert for having had such a long, dull wait, I had to give him that. I let him see another bit of flashlight beam, just so he'd know he hadn't been imagining things, and then I pulled the window shade down, fast. Then I did the same with the other one in the second bedroom. I looked at my fancy new watch. It probably had a stopwatch function, but I didn't know how to work it yet, so I settled for watching the sweep second hand. If the Skokie cops were any good at all, I figured three minutes, maybe three and a half, tops.

"What are you doing down there, Herman? You're starting to make me very nervous."

"Stay put, Rosie. We're about to set the wolves to devouring each other." *Unless, of course, they are all from the same pack, which would not be good at all.*

When my watch rolled up two minutes and fifty seconds, I looked out the back window and saw squad cars converging on both ends of the alley. A large man in a dark coat saw them, too, and headed for the black LTD, running hard. That was as good a diversion as we were likely to get. I ran up the stairs, brushed past a tense-looking Rosie, and went to work on the lock to the roof door. Which didn't budge.

From the alley below came the tinny, rasping sound of a voice on the speaker from one of the prowl cars, saying, "You there by the dumpster! Stop where you are and put your hands where I can see them! Now!" Since nothing around us looked anything like a dumpster, I assumed the cops were talking to somebody else. Poor fellow. I sprayed some oil in the lock and went back to work.

"I said stop!" said the mechanical voice below.

I said open! I thought at the lock. But it remained frozen solid. I hadn't found a single tumbler slot yet. Then I heard the sound I'd been dreading. At the back door downstairs, there was a crash of broken glass and the clicks and clunks of a lockset being hastily jangled open, then the door slamming again. Whoever was down there was inside the building now. And I did not think he was a cop, who just wanted the facts, ma'am.

"Give me a little room," I said. "And cover our backs." She went part way down the stairs and pointed her automatic back at the hallway, taking a braced stance against one wall of the stair shaft. I took a half step back from the roof door and cocked my foot for what I hoped was the kick of a lifetime.

"Whatever you're going to do," said Rosie, "you'd better do it now. I think he's coming up the stairs."

Amen to that. The first kick merely made my foot hurt. On the second one, though, I got my weight behind it better and kept my foot flat to the panel. The door shrieked, splintered, made a sound like a ruptured oil drum, and then flew outward. We ran through and slammed it behind us.

We both blinked at the return of daylight. Crouching low to avoid being seen above the parapet walls, I scrounged up a scrap of wood from the roof and wedged it into the door jamb, then looked around and took stock of our surroundings. Half a block of low roofs stretched out in both directions, all interconnected but set apart by low, fence-like fire walls of dirty red brick. Between each set of walls was another slope-backed little shed with a door in it, like the one we had just come out of.

"I take it we aren't going back down in the tunnel," said Rosie. "Not that I'm complaining, mind you."

I shook my head. "This is better," I said. "Lots better." I could see she wasn't buying a word of it. "We can get further away than the carpet store before we have to go back out in the open."

"Like this isn't out in the open?"

She had a point. "Well, back in plain sight, then. Which direction do you like?"

"You seem to be running on pure luck today. You choose."

I did at that, didn't I? I picked the direction away from the end of the block with Mr. Binoculars, and we scuttled off, hunched down like soldiers under fire. The commotion in the flat below got louder, then more remote.

We went over four more buildings without slowing down to try the doors. On the fifth one, at the end of the block, we stopped and I tried the lock. This time, I oiled it up first and took my time, doing it right. I had two tumblers locked in neatly and was reaching for another pick when the door flew open in my face, nearly smashing my hands. Framed in the dark opening was a very short, dark-complected young man with a very large sawed-off shotgun in his hands. If he'd had a pointy hat, he could have been Chico Marx with a vaudeville prop, sly grin included.

"Um, *Ashlen Devlese, Romale*," I said. Did I mention that I have a good memory, as well as a good ear for dialect?

"Yeah, sure," he said. "Who are you trying to con, *Gadje?*"

But not good enough.

"Anybody I can," I said. *That alone should make me one of your brothers.* "But maybe we should have this conversation someplace a little less conspicuous?"

"Come," he said, backing down the steps but keeping the gun trained on us. "Get off the roof before the *jawndari* see you, and we'll see how much that insult to our language is going to cost you."

Behind me, I knew, Rosie had her gun held inside her purse. She shut the door behind us and we regrouped in an upstairs hall just like the one we had left down the block.

"Look," I said, "I didn't mean any disrespect back there."

"I think you didn't mean to be on the roof, either, did you? But you will pay for both."

"You know Stefan Yonkos?"

"Knew, you mean."

"Yes," I said.

"A great tragedy," said Rosie.

"Women should be silent when the men talk business," he said. "But she shows more respect than you do."

So we were talking business, were we? Things were looking up.

"Of course, I knew Stefan," he said. "Everyone knew Stefan. A great man, a great loss. What do you think that will buy you?"

"The man we are running from is his killer."

"Is that so? The same one who ran away in the alley?"

"The same."

"That might buy you something, after all. How do I know it's true?"

Good question. I wasn't even sure how *I* knew it was true, apart from having seen the black LTD again.

"My name is Herman Jackson," I said. "I had an understanding with Stefan Yonkos. He was going to help me find a killer and clear my name with the police, and I was going to deliver a violin called the Wolf Amati to him." That wasn't quite the deal, of course, but I figured if I got caught in the lie I could always feign confusion. There was damn sure plenty of the stuff to go around.

"That's a good story, Mr. Jackson. But now he is dead."

"Now he is dead." I nodded gravely. "But as far as I'm concerned, it was a good deal when I made it and it still is. And somehow, I'm inclined to believe there's at least one other Rom who still thinks so, too."

"Mmm. You could be right. Let's get someplace further away from the *jawndari* and find out."

"How about putting away the gun?"

"The woman, first," he said. Damn, he didn't miss a trick.

Rosie took her hand out of her purse, the young Rom made the shotgun miraculously vanish under his coat, and I suddenly knew what it felt like to walk away from the brink of Armageddon. We went down the stairs and around a corner, to a back room, where our new guide touched a button on the wall.

"Oh shit, no!" said Rosie. "Not another damn tunnel."

Chapter Eighteen

Revelations

Rosie dozed on the seat beside me while I snacked on beef jerky and salted cashews and watched the dashed white center-line of Illinois Fourteen feed into my headlight beams. In the cracked rearview mirror, Des Plaines, Mount Prospect, and then Arlington Heights suggested themselves one last time and then faded into dim memory. Past Palatine, the countryside opened up into featureless dark prairie, which was fine by me. It looked like a blank slate. Or maybe a threshold.

The battered pickup wasn't as nice as the Pontiac, to say the least, but the engine ran okay, if a bit feebly. The brakes and lights worked, and the steering only wandered if there was a wind from the side. I decided not to take it on the freeway. At anything over sixty miles an hour, the question was not whether a wheel would fall off, but how many of them would stay on. But it would do for the one trip it had to make. If somewhere else, not too far away, there was a black LTD on the Interstate racing us back to the fair city of St. Paul and winning, that was all right, too. In fact, that was better than all right. That would work.

I had needed to give the Rom council, or whatever it was they called the surviving bunch of *kumpania* leaders, something besides my good word and winning smile to get them to rein-state Yonkos' deal, and the rented car was the logical choice. We debated and postured and traded lies for a long time, doing what Yonkos had called "respecting the rhythm of the game," but we all knew where we were going in the end. The junker that they traded me for the Pontiac probably had a thousand miles left in it, max, but that would be enough. The trade was a damned high price to pay for the mere one-time use of an emergency exit, of course, but I had a fairly limited selection and no time to shop.

The other deal, the bigger one, with the promise of the violin, was another matter. I could have done without that, quite possibly didn't even need the help of the Rom anymore. But part of the game wasn't played out yet, and part of me said that wouldn't do. The game had started with Amy Cox, and the Rom were definitely her people. It had to end with them, too. They would never be my allies, but if I left them as happy customers, that would work, too.

Someplace in the middle of Illinois, a state trooper tailed me for a while, but when I didn't break the speed limit, he lost interest and peeled off on a side road. The Gypsies had told me the plates on the pickup were good, not forged or stolen, and that seemed to be the acid test. I thought again about Stefan Yonkos and what he had said about names being so important to those of us who have only one. Good license plates are a sort of face-value proof of identity. *Names and labels, Stefan. Too damn right. Names and labels and identities are everything. That's what this whole chaotic business has been about from the get-go, but I couldn't see it before. First, I needed to get in a junker pickup that even Pud and Ditto, from New Salem, wouldn't be caught dead driving.* I chuckled at the thought of the two hayseeds, and Rosie stirred, sat up, and looked over the dash with one bleary eye.

"Where are we?" she said.

"In the middle of nowhere."

"That's a good place."

"The best."

"For a while, I thought we weren't going to make it."

"Me, too," I said.

"If we ever get to the middle of somewhere, wake me up, will you?"

"That's a promise."

She curled back up, popped a chocolate cherry in her mouth, and chewed it with her eyes closed. The clunker steadily chewed up the miles.

‹›‹›‹›

The sun was well up by the time we rendezvoused with Wide Track Wilkie at a truck stop about twenty miles south of St. Paul on old Highway 55. Rosie and I had anemic-looking fruit plates with yogurt and bran muffins, while Wilkie worked on maintaining his monolithic figure by ordering one item each from the breakfast, dinner, and dessert menus. He was obviously a little embarrassed about it, though. Funny how I had never noticed that in him before: he really didn't function well at all in the presence of a pretty woman. For a while, we sipped black coffee and soaked up the smell of fresh toast and orange juice, and made small talk. I didn't know if Rosie was really interested or just being friendly, but she asked Wilkie a lot about his trade.

"So you're a bounty hunter?" she said. "That's what you do?"

"Sometimes. I do other stuff, too. Whatever comes up that lets me still be my own man. I'm a pretty decent pool hustler. Maybe Herman told you that?"

"No," I said.

"Thanks a lot."

"Tell me about the other thing," said Rosie. "You like it?"

"It's nice, I guess. No health plan or vacation, you know, but no time clock, either. Lots of action, which I personally like, and nobody's ass to kiss. And the work is as steady as you want. There's never any shortage of assholes who think they can run away from their own stupidity. No offense, Herman."

"None taken," I said.

"What do you need?" said Rosie. "To be a bounty hunter."

"You mean like license and bond and that kind of stuff?"

"Well, and..."

"Clean criminal record?"

"Yeah, that one," she said.

"None of that's a problem. Mostly, you just have to be a mean motherfucker and look like it. Um, I mean…"

"I've heard the expression once or twice before," said Rosie. "Is it something I could do?"

"You? Get serious. I mean, you seem like, well…"

"Only seem like? If you mean a woman, Mr. Wilkie, I definitely am. Tell him, Herman."

"I've never known her otherwise," I said. She squeezed my knee under the table.

"It's not that, exactly," said Wilkie. "I once knew a bounty hunter who was a midget, no less, but he gave off menace like a pit bull with rabies. Looked like he'd bite off your kneecap just for arguing with him. So nobody did. You seem too nice. That won't get you very far in the bounty business. If you're nice, you might wind up having to be deadly, too."

"Maybe I am. Herman, tell him…"

"Maybe it's time we did some work," I said. Or anything else that changed the subject. I turned to Wilkie and said, "What have you got for me, Wide?"

He looked relieved. What he had was the full file on one Corporal Gerald Cox, US Army, and it was interesting reading, even in bastardized military non-English.

"Looks like our boy missed all the fun of V-E Day," I said.

"Yeah, they shipped him home just before then, certified him not-quite-sane-but-what-the-hell, or something like that."

"'Battle fatigue with indeterminate prognosis,'" I quoted.

"What I said."

"Where was home?" said Rosie.

"Short Straw, Texas, or some such shithole, but when you muster out, the Army will send you damn near wherever you want to go, if you've got a good reason. Especially back then. They did everything for the vets after that war."

"Not after your war, I take it?"

"Don't get me started, hey?"

"So where did our damaged corporal decide to go?"

"He told them he wanted to go to Chicago, where there was a better VA hospital."

"Or a better something," said Rosie.

"The Gypsy Promised Land," I said. "Did they give him a pension, to boot?"

"Just a little one, 'cause he was only a little crazy. Three hundred bucks and change, every month."

"That was a lot of money back then. He was maybe crazier than we think. Does he still collect it?"

"Would you believe he does? Never did get sane, I guess. Also never died. Or never admitted to it."

"Probably never will, either. Want me to guess where the pension gets sent to?"

"General Delivery, Skokie, Illinois."

"Bingo," said Rosie.

"More bingo than you know," said Wilkie. "That's also where the money for the eighteen hundred dollar check from Amy Cox came from. First Bank of Skokie, Illinois."

"Did we get his mustering-out medicals?" I said.

"I already told you, he was absolutely sort of crazy is all. Everything else was just your normal used-soldier stuff."

"Let's see."

Wilkie pulled the appropriate part of the file, and I looked at the grainy faxes of the even grainier old mimeo forms and found the section headed "Distinguishing Scars or Marks."

"Seems our man Cox had a nasty scar from a burn on his left forearm," I said. "And fairly new, back then."

"This is important?"

"This is the clincher," said Rosie, and I nodded in agreement.

Wilkie gave us a perplexed look and I gave him a short version of the story about the Ardennes Forest. "He had to burn himself to cover the tattoo from the concentration camp," I said. "I thought at the time Yonkos told me the story, he was lying about something, but I couldn't tell what. All that poetic stuff about not knowing where the story came from originally? Hell, he *was* the story."

"Well, part of it," said Rosie.

"Exactly half," I said. "Now the question is…"

"Who was the German?" said Wilkie.

"That's the question, all right."

"I don't think even the Prophet can run that one down for us."

"He doesn't have to. The man will come to us."

"Yeah, I'm so damn sure he wants to," said Wilkie.

"He will?" said Rosie.

"You bet. In a shiny black LTD with a bag of money in it. We're going to accept the last offer from Mr. G. Cox."

"I don't trust him," said Rosie.

"I don't trust him twice as much," said Wilkie. "And when I don't trust people, that's not a good thing. Especially for them."

"Hold onto that thought, both of you," I said. "Hold it really well."

<><><>

Wide Track went back to my office to send the email to Cox accepting his offer, and to wait for a reply. Rosie and I took the limping pickup into town and to the Amtrak depot, to pick up my BMW. It had evolved into a much nicer machine in my absence. Or maybe it just profited by comparison with the 1968 International Harvester pickup. Rosie went inside the terminal to get a schedule, so I would know what train to claim I had come back to town on. I wiped down the pickup, checked it one last time, and left it with the keys in the ignition. It was a sort of feeble, blind payback gesture. The naive but sincere young woman who had rented me the Pontiac might or might not get in trouble when I didn't bring it back. Not a damn thing I could do about that. But some poor bastard fresh off a freight train from North Bumjungle might just get a shot of unexpected good fortune by finding the clunker. It wouldn't really balance the cosmic scales, but it was the best I could do.

Rosie brought me a printed schedule that showed a train arriving from Seattle in about an hour, which meant any time in the next half day, and I made a mental note to come back and hassle the ticket clerk again at the appropriate time. If I had time, that is. But first, we got in the BMW and went to see my friendly pawnbroker.

<>◇<>

Nickel Pete was sitting on his regular perch and, as usual, took his hands from under the counter and smiled when he saw me.

"Herman, my friend! And with a brand new blonde, too. Is this maybe a new feature of the bonding business I didn't know about? I renew my offer to partner with you."

Rosie gave me a raised eyebrow and I told her the last time I had been there was with Amy Cox.

"I hope that time didn't set a precedent," said Rosie.

"Don't give it a thought, young lady." Pete waved a hand dismissively. "Nobody will ever do that to me again, I promise you. But I still got good instruments to show, if you want."

Rosie looked more puzzled than ever at that, with a look that asked, "do *what* to him?" I didn't bother to explain for Pete. He was a big boy; he could extract his own foot from his mouth. Or choke on it. I took the pawn ticket for the Amati out of my wallet and laid it on the counter. "Let's have a look at this one," I said.

"Ah, Herman, what can I say?" He put his hands against the sides of his head, as if it needed to be kept from exploding. "Forget about paying off the ticket. Forget about the vig, even. I owe you way more than that for my stupidity. I don't know how I'm ever going to make it up to you." Apparently simply paying for the lost violin never occurred to him.

"Let's just see it, first," I said.

He went in the back room and returned with the battered black case, which he put down on the counter and opened. I couldn't remember the original one Amy Cox had shown me all that well, but this seemed like a plausible likeness.

"Have you looked at it since we talked on the phone?" I said.

"Why would I do that? To remind myself what a dope I was? This I do not need. I'd be happy if nobody ever looked at it again."

Once again, I had a tiny flash of insight into why some con games work so well. Once the mark decides something is a disaster or a triumph, he never looks at it again.

"It looks old, anyway," I said.

"Sure it looks old. You think I'm going to get taken in by a shiny new plastic one? The broad was slick, Herman. The slickest. She must have made the switch right after she asked if she could kiss her old violin, just for sentimental reasons."

"She did? I didn't see that."

"You were busy scribbling numbers on your little pad or something. It was just so damned corny that I thought I'd be polite and ignore it. And it was a really short time, anyway. Ten seconds, tops. Well, maybe fifteen. But I swear, she never had both cases within easy reach at the same time."

"But she held the Amati up to her face for a little while, with the bottom towards you, hiding what she was doing?"

"Well that would be how you'd kiss the stupid thing, wouldn't it?"

"Maybe. But in this case, I think it was how she changed the label."

"You're a nice guy, Herman, but you're nuts."

"That's a different topic. You got a dentist's mirror and a little flashlight? A long tweezers with a kink or two in the prongs would be good, too. I had a professional lecture about violin labels a while back. I want to see if it was true."

"You mean like, 'labels come and labels go'?"

"Mostly, they accumulate, is what I was told. Get the stuff, will you?"

He went in the back again and returned with an enameled steel box full of tools. I picked a little maglight, shone it in one f-hole, and peeked in the other one. I didn't need a mirror or a magnifying glass to read the name Yamaha.

"This label is oval-shaped and sort of big," I said. "Is that what a Yamaha label should look like?"

"Who the hell knows? The logo is right. Sometimes companies change the shape of the rest of it over the years. And they have been making Yamahas for a while, you know. I don't know them all."

"Uh huh. Give me the tweezers, will you?"

"Sure." He handed me something that looked like a surgical tool. "What are you going to do with it?"

"Peel the label off."

"Excuse me for saying so, Herman, but now you're talking like the amateur you are. Those things aren't meant just to be peeled off. They're stuck on with some damned good glue that has to be steamed or scraped or…"

"It's coming."

"It can't be."

But it did. First one small arc of an edge, then a bigger and bigger blister, and finally the whole thing. The label paper wasn't exactly happy about it, but it didn't pull apart, either, and soon I had it hanging from the jaws of my tool like the skin of a tiny molting reptile. I carefully pulled it out through the f-hole and held it up.

"Looks like stickyback," said Rosie. "Sort of yellowy-colored, but definitely new."

But Pete wasn't looking at the newly peeled label. He was peering intently into the f-hole again, where the faded black script on a crackled paper label could still be clearly seen to say, "Nicolò Amati, A.D. 1643."

"Holy shit," he said.

"No, just an old violin," said Rosie. But she took a look, too.

"Of some kind," I said. "Have you got anything here that will make a small, directable jet of steam?"

"I got a thingy I use to clean complicated jewelry sometimes. What do you want it for?"

"Now we're going to see what's under the Amati label."

Chapter Nineteen

Fiddle Game

Considering that the mighty Mississippi was once the very highway of commerce for St. Paul, it's amazing how much of the present-day waterfront is either undeveloped or abandoned. On the flats below limestone bluffs that hold up downtown are some railroad tracks, an empty warehouse that used to hold huge rolls of paper for the *Pioneer Press*, the back door of the jail, and at the bottom of the appropriately named Steep Street, the County Morgue.

Farther upstream, I'm told there used to be an Italian neighborhood called, not too surprisingly, Little Italy. But it couldn't survive the triple plagues of flood, fire, and the Zoning Board, and by the time I came to St. Paul the area had reverted to a wasteland of weeds, scrubby trees, and surreptitiously dumped junk. There was also a scrapyard and two power plants, one abandoned and one working, but the dominant landscape was urban wilderness. They shot a really awful movie there once, with Keanu Reeves and Cameron Diaz, about small-time crooks. I think the former Little Italy was where they went to bump people off.

Next to the river, there's a couple miles of paved walkway. Nobody ever uses it because it doesn't go anywhere, it's exposed to traffic on the area's only road, and you can't park within half a mile of either end. Also, the police don't patrol it much. And that's where Gerald Cox, which was not his name, chose to trade me eighteen thousand dollars for my violin, which was not really mine. And I didn't even consider refusing. Was the spell of the thing getting to me, too?

Wilkie didn't like the setup, but then, he wouldn't. When he covers my back, he likes to do it from close range, where his sheer physical presence and strength are big advantages, and his lack of speed doesn't matter. He also likes to hear what is going on, and in the time we had to get ready, there was no way we could get a hidden radio rigged up. Somehow, I didn't think the hastily scrounged cell phone in my pocket, even with an open connection, was going to be much help. I had slightly more faith in the nine-millimeter semiauto tucked into the belt clip at the small of my back. Slightly. I didn't have a whole lot of faith in anything just then. But if we quibbled about the setup, we were liable to get another one just as bad, besides making our man more wary and less likely to go through with the deal at all. I didn't want that. I wanted some kind of conclusion. It was time to quit being sneaky and clever and make something happen.

The offer was simple enough:

mr. jackson

bring the violin to the pedestrian walk along shepard road, across from the metal scrapyard, at midnight and walk from the upstream end to the downstream one. You will be given eighteen thousand dollars cash for your violin, and our business will then be at an end. You will not need any assistants or observers.

tonight.

g. cox

And wasn't that just too, too fearsomely cloak and daggerish? Some bored bureaucrat, dying for a bit of drama and intrigue? Wilkie bitched and said it was the perfect setup for a hit. Rosie just rolled her eyes and shook her head sadly. I accepted the offer. Then I went off to the Amtrak depot to wait for the train.

After all, it wouldn't do for me to get killed down by the river if I hadn't yet come back from Seattle.

There weren't a lot of streetlights along Shepard Road to begin with, and several had lamps that needed replacing. The ones that worked made a ragged line from the black parking lot of the abandoned power plant to the illuminated arches of the Robert Street Bridge, some three or more miles distant. The walkway itself wasn't lit at all. It was not as dark as the cellar in Skokie had been, but it damn sure wasn't the Great White Way, either. On my right was a line of concrete freeway barriers about three feet high, which are used to hold sandbags during floods. I touched the tops now and then to keep my spatial orientation. Beyond them, the river rushed and gurgled, occasionally showing a glint of reflected light on its dark, undulating surface. It looked fast, powerful, and very close, and it occurred to me that I would not care to find myself trying to swim in it. No wonder Wilkie hadn't liked the setup. But I had agreed to be there, I reminded myself, and it was too late to back out now. The streetlights beckoned and I went.

Off to my left, the expanse of scrubby brush got wider as I went east, downstream, finally flaring out to a full quarter of a mile. Rosie was out there somewhere, shadowing me as well as she could without being too obvious about it. Our thinking was that if she got spotted, our mystery man, assuming he was local, was not so likely to associate her with me, though the new all-black catburglar outfit she insisted on wearing probably made her more, rather than less, conspicuous. Wilkie, on the other hand, would stand out like Wilkie, no matter what he wore. I didn't know where he was. He had told me I didn't want to know and I had believed him. But wherever my people were, I definitely felt alone. Alone and vulnerable.

I started down the walk exactly at midnight, using one of the flashlights I had bought in Skokie for occasional guidance and moral support, carrying the violin case in my left hand. I walked steadily but not in any hurry, and I stopped from time to time to listen to the river. There was nothing else to listen to. No footsteps, no cocking of guns, no banshees or werewolves.

A thousand yards down the walkway, as I was about to pass under High Bridge, I came upon a leather briefcase sitting on top of one of the flood barriers. It had a tiny flashlight on it which was turned on, presumably so I wouldn't miss the case in the dark. I stopped and played my own flashlight beam over it, and I saw something glint on the side, under the handle. When I went closer, I could see it was a shiny brass plate. Closer still, and I saw my name engraved on it. *Nice touch. A personalized booby trap.* But I didn't think so. I put the violin down on the sidewalk.

From inside my jacket pocket, I could hear a small, tinny version of Wilkie's voice. I think he was trying to whisper and scream at the same time.

"Don't open that thing, Herman! Don't even touch it!"

I popped the latches.

"Goddamn it, Herman, I know you can hear me!"

I opened the lid.

"Get away from that thing, now!"

I looked. Inside the case were several stacks of bundled bills and a note. The bills were all used twenties, and I didn't try to count them, but it seemed like about the right amount of bulk for eighteen grand. The note was not as elegant as the brass plate. Done in magic marker on a plain sheet of typing paper, it simply said:

LEAVE THE VIOLIN WHERE YOU FOUND THE CASE
TAKE THE CASE
GO

Simple enough. I saw no reason to argue with any of those instructions, other than the fact that I had really come there to meet their author. I snapped the case shut, picked it up, placed the violin in the same spot, and stepped back. But I didn't leave right away. I had no urge to kiss the fiddle, or even shake hands with it, but it didn't seem right simply to turn away and never look at it again. Maybe I thought it owed me an apology.

In my pocket, the mechanized Wilkie shouted, "Will you please get the hell out of there?" His voice had less conviction than before, but I knew he was right. As I was about to oblige him, I heard the crack of doom from the jungle to my left. It was loud and high-pitched, and it had that kind of lingering reverberation that comes only from very high-powered, heavy caliber rifles. A deer rifle, I thought. Definitely not one of Rosie's handguns. Not a seven-millimeter, either. I hit the dirt, or rather the sidewalk, and put the briefcase over my head.

The first shot hit the concrete bumper, close to the center, making a distressingly large crater and showering me with shards and powder. *One shot to find the range. The next one will be for real.* The second one hit the violin. It hit it squarely and explosively, smashing both case and instrument into splinters and dust and sending all the pieces spinning off into space. Or rather, into the black river, which swept them away forever. I tipped the briefcase up on edge, making an inadequate wall out of it, and I braced myself for the heavy slug that I was sure would find me next. After a second, I also drew my knees up in front of my torso, thinking it was better to have a shattered leg than a bullet in the gut. Then I drew the nine millimeter from under my jacket, and I waited. And waited. Where the hell were my partners?

There was no third shot.

After what seemed like forever, Rosie came running at me from the bushes, her big revolver at high port, eyes scanning all directions.

"Herman? Herman, if you're dead, I am going to be so damn pissed at you, I'll never let you forget it."

"I'm flattered."

"Flattered? What about shot?"

"No." I rose to a more dignified position and started to stand all the way up.

"Well, maybe you ought to be. I mean, walking into a setup like that, with…"

"Herman? You okay, my man? You catch one?" Wilkie, this time, breaking out of the bushes like a small herd of mammoths. He had some kind of an assault rifle with a night scope, but having no target for it, he didn't quite seem to know what to do with the thing.

"I already had this conversation, Wide. I mean, if you can't come in at the beginning, you could at least…"

"You sure you're not shot?"

"I'm sure. I'd have noticed, you know? Are you sure you didn't catch anybody?"

"Um," said Rosie.

"Well, see…" said Wilkie

I put the nine back in its holster and dusted off my clothes. It definitely wasn't the way I had expected the scene to play out, but I was fairly certain it was over. At least as far as our mysterious Mr. Cox was concerned, it was. He had given us money, bullets, and excitement, but no interview, thank you.

"Anybody see anything?"

"Muzzle flashes off that way," said Wilkie, pointing to a wall of vegetation that looked like the rain forest on the banks of the Amazon, black and impenetrable.

"Let's have a look." I picked up the flashlight from where I had dropped it and headed that way.

"Are you nuts?" said Wilkie.

"He could still be there," said Rosie.

"I don't think so. If he wanted me dead, I'd already be that way. I think he's gone."

"So what did he want?" said Rosie.

"Obviously, he wanted to destroy the violin. And he likes rivers better than bonfires, I guess."

"That's crazy," she said.

"No, but I think it may be tragic, in the classic sense."

"Same thing," said Wilkie. He went ahead for a bit, to beat a trail into the brush. We could smell the cordite now, as sweet as lingering lilacs on the cool night air.

"What's in the case?" he said. "The one that you picked up in spite of all my good advice."

"Money."

"Real money?"

"It sure looks real, anyway. And I'd be willing to bet it's exactly the right amount."

"I don't get it," said Wilkie.

"Me either," said Rosie.

"I think I do. I think in his own way, our Mr. Cox is an honorable man. That's why he offered me eighteen thousand, the exact value of my bond. He was buying the violin back and giving me a chance to get clear of it. Not to get rich or even to make a profit, mind you, just to get clear. And if I took the money, that would show him I was honorable, too, and he would settle for that."

"But why...?"

"It was the final con, the one that got him clear, too. He not only had to destroy the violin, he had to be sure I saw it destroyed. That was the whole point."

"But it's not..."

"Here," said Wilkie, shining his own flashlight on a small clearing in the bushes. The brush was trampled down a bit there, and on the ground lay a very old, heavy rifle. It fit. In fact, everything finally fit.

"Mauser?" I said.

"The man knows his guns."

"No I don't, but I know my history. Sometimes I even know my modern myth. The gun is a throwback to another age, and so is our shooter. Also a romantic. I think he left it here to show us that the affair is over, that he's done with it."

I picked up the rifle and looked at the oiled metal and polished wood, lovingly cared for by professional hands. Hands I had seen. Big, strong hands that could push a carving chisel through a block of hard maple, without using a mallet. Hands that could also break somebody's neck.

"I can't believe how long it took me to figure it out," I said. "I know this man."

"It's the German?" said Wilkie.

"Yes." I nodded. "The German from the Ardennes Forest. Only, now he makes fine violins and even better coffee. He also tells great stories. His name is G. B. Feinstein."

"I don't sell…" he began, not looking up from his work.

"Out of the shop," I finished for him. "I knew that already."

I held up a package of rolls and a bottle. "Actually, I came here hoping for some coffee."

He put down the chisel, stood up, and laughed, the only time I ever saw him do so.

"Ah, coffee," he said. "Well, that would be a different matter altogether. Come in, *mein herr.*"

The cinnamon rolls weren't quite as fresh this time, but they weren't bad. I figured the delivery man from the bakery wouldn't buy my phony cop routine a second time, so I followed his truck to an all-night convenience store and bought the rolls, legit. I also stopped at Lefty's bar and got the bottle, not quite so legit. Lefty's license technically doesn't allow him to sell liquor for consumption off the premises, but he indulged me, for future times' sake. He does enough things outside the law that, while he might not always accommodate a cop or even a wise guy, he won't risk offending his bondsman. Every profession has its perks, they say.

Feinstein brewed the coffee in the same freestyle way as he had when we first met, and as the aroma began to fill his shop and we smeared butter on the warm rolls, it was tempting to think that nothing had happened since that first time. But of course, it had, and we both knew this was as much a farewell as a reunion.

"I didn't expect to see you again, *Herr* Herman."

"A lot of people have had that prejudice, over the years. But I'm not as easy to get rid of as they generally suppose."

"Are you again on the run?"

"I don't think so. It's hard to tell for sure, but the cop who wanted me is dead now, and I think that's the end of it." *But then, you already know that.*

"The coffee is ready, I think."

I held out my cup and he poured steaming black liquid in it, leaving room for the obligatory spike. As he did so, I watched his hands and again saw the steady power and control. No wonder I hadn't noticed his age. I could see it now, easily enough. The shoulders were stooped a bit, even when he wasn't bent over his work, and the slicked back hair was obviously dyed. And he had strong facial bone lines, but like my Uncle Fred, he flashed intelligence and energy from eyes that were nevertheless trapped in a matrix of wrinkles. He poured coffee for himself after serving me, then put the pot down and added booze to both cups, taking a swig directly from the bottle first.

"This is excellent brandy," he said.

"Technically, it's five-star cognac, but I have to admit the distinction is somewhat lost on me. Brandy is brandy. The only difference is who you drink it with."

"I think I like that." He clinked his cup to mine. "To present company."

"To old friends," I said.

"You think so?" He smiled and took a large drink. "I like to think we might have been, in another world. But our history did not go that way, yes? It is a terrible burden, history."

"It can be," I said, meaning it more deeply than he would ever know. I took a gulp of the steaming brew and savored the familiar hot rush. "But are you talking about you and me, or about the history of a place called the Ardennes Forest?"

"You know this story, then? I am impressed."

"I know a version of it, anyway. Shall I tell you?"

He nodded and took a bite of roll, settling down on a corner of a workbench. I retold Stefan Yonkos' story for him, including where and how I came to hear it. As I did so, he alternately shook and nodded his head, smiling sadly the whole time. At one point, he may have blinked back a tear. He waited until I was done before he said anything.

"Well, that's the way he would tell it, wouldn't he? And he's had a long time to polish it up. But he left out the most important part."

"Which was?"

"When he killed the real Gerald Cox."

Chapter Twenty

End Game

March 17, 1945

The American was on the road when they first saw him, walking with his head down and his rifle at sling-arms. They spotted him in the mist before he was aware of them, and they immediately ducked behind a tree.

"Give me your rifle," the Gypsy whispered in German.

"But he is not a Russian. We do not need the charade that you planned."

"We need another one, if we want to be treated well."

"But we..."

"Trust me, this will be better. I will say that I am a partisan, a resistance soldier, and that I have captured you. Then he will take us both to his superiors, not just to a prison camp, and the war will be over for us."

"You think you can convince him of such a story?"

"I speak enough English, and he looks stupid enough. And he will want to believe it."

"If you are sure..."

"I'm sure. Quickly now!"

The German handed over his Mauser and felt the power of it pass to the other man as well. He immediately wondered if he had done a foolish thing, and he felt in his coat pocket for the reassuring bulk of the 7 mm Luger he had taken from a dead SS officer. But he didn't know if he could bring himself to use it, even to save his own life. A gangly youth with a hooked nose and dark hair, trying to be a grown up soldier in an army that worshipped tall, square-featured blond goons, he had never had any confidence in anything. He let the Gypsy push him out onto the road, hands aloft, rifle poking in his spine.

"Hey, GI! I have a prize for you. I make you a hero, okay?"

The American, probably ashamed at being caught off guard, snapped his rifle up to his shoulder and went down on one knee and into a firing position.

"Who the hell are y'all? I mean, who goes there? Halt, is what I mean."

"Okay, Joe. It is okay," the Gypsy crooned, and his voice became progressively lower and more rhythmic. "I am partisan, okay? I capture Nazi bad guy for you. Here he is, you see? He is halt already."

The American got up and advanced warily, keeping his rifle trained on both of them, but mainly pointed at the German.

"He don't look like much of a soldier to me."

"He is a boy, is all. The Nazis are all out of men. Now they send children to fight. You take him for a prisoner, yes?"

"He's all disarmed and all? He ain't got no knife or nothing?"

"I have his rifle," said the Gypsy. "Is all he had."

The German continued to hold his hands up, looking fearful, understanding small bits of the conversation but mostly wondering if both he and the Gypsy were about to be shot. The GI came up close to him, stared into his eyes, spat on the ground, and finally lowered his weapon. The moment he stepped back, the Gypsy raised the Mauser and pressed it to the side of the American's head. "Now you give us your weapon," he said.

"What are you doing?" said the German. "He wasn't going to shoot us. I'm sure of it."

"Take his gun."

"Have you gone mad?"

"Take it, or I'll shoot both of you."

The German lowered his arms and took the US Army carbine, holding it uncertainly. And he noticed the man's name, stenciled on his fatigue jacket: G. B. Cox.

"Do you think this American will give me his clothes now?" said the Gypsy. "Will he give me his identity?"

"Of course not. Why would he do that?"

"I don't think so, either." The Mauser was still at the American's head, and he pulled the trigger, sending the man's helmet flying off into the trees, along with large pieces of his skull and brains.

The German soldier didn't wait to see what would happen next. He fled into the forest as fast as he could run. More shots from his own gun slammed into the trees around him, but he never slowed down and never looked back. Finally, miles later, when he could run no further, he fell to his hands and knees and retched uncontrollably onto the carpet of pine needles. And he wept. He wept the tears of a boy who has realized his own fear and a man who has witnessed an obscene atrocity and was utterly unable to do anything about it. He judged himself and found himself lacking, and he wept and trembled and vomited until he was empty and spent.

He slept then, on the rough forest floor, through the day and into the darkness. When he finally rose again and left that place, he vowed that he would never weep or tremble again.

He may have never trembled again, but he had tears running down his cheeks as he finished the story. He turned his back to me and busied himself with making a fresh pot of coffee.

"Good lord," I said. "You were right about Yonkos leaving out the most important part. What happened after that? Did you also vow to kill the Gypsy?"

"No. That did not happen until much, much later. The rest of my war story is not so interesting, I'm afraid. I went back to the place where Cox had been shot. The Gypsy had left his own clothes there, and I took them. I threw my own uniform away and I became what he had said he was going to pretend to be, a partisan living off the land. I also threw away the American gun, which I didn't know how to use, and found another Mauser. It was a hard life for a while, but I didn't care any more. I found my way to an American army camp, a staging area, and they kept me around, like a mascot. That was when I took the name of Feinstein. I thought they would be more likely to believe I wasn't a Nazi if I had a Jewish-sounding name. And I added the G. B. so I would always remember the name of the dead American."

I poured myself some more coffee and thought of Rosie and her many aliases. *Doesn't anybody or anything in this damn world go by its real name anymore?* Then I remembered my own past and bit my tongue. Feinstein, for that was now his only name, continued.

"I worked on their trucks and did menial jobs, and they taught me bits of English. You wouldn't believe how long it was before I learned that 'fuckin' A' was not the correct way to say 'I agree.' And when the unit was sent back to the United States, I stowed away on the transport ship."

"Along with the Mauser?"

"Yes. And the Luger. There were many, many souvenir guns being taken back. A few more didn't matter. I never got a visa or any citizenship papers, and I never will. Your wonderful government gave me a Social Security card anyway. After you have that, you can get anything."

"Under your assumed name."

"Of course. I got a job cleaning up and doing general labor in a guitar factory, and I decided to teach myself luthiery. It seemed like a way of coming to terms with my great downfall, you see. A calling, if you will. The rest is pretty much what you would expect."

"How old were you, back when you met the Gypsy in the forest?"

"I was born in 1931."

"Jesus, Mary, and Joseph. You really were just a kid."

"Not after that, I was not. After that, I was never young again."

"No. You wouldn't be, would you?" I stopped for a moment, took a deep breath, and braced myself. Sooner or later, somebody had to say the obvious, and I decided it might as well be then.

"So you killed Stefan Yonkos, finally..." I began.

"And his daughter and son, don't forget."

"No. I definitely didn't forget. You killed them all for revenge? Revenge for your lost youth and innocence?"

"Revenge? Oh no, *Herr Herman*. I never thought of it in that way for a moment. It was setting things right, you see, making up for my own past failure. War is all about guilt. People talk these days about post-stress something..."

"Post Traumatic Stress Syndrome," I said.

"Ya ya, that is it. Thank you. But it's always about the guilt of killing. They think that's all there is, the doctors. Backwards, for me, all wrong. All those years, all the places I went, I carried the guilt of who I did *not* kill. I should have killed the Gypsy."

Where had I heard that before?

"You could have been killed yourself, trying to," I said.

"Very true. But then, also, I would have been free of the guilt. And the poor man named Gerald Cox might also have lived."

"Might have, could have, should have," I said. "You take all those 'haves' and put them with three dollars, and you can buy yourself another package of these cinnamon rolls. Why bother with it, after all these years? I mean"—I swept my hand around, indicating the shop behind us—"you have a vocation here, a real life. A calling, even. Most poor working stiffs never find that. Couldn't you let the past go its own way?"

"You would think so, wouldn't you? And believe it or not, I tried. But the past would not let me go. Twenty some years ago, it came to claim me."

"The certificate of authenticity," I said.

"Exactly so. It was 1975, as I recall. The blonde—I forget what she was calling herself back then—wanted me to appraise her old violin, certify it as a real Amati. Which it was, of course. And from what she told me of its story, I knew it had to be the violin from the Ardennes."

"And she was the Gypsy's daughter."

"She said as much, and I had no reason to doubt it."

"Was that when you switched the violins?"

"*Mein Gott!* You figured that out, also? *Wünderbar!* How?"

"I took off the label. Somebody told me once that the real trademark would be burned in the wood, under it."

"Ah, so he did, *Herr* Herman. That's what comes of revealing trade secrets, *ya*? Still, it had to take a lot of confidence to remove a fragile piece of history. But you have surprised me many times now. You are, as you say, not so easy to dispose of. Yes, I switched the violins then. I told the woman I had to keep the Amati for a few days, to do some tests. That gave me enough time to make one of the others in my collection into a very good likeness. It was a small enough bit of sabotage, considering what her family had done. And for a time, I thought it would be enough for me. More brandy?"

"Thank you," I said. "For the brandy and the compliments. Are we out of coffee?"

"I thought perhaps it was time to get down to essentials."

"Maybe it is, at that."

We both took another shot, clinking our cups again.

"But you must have assumed I'd look under the label sooner or later," I said. "And when I saw the burned-in brand of Roger Baldwin, written backwards, it would point me straight to you."

"I assumed later, rather than sooner," he said. "Or possibly not at all. Maybe someday another appraiser would do it, say. In the meantime, it was possible to do one last, um…"

"Con."

"Yes, thank you. A last con in a world of cons. If I destroyed the instrument that you thought was the Amati and made good on your cash losses, then that would be the end of it. The curse, the killing, and even the past. I wanted you to be free of it, you see."

"I picked up on that, yes. Thank you so much. Why?"

He shrugged. "I told you when we first met that I liked you. That buffoon, Evans, died just because he got in the way. I didn't want that to happen to you."

"Are you saying you didn't tip him off that I was in Skokie?"

"Tip him off? Oh, no. I was never in league with him or any of them. As far as they knew, I was just a disinterested appraiser, used once and forgotten."

"You know, that's really rather wonderfully ironic." I had another sip from the tin cup, and it seemed even more so.

"It is, isn't it? The violin that led me to become a fine luthier also led the Gypsy family back to me for a final accounting, and they didn't even know it."

"I believe I led you to Skokie, though."

"On the contrary, I followed Evans to Skokie, not you. He was what the Gypsies call the cop-in-the-pocket, you see. The woman, Amy, was the bait in a sweet fish hook, I think? No, that's not quite right."

"A honey trap."

"*Ya, ya*, that's it. Thank you again. She was supposed to compromise him, seduce him and make him pliable. But I think she succeeded beyond her own hopes. He not only became her lover, he became insanely protective and jealous of her. And he really did think you had killed her. So when you were looking for the Gypsy connection, he was looking for you, to kill you, I'm sure. I was merely looking for her father, looking to be sure that Yonkos *was* her father. And Evans was so very easy to follow. The man couldn't go for an hour without calling somebody or other on the radio or phone. Not like you, *Herr* Herman. You were really very clever."

"Not so clever that you didn't almost trap me and kill me when I went back to the *officia*."

"That was you?"

"Me and a friend."

"Ah, yes, the pretty woman. Perhaps I spent too much time looking at her. Anyway, that was a mistake. I wasn't sure you hadn't given your violin to Yonkos, and I thought it might be more of the Gypsy gang, come back to retrieve it. And to be honest, the killing had almost become a habit by then. It wanted to have a life of its own. An evil life, just like the violin that started it all. The hunter of evil becomes evil himself."

"So you really weren't part of the original con game at all?"

"Never. Not that one, nor any of the others the brother and sister ran over the years. And there were many."

"So how did you know about them?"

"Well, I wouldn't know about the ones before I did the appraisal, would I? After that, I followed their career from a distance, you might say. An insurance adjustor or a policeman would come to me to verify the certificate, and so I would get a new set of bogus names, a new bit of a trail. I never knew exactly how the fraud worked or how they kept getting the Amati back. And I didn't care. I waited and waited for them to lead me back to the father. Finally, when they started using the name Cox for their scams, the name they had stolen, it was just too much. I decided if I couldn't kill the father, I would kill the children

230 Richard A. Thompson

instead. After all, they were my mistake, too. He shouldn't have lived to sire them in the first place."

"So you stalked Amy Cox?"

"An ugly word, but yes, I suppose I did. I followed her to your office, and when she finally left with a violin under her arm, I seized my chance. But as you know, that killing was a beginning, not an end."

"It was an end for her."

"True enough."

"Did you really break her neck, or was Evans just telling me that to rattle me?"

"Oh, I broke her neck, all right. I wanted her dead, but I didn't want her to suffer, after all. It was always Yonkos I was after. And when I finally found him, he didn't even remember who I was. Can you believe that?"

"Well, he was under rather a lot of stress at the time. And he was also blind, remember."

"Hmm. Or he pretended to be. I tell you one thing, though: After I finally killed him, I slept without dreams for the first time in fifty years."

"And the real Amati?"

"Can't you guess?" He grinned slyly and chuckled. "A clever fellow like yourself?"

I let my gaze drift pointedly to the Baldwin hanging on his wall, the one he had shown me that first night. Feinstein saw my gaze and nodded in silent confirmation. And it may have been the booze at work, but I felt obliged to chuckle, too.

"Why is it called the Wolf?" I said.

"Because it has a wolf note, of course."

"Say what?"

"You do not know this thing? It is every violin maker's worst nightmare. It is an unplanned harmonic, a note that emerges without being played, a squawk in the middle of an otherwise flawless performance. It is a rogue harmony that the box will produce, again and again."

"But the whole art of making violins is harmonics, I thought. How can this happen?"

"It only happens among the very best ones. It's rare and unpredictable, and it seldom shows itself when the instrument is new. But once it emerges, there is no remedy for it at all. The instrument becomes worthless for professional play. Some museum might give a few thousand for it, since it is still an Amati, but that's all."

"So after that, it's only good for con games."

"Or hanging on my wall. Fitting, is it not?"

And that may have also been the booze, but I had to admit that it was. I couldn't let it stay there, but it was very fitting.

We drank and talked for a long time then, telling each other trivial or monumental stories, both of us avoiding the obvious question. Feinstein produced another bottle and we slipped into it seamlessly. Finally, it was he who broached the unspeakable.

"You talked a while ago about me having a true vocation, I think?"

"I did," I said, nodding with intoxicated exaggeration. "Many people would envy it."

"And I would trade it for a good night's sleep, as it turned out. Amusing. But the problem, I think, is not my profession, but yours."

"How do you mean?"

"You work for the law. You have personal knowledge of four killings. Surely, you have to do something about that?"

"Do I?" I said.

"Don't you?"

"I work for the law, I suppose." I sighed. That's a fact that I've never really come to terms with. "But I'm not a lawman. I'm not always sure just what I am, but it's not that. A referee, maybe. I make sure everybody plays by the rules."

"And the rules in this case?"

"Are simple. The police are entitled to arrest you, and the DA is entitled to try to convict you. But I don't have to help them. I won't lie to them, but I won't do their jobs for them, either.

And I won't call them. If they want you, they have to do their own homework."

He looked astonished. Maybe I did, too, since I had just then figured it all out.

"But this is very generous!" he said.

"Not as generous as you think. I do still have to give the violin back."

"Now you joke, I think. The violin you had is dust on the river, and its owner is dead."

"But her people are still alive. And the violin she *thought* she had is still around, too. One way or another, we both need to be clear of it. If you don't pay off all your debts, they just go back to accumulating interest."

"No, Herman, you cannot mean this. You cannot ask me to do this thing."

"That's the deal I made with the *familyia* in Skokie," I said. "And it's also what I owe to Amy Cox. The duty of my office, if you like that better. What you called my vocation."

"They will only use it to swindle more people, you know."

"They will swindle more people, no matter what. It's what they do. I'm only responsible for what I do. And I have to do this."

"I could still kill you, you know." His powerful hand reached deep in the pocket of his smock, and I had no doubt of what it found there.

"You could, yes. Is that the same Luger you had in the forest?" I said. "The one that has kept you from sleeping for fifty years?"

"Of course."

"I don't think you want to let it do that to you again."

"I... But you can't..." The hand came back out of the pocket, and the gun was in it, but he wasn't pointing it at me. He waved it around aimlessly, as if looking for a correct gesture. Then he laid it on a bench and began to weep. Maybe he also trembled, I'm not sure. I turned away and walked toward the door.

"It's been a long night, G.B., and a lot of heavy talk. And I have drunk more than I need or can handle. I'm going out to my car, the gray BMW across the street. I'm going to tip the seat back and have a very long sleep. Maybe I'll have a dream that tells me what to do about you. Good night, and thanks for everything. Especially the coffee."

I waited for the gunshot that would end my life or his, but it did not come. Instead, as I was almost out the door, I heard him say very quietly, "It has been my pleasure, *Herr* Herman."

I went down to my car and did exactly what I had said I would. The long sleep part was very easy.

The next morning, I found a violin case on the seat beside me. So I knew what to do about Feinstein. Back in the building, his shop was deserted, the walls and benches partially stripped, the door unlocked. He wasn't there.

I never saw the man again.

Epilogue

The police never did come to question me, about Feinstein or Amy Cox, or anything else that had to do with old violins and even older passions. Maybe my uneasy allies, the Rom, had done their jobs, at that. The day after the long night of brandy and soul baring, I met Wilkie in my office and gave him the violin case.

"I've got one last job for you, Wide."

"I'm not going in any more jungles."

"That was a City park, sort of," I said.

"That's its problem."

"This jungle has naked ladies in it."

"Yeah? I'm listening."

"Go find a strip joint in Chicago called the New Lost City, and give this to the night bartender, named Joe Paterno. Tell him it's the Wolf, and it will make him clean if anything can." Joe wasn't really Amy Cox's heir, of course. But then, the Gypsies hadn't really said what they were going to do for me, and in return, I hadn't exactly said who in the *familyia* I was going to give the fiddle back to. Fair is fair.

"Everybody talks in riddles today," he said. But he took the case. "Your girlfriend, Rosie, is talking in riddles, too."

"You saw her today?"

"Just for a bit, this morning at the coffee shop. She says to tell you she's all square with your uncle Fred now. I told her you don't have an uncle, Fred or anything else, but she just laughs, says her markers are all paid off now and she's heading out. What the hell's she talking about?"

"Beats me," I said. "She's crazy." And she had told me as much, more than once. But not as crazy as she seemed at times. Nor was she merely a restless soul running away from a dinky town diner. She was a pro of some kind, one of Uncle Fred's people, and he had sent her to look after me, no less. I always did say he was a good judge of talent.

"When did she leave?" I said. I looked at my watch and suddenly the meaning of the shopping trip in Chicago soaked in. The fancy watch that I would never have bought for myself was Rosie's goodbye gift, given in advance to tell me later that I had not been just an assignment or a debt. Now, when it was almost certainly too late to say so, I was touched.

"About fifteen minutes ago," said Wilkie. "But you aren't going to catch her."

"Why not?"

"She's driving your BMW."

I laughed, in spite of myself. I wouldn't say it to Wilkie, but I felt that she had earned it, wherever she wanted to go with the thing. "Well," I said, "she definitely knows how to do that."

"Yeah?"

"Oh, yeah."

"Whatever," said Wilkie. He left with his signature coattails billowing out behind him. He disappeared into the morning fog, and I watched him do so from the same spot where I had been when Amy Cox had first appeared out of the rain. And I thought about appearances and disappearances and names and labels and illusions and scams and how very muddled they all get at times. I thought about the violin case under Wilkie's huge arm and wondered what was really inside it. Evil? Salvation? Or just an old fiddle? I hadn't looked inside the case, and I didn't intend to.

Finally, I thought about the story Uncle Fred had reminded me of, as I was leaving the visitors room at Redrock, the one he had said to use as my guide. It was an old story, one he had told me many times over the years. I remembered it well.

It happens in the marketplace in ancient Constantinople, a crossroads of commerce and deceit. A young boy, always eager to learn about the ways of the world, is watching the people coming and going when he sees a Turkish merchant, whom he knows, meet a Gypsy who is leading a fine-looking horse. There is lively discussion, money changes hands, and the merchant walks away with the horse. The boy runs after the Gypsy, who is now leaving at a brisk pace.

"Ho, there, Gypsy! Tell me, for my education: did you sell that horse to the Turk?"

"I did," says the Gypsy. "I charged him 54 *sisterces* for it."

"Is that a good price?" says the boy.

"Boy, that is a huge price. That fool of a Turk doesn't know it, but that horse is lame."

The boy then runs the other way and catches up with the merchant, who is leading the horse to a stable.

"Ho, there, Turk! You are the fool of fools. The Gypsy has sold you a lame horse."

"No, no, boy," says the merchant. "It is the Gypsy who is the fool. This horse only walks like he's lame because he has a stone in his shoe. At 54 *sisterces*, I stole this horse."

So the boy runs back to the Gypsy, who is now almost out of town.

"Ho, there, Gypsy! You are the fool of fools. That horse only walks like he's lame because he has a stone in his shoe. The Turk has robbed you."

"Listen to me, boy, for your education. I put that stone in the horse's shoe so the Turk would think that's why he walks that way. That horse really is lame."

Again, the boy runs back to the merchant.

"Ho, Turk! The Gypsy has cheated you, after all. He put the stone in the horse's shoe to deceive you, and you believed what you saw and became a fool."

"This is true?" says the Turk.

"He told me himself, sir."

"Well. A curse on him for a thief, then. Good thing I paid him with counterfeit coins."

To receive a free catalog of Poisoned Pen Press titles, please contact us in one of the following ways:

Phone: 1-800-421-3976
Facsimile: 1-480-949-1707
Email: info@poisonedpenpress.com
Website: www.poisonedpenpress.com

Poisoned Pen Press
6962 E. First Ave. Ste. 103
Scottsdale, AZ 85251

8 VASOS AL DÍA NO SON LA SOLUCIÓN

APAGA TU SED

PLAN DE HIDRATACIÓN PROFUNDA

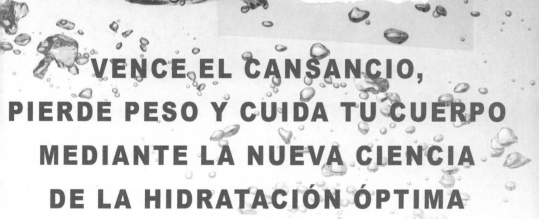

VENCE EL CANSANCIO, PIERDE PESO Y CUIDA TU CUERPO MEDIANTE LA NUEVA CIENCIA DE LA HIDRATACIÓN ÓPTIMA

DANA COHEN · GINA BRIA

edaf

APAGA TU SED

VENCE EL CANSANCIO, PIERDE PESO
Y CUIDA TU CUERPO MEDIANTE LA NUEVA CIENCIA
DE LA HIDRATACIÓN ÓPTIMA

Dana Cohen
Gina Bria

Traducción de Mamen Escudero Millán

www.edaf.net

MADRID · MÉXICO · BUENOS AIRES · SANTIAGO
2018

Título original: *Quench. Beat fatigue, drop weight, and heal your body through the new science of optimum hidration*

© 2017. Dana Cohen · Gina Bria

© 2018. De esta edición, Editorial EDAF, S.L.U., por acuerdo con Hachette Book Group, Inc., representados por A.C.E.R. Agencia Literaria, c/. Amor de Dios, 1, Madrid, 28014, España.

© 2018. De la traducción: Mamen Escudero Millán

Diseño de la cubierta: Marta Elzaurdía López

Maquetación y diseño de interior: Diseño y Control Gráfico, S.L.

Editorial Edaf, S.L.U.
Jorge Juan, 68,
28009 Madrid, España
Teléf.: (34) 91 435 82 60
www.edaf.net
edaf@edaf.net

Ediciones Algaba, S.A. de C.V.
Calle 21, Poniente 3323 - Entre la 33 sur y la 35 sur
Colonia Belisario Domínguez
Puebla 72180 México
Telf.: 52 22 22 11 13 87
jaime.breton@edaf.com.mx

Edaf del Plata, S.A.
Chile, 2222
1227 Buenos Aires (Argentina)
edaf4@speedy.com.ar

Edaf Chile, S.A.
Coyancura, 2270, oficina 914, Providencia
Santiago - Chile
comercialedafchile@edafchile.cl

Octubre de 2018

ISBN: 978-84-414-3884-2
Depósito legal: M-23087-2018

PRINTED IN SPAIN   IMPRESO EN ESPAÑA
COFÁS

A nuestras madres,

Bunny bunbuns

y

Stephanie

Contenido

Prefacio

Mni Wiconi.

«El agua es vida», lema de los sioux lakota.

Este libro sobre la hidratación nació de la mano de dos autoras procedentes de muy diferentes tradiciones: la antropóloga Gina Bria y la doctora Dana Cohen. Cada una de ellas aportó su preparación y su propia experiencia a esta cuestión de vital importancia.

Gina estaba realizando un trabajo de investigación sobre tribus indígenas de regiones desérticas de todo el mundo y sobre el modo en el que lograban sobrevivir en tales condiciones de sequía. Al mismo tiempo, trataba de ocuparse de su anciana madre, que vivía en una residencia de ancianos a más de 1.000 kilómetros de distancia de su casa. Más tarde Gina se daría cuenta de que su madre sufría deshidratación crónica, un problema de salud frecuente entre muchas personas mayores que viven en residencias de ancianos. Como muchos de nosotros, su madre sufría los efectos deshidratantes de vivir en ambientes cerrados: luz artificial, largas horas de inmovilidad, alimentos procesados, medicamentos, escasez de aire fresco y de luz solar, condiciones casi de sequía por su efecto desecante.

Gina necesitaba hallar la manera de aportar a su madre la hidratación que tan desesperadamente necesitaba. Y, de hecho, la respuesta le llegó de los habitantes del desierto a los que estaba estudiando. Eran unos expertos en hidratación. En lugar de buscar agua en su árido entorno, encontraban el agua de otra manera. Practicaban lo que muchos de nosotros hemos olvidado hoy en día: utilizaban, para hidratarse, el agua que contienen *las plantas*. Gina comenzó centrándose en el agua que poseen los alimentos frescos, como las manzanas, para ayudar a su madre a conseguir la hidratación que necesitaba, y los resultados fueron espectaculares. Su madre no volvió a tener ningún percance debido a la deshidratación. A Gina le asombraba que nadie hablara de esta estrategia de bienestar tan sencilla y a la a vez tan absolutamente eficaz, de modo que comenzó a compartir su relato sobre el poder del agua —en especial de la eficacia del agua de las plantas— en el ámbito de la salud.

En el extremo del mundo opuesto a las tierras desérticas en las que vivían esas tribus, en la isla de Manhattan, la doctora Dana Cohen trabajaba al mismo tiempo en su consulta de medicina del Midtown. La doctora Cohen es especialista en medicina integral, dentro del reducido aunque creciente círculo de médicos de la ciudad de Nueva York que evitan prescribir medicamentos para cualquier dolencia. Su enfoque holístico estaba ligado a los últimos conocimientos en ciencias de la nutrición, que ella ofrecía a sus pacientes como una forma innovadora de promover la salud. Siempre estaba buscando métodos nuevos para tratar a sus pacientes e incluso se planteaba escribir un libro sobre el tema. No quería escribir otro título genérico sobre alimentación y salud que se centrara en un área del bienestar o en un pequeño segmento de su población de pacientes. Buscaba un mensaje mucho más universal para acelerar la curación de *todos* sus pacientes. Y estaba empezando a experimentar con un nuevo protocolo en algunos de ellos, tratándolos no solo a través de la nutrición, sino también de la hidratación. Los resultados eran prometedores, y quería ampliarlos.

Un día, Gina y Dana coincidieron en una pequeña consulta después de que varios conocidos comunes en el ámbito profesional insistieran en que se conocieran. Enseguida se dieron cuenta de que ambas habían estado observando los mismos indicios. De hecho, casi nadie entraba en la consulta de Dana sin hablar sobre su inexplicable fatiga y falta de energía. ¿Estaría la deshidratación detrás de tantas dolencias generalizadas? ¿Podría una mejor hidratación ser la solución en origen, al interceptar el declive de las funciones orgánicas? Gina hablaba con apasionamiento de su trabajo de investigación. Los habitantes del desierto utilizaban de manera inteligente las plantas para mantenerse hidratados, y lo conseguían durante mucho más tiempo que los habitantes de las ciudades. No era el volumen de agua en lo que hacían hincapié, sino en la absorción y la retención. Comían plantas que *estaban ya bien hidratadas*.

Gina contó su propia experiencia personal, es decir, el asombroso efecto que la hidratación «absorbida» había tenido en su madre. Dana supo inmediatamente que Gina iba por buen camino en sus investigaciones.

«Piensa en un cactus», dijo Gina a Dana, y continuó contándole cómo había resuelto la deshidratación de su madre. «La animé a tomarse su zumo de naranja mezclado con semillas de chía, para multiplicar por dos la retención de humedad».

Dana tenía también su propia experiencia personal: su madre, enferma de Alzheimer, había fallecido hacía quince años en una residencia de ancianos, dejándola con un terrible sentimiento de frustración como médico y con un dolor tremendo por no haber podido ayudarla. Además, ella veía cómo a diario acudían a su consulta pacientes consumidos, cansados y enfermos y había sido testigo presencial de que la recuperación de un adecuado nivel de hidratación podía curarlos. Sin embargo, hasta ese momento, no había pensado en utilizar la comida como recurso de hidratación.

Mientras iba dando sorbitos al batido que Gina le había llevado, Dana miró a su nueva amiga y afirmó: «Escribamos un libro sobre lo último en hidratación».

Aquel encuentro fue la semilla de una idea, y floreció de un modo asombroso. En la actualidad Gina es la directora de la Hydratation Foundation, una organización sin ánimo de lucro que promueve el poder curativo de la hidratación y la nueva ciencia que se aborda en *Apaga tu sed*. Y Dana continúa ejerciendo en su consulta médica, incorporando estas ideas a su práctica diaria con cientos de pacientes y siendo testigo directo de los asombrosos resultados de la técnica.

El libro que tienes en tus manos podría ser la respuesta a tu cansancio. O a dolores de cabeza, confusión mental, aumento de peso, insomnio, dolor de estómago, dolores articulares... En definitiva, esta obra puede aumentar tu rendimiento intelectual y cognitivo en los estudios y en el trabajo y protegerte frente a lesiones deportivas y conmoción cerebral. A menudo pensamos erróneamente que estas y otras frecuentes dolencias modernas se deben a la ingesta de gluten o de demasiado azúcar o a que hacemos muy poco ejercicio. Pero hemos identificado una pieza crucial y que suele pasarse por alto en el rompecabezas de nuestra salud. La *hidra-*

tación es la clave. En *Apaga tu sed* te proporcionamos estrategias senci-llas y absolutamente novedosas, basadas en una ciencia de vanguardia y avaladas por antiguas tradiciones. Y toda esta información la hemos agrupado en un plan inicial de cinco días, el *Plan Quench*, agradable y fácil de seguir, todo ello para alcanzar una hidratación óptima.

Hemos podido asistir a los asombrosos y poderosos efectos que tiene el llegar a comprender que una hidratación óptima puede curar. Y esta-mos encantadas de poder compartir estas técnicas de curación. Sigue leyendo y comienza a sentirte mejor… ¡Hoy mismo!

Hidratación: ¿Cómo podemos mejorarla?

El agua es materia y matriz de vida, es madre y medio. Sin agua no hay vida.

Albert Szent-Györyi, ganador del Premio Nobel.

Durante años te han estado diciendo que es necesario beber ocho vasos de agua al día para mantener la hidratación del cuerpo. Y si estás intentando perder peso, te encuentras mal o estás entrenando para un gran evento deportivo, ocho vasos de agua son solo la punta (derretida) del iceberg. Es extraño: en la mayoría de los aspectos de nuestra salud se nos enseña que la clave está en la moderación. Sin embargo, en lo referente al agua, el mensaje ha sido siempre que hay que beber más y más y más. En nuestra búsqueda de la salud, siempre hemos pensado que era imposible beber demasiada agua.

La sabiduría popular tiene razón a medias. Una adecuada hidratación es la clave para alcanzar una salud óptima. Pero debemos empezar a considerar la hidratación por lo que es: la esencia misma de nuestra salud. Cada uno de nosotros somos un cuerpo de agua. De hecho, según las más modestas estimaciones tradicionales, alrededor del 65% de nuestro cuerpo es agua. Si no estás hidratado, cualquier cosa que hagas para estar sano (hacer ejercicio, comer correctamente, abordar debidamente el estrés, dormir) no tendrá el efecto esperado.

Se sabe que el ser humano puede sobrevivir cerca de dos meses sin comida, pero unos días sin agua nos llevan a la muerte. Sorprende por ello que la mayoría estemos deshidratados —de hecho, hay doctores que piensan que el 75% de los estadounidenses sufren deshidratación[1]. Una deshidratación de grado leve es la mayor de las epidemias, un dilema omnipresente, aunque invisible, que está alcanzando niveles de urgencia en las modernas condiciones de vida. El tipo de alimentos que consumimos —incluidos los alimentos procesados, cargados de sal y deshidratados— hace que nuestro organismo tenga que trabajar más para metabolizarlos. Y la ausencia de frutas y verduras de acción hidratante nos deja deshidratados, incluso resecos. Además, nos encontramos cada día más expuestos a luces fluorescentes, al calor seco y al aire acondicionado... por no hablar de todos los dispositivos electrónicos que usamos a diario y que acrecientan la deshidratación orgánica. Y para rematar la situación, los medicamentos que compramos, con o sin receta, para reducir el dolor, la rigidez articular, las alergias o ciertas dolencias crónicas también tienen un potente efecto deshidratante. Existe una larga lista de medicamentos —de la que es conocedora la FDA estadounidense reguladora de alimentos y medicamentos— que provocan deshidratación clínica. Es posible que estés utilizando alguno ahora mismo. Piensa en la última vez que tomaste difenhidramina o pseudoefedrina para la alergia; seguro que notaste los efectos deshidratantes de estos medicamentos. ¿Estás tomando aspirina o paracetamol para el dolor de cabeza? ¿Alprazolam o zolpidem para dormir? ¿Alguien te prescribió que bebieras más agua de la habitual con cualquiera de estos fármacos?

Añade ahora otra sorprendente fuente de deshidratación: la inmovilidad, que frena o corta el suministro de agua a las células, así como el importante flujo de salida de las partículas de desecho. Todo lo que la mayoría hacemos sentados —generalmente en un ambiente de oficina artificial y cerrado o conduciendo el coche durante horas— literalmente nos está deshidratando, al frenar el flujo de agua y energía en nuestro cuerpo.

Como resultado de todos estos factores, la mayoría de nosotros vivimos en un estado de deshidratación crónica, que se manifiesta en forma de fatiga, falta de concentración y ánimo bajo, así como sueño deficiente[2] y, sorprendentemente, incluso exceso de peso.

De hecho, de acuerdo con un estudio llevado a cabo por Tammy Chang y colaboradores[3] de la Universidad de Michigan, es más probable que las personas obesas no estén debidamente hidratadas. Y otro estudio, esta vez del Departamento de Nutrición Humana, alimentos y ejercicio de La Universidad estadounidense de Virginia Tech[4] ha puesto de manifiesto que beber agua antes de las comidas favorece la pérdida de peso. Brenda Davy, investigadora principal del estudio, afirma: «Encontramos que a lo largo de las doce semanas de estudio, las personas que seguían dieta y bebían antes de las comidas, tres veces al día, habían perdido en torno a dos kilos más que quienes no habían aumentado su ingesta de agua».

Los efectos de una deshidratación crónica de grado bajo son reales, de larga duración y potencialmente muy debilitantes. Nosotras pensamos que esta hipohidratación es la madre de todas las epidemias y podría estar ligada a muchas dolencias comunes. Las señales son fatiga por la tarde, declive del rendimiento cognitivo, dolores de cabeza, debilidad, infecciones de las vías urinarias y estreñimiento. Sin embargo, otros trastornos debidos a la deshidratación pueden sorprendernos: sueño deficiente, disminución de la inmunidad, dolores articulares, enfermedades crónicas como fibromialgia, diabetes tipo 2, reflujo e incluso Alzheimer. Hablaremos más acerca de ello en el capítulo 1, pero baste decir que la deshidratación puede tener un efecto importante y persistente sobre nuestra salud general.

Entonces, admitiendo que nos hidratamos de manera inadecuada, ¿qué podemos hacer para evitarlo? De eso trata este libro. Somos conscientes de que no existe un método único para alcanzar una salud perfecta. Pero ¿y si hubiera algo que nos acercara más a ese estado? Existe una manera *mejor* de hidratarnos... y los efectos beneficiosos de una hidratación adecuada pueden tener un asombroso efecto sobre la salud, la vitalidad y, en general, sobre la calidad de vida de la persona.

UNA MANERA MEJOR DE HIDRATARNOS

Vamos a presentarte una nueva manera de reivindicar el poder del agua. *Apaga tu sed* te ayudará a determinar cómo hidratarte correctamente (pista: no supone beber cuatro litros de agua al día) y, luego, a que el agua que bebes llegue en profundidad a tus músculos, células y fascias (el tejido conjuntivo de tu cuerpo), donde es más necesaria. Cuando se habla de beber una cantidad suficiente de agua no se está teniendo en cuenta necesariamente su calidad. De ella depende la absorción, y esta es la razón por la cual nuestro plan no te anima simplemente a beber más. ¿Por qué? Porque contar solamente con el agua de bebida para hidratar tu organismo es ineficaz, e incluso podría perjudicarte. Beber demasiada agua puede lavar y eliminar nutrientes esenciales y electrolitos de células y tejidos, dañando en realidad tu salud y limitando la capacidad de rendimiento de tu organismo. En el capítulo 2 te mostraremos por qué tienes que incorporar una mayor hidratación a tu dieta, no solo a través del agua, sino también a través de plantas, como frutas y verduras, semillas y otros alimentos que hidratan. Los efectos de la hidratación pueden ser transformadores y, cuando los hayas notado, nunca volverás a mirar de la misma manera un simple vaso de H_2O.

¿Cuáles son entonces los efectos beneficiosos de una hidratación adecuada? En el caso de los niños puede suponer mejor humor y favorecer la inteligencia. Para los deportistas que buscan potenciar su rendimiento, su fuerza o su velocidad, una hidratación adecuada puede decidir el juego. Para todas aquellas personas que luchan con problemas de salud como dolores de cabeza, hinchazón e incluso enfermedades crónicas, tomar el tipo adecuado de agua puede aliviar sus síntomas y recargar su vida de energía. Y en el caso de las personas mayores con dificultad para mantener una nutrición y una hidratación adecuadas, esta información puede realmente salvarles la vida. Podemos incorporar alimentos superhidratantes a nuestra dieta de forma sencilla. Te ayudaremos a encontrar la mejor manera de hidratarte profunda y completamente, de manera que todas tus células calmen su sed.

Hemos creado un plan de inicio rápido de cinco días que te ofrece una deliciosa variedad de bebidas, platos y *smoothies*, que constituyen la clave de nuestro programa y que reúnen todas las ventajas de los alimentos más hidratantes y ricos en nutrientes, para hidratarte de manera más profunda, completa y duradera. Existe un segundo componente de este plan que en realidad es la parte olvidada de la hidratación. Y es el movimiento del agua hasta el interior de los tejidos. En el capítulo 3 te explicamos el modo en que el movimiento proporciona hidratación. Un aspecto clave de este programa es la inclusión de micromovimientos: movimientos pequeños y sencillos que puedes realizar unas cuantas veces al día para llevar la hidratación a los tejidos y órganos que más la necesitan. El capítulo 4 describe las líneas fundamentales de la ciencia de los micromovimientos. Si sigues nuestro sencillo plan durante cinco días notarás más energía, mayor concentración y mejores digestiones. Te prometemos que querrás incorporar nuestras estrategias de hidratación y movimientos a tu vida, pues pronto te darás cuenta de que te permiten moverte sin dolor y vivir con fuerzas renovadas, con una energía que ni tan siquiera tú sabías que tenías.

¿Estás deshidratado?

Responde a este cuestionario de autoevaluación para saber si la deshidratación te está afectando:

¿Has notado que no pierdes peso, aunque lo intentes?
¿Tienes más sed?
¿Te parece que sufres estreñimiento?
¿Has notado una disminución de la micción?
¿Sientes hinchazón?
¿Notas cierta confusión mental?
¿Tienes cansancio por la tarde?
¿Luchas por vencer la somnolencia diurna?
¿Has notado algún mareo?
¿Duermes mal?
¿Sientes rigidez muscular?
¿Sientes dolor en las articulaciones?
¿Tienes dolores de cabeza?
¿Tienes la piel seca?
¿Tienes a menudo los labios agrietados?
¿Has notado que tienes los ojos secos?
¿Percibes la boca seca?
¿Tienes mal aliento?

¿Notas la garganta seca?
¿Crees que necesitas beber más agua?

Si has respondido afirmativamente a alguna de estas preguntas, tu cuerpo puede estar diciéndote que necesita hidratación. Considérala tu primera línea de terapia. El agua del grifo no es suficiente.

Sigue leyendo para descubrir cómo conseguir y mantener la hidratación de tu cuerpo. Tu salud depende de ello.

NUESTRO ENTORNO ES DESHIDRATANTE

«¡Pero si yo bebo mucha agua!», puede que estés pensando. «¿Cómo es posible que esté deshidratado?».

Aunque pensemos que consumimos suficiente agua, soportamos a diario un cansancio de grado bajo y, en tales condiciones, hemos de enfrentarnos al desafío de múltiples factores de la vida moderna, que nos roban humedad. Si pensamos en un cuerpo sano como en una planta —con raíces en un suelo rico en nutrientes, absorbiendo minerales y agua y captando la luz solar y convirtiéndolo todo en abundante materia vegetal—, entonces, en comparación, nuestro cuerpo, privado de hidratación, sería como una planta de hojas marchitas y tallos secos y arrugados. ¿Te sientes así a veces?

Se estima que el ser humano pierde al día entre dos y tres litros de agua a través de la respiración y del sudor, de la orina y las deposiciones. Recuerda esta frase: todo lo que entra tiene que salir, y viceversa. Para mantener el delicado equilibrio (u homeóstasis) orgánico el agua ingerida debe ser equivalente al agua que pierde el cuerpo.

Si no se repone esa pérdida de agua, el cerebro envía señales hormonales para desviar el agua de áreas no vitales y poder así regular la función de órganos más importantes, como el cerebro, el corazón y el hígado. La sed no es siempre un indicador temprano de alarma por deshidratación, de modo que es muy fácil caer sin darnos cuenta en un estado de deshidratación de grado bajo[5]. La deshidratación puede estar acechándote.

¿Cómo puedo saber si sufro deshidratación?

Por desgracia, no existe una ciencia exacta para determinar si sufres deshidratación crónica: no existe tampoco una prueba fiable que tu médico pueda ofrecerte o una escala en la que poder medir tu nivel de agua. Pero existen algunos buenos indicadores de que es posible que tu cuerpo necesite más líquido: realiza estas sencillas pruebas en casa para empezar a valorar si puedes mejorar su estado de hidratación.

- **Observa tu orina.** Como regla general, el color de la orina es un buen «indicador» de ingesta de agua. La orina está compuesta de agua, urea (desecho metabólico), material orgánico como carbohidratos, enzimas y ácidos grasos y hormonas, y algunos electrolitos. La orina normal es clara o ligeramente amarilla. A menudo es más amarilla si se están tomando vitaminas o ciertos medicamentos. La orina de color amarillo oscuro es un indicador de deshidratación. Observa también si la orina es escasa.
- **Pellízcate la piel.** Si el pellizco se mantiene, es decir, si la piel no vuelve a la normalidad, especialmente en el dorso de la mano, significa que sufres deshidratación.
- **Aplica presión sobre la uña de un dedo de la mano durante cinco segundos.** Suelta y observa cuánto tiempo tarda el color en restablecerse. En buen estado de hidratación, el color vuelve en uno a tres segundos. Si tarda más de cinco segundos, es probable que estés deshidratado.
- **Vigila tu peso.** Pesarse antes y después de hacer ejercicio puede parecer un poco obsesivo, pero si estás haciendo ejercicio en un ambiente en el que hace mucho calor o estás realizando una actividad particularmente larga o extenuante, puede que sea prudente vigilar cuánta agua estás perdiendo. Es lo que hacen los deportistas de élite. Si haces ejercicio o realizas entrenamiento de resistencia durante más de una hora, asegúrate de que no pierdes demasiada agua y, lo que es más importante, de que repones el agua que pierdes (consulta nuestras recomendaciones en el capítulo 6).

Piensa ahora en el típico día de oficina, en el que prácticamente no te levantas de la silla. Tal vez incluso pidas la comida por teléfono. Cuando no te mueves durante largos períodos de tiempo, a tu cuerpo le cuesta suministrar agua a sus células y eliminar las partículas de desecho. Todo ese tiempo que pasamos sentados está literalmente deshidratándonos, al reducir la circulación de agua por el cuerpo.

¿Deberías, entonces, beber el doble de H_2O que bebes ahora? No tan deprisa. Recientes estudios revelan que puedes hidratarte mejor y de manera más inteligente abordando el tema de la hidratación con un enfoque de salud global.

De esta manera te sentirás mejor, tu organismo funcionará también de forma más precisa y tu aspecto será óptimo. En *Apaga tu sed* abordamos la deshidratación del día a día, no la deshidratación avanzada, que puede acabar en un hospital con un goteo intravenoso. Estamos aquí para enseñarte a reponer el agua que pierdes por tus funciones diarias: visitas al baño, sudoración, estrés y agresiones ambientales como habitaciones en las que hace demasiado calor, atascos de tráfico, comida procesada y seca, medicamentos... sencillamente, la vida moderna.

Incluso el grado más leve de deshidratación puede tener un gran impacto: una pérdida de hidratación de apenas un dos por ciento conduce a un deterioro mensurable de la función cognitiva[6]. Ello equivale a una pérdida de menos de un litro de agua. Suficiente para que tus capacidades sensitivas disminuyan. La capacidad de comprensión y de apreciación caen. La vida pierde colorido. Tu cerebro se seca en un dos por ciento. Y esto nos ocurre a la mayoría en algún momento a lo largo del día. A menudo, cuando llegan las tres de la tarde, nos encontramos flotando en una deshidratación de grado bajo, y a las 9 de la tarde estamos ya casi vacíos de agua. Y así, una y otra vez, todos los días, durante toda la vida, nos vamos secando. Y ello acelera el envejecimiento día a día.

La deshidratación afecta negativamente a casi todos los aspectos de la salud. Estudios recientes llevados a cabo en las principales universidades, instituciones médicas y hasta en el ejército de Estados Unidos revelan que una deshidratación menor puede provocar un empeoramiento de dolores mayores y menores, como dolor articular, migrañas y dolor después de una intervención quirúrgica[7]. Además, ofusca la capacidad de concentración[8] y dispara el apetito.

Pero no tiene por qué ser así.

LA BOTELLA DE AGUA NO ES LA SOLUCIÓN

Con todo lo que sabemos acerca de la importancia de beber agua, bien podríamos mantenernos perfectamente hidratados, pensarás. La verdad es que *deberíamos* estar más hidratados que nunca. Después de todo, para la mayoría de los habitantes del mundo occidental, el agua limpia es omnipresente, si no es del grifo es en botella. De acuerdo con la Beverage Marketing Corporation, las ventas de agua embotellada aumentaron un 7,9% en 2015, por encima del incremento del 7% de 2014. En 2016, los estadounidenses compraron cerca de 48.500 millones de litros de agua embotellada. El agua embotellada está en todas partes: ya sea en una máquina expendedora o en las estanterías de una tienda de alimentación, puedes encontrar agua de manantiales naturales, agua que ha sido depurada por ósmosis inversa, agua con electrolitos añadidos y agua mezclada con zumo de coco o aloe. ¿Existe alguna base científica tras estas mezclas y tras las afirmaciones de que «son buenas para nuestra salud»? ¿Son realmente estas costosas opciones tu única posibilidad —y representan la mejor elección— para una hidratación saludable?

El agua embotellada es una alternativa saludable y cada vez más habitual a los refrescos, pero las botellas de plástico tienen un oscuro lado oculto, ligado al consumo de energía, a la eliminación de residuos y a otros problemas medioambientales. A medida que aumenta la popularidad del agua embotellada, proliferan los problemas. Sabías que...

- Hacen falta tres litros de agua para producir una botella de agua de un litro.
- En todo el mundo, el consumo de agua embotellada se multiplicó por más de dos entre 1997 y 2005, siendo los residentes en Estados Unidos los mayores responsables —en torno a 30.000 millones de litros en total, o 98,5 litros por persona, en 2005—.
- El agua embotellada puede llegar a costar en Estados Unidos hasta 10 dólares el galón (3,78 litros), frente al agua del grifo, que cuesta menos de un centavo por galón.
- El 14% de toda la basura que producimos procede de envases de bebidas[9].

¡Qué paradoja que bebamos tanta agua pero que no podamos hacer frente a los efectos deshidratantes de la vida moderna! La verdad es que toda esta agua no ha acabado con los problemas de deshidratación y el agua embotellada no es una solución viable ni a corto ni a largo plazo. La escasez de agua, sequías que baten récords y una creciente preocupación por la contaminación del agua son recordatorios constantes de que no podemos subestimar el agua, ese elemento fundamental para la vida. Necesitamos urgentemente un nuevo enfoque en lo referente a la obtención del agua diaria. Al beber de manera habitual agua embotellada, nuestra sociedad está sosteniendo una industria que en realidad contamina el medioambiente y contempla el agua como un producto de lujo, más que como un derecho o como un elemento indispensable para la salud de todos los seres vivos. El agua embotellada no solo es una manera menos eficaz de mantener la hidratación en el día a día, sino que además agota acuíferos y otras fuentes de agua, produce residuos innecesarios y tiene un precio desorbitado.

Como alternativa, el plan de hidratación profunda que te presentamos en estas páginas, basado en la constatación de que el *momento en el que* bebemos es tan importante como *lo que* bebemos y como *la cantidad* que bebemos, reconfigura nuestra actitud ante este valioso recurso, al mismo tiempo que rompe nuestra dependencia del agua embotellada. Hemos llamado a nuestro Plan Quench, que en inglés vendría a significar «aplacar», «saciar», «apagar», pues eso es lo que consigue, apagar la sed de nuestro cuerpo. Se trata de un plan sostenible, que anima a la gente a pensar de manera más crítica en el impacto global de sus hábitos de bebida y que sienta las bases de un futuro más saludable para un mundo en el que las reservas de agua representan actualmente un desafío.

¿CÓMO SE NOTA LA DESHIDRATACIÓN?

Junto con los problemas ligados al agua y a las bebidas embotelladas, abunda la información errónea sobre lo que deberíamos beber, cómo y cuándo. Como ya hemos mencionado, la sed no es siempre el aviso más fiable de baja hidratación. A menudo, cuando nos sentimos cansados y nos duele la cabeza, pensamos que necesitamos comer, cuando lo que realmente necesitamos es beber. Los investigadores consideran ahora que estos efectos negativos son el «sistema de alarma» integrado del cerebro, que te avisa de que tu cuerpo necesita hidratación inmediata. Si te duele la cabeza, estás de mal humor, no consigues concentrarte o te sientes de todo menos genial, es muy probable que estés deshidratado.

Y los problemas van más allá de cierta sensación de cabeza pesada y boca seca. La investigación sugiere que la deshidratación está relacionada con muchas dolencias, cuando no con la mayoría. Como comentaremos más adelante en el capítulo 1, la deshidratación contribuye directamente a toda una serie de dolencias, entre ellas:

- Dolores de cabeza, incluidas migrañas
- Debilidad y fatiga, diariamente y relacionadas con enfermedades como la fibromialgia
- Pensamiento embotado y falta de concentración
- Infecciones de vías urinarias
- Estreñimiento
- Trastornos del sueño
- Disminución de la inmunidad
- Enfermedades cardíacas
- Diabetes tipo 2
- Reflujo ácido
- Demencia, incluida la enfermedad de Alzheimer

UNA HIDRATACIÓN MÁS INTELIGENTE

¿Cómo se hidratan las culturas del desierto?

Los beduinos, pueblo árabe y nómada del desierto, saben «algo» de deshidratación. Ellos se tragan el líquido que beben, no lo toman a sorbitos. Lo primero que hacen por la mañana es «empapar» bien sus órganos, y después continúan con su jornada de viaje. Esta es una de las estrategias clave de este pueblo nómada, que da como resultado la necesidad de menos líquido. Dado que la ingesta diaria media de agua de los beduinos adultos es de apenas un litro, a los antropólogos les costó comprender cómo era posible que sobrevivieran a las condiciones de sequía del desierto. Y es que no tenían en cuenta su ingesta de alimentos. La leche de cabra o de camello es la base de la hidratación de este pueblo, junto con un tipo de mantequillla de cabra o *ghee* que untan en pan ázimo y que utilizan también para cocinar. Tanto la leche como la mantequilla proporcionan altos niveles de electrolitos. Los estudios etnográficos han revelado además que los beduinos, gracias a sus pesadas ropas negras, forman, con su respiración y sudoración, algo así como una tienda humidificadora, creando en definitiva un microambiente húmedo portátil.

No sabemos lo suficiente acerca del agua, el elemento vital más común. Científicos y médicos siguen investigando cómo funciona exactamente la molécula de agua, de qué forma contribuye a la salud y en qué medida es realmente necesaria para mantener el cuerpo hidratado. No se ha dado aún con un método estandarizado que permita medir la hidratación del cuerpo y saber cuál es la adecuada. Pero lo que se está descubriendo es que la hidratación es más esencial para nuestra salud de lo que creíamos, y ahora más que nunca.

Afortunadamente, cada día se emprenden nuevos e interesantes estudios de investigación. Un hallazgo muy importante es el de los efectos del agua sobre la salud general, al interceptar las enfermedades crónicas. Hemos profundizado en esta línea de investigación y hemos creado para ti una visión global de cómo beber de forma más inteligente. Protegerte de las enfermedades crónicas no significa aumentar la ingesta de agua, sino conseguir que tu cuerpo la absorba mejor. Novedosos estudios aún en marcha, dentro y fuera de los laboratorios, muestran que el agua contenida en las plantas hidrata de forma más eficaz y completa que el agua del grifo por sí sola. ¿Cómo? Las fibras vegetales nos ayudan a absorber el líquido y este concepto ha revolucionado lo que pensábamos acerca de la hidratación.

EL AGUA DE LAS PLANTAS ES LA QUE MÁS HIDRATA

Siempre se ha sabido que las plantas —verduras y hortalizas, frutas, raíces y semillas— son una excelente fuente de nutrientes. Pero ahora se está descubriendo que tomar el agua contenida en las plantas es mejor que simplemente beber agua. Ya está depurada, es alcalina, tiene un pH perfecto, está mineralizada, es rica en nutrientes, está estructurada (ampliaremos este aspecto más adelante) y cargada de energía lista para ser absorbida por nuestras células. Piensa en ello la próxima vez que te comas un melocotón maduro. El jugo que te resbala por la barbilla es un tipo diferente y más poderoso de agua. Hemos tenido la oportunidad de conocer los primeros hallazgos de los investigadores que muestran que esta agua vegetal puede ser la modalidad de agua más eficaz en términos de hidratación. La Madre Naturaleza siempre es sabia. ¡Y el «envase» es excelente!

Dado que dichos estudios son muy recientes, no se cuenta aún con un trabajo clínico adecuado cuyos resultados confirmen la buena hidratación que ofrece el agua de las plantas. Pero el Plan Quench puede ser el pistoletazo de salida para este interesante estudio de investigación. A lo largo de los últimos dos años y medio, hemos trabajado con más de cuatrocientos pacientes para mejorar su estado de hidratación y hemos observado asombrosos resultados en términos de mejoría de su salud y de su calidad de vida.

Lo que tienes en tus manos es la culminación de nuestro trabajo de investigación y de los estudios de casos que han hecho que nuestro Programa Quench sea tan eficaz.

EL PROGRAMA QUENCH

Nosotras —como doctora especializada en medicina integral una y antropóloga cultural la otra— hemos combinado nuestro trabajo de investigación y nuestros años de experiencia con estos datos novedosos. El plan que te proponemos en *Apaga tu sed* te ayudará a suministrar más agua a tu cuerpo combinando frutas, verduras y otros ingredientes con agua, todo ello diseñado para lograr una hidratación máxima.

La dieta saludable de base vegetal de este plan, que incluye *smoothies*, sopas y otras comidas hidratantes, se ve complementada por nuestras «recetas» de sencillos micromovimientos, pensados para impulsar la hidratación en profundidad, hasta el interior de las células de tu cuerpo. Sin darte cuenta, irás incorporando los movimientos a tu vida diaria, sin importar dónde te encuentres ni tu nivel de forma física.

Mientras la comunidad científica sigue tratando de identificar el modo en el que las plantas mejoran la hidratación en las células, nosotras hemos sido testigos de resultados en aquellas personas que ya han aplicado el Plan Quench. Lo que nosotras y otras personas hemos visto es que, utilizando el agua de las plantas, no solo obtenemos nutrientes, sino que además nos beneficiamos de una mejor hidratación por absorción.

Te darás cuenta de que tus niveles de energía aumentan porque finalmente tu cuerpo ha absorbido agua suficiente. Pero lo más importante es que el agua mejorará tus funciones orgánicas en todos los sentidos y fortalecerá tu cuerpo, ayudándote a evitar el aumento de peso, ralentizando el envejecimiento y protegiéndote frente a la enfermedad. No es cuestión de que creas ciegamente en nuestra palabra: en este libro incluimos estudios de casos de pacientes que se han visto beneficiados por el Plan Quench y que han querido compartir su experiencia y contar cómo sus vidas cambiaron para mejorar. También ofrecemos fascinantes conclusiones de investigación antropológica que confirman que numerosos pueblos antiguos y muchas tribus indígenas encontraron una manera óptima de hidratarse mejor: mediante las plantas. El objetivo es reunir todas estas prácticas ancestrales y considerarlas de nuevo a la luz de los conocimientos científicos y los resultados clínicos actuales.

Notarás enseguida los efectos de nuestro programa de cinco días y verás resultados concretos durante las semanas y los meses siguientes. Hemos basado nuestro método en técnicas tradicionales utilizadas en culturas de todo el mundo —que, a su manera, han llevado a cabo ensayos clínicos a lo largo de años y años de uso— y nosotras únicamente las hemos confirmado, de la mano de otros científicos y profesionales de la salud.

Nosotras mismas hemos utilizado estos métodos y hemos ayudado a cientos de personas a sentirse mejor y a tener mejor aspecto siguiendo una correcta rutina de hidratación, una rutina que favorece la absorción del agua por parte del organismo. Nuestras recomendaciones para una buena hidratación no solo apagan la sed, sino que además infunden al cuerpo nutrientes vitales. De la mano de nuestro plan, crearás una rutina práctica y saludable que elevará tu hidratación a niveles desconocidos para ti.

Para comenzar, he aquí las reglas fundamentales de nuestro Plan Quench, que se basa en los siguientes tres principios de hidratación. Describiremos todos los detalles en los siguientes capítulos:

1. **Bebe para una absorción máxima.** Consigue la máxima absorción del agua que bebes y aumenta su disponibilidad para todas las células. ¿Cómo lograrlo?
   - Cuando te levantes por la mañana, bebe entre 240 ml y 480 ml de agua con una pizca de sal marina y el zumo de un limón para empapar bien tu interior.
   - Bebe al menos un *smoothie* verde todos los días.
   - Bebe entre 180 y 240 ml de agua antes de cada comida.
   - Muévete.
2. **Obtén más agua de los alimentos.** Comer alimentos con alto contenido de agua favorece una hidratación profunda —nuestros *smoothies* vegetales, por ejemplo, hidratan mucho más que la *misma cantidad de agua embotellada*. Te enseñaremos la manera de incorporar más alimentos hidratantes a tus comidas.
3. **Utiliza el movimiento para distribuir la hidratación.** Te mostraremos micromovimientos esenciales y de fácil realización que te ayudarán a llevar la hidratación hasta los tejidos más profundos, favorecerán tu flexibilidad y te librarán del dolor.

ESTUDIO DE CASO DE LA DRA. DANA COHEN

Elizabeth

Elizabeth es una auxiliar de vuelo de cincuenta y seis años que, en general, goza de buena salud, aunque los continuos viajes en avión han hecho mella en su cuerpo. Como todos sabemos, volar resulta extremadamente deshidratante: da lugar a piel seca, fatiga, embotamiento mental, dolores musculares. Pues Elizabeth lo tenía todo. Dada su edad, le preocupaba la menopausia, aunque no tenía síntomas importantes, como sofocos o sequedad vaginal. Otras mujeres podrían exclamar: «¡Qué suerte!». De todas formas, Elizabeth había oído hablar de la terapia de sustitución hormonal y pensaba que podría ayudarle a aliviar su sensación general de «desgana». Pero cuando vino a verme para que le recetara hormonas, le sugerí que indagáramos un poco más profundamente en sus síntomas antes de instaurar una terapia de sustitución hormonal (TSH). Aunque las hormonas que yo prescribo son bioidénticas, mi filosofía es siempre «menos es más», y no tenía claro que Elizabeth necesitara una terapia hormonal, de manera que decidimos realizar antes algunas pruebas.

Mientras esperábamos los resultados propuse a Elizabeth el Programa Quench. Cuando volvió tres semanas más tarde a consulta para su seguimiento, ni ella misma podía creerse los resultados. La fatiga había desaparecido. El embotamiento mental se había esfumado. Y no le dolía nada. También me di cuenta de que Elizabeth tenía una piel resplandeciente. «No puedo creerlo. Simplemente siento que he recuperado energía y me he dado cuenta de que ya no estoy tan cansada después de un vuelo largo. ¡Y tengo más paciencia con los pasajeros difíciles!».

Hablamos sobre la TSH. Todos los resultados de las pruebas sanguíneas eran normales y el Programa Quench le estaba dando tan buen resultado que no nos pareció que necesitara un tratamiento de sustitución hormonal. De modo que continuó con el programa, y lo compartió además con sus compañeras auxiliares de vuelo. En el siguiente control, unos meses más tarde, Elizabeth me contó que todo el mundo que lo había probado había experimentado un notable aumento de energía y había notado una piel más radiante, mayor claridad mental y menos dolores en general. Todas estas personas seguían ya el plan e incluso bromeaban entre ellas sobre dónde tenían escondidas en el avión sus semillas de chía, para tomarlas con sus bebidas durante los vuelos.

¿Por qué tengo tanta sed cuando vuelo?

Podemos afirmar que los aviones representan sin duda uno de los ambientes más deshidratantes de la vida moderna. Todo el mundo lo sabe; todo el mundo lo nota. La deshidratación, no el *jet lag*, es la razón principal por la que volar resulta tan agotador. Además, el aire que recircula en los aviones tiene menos humedad de la habitual, de modo que nos deshidrata más. Las cabinas de los aviones tienen a menudo menos de un 20% de humedad, a diferencia del 50% de humedad que necesitamos para tener una sensación agradable. Y los viajes largos son aún peor: en un vuelo transcontinental o de costa a costa en Estados Unidos, por ejemplo, la humedad puede ser del uno por ciento. Ello produce sed y reseca labios, nariz y ojos. He aquí algunos buenos consejos que puedes tener en cuenta la próxima vez que viajes en avión:

- **Como regla general, bebe un vaso de agua: 220 ml de agua cada hora, mientras dure el vuelo.** Añádele un poco de sal natural. Si no repones electrolitos, estarás perdiendo minerales. Lleva un paquetito o una bolsita hermética de congelados con sales naturales y añade un pellizco a tu botella de agua. Nosotras somos más partidarias de una botella de agua con sal natural añadida y una manzana que de dos botellas de agua. La fibra de una manzana te ayudará a mantener la hidratación durante más tiempo.
- **Lleva una bolsita con semillas de chía, calabaza, cáñamo o girasol.** Una medida estupenda consiste en moler estas semillas en el molinillo de café y añadir y mezclar al menos una cucharada directamente en tu bebida. O puedes tomarlas como aperitivo mientras bebes. Ayudan a absorber el agua y añaden energía al agua de bebida.
- **La postura en el avión es un factor muy importante durante el vuelo.** Te presentamos un truco para mantener una mejor postura en el avión: siéntate con la espalda recta y después coloca una americana, un jersey, una almohada o incluso un libro entre la espalda y el asiento del avión. Coloca este elemento en línea

con el ombligo. Este es el punto que ejerce presión sobre toda la columna para enderezar el canal medular y alinear bien las vértebras, favoreciendo al máximo la circulación del líquido sinovial. Ahora podrás trabajar en perfecta concentración.

- **Levántate y ve al baño, aunque no tengas ninguna necesidad.** Moverte y estirar las piernas al menos cada hora te ayudará a no aterrizar cansado. Si tu vecino de asiento parece molesto porque te muevas tanto, alégrate en secreto de que, probablemente, estés salvando también a esa persona de la posterior sensación de cansancio o incluso de un ataque de trombosis venosa profunda, pues los coágulos de sangre son un riesgo real después de largos períodos de inmovilidad. En el capítulo 1 encontrarás más detalles al respecto.
- **Realiza micromovimientos durante todo el vuelo.** Barbilla al pecho, hombros hacia las orejas y usa los omóplatos para masajear la espalda. Consulta los micromovimientos del Plan Quench, capítulo 8.
- **Aplícate un tratamiento facial.** Date un masaje en las sienes y detrás de las orejas. Parecerá que te duele la cabeza, pero estarás moviendo líquidos en puntos clave para reducir la fatiga.
- **Hidrata cara y manos.** Cualquier crema con aloe vera es un «súper búfer» contra el aire seco recirculante del avión. Actúa como una barrera para mantener la hidratación, pero no solo tiene efecto emoliente, sino también propiedades antibacterianas y antivíricas. Puedes aplicarte también crema en el área de la nariz para mantener los orificios nasales hidratados, lo cual ayuda a combatir los contaminantes presentes en el aire[10].

Te sorprenderán los efectos que tiene una hidratación óptima sobre tu cuerpo:

- Te concentrarás mejor y perderás esa sensación de torpeza mental que nos afecta a tantos.
- Recuperarás energía, superando la fatiga que a menudo trae consigo la deshidratación.

- Notarás que mejoran tus digestiones, el tránsito intestinal y la eliminación de toxinas, puesto que las funciones celulares en todos sus sistemas orgánicos serán más eficaces.
- Dormirás mejor y más profundamente. De verdad. Deja que el agua haga lo que ningún remedio de hierbas o fármaco puede conseguir.
- Tu flexibilidad aumentará, pues articulaciones, músculos y sistema facial estarán bien lubricados. Lo creas o no, incluso nuestros huesos son agua en un 31%.
- Tu plan de adelgazamiento por fin funcionará. El agua es una de las mejores herramientas para perder peso, de modo que las dietas yo-yo quedarán en el pasado.
- Desaparecerá la hinchazón. ¡Adiós a los tobillos hinchados! La ropa sentará mejor.
- Tu piel tendrá un aspecto radiante y más joven, pues el agua «rellena» la piel a través de la hidratación.
- La inflamación disminuirá, al mejorar el funcionamiento de los sistemas de eliminación de residuos.

LAS PLANTAS Y LA TIERRA

El descubrimiento de que las plantas tienen un papel esencial en la hidratación no podría haber llegado en un momento más crítico. El acceso a agua potable en cantidad suficiente es una cuestión social apremiante y la preocupación por la escasez y la calidad del agua es cada día mayor. Las sequías severas son cada vez más frecuentes y ponen a prueba las fuentes de agua en el planeta. Para alcanzar una hidratación más eficaz, el Plan Quench combina viejas estrategias utilizadas por antiguas tradiciones con la nueva ciencia del agua. Siguiendo nuestro plan, beberás menos agua pero sentirás que estás mejor hidratado, nutrido y flexible. Al mismo tiempo, este eficiente abordaje del consumo de agua ayuda a nuestro cuerpo y a nuestro planeta. *Apaga tu sed* supone un nuevo enfoque de la cuestión del agua y de la hidratación, de importancia esencial en el marco de una solución natural, permanente y disponible para todos.

Sigue leyendo y experimenta lo que el Plan Quench puede hacer por ti.

La nueva ciencia del agua

Conexión entre hidratación y salud

No hay nada más suave y flexible que el agua, y sin embargo nada se resiste a ella.

Lao Tse

La hidratación es una necesidad primordial del ser humano, aun cuando sigamos subestimando su importancia. El grado de hidratación influye en la resistencia del sistema inmunitario, en la elasticidad de la piel, en el nivel de energía, en la facilidad de movimiento y en la resistencia general del cuerpo al envejecimiento y a la enfermedad. Incluso determina tu sensación de bienestar cuando te levantas por la mañana.

A medida que la ciencia va avanzando en el conocimiento del modo en el que actúa la hidratación —y como no nos cansaremos de repetir en este libro, no se trata simplemente de beber ocho vasos de agua al día—, nos vamos dando cuenta de que la cantidad de agua que bebemos es solo la primera parte de la historia. Ahora sabemos que lo que bebemos, el momento en el que bebemos y la manera en la que nuestro organismo moviliza el líquido hacia el interior de las células son factores cruciales para sentirse bien y alcanzar una salud óptima. Abordamos a continuación más detenidamente algunos de los aspectos fundamentales de la ciencia del agua y de la hidratación.

LA MEDICIÓN DEL AGUA EN NUESTRO CUERPO

Existen muchas maneras de determinar de cuánta agua estamos hechos, si bien todo depende de cuándo y de dónde se mida. Por ejemplo, los bebés son un 75 % agua, mientras que los ancianos pueden serlo en menos de un 55 % —perdemos hidratación al envejecer—. En nuestro interior, el agua se mueve y cambia de forma y función, convirtiéndose en sangre o vapor o líquido articular. Para comprender todas estas funciones, necesitamos disponer de un modo más sofisticado de medir el agua.

Brian Ritcher, reconocido científico en el terreno de la investigación del agua, lo intentó con las matemáticas. En una publicación de 2012 en la página web de *National Geographic* llamada «Walking Water», postulaba lo siguiente:

> Imagina que vas por ahí cargando con unos 50 litros de agua… todo el día, todos los días del año. No sería de extrañar que estuvieras cansado al final del día… Añade 10 kilos de piel y lo que obtendrás básicamente serán cientos de miles de años de evolución humana produciendo un balón de agua andante envuelto en carne… En un día normal eliminamos a través de la respiración, la orina y el sudor en torno a 2,5-2,8 litros de agua, es decir, alrededor de un cinco-diez por ciento de nuestra agua corporal.

Con la eliminación de un litro de agua, explica Ritcher, es probable que estés perdiendo ya algo de función cognitiva, de estado de alerta y de capacidad de concentración. «Si pierdes tres litros… es probable que te duela la cabeza. Si tienes seis litros menos, te sentirás tan mal que tendrás que ir al hospital y si son diez irás directo a la morgue».

Para comprender realmente cómo funciona el agua, echemos un vistazo a sus efectos en el plano molecular. El ser humano está integrado no por un 60% de agua, ni por un 70%, ni tan siquiera por un 75%, sino por un 99%. ¿Cómo puede ser? Si esto fuera cierto ¡seríamos más bien un charco! Para llegar a ese 99%, se tienen en cuenta todas las moléculas de materia del cuerpo. Cuando lo hacemos, encontramos que 99 de cada 100 de estas moléculas son agua. Ello se debe a que la molécula de H_2O es la más pequeña de todas. Analicemos qué hace toda esa agua.

EL AGUA ES BUENA PARA EL CUERPO

¿Cómo pueden hacer tanto un simple átomo de oxígeno y dos átomos de hidrógeno? Las moléculas de agua presentan una disposición polar de sus átomos de oxígeno e hidrógeno —el hidrógeno tiene carga eléctrica positiva y el oxígeno negativa—. Ello hace posible que la molécula atraiga muchos otros tipos de moléculas, como por ejemplo de sal (NaCl). El agua puede disolver la sal, porque el hidrógeno atrae los iones cloruro negativos y el oxígeno negativo atrae los iones sodio positivos. Sustancias que se disuelven fácilmente en agua, como el azúcar y la sal, son hidrófilas, mientras que las que no se disuelven tan fácilmente en agua —como el aceite— son hidrófobas.

No es solo la composición *química* del agua lo que hace que sea un excelente disolvente —lo cual quiere decir que, viaje adonde viaje, ya sea a través del suelo o a través de nuestro cuerpo, transporta valiosos elementos químicos, minerales y nutrientes hasta el interior de nuestras células—. La configuración *molecular* de H_2O hace posible este transporte de elementos hasta el interior de las células y desde estas hacia fuera. De hecho, el agua desensambla material en un nivel molecular.

Y esta sencilla pero a la vez compleja molécula representa la primera línea de defensa de nuestro organismo, pues ayuda a mantener la homeostasis en las células. El agua interviene en este equilibrio esencial mediante cinco funciones vitales:

1. **Favorece las funciones celulares.** Es como un sistema de riego; ayuda a llevar nutrientes (vitaminas, minerales, carbohidratos) y oxígeno a todas las células, en un flujo de doble sentido. Sin agua, las células morirían.
2. **Ayuda a regular la temperatura.** Cuando nuestra temperatura corporal aumenta, producimos sudor, que enfría el cuerpo.
3. **Elimina los productos de desecho** del cuerpo a través de la orina y del sudor, por supuesto, pero también ayuda a nuestro cuerpo a eliminar residuos sólidos.
4. **Es un excelente lubricante.** Ayuda a absorber los golpes, actúa como amortiguador en articulaciones y tejidos, protege nuestros

órganos, «mece» al cerebro en el interior del cráneo y lubrica ojos, nariz y boca, haciendo que nos resulte más fácil comer, respirar y llorar.

5. **Es esencial para las reacciones metabólicas** y químicas de nuestro organismo. El agua participa en la descomposición bioquímica de lo que comemos en proteínas, lípidos y carbohidratos. Básicamente, nos ayuda a obtener de los alimentos los nutrientes que necesitamos y también energía y participa en la eliminación de lo que no necesitamos.

EL SISTEMA DE RIEGO INTERNO DEL CUERPO

Ya estés bebiendo agua, ya estés comiendo alimentos ricos en agua, todo ese líquido acaba en tu estómago, desde donde una parte es enviada al torrente sanguíneo para nutrir los tejidos y otra parte continúa su periplo por el sistema digestivo.

El torrente sanguíneo no es el único medio por el que el agua llega a los órganos y otras áreas del cuerpo donde es necesaria. Interesantes estudios recientes revelan que las fascias —láminas de tejido conjuntivo presentes no solo bajo la piel sino también alrededor de órganos, músculos, nervios, vasos sanguíneos y huesos— no solo envuelven y mantienen unidas las distintas partes del cuerpo. Constituyen además un intrincado sistema de suministro que envía agua directamente a las áreas en las que es necesaria. En el capítulo 3 nos detendremos un poco más en la importancia de la hidratación y de las fascias, pero has de saber que, cada vez que bebes agua, estás alimentando el complejo y hermoso tejido fascial de tu cuerpo.

HIDRATACIÓN Y ENFERMEDAD

En un nivel más macroscópico, sabemos que el agua ayuda al organismo en diferentes enfermedades crónicas. Tanto es así que nosotras, como muchos otros expertos, vamos más lejos y nos atrevemos a afirmar que el agua es cuantitativamente el nutriente más importante a tener en cuenta cuando se investiga el origen de problemas crónicos. Definitivamente interviene en numerosos problemas de salud a los que nos enfrentamos al envejecer.

Enfermedades cardiovasculares, entre ellas cardiopatías coronarias, ictus e hipertensión

Aunque te cueste creerlo, una deshidratación leve —del rango de una disminución de apenas un dos por ciento en los niveles de hidratación— puede afectar a los vasos sanguíneos del mismo modo que fumar un cigarrillo. Un reciente estudio de la Universidad de Arkansas ha encontrado que hombres jóvenes que no se hidratan de forma óptima experimentan una reducción inmediata de la capacidad de contracción y dilatación del endotelio, que es el revestimiento celular de los vasos sanguíneos, funciones esenciales para un buen flujo sanguíneo[1]. Si esto les sucede a hombres en buen estado de salud, imagina cuáles puedes ser los efectos en hombres mayores o con factores de riesgo de enfermedad cardiovascular, como la diabetes. No sorprende por ello que expertos de Harvard afirmen que niveles bajos de hidratación elevan la probabilidad de sufrir un ataque cardíaco[2].

¿Por qué? En realidad se trata de una cuestión muy fácil de visualizar: cuando hay poca agua en la sangre, esta se vuelve más espesa. Como apunta el cardiólogo Stephen Sinatra, una sangre sana tiene la consistencia del vino; no debe ser como una versión aguada de kétchup. Sin embargo, este es el aspecto que puede adquirir tu sangre —y muy rápidamente— si no te hidratas como debes. La sangre espesa hace que el corazón tenga que trabajar más para poder bombearla, lo cual puede dañar el músculo cardíaco y contribuir a la aparición de hipertensión arterial. Además, obliga al organismo a utilizar más energía para que la sangre pueda fluir por arterias y capilares, energía que podría ser utilizada por otras partes del cuerpo, como por ejemplo el cerebro. El resultado es una combinación de inflamación celular y problemas cardíacos y sanguíneos que crean el escenario idóneo para las enfermedades cardiovasculares. El trabajo del doctor Sinatra en medicina integral le llevó a ampliar sus estudios de investigación sobre impulsos eléctricos en el organismo más allá del corazón y del modo en el que el agua afecta a la conducción de dichos impulsos. Más adelante hablaremos de la importancia vital del agua y de los impulsos eléctricos.

Diabetes

Si tienes diabetes de tipo 1 o 2 corres un riesgo más alto de sufrir deshidratación. Ello se debe a que tu organismo no es capaz de fabricar insulina (como en la diabetes de tipo 1 y en la diabetes de tipo 2 avanzada) o no es sensible a la insulina (tipo 2), lo cual conduce a niveles más altos de azúcar en sangre, lo que se conoce como hiperglucemia. ¿Y por qué es esto un problema? Cuando los niveles de azúcar en sangre aumentan, los riñones intentan eliminarlo del torrente sanguíneo produciendo orina adicional y ello —adivina— provoca deshidratación.

Es un círculo vicioso: cuanto más espesa es la sangre y más deshidratada está, mayor es la probabilidad de tener niveles altos de azúcar en sangre, por el simple hecho de que no existe suficiente agua para diluir todo ese azúcar. Como resultado de ello, puede aumentar la deshidratación, lo cual conduce a problemas adicionales de azúcar en sangre.

La consecuencia puede ser una enfermedad grave llamada cetoacidosis que aparece cuando los niveles de azúcar en sangre son demasiado altos, los niveles de insulina demasiado bajos y el organismo empieza a quemar grasa para obtener energía, dejando en este proceso niveles sanguíneos altos y potencialmente tóxicos de unos compuestos llamados cetonas. Tal vez hayas oído hablar de las cetonas como una estrategia para perder peso que aprovechan las dietas ricas en proteínas, pero para las personas con diabetes esas cetonas pueden ser mortales[3].

¿Cómo se puede prevenir este círculo vicioso? Con un ingesta adecuada de líquido, por supuesto. El mantenimiento de una adecuada hidratación reduce además el riesgo de enfermedad cardíaca e hipertensión arterial, que se encuentra por encima de la media en personas con diabetes insulinodependiente[4].

Algunos expertos consideran incluso que la hidratación puede reducir el riesgo de *desarrollo* de diabetes de tipo 2. Cuando se sufre una deshidratación crónica, la escasa agua que se consume va directa al órgano posiblemente más vital: el cerebro. Por ello, el volumen de agua presente en el torrente sanguíneo disminuye, dando lugar, por una serie de procesos metabólicos, a una elevación de los niveles de azúcar en sangre. Si esto sucede muy de vez en cuando, es poco probable que la salud de la persona se vea afectada. Pero si se repite día tras día, semana tras semana, la deshidratación da lugar de forma crónica a niveles elevados de azúcar en sangre, los cuales acaban dañando las células sensibles del cuerpo, cuya respuesta a la insulina disminuye. En esto consiste la resistencia a la insulina, que rápidamente puede convertirse en una diabetes de tipo 2[5].

Problemas digestivos

Si sufres estreñimiento o tienes a menudo dolores, cólicos (o ambas cosas), incrementa tu ingesta de agua y llena tu dieta de alimentos ricos en agua que pongan de nuevo en movimiento tus intestinos. El agua y los alimentos ricos en agua, como las semillas de chía y las verduras (que además tienen abundante fibra que favorece la digestión), ablandan los alimentos y también las deposiciones. Y cuando las deposiciones son más blandas, pasan más rápida y fácilmente por el tubo digestivo, evitando los dolores intestinales y la sensación de hinchazón y mejorando la evacuación sin esfuerzo y sin tener que recurrir a laxantes. De acuerdo con los profesionales del Barnard College, los laxantes son en sí mismos deshidratantes y provocan retención de agua y, por consiguiente, mayor hinchazón[6].

El agua puede resultar de ayuda también en problemas digestivos más graves, como reflujo ácido o úlceras, tal y como apunta el doctor Batmanghelidj en su libro *Your Body's Many Cries for Water* (traducido al español con el título *Los muchos clamores de su cuerpo por el agua*). Batmanghelidj fue preso político en Irán a finales de la década de 1970. Durante ese tiempo trató y curó a miles de compañeros prisioneros —muchos de los cuales padecían úlcera péptica— solo con agua y electrolitos en forma de sal o azúcar[7].

El poder hidratante de las semillas de chía

El libro *Nacidos para correr: la historia de una tribu oculta, un grupo de superatletas y la mayor carrera de la historia,* de Chris McDougall, ha sido superventas en Estados Unidos. En él su autor nos presenta a la tribu de los tarahumara, que vive en los cañones del desierto de Sierra Madre, en México, y en la que los hombres jóvenes corren maratones de 80 kilómetros por diversión. En el libro, McDougall describe cómo los tarahumara se preparan para las maratones comiendo semillas de chía. Antes de la carrera, beben una mezcla de cerveza de maíz fermentado y semillas de chía y luego, en un saquito, llevan otras dos cucharadas más de semillas de chía. Increíble pero cierto: he aquí un pueblo del desierto que muestra una resistencia enorme corriendo una distancia que excede en principio lo humanamente posible —sin hidratarse con litros de agua, sino simplemente comiendo unas pequeñas semillas locales—. Hemos descubierto que cada semilla aporta al cuerpo de estos corredores de grandes distancias una poderosa hidratación de liberación lenta mientras corren. Estas semillas de chía de aspecto engañosamente seco encierran un ingrediente necesario para los corredores: cuando se mezclan con líquido, liberan una forma de agua gelificada que hidrata de manera más lenta y eficaz que solamente el líquido.

Si tienes un problema digestivo crónico, como enfermedad de Crohn, colitis o síndrome de intestino irritable, una ingesta adecuada de agua es obligada, porque todas estas enfermedades cursan con diarrea, que hace que tu organismo pierda más agua de lo normal.

Trombosis venosa profunda

La trombosis venosa profunda (TVP) puede aparecer cuando se forma un coágulo sanguíneo en venas profundas del cuerpo (de forma característica, en las venas de las piernas). Afecta sobre todo a los viajeros, aunque si estás embarazada, estás utilizando anticonceptivos con estrógenos, tienes sobrepeso u obesidad, eres una persona de edad avanzada, presentas mala circulación en las piernas o te has sometido recientemente a una intervención quirúrgica, también corres alto riesgo.

La TVP es una enfermedad grave que puede conducir a embolia pulmonar, que es el bloqueo de un vaso sanguíneo en los pulmones; a menudo resulta mortal. La hidratación ayuda a prevenir la TVP de dos maneras: una, evitando que la sangre espese y se formen coágulos; y dos, aumentando la necesidad de orinar, lo cual nos obliga a movernos más a menudo. Incluso pequeños momentos de actividad física reducen el riesgo de TVP.

Esa es la razón por la cual es tan importante evitar las bebidas alcohólicas, que son deshidratantes, y optar por el agua —y en gran cantidad— cuando se viaja en avión o se realizan viajes largos en coche. Y lo mismo puede decirse si presentas algunos de los factores de riesgo de TVP que acabamos de mencionar[8].

Enfermedades pulmonares, como enfermedad pulmonar obstructiva crónica (EPOC) y asma

El agua mantiene todos los sistemas orgánicos internos lubricados y en buenas condiciones de funcionamiento, y tus vías respiratorias y pulmones no son una excepción. El agua diluye el moco que reviste pulmones y garganta. Esta mucosidad ayuda a procesar y eliminar agentes contaminantes inhalados, toxinas y otras sustancias que pueden suponer un riesgo (tanto para pulmones sanos como para los afectados por enfermedades como la EPOC). Un moco espeso y alterado filtra menos sustancias perjudiciales para la respiración, lo cual explica por qué la deshidratación produce un empeoramiento de la EPOC (en forma de bronquitis crónica o enfisema). Algunas investigaciones indican que la deshidratación podría contribuir a la inflamación de las vías respiratorias, que dificulta la respiración[9].

ESTUDIO DE CASO DE LA DRA. DANA COHEN

Hank

Hank es un analista informático de treinta años. Siempre anda peleándose con su peso, que ha fluctuado ampliamente desde la adolescencia. Cuando tenía veinte años llegó a pesar más 100 kilos: con su metro ochenta de estatura, era obeso.

Aquel fue un punto de inflexión para Hank. Decidido a perder peso, emprendió un régimen de intenso ejercicio físico y una estricta dieta pobre en carbohidratos y rica en proteínas. Perdió 30 kilos en un año. Llegó un momento en el que empezó a preocuparse por estar en la frontera de la anorexia, pues había adelgazado hasta quedarse en 68 kilos. Pero luego cayó de nuevo en los viejos malos hábitos y volvió a superar los 100 kilos de peso.

Más que frustrado, vino a visitarme.

«Ayúdeme. No entiendo por qué tengo tantos problemas con el peso».

«Veamos qué es lo que está pasando», le dije para tranquilizarle.

Tras realizar una analítica sanguínea y una exploración física, pasé a considerar su medicación. Hank había tenido siempre asma, hasta donde le alcanzaba la memoria, y utilizaba a diario un inhalador de albuterol (un inhalador de rescate). También tomaba medicación para la ansiedad. Fumaba medio paquete de cigarrillos al día, hacía ejercicio dos veces por semana, combinando pesas y cardio. Su menú diario típico era el siguiente:

- Desayuno: una barrita de pan pequeña con queso untado, dos tazas de café solo.
- Comida: ensalada con pollo a la plancha y queso feta, aliñada con aceite de oliva.
- Cena: un bocadillo de pavo de Subway.

Me preocupaba que alguna sensibilidad alimentaria pudiera ser la causa de sus fluctuaciones de peso y que estuviera influyendo en su asma, de modo que decidí someterlo a una dieta de eliminación (hablaremos más sobre ello en las siguientes páginas). También le sugerí que incrementara su hidratación bebiendo dos vasos de agua con limón y sal marina por las mañanas, así como un vaso de agua antes de cada comida y uno o dos vasos más después de cada sesión de ejercicio. Le di además una receta de un *smoothie* para el desayuno que incluía verduras acordes con una dieta de eliminación, proteína de guisante, frutos del bosque, leche de coco y chía hidratante.

El paciente volvió tres semanas más tarde ¡con *cuatro* kilos menos! Ni él mismo se lo creía, y también yo me llevé una grata sorpresa. Me dijo que se sentía más ligero y con más energía y, lo que es más importante, se sentía *mejor*. Se sentía como si se hubiera quitado de encima un gran peso. Miramos los resultados de sus análisis, que eran todos normales, salvo por sus alergias ambientales, que se salían de los parámetros de normalidad.

Ahora que ha pasado un año, Hank es una versión mucho más delgada de sí mismo, pues pesa 88 kilos. Usa dos veces al día un inhalador diferente, un medicamento no esteroideo llamado salmeterol. Y no ha tenido que volver a usar su inhalador de rescate. Le receté montelukast, un medicamento antialérgico que reduce la inflamación pulmonar y que tiene muy pocos efectos secundarios. Y lo mejor de todo es que ha dejado de fumar, aunque sigue usando chicles de nicotina. Con esta plétora de energía, hace ejercicio religiosamente cuatro días a la semana. Se hidrata de manera eficaz y dice que nota la diferencia si se salta su *smoothie* de la mañana. Poco a poco ha ido incorporando de nuevo muchos alimentos a su dieta (salvo el marisco, porque le produce mucha alergia), pero sigue evitando el gluten y los lácteos. ¡Una auténtica historia de éxito de *Quench*!

NOTA: La dieta de eliminación es una forma excelente de abordar cualquier dolencia crónica no diagnosticada, pues las sensibilidades alimentarias son causa frecuente de una amplia serie de problemas médicos[10]. De hecho, yo animo a casi todos los pacientes que entran por la puerta de mi consulta a que sigan una dieta de eliminación. Y he visto resultados que han cambiado la vida de las personas. ¿Por qué? Las sensibilidades alimentarias son una causa no del todo conocida de enfermedades crónicas, como intestino irritable, migrañas, asma, alergias y dolor muscular y articular. Y lo que tal vez es más importante: estas sensibilidades a menudo conducen a una enfermedad crónica. Creo que si evitamos alimentos que suponen una agresión para nuestro organismo, podríamos estar evitando posibles desencadenantes de enfermedades, como trastornos autoinmunes y posiblemente la gran «C», el cáncer.

Las sensibilidades alimentarias son diferentes de las verdaderas alergias alimentarias, como la alergia a los cacahuetes, que hace que la garganta se irrite o, aún peor, que se hinche. La mayoría de los adultos saben si pueden o no tener estas reacciones agudas a determinados alimentos, pero las sensibilidades alimentarias no son tan fáciles de detectar o de identificar mediante pruebas. Es entonces cuando entra en juego una dieta de eliminación.

Hemos incluido en el apéndice una dieta de eliminación muy completa para alergias del doctor Alan Gaby, pero para una dieta de eliminación rápida e inmediata animo a mis pacientes a prescindir, durante veintiún días, de los cinco alimentos que con mayor frecuencia producen sensibilidad: gluten, lácteos, huevos, maíz y soja. Después de ese período de tres semanas, se va reintroduciendo cada alimento, uno por uno. Yo les digo que coman el alimento reintroducido dos veces al día durante tres días y anoten lo que les ocurre. Los síntomas pueden ser desde gases, hinchazón, diarrea, estreñimiento o fatiga, hasta dolor de cabeza, erupción cutánea, dolor muscular o articular o embotamiento mental. Si al cabo de tres días el alimento a prueba no ha producido síntomas, el paciente puede pasar al siguiente alimento, reintroduciéndolo de la misma manera que el anterior y tomando nota de los síntomas. Si se presentan síntomas, el paciente elimina ese alimento de su dieta y pasa al siguiente, y así sucesivamente.

Puede que te estés preguntando: «Todo eso suena genial, pero ¿qué pinta una dieta de eliminación en un libro sobre hidratación?». Tal y como hemos apuntado, todo lo referente a hidratación tiene que ver también con reparar el cuerpo después de una lesión y de protegerlo de la enfermedad. Piensa en nuestro Plan Quench y en la dieta de eliminación como en un doble golpe de boxeo. Juntos, constituyen una poderosa protección frente a enfermedades crónicas. Incluimos ambas estrategias en el libro con la intención de que las apliques juntas. Para elaborar las comidas, puedes elegir de entre todos los alimentos permitidos en la dieta. Para muchos pacientes, las dos estrategias, aplicadas juntas, han supuesto una experiencia que les ha cambiado la vida.

Recomendamos encarecidamente que, antes de comenzar la dieta de eliminación, consultes a un profesional sanitario con experiencia y que conozca tus antecedentes médicos, pues si no se sigue correctamente, el régimen puede causar deficiencias nutricionales. En personas con asma o eccema grave puede no ser recomendable seguir una dieta de eliminación. Por supuesto, siempre puedes comenzar con el Plan Quench de cinco días, que es muy suave, pero con el que obtendrás sorprendentes resultados.

Cerebro y cognición

De acuerdo, quieres mejorar tu salud. Pero lo que en realidad nos motiva a la mayoría para empezar a actuar al respecto es el deseo de sentirnos mejor. Y el agua puede hacer esto por ti... y de muchas maneras. Si notas que no te concentras, que tienes la mente dispersa, el agua es un remedio casi inmediato. Un estudio de 2012 publicado en la revista científica *Journal of Nutrition* llegó a la conclusión de que la deshidratación, aun siendo leve, reducía los niveles de concentración en las mujeres, que alcanzaron peores resultados en los tests de evaluación de concentración y cognición[11]. En cambio, realizaban bien estos tests cuando estaban perfectamente hidratadas. La deshidratación influía además a su estado de ánimo. Pero las mujeres no son las únicas afectadas por la deshidratación: otro estudio muestra que beber agua mejora la memoria y la concentración también en hombres, en niños y niñas[12].

¿Por qué los hombres tienen un porcentaje más alto de agua que las mujeres? Los músculos son agua en un 75% y los hombres tienen un porcentaje más elevado de masa muscular en su cuerpo que las mujeres. Por consiguiente, para una función metabólica y una hidratación eficaces, es muy importante que la mujer desarrolle y mantenga su masa muscular.

Numerosos científicos piensan que la sensación de falta de concentración y de vaga confusión mental que acompaña a una ligera deshidratación es la forma que tiene el cerebro de decir: «¡Oye, dame agua!». Es sencillo: es una forma efectiva e inmediata que tiene tu cuerpo de decirte que tus reservas de agua se están agotando. En efecto, las investigaciones muestran que las neuronas del cerebro son capaces de detectar las señales tempranas de aviso de deshidratación y, cuando lo hacen, activan otras neuronas y regiones del cerebro que regulan el estado de ánimo, poniendo en marcha este sistema interno de alarma.

Un aspecto aún más importante es la existencia de estudios tempranos que vinculan la deshidratación crónica con el desarrollo de enfermedad de Alzheimer. Ahora sabemos que la enfermedad de Alzheimer y la diabetes comparten aspectos patológicos y muchos médicos se refieren incluso al Alzheimer como «diabetes de tipo 3»[13]. Algunas relaciones causales son resistencia a la insulina, inflamación, estrés oxidativo, obesidad y síndrome metabólico. ¡Y nosotras pensamos que la hidratación es el primer paso en la protección frente a todas estas cosas!

El doctor Simon Thornton, profesor de neurociencia en la Universidad de Lorena, en Francia, está de acuerdo con nosotras. Cree que la deshidratación crónica de grado bajo es una de las principales causas de desarrollo de obesidad, diabetes, hipertensión e incluso enfermedad de Alzheimer[14]. De ser así, una baja hidratación contribuiría a un menor volumen (hipovolemia) y a una menor función del cerebro[15]. Avalan esta teoría de la deshidratación trabajos que ponen de manifiesto que el agua corporal total disminuye con la edad[16] y con el aumento del índice de masa corporal[17]. Esto sugiere que los pacientes obesos y/o diabéticos y/o ancianos podrían sufrir deshidratación crónica. Por otro lado, la mayor parte de los medicamentos utilizados para tratar las enfermedades cardiovasculares bloquean la capacidad de hidratación de las células. En otras palabras, estos fármacos frenan la capacidad del organismo para activar un sistema que mantiene la hidratación donde más se necesita[18]. Los valores altos de presión arterial se han asociado a disminuciones del volumen cerebral[19]. Todo ello apoya el nuevo paradigma de patologías inducidas por deshidratación.

Hidratación, prevención de lesiones y conmoción cerebral

La hidratación no se menciona en ninguna parte en la web de la agencia de Centros para el Control de Enfermedades (Centers for Disease Control) de Estados Unidos, en el enlace sobre consejos de seguridad y prevención de lesiones cerebrales. Tampoco se habla de deshidratación en la página web de la Clínica Mayo cuando se aborda la conmoción cerebral. Nosotras nos hemos propuesto cambiar esto, pues creemos que una buena y adecuada hidratación es el tratamiento de primera línea para la prevención de numerosas cuestiones de salud, incluida la conmoción cerebral (conocida como lesión traumática cerebral, LTC, leve). Esta es una cuestión importante, en especial si se relaciona con los niños y el deporte.

El cerebro tiene una consistencia gelatinosa. El líquido cefalorraquídeo contenido en el cráneo lo mantiene protegido de los pequeños golpes y sacudidas del día a día. Un golpe violento en la cabeza y el cuello o en la parte superior del cuerpo puede dar lugar a que el cerebro se golpee hacia delante y hacia atrás contra las paredes internas del cráneo. Una aceleración o desaceleración repentina, causada por una súbita colisión o caída, por ejemplo, también puede dar lugar a lesión cerebral. Y en este contexto, más agua equivale a mayor amortiguación y protección.

Las LTC leves representan una carga enorme en los servicios de urgencias de Estados Unidos[20]. En los últimos diez años se ha registrado un incremento mayor del 100% (y, en algunos grupos de edad, de más del 200%) en el número de pacientes recibidos en urgencia por conmoción cerebral por traumatismos relacionados con el deporte.

En un artículo publicado en Surgical Neurology International[21], la doctora Stephanie Seneff, investigadora del MIT, el Instituto Tecnológico de Massachusetts, y sus colaboradores llegaban a la importante conclusión de que el aumento de los casos de conmoción cerebral relacionados con el deporte podría guardar relación con una disminución preexistente de la elasticidad del cerebro debida a persistencia masiva de toxinas ambientales y a deficiencia de nutrientes en los deportistas. Estos trastornos conducirían a un «aumento de la sensibilidad ante contusiones antes consideradas inocuas» y reflejan la incapacidad del cuerpo para recuperar el equilibrio. En este nuevo marco de conocimientos la hidratación se torna esencial para la protección del cerebro y para el mantenimiento de la homeostasis, la función número uno del agua.

ETC e hidratación

Las LTC repetidas y a largo plazo, cuando no cuentan con tiempo suficiente para su recuperación, tienen consecuencias devastadoras. Puede que recuerdes un suceso terrible que sucedió en 2011: la noticia
de la muerte del famoso jugador de hockey Derexk Boogaard supues-
tamente por sobredosis a la edad de veintiochos años causó mucha
impresión en mundo del deporte. El reconocido jugador del Minnesota Wild y del New York Rangers se había convertido en el favorito de
los aficionados al hockey sobre hielo por su habilidad para luchar por
el disco y su capacidad de intimidación sobre el hielo, que le valió el
apodo de «The Boogeyman». Pero años de golpes en la cabeza y leves
lesiones traumáticas le llevaron a necesitar la prescripción de fármacos y, aunque siguió cosechando victorias sobre el hielo y jugando de
manera muy agresiva, empezó a sufrir cada vez más cambios de humor
y de conducta y se volvió olvidadizo y antisocial. Cuando falleció, amigos y familiares achacaron estos cambios de comportamiento a años
de consumo de drogas y de vida desenfrenada. Pero el informe de la
autopsia reveló un cuadro diferente: Boogaard había muerto por ence-
falopatía traumática crónica, también conocida como ETC, una enfermedad hermana del Alzheimer y cuya causa son los golpes repetidos
en la cabeza. Es difícil de diagnosticar y solo se detecta post mortem,
pero lo que realmente sorprendió fue lo avanzado de la enfermedad en
el caso de Boogaard. Fue muy impactante ver una progresión tan rápida de la enfermedad —más avanzada que en ningún otro jugador de
la National Hockey League (NHL) de Estados Unidos fallecido por esta
misma causa— a una edad tan joven. Aun cuando el diagnóstico de
Boogaard ocupó muchos titulares, la NHL no reconocería jamás relación alguna entre el hockey y las lesiones de la cabeza que acaban en
una ETC como consecuencia del juego. La buena noticia es que recientemente la National Football League ha donado millones de dólares
a la Universidad de Carolina del Norte en Chapel Hill para financiar la
investigación en estrategias activas de rehabilitación de deportistas
que sufren traumatismos cerebrales[22].

Los deportistas que sufren un traumatismo craneal pueden perder el conocimiento de forma temporal, sentir confusión, mareos, náuseas y cansancio y presentar dificultad para hablar, problemas de sueño y de concentración, irritabilidad y/o depresión y sensibilidad a la luz, por citar algunos de los trastornos presentados. Estos *síntomas* pueden observarse inmediatamente después del traumatismo, o pueden salir a la luz horas, días o incluso años después del mismo. Una vez que se ha sufrido una LTC leve, el riesgo de sufrir otra es mayor[23]. El médico puede diagnosticar una conmoción basándose en estos síntomas con o sin ayuda de pruebas de diagnóstico por imagen, como una RMN o un TAC. Sin embargo, el diagnóstico puede confundirse con el de deshidratación, que en ocasiones tiene una presentación similar. Por consiguiente, *antes de evaluar* una posible conmoción cerebral, es importante para el deportista llevar unas excelentes prácticas de hidratación y, para el médico, asegurarse de que el paciente se encuentra debidamente hidratado. Hacemos hincapié en este importante hecho para que los médicos que puedan estar leyendo este libro se fijen en modo especial.

En el novedoso artículo que ya hemos mencionado, la doctora Seneff y sus colaboradores llegaron a la conclusión de que la conmoción cerebral relacionada con el deporte es un problema moderno favorecido por una menor elasticidad del cerebro y relaciona las causas con la siguiente lista, cuyos elementos son abordados en su totalidad en el Programa Quench, al mismo tiempo que se proponen distintos *smoothies,* por ser una bebida magnífica para tomar antes de hacer deporte.

- Exposición a pesticidas y agentes químicos.
- Exposición reducida a luz solar natural.
- Deficiente relación omega 3:6 en la dieta.
- Consumo excesivo de alimentos procesados[24].

Aunque en la mayor parte de los recursos sobre salud, como la página web de la Clínica Mayo, nunca mencionan la hidratación como *tratamiento* de la conmoción cerebral, nosotras pensamos que el Programa Quench es un excelente complemento del necesario reposo en la recuperación de una lesión cerebral[25].

Dolor crónico

Al menos una de cada cinco personas sufren dolor crónico —y muchas más presentan dolor periódico—. La deshidratación puede estar en la raíz de ciertas formas de dolor, como en migraña o los calambres musculares, de modo que para estos problemas, beber agua puede ser, a la vez, bálsamo y cura. Pero incluso en casos más complejos de dolor, como traumatismos agudos o dolores articulares y menstruales, la hidratación puede ser de ayuda. Las investigaciones muestran que la deshidratación hace que el dolor empeore[26]. Y tiene sentido. Cuando estás deshidratado, el agua se desvía: en lugar de dirigirse a tejidos y articulaciones, se dirige directamente al cerebro, al corazón y a otros órganos vitales que necesitan agua para mantenerte vivo. Esto puede aumentar la rigidez de tejidos y articulaciones, causar acumulación de productos residuales, como el ácido láctico, y contribuir a la inflamación, causante también de dolor.

Y lo que es más: la deshidratación incrementa la actividad cerebral ligada al dolor, mientras que una hidratación adecuada calma esa actividad, conduciendo a niveles de dolor más bajos[27]. Esa puede ser la razón por la cual muchos médicos especialistas en medicina funcional recomiendan a los pacientes con fibromialgia una hidratación «extra», en ocasiones en forma de líquidos intravenosos. El simple hecho de llevar la hidratación a un nivel óptimo ayuda a aliviar la fatiga y el estado de agonía general de esta enfermedad crónica.

ESTUDIO DE CASO DE LA DRA. DANA COHEN

Betty

Cuando acudió por primera vez a mi consulta, Betty, una mujer de cincuenta y cuatro año residente en Nantucket, Estados Unidos, sufría una fibromialgia tan grave que no podía trabajar. Contaba que «le dolía todo», tanto que se bebía entre dos y cuatro vasos de vino por la noche para aguantar el dolor y poder dormir. El vino la ayudaba a aguantar, pero no podía dormir toda al noche.

No es de extrañar que Betty sufriera depresión y sobrepeso. Acudió a mi consulta pensando en una terapia de sustitución de hormonas bioidénticas que la ayudaran con sus síntomas de menopausia. Al final de la visita, me quedó muy claro que teníamos que abordar algo más que unos sofocos. Le sugerí que probara el Programa Quench y que redujera de manera drástica su consumo de alcohol. Y ella, deseosa de realizar un cambio en su vida, estuvo de acuerdo.

Tres semanas más tarde, Betty entró dando saltos de alegría en la consulta, diciendo: «*¡Dra. Cohen, me encuentro mucho mejor!*». Actualmente (un año después), se describe a sí misma como una persona nueva: en lugar de alcohol, bebe agua y batidos. Ha cambiado su dieta y ha empezado a hacer ejercicio, después de pensar durante mucho tiempo que la fibromialgia le impedía hacerlo. Ha experimentado una drástica disminución del dolor y un aumento de energía por primera vez en décadas. El Programa Quench, con sus pequeños cambios, ha supuesto el impulso que necesitaba para conseguir esos cambios mayores. Además, ha sido capaz de dejar el alcohol, que ya no necesita para olvidarse del dolor, y duerme mejor.

Dormir

¿No duermes tanto ni tan profundamente como te gustaría? Bienvenido al club. Casi la mitad de la población estadounidense no duerme lo suficiente[28]. Tomarse una pastilla no es una buena solución a largo plazo y además entraña todo tipo de riesgos. Olvídate de los fármacos y opta en cambio por el agua. La hidratación tiene varios efectos beneficiosos sobre el sueño. Para empezar, mantiene la humead de la boca y los orificios nasales, lo cual reduce los ronquidos que interrumpen el sueño. Además, una adecuada hidratación previene los calambres en las piernas, que pueden despertarte, aunque por la mañana no te acuerdes de ellos. Aunque no muestres tendencia a roncar ni a despertarte con sed en mitad de la noche, beber durante el día es importante para dormir luego mejor.

¿Por qué? Está en juego una gran respuesta, aunque poco estudiada. La mayor parte del proceso de desintoxicación del cuerpo tiene lugar sin que seamos conscientes de ello. Y el agua es el centro de ese proceso de desintoxicación. Por eso el sueño es tan reparador: te despiertas literalmente con un sistema operativo más limpio y eficaz. Nuevas investigaciones ponen de manifiesto que, cuando estás despierto, el organismo incrementa el movimiento de varios líquidos clave, como el líquido intersticial y el líquido cefalorraquídeo, en el cerebro, la columna vertebral, el sistema linfático y otras áreas clave. Este incremento del movimiento de líquido ayuda al cerebro y al cuerpo en general a eliminar ciertos metabolitos y toxinas, como la proteína beta amiloidea, que contribuye a la enfermedad de Alzheimer. Y cuanto mejor hidratado está el organismo, mejor funciona todo el proceso[29-31].

Por fortuna, dormir mejor no requiere beber dos litros de agua antes de irse a la cama (consulta el apartado sobre micción para saber algo más sobre por qué la hidratación durante el día no tiene por qué sabotear la noche). Si bebes agua y optas por alimentos hidratantes a lo largo del día, ya estás haciendo lo debido para ayudar a tu organismo a desintoxicarte y lograr un sueño profundo y reparador. ¿Te sigue preocupando tener que levantarte de madrugada para ir al baño? No bebas más de media taza de líquido en torno a una hora antes de irte a la cama y sáltate también la copa de por la noche. Además de deshidratar, el alcohol altera el sueño e irrita la vejiga.

¿Y qué hay de las visitas al baño?

Efectivamente, beber suficiente agua va a llevarte más a menudo al cuarto de baño, pero eso es bueno. Deberías ir al menos cada tres horas, y algunos médicos (como el especialista en medicina holística Gabriel Cousens, autor de *Spiritual Nutrition*) dice incluso que cada dos horas. Tal vez tú, como el resto de la sociedad moderna, pases demasiadas horas sentado. Levantarte para ir al baño es una manera sencilla de bombear sangre y oxígeno y de permitirte combatir los numerosos efectos negativos del sedentarismo.

La micción tiene en sí misma mala reputación, pero en realidad es una de las mejores cosas que puedes hacer para tu vejiga y tus riñones: cada vez que haces pis, eliminas bacterias persistentes, productos de desecho y otros compuestos presentes en el sistema «de filtración» de tu organismo.

Tal vez te estés preguntando cómo puedes hacer pis ocho o más veces al día y pasar en cambio entre siete y nueve horas por la noche sin ir al baño. Tienes que agradecérselo a tu cerebro. Cuando duermes, el cerebro libera una hormona antidiurética (ADH) que ayuda a tus riñones a concentrar la orina, en lugar de llenar excesivamente la vejiga y despertarte con sensación de urgencia miccional. Esta es también la razón por la cual la orina puede tener un color más oscuro por la mañana: está ultraconcentrada.

Al envejecer, el organismo produce menos ADH y este es el motivo por el cual muchos mayores se pasan toda la noche yendo al baño, cuando no lo hacían siendo más jóvenes. Y por eso también es clave ir al baño justo antes de apagar la luz por la noche, a cualquier edad. Deberás asegurarte de no dejar la mayor ingesta de agua justo para antes de acostarte. Además, si te hidratas a lo largo del día, no tendrás necesidad de hacerlo a última hora. Si tienes una buena higiene del sueño y anticipas tu ingesta de agua pero, aun así, te despiertas de noche para ir al baño, prueba a evitar el alcohol y la cafeína en exceso, y consulta al médico. Prueba también a tomar una cucharadita de semillas de chía molidas en media taza de té aproximadamente una hora antes de acostarte. Para algunos, esta receta actúa como una esponja y ayuda a retener más tiempo la orina durante el sueño.

Cáncer

No, el agua por sí sola no cura el cáncer. Pero recientes trabajos de investigación muestran que la hidratación tiene un papel clave en la reducción del riesgo de diversas formas comunes de esta enfermedad. Investigadores italianos han encontrado que los adultos que beben menos agua arrojan una probabilidad más alta de presentar cáncer de vejiga y de vías urinarias inferiores. Han propuesto la hipótesis de que el aumento de la ingesta de agua ayuda a impulsar los carcinógenos por el tracto urinario. Cuanto menor contacto tengan estas sustancias dañinas con los tejidos, menos probable será que causen cáncer[32].

El mismo equipo de investigadores encontró que un aumento de la ingesta de agua puede reducir el riesgo de cáncer colorrectal. El mecanismo es el mismo, aunque sean distintas las regiones orgánicas: el agua acelera el tránsito intestinal en el colon y el recto, los últimos 15 centímetros del intestino grueso, limitando en consecuencia el contacto en estas área con carcinógenos procedentes de la dieta y del entorno.

Pérdida de peso

La hidratación es esencial para perder peso. Ya hemos mencionado que un estudio de 2010 mostró que beber agua antes de cada comida puede ayudar a perder más de dos kilos en tres meses. Otros estudios han llegado a resultados similares. A menudo los investigadores atribuyen este fenómeno a la reducción de la ingesta calórica —el agua llena el estómago, lo que hace más difícil que se coma en exceso— pero puede que, además, quite el hambre. Y el agua no tiene valor calórico. Cuando se sustituyen por agua otras bebidas de escaso valor nutritivo o, lo que es peor, con edulcorantes añadidos como jarabe de maíz rico en fructosa o sacarosa, se reducen de manera natural las calorías añadidas.

Pero otros mecanismos están en juego. Un estudio de 2010 de la Universidad de Vanderbilt, en Tennessee, Estados Unidos, encontró que el agua aumenta la actividad del sistema nervioso simpático, lo cual da lugar a que nuestro organismo queme más calorías. De hecho, dicen los investigadores que beber incluso tres vasos de 48 cl de agua al día incrementa las calorías quemadas al día en medida suficiente para ayudar a perder dos kilos en un año sin hacer ningún otro cambio de estilo de vida[33]. Un estudio similar de investigadores alemanes encontró que beber 480 ml de agua estimulaba en un 30% el índice metabólico —esto es una media de doscientas calorías adicionales al día—[34].

Dicho esto, cuando optas por beber agua estás desechando otras bebidas que pueden contribuir a un aumento de peso, como refrescos azucarados, bebidas alcohólicas cargadas de calorías e incluso refrescos con edulcorantes artificiales —especialmente los refrescos «dietéticos», que las investigaciones han ligado repetidas veces a aumento de peso y a un montón de problemas de salud[35], como osteoporosis, ictus y demencia—[36].

CIENCIAS EMERGENTES EN LA INVESTIGACIÓN DEL AGUA

El agua es un tema resbaladizo. Aunque sabemos mucho acerca de sus propiedades, hay también muchos aspectos que desconocemos. Al mismo tiempo que los científicos siguen tratando de comprender cómo actúa esta esquiva molécula, en laboratorios de todo el mundo se llevan a cabo estudios sobre el agua y la eficiencia celular. La ciencia del agua en el ámbito molecular ha puesto manos a la obra a la comunidad científica y está dando forma a nuestros conocimientos sobre las funciones del agua. Y, lo que es más importante para ti, la ciencia del agua es la base de *Apaga tu sed*.

Esta nueva ciencia revela que el agua de nuestras células es un tipo distinto de agua: es del mismo tipo que podemos encontrar en las plantas. Ya sabemos que el agua existe en forma de líquido, gas o sólido, pero nuevos hallazgos están descubriendo un cuarto estado del agua similar al gel, apenas un diez por ciento más viscoso que el estado líquido. Este cambio en las fases del agua tiene lugar a nivel molecular. No podemos ver el cambio molecular a simple vista, pero en ese estado, el agua hidrata de manera más eficaz. Para ti significa que puedes beber menos líquido y, aun así, estar más hidratado. No es posible determinar con exactitud en qué medida es más eficaz esta agua similar a un gel, pero, realizando una extrapolación de ambientes extremos como el desierto, donde esta forma de hidratación se emplea desde tiempos ancestrales, parece que la diferencia es considerable.

Estrategias ancestrales en el mundo

Algunas de nuestras mejores pistas sobre qué alimentos hidratan de manera más eficaz proceden de ambientes extremos, donde el acceso a agua abundante es limitado. Es en tales condiciones cuando más vemos al ser humano recurrir a alimentos para suplementar las fuentes de agua y las necesidades de hidratación. Más allá de nuestros relatos sobre desiertos actuales, otros ambientes extremos que requieren adaptación del hombre son las regiones situadas a gran altitud, como el Himalaya y el altiplano de Perú.

Análisis arqueológicos y forenses de vasijas antiguas procedentes de Hualcayan, en los Altos Andes, muestran una evidencia sorprendente de que, en esas tierras, los guisos eran la piedra angular de la hidratación de las personas. Estos guisos contenían gelatinas liberadas por los cereales. La antropóloga Rebecca Bria afirma: «Al interpretar mis datos microbotánicos mediante análisis botánico, lo que en realidad encontramos fueron almidones «gelatinizados» e incrustados en la cerámica»[37].

El científico Harold McGee, autor del libro *On Food and Cooking* (1984) publicado en España con el título *La cocina y los alimentos,* en el que escribe sobre la ciencia y las características moleculares de los alimentos, afirma que el calentamiento de los cereales con almidón en presencia de agua descompone las capas cristalinas y da lugar a la gelatinización de los almidones o forma un complejo viscoso con el agua. Estas gelatinas liberadas a partir de los cereales potencian luego el poder de absorción y, por consiguiente, de hidratación del agua de cocción presente en los guisos. De hecho, estas antiguas estrategias que alteran el poder hidratante del agua añadiendo plantas como cereales, hierbas, semillas o raíces fueron extendiéndose con el tiempo por todos los continentes. A este respecto, una abrumadora evidencia procede de registros etnográficos y medievales que ponen de manifiesto que las plantas eran utilizadas para la hidratación y la depuración del agua. Los guisos y potajes cocinados a fuego lento liberaban más gelatina, alterando la estructura molecular del líquido de cocción. La cerveza y el hidromiel daban lugar al mismo cambio a través de la fermentación y fueron utilizados en todo el mundo para depurar, o reemplazar por completo, aguas sucias o contaminadas.

NUEVOS ESTADOS DEL AGUA

Estos nuevos estados o fases del agua están siendo debatidos en algunas de las más prestigiosas instituciones del mundo. Estudios recientes confirman estados del agua que antes no se reconocían.

El verano de 2017, trabajando en su laboratorio de la Universidad de Estocolmo, Katrin Amann-Winkel identificó una fase nueva y diferente del agua. Observó que «se transforma en un líquido viscoso, que a su vez se transforma prácticamente al instante en un líquido diferente e incluso más viscoso, de densidad mucho menor que la del hielo»[38]. Laura Maestro y los científicos que colaboran con ella en la Universidad de Oxford confirman asimismo que el agua cambia de un estado a otro[39]. Maestro ha afirmado: «La existencia de estos dos estados en el agua líquida tiene un importante papel en los sistemas biológicos».

El aspecto clave en este asunto es que el nuevo estado del agua es esencial para la función molecular —con consecuencias ahora identificadas sobre el funcionamiento de nuestro organismo—. Este diferente estado del agua está más organizado y las moléculas organizadas son más eficaces en su trabajo, como una orquesta con director, que interpreta las piezas de manera mucho más eficaz que músicos tocando cada uno por su cuenta. Esta ciencia emergente es tan nueva que la comunidad científica todavía no ha llegado a un acuerdo sobre la denominación de esta nueva fase del agua. Se la ha llamado agua estructurada, agua EZ o en gel, agua cristalina líquida o agua ordenada o coherente. A lo largo del libro nos referiremos a ella sobre todo como agua estructurada o agua en gel.

El Saykally Group de la Universidad de California, en Berkeley, está utilizando espectroscopia de láser ultrarrápido para estudiar las moléculas de agua y sus hallazgos muestran que el agua existe también en otros estados, además de los estados líquido, gaseoso y sólido. R. J. Saykally, principal autor del estudio, apunta: «El agua es la sustancia más importante del planeta. Su red única y versátil de enlaces de hidrógeno subyace a muchos de los procesos responsables de la vida. Aun así, y a pesar de siglos de estudio, cuestiones vitales referentes a la naturaleza intrínseca del agua siguen irresueltas»[40].

Un grupo de investigación de la Universidad de Cornell ha encontrado que el agua forma una «columna de hidratación» en torno al ADN. Lars Petersen, autor principal del estudio, afirma lo siguiente: «Nuevos resultados respaldan con fuerza un escenario en el que el agua a temperatura ambiente no puede decidir en cuál de las dos formas estar, de alta o baja densidad, lo cual da lugar a fluctuaciones locales entre ambas. El agua no es un líquido complicado, sino dos líquidos simples con una relación complicada». Petersen concluye que «un cambio en el estado de hidratación puede conducir a cambios importantes en la estructura del ADN».

Como puedes ver, los científicos están de acuerdo en que algo insólito y desconocido hasta ahora está pasando con la molécula de agua, que no se contempla ya como una simple fórmula química o molécula de H_2O.

AGUA ESTRUCTURADA

Uno de los conocimientos científicos más emocionantes de los últimos años ha sido el que se ha desprendido de los trabajos llevados a cabo en el laboratorio del doctor Gerald Pollack, que fue el primero en identificar de manera indiscutible, mediante experimentos documentados, este nuevo estado de gel del agua. Pollack, de la Universidad de Washington Seattle, es doctor en bioingeniería. Con treinta años de experimentos a su espalda, cuenta con reconocimiento mundial.

Los experimentos del laboratorio de Pollack identificaron lo que él denomina agua EZ, iniciales en inglés de «*exclusionary zone*», o zona de exclusión, en referencia a su capacidad para eliminar toda las partículas del interior de esa zona.

En la «zona de exclusión» del agua en gel, el doctor Pollack vio que las moléculas de agua pueden empezar a adherirse o cohesionarse y expulsar cualquier otra molécula más grande que las propias. Recuerda que las moléculas de agua se encuentran entre las más pequeñas del mundo y sirven de filtro para otras partículas más grandes, pero aun así diminutas, como las de toxinas y otras sustancias no deseadas. Nadie había observado este mecanismo hasta que Pollack encontró una manera de demostrarlo en laboratorio. En su forma de gel más denso, o fase EZ, las moléculas se unen para expulsar o excluir cualquier partícula más grande. El agua EZ es, digámoslo así, agua que se filtra a sí misma.

Según Pollack, el agua de la zona de exclusión presenta *diferencias de vital importancia* respecto del agua líquida simple, el H_2O. Es más densa y tiene más oxígeno. Pero he aquí la diferencia más sorprendente: si por un lado el agua líquida tiene carga neutra, por otro el agua EZ tiene carga negativa. Aunque el hecho de tener carga negativa puede parecer algo malo, en realidad es la manera que tiene el agua de formar una batería y de comenzar a producir y a almacenar energía en nuestro interior, la energía que necesitamos para movernos, pensar, reparar tejidos y curarnos.

Esta agua no solo es más densa, sino que además tiene mayor capacidad de conducción de los impulsos eléctricos para las funciones de nuestro organismo. Mediante estos experimentos se ha podido medir en el agua la cantidad de fuerza electromagnética, o aumento de energía.

CÓMO ACTÚA EL AGUA EN GEL

Nuestra historia favorita sobre cómo comenzó todo nos llega de la mano del propio Dr. Pollack. Mientras estudiaba una célula de músculo cardíaco, perforó sin querer la pared celular y observó que el agua contenida dentro de la célula no salía, ni tan siquiera goteaba. Se preguntó entonces: ¿por qué cuando rompes la membrana celular el agua permanece dentro? «Esa agua debe ser diferente», pensó.

Comenzó a preguntar a su alrededor y se dio cuenta de que nadie conocía el por qué. Esta cuestión le llevó hasta la Conferencia internacional sobre física, biología y química del agua, en su duodécima edición, que convoca a científicos y pensadores para compartir las teorías actuales sobre el comportamiento del agua y buscar nuevas respuestas. Aunque, en general, se piensa que el agua tiene un efecto de dilución, esta nueva línea de investigación muestra que también puede dar lugar a cohesión. El rompedor trabajo de Pollack se desarrolló al darse cuenta de lo diferente que era el agua cuando sus moléculas se unían en el tiempo y en el espacio. Juntas, las moléculas se tornaban más y más estrechamente unidas, pero no como cristales de hielo estables o como copos de nieve, sino más bien como cristales solapados o entrelazados, como una redecilla de ganchillo, pero aún en estado líquido. Este se conoce también como estado líquido cristalino. Se forma así, no una conexión de H_2O solitaria, sino una conexión más compleja: H_3O_2. Estos hallazgos siguen siendo objeto de debate; después de todo, llevamos demasiado tiempo considerando el agua como una simple molécula de H_2O, aunque son ya numerosos los científicos que están de acuerdo en que ahora ya se puede explicar cómo funciona el agua en la naturaleza.

Además, como ya hemos dicho, existe un consenso cada día mayor en torno a la idea de que el agua existe en fases diferentes de las de líquido, vapor y hielo. Un grupo de investigación de la Universidad de Harvard llegó a la conclusión en 2008 de que el agua dentro de las proteínas celulares es diferente del agua líquida y da lugar a una forma hexagonal organizada en muchas láminas o capas. Se trata de una descripción llamativamente similar a la de la estructura del agua EZ[41].

Lo que se deduce del trabajo de Pollack y de otros estudios es que el agua es un compuesto sofisticado, más sofisticado de lo que pensábamos. El agua no volverá a ser considerada nunca un material de fondo, ni un disolvente universal, sino el mayor activador de ignición química y eléctrica. En este entorno molecular, el agua es un *continuum vibrante*, que pasa de una fase y una forma a otra, aun cuando a simple vista parezca simplemente eso... agua. Cuando pasa del estado líquido al estado de gel —y ya te mostraremos cómo ocurre esto— las propiedades vitales del agua se amplifican. Lo más importante que debes saber sobre esta increíble nueva ciencia del agua es que existe un agua que es más densa, se activa por efecto de ondas de luz y tiene más energía mensurable. Todavía queda por descubrir cómo funciona todo esto, pero se intuye que podría acelerar la capacidad de nuestras células de reparación y regeneración y, en última instancia, suponer mayor vitalidad.

DÓNDE SE ENCUENTRA EL AGUA ESTRUCTURADA

El agua en gel está presente en todas las células vivas, incluso en las plantas. Podemos sentir y probar la diferencia. El agua en gel puede parecer tan fluida como el líquido, aunque ligeramente más suave, y puede expandirse y llegar a ser tan densa como la gelatina. Está presente en todo tipo de alimentos. Por ejemplo, la lechuga iceberg es en realidad un alimento superhidratante. Dentro de la lechuga, el agua se encuentra estructurada. El agua en gel presente en el caldo de huesos resulta muy restauradora, como todos sabemos. Y si dejas en remojo semillas de chía, verás cómo se forma el gel.

La pregunta ahora sería: ¿en qué sentido el agua en gel hidrata de forma diferente del agua en su estado corriente? Por lo que sabemos a día de hoy, y teniendo en cuenta que todavía queda mucho por descubrir, el agua en gel hidrata de manera diferente porque es un estado diferente del agua y, no solo aporta una hidratación más duradera, sino que además conduce los impulsos eléctricos en nuestro cuerpo de modo mucho más eficaz. Un ejemplo excelente se tiene cuando el médico aplica un gel en la piel para obtener una mejor lectura en las pruebas ecográficas y electrocardiográficas. Ello se debe a que el gel más denso es un excelente conductor. La conducción eléctrica guarda relación con todos esos electrolitos de los que has oído hablar, que son minerales y que están presentes en abundancia en las plantas. Disueltos en agua, liberan su carga eléctrica. Dado que la densidad y la carga tienen mucho que ver con una conducción eficaz, el agua en gel conduce la electricidad de manera muy eficaz. Y a más energía, menos fatiga y más poder de curación. Esto equivale a decir que, si comemos frutas y verduras frescas, estamos tomando alimentos con más energía mensurable y con mayor capacidad hidratante que una botella de agua.

Infusiones de yerba para los vaqueros del desierto

Para hidratarse bien con una dieta basada principalmente en la carne de vacuno, los célebres vaqueros nómadas de las llanuras de la pampa uruguaya —gauchos— utilizaban una infusión de yerba mate, una infusión muy intensa de hojas de un arbusto llamado *Ilex paraguarensis*. Estas infusiones estaban cargadas de nutrientes y minerales vegetales y, tal y como evidencia la salud de hierro de los gauchos que vivían en tan áridas condiciones, proporcionan una hidratación óptima. En la década de 1960 la infusión de mate fue extensamente estudiada en el Instituto Pasteur de París, que llegó a la conclusión de que «Es difícil encontrar en el mundo una planta que iguale a esta yerba en cuanto a valor nutricional, pues contiene prácticamente todas las vitaminas necesarias para la vida». Otro estudio reveló que la yerba mate tiene un contenido muy alto de elementos minerales y un correcto equilibrio de electrolitos. Y ahora tenemos también alguna pruebas de que la yerba mate contribuye al equilibrio de peso e incluso a la pérdida de peso[42].

Una cosa está clara: las plantas encierran nutrientes, muchos de los cuales solo pueden ser liberados gracias a la acción disolvente de las moléculas de agua. De modo que, gracias al poder de disolución del agua, las plantas aportan nutrientes a nuestro cuerpo, además del agua hidratante que encierran.

EN REALIDAD NOS CARGA EL SOL

Puede parecer una ironía, pero la hidratación comienza con el sol. La relación entre el sol y el agua es original y originaria. Se produce hidratación cuando la luz solar incide en las moléculas de agua, incluso a través de la piel. El doctor Pollack propone que, cuando las ondas luminosas llegan al agua —incluso en nuestro interior, en un nivel celular— la molécula de agua se divide, dando lugar a una carga más negativa y convirtiendo el agua en una batería energética. Las baterías retienen y almacenan la carga eléctrica para que sea utilizada como energía y las células hacen lo mismo. Juntos, el sol y el agua nos convierten en baterías. La luz solar y la luz infrarroja, y todos los espectros entre ambas, determinan nuestra energía y la calidad de nuestra hidratación. Además de los alimentos, la luz solar es la manera más natural y accesible de contribuir a la función celular. La exposición a la luz, bien sea en forma de luz visible bien sea en forma de luz infrarroja (la luz que no puedes ver), ayuda a que se forme o que crezca el agua en gel dentro del cuerpo. Según Pollack «la energía para construir la estructura del agua procede del sol. La energía radiante a partir de longitudes de onda que abarcan desde la luz ultravioleta hasta la infrarroja, pasando por el espectro de luz visible, convierte el agua líquida o corriente en agua organizada». Mediante experimentos, Pollack demuestra que el agua absorbe la energía luminosa libre del medio y utiliza esa energía para construir agua EZ. La entrada adicional de energía, ya sea a partir del sol o de alimentos vegetales, forma EZ adicional.

Por esta razón Pollack describe esa cuarta fase del agua con una ecuación química diferente. En el agua EZ, los electrones comparten una carga positiva y una carga negativa para formar esta nueva H_3O_2. «La energía radiante absorbida divide las moléculas de agua; la fracción negativa constituye la unidad básica de construcción de EZ, mientras que la fracción positiva se une a moléculas de agua para formar iones hidronio libres (H_3O^+), que se difunden a través del agua. La luz adicional (energía radiante) estimula la separación de carga», dando lugar en consecuencia a más agua estructurada[43].

Pollack no es la única persona que estudia el modo en el que nuestro cuerpo utiliza la luz para generar energía. De hecho, en 2014 se publicó un estudio nuevo que integraba el papel de la luz, del agua y de las plantas en el organismo de los mamíferos. Este reciente estudio, publicado en la revista *Journal of Cell Science*, documenta el modo en que la molécula de clorofila interactúa en el organismo con la luz para producir ATP, que es una molécula que almacena la energía en nuestras células[44]. Por primera vez los autores muestran que las moléculas vegetales ingeridas captan la luz en el interior del cuerpo del mamífero y producen energía en forma de ATP. ¿Te resulta familiar? Como ocurre con la fotosíntesis de las plantas, los autores proponen que, al comer plantas verdes (clorofila), los mamíferos pueden obtener energía de la luz solar.

Al incidir sobre la piel, la luz pone en marcha una reacción en cadena en todas las células y esa reacción en cadena va trasmitiendo la carga y nos aporta energía. Piensa en la frase: «Necesito cargar pilas». Es como enchufar el móvil o el ordenador: estamos recargándonos con nuestra fuente de luz y un cuerpo bien hidratado conduce esa carga.

Al margen de la exposición a la luz para seguir formando agua en gel dentro del cuerpo, también debes *ingerir alimentos* que contienen esta forma de agua estructurada. Así contribuyes a la carga eléctrica. Un tipo de alimento es el agua exprimida de las plantas. Cuando preparas zumos o batidos vegetales, lo que obtienes es agua estructurada. Como apunta Pollack, «estás introduciendo en tu cuerpo lo que este más necesita. Desde mi punto de vista, esta es la mayor revolución en la medicina. Simplemente bebiendo el tipo adecuado de agua puedes mejorar tu salud e incluso invertir el curso de una patología».

UNE TODOS LOS PUNTOS

Esta nueva ciencia supone un estímulo para nuestra hidratación, favoreciendo la salud y la vitalidad en momentos difíciles. Una mejor hidratación mejora la función y ello protege todos nuestros sistemas y tejidos. La deshidratación nos perjudica. Ahora más que nunca todos sufrimos los efectos negativos de un entorno artificial. Pero esta nueva ciencia ha llegado justo a tiempo para identificar una fase diferente del agua, presente tanto en nuestras células como en las células vegetales. Podemos mejorar fácilmente nuestra función celular manteniendo y favoreciendo el volumen de gel a partir de fuentes naturales. Podemos incorporar alimentos hidratantes a nuestra dieta para generar más energía. Nuestro Plan Quench te presenta esta nueva ciencia a través de sencillas recetas de *smoothies* para hidratar el organismo en el plano celular, dado que vivimos en condiciones cada día más deshidratantes.

Cómete el agua

Alimentos para una hidratación óptima

Sin agua no hay vida. Sin azul no hay verde.

Sylvia Earle

¿**S**abías que lo que comes puede absorber tu humedad? ¿O que, por el contrario, puede rehidratarte? ¿Y que hay alimentos que rehidratan de manera incluso más profunda que el agua por sí sola? Por ejemplo, una manzana con una botella de agua hidrata más que dos botellas de agua. Funciona así: la fibra de esa manzana actúa como una esponja, ayudando a retener la humedad durante más tiempo en su interior, y también durante más tiempo dentro de ti.

Pero antes de empezar a hablar de comida, queremos hablar de cambio. El ser humano está hecho para el cambio, en términos de crecimiento y adaptación. Es la cualidad humana más común, es parte de tu herencia y te corresponde. Los alimentos que decidas comer pueden acabar con parte del cansancio inherente a la vida moderna. Pero tenemos que dejar atrás nuestra vieja manera de comer. Si no has cambiado ya tus hábitos alimentarios, es hora de hacerlo. Ha llegado el momento de «comerte el agua».

¿Por qué? Realmente nos hallamos en un entorno nuevo. Nuestros actuales patrones de vida, incluida la comida preparada, nos «barren» por dentro. Generan fatiga y, lo que es más importante, nos roban alegría. El motivo por el que tenemos que hidratarnos y utilizar la comida para tal fin es, en última instancia, un motivo alegre: para conseguir más vida. Más vitalidad. Una mejor función cognitiva y una mayor capacidad de apreciación. Y resulta que la estrategia más inteligente consiste en combinar agua y alimentos, siendo la propia naturaleza la que la diseña ¿En qué momento se produjo la separación de hidratación y alimentos en dos categorías distintas? La naturaleza los envasa juntos en un sistema de suministro supereficaz.

Trucos para evitar la deshidratación ambiental

Problema: el calor deshidrata. Piensa en todas esas luces y dispositivos electrónicos que se calientan solo con encenderlos. ¿Te has dado cuenta de cuánto llegan a calentarse tu ordenador o tu móvil?

Truco de hidratación: pon el móvil y el ordenador en modo luz azul —calienta menos—. Mejor aún, aléjate de cualquier dispositivo electrónico durante cinco minutos cada hora. Trabaja con luz natural tanto tiempo como puedas. Considera la posibilidad de llevarte a la oficina una bonita lámpara de escritorio y apagar las luces del techo. Queda con la gente al aire libre, para dar un paseo. Un perímetro seguro para el móvil es de 60 centímetros, de modo que mantenlo a esa distancia de tu cuerpo y, siempre que puedas, utiliza auriculares o, mejor aún, el altavoz.

Problema: el estar tanto tiempo sentados y encorvados sobre el teclado del ordenador o sobre el móvil reduce e inhibe el flujo vital de líquido por todo el organismo.

Truco de hidratación: realiza unos pequeños movimientos y comprueba tu postura cada hora. ¿Encorvado? Hombros abajo, pecho arriba. ¿No te sientes mejor?

Problema: puede parecer que el aire acondicionado nos ayuda con el calor, y lo hace, pero también nos deshidrata, absorbiendo la humedad del ambiente. Objetos como alfombras, cortinas sintéticas, muebles y ambientes muy cerrados parecen aliarse para absorber el vapor del aire. Echa un vistazo a tu alrededor en la habitación o en la oficina y fíjate en todas las cosas que compiten contigo para absorber la escasa humedad existente en los ambientes interiores.

Truco de hidratación: podemos reequilibrar estos ambientes devolviéndoles la humedad. Pero humidificar toda una habitación puede requerir un equipo costoso. Un truco fácil consiste en poner un difusor cerca de ti, de modo que estarás humidificando tu cuerpo, aunque no toda la habitación. Gestos tan simples como poner una jarra de agua abierta encima del escritorio o colocar plantas en tu lugar de trabajo o en casa suponen una diferencia que se nota.

Los aceites esenciales añadidos al difusor aportan las moléculas de la planta aromática, una manera ingeniosa aunque no siempre reconocida de rehidratar. Y el vapor llega a los orificios nasales y a los pulmones, es una manera de aportar hidratación justo ahí. Un simple truco, ya sea en la oficina o en reuniones, consiste en colocar cerca de ti una bonita taza de té para inhalar los vapores de vez en cuando, aunque no llegues a beberte el té.

Problema: coches, aviones, trenes e incluso el metro son cápsulas deshidratantes. Se cuentan entre los ambientes más secos, ocupando en este sentido los aviones el primer puesto. En un ambiente cerrado, se considera saludable una humedad comprendida entre un 50 y un 60 %, pero en los aviones la humedad puede ser inferior al 20 %, bajando en ocasiones hasta el uno por ciento. Los coches son un peligro también: por cada hora que pasas dentro del coche, tu grado de hidratación disminuye, pues el aire húmedo es sustituido por aire desoxigenado y seco. La deshidratación durante los viajes puede acelerar la sequedad y la descamación de la piel, todo ello sumado al hecho de tener que permanecer sentado y con muy poco movimiento en un ambiente deshumidificado.

Truco de hidratación: nunca viajes sin algo para beber en el coche, abre las ventanas de vez en cuando para que entre aire fresco en el coche y realiza micromovimientos en los semáforos.

Problema: la ausencia de luz natural en los interiores, en casa y en la oficina, nos cuesta nuestra hidratación de un modo insospechado. No solo vivimos una vida sumamente estresante en habitaciones intencionadamente deshumidificadas, sino que vivimos fuera del alcance de la luz del sol, que tiene mucho que ver con nuestra hidratación, además de calentarnos y de calmar todo nuestro sistema nervioso.

Truco de hidratación: mantente alerta para detectar tu necesidad de luz solar, tómate descansos de diez a quince minutos al aire libre y pasa también al sol tu hora de comer. No podemos decir cuánto sol debe tomar todo el mundo, ya que probablemente cada persona necesite un grado diferente de exposición; pero ese tiempo de la comida te vendrá bien (contando siempre con la autorización del médico si tienes algún problema, por supuesto). Te beneficiarás de las ondas luminosas incluso los días nublados. Por último, existen nuevas evidencias de que necesitamos la información de la luz solar para poner debidamente en hora nuestro reloj interno cada día. Esa primera hora de luz diurna puede ser mucho más crucial de lo que pensamos.

Problema: el estrés y la presión que nos ocasiona la ajetreada vida moderna activan la liberación de sustancias neuroquímicas en nuestros sistemas, lo cual supone un sobreesfuerzo para el organismo, que ha de hacer un mayor uso de sus reservas de agua.

Truco de hidratación: los *smoothies* y los alimentos hidratantes aportan nutrientes protectores que combaten esa falta de agua. Un hábito regular de respiraciones profundas ayuda a restablecer el equilibrio y conduce hasta el interior aire hidratante.

En nuestro programa de hidratación profunda volvemos a juntar los elementos que la naturaleza aporta ya combinados. Por tu parte, solo te pedimos un poco de adaptación. Realizaremos pequeños cambios para llevarlo a cabo. Después de todo, solo te pedimos que introduzcas en tu rutina diaria algunos batidos, que bebas en momentos clave del día y añadas alimentos hidratantes para compensar ciertas comidas deshidratantes. ¿Puede haber algo más sencillo que esto?

Por ejemplo, si te comes dos manzanas en lugar de dos porciones de pizza... de acuerdo, es poco probable. Pero ¿qué tal un pedazo de pizza y una manzana? Acabas de reequilibrar los cálculos internos de tu organismo sobre cómo emplear la energía de la digestión. Tu cuerpo sabe que va a obtener ayuda hidratante de esa manzana. Y acabas de recargar tu batería tomando la carga eléctrica que proviene del agua en gel de esa manzana.

En este capítulo te proporcionamos información para el cambio. La hidratación en profundidad te permite cambiar tus opciones alimentarias sabiendo lo que haces y por qué lo haces, de manera agradable y con resultados. En nuestro plan te ofrecemos consejos vitalizantes y te enseñamos técnicas prácticas.

EL AGUA NO ES AZUL: ES VERDE

Es posible que sea la primera vez que oyes hablar del agua como alimento. En general, el agua no es considerada como un nutriente; en lugar de ello, pensamos que es un elemento funcional, humectante. Y te habrán dicho una y otra vez que una buena hidratación requiere ocho vasos de agua al día, o la mitad de tu peso corporal (medido en libras) en agua (medida en onzas) según directrices oficiales en Estados Unidos. De hecho, la ampliamente conocida recomendación de los ocho vasos al día fue una sugerencia originariamente gubernamental, que basaba las pautas de hidratación en cantidades totales[1]. Lo sorprendente es que, en las directrices originales, el 45% de esa cantidad recomendada provenía de *alimentos*. Con el paso de los años, la leyenda urbana convirtió aquellas onzas en líquido únicamente y, al final, solo en agua. Sin embargo, obtener nuestra hidratación del agua y de los alimentos constituye la estrategia más inteligente que existe en el planeta, pues es la diseñada por la naturaleza. La naturaleza creó juntos agua y alimentos, en un sistema supereficiente de suministro.

He oído que lo que tengo que hacer es beber la mitad de mi peso corporal (en libras) en agua (en onzas): ¿es eso cierto?

Beber la mitad de tu peso corporal en agua (utilizando la onza como unidad de medida) es una recomendación general lanzada en su día en Estados Unidos y ampliamente utilizada, porque es sencilla. Por ejemplo, según estas directrices, una mujer con un peso de 120 libras (unos 54,5 kilos) debería beber 60 onzas (cerca de 1,77 litros) de agua al día. No es una mala regla general, pero está lejos de la verdad absoluta. En realidad, la hidratación depende de muchos factores, no solo del peso corporal. Puede ser que te encuentres en circunstancias de sequedad ambiental, que seas joven, que estés en muy buena forma o que estés siguiendo alguna medicación, y cada situación requiere una medida diferente de hidratación. O puede que seas una persona anciana y tengas menos músculo (el tejido que mejor mantiene la hidratación del cuerpo). También es posible que estés sudando mucho.

Pero, por encima de todo, lo que comes es crucial para una adecuada hidratación.

En *Apaga tu sed,* te pedimos que prestes atención a las señales que te lanza tu cuerpo para que bebas, no te indicamos una cantidad fija. Nuestras dos señales principales son cansancio, especialmente al caer la tarde, y falta de claridad mental. Detrás de esto vienen los dolores de cabeza, la rigidez y el dolor articular, la irritabilidad y un bajo estado de ánimo. La sequedad de lengua, garganta y orificios nasales es también un signo temprano. Te recomendamos que te hidrates de manera más eficaz cargándote de agua a primera hora de la mañana y que incluyas zumos de frutas y verduras, que proporcionan fibra, para mantener la hidratación durante más tiempo.

Con un 80 a un 98% de volumen de agua, las plantas son el envase biológico perfecto. La próxima vez que des un mordisco a una manzana o a una pera, piensa que esa pieza de fruta te está aportando agua que no solo es pura, o más pura, sino que te hidrata en profundidad, además de proporcionarte nutrientes y minerales. Su secreto reside en el equilibrio funcional perfecto de nutrientes e hidratación de su estructura natural. Ni mucho ni

Las 12 verduras más hidratantes (porcentaje de agua)	Las 12 frutas más hidratantes (porcentaje de agua)
1. Pepinos 96,7%	1. Carambola 91,4%
2. Lechuga romana 95,6%	2. Sandía 91,4%
3. Apio 95,4%	3. Fresas 91%
4. Rábanos 95,3%	4. Pomelo 90,5%
5. Calabacines 95%	5. Melón 90,2%
6. Tomates 94,5%	6. Piña 87%
7. Pimientos 93,9%	7. Frambuesas 87%
8. Coliflor 92,1%	8. Arándanos 85%
9. Espinacas 91,4%	9. Kiwi 84,2%
10. Brécol 90,7%	10. Manzanas 84%
11. Zanahorias 90%	11. Peras 84%
12. Coles de Bruselas 86,5%	12. Uvas 81,5%

poco: son ricas en nutrientes, ricas en fibra y están llenas de agua. Cada vez que te comes un vegetal, ya sea una verdura de hoja, una pera o incluso semillas de chía, estás tomando una forma de agua.

Los alimentos ricos en agua son también ricos en nutrientes, en forma de antioxidantes, proteínas y sus aminoácidos, minerales y vitaminas. También aportan nutrientes como calcio, magnesio, potasio y sodio que, activados por la carga eléctrica del agua, se conocen como electrolitos. Pero de lo que nos alerta la nueva ciencia es de que el agua, rica en todos estos electrolitos, está también *llena de electrones* que hacen posible la conducción de impulsos eléctricos. El agua conduce electricidad, no solo como fuente de energía, sino también para la función mental y el estado de ánimo. Recuerda que la calidad de nuestra hidratación está muy relacionada con la calidad de la conducción eléctrica. No nos cansaremos de decirlo: el agua conduce electricidad y la hidratación pone en marcha nuestra función eléctrica.

Esto hace que el agua pase de ser considerada un agente simplemente humectante o limpiador a ser considerada una fuente de energía. Y quédate con esto: gracias a la fibra de las plantas, el agua permanece en nuestro sistema más tiempo, pues la absorbemos más lentamente. Es una triple jugada de salud: agua pura, fibra absorbente y no solo nutrientes necesarios, sino también electrolitos. *Por todos estos efectos, pensamos que las plantas hidratan de manera más eficaz que un simple vaso de agua.*

Cómo se hidratan las vacas

Las vacas se pasan la vida comiendo hierba cargada de agua en un 97%, y se mantienen hidratadas. Aun así, por supuesto, necesitan beber, pero esta fabulosa combinación de agua y fibra digestiva que es el pasto cubre en gran parte las necesidades de hidratación de estos animales. Ello contrasta con las vacas que se alimentan con pienso y que todos sabemos que necesitan beber más agua y que están peor nutridas.

Las vacas alimentadas con pastos beben menos agua. Las mediciones realizadas el verano de 2009 en la Save Your Dairy Farm, en Arizona, pusieron de manifiesto que sus 130 vacas de pasto bebían en conjunto una media de 6.800 litros de agua al día. Sin embargo, un estable similar de vacas alimentadas con pienso consumirían entre 11.350 y 15.140 litros al día[2].

En el momento de la publicación de este libro, estudios aún no publicados han llegado a la conclusión de que las plantas pueden resultar el doble de hidratantes que un vaso de agua. ¡Imagínate!

A PROPÓSITO DE LA PIZZA

¿Te acuerdas de cuando hablamos de pizzas y manzanas? ¿Por qué reemplazamos una porción de pizza por una manzana? Porque la pizza tiene efecto deshidratante. ¿Cómo es esto exactamente?

La respuesta es sencillamente que la pizza está cargada del tipo inadecuado de sal, que hace que pierdas más líquido del que tomas y que tu cuerpo no disponga de agua ni de otros líquidos en cantidad suficiente para llevar a cabo las funciones orgánicas normales. Si no repones los líquidos perdidos, evidentemente sufrirás deshidratación, en mayor o menor medida.

La respuesta ampliada es que nuestras células utilizan y almacenan el agua en dos compartimentos: el líquido intracelular (LIC) y el líquido extracelular (LEC). El LIC supone el 60 al 65% de toda el agua del interior de las células de nuestro cuerpo y el LEC supone en torno al 35 al 40% del agua que rodea las células. Los nutrientes como el cloro, el potasio, el magnesio y el sodio ayudan a mantener el equilibrio entre LEC y LIC. Si una molécula presenta una concentración demasiado alta en uno de los compartimentos, tomará agua del otro para diluirla.

Pero volvamos a la pizza: el sodio de la salsa de tomate, del queso, de los pimientos y de otros ingredientes salados se acumula en el LEC, que toma agua del LIC. Este mecanismo envía señales al cerebro de que las células se están deshidratando. Y el cerebro envía a su vez señales para que bebas agua. De hecho, la hinchazón que puedes notar se debe precisamente a este desequilibrio.

LA SAL: UNA SOLUCIÓN HIDRATANTE

¿Cómo? ¿Que la sal puede ayudar a mantener una buena hidratación?

Acabamos de ver que el sodio (o sea, la sal) tiene efecto deshidratante. Es verdad que una cantidad excesiva de sal común de mesa, procesada, no es buena para la salud. Los riñones utilizan el agua para filtrar la sal y eliminarla del organismo con la orina. Es algo normal, es un proceso cotidiano. Pero si tienes ya cierta escasez de agua y en tu dieta abunda la sal procesada añadida, esta combinación puede conducir a deshidratación y a posibles problemas renales.

No obstante, evitar la sal tampoco es la solución. De hecho, puede ser perjudicial para la salud. El sodio es un electrolito clave. Con ayuda del potasio, el sodio es necesario para mantener el equilibrio interno de cargas eléctricas en el organismo. El sodio y el potasio disueltos en el agua tienen una función celular esencial, que se conoce como bomba celular de sodio-potasio. En nuestro cuerpo, el sodio proporciona iones con carga positiva, mientras que el potasio proporciona iones con carga negativa, y esta combinación genera potenciales eléctricos en las membranas celulares. Se trata de un proceso constante de paso de un lado a otro, que mantiene el funcionamiento de las células incluidas células nerviosas y neurotransmisores. Si el organismo no dispone de sal suficiente, el equilibrio eléctrico interno se rompe y las células no pueden recibir ni trasmitir impulsos como deberían. Una pequeña cantidad de sal natural es absolutamente esencial para la hidratación.

Esta es la razón por la cual, a menudo, puede verse a la gente que hace ejercicio a diario y a los deportistas profesionales pegados a alguna bebida deportiva durante y después de competir. No solo están reponiendo el agua que han perdido; también están reabasteciendo sus depósitos orgánicos de sodio y potasio. Si haces ejercicio, deja a un lado las bebidas deportivas cargadas de edulcorantes artificiales, productos químicos sintéticos, colorantes alimentarios y otros aditivos innecesarios.

¿Por qué cada día son menos populares las bebidas deportivas como forma de hidratación?

Las bebidas deportivas y otras soluciones «hidratantes» tiene cada día peor fama, y por una buena razón. Este tipo de refrescos están cargados de azúcares, que nunca son bienvenidos para una bebida saludable. Después de pasar todo el día fuera de casa, solo quieres beber algo agradable, sin tener que sufrir un subidón de azúcar en sangre. Las bebida deportivas se elaboran no solo con azúcares indeseados o edulcorantes, sino que además incluyen electrolitos sintéticos, es decir, minerales fabricados, no naturales. Y con los minerales sintéticos las bebidas deportivas pierden el amplio espectro de minerales traza, cuya labor favorecedora de la hidratación empieza ahora a conocerse, pues han sido identificados como reguladores importantes de la función metabólica. Y lo mismo puede decirse a propósito de las bebidas con vitaminas añadidas. Esas vitaminas también son sintéticas, no naturales, y a menudo están cargadas de azúcar para mejorar su sabor. Prueba nuestra receta de bebida deportiva natural del capítulo 6.

Una reciente revisión Cochrane (que es una extensa revisión de la literatura científica, referencia de evidencia científica en materia de salud) ha llegado a la conclusión de que, en realidad, una dieta baja en sodio aumenta la producción de hormonas renales y puede elevar la presión arterial. También se ha puesto de manifiesto que las dietas bajas en sodio aumentan los niveles de catecolaminas —neurotransmisores que intervienen en la reacción de lucha o huida y que aceleran el ritmo cardíaco y producen vasoconstricción—. Así pues, hay que considerar que una dieta baja en sodio puede no ser la cura para una presión arterial alta y que incluso puede contribuir a la hipertensión.

EL VÍNCULO SODIO-HIDRATACIÓN

En lo referente a la sal, hay que pensar en la calidad, y no en la cantidad, cuando se trata de velar por la hidratación y la salud. La sal de mesa no tiene las propiedades adecuadas para contribuir a la hidratación y mantener la salud. Pero otros tipos más sanos de sal —es decir, la sal natural, mínimamente procesada— tienen un papel crucial en la hidratación. Ello se debe a que la sal natural contiene algo más que sodio. Encierra además minerales traza, como yodo, hierro, potasio, magnesio y calcio. Algunos de ellos, como el potasio y el calcio, mantienen el equilibrio electrolítico y el buen funcionamiento celular cuando aportas agua a tu organismo.

Opta por:

- Sal marina
- Sal céltica
- Sal de roca
- Sal del Himalaya

Estas sales realzarán el sabor de tus comidas. Pero puedes hacer algo aún mejor: comenzar a salar el agua en lugar de la comida. Añadir una pizca de una sal saludable a tu vaso de agua o *smoothie* es una manera sencilla de garantizar el intercambio electrolítico ideal para mantener tu hidratación interna.

Nosotras recomendamos cambiar la sal de tu salero por otra forma más saludable de sal natural, aunque es conveniente señalar que incluso la sal común de mesa puede no ser el enemigo de la salud que los expertos se han empeñado en combatir durante décadas. Por ejemplo, un reciente estudio de la Universidad Emory, en Atlanta, en el que participaron más de 2.600 adultos encontró que la ingesta de 1.500 a 2.000 mg de sodio al día no solo no se asociaba a un riesgo más alto de cardiopatías, sino que esas personas arrojaban una probabilidad ligeramente mayor de vivir más tiempo que las que consumían una media inferior a 1.500 mg al día. Es correcto: en realidad el sodio estaba ligado a una mayor *longevidad*. Otro estudio, en este caso francés, en el que participaron ocho mil adultos encontró que la ingesta de sodio no estaba ligada a la presión arterial sistólica, lo cual llevó a los investigadores a afirmar que la relación entre sal y presión arterial se había «sobreestimado». Ni que decir tiene que los franceses son famosos por su uso de sales marinas.

Hiponatremia

Es *posible* beber demasiada agua. La intoxicación por agua es peligrosa, porque puede diluir el sodio en sangre. Para complicar esta situación, el sodio, además, se pierde con el sudor. Mientras tanto, los niveles de sodio en el interior de otras células —piel, músculos y órganos internos— se mantienen constantes. Para corregir el desequilibrio, la ósmosis dirige el agua fuera del líquido extracelular, dando lugar a que las células se llenen. Manos y pies se hinchan. No ocurre a menudo, porque nuestros riñones pueden producir una gran cantidad de orina en muy poco tiempo para corregir este desequilibrio en los niveles de sodio. Sin embargo, los deportistas pueden presentar hiponatremia en competiciones prolongadas que requieren mucha resistencia, como los maratones. Los síntomas son vómitos, dolor de cabeza, abotargamiento, pies y manos hinchados, desorientación, cansancio y respiración sibilante. El edema por hiponatremia es infrecuente, pero creemos que beber demasiada agua provoca en el organismo un agotamiento de minerales y electrolitos esenciales. No solo los deportistas tienen que tener cuidado; puede ocurrirles a quienes practican el Bikram yoga e incluso a niños que realizan actividades deportivas después de la escuela. Por esta razón hay que protegerse con bebidas a base de vegetales, como las que te enseñamos a preparar aquí.

La mayor parte de las personas en buen estado de salud pueden manejar los más de 1.500 mg de sal al día que recomiendan muchas organizaciones para la salud. Pero lo que quizá sea más importante es que la sal misma puede no ser la razón por la que algunos estudios vinculan la hipertensión arterial y los problemas cardíacos con el sodio. En lugar de ello, es posible que los alimentos procesados, ricos en sal procesada —piensa en la comida rápida y en los precocinados, en la comida que se calienta en el microondas y en comida basura como las patatas fritas de bolsa— sean los verdaderos culpables.

Dana lleva años sugiriendo a muchos de sus pacientes que añadan una pizca de sal a un vaso de agua, especialmente por la mañana. Da sabor, ayuda a mantener la hidratación y resulta especialmente adecuada para las personas que tienen una presión arterial anormalmente baja y para aquellas que se deshidratan con facilidad. Convierte este gesto en parte de tu rutina diaria.

Alimentos deshidratantes

Alimentos cuyo consumo debes limitar, evitar o compensar:

Alcohol: el alcohol requiere gran parte de tu hidratación interna para su procesamiento. Tu estrategia ha de ser siempre la de beber un vaso de agua por cada bebida alcohólica que consumes. ¡Y además ahorrarás dinero!

Azúcar: necesitas mucha hidratación para metabolizar y filtrar el azúcar y esto sin tener en cuenta los efectos en cascada del azúcar, que reduce aún más tus reservas de hidratación y que tiene impacto sobre la insulina. Si optas por un donut, un helado o un pastel de vez en cuando, compensa luego tu elección bebiendo un poco de agua extra. (Consulta también el apartado «Un toque dulce», en el capítulo 8).

Legumbres, almidones, carnes y quesos: ¿te has sentido alguna vez abotargado después de una comida de celebración o de un almuerzo de trabajo y ello te ha obligado a una siesta no programada? Un truco fácil consiste en comer una ración más grande de ensalada o sopa y una ración más pequeña de legumbres, almidón o carne. Recuerda: no te estamos pidiendo que evites estos deliciosos alimentos, sino solo que reduzca las raciones y compenses con hidratación adicional.

Café e infusiones: si bebes una cantidad excesiva de estas bebidas, en el rango de cuatro a seis tazas, sentirás seguro sus efectos diuréticos, que conducen a deshidratación. Después de la taza número dos, añade solo agua caliente. A menudo lo que buscamos es simplemente esa reconfortante sensación cálida. Puedes añadir una cucharadita de mantequilla ecológica o ghee —una costumbre de los pueblos del Himalaya que frena el impacto de la cafeína—.

MICROBIOMAS

Se cuenta que Benjamin Franklin bromeaba diciendo: «En el vino hay sabiduría, en la cerveza hay libertad, en el agua hay bacterias».

Franklin tenía razón, pero se olvidaba de que las bacterias pueden ser buenas para el organismo humano. Si no has seguido los nuevos conocimientos sobre la necesidad de que tengamos bacterias «buenas» en nuestro interior, has de saber que los microbios, cuando se encuentran en equilibrio —e hidratados— son literalmente tus mejores aliados en la vida. Cuando bebemos más agua en forma de materia vegetal, estamos ayudando a nuestro microbioma a hacer su trabajo, pues estamos alimentando a esos microbios con los nutrientes, la fibra y el agua que necesitan. Como nosotros, necesitan más y mejores nutrientes. Y, como nosotros, requieren una buena hidratación. Las bacterias están llenas de agua, como nosotros. En definitiva, la eficacia de toda tu ecología interna aumenta cuando hidratación y nutrición van de la mano. No es más que sentido común.

¿La fermentación como forma de filtración?

Los peregrinos que viajaban por España en el siglo XII se recuperaban bebiendo por la noche aguamiel, o hidromiel, una bebida fermentada que limpia el agua contaminada y al mismo tiempo refuerza el sistema inmunitario. Los probióticos presentes en bebidas fermentadas se unen a toxinas, mohos y metales pesados y los transportan fuera del organismo, sin permitir su absorción[3]. De hecho, la ingesta de bebidas y alimentos fermentados contribuye al correcto funcionamiento de nuestro organismo, mucho mejor de cómo lo hacen los filtros de agua.

Es posible que hayas oído hablar de la importancia del microbioma en la salud intestinal; de hecho, es en el intestino donde residen la mayoría de las bacterias de nuestro organismo. Las bacterias ayudan a que las partículas alimentarias demasiado grandes o sin digerir pasen al torrente sanguíneo. La microbiota interviene en el desarrollo del revestimiento intestinal. Incrementa la densidad de los pequeños capilares intestinales y, al hacerlo, influye en la fisiología y en la motilidad intestinales. Ahora sabemos que la microbiota intestinal interviene en la digestión, en la estimulación inmunitaria y en el metabolismo del huésped (que eres tú)[4].

Para comprender cómo actúa la microbiota, piensa en tu cuerpo como si fuera un acuario, lleno de pequeños elementos flotantes que necesitan agua circulante muy oxigenada, con carga negativa y rica en nutrientes.

MICROBIOS ESTACIONALES

Del mismo modo que nuestro cuerpo reacciona a los cambios de estación, los microbios también siguen patrones estacionales. Cada alimento de temporada viene con un tipo nuevo de microbios y cuantos más alimentos de temporada cercanos a nuestro entorno consumamos, más fácil será que nuestro medio interno natural nos ayude a afrontar entornos artificiales. La doctora Lara Hooper dirige uno de los laboratorios más innovadores en investigación sobre el microbioma, en el Southwestern Medical Center de la Universidad de Texas. La doctora ha revelado otro importante descubrimiento: las microbacterias actúan también siguiendo los ritmos circadianos... así que ¡también duermen! Necesitan que salgamos al aire libre, para saber cuándo es de día y cuándo es de noche. Incluso en nuestro interior, en esa total oscuridad, pueden leer el ángulo de incidencia de las ondas luminosas y saber qué hora es y en qué estación nos encontramos. Poco a poco estamos averiguando de qué modo nuestra vida en ambientes interiores afecta a nuestro medio interno. Comer alimentos de temporada tiene más importancia de la que pensábamos y un reciente estudio de la Universidad de Stanford parece demostrarlo. Investigadores de esta universidad revisaron los hábitos de los hadza, una tribu nómada de Tanzania que sigue antiguos hábitos de alimentación. Los hazda viven cada estación en un paisaje diferente y, por consiguiente, con diferentes alimentos. Comen alimentos de temporada y esta estrategia no solo les proporciona un espectro más amplio de nutrientes, sino también un espectro más amplio de bacterias «buenas». Al tener una mayor diversidad de microorganismos en su microbiota, su inmunidad y su resistencia a la enfermedad también son altas, y todo por esa costumbre suya de comer de temporada.

Además, todo lo que comen contribuye a la digestión y a la absorción de estos nuevos y diversos microbios. Las bacterias vienen de la mano de los alimentos más disponibles. Samuel Smits, el principal autor del estudio, encontró diferencias muy llamativas, de tal manera que ciertos microbios desaparecían y reaparecían en las diferentes estaciones[5].

John Douillard, reconocido experto en nutrición y medicina ayurvédica, confirma que los microbios de nuestro intestino cambian de manera natural con las estaciones. Existe un motivo por el que a Douillard le entusiasma el mencionado estudio de Stanford. Lleva mucho tiempo defendiendo los alimentos de temporada. Como autor de *The 3-Season Diet*, ha desarrollado un moderno plan de tres estaciones para comprar alimentos en los supermercados habituales. Nuestro Plan Quench, al ofrecer opciones de alimentos de temporada, potencia al máximo su contenido de nutrientes. El comer alimentos locales en la medida de lo posible permite que nos beneficiemos de esos efectos recién descubiertos. La fruta empieza a perder su contenido nutritivo nada más ser recolectada. Por no hablar de que se estropea y del coste que supone transportarla a miles de kilómetros de distancia. Hemos consultado el importante trabajo de Douillard sobre el consumo de alimentos según las estaciones para preparar *smoothies* fríos y calientes, para todos los climas. Dice Duillard: «Cuando no comemos productos de temporada, nuestro microbioma queda inmediatamente desconectado de la inteligencia de la naturaleza y perdemos en gran medida nuestra dependencia genética de los microbios estacionales».

LOS BENEFICIOSOS EFECTOS DE ZUMOS Y *SMOOTHIES*

En nuestro Plan Quench recomendamos los *smoothies* mejor que los zumos. No tenemos nada en contra de los zumos, pues son portadores de agua en gel de las plantas y, en muchas situaciones, siguen siendo más nutritivos e hidratando mejor que una botella de agua. Sin embargo, nuestro plan busca una hidratación óptima. Al elaborar un zumo, se extrae el líquido y se filtra la pulpa, mientras que los *smoothies* se preparan triturando toda la verdura o la fruta, conservándose así la fibra. Los *smoothies* permiten que la bebida conserve todos los efectos nutritivos del vegetal. El efecto esponja de las fibras vegetales propicia una absorción de larga duración y una liberación lenta del agua y es por esto la mejor estrategia posible para mantenerse hidratado y joven por dentro.

ESTUDIO DE CASO DE LA DRA. DANA COHEN

Evelyn

Evelyn es una mujer de treinta y nueve años con bastante buena salud. Cuando acudió a la consulta de la Dra. Cohen se cuidaba, vigilaba su alimentación y no tenía antecedentes médicos importantes ni tomaba medicamentos, salvo algún suplemento.

Pero, a pesar de todo esto, se quejaba de un inexplicable dolor en la cara posterior de la rodilla derecha, que llevaba molestándola desde hacía un año. (Nota: ¡No esperes un año con dolor para ir al médico!). El dolor empeoraba cuando permanecía mucho tiempo sentada, de manera que, cuando se ponía de pie para salir a caminar después de haber estado sentada mucho tiempo, su mente se anticipaba al dolor, hasta tal punto que se había vuelto más sedentaria con el paso del tiempo. El ejercicio físico que practicaba consistía básicamente en caminar y en una clase de Pilates una vez por semana, lo cual provocaba a veces que, al día siguiente, el dolor empeorara.

Tras una exploración física y un análisis de sangre, abordamos su alimentación. Le pregunté si pensaba que bebía suficiente agua. Me respondió que probablemente no, que es la respuesta que suelen darme la mayoría de los pacientes. La mandé a su casa con el Programa Quench, consistente en un *smoothie* al día, micromovimientos y un vaso de agua con limón y sal marina por la mañana.

Volvió a consulta para una visita de control al cabo de dos semanas y le pregunté cómo se encontraba. Me dijo que se encontraba bien. Cuando le pregunté por el dolor, se quedó estupefacta, pues se dio cuenta de que se había esfumado. ¡Realmente se había olvidado de él! En otra visita de seguimiento unos seis meses más tarde, me dijo que no había tenido más dolores y que, además, había adelgazado cuatro kilos y medio. No volvió a tener ningún dolor.

Lo que hacen las fibras vegetales, o la celulosa, es básicamente eliminar las toxinas microscópicas, los desechos celulares y los detritos que se producen constantemente en nuestro entorno industrial. Los compuestos vegetales pueden incluso protegernos frente a las agresiones electromagnéticas que sufre nuestro cuerpo y que pueden dar lugar a desequilibrios minerales[6]. Con los *smoothies* no se desperdicia la valiosa pulpa. Los numerosos cofactores biológicos y compuestos vegetales sinérgicos que encierra la pulpa no se pierden ni se estropean. Todavía no se ha identificado todo lo que tiene para ofrecernos la Madre Naturaleza. Los *smoothies* nos proporcionan toda esa fibra tan importante que falta en las dietas habituales. Las fibras vegetales crean el medio óptimo para nuestro microbioma y para todas las bacterias buenas que ¡también necesitan hidratación! Los *smoothies* nos sacian de forma agradable y hacen que nuestros sistemas orgánicos funcionen de manera eficaz y con un coste menor que los zumos. Nos alimentan y nos nutren, a nosotros y a nuestro microbioma, y por consiguiente reducen los antojos entre horas y evitan el sobrepeso debido a esos caprichos insaciables. ¡Ahógalos a base de *smoothies*!

Los *smoothies* aportan:

- Absorción de la hidratación
- Hidratación prolongada en el tiempo
- Densidad de nutrientes
- Fibra densa
- Alimento para nosotros
- Alimento para nuestro microbioma
- Microlimpieza
- Neutralización de toxinas ambientales y electromagnéticas
- Ningún residuo
- Nutrición eficaz con respecto al coste
- Menos antojos

Los zumos aportan:

- Hidratación nutritiva
- Minerales y vitaminas de fácil absorción

- Biodisponibilidad inmediata
- Una posible mayor absorción de azúcar, que debes vigilar

La dieta de hace un millón de años

Los hadza del norte de Tanzania son una de las comunidades que Gina estudió para su trabajo de investigación antropológica sobre cómo sobreviven las poblaciones del desierto o de ambientes muy secos con muy poca agua. Los hazda viven en una región de sabana en su mayor parte árida y, aunque tienen contacto con otras culturas, la mayoría opta por seguir su forma de vida ancestral.

El profesor Tim Spector, del departamento de Epidemiología genética del King's College de Londres, pasó tres días con los hadza, comiendo solo lo que comían ellos. De hecho, la dieta que siguió coincidía con los informes del estudio original de Gina; Spector contó que, por la mañana, bebía un «smoothie» que le proporcionaba un alto nivel de hidratación y nutrición. El relato de su dieta fue fascinante[7].

Hablaba del fruto del baobab como de la piedra angular de la dieta hadza. Rico en vitaminas, grasas y fibra, este fruto tiene una corteza dura similar a la del coco y una carne interior blancuzca, rodeando la semilla. Spector describió cómo los hadza mezclaban esa sustancia blanquecina con agua hasta que conseguían una consistencia de leche densa. Ese era su desayuno típico. También describió que comían bayas silvestres llamadas bayas de kongorobi, que tienen veinte veces más fibra y polifenoles que los frutos del bosque que compramos en nuestras tiendas. Su cena consistía en unos cuantos tubérculos ricos en fibra.

En su relato, Spector describe con todo detalle una dieta que, desde el punto de vista funcional, coincide con las recomendaciones del Plan Quench, comenzando por el *smoothie* de la mañana. El alto contenido en fibra y grasa, mezcladas con agua, proporciona una hidratación profunda y de larga duración en condiciones secas y, además, tiene efecto saciante. Asistimos en nuestros días a un gran auge de las dietas que retoman las costumbres de nuestros ancestros, como las paleodietas, pero existe un aspecto que no se suele conocer: como los hadza, los pueblos más distantes en el tiempo comían gran cantidad de plantas.

En medida mucho mayor que carne. Estas dietas con alto contenido vegetal servían para complementar la hidratación, una estrategia utilizada especialmente en ambientes áridos.

Spector cuenta que los hadza comían una gran diversidad de plantas y animales, si bien no dedicaban mucho tiempo ni a la caza ni a la recolección. Cabe preguntarse qué sociedad es más avanzada: las sociedades cazadoras-recolectoras que trabajan menos horas al día para alimentar a su familia o nuestra sociedad moderna, que trabaja más de ocho horas al día[8].

El consumo de alimentos de temporada proporciona a nuestros mecanismos internos un montón de indicaciones para funcionar de manera eficaz a lo largo de todo el año. Puede que no sepamos aún cómo se desarrollan estas relaciones, pero si comemos siguiendo el curso de las estaciones y salimos al aire libre a menudo, no tenemos por qué saberlo todo acerca de la simbiosis ambiental para aprovecharnos de sus beneficiosos efectos.

LA FERMENTACIÓN

Es muy probable que últimamente hayas oído hablar de los alimentos fermentados, y por una buena razón. Como consecuencia del proceso de fermentación, estos alimentos adquieren propiedades que amplifican su valor nutricional. La fermentación es la técnica más antigua para enriquecer y conservar los alimentos. Los alimentos fermentados han pasado por un proceso en el que bacterias naturales se alimentan de azúcares y carbohidratos, generando ácido láctico. Este proceso genera además enzimas y bacterias beneficiosas y contribuye a la unión de ácidos grasos omega 3, además de ayudar al tubo digestivo en su trabajo.

Sin embargo, hoy en día, estamos reduciendo nuestras bacterias naturales debido al uso de antibióticos y a las técnicas de esterilización y aniquilación de gérmenes. La fermentación de los alimentos es una técnica muy, muy antigua, presente en todas las culturas y que potencia y conserva los nutrientes esenciales. Los alimentos fermentados fueron las primeras conservas. La fermentación hacía innecesaria la refrigeración. Nosotros coevolucionamos con estas bacterias y ellas ponen en marcha

funciones para que nuestros sistemas funcionen bien. De modo que rein-
corporémoslas a nuestras dietas diarias. Las bacterias se adaptan enseguida y descubren rápidamente cuál es la mejor manera de ayudarnos,
porque al hacerlo se están ayudando a sí mismas ¡Son unos excelentes
huéspedes!

¿Son las plantas medicamentos?

¿Sabías que la palabra «droga», en el sentido de sustancia empleada
en medicina, deriva del francés drogue, que significa «hierba seca»? El
origen de la palabra sugiere que las primeras sustancias medicamento-
sas, o drogas, debieron extraerse de las plantas. Sin embargo, es posible que te sorprenda que tales medicamentos siguen representando
alrededor del 40% de los productos farmacéuticos que se venden en
Estados Unidos. Si tenemos en cuenta todo el dinero que genera esta
industria, no nos queda más remedio que pensar que debe ser por algo.
Y así es: las plantas son beneficiosas para el cuerpo y estamos averiguando en qué medida.

No todas nuestras recetas de *smoothies* tienen ingredientes fermentados, pero vamos a compartir contigo trucos que puedes utilizar siempre
que quieras. Y recuerda que la fibra de nuestros *smoothies* es alimento
para tu microbioma —esa fibra se conoce a menudo con el nombre de
«prebióticos»—. Ahora ya no te preguntarás por el motivo de beber
smoothies con ingredientes fermentados. Y te sorprenderá lo deliciosos
que pueden llegar a ser.

Nuestra estrategia de hidratación profunda, tanto antigua como
moderna, nos ayuda a conservar y proteger el agua en la Tierra. El agua
que extraemos de los alimentos, de las plantas, y no de acuíferos, supone que hemos utilizado agua para nutrir esas plantas. Dejamos que las
plantas transformen el agua, y a cambio obtenemos un agua de mejor
calidad de las plantas que comemos. Así pues: ¡cómete el agua!

Mueve tu agua

Fascia e hidratación

Si hay magia en el planeta, está encerrada en el agua.

Loren Eiseley

¿Cómo llega realmente el agua adonde se necesita, para hidratar la piel y saturar cerebro, músculo y demás órganos y tejidos? Tenemos una hermosa y novedosa respuesta a estas preguntas: se llama fascia.

Fascia, en su definición más corta posible, significa tejido. Se trata de un tejido especializado, extraordinariamente fino, como una gasa, que se extiende no solo bajo la piel, sino también entre y alrededor de órganos y huesos. Y se extiende por todo el cuerpo, de un lado a otro, a lo largo de kilómetros. Es uno de los misterios anatómicos más profundos que los científicos están estudiando en la actualidad. Este misterioso campo de investigación resulta ahora tan emocionante como cuando se examinó el primer cuerpo humano. El doctor James Oschman, biofísico estadounidense que llevó a cabo un estudio de cuatro años de duración en la Universidad de Cambridge para investigar el transporte de líquidos y electrolitos en la célula, dice: «La fascia integra el sistema más grande del cuerpo, pues es el sistema en contacto con todos los demás sistemas»[1]. Y, según estamos sabiendo, la función de la fascia es clave para la hidratación. Es posible que no hayas oído hablar nunca antes de la fascia, a menos que hayas sufrido una fascitis plantar, una frecuente pero dolorosa inflamación del tejido conjuntivo del arco del pie. Los movimientos que estiran esta fascia rehidratan el tejido y aceleran la recuperación.

Hasta hace poco tiempo, la fascia eran considerada una envoltura meramente protectora que mantenía en su lugar órganos y músculos, como si fuera film de cocina. Los anatomistas, en su trabajo de disección, debían retirarla y desecharla, como haces tú con el film transparente, para quedarse con lo importante: órganos y sistemas esquelético, vascular, muscular y nervioso. Esta envoltura similar a un plástico se encontraba ya seca y deshidratada cuando los estudiantes de anatomía acometían la disección. No parecía importante. No fue hasta el año 2005 cuando los científicos pudieron observar la fascia plenamente viva e hidratada. Se grabó un vídeo asombroso, que se hizo viral inmediatamente.

ESTUDIO DE CASO DE LA DRA. DANA COHEN

Jeffrey

Un fisiatra del centro médico en el que trabajaba me pidió que viera a Jeffrey, de treinta años. Había estado tratándole por problemas en los pies, concretamente por una fascitis plantar muy dolorosa. Jeffrey había estado haciendo los ejercicios recomendados y se había comprado unas plantillas a medida para los zapatos, pero dos meses más tarde su dolor de pies no había apenas mejorado. Tenía mucho sobrepeso y mi compañero pensaba que esa podía ser la razón.

Cuando vino a mi consulta, hablamos sobre sus antecedentes.

«Siempre he tenido sobrepeso, incluso cuando era niño. He llegado a pesar 150 kilos, pero ahora estoy en 114, gracias sobre todo a que he prescindido de los carbohidratos. Pero han pasado ya varios meses y no he vuelto a perder ni un kilo. Me gustaría hacer más ejercicio, pero los pies...».

Según fuimos avanzando en la entrevista, me contó que se había desmayado en dos ocasiones por deshidratación. Le hice un análisis de sangre y, mientras esperábamos los resultados, le pregunté si quería comenzar con el Programa Quench. Dudó un poco, pues se había acostumbrado a pensar que lo único que le funcionaba era una dieta muy baja en carbohidratos; le daba miedo comer fruta e incluso ciertas verduras, debido a su contenido de carbohidratos. Le garanticé que no iba a hacerle daño, que había carbohidratos «buenos», y le sugerí un plan de alimentación saludable, similar al que recomendamos en este libro.

Cuando volvimos a vernos para una consulta el seguimiento dos semanas más tarde, había adelgazado dos kilos y medio y estaba haciendo más ejercicio, porque se encontraba mejor de los pies. Seis meses después, había bajado a 98 kilos, haciendo ejercicio de manera regular y siguiendo religiosamente una dieta de alimentos naturales enteros y las reglas de la hidratación profunda. Su fascitis plantar es ya historia. Su día a día incluye un gran vaso de agua y sal marina nada más levantarse por la mañana, un vaso de agua justo antes de cada comida y generalmente dos smoothies al día.

Aquel fue el año en el que el doctor Jean-Claude Guimberteau, un reconocido cirujano francés experto en reconstrucción de manos, llevó a cabo una delicada operación. Para visualizar mejor los tejidos durante la intervención, pegó una cámara de fibra óptica bajo la piel del paciente. La sangre roja habría ocultado normalmente la complicada capa inferior de fascia, pero esta vez el cirujano pinzó y retiró los vasos sanguíneos para poder ver mejor el tejido fascial. La cámara de fibra óptica grabó y permitió ver un magnífico tejido que latía y se movía, casi como si estuviera respirando. Esta malla transparente *transportaba gotitas de agua*, revelando por primera vez que la fascia constituye uno de los principales sistemas de transporte de agua del cuerpo[2]. El vídeo reveló que se trataba de un auténtico «sistema de riego» que se expandía y contraía para impulsar el paso de agua. Por fin pudimos ver el modo en que la fascia proporciona agua a nuestros tejidos, como si estuvieran regando un jardín.

Junto con el agua en gel, la identificación de la fascia en el cuerpo debe considerarse como uno de los descubrimientos más importantes de nuestro tiempo. Este «momento eureka» alteró de inmediato nuestra visión del modo en el que el organismo retiene el agua y la moviliza en su interior. La cámara mostró con total claridad que la fascia presenta tubos huecos y láminas, que envían el agua que bebes a los tejidos. En las páginas finales del libro, en la sección Recursos, encontrarás el *link* del vídeo, por si quieres verlo y comprobar lo que aquí te contamos[3].

Este descubrimiento es una prueba de que las fascia[8] tienen un papel esencial en la relación entre hidratación y movimiento corporal. Cualquier movimiento —torsión, estiramiento, giro— activa este sistema de suministro de agua. La fascia actúa como una bomba hidráulica, mediante constricción y relajación. De hecho, el término hidráulico significa literalmente «movimiento por el agua».

Se trata de una magnífica revelación. La fascia no es meramente un tejido de relleno, un sistema de revestimiento de las distintas partes de nuestro cuerpo: es en sí misma un sistema hidráulico recién descubierto. La fascia, un sistema móvil transparente, casi invisible, es clave en el transporte de agua en nuestro organismo. Ahora podemos seguir la pista al agua hasta su llegada a tejidos y células. De hecho, después de beber, el movimiento es el siguiente paso necesario en la hidratación. El movimiento dirige la hidratación hasta las células[4]. Es prácticamente la otra mitad de la hidratación. Con el acto de beber comienza el proceso de hidratación, pero el movimiento lo completa.

TODO LO QUE HACE LA FASCIA

La fascia tiene múltiples funciones, algunas de ellas casi milagrosas. Es la red que mantiene los músculos sobre los huesos y los globos oculares dentro de las órbitas. Pero esta extraordinaria nueva visión de la fascia como sistema de riego encierra otra sorpresa. La fascia no solo transporta agua, sino que realmente está integrada por agua —agua en gel, mas colágeno— la proteína más abundante en el cuerpo. Juntos integran la estructura flexible y maleable del cuerpo. Pero ¿qué hace en realidad la fascia?

La fascia es un sistema eléctrico, integrado por agua y que funciona gracias a ella. La medicina tradicional consideraba que el sistema nervioso era el único transmisor de impulsos eléctricos del cuerpo, pero ahora se sabe que la fascia transmite también cargas eléctricas. ¿Cómo es posible que no haya sido identificado hasta ahora un sistema eléctrico esencial del cuerpo? El agua conduce electricidad, de modo que tiene sentido que la fascia, integrada por agua, también lo haga. De hecho, ahora sabemos que la fascia conduce electricidad a un ritmo exponencialmente mayor. En el cuerpo humano existen setenta y cinco kilómetros de nervios, pero hay muchos más kilómetros de fascia. La fascia rodea todos los órganos y vasos, y ello incluye nervios. Y dada su velocidad de conducción, podría decirse que la fascia es como el sistema de fibra óptica de comunicación e información del cuerpo.

La doctora Mae-Wan Ho, biofísica y científica experta en nanopartículas y fundadora del Institute for Science and Society de Londres, señaló que los nanotubos, presentes en el interior de microscópicos cristales del agua de la fascia, se encuentran alineados con fibras de colágeno. Esta combinación, apunta la doctora, cumple con todos los criterios de la superconducción. Su teoría es que, aunque no conozcamos el mecanismo exacto en virtud del cual el agua en gel genera electricidad, en cada uno de nosotros tiene lugar constantemente un proceso de superconducción[5]. Esto acelera el «servicio de comunicación», desde y hacia nuestras células, que se autocargan simplemente por movimiento. ¡Oh, quién tuviera este sistema para cargar el móvil!

La fascia constituye además un sistema sónico, que aprovecha la energía vibracional y la energía sonora. Esto abre ante nosotros todo un mundo de posibilidades diagnósticas y terapéuticas de curación y vitalidad. Los médicos están usando ya la terapia mediante ultrasonidos para el dolor de tendones. Una fascia sana, bien hidratada, responde a las vibraciones. El doctor Sungchul Ji, de la Universidad Rutgers, en Nueva Jersey, propone una sencilla y al mismo tiempo brillante analogía para comprender el modo en el que las moléculas de agua podrían ser más eficientes. Propone que el agua en gel, con su alineación cristalina única, actúa como un diapasón. Todas las ondas vibracionales se sincronizan y se tornan coherentes, como un láser, y menos dispersas. Se mueven juntas, creando una nueva resonancia.

Incluso Albert Einstein afirmaba: «Todo en la vida es vibración». De modo que ¿por qué el agua no habría de serlo? Esta sincronización o coherencia da lugar a una función más eficaz. Es posible que pueda organizar y amplificar la carga eléctrica, «debido a la extrema sensibilidad de las moléculas de agua a la vibración del sonido y a los cambios del medio molecular», dice Ji[6].

Para despertar en el público general interés por la fascia, muchos investigadores de distintas disciplinas tuvieron que ponerse manos a la obra, y en ello siguen. Profesionales de la salud holística, bailarines y fisioterapeutas especializados en masaje sabían, por su experiencia profesional, que algo ocurría en la fascia que estaba aún por definir. Incluso ahora, el campo de la investigación sobre la fascia es como la parábola de los ciegos que describen a un elefante: cada uno describe solo una parte del elefante. Y, como el elefante, la fascia es enormemente compleja.

Todavía quedan muchas incógnitas por resolver sobre la fascia, pero una cosa es segura: requiere hidratación para realizar sus múltiples funciones. La investigación sobre la fascia es nueva y revolucionaria, pero las técnicas de manipulación de la fascia y de mantenimiento de su elasticidad son antiguas. El yoga, el tai chi y el qi gong y, por supuesto, la danza, son solo algunas de las prácticas más comunes que hacen que podamos ver a personas centenarias con una asombrosa flexibilidad.

Para ejercitar la fascia mientras trabajas, prueba lo siguiente: estira el brazo hacia fuera, con el codo rígido, la palma hacia arriba y los dedos todo lo separados que puedas.

Comienza con la palma hacia arriba y luego, suavemente, gírala tanto como puedas. Intenta trazar en el aire un círculo completo con el pulgar. Ahora comprueba lo lejos que has llegado en la rotación. Sentirás la torsión desde las puntas de los dedos hasta la escápula en la espalda. Con este estiramiento, ejercitas más tu fascia que tus músculos, tendones y nervios. Esperamos que te des cuenta de que, aunque aparentemente solo estés estirando el pulgar, en realidad estás estirando todo el cuerpo.

Otra forma de tomar consciencia de tu sistema fascial consiste en revisar tu columna a lo largo del día. ¿Te sientas, en general, con la espalda recta o encorvada? Corrige tu postura, que depende más de la fascia que de la columna. Cuanto más a menudo lo hagas, más mejorará el flujo de agua ¡Y, además, tendrás mejor aspecto! La hidratación y la vitalidad también están ligadas a la longevidad. Cuando encorvas la espalda, estás constriñendo tus tejidos y tu respiración y por consiguiente restringiendo la circulación de agua en tu cuerpo. No queremos tratar nuestra columna como una manguera doblada, apretada y constreñida, que bloquea el flujo de agua e interfiriere en nuestra capacidad respiratoria. La respiración, al tomar vapor del aire, es otra fuente de hidratación, aunque poco conocida. Por otro lado, una postura encorvada hace presión sobre el tubo intestinal, obstaculizando una vez más la función digestiva y el flujo. Así pues, la postura afecta a todas las funciones corporales. Este flujo, recuerda, no solo es hidráulico por naturaleza, sino que también es eléctrico, porque el flujo de agua es flujo eléctrico. El agua es movimiento. De hecho, si no se moviera, no estaría viva, y tampoco lo estaríamos nosotros. Tal vez esto te ayude a pensar en el ejercicio y en el movimiento de otra manera, sabiendo que puedes influir más en tu salud y bienestar si realizas frecuentes estiramientos suaves que con maratonianas sesiones de flexiones y abdominales.

Los pequeños estiramientos y torsiones del cuerpo realizados aquí y allá a lo largo del día tienen ahora mucho más sentido.

FASCIA Y DEPORTE

La moderna medicina deportiva ha desarrollado también técnicas para restablecer la salud de las fascias. Es en el mundo del deporte de alto rendimiento donde recogemos más información práctica sobre la fascia y sobre cómo tratar las lesiones. El fisioterapeuta deportivo de las estrellas de fútbol en Estados Unidos, Klaus Eder, trabaja con fascias dañadas. Se ha dado cuenta, mediante ecografía especializada, que entre las capas de la fascia se interpone una película de gel. De modo que lo que hace Klaus Eder es separar despacio y con cuidado las capas apelmazadas por una lesión, lo cual permite que la película de gel vuelva al ocupar el espacio entre los tejidos. Este estrato de gel favorece el deslizamiento libre de los tejidos, haciendo posible que los deportistas vuelvan a la competición más rápidamente. Para ayudar a la gente a comprender el funcionamiento de la fascia desde su perspectiva, Eder describe la fascia lesionada como si se tratara de un suéter que se ha lavado en agua demasiado caliente y que, por tanto, ha perdido su elasticidad. Cuando la fascia está apelmazada o endurecida, es más propensa a las lesiones y reduce el acceso de nutrientes, sangre y oxígeno a la zona. La hidratación es tu primera intervención en caso de lesión deportiva. Además de hacerte con una bolsa de hielo, debes beber un vaso de agua.

LA FASCIA ES ARQUITECTURA DE SUSPENSIÓN

Cada fibra muscular está revestida por una fina lámina de fascia amortiguadora, como una envoltura elástica. Pero más allá de eso, la fascia tiene una función de soporte biomecánico. Thomas Myers, pionero en el estudio de la conexión miofascial (músculo-fascia), tiene una palabra maravillosa para esto: *tensegridad*[7]. El término fue acuñado en origen por el legendario arquitecto e ingeniero Buckminster Fuller, que lo utilizó para referirse a la resistencia de estructuras arquitectónicas usando cables equilibrados. Myers aplica este concepto al cuerpo, comparando la fascia con cables de puentes. «En un estado normal de salud, la fascia está relajada y tiene una configuración ondulada. Tiene la capacidad de estirarse y moverse sin restricciones. Sin embargo, cuando se sufre un traumatismo físico o un trauma emocional, un proceso de cicatrización o de inflamación, la fascia pierde elasticidad. Se vuelve tensa y apretada y se convierte en una fuente de tensión para el resto del cuerpo»[8]. Explica, además, que cualquier cosa, desde un traumatismo mayor, como un accidente de tráfico o una intervención quirúrgica, hasta agresiones menores, como una mala postura o un uso excesivo y repetitivo de una parte corporal, puede tener efectos acumulativos sobre el cuerpo, y en particular sobre el sistema fascial. Los cambios causados por el traumatismo en el sistema fascial influyen en el bienestar y en la función de nuestro cuerpo. Cuando se produce una lesión o un traumatismo, pueden aparecer constricciones en la fascia que afectan a la amplitud de los movimientos, a la flexibilidad y a la estabilidad y que pueden causar una gran cantidad de síntomas como dolores, entre ellos cefaleas. La hidratación debe ser el primer paso hacia la reparación de la fascia, junto con fisioterapia y otras modalidades terapéuticas. La hidratación devuelve a la fascia su elasticidad.

LA FASCIA SE MANTIENE ALERTA

Otro asombroso descubrimiento, obra del alemán Robert Schleip, ha puesto de manifiesto que la fascia presenta receptores y terminaciones nerviosas[9]. Es la localización orgánica con mayor densidad de receptores espaciales. Estos sensores o receptores se activan cuando el tejido se estira y permiten así que nuestro cerebro y cuerpo registren nuestra localización en el espacio. Así pues, parece ser que la fascia y el sistema nervioso autónomo están íntimamente conectados. Nuestro sentido de propiocepción —ese GPS interno— es el que nos ofrece información como seres tridimensionales en el espacio. Ahora imagina que nuestra consciencia espacial depende del nivel de hidratación.

¿Que has sufrido una torpe caída? Los músculos son los últimos en enterarse de la noticia. El sistema de receptores de la fascia es el primero en tomar nota de lo ocurrido. Pues bien, la deshidratación reduce nuestra percepción del espacio y del equilibrio, que es el motivo por el cual una fascia debidamente hidratada es clave para que los jóvenes alcancen un óptimo rendimiento deportivo, así como para que la gente mayor evite desagradables caídas.

He aquí un ejemplo del sistema fascial en funcionamiento: para entrenar la consciencia espacial en los niños que carecen de ella, los terapeutas ocupacionales les ponen unos chalecos muy ceñidos. De este modo los niños pueden sentir dónde está su cuerpo. Quizá ahora nos resulte más fácil comprender el sentido de esta técnica: al tocar y hacer presión sobre el chaleco, los terapeutas estimulan en mayor grado los receptores fasciales.

Esta terapia del chaleco nos recuerda a otra terapia estimuladora por tacto: el cepillado en seco de la piel. La técnica es conocida sobre todo por su efecto exfoliante, que favorece la circulación sanguínea en toda la piel, y por favorecer el drenaje linfático. El cepillado en seco tiene sin duda tales efectos, pero además favorece la función fascial en tres frentes. Piensa en lo que el cepillado en seco desencadena bajo la piel: estimula receptores de distinto tipo y terminaciones nerviosas; ejerce una compresión puntual, ejercida por las cerdas del cepillo, de forma no muy distinta de la acción ejercida mediante acupuntura superficial; y cuando pasas el cepillo seco por la piel seca, el cepillado impulsa el líquido a través de la red fascial. Un efecto beneficioso tipo «tres en uno».

Cepillado

Puedes comprarte un cepillo corporal de cerdas naturales en cualquier perfumería o tienda de productos naturales para la salud. Suelen tener una etiqueta que indica su uso para el cepillado corporal en seco. La técnica de cepillado en seco consiste en realizar pasadas largas hacia arriba en las extremidades, dirigiendo el líquido hacia los ganglios linfáticos de ingles y axilas. Después se cepillan glúteos, torso y espalda, siempre con movimientos largos y hacia la cabeza. Cuando flexiones el cuerpo o lo estires para llegar a estas áreas, también estarás provocando un beneficioso estiramiento de la fascia.

Otra versión del cepillado en seco consiste en un sencillo automasaje. En el capítulo 7 compartiremos contigo varias técnicas de automasaje tomadas de las antiguas tradiciones china e india.

FASCIA Y ACUPUNTURA

La acupuntura se ha asociado siempre con el tratamiento del dolor. Estos nuevos descubrimientos sobre la fascia vienen a corroborar las teorías en las que se basa esta antigua técnica. Estudios recientes documentan que los neurorreceptores no se encuentran uniformemente distribuidos por la fascia, sino que se localizan concentrados en canales. Helene Langevin, neuróloga de la Universidad de Vermont, considera que existe un solapamiento del 80% entre los puntos de concentración fascial y los antiguos mapas que ilustran los meridianos en acupuntura. Estas áreas superpuestas presentan una gran densidad de receptores y terminaciones nerviosas. Y lo que es aún más asombroso, el equipo de la reconocida neuróloga fue capaz de grabar en vídeo cómo reaccionaba la fascia a la inserción de la aguja de acupuntura. Fueron testigos de una escena única: la fascia reacciona a la inserción de agujas engrosándose alrededor de la punta de la aguja, dando lugar de hecho a una malla más fuerte o a una mayor densidad de fibras de colágeno[10]. ¿Sabemos ya lo que significa esto? No. Pensamos que este efecto debe ser lo que hace que la acupuntura ayude frente al dolor. Se trata de un mundo absolutamente nuevo, pero puede que esa investigación conduzca a una mejor comprensión de la eficacia de las técnicas de la medicina oriental.

LA FASCIA COMO FUENTE DE VITALIDAD

La fascia sigue planteándonos multitud de interrogantes, pero una cosa es segura: requiere hidratación para hacer su trabajo. Los estudios de investigación sobre la fascia son bastante recientes, aun cuando las técnicas de manipulación y de mantenimiento de su elasticidad son antiguas. El yoga, el tai chi, el qi gong y, por supuesto, la danza, son algunas de las prácticas más populares que favorecen la flexibilidad, así como la longevidad.

¿Te sentirás de otra manera ahora que sabes que estás lleno de fascias? Esperamos que sí y aquí te enseñamos a activarlas. Incluso nosotras mismas hemos sentido nuestro cuerpo de forma diferente solo con investigar y escribir sobre la fascia. Por ejemplo, ya no permanecemos sentadas frente al ordenador durante largas sesiones sin intercalar numerosos intervalos de pequeños movimientos y estiramientos. Ahora somos más conscientes del sistema fascial vivo que albergamos en nuestro interior y sabemos que podemos activarlo simplemente prestándole atención y concediendo a nuestro cuerpo pequeños descansos. Son descansos para recargar. Nuestro sistema de fascias y nuestro cuerpo nos recompensarán a su vez con más energía y vitalidad. Qué interesante es descubrir un nuevo sistema de riego oculto en nuestro interior.

CAPÍTULO 4

El movimiento mantiene la hidratación

La ciencia de los micromovimientos

El agua es la fuerza motriz de la naturaleza.

Leonardo da Vinci

La gran sorpresa que queremos compartir contigo es que el *movimiento nos mantiene hidratados*. Tal vez pienses que el ejercicio te deshidrata, y en ocasiones es así. Pero el movimiento es necesario para una adecuada hidratación. Tenemos ya conocimiento de cientos de estudios que demuestran la importancia del ejercicio y del movimiento para nuestra salud. No es nada nuevo. Pero la gran noticia es que el movimiento tiene un papel esencial que es incluso más importante: el movimiento activa la hidratación en el plano celular. Y estamos constatando que no es necesario mucho movimiento, en absoluto; el movimiento más ligero y sencillo puede ayudar a que el agua llegue a todas las partes del organismo. El movimiento es la segunda mitad de la fórmula de hidratación. Sin movimiento, la hidratación no llega a nuestra fascia y, en última instancia, a las células.

En 2016 se publicó un importante estudio en el que habían participado 12.776 mujeres británicas, que fueron sometidas a un estrecho seguimiento para investigar una sola cosa: ¿actuaban los pequeños movimientos nerviosos como un factor protector de la longevidad?[1] La conclusión fue que así era. Las mujeres sin este tipo de movimientos inquietos y que permanecían sentadas durante siete horas o más al día, arrojaron un asombroso *aumento* del 43% del riesgo de *mortalidad por cualquier causa*. Se compararon estos resultados con los de las mujeres que podrían clasificarse dentro de la categoría media o alta de actividad inquieta. En su caso, el riesgo de muerte no aumentó, aun cuando *permanecieran sentadas durante más de siete horas al día*. Todo viene a poner de manifiesto que el movimiento conduce a la salud, incluso los más pequeños movimientos. Incluso estando sentados. Incluso si es un jugueteo inquieto.

Otro peculiar estudio esclarece al cien por cien estas noticias. Tal y como recoge la revista *American Journal of Physiology* de 2016[2], se pidió a once hombres jóvenes que se sentaran durante tres horas y movieran simplemente una pierna ¡Qué gran esfuerzo para un estudio de investigación! Pero obtuvieron resultados muy desconcertantes. Un minuto de movimiento inquieto cada cuatro minutos *mejoraba* la circulación en la pierna en movimiento, mientras que la *rigidez* vascular de la pierna inmóvil aumentó en relación con el valor inicial. Los autores llegaron a la conclusión de que el «simple hecho de mantener cierto grado de inquietud corporal es suficiente para contrarrestar los efectos negativos del sedentarismo». Así pues, aportaron la original evidencia según la cual el impacto negativo de la inmovilidad durante períodos prolongados puede evitarse mediante pequeños movimientos.

LAS CÉLULAS COMO DETECTORES DE MOVIMIENTO

El aspecto más importante que se aborda en este capítulo es que el movimiento activa la función celular. Las células son literalmente detectores de movimiento. Tú eres tu propio motor, diseñado para impulsarte gracias al movimiento. Cualquier tipo de movimiento. Si no te mueves, tus células no están en modo de alto rendimiento. No están hidratadas ni cargadas. El *tipo* de movimiento es importante —no estamos hablando de correr una maratón o de pasar horas y horas en el gimnasio—. El movimiento más sencillo, el más pequeño, puede contribuir a que el agua y la carga eléctrica lleguen a todos los rincones del cuerpo. En *Apaga tu sed* te enseñamos algunos de estos sencillos movimientos.

¿Cómo es todo este asunto del movimiento y de la hidratación? Pues tiene que ver de nuevo con esa asombrosa red que tenemos bajo la piel: la fascia. Al moverte, la acción de polea de músculo, fascia y piel, al estirar tu arquitectura esquelética, impulsa la hidratación más profundamente en los tejidos y activa las células del cuerpo.

Cualquier movimiento, sea grande o pequeño —una inclinación de la cabeza, una ligera elevación de los hombros o una gran zancada— estira los tejidos y genera electricidad. Este es un principio que rige en toda la naturaleza y que se basa en la tensión mecánica directa. El nombre científico para este proceso es piezoelectricidad o «electricidad de presión». El movimiento piezoeléctrico ayuda a que la hidratación penetre en los tejidos y cargue las células. Los movimientos no tienen que ser amplios ni persistentes. Las células son diminutas, de manera que un pequeño movimiento es un gran movimiento para cualquier célula.

Pierre y Jacques Curie identificaron el efecto piezoeléctrico en 1880, demostrando que la tensión mecánica puede convertirse en voltaje. Recientemente los investigadores han identificado que este mismo principio es aplicable en los planos celular y molecular. Investigadores de la Universidad de Yale ponen de manifiesto en la revista *Cellular Neuroscience, Neurodegeneration and Repair* que existen proteínas piezoeléctricas en el interior de la célula. Estas proteínas son responsables de la percepción de movimiento y estiramiento y esos pequeños movimientos activan numerosas funciones en la célula[3].

La presión genera energía

¿Sabías que solo con apretar un cristal de cuarzo entre los dedos estás generando electricidad? Más o menos así es como funcionan las pantallas táctiles de ordenador, ya que están hechas de cristal líquido, cuya estructura, exactamente igual que la del agua en gel, responde a la presión.

INTRODUCCIÓN A LOS MICROMOVIMIENTOS

Si todos los días te mueves de la misma manera, siguiendo los mismos hábitos, probablemente la mitad de ti estará inactiva. Somos criaturas tridimensionales. De hecho, vías nuevas de movimiento estiran las fascias y sacan a las células de ese estado de indolencia, que incluye pasarse el día sentado. A menudo pensamos que dejar quieto un músculo que nos duele es la mejor de manera de favorecer su curación. Se trata de un instinto de protección, pero la realización de suaves y pequeños movimientos para estirar partes del cuerpo doloridas es lo que realmente puede acelerar la curación.

¿Sientes pereza? Si te parece que te falta energía, probablemente no sea culpa tuya. No es un defecto de carácter. No es que seas vaga o vago. Lo que ocurre es que vivimos condicionados por la cultura contemporánea de no moverse, y nos está costando la vida. Comienza en la infancia, cuando nos sientan delante de una mesa en la escuela, y continúa en la edad adulta, cuando la mayor parte de nosotros permanecemos pegados a un ordenador, una silla y un coche durante ocho o más horas al día. Si no te mueves, no te cargas de energía. No te culpes si no te mueves tanto como deberías por naturaleza. Pero quizá puedas descubrir cuánta vida y energía tienes todavía. Tal vez haya una manera de poner de nuevo un poco más de movimiento en tu vida, para hidratar plenamente tus células y devolver algo de energía a tu día a día, sin importar tu trabajo ni tu edad.

No tienes que levantarte y correr una maratón para activar tus células. Puedes realizar micromovimientos. Fíjate en que no estamos utilizando la palabra «ejercicio», sino «movimiento», por una razón. El movimiento y la energía que genera pueden llevarte más lejos en la persecución del objetivo final que el ejercicio regular. Pero eso no es lo que nos ocupa ahora. Y si ya eres aficionado al ejercicio, también es importante que mantengas un cuerpo flexible mediante micromovimientos de 360 grados. Lo que aquí nos interesa destacar es este nuevo conocimiento, a saber, que la energía que los micromovimientos aportan a nuestras células procede de la hidratación.

A lo largo del día es conveniente que evites que tu sistema entre «en reposo», como hacen los ordenadores cuando no se usan. Los micromovimientos son la solución para que tus células y tu cuerpo se mantengan en modo «on» hasta el final del día.

PEQUEÑOS MOVIMIENTOS CONDUCEN A GRANDES MOVIMIENTOS

No estamos en contra del ejercicio. Nuestro objetivo en este capítulo es conectar incluso el más pequeño movimiento con la activación celular, basada en la capacidad de hidratación para aportar energía. Existen multitud de libros escritos sobre los beneficiosos efectos físicos y fisiológicos del ejercicio, algunos de los cuales mencionamos en la sección de recursos. Para aquellos que no pueden o no quieren hacer ejercicio, estos pequeños micromovimientos pueden ser el impulso para que hagas ejercicio de manera más formal. Solo necesitas un pequeño movimiento para conseguir mucho… Tal como indica su nombre, los micromovimientos son pequeños movimientos orientados a ayudar al cuerpo a funcionar mejor, aunque sea solo cierta inquietud. Pero los micromovimientos que te proponemos aquí te aportarán incluso más energía.

FLUJO CORPORAL DE ENTRADA Y SALIDA

En *Apaga tu sed* te enseñamos una serie estratégica de pequeños movimientos dirigidos para movilizar el cuerpo de la cabeza a los pies. Hemos ideado estos micromovimientos sobre la base de los más recientes descubrimientos en el campo de la relación entre actividad e hidratación, que confirman el gran poder del movimiento, aunque sea mínimo. *Apaga tu sed* te lleva al terreno de la consciencia tridimensional, con el propósito de que el tejido no utilizado no se torne rígido, no se duerma o entre en reposo como tu ordenador. Nos referimos a movimientos de rotación, como mirar hacia atrás, rotar hombros, tobillos, caderas e incluso los ojos, para conseguir una mayor hidratación. Ahora que ya has comprendido el concepto de micromovimiento, puede que quieras buscar puntos rígidos de tu cuerpo y dirigir hacia esas áreas algunos pequeños movimientos. Luego podrás idear tus propios micromovimientos personalizados. Una vez que te des cuenta de que puedes realizar estos pequeños y discretos movimientos en cualquier lugar, en la cama, en la silla, en el coche o en la cola del autobús, y te des cuenta de que te encuentras mejor, no podrás prescindir de ellos.

Además, los micromovimientos favorecen el trabajo de eliminación de líquidos cargados de desechos celulares. La limitación de la movilidad comienza con la falta de uso, que da lugar a la acumulación de desechos celulares y a inflamación. Todos deseamos tener un rango completo de movimiento en nuestras articulaciones, para lo cual todos los tejidos del cuerpo deben contar con un eficiente flujo de entrada y salida.

Hasta ahora nos hemos centrado en el concepto de hacer llegar la hidratación a las células. A continuación queremos centrarnos en el poder del agua para arrastrar los desechos fuera de la células y, en consecuencia, fuera de nuestros tejidos. La auténtica hidratación no solo está dentro de la célula, sino también fuera. Todo el sistema linfático, nuestro servicio interno de saneamiento, depende en última instancia de nuestro movimiento. Si no recurres a pequeños movimientos a lo largo del día, estarás acumulando desechos. Tu sistema volverá a caer en la pereza y quedará a la espera de que te pongas de nuevo en movimiento. Si no te comprometes de forma activa en este proceso natural, el material de desecho comenzará poco a poco a inflamar los tejidos, a interferir en las funciones, restándoles eficacia, y hará que envejezcas antes de tiempo.

Llegado este momento, te presentamos una estrategia especial: la torsión. Al final del capítulo te ofrecemos una guía de micromovimientos de todo el cuerpo, que puedes realizar en cualquier lugar.

LA TÉCNICA DE TORSIÓN

El movimiento de torsión, ya sea de brazos, piernas, cuello o columna, representa una técnica muy eficaz para la gestión de residuos. Piensa en la torsión como en la acción de estar retorciendo un trapo mojado, escurriendo toda el agua que sobra. La torsión o giro en espiral, muy presente en el tai chi clásico, en el yoga y en otras disciplinas, como la danza, induce un movimiento de rotación en la columna y da lugar a un fabuloso efecto exprimidor en espiral. Y cuando terminas la torsión, tu organismo atrae líquidos nuevos, cargados de oxígeno y nutrientes. En efecto, el movimiento de torsión es una eficiente técnica antiinflamatoria.

MICROMOVIMIENTOS EN TU DÍA A DÍA

Identifica esos momentos del día en los que sientes cansancio y, por ejemplo, aprovecha mientras hablas por el móvil para estirar la barbilla por encima del hombro un par de veces, o para dibujar varios círculos con los tobillos. A diferencia del ejercicio aeróbico, donde el lema parece ser «sin dolor no hay resultados», los micromovimientos de torsión tienen un importante efecto con muy poco esfuerzo. Recuerda los estudios sobre pequeños movimientos inquietos que ya hemos comentado.

Resulta interesante descubrir que los micromovimientos pueden realizarse en cualquier lugar y en cualquier momento. ¿Con qué frecuencia giras la cabeza por encima del hombro, salvo quizá para sacar el coche del aparcamiento? Prueba a hacerlo ahora: procede despacio y sin sentir molestia alguna, pero procura mantener la barbilla en línea con el hombro y date cuenta de cómo ese simple movimiento activa todos los grupos de músculos de tu espalda, músculos que no usas habitualmente en tu rutina diaria. Aprovecha momentos como cuando vas en el coche o hablas por el móvil para realizar micromovimientos: te ayudarán a corregir tus malas posturas habituales que, con el tiempo, desembocan en rigidez, falta de flexibilidad y menor movilidad.

Si sufres una tensión continua en cuello y hombros (¡y quién no, cuando estamos constantemente inclinados sobre un teclado o una pantalla!), estos sencillos movimientos te ayudarán. Piensa en ellos como en una sesión de fisioterapia para la que no hay que acudir a la consulta de un profesional, sino que puedes autoaplicártela a lo largo del día. La tensión en cuello y hombros nos afecta a todos los que pasamos 24/7 enviando mensajes de móvil.

El movimiento diario es el primer elemento de la lista de las nueve prácticas saludables identificadas en las «zonas azules» del mundo, esos puntos del planeta con las más alta tasas de longevidad. Los ancianos que viven en estas zonas azules caminan y trabajan con la azada y cargan peso y cuidan del jardín, compartiendo estas actividades con miembros de la familia de todas las edades. Deseamos llegar a la vejez como esos ancianos, independientes, despiertos, ágiles, con buena actitud ante la vida y capaces aún de cuidar de otros. ¿Se te ocurre un final mejor? Tu cuerpo es capaz de infinidad de movimientos que nunca has intentado realizar y tus células están listas para responder, siempre y cuando les des un pequeño empujón o estrujón. ¿Sabías que la hidratación —y la hidratación trasladada a nuestras células a través del movimiento— puede llevarnos a este nivel de vital longevidad? El agua ha sido siempre, y seguirá siéndolo, fuente de juventud.

MICROMOVIMIENTOS EN LÍNEA CON LA MICROMEMORIA

Norman Doidge, neurólogo y autor del rompedor libro *The Brain That Changes Itself* (traducido al español con el título *El cerebro que se cambia a sí mismo*)[4], afirma que, cuando las neuronas se activan a la vez, se establecen conexiones más fuertes, como por ejemplo cuando se activan al mismo tiempo el movimiento y la memoria.

De modo que pregúntate: «¿Cuándo fue la última vez que te sentiste *realmente* bien? ¿Lleno de salud y vitalidad? ¿Y con un montón de energía? ¿En qué circunstancias? ¿ Eres capaz de identificar o recordar si fue en un momento en que eras más activo? Quédate con esa imagen y considera si puedes reactivar ese recuerdo corporal realizando pequeños movimientos a lo largo del día. Utiliza nuestros movimientos supersencillos, que cualquiera puede realizar, y combínalos con el recuerdo de momentos de actividad que te han aportado felicidad. Esta combinación, al despertar un recuerdo feliz, es siempre una combinación ganadora, y activa las células del cerebro y las sitúa en línea con el movimiento corporal. ¿Y has oído hablar de la técnica del golpeteo (*tapping* en inglés)?[5] Se utiliza para aliviar el dolor físico y emocional y consiste en darte ligeros golpecitos en puntos clave de la cara, la cabeza y el cuerpo al mismo tiempo que pronuncias afirmaciones positivas. Los veteranos utilizan esta técnica con una alta tasa de recuperación de trastornos de estrés postraumático, a menudo en menos de diez sesiones. Se ha documentado una tasa de recuperación del 69%, más alta que la de cualquier actuación médica[6].

ESTUDIO DE CASO DE LA DRA. DANA COHEN

Patricia

Patricia, de cincuenta y tres años, editora de una revista, vuela a menudo por motivos de trabajo. Recientemente, a su regreso de un viaje en avión desde Londres, se dio cuenta de que tenía los pies hinchados. Le apretaban los zapatos y sentía un gran peso en los tobillos y las pantorrillas, una sensación muy desagradable. Vino a verme en busca de algo que aliviara sus molestias. La tranquilicé diciéndole que no se trataba de nada grave, pero era un claro caso de edema, una acumulación de líquido en exceso en los tejidos corporales. Una causa importante de edema puede ser la deshidratación y, como habrás leído, volar puede ser un gran desencadenante de deshidratación. (Consulta el apartado «¿Por qué tengo tanta sed cuando vuelo?» en la Introducción y encontrarás consejos sobre hidratación y viajes en avión).

Di a Patricia unos cuantos consejos sobre hidratación y le enseñé a realizar una serie de sencillos movimientos que la ayudarían con la hinchazón, entre ellos las clásicas elevaciones de pelvis. Patricia observó inmediatamente resultados, y me envió un correo electrónico pocos días más tarde para decirme «¡No puedo creerlo! ¡Tengo tobillos!».

Estaba asombrada por lo rápidamente que había bajado la hinchazón después de aplicar las técnicas de movimiento todos los días.

Describimos a continuación el movimiento de la pelvis que activa la circulación en las extremidades inferiores: túmbate sobre la espalda con las rodillas flexionadas y las plantas de los pies apoyadas en el suelo. Coloca las palmas de las manos también sobre el suelo y sube y baja la cadera. Realiza tres series de cinco elevaciones. Las elevaciones pélvicas pueden realizarse también en la cama y puedes añadirlas a tus micromovimientos de la mañana.

Quítate de encima años y enfermedades

Sanford Bennett, conocido como «el hombre que se hizo joven a los setenta», tomó la decisión de cambiar su vida después de sufrir una serie de enfermedades crónicas que le habían dejado prácticamente postrado en la cama. A los cincuenta años se encontraba totalmente recuperado y en 1907 publicó un libro titulado *Exercising in Bed,* en el que relataba su transformación. Pues bien, su crónica nos ha servido de inspiración para algunos de nuestros micromovimientos. Bennett, convencido de que estaba envejeciendo de forma prematura debido a la acumulación de residuos en sus tejidos, pensó que si retorcía, contraía y relajaba sus músculos, podía movilizar y eliminar esos productos de desecho de su sistema sanguíneo. Puede que Bennett no tuviera muy claros los detalles, pero no estaba equivocado en lo que respecta a los principios fundamentales, y su cuerpo se convirtió en la prueba viviente. A los setenta años de edad, era visiblemente un hombre más joven. Este es un magnífico ejemplo de cómo los movimientos de torsión pueden ser muy beneficiosos, incluso si se realizan en la cama.

Joseph Pilates es otro gran pionero en el terreno del ejercicio físico. Creció con numerosos problemas de salud, entre ellos raquitismo y asma, y abrazó el ejercicio y la potenciación de la fuerza como armas para superar sus enfermedades. Durante la Primera Guerra Mundial, al ver en el hospital de un campo de internamiento a soldados que estaban demasiado débiles para salir de la cama, diseñó un sencillo sistema de poleas anclado a la cama. Les hacía realizar pequeños movimientos dirigidos, convencido de que estos movimientos eran esenciales para impulsar su salud física y emocional y su actividad mental. Hoy en día el método Pilates es utilizado como una modalidad más de ejercicio tonificante por madres de familia, del mismo modo que se utilizó en el pasado para recuperar a veteranos de guerra. En cualquier caso, sigue ayudando a millones de seguidores a mantenerse en forma. Y, una hermosa ironía: hoy en día algunos de los más innovadores hospitales utilizan el método Pilates, que ha recuperado así sus orígenes.

ESQUEMA DE MICROMOVIMIENTOS PARA TODO EL CUERPO Y PARA TODO EL DÍA

El movimiento potencia todos los efectos positivos de la hidratación. Imagínate por un momento a ti mismo levantándote de la cama por la mañana sin rigidez, sin dolores. Piensa en ti levantándote ágilmente de la silla en la oficina, cogiendo con facilidad a tu hijo en brazos o mirando hacia atrás por encima del hombro sin rigidez para aparcar el coche. La hidratación, junto con los movimientos correctos, te ayudará con todo esto. Más adelante, en el Plan Quench de cinco días, te sugeriremos movimientos específicos que cambiarán tu forma de sentirte, frenando tu trayectoria de envejecimiento e incrementando tu vitalidad, pero este esquema corporal diario está diseñado para que te sirva cuando acabes con el Plan Quench de cinco días, para toda una vida de movimientos corporales sencillos pero integrales.

ESQUEMA DE MOVIMIENTOS CORPORALES DIARIOS

Descomponemos a continuación estos ejercicios en dos series: la serie de la mañana para la mitad superior del cuerpo y la serie de la tarde, que trabaja la mitad inferior del cuerpo.

Serie de la mañana: parte superior del cuerpo

En posición sentada o de pie, comienza bajando la barbilla hacia el pecho, tres veces.

Sentirás una ligera tensión en los hombros y en el cuello.

Dibuja unos círculos en el aire con la barbilla, primero pequeños, después cada vez más grandes y sueltos.

Dibuja en el aire una figura en ocho con la barbilla. Ahora intenta hacerlo con la nariz. Alterna entre nariz y barbilla para una experiencia avanzada de percepción.

Baja una oreja hacia el hombro un par de veces, lo mejor que puedas, solo hasta donde te resulte cómodo.

No es necesario que la oreja toque tu hombro; lo único que se pretende es activar todos los músculos entre estos dos elementos corporales. Explora diferentes posiciones, elevando o bajando uno o ambos hombros.

Gira la cabeza llevando la barbilla por encima de un hombro, mira hacia abajo, mira hacia arriba y gira hacia el otro hombro.

Con los brazos flexionados, lleva los codos hacia atrás como si quisieras juntarlos, hasta que sientas cómo estrujas las escápulas, dos o tres veces.

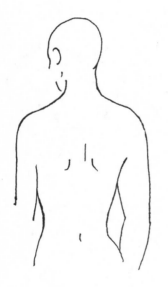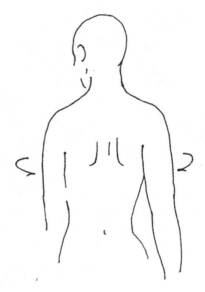

Si lo deseas, eleva la barbilla al mismo tiempo que diriges hacia atrás los codos, pero solo en la medida en que te resulte cómodo.

Baja la barbilla hacia el pecho, expulsa el aire, y después eleva los hombros, encogiéndolos hacia las orejas. Baja rápidamente los hombros.

¡La mitad superior de tu cuerpo ya está lista! Luego, por la tarde, trabaja la mitad inferior.

Serie de la tarde: parte inferior del cuerpo

De pie, o en posición sentada, con la cadera de frente, gira el tronco hacia la derecha, tratando de mantener los hombros sobre la caderas, y mantén la posición tanto tiempo como te resulte cómodo. Puedes hacer presión en el borde de una mesa o de un escritorio para mantenerte o incluso para empujar un poco.

Ahora hacia el otro lado: gira a la izquierda, con la cadera de frente, y una vez más mantén los hombros sobre las caderas, agarrándote quizá al respaldo de la silla o al marco de la puerta para ayudarte un poco.

De pie en el hueco de una puerta, levanta la mano por encima de la
cabeza para situarla en el marco de
la puerta. Gira hacia delante y hacia
atrás hasta que sientas tensión en la
axila. Este ejercicio es especialmente
bueno para la mujer, al drenar residuos del área de la mama y mejorar
la circulación.

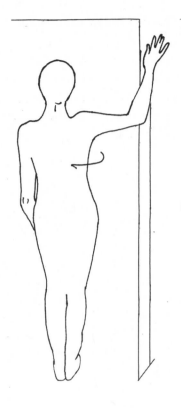

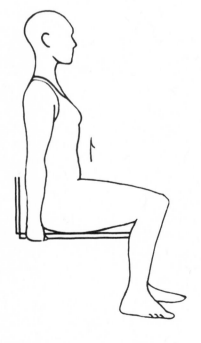

Sentado en una silla, sitúa las
manos en los laterales, agárrate al
asiento y tira hacia arriba para enderezar el tronco. Hazlo tres o cuatro
veces.

Mientras permaneces sentado,
eleva una rodilla y describe un círculo con el tobillo. No te olvides de
repetir con la otra pierna. Recuerda los estudios sobre movimientos
inquietos de piernas.

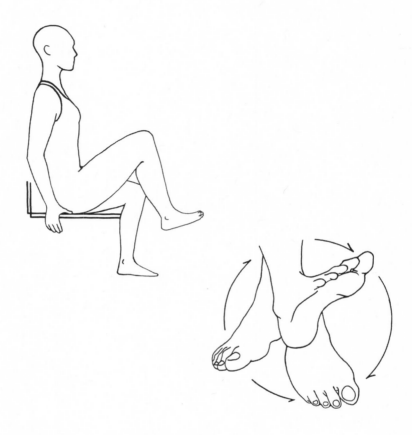

Mueve varias veces los dedos de los pies.

De pie, con los talones firmemente apoyados en el suelo, eleva el dedo gordo. Trabaja solo un pie, luego el otro y, finalmente, los dos.

Grasa e hidratación

El aceite y el agua sí se mezclan

Fórmula para el éxito: levántate temprano, trabaja duro, combate la grasa.

J. Paul Getty

Tu salud y tu juventud están ligadas directamente no solo a la cantidad de agua que bebes, sino también al modo en el que tu cuerpo obtiene agua para sus células. Los aceites y las grasas hacen posible la hidratación celular. Para entrar en las células, el agua tiene que atravesar, literalmente, una barrera guardada por aceite. Puedes beber todo lo que quieras, pero si el agua no atraviesa esa membrana, no se produce hidratación.

Las membranas celulares están formadas en esencia por ácidos grasos, llamados lípidos, que ayudan a mantener la elasticidad de la membrana para que las células puedan absorber el agua. Nuevos e importantes estudios documentan que los ácidos grasos omega 3 tienen un papel esencial en el mantenimiento de la elasticidad de las membranas celulares y en la hidratación de las células[1]. Pero eso no es todo. Los omega 3 ayudan también a incrementar el área de la superficie de la membrana celular para que más agua y más nutrientes puedan pasar al otro lado[2].

Una dieta cargada de perjudiciales grasas trans o grasas alteradas por el calor da lugar a una acumulación de colesterol y grasas perjudiciales en el interior de la célula.

La acumulación de desechos y tóxicos altera la comunicación celular[3] y obstaculiza la captación de nutrientes y la eliminación de desechos celulares. Esta pereza intracelular trastoca con el tiempo el funcionamiento de la célula y conduce a un incremento de la deshidratación celular.

La deshidratación celular se produce por acumulación de desechos y toxinas. Al envejecer, las membranas celulares se tornan más rígidas y bloquean no solo la hidratación, sino también la entrada de nutrientes esenciales y de oxígeno. Todos estos elementos son, por supuesto, esenciales para que la célula pueda eliminar los productos de desecho. Acumulación de desechos y rigidez: estos son los dos puntos a combatir. ¡Grasas al rescate!

GRASAS: SON BUENAS PARA EL CUERPO

¿Piensas en las *grasas* como algo malo? Es habitual. Una reciente encuesta llevada a cabo por el International Food Information Council encontró que la mayoría de los estadounidenses no saben bien qué tipos de grasas son saludables. Durante años, muchos de nosotros simplemente evitamos todo tipo de grasas, pensando que estábamos haciéndoles un favor a nuestro corazón y a nuestra cintura[4]. Pero eso es un error. Los expertos nos dijeron durante décadas que, evitando las grasas, estábamos protegiendo nuestro corazón al mismo tiempo que manteníamos la línea, mientras que actualmente multitud de estudios revelan lo contrario. La mayor parte de las grasas no solo son buenas como parte de nuestra alimentación. Son realmente esenciales para la salud.

Las grasas alimentarias —esto es, las grasas que se obtienen de alimentos como aguacates, aceite de oliva, frutos secos e incluso la carne y los productos lácteos— son una poderosa fuente de energía. Tu cuerpo quema la grasa buena como combustible, lo cual favorece la función cerebral y el funcionamiento de todo el organismo en general. Además, las grasas frenan la velocidad a la cual el cuerpo digiere el resto de la comida, contribuyendo a la sensación de saciedad y evitando las fluctuaciones de los niveles de azúcar en sangre, que alteran el apetito y hacen que te sientas débil y descentrado.

Y lo que es más importante: la grasa forma parte de las membranas celulares, y el cuerpo humano tiene muchísimas células. Cada célula —sin importar el tipo— está formada por lípidos, que es como decir grasas, y tiene dos capas de ácidos grasos. Tu cuerpo utiliza la grasa que consumes para formar estas membranas celulares. Si consumes muy poca grasa, tus tejidos y órganos no funcionan debidamente porque tus membranas celulares no están siendo «alimentadas». De hecho, multitud de estudios recientes de investigación muestran que una alimentación rica en grasas y pobre en carbohidratos mejora la función de las mitocondrias, es decir, de ese microscópico sistema de energía existente dentro de cada una de nuestras células. Unas mitocondrias sanas mejoran la salud general de las células y aumentan la esperanza de vida, lo cual ayudaría a explicar por qué nuevas investigaciones llevadas a cabo por la UC Davis School of Veterinary Medicine encontraron que los ratones alimentados con una dieta rica en grasas vivían más tiempo que los que consumían menos grasa[5].

Frutos grasos

La medicina china ha utilizado los frutos y la corteza de la morera durante literalmente miles de años para tratar enfermedades circulatorias como cardiopatías, diabetes, anemia y artritis. Los ácidos linoleicos presentes en la mora y en la corteza interna favorecen la hidratación y ayudan a absorber los nutrientes solubles en grasas de nuestra dieta. La infusión de moras se sirve en toda Asia al caer la tarde, cuando a menudo los niveles de hidratación caen también[6]. Las moreras crecen asimismo en el este de Estados Unidos y los indígenas norteamericanos utilizaban también el fruto y la corteza, como en la tradición china.

La grasa no es merecedora de su mala fama. Una serie de estudios publicados en la revista *Journal of the American Medical Association* pusieron de manifiesto que las mujeres que obtenían el 32% de sus calorías de las grasas presentaban las mismas tasas de cáncer de mama y de colon, ataques cardíacos e ictus que las mujeres cuya alimentación contenía un 20% de grasa[7]. De hecho, varios estudios recientes, entre ellos el proyecto *Prospective Urban Rural Epidemiology*, están observando que una ingesta más elevada de grasas insaturadas y saturadas (no es un error tipográfico) está ligada a una salud mejor. Por otro lado, una dieta rica en carbohidratos, eleva la probabilidad de enfermedades como cardiopatías, diabetes y obesidad[8]. En su consulta de medicina, Dana Cohen ha visto como miles de personas han perdido peso, han mejorado sus valores de presión arterial y de colesterol y han dado un giro a su salud siguiendo una dieta baja en carbohidratos y rica en grasas saludables[9].

La grasa tiene otro importante cometido: ayuda al cuerpo a absorber las vitaminas liposolubles (solubles en grasas) que favorecen la salud y combaten las enfermedades, como son las vitaminas A, D, E y K. Como prueba: un estudio de la Universidad Estatal de Ohio puso de manifiesto que las personas que comían un aliño preparado con aguacate absorbían cuatro veces más licopenos de los tomates y cerca de tres veces más vitamina A que aquellos que comían la versión sin aguacate[10].

Y por si todo esto no fuera motivo suficiente para empezar a decir «sí» a las grasas, las pruebas de laboratorio del doctor Gerald Pollack han demostrado que el ghee —una mantequilla clarificada que ha resultado ser una forma de grasa muy saludable— está cargado de agua ultrahidratante, lo cual sugiere la posibilidad de que otras formas de grasas tengan también un papel fundamental en la hidratación. También podría ser este el motivo por el que las jorobas de los camellos tienen tanta grasa —¡sí, grasa!— y no precisamente agua, como se nos contaba de niños. Esto puede hacer que te preguntes si la grasa tiene algún papel en la legendaria capacidad de estos animales para recorrer kilómetros y kilómetros a temperaturas muy elevadas y sin fuente alguna de agua.

Si para desayunar tomas claras de huevo, a mediodía comes una ensalada acompañada con lomo magro y un aliño sin grasa y por la tarde cenas pasta con salsa de tomate, te alegrará saber que si añades un poco de sabor, por ejemplo en forma de yema de huevo, un chorrito de aceite de oliva e incluso un poco de carne roja y de queso, podrás incluso mejorar tu salud y favorecer una hidratación óptima.

NO TODAS LAS GRASAS SE FORMAN DE LA MISMA MANERA

La mayoría de las grasas son en realidad una mezcla de ácidos grasos. Suelen definirse como saturadas, poliinsaturadas, etc. en función del ácido graso que tengan en mayor medida. Como probablemente sabrás, existen dos grupos principales de grasas: saturadas e insaturadas. Estas son las diferencias.

¿Pero no comer grasa engorda?

Lo habrás escuchado un millón de veces: la grasa de la dieta se convierte en grasa corporal más deprisa que los carbohidratos y las proteínas. Es una leyenda. Si es verdad que las grasas encierran más del doble de calorías que las proteínas y los carbohidratos (nueve calorías de las grasas frente a cuatro calorías de proteínas y carbohidratos), incluir una cantidad moderada de grasas en tu dieta no echará por tierra tus esfuerzos por perder peso. De hecho, las investigaciones muestran que un aumento de la ingesta puede en realidad ayudar a adelgazar. Un estudio reciente de la Universidad de Stanford encontró que las personas que obtenían de las grasas de su dieta en torno al 40 % de las calorías habían perdido el doble de peso que aquellas que obtenían de las grasas alimentarias el 20 % del total de sus calorías, a lo largo de ocho semanas[11].

¿Por qué? La grasa hace que el estómago digiera los alimentos más despacio y da lugar a que te sientas más lleno durante más tiempo. Se puede afirmar que es posible adelgazar simplemente aumentando la ingesta de agua y añadiendo una ración de grasa saludable, como medio aguacate o un poco de aceite de oliva, a cada comida. Esta es la razón por la cual las dietas con muy bajo contenido en grasas son, en ocasiones, tan difíciles de seguir. En efecto, incluso si estás tomando suficientes calorías, si no tomas suficientes grasas cabe la posibilidad de que experimentes sensación persistente de hambre, que podría llevarte a comer en exceso más tarde o directamente a saltarte la dieta.

Las **grasas insaturadas** son un tipo de grasas que tienen una elevada proporción de moléculas de ácidos grasos con al menos un doble enlace. Todas las grasas insaturadas son buenas para la salud. Pero cada grupo —monoinsaturadas y poliinsaturadas— es saludable por diferentes razones.

Las **grasas monoinsaturadas** están presentes en semillas, plantas y aceites vegetales, como el aceite de oliva, los aguacates, las semillas de calabaza y los cacahuetes.

Todas las grasas monoinsaturadas son ácidos grasos omega 9. Deben su nombre al primer doble enlace en la cadena de ácido graso y se ha demostrado que reducen el riesgo de enfermedad cardiovascular. La superestrella de esta categoría de grasas es el aceite de oliva, que posee una elevada concentración de ácidos grasos monoinsaturados y que es rico en ácido oleico, un tipo de omega 9 con efectos particularmente cardioprotectores.

No corras al supermercado para comprar cualquier aceite de oliva. Escoge uno virgen extra, lo cual significa que se ha obtenido por presión, sin agentes químicos. Recomendamos asimismo que sea un aceite ecológico y prensado en frío, lo cual garantiza que ha estado protegido de la luz, reduciendo así la oxidación durante el proceso de prensado. La obtención del aceite por presión en las seis horas siguientes a la recolección de la aceituna da lugar a la más alta concentración de nutrientes. Ten en cuenta también el aceite de nuez de macadamia. Es incluso más rico en ácidos grasos monoinsaturados que el aceite de oliva y, aunque su precio puede ser elevado, tiene un punto de humo muy alto (211 °C) y un sabor delicioso que lo convierten en el héroe olvidado del reino del aceite para cocinar.

Las grasas poliinsaturadas están presentes en aceites vegetales como son los de cártamo, maíz, soja y girasol, ciertos frutos como las nueces y en pescados grasos como el salmón y la sardina, así como en la carne roja ecológica de animales alimentados con pastos y huevos también ecológicos.

Existen dos tipos de grasas poliinsaturadas: ácidos grasos omega 3 y omega 6. Multitud de estudios ponen de manifiesto que los ácidos grasos omega 3 son especialmente importantes para nuestra salud y tienes que obtenerlos de los alimentos, porque tu cuerpo no puede fabricarlos por sí solo. Los alimentos ricos en omega 3 son pescados grasos como el salmón, el atún y las sardinas, semilla de linaza, chía, nueces, huevos ecológicos y carne roja de animales alimentados con pastos.

En las últimas dos décadas, los trabajos de investigación han revelado que los omega 3 intervienen en todo, desde bajar la presión arterial y contribuir al equilibrio del colesterol hasta combatir la pérdida de memoria relacionada con el envejecimiento y la enfermedad de Alzheimer. Algunos expertos afirman incluso que los ácidos grasos omega 3 pueden mejorar el estado de ánimo y defendernos de la depresión. Son como generadores de nutrientes: no solo contribuyen a que el organismo absorba los nutrientes más fácilmente, sino que, además, una vez que están en las células, reducen la inflamación que conduce a enfermedades crónicas. Por ejemplo, una revisión de cuarenta y seis estudios distintos de investigadores de la Universidad Tufts, Massachusetts, encontró que las personas que aumentaban su ingesta de ácidos grasos omega 3 EPA y DHA mediante suplementos y/o pescado corrían un riesgo menor de parada cardíaca y muerte por cualquier causa.

Existen diferentes tipos de ácidos grasos omega 3, que tiene también efectos diferentes. Mientras que las tres principales variedades —ALA, DHA Y EPA— tienen un impacto positivo sobre la salud, las otras dos muestran un efecto más potente contra las enfermedades. ALA procede de fuentes vegetales, como verduras y semillas, entre ellas la chía; DHA y EPA proceden de fuentes marinas, entre ellas el marisco y las algas. Si no te gusta mucho el pescado, opta por las cápsulas de aceite de pescado, o toma un suplemento de DHA integrado por algas o aceite de krill, que son más respetuosos con el medio oceánico.

En cuanto a los omega 6, también son saludables —especialmente un tipo de omega 6 llamado GLA, presente en el aceite de onagra y en el de borraja—. Son importantes para la síntesis de hormonas sexuales. En su consulta, la doctora Dana Cohen ve a menudo a mujeres jóvenes con amenorrea, es decir ausencia de menstruación. Ella considera que el truco para las molestias de estas mujeres está en añadir a la dieta un suplemento de estos ácidos grasos o en incrementar el consumo de estas grasas con la dieta. Milagrosamente el ciclo menstrual se normaliza sin más intervenciones. Es este un problema mucho más frecuente de lo que imaginas y no estamos hablando de pacientes con trastornos de la alimentación que han dejado de tener la menstruación. Son muchas las personas con un estilo de vida de dieta baja en grasas.

Los omega 6 son el tipo de ácidos grasos más abundante en la dieta de los estadounidenses. Y, por ello, la mayoría comemos demasiados omega 6 y muy pocos omega 3, lo que nos impide obtener los máximos beneficios para la salud que ofrece un correcto equilibrio entre omega 3, omega 6 y omega 9. Es una razón más para limitar nuestra ingesta de alimentos procesados —muchos de los cuales están cargados de omega 6— y para centrarnos en obtener omega 3 de fuentes alimentarias naturales, como el salmón, las nueces y las semillas de chía molidas.

GRASAS SATURADAS

Las grasas saturadas son un tipo de grasa presente principalmente en alimentos de origen animal y, en menor medida, en otros alimentos, como el coco. Son diferentes de las grasas insaturadas, porque cada uno de sus átomos de carbono está cargado con una molécula de hidrógeno, que forma una cadena recta. Las grasas insaturadas, en cambio, tienen al menos un «codo» en la cadena. La mayor parte de las veces solidifican a temperatura ambiente y se licúan con el calor; tal es el caso, por ejemplo, de la mantequilla y del aceite de coco.

Durante años los expertos en salud afirmaron que las grasas saturadas eran un grave factor de riesgo de cardiopatía y obesidad, entre otras enfermedades. Pero en la última década, la marea ha empezado a bajar. Entre otras evidencias, un estudio control aleatorizado —es decir, un estudio de referencia— realizado entre cuarenta y seis hombres con sobrepeso y publicado en la revista *American Journal of Clinical Nutrition* encontró que las personas que habían seguido una dieta de alto contenido graso tenían realmente mejor salud: el régimen de grasas altas había dado como resultado menor presión arterial, reducción de grasa abdominal y mejor control de insulina y azúcar en sangre.

Por otro lado, evitar las grasas saturadas es malo para el cerebro. La materia blanca del cerebro contiene fosfolípidos, un tipo de grasa que constituye un componente esencial de toda las membranas celulares. Los fosfolípidos intervienen en numerosos procesos metabólicos y están integrados por grasas saturadas y monoinsaturadas. Dado que nuestro organismo no puede fabricar grasas saturadas, tiene que conseguirlas de la alimentación, para obtener esos fosfolípidos y mantener la salud cerebral.

Pero no solo se trata de estudios de investigación. Entra en cualquier página web o blog sobre dietas de tipo paleo y encontrarás a multitud de gente que opina que más proteínas y grasas saturadas y menos carbohidratos les suponen más energía, mejor salud y más cintura.

El debate sigue abierto: en Estados Unidos, The National Institutes of Health, grupo de instituciones del gobierno volcadas en la investigación para la salud, sigue recomendando sustituir las grasas saturadas por aceites vegetales monoinsaturados, quedando aún por resolver algunas preguntas sobre las grasas saturadas. Nosotras pensamos que el problema reside en el hecho de que la mayor parte de la investigación sobre grasas saturadas no hace distinción entre los distintos tipos (ampliamos este punto enseguida).

Pero podemos decir con seguridad que, si te centras en eliminar las grasas saturadas pero insistes en comer pasta cargada de carbohidratos, pan y azúcar, estarás perdiendo la visión de conjunto. Un cuerpo sano necesita una dieta completa y centrada en alimentos no procesados. Y sí, efectivamente, mucha agua.

EL MEJOR TIPO DE GRASA SATURADA

Aun a riesgo de sonar como un disco rayado, hemos de decir que las grasas saturadas —y las demás grasas— no son todas iguales. Es posible subdividirlas en categorías en función de la longitud de sus moléculas.

Algunas de la grasas saturadas más sanas son ácidos **grasos de cadena corta (AGCC)**. Están presentes en la mantequilla, el ghee y los productos lácteos de alto contenido graso. Estas grasas saturadas son especialmente ricas en butirato, un AGCC que protege frente al cáncer de colon, sirve como poderosa fuente de energía para las células del tubo gastrointestinal e incluso reduce la inflamación, de manera que es importante en el terreno de la prevención y del tratamiento de las enfermedades autoinmunes. Estudios tempranos muestran que los AGCC pueden mejorar el metabolismo, favoreciendo la pérdida de peso.

ESTUDIO DE CASO DE LA DRA. DANA COHEN

Lisa

Lisa, de cuarenta y nueve años, redactora en una empresa de publicidad, llegó a mi consulta con un montón de problemas por la enfermedad de Sjörgren, un trastorno autoinmune que, entre otros síntomas, causa artritis y sequedad de ojos y boca, al deshidratar las glándulas que proporcionan humedad al cuerpo. Estaba angustiada por esa sequedad crónica que a veces le resultaba hasta dolorosa y que le afectaba a los ojos y a la piel, que en ocasiones sentía tensa en torno a las articulaciones. Y estaba cansada de que su dolencia interfiriera en su trabajo y le impidiera ir al gimnasio o hacer más vida social. Con lágrimas en los ojos, me contó que un reumatólogo tras otro le habían dicho que su enfermedad solo empeoraría con los años y que los fármacos y los esteroides eran la única opción de tratamiento —eso y suero salino—. Pero el uso de esteroides a largo plazo tiene graves consecuencias, como diabetes y osteoporosis, y Lisa estaba lógicamente preocupada.

Yo quería aliviar sus molestias y, dado que la deshidratación era una parte importante de su enfermedad, le pregunté si querría intentar como primer paso hidratarse mejor. En un primer momento asintió, pero después pareció dudar. «¿Supondrá mucho trabajo?», me preguntó. estaba ya sobrecargada de trabajo y un plan complicado sería demasiado para ella. Podía palpar su estrés cuando dijo: «El exceso de trabajo deshidrata», y vi cómo las lágrimas empezaban a formarse en sus ojos. La tranquilicé, diciéndole que le resultaría fácil integrar el plan en su ajetreada rutina diaria.

Lo primero que me preguntó fue si tendría que dejar el café. Ella vivía de la cafeína como combustible; bebía al menos cinco tazas de café al día. La cafeína en ese nivel es un diurético suave, de modo que deshidrata. No, le dije, no tendría que dejarlo, pero sí reducir el consumo. Y la forma más sencilla de hacerlo era con ghee. «¿Ghee?», me preguntó. *Sip*, Ghee. Ghee es un tipo de grasa que aumenta la energía orgánica, al mismo tiempo que frena la absorción de cafeína. Eso significa que Lisa no necesitaría tomar cinco tazas de café para superar la mañana, ni tan siquiera para todo el día. Además, el ghee favorece la función mental y la claridad de ideas.

Establecimos un programa de tres semanas, incluido el plan de inicio rápido, seguido de dos semanas más de comidas hidratantes consistentes en dos raciones de verduras en cada comida. El trabajo diario de Lisa consistía en sentarse delante del ordenador durante muchas horas al día, a menudo incluso comía su almuerzo en el puesto de trabajo. De manera que necesitaba un menú mejor equilibrado: no más burritos congelados, su comida comodín, pues tienen el 20% del contenido total de sodio recomendado como ingesta diaria. Los alimentos congelados tienen a menudo demasiada sal. Lisa esperaba poder sustituir su bebida favorita —la coca cola— por un zumo.

«¿No son hidratantes los zumos?», me preguntó.

Le conté que, por desgracia, los zumos tienen tanto azúcar como los refrescos, pero que podía tomar *smoothies,* que son el pilar del Plan Quench. Eso le gustó, había un sitio de *smoothies* justo al lado de su oficina. Revisamos juntas el menú online y redactamos un plan de comidas para cinco días.

En lo referente a la actividad física, le enseñé algunos sencillos micromovimientos para realizar mientras viajaba en el metro, como giros de cuello y giros de tobillos. También le enseñé unas técnicas de respiración, que podía aplicar cuando estuviera estresada, junto con sencillos estiramientos y paseos que podía realizar en la oficina. Conocía algo el «yoga de escritorio», pero para ella fue toda una revelación que los movimientos pudieran ayudar a movilizar los líquidos en su cuerpo.

Concertamos una revisión para tres semanas más tarde. Cuando Lisa volvió a la consulta, pude ver con claridad el cambio: sonreía y hablaba con más energía. Me contó que se sentía menos deprimida y agobiada. Y los síntomas de su enfermedad de Sjögren habían disminuido también, había pasado a usar menos de la mitad de la cantidad de suero salino en gotas para los ojos (antes gastaba un frasco pequeño al día) y ya no tenía la piel y los labios descamados. Y me contó que ya no se encontraba cansada por la tarde. Salía con amigos dos días a la semana. ¡Y había perdido 1 kilo y 360 gramos!

Con tan excelentes resultados, diseñamos un plan más a largo plazo, que incluía diversos *smoothies,* de manera que no se aburriera hasta conseguir una hidratación óptima. Puedes encontrar algunos de estos *smoothies* en la sección de recetas del libro. Además, le di una receta de caldo de hueso y le recomendé que bebiera caldo en lugar de ese café de media mañana al que recurría siempre. Lisa sigue hidratada y mantiene a raya sus síntomas.

Otro tipo saludable de grasa saturada es el de los ácidos grasos de cadena media, también conocidos como **triglicéridos de cadena media (TCM)**. La mantequilla contiene algunos TCM, pero el aceite de coco y el aceite de nuez de palma tienen concentraciones más altas. Existe una razón por la cual muchas personas preocupadas por la salud alaban las propiedades del aceite de coco: las investigaciones muestran que los TCM estimulan el metabolismo, mejoran la sensibilidad a la insulina e incluso ayudan a mejorar el pensamiento crítico y la memoria.

Por último, existen ácidos grasos de cadena larga (AGCL) y ácidos grasos de cadena muy larga (AGCML), que se encuentran en la mayoría de los alimentos de origen animal (aunque estos ácidos están presentes también en grasas moninsaturadas y poliinsaturadas). Aunque no son el enemigo de la salud que siempre se ha dicho que eran, tienen menos efectos beneficiosos que los AGCC y que los TCM. Una de las razones principales es que no pueden atravesar la barrera hematoencefálica, que es como decir que el cerebro no puede utilizarlos como combustible.

Los AGCL abundan en la dieta estadounidense, especialmente en los aceites procesados que han sufrido enranciamiento por exposición a la luz o por sobrecalentamiento, así como en la grasa de la carne y en productos lácteos elaborados a partir de leche de animales no alimentados con pastos. Este es el motivo por el cual recomendamos optar por cortes magros, recortar la grasa de la carne roja y comer pescado y pollo más a menudo.

¿Y QUÉ HAY DEL ACEITE PARA COCINAR?

Cuando se trata de elegir un aceite con el que cocinar, existen miles de opciones: canola (colza), oliva, coco, cacahuete, aguacate, soja y muchas más.

Lo primero en lo que hay que pensar cuando se va a elegir un aceite es el punto de humo, es decir, la temperatura a la cual el aceite empieza a humear. Para decirlo en pocas palabras, cuanto más alto sea el punto de humo, mejor. Cuando un aceite empieza a humear quiere decir que ha empezado a oxidarse y a liberar grasas trans, que no son saludables. También es el punto en el que se torna inestable y libera moléculas perjudiciales para la salud, como aldehídos y alcoholes. Este proceso recibe el nombre de peroxidación lipídica y, además de dar mal sabor a la comida, ocasiona daño celular, que contribuye a un montón de enfermedades, como por ejemplo asma, enfermedad de Parkinson y enfermedad inflamatoria, por citar algunas[12].

Los aceites más saludables para cocinar, con punto de humo más alto, son ricos en compuestos vegetales saludables. Cabe citar entre ellos los siguientes:

- Aceite de aguacate.
- Aceite de cacahuete. Hay que decir que tiene un sabor neutro y que no contiene la proteína de cacahuete causante de alergias. Si tienes alergia grave al cacahuete, por favor, consulta antes al alergólogo.
- Aceite de coco. Por regla general, con un fuerte sabor a coco.
- Aceite de oliva virgen extra. Es la opción más sana, tiene un punto de humo ligeramente más bajo, de manera que debe utilizarse cuando se cocine a temperaturas por debajo de los 160 °C o, mejor aún, regar con él ligeramente el alimento cuando ya esté cocinado.
- Aceite de nuez de macadamia. Es delicioso y de sabor neutro, pero caro.
- Ghee.
- Aceite de semilla de uva.
- Aceite de sésamo.

Importante: el aceite de linaza es saludable, pero resérvalo para aliñar ensaladas o para añadirlo a *smoothies* y nunca cocines con él ni lo calientes, pues el calor provoca la rápida liberación de peróxidos lipídicos, que son perjudiciales.

Puede que estés preguntándote: *¿y qué ocurre con el aceite de canola?* Lo encontramos en forma de spray para cocinar y en recetas que requieren aceite. Si bien tiene un alto punto de humo y está integrado por grasas monoinsaturadas, la mayoría de los aceites y productos de canola están genéticamente modificados. Por otro lado, el aceite de canola se obtiene de la semilla de la colza, una planta de flores de color amarillo perteneciente a la familia de la mostaza y de la col y que suele rociarse con pesticidas justo antes de la cosecha. Dados los conocimientos actuales sobre la relación entre pesticidas y problemas de salud como el cáncer y el síndrome metabólico, el aceite de canola se nos presenta de repente como una opción poco saludable.

Guía rápida para elegir la grasa adecuada

Sigue una alimentación variada y llena de alimentos naturales y frescos y no tendrás que preocuparte por la posibilidad de estar comiendo grasas en exceso o del tipo incorrecto. Realmente es así de sencillo: si optas por alimentos «reales», en lugar de por el tipo de alimentos que vienen envasados o empaquetados para calentar en el microondas, estarás evitando las insanas grasas trans. Sabemos que las grasas hidrogenadas están ligadas a numerosos problemas de salud, desde obesidad hasta diabetes e ictus. Aléjate de las grasas menos saludables, del tipo de la grasas que abundan en alimentos procesados como patatas fritas de bolsa, galletas, muffins y galletitas saladas.

Las grasas tienen más que ver con la hidratación de lo que pensábamos, de modo que digamos adiós a los días de la fobia a las grasas y tomemos las decisiones correctas relacionadas con añadir de nuevo grasas saludables a nuestra dieta. En este caso, el aceite y el agua sí se mezclan.

¿Quién necesita más el agua?

La hidratación ideal para poblaciones con altas necesidades

La cura para todo es el agua salada: sudor, lágrimas o el mar.

Isak Dinesen

Aun cuando es necesario que todo el mundo sea mucho más consciente de la importancia de la hidratación, existen grupos que deben prestar especial atención a este aspecto: los niños, los deportistas y los ancianos. En el caso de los niños, la hidratación es esencial para su cuerpo y su mente en crecimiento. A los deportistas, una adecuada hidratación les ayuda a alcanzar un mejor rendimiento, a ser más fuertes y más rápidos y a evitar las lesiones. Por cuanto respecta a los ancianos, la hidratación es más difícil de mantener, ya que, a medida que envejecemos, el contenido de agua de nuestro cuerpo disminuye y, en consecuencia, la probabilidad de deshidratación aumenta. Por todo ello, profundicemos un poco más en cómo podemos estar seguros de que nuestros seres queridos cuentan con el agua que necesitan.

NIÑOS

Los niños son especialmente propensos a la deshidratación, porque su cuerpo en crecimiento necesita agua para desarrollarse y madurar. Los lactantes, en especial, pueden sufrir deshidratación apenas unas horas después de caer enfermos y la deshidratación es causa importante de enfermedad y muerte del lactante en todo el mundo.

Cuando se trata de niños mayores, todo lo que corren y todo lo que juegan supone una gran pérdida de agua. Además, los niños tienden a no beber agua en cantidad suficiente para compensar la pérdida. Cualquier madre te dirá que tiene que recordar a su hijo que beba —¡están demasiado ocupados jugando!— Si tenemos en cuenta un reciente estudio de Harvard T. H. Chan School of Public Health, más de la mitad de todos los niños y adolescentes de Estados Unidos no están suficientemente hidratados. La hidratación tiene importantes consecuencias para sus funciones físicas, cognitivas y emocionales, aún en fase de formación. El estudio encontró otro dato interesante: los niños de raza negra corrían un riesgo más alto de deshidratación que los de raza blanca. Además, los niños corrían más riesgo que las niñas. Y lo que es más sorprendente: cerca del 25% de los niños refirieron que no bebían agua. Lo cual nos lleva a preguntarnos qué es lo que beben.

Aunque puede resultar difícil conseguir que los niños beban en la escuela, existen varias maneras de garantizar una adecuada hidratación de los más pequeños. Consideremos, por ejemplo, el Hydratation Pilot Project at the Ideal School (proyecto piloto de hidratación en la escuela ideal) llevado a cabo en colaboración con la Hydratation Foundation en una escuela privada de Manhattan, durante el año 2014. El personal dibujó el mapa de la escuela como si fuera un «oasis», para saber dónde estaban situadas las fuentes y otros puntos de agua. Al elaborar el mapa, el personal de la escuela se dio cuenta de los puntos en los que no existía acceso amplio y fácil al agua y, como solución, instalaron dispensadores de agua en las clases. ¿Hubo derramamientos de agua? Efectivamente ¿Mejoraron las calificaciones en las pruebas? También. Además los niños se hidrataban bien antes y después de la clase de gimnasia. Y, en un sorprendente hallazgo, cuanto mayor era el acceso de los niños al agua de bebida, más fácil resultaba moldear su comportamiento. La concentración por las tardes mejoró considerablemente. Y, después de la escuela, los niños acudían a sus actividades extraescolares mejor protegidos frente a posibles lesiones gracias a una mayor hidratación. La planificación de un descanso para beber para todos y cada uno de los estudiantes se convirtió en parte de la cultura de la escuela y sentó además las bases para que los niños crecieran con el hábito de beber agua con regularidad.

Los móviles deshidratan

Nos pasamos el día pegados al móvil, mirando la pantalla o hablando. Miramos el móvil para mantenernos al día en Facebook y Twitter, obtener direcciones y decir a alguien que vamos a llegar tarde. Los adolescentes dependen especialmente del móvil. Pero ¿sabías que el uso del móvil deshidrata? Existen dos razones: en primer lugar, cada vez que cambiamos de foco de atención tenemos que fabricar una nueva ronda de sustancias neuroquímicas, haciendo uso de nuestra hidratación. Todas esas miradas hacia arriba y hacia abajo y todas esas interrupciones nos hace recurrir a nuestras reservas de agua y nutrientes para resintetizar y reproducir la siguiente serie de sustancias químicas necesarias para fijar la atención. En segundo lugar, al mantener la cabeza inclinada hacia abajo y hacia delante, esa presión añadida sobre el cuello, supone que el líquido sinovial que pasa al cerebro desde el canal vertebral resulte comprimido y que su circulación se ralentice. Cada uso supone un pequeño porcentaje de disminución y agotamiento de tus reservas de agua, que se produce de forma repetida a lo largo del día. Consulta el Plan Quench para descubrir sencillos micromovimientos que restablecen el flujo en los usuarios de móvil.

Una amiga de Gina estaba preocupada porque su hijo presentaba trastorno de déficit de atención e hiperactividad y le costaba centrarse en el colegio. Gina le habló del proyecto piloto de hidratación. Sobre la base del éxito del proyecto, la madre pidió cita con la profesora de su hijo en la escuela y compartió con ella los resultados. Convencida por el éxito del proyecto, la maestra aplicó algunas de estas nuevas estrategias. Concretamente, en lugar de pedir una y otra vez al niño que tratara de centrarse, le mandaba fuera de clase a beber a la fuente. Y el niño regresaba tras ese breve descanso más dispuesto a trabajar.

Su concentración y su comportamiento mejoraron notablemente. ¿Por qué? Porque el niño estaba más hidratado y se movía más. Este es un bonito ejemplo del modo en el que la combinación entre hidratación y el movimiento favorece la concentración.

En el estudio piloto, cuando el equipo de la Hydratation Foundation explicó a los estudiantes que el agua conducía electricidad y que, por tanto, era necesaria para llevar más impulsos elétricos al cerebro, los estudiantes se mostraron fascinados y bebieron más voluntariosos y con mayor intención de centrarse en el trabajo de la escuela. Durante una clase de dibujo, un estudiante pidió ir a beber para que su trabajo «le saliera mejor». Estaba claro que habían comprendido la conexión entre beber y concentrarse en el trabajo[1]. ¡Chicos listos!

La buena noticia es que el problema de salud publica de los niños y la deshidratación tiene una solución sencilla, según las conclusiones de Steven Gortmaker, profesor de Sociología de la salud en Harvard. «Si somos capaces de centrarnos en ayudar a los niños a beber más agua —una bebida barata y acalórica— podemos mejorar su estado de hidratación, que puede permitir a muchos niños sentirse mejor durante todo el día y rendir más en la escuela»[2].

Nosotras tenemos una solución aún más ventajosa. Dado que los típicos tentempiés de las escuelas, como galletitas saladas, bollos o barritas de cereales, se suman al problema, reemplacémoslos por alimentos frescos ricos en agua como manzana en rodajas, pepino en rodajas, apio, melocotones, melón, fresas y uvas —¡y por los *smoothies* y helados de fruta del Plan Quench!—. En preescolar, a los más pequeños les encanta preparar platos de frutas. Déjales que sean creativos, que elijan qué frutas quieren usar y que pongan nombre a sus creaciones.

SUDAR LA CAMISETA

El deporte y el ejercicio físico deben formar parte de nuestra vida diaria. Unos trabajan un poco más que otros y unos sudan un poco más que otros. Y los hay que sudan *mucho más*. Por supuesto, los adictos al gimnasio tienen que estar más atentos a su hidratación. Nos referimos especialmente a los aficionados al Bikram yoga. ¡Chico, tú también sudas! He aquí por qué es una función maravillosa.

El sudor no se considera con respeto. Y, sin embargo, requiere un complicado y delicado sistema esencial de eliminación, que colabora con muchos otros sistemas orgánicos. Para sudar hace falta energía, y este es un proceso complejo. Dependiendo de tu índice metabólico en reposo (es decir, de cuántas calorías quemes en reposo), tus riñones, por sí solos, pueden quemar más de cuatrocientas calorías al día —y gran parte de esa energía se emplea en equilibrar el flujo corporal de líquido entre células y órganos[3].

La sudoración es un componente esencial del termostato interno del cuerpo; le permite enfriarse rápidamente, lo cual evita el sobrecalentamiento de órganos, sangre y tejidos[4]. La sudoración es una de las múltiples maneras que tiene tu cuerpo de desintoxicarse de manera natural; ayuda a eliminar ciertos compuestos del torrente sanguíneo. Es además el sistema de trasporte de las feromonas naturales, «hormonas sexuales» del olor que influyen en las personas a las que atraes y por las que sientes atracción[5].

El sudor se produce en glándulas que se localizan en la dermis, la capa que se encuentra justo por debajo de la superficie de piel que tocas. Las glándulas sudoríparas están distribuidas por toda la superficie corporal, pero la frente, las axilas, las palmas de las manos y las plantas de los pies presentan una mayor concentración de las mismas.

PERO... ¿QUÉ ES EXACTAMENTE?

La composición exacta del sudor varía de una persona a otra y de un día a otro. Pero es agua aproximadamente en un 99%. El uno por ciento restante está integrado por los electrolitos sodio y cloro, así como por amoníaco, azúcar y cantidades muy pequeña, de minerales como calcio, potasio, magnesio, hierro, cinc, cobre y ciertas vitaminas solubles en agua[6]. Para reponer debidamente lo que perdemos con el sudor, necesitamos no solo reponer agua, sino también electrolitos. Añadir un poco de sal de mar natural a nuestra botella de agua cumple perfectamente con esta función.

REPONER DESPUÉS DE UNA SESIÓN DE SUDOR

Hay ciertas cosas que no es posible controlar por completo —como la menopausia, el estrés y los nervios previos a una competición— y que pueden desencadenar sudoración. La genética y ciertos trastornos de la salud influyen también en la cantidad de sudor. Lo mismo puede decirse a propósito del peso: cuanto mayor es el peso, más tendrá que trabajar el organismo para mantenerse fresco, lo que conduce a su vez a sudoración.

Con todo, la cantidad de sudor está ligada directamente a los niveles de actividad física. Si realizas una modalidad suave de ejercicio, como caminar o montar tranquilamente en bicicleta, en un ambiente de temperatura fresca o templada, es posible que sudes apenas cien mililitros de sudor en una hora. Si haces ejercicio intenso, como correr, y en un ambiente cálido o bochornoso, puede que pierdas más de tres mil mililitros de sudor en una hora[7].

Como regla general, Tum Coyle, fisiólogo experto en actividad física y compañero de trabajo de Dana, recomienda las siguientes pautas para reponer agua de forma adecuada:

- Bebe entre 120 y 240 ml de agua por cada quince minutos de actividad física mientras haces ejercicio. Guíate por la sed, pero ten cuidado de no beber más de 350 ml de agua cada quince minutos, pues correrías el riesgo de sobrehidratarte.
- Si estás realizando un deporte extremo, como correr una maratón o entrenar, bebe en torno a 2,5 vasos (600 ml) de agua 2,5 horas antes de hacer ejercicio, y 1,5 vasos (o 350 ml) 15 minutos antes de hacer ejercicio. Esto garantiza que no te deshidratarás mientras desarrollas tu actividad física.

Puede que sea necesario pasar por una etapa de «prueba y error» hasta llegar a saber qué es lo adecuado en tu caso. Otra manera bastante sencilla de averiguar si estás hidratándote bien cuando realizas ejercicio físico es la siguiente: súbete a una báscula antes de empezar, y luego otra vez cuando acabes. Según el American College of Sports Medicine, un incremento o una disminución de peso puede indicar si tienes o no líquido suficiente en tu sistema.

- **Bien hidratado:** una variación de uno a más de uno por ciento de tu peso corporal. Por ejemplo, si pesas 68 kilos, no debes haber perdido ni ganado más de 680 gramos inmediatamente después de la actividad física.

- **Ligeramente deshidratado:** de uno a tres por ciento —si pesas 68 kilos, has perdido entre 68 gramos y 2 kilos de peso inmediatamente después de la actividad física.
- **Considerablemente deshidratado:** de tres a cinco por ciento —si pesas 68 kilos, has perdido entre 2 kilos y 3,4 kilos inmediatamente después de la actividad física.
- **Gravemente deshidratado:** cinco por ciento o más —si pesas 68 kilos, has perdido 3,4 kilos o más inmediatamente después de la actividad física[8].

DEJA QUE LA SED TE GUÍE... HASTA CIERTO PUNTO

Aunque el lema «Deja que la sed te guíe» sea en general un buen consejo, tienes que tener cuidado y no dejar que la sed te lleve a beber demasiada agua —especialmente durante y después de una dura sesión de ejercicio, como un triatlón, o si hace un calor extremo—. La hidratación en exceso puede conducir a una enfermedad llamada hiponatremia, que se presenta cuando los niveles de sodio en sangre alcanzan niveles bajos críticos porque hay demasiada agua circulando en el sistema. Esto hace que las células se hinchen, lo cual puede causar graves problemas e incluso puede poner en peligro la vida de la persona[9]. Se estima que un 13% de la gente que compite en la maratón de Boston desarrolla hiponatremia, que es una de las múltiples razones por las que se cuenta con un equipo de médicos para asistir a los corredores[10].

Deshidratación y trastornos por calor

Los primeros signos de deshidratación pueden ser sed, mareo, debilidad, cansancio, dolor de cabeza, piel seca, boca seca y orina concentrada o color ámbar o menor producción de orina. Una deshidratación más grave puede presentarse con anuria (ausencia de producción de orina), mareos que impiden a la persona mantenerse en pie o caminar normalmente, baja presión arterial, aumento de la frecuencia cardíaca, fiebre, aletargamiento y confusión, y ello puede conducir a convulsiones, shock o coma. Estos síntomas requieren atención médica inmediata.

A las personas que están deshidratadas y vomitan hay que tratar de darles sorbitos de agua muy despacio u ofrecerles un helado de zumo o bebidas con electrolitos. Si la persona está deshidratada y no vomita, un tratamiento inmediato y eficaz contra la deshidratación consiste en reponer los líquidos perdidos dándole de beber agua fresca a la que se haya añadido un pellizco de sal. Además, habrá que enfriar su cuerpo con una toalla húmeda o rociarle la piel con agua mediante un aerosol. Si es una urgencia, se puede recurrir a una bebida deportiva o una solución tipo Pedialyte. Ante este grado de deshidratación, no hay que preocuparse por detalles como el consumo de azúcar. La hidratación es urgente y crítica.

Tres síndromes debidos al calor y que cursan con deshidratación son los calambres por calor, el agotamiento por calor y el golpe de calor. Los **calambres por calor** son breves contracturas musculares dolorosas. Se deben a la pérdida de electrolitos por ejercicio intenso y a la inapropiada reposición de los mismos. Pueden afectar a las pantorrillas, los muslos, el abdomen y los hombros. El **agotamiento por calor** es evitable y los síntomas son piel fría, intensa sudoración, sensación de desmayo, mareo, cansancio, debilidad, aumento de la frecuencia cardíaca, baja presión arterial al ponerse de pie, calambres musculares, náuseas y dolor de cabeza. Puede prevenirse mediante una hidratación adecuada durante el ejercicio y con medidas de precaución, como llevar ropa ligera, comprobar la temperatura ambiental y evitar el ejercicio cuando haga excesivo calor. El agotamiento por calor, si no se trata, puede conducir al **golpe de calor,** que es un trastorno potencialmente mortal que requiere atención médica inmediata. Su signo revelador es una fiebre de más de 40 grados.

¿Y QUÉ HAY DE LAS BEBIDAS DEPORTIVAS?

Aunque a los publicistas les gustaría que pensaras de otra manera, en realidad no necesitas beber un Gatorade después de pasar media hora en la elíptica o veinte minutos levantando pesas. Siempre que no estés evitando el sodio y que sigas una dieta con abundantes alimentos frescos, tu cuerpo será capaz de restablecer el equilibrio de electrolitos después de una sesión «normal» de ejercicio. Un vaso de agua —y no una bebida deportiva especial— cumplirá perfectamente con su cometido de calmar tu sed y reponer las reservas de agua de tu cuerpo.

Si haces ejercicio durante más de una hora, será una buena idea comer y/o beber algo que te aporte glucosa (es decir, combustible) en forma de carbohidratos y electrolitos (especialmente sodio). Dana aconseja a los deportistas de resistencia que tiene como pacientes que se alejen de cualquier bebida cargada de colorantes artificiales y azúcares añadidos y que, en su lugar, opten por la siguiente bebida, que puede prepararse en casa.

SORBOS INTELIGENTES: PREPARA TU PROPIA BEBIDA DEPORTIVA

Con esta bebida, preparada únicamente con ingredientes naturales, puedes reponer electrolitos, agua y carbohidratos.

- 240 a 350 ml de agua o de agua de coco
- Una pizca de sal natural (como sal de mar o céltica)
- Un chorrito (15 a 30 ml) de zumo de limón o de lima
- Una cucharadita de miel o de jarabe de arce

EL DEPORTE DESPUÉS DE LA ESCUELA

La hidratación —que ha de incluir un poco de sal y electrolitos esenciales— es fundamental después de la escuela para los jóvenes deportistas, como medida de protección frente a las lesiones. Piensa en la hidratación simplemente como en una reposición de líquido e imagina que se almacena en tejidos y células. El agua, que siempre es una bendición, no solo proporciona energía sino también esponjosidad, muy necesaria si pensamos que los jóvenes deportistas se enfrentan a todo tipo de golpes y choques. La hidratación a lo largo de todo el día es esencial para mantener el cerebro despierto a última hora en clase (y, a propósito ¿podría alguien explicar por qué la clase de química siempre es a última hora en los institutos?), pero también es fundamental para los niños que practican deporte después de la escuela, pues la hidratación protege los tejidos en general, y en particular frente a la conmoción cerebral.

No queremos asustar a nadie con estadísticas sobre conmoción cerebral en jóvenes deportistas y sobre las consecuencias ocultas pero prolongadas, de modo que iremos directas a la solución. La hidratación es la primera y más importante manera de proteger y precargar, ofreciendo un medio amortiguador al músculo y al cerebro. Y si la combinas con aceites, especialmente omega 3, estarás enviando estratégicamente un equipo de defensa, listo para repeler una lesión o una conmoción cerebral. Los datos que avalan la protección del cerebro y el tratamiento de la conmoción cerebral mediante omega 3 son ahora una legión. La investigación fue iniciada por el Ejército de Estados Unidos. Michael Lewis, por entonces coronel del Cuerpo de Médicos del Ejército de EE.UU., documentó el modo en el que los suplementos de omega 3 antes de un accidente tenían efecto protector frente a la lesión cerebral y aceleraban la recuperación[11].

¿Y si hubiera una bebida deportiva que cumpliera con este cometido? ¿Una bebida que proporcionara hidratación, electrolitos y omega 3 al mismo tiempo? Hemos desarrollado una receta *Quench* precisamente para esto y la hemos llamado *Bebida Tara* (véase la siguiente receta) en honor de la antigua tribu de los tarahumara, que se hicieron famosos gracias al libro que ya hemos mencionado *Nacidos para correr*. Este pueblo utiliza como combustible para sus carreras semillas de chía, de modo que regresamos al punto en el que iniciamos nuestra investigación sobre la hidratación profunda: las estrategias alternativas de hidratación abundan en muchas culturas. Los pueblos del desierto tienen mucho que compartir a propósito de la hidratación.

Bebida Tara

PARA UNA PERSONA

- 350 ml de agua
- 1 o 2 cucharaditas de semillas de chía molidas (omega 3)
- 120 ml de kombucha, de tu sabor favorito; el de jengibre va genial. Los tarahumara mezclaban chía con su cerveza casera de maíz fermentado. La kombucha es nuestro sustituto.
- 1 pellizco de sal de mar o de roca

Preparación: Mezcla los ingredientes en una botella de agua. Tapa la botella, agita con fuerza y... disfruta.

La falta de pescado en el desierto

Los aceites omega 3 están presentes sobre todo en el pescado. Pero ¿y las tribus que no tienen acceso al pescado? La adaptación evolutiva al medio permite a los habitantes del desierto convertir de manera más eficaz los ácidos grasos ALA, presentes en semillas, nueces e incluso en algas de lagos estacionales, en EPA y DHA. Recuerda que los habitantes del desierto son en su mayor parte nómadas. Las tribus centroafricanas se concentran en primavera alrededor del lago Victoria. Los antropólogos observaron que la mayor parte de los matrimonios, festejos, bailes y celebraciones de estas poblaciones tenían lugar durante estas grandes concentraciones estacionales. Pero adivina qué. Coincidiendo con todas estas celebraciones, las mujeres iban recogiendo algas del lago, las secaban y las empacaban para conservarlas hasta la siguiente estación difícil. Ahí lo tienes: omega 3 en la dieta a partir de algas.

Para nosotros, es fácil obtener ácidos grasos omega 3 del pescado o incluso del krill envasado del supermercado. Pero nunca nos cansaremos de resaltar la importancia de la ingesta de omega 3. Ahora sabes que otros pueblos en otra época recorrían grandes distancias con gran

esfuerzo para obtener estas grasas en su alimentación. Y, a los vega-
nos que hay entre nosotros, les recomiendo combinar la ingesta de
ALA (presente en las semillas de lino, las nueces o la chía) con aceite
de coco, que ayuda a convertir el ALA en EPA y DHA de manera más
eficaz.

DEPORTISTAS DE OFICINA

Para la mayoría de la gente, el trabajo es como una competición deportiva. Mantenerse fresco, atento, flexible y estar siempre listo para responder con prontitud exige tanto como competir en un campo de juego. Es notorio que los ambientes de trabajo resecan mucho. Pensemos
en nuestra jornada laboral como en una jornada deportiva y utilicemos
todos los nuevos trucos que ahora conocemos, introduciendo además los
micromovimientos como hábito diario. Incluso corporaciones con grandes edificios de oficinas están poco a poco apuntándose a esta estrategia.
Hace no mucho tiempo, un importante banco retiró las papeleras personales a sus empleados, no como medida punitiva, sino para obligarles a
levantarse y moverse. Pero no necesitas a tu jefe para hacer deporte en tu
lugar de trabajo. Opta por ser un deportista de días laborables, en lugar
de un deportista de fin de semana. Realiza micromovimientos e hidrátate
como si estuvieras en el gimnasio.

LA HIDRATACIÓN EN LOS ANCIANOS

Con la edad, la hidratación tiene consecuencias mucho más pronuncia-
das. Según Barry Popkin, experto en deshidratación, nuestro mecanismo
de la sed disminuye con la edad, lo cual coincide con la pérdida de masa
muscular[12]. El tejido muscular es uno de los sitios de almacenamiento
de agua de nuestro organismo, de manera que nuestra capacidad para
almacenar agua disminuye más o menos al mismo tiempo que la señal
de nuestro cuerpo para beber. Se trata pues de un agravante, que con frecuencia da lugar a infecciones del aparato urinario, trastornos gastroin-
testinales, pérdida de facultades cognitivas, confusión, cansancio, pérdida

de equilibrio y una cascada de consecuencias, que es posible interrumpir mediante una adecuada hidratación. Y los jubilados que se mudan para pasar el invierno —o para siempre— a lugares de clima más cálido son también más propensos a sufrir deshidratación.

ESTUDIO DE CASO DE LA DRA. DANA COHEN

Havie

Una de mis pacientes, Havie, es una diseñadora de moda de setenta y cuatro años asombrosamente llena de energía y muy activa para su edad. Lo único que la frena es la osteoartritis cervical que padece. Se sometió a una intervención quirúrgica de cuello hace más de quince años, pero sigue sintiendo molestias en toda la parte superior de la columna. Ha consultado a ortopedas, quiroprácticos, fisioterapeutas, especialistas en acupuntura y en masaje. Toma ibuprofeno con bastante regularidad y tiene que lidiar con el dolor para superar el día a día.

Por otro lado, tras someterse a una endoscopia hace un año y diagnosticársele una hernia de hiato, se le prescribió omeprazol —un inhibidor de la bomba de protones—. Toma la medicación religiosamente todos los días y, aunque le ha resultado de ayuda, siente amargor en la boca y tiene unas desagradables y densas flemas. Ha llegado también a sentir presión en el pecho, pero ha acudido a un cardiólogo y todas las pruebas han sido normales.

Además de tomar medicamentos sin receta para el dolor y de utilizar un inhalador, toma un fármaco para bajar el colesterol (Zetia), aun cuando no tiene antecedentes de cardiopatía: su médico se lo prescribió hace unos años como medida preventiva, porque sus niveles de colesterol estaban en el límite más alto.

Una vez que hube recopilado todos sus antecedentes médicos, le pregunté cuál era su dieta habitual, que consistía en lo siguiente.

Desayuno: café, a veces dos tazas. Durante la semana nunca come nada para desayunar; los fines de semana puede comerse una barrita de cereales y yogur o huevos.

Comida: ensalada, a veces con pollo a la plancha, y un té helado envasado.

Cena: salmón y verduras, agua. No suele tomar postre.

Le pregunté si pensaba que bebía suficiente agua.

«Probablemente no», me contestó. «Si bebo demasiado, ¡me paso el día haciendo pis!».

«Como primera medida, me gustaría que te hidrataras mejor», le dije. «Vamos a retirar los medicamentos innecesarios y a proporcionarte una dieta más adecuada».

Cuando le describí los posibles efectos secundarios —entre ellos dolor articular y reflujo— de algunos de los fármacos, incluso de los menos perjudiciales, como por ejemplo el omeprazol, y le expliqué que podrían estar contribuyendo al dolor y al cansancio que sufría, estuvo de acuerdo en prescindir de ellos.

Mientras esperábamos los resultados de los primeros análisis de sangre, le presenté a Havie el Programa Quench de inicio rápido. Su dieta era buena, pero era necesario que hiciera algunos sencillos cambios. Tenía que beber un vaso de agua antes de cada comida, pero las mañanas eran las que iban a requerir más trabajo por su parte. En lugar de saltarse el desayuno, tenía que comenzar el día con un *smoothie*, junto con un gran vaso de agua con limón y un pellizco de sal marina.

A Havie le llamó la atención esta sugerencia: «Siempre había pensado que la sal era mala para mí, ¡y la evitaba como la peste!».

Le expliqué lo siguiente: existe una gran diferencia entre una buena sal como es la sal marina, cargada de minerales, y la sal corriente, que es mejor que utilices para esparcir delante de la puerta de casa cuando hiele.

Incorporé además a su dieta un *smoothie* por la tarde para una hidratación adicional, pues sospechaba que sus raciones de comida eran muy pequeñas y que le vendría bien ese batido.

Debido a su dolor de cuello, le sugerí algunos micromovimientos como tabla de ejercicios. Debía realizar algunos estiramientos por la mañana, tumbada en la cama, como *Barbilla al pecho* (véase capítulo 8) y *Estiramiento de todo el cuerpo*, descritos en el Plan Quench. También le sugerí la realización de algunos sencillos estiramientos a lo largo del día, como suaves movimientos de cabeza hacia arriba y hacia abajo mientras subía o bajaba en el ascensor y sencillas elevaciones de hombros.

Havie regresó a mi consulta para una revisión tres semanas más tarde. Su aspecto era magnífico. Tenía brillo en los ojos.

«¿Cómo te encuentras?», le pregunté.

«No me sentía tan bien desde hacía diez años. Mi rigidez ha mejorado muchísimo», me contestó.

«¿Cuánto ha mejorado?».

«¡Un ochenta por cien! Todavía tengo que tomar paracetamol por la mañana, pero no he necesitado tomar omeprazol en dos semanas. El reflujo ha desaparecido por completo. El sabor amargo en la boca también. Y el moco denso… ¡también!».

Llegaron los resultados de las pruebas de laboratorio y todo era normal, salvo la vitamina D, que estaba un poco baja, y el colesterol total, que estaba en 160, por debajo de los nieles normales. Me alegraba mucho por haber podido retirar a Havie el medicamento para bajar el colesterol y por ver que el Plan Quench le daba resultado. Y ella estaba de acuerdo y entusiasmada.

En la revisión de Havie de los seis meses, el Plan Quench ya constituía para ella un hábito diario. Ahora que se ha quitado la medicación, su colesterol ha vuelto a 190 —aún por debajo de los valores normales—. Todas las mañanas prepara un *smoothie* para ella y otro para su marido. Los hombros y el cuello han mejorado considerablemente, presentando ahora una amplitud de movimiento mucho mayor. Sigue utilizando paracetamol para el dolor, pero no todos los días. También dice que utiliza las escaleras para subir a su casa, en un tercer piso, y que sigue realizando los ejercicios de cuello por la mañana y en el ascensor. Al hidratarse de forma más inteligente a través de la alimentación y del movimiento, ahora tiene más líquido y menos dolor y toma menos fármacos, y ese mal sabor de boca misteriosamente ha desaparecido.

Tal y como esperaba, cuando empezó a hidratarse mejor y de manera más inteligente, combinando alimentos hidratantes, agua y movimiento, las articulaciones y los músculos de hombros, brazos y cuello resultaron mejor lubricados y el dolor disminuyó considerablemente. Dados los excelentes resultados, Havie mantiene estos cambios en su alimentación y en su estilo de vida.

La medicación es también un factor de riesgo, pues la gente mayor tiende a tomar más fármacos para distintos achaques. Este uso simultáneo de medicamentos, lo creas o no, tiene un nombre: polimedicación. Lee Hooper, Diane Bunn y Suzan Whitelock, enfermeras de investigación, fueron las primeras en llevar a cabo un estudio de valoración del modo en que la polimedicación influye en la deshidratación de las personas mayores[13]. Observaron que los cuidadores debían estar más atentos y vigilar si los ancianos bebían lo suficiente y tomar las medidas necesarias para que bebieran más. Existe toda una logística que complica el asunto, como la movilidad de los pacientes y su preocupación por no llegar a tiempo al baño. La gente mayor también sufre discapacidades físicas que dificultan su acceso a la bebida o tienen con frecuencia problemas de deglución. Un truco ridículamente sencillo para conseguir que la gente mayor, o cualquiera, beba más consiste en utilizar dos pajitas para beber, en lugar de una. Gina solía pegar con papel celo dos pajas juntas para que su madre bebiera más de un solo sorbo. También pueden ser de ayuda las pajas de diámetro mayor, de las que se utilizan para el *bubble tea* (té de frutas con perlas de gelatina).

La rosa

Tradiciones de todo el mundo contemplan el uso de la rosa por sus poderes curativos. En origen las rosas se cultivaban por sus propiedades medicinales, siendo su belleza un valor añadido. Desde Persia hasta la India, se tiene conocimiento de antiguas recetas para la preparación de mermeladas y jaleas dulces a partir del contenido rico en pectina de los pétalos. Los efectos hidratantes de la rosa se han aprovechado para tratar la sobreexposición al calor, el cansancio y todos los síntomas típicamente asociados a la deshidratación, como dolores de cabeza y musculares, ojos secos, mareos y falta de claridad mental. El gulqand, una conserva dulce de pétalos de rosa, es un alimento básico en cualquier despensa tradicional del subcontinente indio. La rosa de Damasco, o *Rosa damascena,* ha sido siempre utilizada por sus propiedades purificadoras y porque contribuye a la memoria. A principios de la Edad Media, la rosa de Francia (*Rosa gallica*) aparecía en todos los manuscritos sobre hierbas e inventarios de plantas comunes de jardines medicinales. Los tés de rosas se hicieron populares y se convirtieron en todo un placer, y se recomendaban además por su gran poder de hidratación.

¿Sabías que los antiguos persas de Kashan utilizaban gelatina de rosa para curar enfermedades? La gelatina se elaboraba a partir de pétalos de rosa, tenía un alto contenido en pectina y aportaba humedad a los tejidos. Los antiguos médicos persas utilizaban la mermelada de pétalos de rosa especialmente para los ancianos; la administraban bajo la lengua, por el gran poder hidratante de la pectina y por sus efectos medicinales, todo ello con una agradable forma de administración. Se sabía concretamente que la jalea de rosa regeneraba las membranas mucosas que recubren el tubo digestivo. El moco, para formarse, requiere hidratación. De hecho, las rosas se cultivaban en Persia en jardines de hierbas, junto con otras plantas de uso en farmacología. Celebradas por su belleza, hemos olvidado que las rosas contienen agentes medicinales. La ciencia moderna[14] ha analizado los elementos medicinales de los pétalos de rosa y los experimentos han puesto de manifiesto que las bacterias mueren en un plazo de cinco minutos tras el contacto con los pétalos frescos de la flor. Se ha demostrado asimismo que las rosas tienen múltiples propiedades beneficiosas, entre ellas antibacterianas y antioxidantes, así como un efecto relajante.

Las enfermeras de investigación mencionadas con anterioridad idearon un sencillo plan: conseguir que, al final del tiempo destinado para el desayuno, sus pacientes hubieran bebido un litro de agua, o cerca de cuatro tazas. Al ampliar el tiempo social dedicado al desayuno, los residentes bebían más. Así pues, las enfermeras, en sus labores de asistencia por la mañana temprano, «precargaban» de agua a los ancianos, y nosotras recomendamos hacer lo mismo en nuestro Plan Quench (véase capítulo 8).

Las enfermeras pudieron establecer una relación entre esta estrategia de hidratación y la reducción de las intervenciones paramédicas y de los ingresos hospitalarios[15].

Membrillo

El membrillo es una fruta conocida tradicionalmente por sus propiedades hidratantes. Sus consistencia blanda y gelatinosa ha sido apreciada en todo el mundo, desde su tierra de cultivo original en Turquía, pasando por la península ibérica hasta Inglaterra en el siglo XIV y más tarde el Nuevo Mundo. En Chile, las mujeres de aldeas tradicionales al cuidado de sus padres mayores utilizaban una dosis diaria de pasta de membrillo dulce para que los ancianos se sintieran bien mientras ellas atendían a los niños. Daban a la pasta forma de comprimido y la depositaban en la lengua del anciano, para que se disolviera lentamente. Y pasta de membrillo era también el último alimento que se daba para que el tránsito a la muerte fuera más fácil. Los pequeños morteros de madera o prensas de pasta de membrillo se decoraban con bendiciones o deseos de despedida. Esta costumbre se conserva en sus distintas versiones y la jalea de membrillo sigue ofreciéndose en Argentina en las residencias de ancianos para conseguir una mayor hidratación cuando existe dificultad para beber.

Vivimos rodeados de personas a las que amamos, de modo que asegurémonos de que gozan de buena salud y de que están hidratadas. En nuestro Plan Quench te enseñamos la manera de ayudarlas a hidratarse de forma adecuada.

CAPÍTULO 7

Piel, belleza y antienvejecimiento

Haré agua, hermosa agua azul.

Claude Monet

Nosotras detestamos la palabra *antienvejecimiento*. Porque envejecer es precisamente lo que *queremos* hacer. Envejecer es lo que cada día nos acerca más y más a quienes somos. Nos referimos al crecimiento constante, a la suma y al desarrollo que nos conducen a nuevos niveles de sabiduría y que determinan nuestra capacidad para abordar la vida. Con el tiempo, acumulamos experiencia, historias de vida, golpes y celebraciones y, por encima de todo, la sabiduría que encierran. Son lecciones de vida y emociona ver todo lo que hemos aprendido de ellas. Eso se llama envejecer. La cuestión no es «cómo no envejecer», sino cómo *envejecer bien*. La respuesta, una vez más, está en la hidratación.

De la capacidad para seguir siendo una persona vital y llena de energía a medida que se envejece es de lo que trata este libro. ¿Cómo podría la hidratación no tener un efecto rejuvenecedor? Es como regar una planta mustia. La nueva ciencia de la hidratación sitúa en el mismo nivel la ingesta de agua y la ingesta de energía. En este libro encontrarás la explicación científica de por qué es así. La hidratación es la mejor y la más potente fórmula de… no diremos de antienvejecimiento, sino más bien de aumento de nuestras *expectativas* de vida, de una vida llena de energía. La vida que todos esperamos tener es una vida vibrante, de lucidez y consciencia, percibiendo en todo momento la exquisita red de conexiones que es nuestro cuerpo. Y el agua es lo que orquesta los elementos en nuestro interior. ¡Eso es belleza!

Si no cuentas en tu interior con la debida hidratación, entonces todas esas cremas de belleza, hidratantes, serums y cápsulas no te servirán de mucho. Esos productos son importantes, pero lo más importante de su trabajo es favorecer la hidratación que tú ya tienes. Cualquier esteticista sabe que la hidratación y una buena piel vienen de dentro, de manera que la primera recomendación de los mejores profesionales es siempre hidratar. Agua y sabiduría van de la mano.

HIDRATACIÓN Y PIEL

La piel es el órgano más grande del cuerpo, protege nuestros valiosos órganos de agresiones del entorno y, lo que es más importante para nuestros propósitos, conserva el agua corporal. Y aunque puedas estar pensando que la piel actúa como defensa, en realidad su principal labor es jugar al ataque, eliminando materiales no deseados a través de los poros. No solemos pensar en la piel de esta manera, pero precisamente así es como trabajan los poros de la piel. Y esta es la razón por la cual la piel es un importante órgano de hidratación, al retener la humedad y eliminar los desechos. El flujo de salida es tan importante como lo que bebemos. La piel tiene en torno a 150 poros por centímetro cuadrado, a través de los cuales sudamos.

La función del poro cutáneo puede ser de ayuda si mantiene su eficacia y la mejor manera de favorecer su función es induciendo la sudoración. Anteriormente hemos hablado del sudor en el deporte, sobre todo como mecanismo de enfriamiento. Pero aquí estamos hablando de sudar como terapia, no solo para la salud de la piel, sino para la hidratación de todo el cuerpo. De modo que ¡empecemos a sudar!

SUDAR POR BELLEZA

El sudor transforma los desechos orgánicos de una sustancia química liposoluble —o soluble en grasa— en una sustancia química hidrosoluble —o soluble en agua— que se elimina por los poros. El papel de la piel en la hidratación es tan esencial como la función de la fascia, la circulación sanguínea o la circulación linfática. El doctor Stephen Genuis, de la Universidad de Alberta, en Canadá, ha publicado algunos estudios en los que el sudor es reconocido como sistema de eliminación de desechos. Concretamente, la sudoración puede incrementar la eliminación de metales pesados, como mercurio, plomo y cadmio, y de algunos tóxicos químicos como bisfenol A y ftalatos[1]. El sudor posee además propiedades antimicrobianas, en la medida en que su pH puede impedir que las bacterias se asienten en los poros y causen acné. Una sudoración entre ligera y moderada abre los poros y permite la liberación de las grasas y de la suciedad que los obtura. No obstante, es importante limpiar la piel inmediatamente después de sudar, de modo que la suciedad y las toxinas presentes en el sudor no sean reabsorbidas por la piel. La piel reclama que le prestemos atención y que la renovemos, por dentro y por fuera. Tal vez ahora comprendamos que debemos cuidarla desde ambos frentes.

ESTUDIO DE CASO DE LA DRA. DANA COHEN

Irene

«¡Doctora, necesito tener buen aspecto para mi primer día de universidad!»

Irene, una estudiante de dieciocho años, vino a la consulta con su madre, también paciente mía, para una revisión. Era una estudiante modelo y en otoño iba a comenzar sus estudios en Ivy League. Como cualquier adolescente, le preocupaba mucho su aspecto y luchaba contra el acné y la báscula. Estaba nerviosa porque quería que la ayudara antes de ir a la universidad. Toda esta ansiedad le había provocado síndrome de intestino irritable; le dolía a menudo el estómago y sufría alternancia de episodios de diarrea y estreñimiento. Los dolores de estómago no eran nada nuevo: su madre me dijo que los había sufrido de niña y que había tenido cólicos cuando era un bebé.

Primero le pregunté por su alimentación.

«Soy vegetariana». Cuando indagué más en su dieta, me encontré con que comía mucha pasta, pan, queso y productos lácteos.

Sabiendo que los derivados lácteos pueden causar inflamación y problemas de estómago, le pedí que los eliminara de la dieta durante tres semanas. Le entregué una lista de sustitutos de los lácteos y le pedí que sustituyera los carbohidratos que tomaba por cereales como la quinoa o el arroz integral. También le pedí que comiera pescado para elevar sus niveles de omega 3, que sospechaba que debían estar bajos pero que no conocía pues había que esperar a que llegaran los resultados del laboratorio. Para gran alegría mía, la joven se mostró dispuesta a incluir pescado en la dieta, porque realmente quería tener la piel limpia. Le di algunas sencillas ideas de platos de pescado para que probara y entonces ella recordó que antes le encantaban las gambas y otros mariscos, de modo que prometió que los combinaría. Le entregué también el Programa Quench de cinco días.

Cuando volvió a consulta dos semanas más tarde, su piel había mejorado notablemente. No tenía granos e iba al baño con regularidad, y sin dolores. Estaba eufórica por verse y sentirse tan bien después de haberse sentido tan mal durante tanto tiempo. Los resultados de los análisis de sangre volvieron a ser normales, excepto su perfil de ácidos grasos. Sus omega 3 estaban bajos, como había sospechado, pero le había venido bien aumentar su consumo de pescado e incluso había añadido salmón a su menú.

Estábamos encantadas con los resultados, pero la pregunta que inmediatamente se nos ocurrió fue la siguiente: ¿Cómo iba a continuar con el plan en la universidad? Hablamos largo y tendido sobre cómo abordar el año escolar que Irene tenía por delante. Comprometida con su salud, preguntó en el departamento de alojamiento de la universidad si podía tener en su habitación una licuadora y un pequeño frigorífico. También se interesó por la ubicación de mercados de productos locales cerca de la universidad y, por supuesto, se llevó una copia de bolsillo del Plan Quench. Irene sigue feliz y rebosante de salud; tiene una piel hermosa y sigue siendo una chica de dieces.

Aspectos antropológicos de la sauna

En el mundo, cada cultura tiene su propia estrategia de limpieza, renovación y rejuvenecimiento, siempre de la mano de la hidratación. Antiguos pueblos de Asia Menor desarrollaron los famosos baños turcos de vapor; los antiguos romanos construyeron sus «thermae», centro de la vida cívica; los rusos tenían sus «banya» relajantes. La tradición japonesa elevó con los «onsen» la categoría de los baños y del sudor al más alto nivel de cuidado de la salud y de la belleza corporal. Y en las culturas indígenas las saunas siempre han sido un elemento obligado, un lugar de reunión para la salud y la elevación mediante rituales sagrados celebrados en comunidad. Los indígenas norteamericanos ya utilizaban sus tiendas o tipis para sudar; los lenape de la isla de Manhattan construían sus tipis con la duradera madera del árbol tulipero, cuya corteza interna impregnaba el vapor de una resina curativa. Los incas utilizaban baños de hierbas medicinales como parte de su tradición del sudor. Sin embargo, una de las técnicas para favorecer la salud a través de la sudoración más estudiadas clínicamente es la famosa sauna finlandesa. La doctora Rhonda Patrick, científica biomédica y fundadora de la página web FoundMyFitness.com, es una experta en los efectos de la sauna sobre la salud y recientemente ha documentado que los efectos positivos del calor sobre nuestros sistemas provienen de la estimulación de las proteínas del choque térmico del interior celular[2]. Además, las inmersiones en agua fría después de una sauna muy caliente están ampliamente documentadas en las culturas del norte, pues aclimatan a las personas al medio invernal. En efecto, salir de nuestra «zona de confort» proporciona resistencia celular.

SAUNAS Y LUZ INFRARROJA

Sin duda se ha escrito mucho sobre la hidratación y el cuidado de la piel, pero nosotras ponemos ahora sobre la mesa la nueva ciencia de las moléculas de agua.

La aplicación sobre la piel de luz infrarroja mediante lámparas tiene efectos hidratantes reales y clínicamente establecidos. Esto tiene sentido, si pensamos que, efectivamente, las ondas de luz favorecen la formación de agua en gel en nuestro cuerpo. Como ya hemos mencionado, el trabajo del Dr. Pollack ha revelado que la luz infrarroja es el productor más potente de agua EZ. Cuantos más infrarrojos, más agua en gel. La mejoría observada en la piel gracias al uso de una sencilla lámpara de infrarrojos puede medirse. Así, en un estudio de 2014, Alexander Wunsch y su equipo trataron con luz infrarroja a una serie de pacientes, que experimentaron una considerable mejoría de piel. Este estudio alemán realizó mediciones muy precisas sobre y bajo la piel y empleó el estudio ecográfico para medir la densidad de colágeno. Las pruebas confirmaron no solo una importante mejoría de la propia piel, sino un incremento medible del colágeno intradérmico. Se comprobó asimismo la seguridad del rejuvenecimiento de la piel mediante infrarrojos. Para conseguir estos efectos, el paciente únicamente debía permanecer sentado bajo la lámpara de luz infrarroja[3].

Para nosotras, esto significa piel rejuvenecida utilizando luz y agua. El ser humano siempre ha estado buscando la fuente de la eterna juventud. ¿Podría ser la combinación de agua y luz?

ESTUDIO DE CASO DE LA DRA. DANA COHEN

Denise

Denise, profesora de yoga de cuarenta y cinco años, goza de muy buena salud y sigue una excelente alimentación de base vegetal. Vino a mi consulta en busca de tratamiento para la enfermedad de Hashimoto, un trastorno de la glándula tiroides que padecía desde los veinte años. Siempre había tenido cuidado para mantener la enfermedad a raya y comentaba que se sentía sana y no tenía achaques, como siempre. Aunque Denise no era la típica candidata al plan, decidí proponerle el Programa Quench, pues sospechaba que no debía estar hidratada de manera óptima —la mayor parte de las personas no lo están— y quería ver si podíamos conseguir un perfil de salud todavía mejor.

Al cabo de pocas semanas, me escribió un correo electrónico para contarme cómo estaba. ¡No podía creer lo bien que se encontraba desde que su cuerpo tenía más líquido! «¡Mi piel está radiante!». Se había dado cuenta de que probablemente no estaba bebiendo suficiente agua durante el día. «Qué inocente parece la hidratación» —escribía— «pero los increíbles resultados de cambiar ligeramente mis hábitos han sido alucinantes». Terminaba el correo diciendo que, desde que estaba más hidratada, sus ejercicios de yoga eran «la bomba». Y, por supuesto, ahora enseña a sus estudiantes lo que ha aprendido. ¡Una bonita manera de devolver el favor recibido!

LA BELLEZA DEL SUEÑO

Belleza y sueño están conectados. Habrás oído un millón de veces la frase «Tómate un descanso de belleza», ¿verdad? Existe una razón nueva detrás de esta afirmación, y es la desintoxicación. El doctor Maiken Nedergaard y sus colaboradores en el University of Rochester Medical Center asombraron a los científicos al descubrir todo un sistema de drenaje oculto en células especializadas del cerebro[4]. Este sistema funciona de forma similar al sistema linfático, pero drena los productos de desecho solo del cerebro. Lo llamaron sistema glinfático. Y funciona por la noche, durante el sueño, creando un aumento del flujo del 60%, como un equipo nocturno de saneamiento. Es un reciente e importante descubrimiento. Es como si el cerebro, una vez libre del «tráfico de pensamiento», utilizara este momento perfecto para eliminar residuos. Nedergaard dice: «El conocer exactamente cómo y cuándo el cerebro activa el sistema glinfático y elimina los desechos es un primer paso esencial en el esfuerzo por conseguir que potencialmente trabaje de manera más eficaz». Todo ese flujo y esa circulación dependen de unos niveles adecuados de hidratación. ¿Quién podía pensar que tumbarse, cerrar los ojos y dejarse llevar iban a formar parte de nuestro relato sobre la hidratación?

MASAJE

No ha habido ningún momento en la historia de la humanidad en el que el masaje no haya sido utilizado por distintos pueblos. El masaje terapéutico es una técnica más antigua que el registro histórico. Lo utilizan incluso los monos. Existen, por supuesto, una gran variedad de tradiciones. En muchas culturas, los masajes se aplicaban al final del día, bien en forma de automasaje bien entre dos personas. Era la recompensa tras el trabajo del día. Y no deberíamos abandonar esta ancestral y saludable tradición.

Por qué los masajes hidratan

Cualquier masaje tiene que ver con movilizar líquidos por el cuerpo. Sabemos desde hace tiempo que el masaje mueve la sangre por el sistema circulatorio, pero recientes investigaciones sobre el sistema fascial muestran que el masaje activa también la hidratación. Recordemos el trabajo del doctor Jean-Claude Guimberteau, en cuyo vídeo, presentado en el capítulo 3, aparecían gotas de agua moviéndose por el sistema fascial. El masaje con las manos impulsa la hidratación a través de las fascias, así como a través de los sistemas linfático y sanguíneo, de modo que actúa a la vez sobre distintos sistemas. Los masajes especializados, como el masaje linfático o el facial, movilizan los desechos para una más rápida eliminación.

Efectos beneficiosos del masaje

Sabemos que el masaje tiene efectos terapéuticos demostrados. Es una industria que mueve mucho dinero, precisamente por sus efectos positivos sobre la salud. Se ha demostrado que mejora la inmunidad en los pacientes de cáncer de mama y prueba de ello es que el centro oncológico Memorial Sloan Kettering Center de Nueva York lo ofrece como parte de su estrategia de tratamiento del cáncer. Sin embargo, en las revistas médicas se han publicado muy pocos estudios serios sobre el masaje terapéutico.

Pregunta a cualquiera que haya recibido un masaje: tendrá claro cuáles han sido los efectos beneficiosos. Su piel estará radiante, lo dolores habrán cedido, la ira y la ansiedad habrán disminuido y su nivel de energía habrá aumentado. Cuando recibes un masaje, ocurren muchas cosas en tus sistemas orgánicos. Aparte del movimiento de líquido por todo el cuerpo, se activa la producción de proteínas del colágeno, se favorece la respuesta de relajación (pero esto ya lo sabías), se eliminan desechos y probablemente los movimientos respiratorios se vuelven más profundos.

Automasaje

No es necesario que recurras a masajistas profesionales; el automasaje también funciona. Puedes aplicar presión, para así movilizar el líquido y estirar los tejidos, activando las células para que tu estado sea el óptimo. Ahora ya tienes una motivación para masajearte las piernas mientras ves la televisión. Lo mejor del automasaje es la rápida respuesta del cuerpo. «Tómate un tiempo para sentarte y concentrarte en ti mismo», dice Masae Shimomoto, terapeuta masajista en Complete Wellness, Nueva York. Para iniciarte en el automasaje, Shimomoto recomienda comenzar por los dedos, las manos y los pies. Variaciones de este tipo de automasaje se encuentran por toda Asia y son en todos los casos técnicas ancestrales. Los usuarios del Plan Quench afirman haberse dado cuenta de que se masajean con mayor frecuencia. Una técnica aplicable durante la jornada laboral es el masaje de manos y dedos.

El movimiento como forma de automasaje

Sabiendo ya cómo funciona la fascia y cómo se activan las células, puedes reinterpretar cualquier movimiento como una forma de automasaje, o masaje celular, ya lo hagas desde fuera, con tus propias manos, o desde dentro, mediante autoestiramiento generador de movimiento. El autoestiramiento, cuando se practica a a lo largo del día, aporta nuevos niveles de fluidez, pero también nuevos niveles de función cerebral, función celular y vitalidad corporal ¿Hemos mencionado la hidratación?

El cepillado en el cuidado tradicional de la piel

El cepillado en seco es una técnica tan antigua como la historia de la humanidad. Frotar la piel con hojas, flores, palos (que en realidad es una interpretación temprana de un cepillo), algas, arena, arcillas, guijarros y telas ha sido una forma natural de tratar la piel desde que el ser humano comenzó a caminar erguido y dejó libres sus manos. Estas técnicas existen en todas las culturas y a menudo forman parte de rituales y procesos de renovación, y no sin razón. Desde nuestra nueva perspectiva podemos firmar que frotar el cuerpo funciona en muchos sentidos, pues estimula el crecimiento de colágeno en la piel, exfolia la piel muerta, descubre células nuevas, moviliza líquidos y acelera la eliminación de material de desecho. En la ducha, antes de abrir el grifo, es el momento perfecto para un cepillado en seco.

Masaje de cara

A algunas personas les preocupa que masajear y estirar la piel de la cara provoque en realidad envejecimiento y flaccidez de forma prematura, pero ahora sabemos que ocurre exactamente todo lo contrario. Las células producen colágeno bajo presión, y el colágeno es la estructura subyacente a la piel. Masajearla literalmente la renueva. Existen técnicas fascinantes de masaje de cara que proceden de tradiciones ancestrales y que dan un resultado magnífico.

Tonya Zavasta, autora de *Beautiful on Raw* y experta en piel y envejecimiento, actualiza las viejas tradiciones rusas sobre masaje de cara y cuidado de la piel recomendando el cepillado en seco del rostro, una idea nueva para mucha gente. No obstante, advierte que debe utilizarse un cepillo más suave de los que se emplean habitualmente para el cepillado en seco del cuerpo y que hay que describir con él círculos pequeños.

En la tradición hindú, la cara no se cepilla en seco, sino que se masajea con aceites, al mismo tiempo que se practican formas de acupresión y se dan palmaditas en la cara.

Siguiendo la tradición china del qigong, técnica famosa por la belleza de sus movimientos y que propician una mayor resistencia y una mayor esperanza de vida, grandes grupos de ancianos se reúnen todas las mañanas en los parques de China. Pocos saben, sin embargo, que también son expertos en masaje facial, que se considera una extensión natural del movimiento corporal completo. Simplemente se frotan la cara y el cuello en movimientos rápidos con el dorso de las manos. Y nunca comienzan el día sin este gesto.

Por qué la postura es un acto de belleza y una forma de micromasaje

Cuando estás de pie con el cuerpo perfectamente alineado, estás activando toda una serie de micromovimientos. Una buena postura es un acto dinámico. Piensa en la postura como en una forma dinámica de estar, con minúsculos movimientos concentrados, pero relajados, como un puente colgante mecido por el viento. Este concepto de equilibrio es realmente una nueva visión de la postura, que la vincula además con la hidratación a través precisamente de esos micromovimientos de ajuste. Una buena postura no solo incrementa el flujo de líquido a través de los tejidos fasciales y la circulación sanguínea, sino que además abre nuestros pulmones para una respiración más profunda y resta presión a todo el sistema digestivo. Comprueba la postura y la columna a lo largo del día. Si llevas una postura encorvada, sé consciente de ello y corrígela con los siguientes micromovimientos.

Daniel Fenster es médico desde hace más de treinta años, director clínico de Complete Wellness y autor de un libro de próxima publicación sobre la postura. Afirma que «todo el mundo sabe que la postura es importante, ¡nuestras madres nos lo decían! Pero ¿por qué es importante la postura? ¿Y por qué es importante para la hidratación? Cuando se mantiene una buena postura, también llamada alineación correcta, todo en el cuerpo funciona mejor. Además, la musculatura se encuentra sometida a menos estrés y, en consecuencia, retiene mejor una hidratación normal». El doctor está de acuerdo con nosotras en el problema que supone en la actualidad el estar todo el día encorvado sobre un escritorio o poniendo mensajes, una postura que resulta muy deshidratante porque el cuerpo pierde su alineación.

Otro experto en materia de postura, el doctor Guy Voyer, creador del Método ELDOA de terapia fascial, también profundiza en la importancia de la alineación vertebral para la hidratación. Sin alineación, dice, «el disco intervertebral pierde su contenido de agua (se deshidrata) y también su presión hidrostática (presión osmótica)». En pocas palabras, incluso si estamos bien hidratados, sin presión osmótica es más difícil llevar líquido hasta donde se necesita. Por consiguiente, la postura dinámica es una estrategia de hidratación muy importante.

Flujo postural

En 2012 la psicóloga social Amy Cuddy dio la charla TED «Your Body Language May Shape Who You Are» (Tu lenguaje corporal da forma a tu identidad), que se haría viral. En ella recurrió a la ciencia para cambiar la mentalidad sobre el modo en que la postura nos afecta, a nosotros y a aquellos que nos miran. En aquella charla explicó el experimento que había llevado a cabo para comprobar si las «posturas de poder» reducían los niveles de sustancias químicas ligadas al estrés. Había analizado la saliva de estudiantes para determinar si el permanecer de pie durante dos minutos en ciertas posturas que denotaban poder reducía, entre otras sustancia químicas, el cortisol. Efectivamente, en dos minutos, el cortisol caía entre un 15 y un 25%. De modo que el cambio de postura, por sí solo, conduce a cambios químicos que configuran el cerebro para una mayor sensación de confianza y comodidad[5].

En muchos aspectos, la postura se convierte en una estrategia hidratante, no solo en algo que le gusta o no a tu madre. Te proponemos un recurso visual para ayudarte a pensar en la alineación de la cabeza en relación con la columna vertebral: imagina que tu cabeza en un balón atado en el extremo de un palo, balanceándose libremente. Es una buena imagen por la que empezar. Alargar o estirar el espacio entre tu cadera y tus costillas también te llevará a adoptar una buena postura y, además, estrecha la cintura.

Desde un punto de vista antropológico, nuestra percepción de la belleza incluye la postura. En general, las mujeres y los hombres que mantienen una posición erguida son considerados más atractivos y son percibidos en mayor medida como líderes.

Pero, a través de la postura, es posible restablecer una hidratación óptima. Adalbert I. Kapandji, reconocido cirujano ortopédico, afirma lo siguiente: «Por cada pulgada (2,5 cm) de inclinación de la cabeza hacia delante, el peso de la cabeza sobre la columna aumenta en 10 libras (4,5 kilos)»[6]. Cuando mantenemos una postura encorvada hacia delante no solo estamos cargando con una cabeza más pesada, sino que además estamos estrechando considerablemente el paso de líquido hacia el cerebro, y mermando su función.

Para lograr una postura perfecta en poco tiempo, a nosotras nos encanta el Método Egoscue, desarrollado por Pete Egoscue en la década de 1970. Su terapia postural ofrece una breve pero completa tabla de ejercicios para entrenar tu consciencia. Nos gusta porque esta técnica tiene en cuenta la relación entre hidratación y drenaje del sistema linfático y es uno de los pocos programas posturales que solo requiere que te tumbes boca arriba con los pies levantados y apoyados en una silla. ¡Era el tipo de ejercicio que nosotras buscábamos! Puedes modificarlo con almohadas para realizarlo en·la cama por la noche mientras lees. Y añade al mismo tiempo algunos micromovimientos.

MICROMOVIMIENTOS EN MARCHA

Ahora que ya hemos hablado de la posición erguida, ¿qué tal si la practicamos en marcha? La mejor manera de asentar una buena postura es caminando. Caminar con una postura alineada es una actividad dinámica, no un episodio de un momento conteniendo la respiración. Otra manera rápida de conseguir una postura excelente es la que propone Teresa Tapp, creadora del programa de ejercicios T-Tapp y autora de *Fit and Fabulous in Fifteen Minutes*. Teresa Tapp se dio cuenta enseguida en su profesión como preparadora física que pequeños movimientos hacían un gran trabajo. También se dio cuenta de que todos tratamos de llegar a una buena postura desde un punto de partida equivocado. «No saques pecho», suplica, «Eleva las costillas e inmediatamente sentirás que los músculos de tu espalda entran en juego». Esos músculos de la espalda están ahí para sujetar la columna mientras caminas.

Por otro lado, Mary Bond, autora de *Las nuevas reglas de la postura*, relaciona la postura con una mejor función cognitiva, al potenciar el estado de alerta y de concentración. Dado que este tipo de buena postura dinámica moviliza de manera natural los materiales de desecho en nuestro sistema, ¿cómo no habría de afectar positivamente a nuestro pensamiento?

300 movimientos

Esther Gokhale ha indagado en la postura desde el punto de vista antropológico. Ha estudiado las tradiciones de la gente en todo el mundo y ha considerado el modo en el que los bebés consiguen el equilibrio. Desde el punto de vista anatómico, somos capaces de más de trescientos tipos distintos de movimiento, si bien en nuestra cultura moderna, cuando alcanzamos la edad adulta, bajamos a un rango de alrededor de treinta. Esto es realmente sorprendente y además provoca dolor, especialmente lumbalgia. En el libro de Gokhale, *8 Steps to a Pain-Free Back* (8 pasos para una espalda sin dolor), asume el reto del limitado rango de movimientos que la vida moderna nos exige y ayuda a revertir las consecuencias del escritorio, del coche y, en general, de una vida aferrada a la inmovilidad.

POR QUÉ LA MEDITACIÓN ES HIDRATANTE

El Dr. Roger Jahnke, fundador del Institute of Integral Qigong and Tai Chi y autor del influyente libro *The Healer Within*, ha sido un defensor incansable de la aplicación en los países occidentales de estrategias de salud y de manejo del estrés de tradición oriental. Nos habla de las antiguas técnicas asiáticas que bloquean las señales de estrés, es decir, las hormonas y sustancias neuroquímicas que se liberan como consecuencia del estrés y que tienen un poderoso efecto deshidratante. Si nos acordamos de soltar el estrés y la tensión varias veces al día, estaremos cambiando la bioquímica de nuestro organismo, al alterar los neurotransmisores. No esperes a llegar a casa para descargarte del estrés de todo el día: practica la micromeditación del mismo modo, o incluso al mismo tiempo, que los micromovimientos. Los círculos con la barbilla o los giros de cabeza representan ocasiones excelentes para una breve meditación. A lo largo del día, amortigua de forma consciente el estrés y la tensión y de esta manera reducirás la carga acumulada. Despréndete de un poco de estrés aquí y de otro poco allí. Tal vez mientras bebes algo despacio, a sorbitos.

Vivimos en una cultura de alto estrés sostenido; nadie escapa a la locura del tráfico, a los plazos sin sentido, a las continuas interrupciones, a las contraseñas online y a otros desasosiegos de la vida moderna. Cuando estamos estresados, nuestros niveles de cortisol y de otras hormonas del estrés aumentan. ¿Y sabes qué? Esas hormonas se encuentran en todos los líquidos corporales y pueden medirse en la sangre y en la saliva. Y esas hormonas, con el tiempo, pueden dañar nuestro organismo, en forma de hipertensión arterial, sobrepeso y depresión de la función inmunitaria. Sin embargo, es posible diluir esas sustancia químicas mediante una hidratación potente. De verdad. Recuerda que somos un 99% agua —en número de moléculas—, de modo que no te «ahogues» en preocupaciones. En lugar de ello, usa el agua y la meditación para diluir las sustancias químicas ligadas al estrés. Te ofrecemos aquí dos formas de meditación para romper el círculo vicioso del estrés.

SUMÉRGETE

Pero volvamos al doctor Roger Jahnke, un extraordinario visionario en lo que se refiere a la fusión entre formas orientales y occidentales de abordar la salud y pionero también en la introducción de técnicas antiestrés en hospitales y comunidades de todo el mundo. En su libro *The Healer within* fusiona movimiento y meditación. Nosotras incluimos aquí nuestra propia versión de la técnica de meditación «Remembering Breath» de Jahnke, con nuestro toque de «agua» al final para convertirla al mismo tiempo en una experiencia de hidratación.

Sentado o de pie, adopta una postura erguida en la que te encuentres cómodo. Coloca la cabeza alta y la barbilla hacia dentro para sentir la alineación de la columna vertebral arriba y en la parte posterior del cráneo, como si alguien estuviera tirando de ti hacia arriba con una cuerda. Realiza una respiración profunda, algo que te resultará más fácil ahora que tus pulmones están libres de todo ese encogimiento. Cierra los ojos e imagina que estás en una piscina, un lago o un mar, con el agua hasta el pecho o el cuello. Al inspirar, imagina que lentamente vas hundiéndote bajo la superficie. Imagina cómo el mundo se desdibuja a medida que te hundes, solos tú, tu respiración y el silencio. Puedes soltar el aire cuando lo desees.

Este ejercicio de meditación dura el tiempo que dura una respiración profunda, aunque puedes practicar la técnica de «desaparición» varias veces a lo largo del día, mientras pasas de una tarea a la siguiente. Esta sencilla secuencia respiratoria rompe el bucle de la preocupación y reinicia tu sistema nervioso autónomo. Es asombroso lo que puede hacer una respiración, aunque tal vez encuentres que quieres quedarte «ahí abajo» más tiempo. Recuerda que la respiración profunda aporta hidratación en forma de vapor a tus pulmones.

AGUA DE BELLEZA

Si tienes la costumbre de llevar una botella de agua, queremos que esa botella de agua sea más hidratante. Las recetas de agua de belleza están pensadas para ser sencillas y no requieren ningún aparato, aportando más agua en gel a tu botella de agua habitual. Cualquier planta puede ayudar a tu agua a aportar más gel. Añadir bayas, cítricos, pepino, ramitas de hierbas y otros vegetales al agua hace más fácil que consumas el agua que realmente necesitas para mantener un buen estado de hidratación.

Te sugerimos que, antes de combinar todos los ingredientes, pruebes cada uno de ellos por separado en agua, para apreciar mejor los sabores. Después podrás mezclarlos. Añade cualquiera de los siguientes ingredientes a 480 ml de agua. Revuelve bien.

- ½ cucharadita de granada en polvo o 1 cucharadita de concentrado líquido de granada
- 1 cucharadita de mermelada de pétalos de rosa
- 1 cucharadita de miel, más una ramita de albahaca, romero o tomillo
- 10 bayas de goji
- 10 arándanos, frambuesas u otras bayas, frescas o congeladas
- 1 chorrito de vinagre balsámico añadido al agua con bayas

- ½ cucharadita de cúrcuma molida y 1 cucharadita de jarabe de arce
- Un trocito de jengibre de 1 a 2,5 cm, al gusto, en daditos
- ½ cucharadita de raíz de remolacha en polvo

Agua de belleza de granada

Las granadas están cargadas de poderosos antioxidantes, vitaminas y minerales. Además, se ha demostrado que el aceite de las semillas tiene beneficiosos efectos antiinflamatorios y que incrementa el colágeno en la piel[7].

- 2 cucharadas de semillas de granada
- 1/8 cucharadita de sal marina gruesa
- 3½ tazas de agua mineral o filtrada

Preparación: Machaca un poco las semillas de granada con el dorso de una cuchara de madera y trasládalas a un frasco de 1 litro de boca ancha. Añade la sal y el agua. Puedes enfriarla en el frigorífico o tomarla a temperatura ambiente, sin necesidad de colar el agua.

No existe una crema tópica que iguale la hidratación interna. En el siguiente capítulo, nuestro Plan Quench te guiará por el buen camino para tener un aspecto vital y disfrutar con salud de la vida.

CAPÍTULO 8

El Plan Quench

En cualquier circunstancia, simplemente haz las cosas lo
mejor que puedas y evitarás la autocrítica, el autocastigo y el
arrepentimiento.

Dr. Miguel Ruiz

La hidratación es la acción más poderosa a tu alcance ya que, en número de moléculas, somos agua en un 99%. ¿Quieres sentirte más centrado en el trabajo? ¿Quieres tener más energía para poder superar el día sin pasar por el bajón de la tarde? ¿Quieres acabar tu jornada laboral y que todavía te quede energía para disfrutar de la noche?

Con el Plan Quench conocerás un nuevo nivel de hidratación, salud y energía, a través de instrucciones fáciles de seguir y que te permitirán preparar bebidas «inteligentes». Recuerda los tres principios esenciales de la hidratación que te presentamos en los capítulos anteriores:

1. **Absorción:** obtén el máximo de absorción del agua que bebes para que alcance el mayor nivel celular y produzca energía.
2. **Agua de los alimentos:** comer alimentos con un alto contenido de agua favorece una hidratación profunda. Nuestros *smoothies* vegetales, por ejemplo, hidratan mejor que la misma cantidad de agua embotellada y aportan un alto nivel de nutrición.
3. **Movimiento:** te enseñaremos micromovimientos esenciales y de fácil realización, que llevan la hidratación directamente a puntos clave, como cuello y articulaciones, para mantenerlos flexibles y sin dolor.

¿Cómo puedes conseguir mayor hidratación en tu día a día? Pues bien, es fácil:

1. Bebe a sorbitos un «*smoothie* inteligente». Un vaso tiene más poder hidratante que el agua.
2. Añade unas cuantas bebidas en momentos clave del día.
3. Come alimentos que hidratan, y no alimentos que deshidratan.

Hemos diseñado el Plan Quench en cinco días para potenciar la hidratación: no es un plan para perder peso ni centímetros, aunque puede tener también este efecto. Y no se trata de contar calorías; se trata de conseguir por fin una hidratación óptima. Es un plan que proporciona a todo tu organismo lo que necesita para funcionar de manera óptima. Te sentirás mejor, dormirás mejor, te moverás mejor e incluso envejecerás mejor. Tu rendimiento mental y tu rendimiento físico mejorarán, así como tu piel, tus digestiones y tu movilidad. Y no te extrañe si pierdes algún que otro kilo. Pero ese número en la báscula es menos importante que cómo te sientes. Este plan de cinco días te enseña la manera de empezar, pero su aplicación a largo plazo equilibrará tu peso y mejorará tu salud en todos los frentes. Para que te resulte más fácil, hemos diseñado el plan de manera que solo tendrás que introducir en tu vida diaria algunos pequeños hábitos, pensados para impulsar cambios a largo plazo en tu nivel de energía y en tu salud.

¿Por qué cinco días? Es el período de una jornada laboral típica, de modo que podrás incorporar fácilmente el plan a tu rutina diaria. Y cuando llegue el día cinco, empezarás a notar la diferencia. Cuando veas los resultados, querrás seguir «apagando tu sed». Y si te caes del «tren del agua», como nos ha pasado a todos, lo sabrás y tendrás ahí tu plan de recuperación, listo para reemprenderlo. Pero volvamos al plan.

Ofrecemos aquí instrucciones claras, fáciles y sencillas así como recetas y consejos que te acompañarán a lo largo de cinco días completos, para llevarte a un lugar realmente nuevo y necesario en nuestro mundo moderno. El agua es el combustible de nuestro organismo y nosotras vamos a enseñarte dónde y cómo puedes «repostar» para obtener los niveles más altos de energía y concentración. Te damos la opción de elegir entre uno o dos *smoothies*, te sugerimos cuáles son los mejores momentos para beber, te facilitamos instrucciones para tus movimientos diarios y te proponemos ejemplos de comidas sanas e hidratantes.

Añadimos un ingrediente nuevo cada día, porque queremos que tus papilas gustativas disfruten durante todo el plan de cinco días. Si en algún momento te aburres, utiliza la segunda receta que te proponemos cada día. Tú eliges: puedes optar por la modalidad sencilla de cinco días con la receta propuesta para cada día o diseñar tu propio plan eligiendo una receta de nuestra sección de recetas para cada uno de los cinco días. Cualquiera de las dos modalidades hidrata de manera óptima. Combina y mezcla durante los cinco días y también en el futuro.

Lo mejor del Plan Quench es que es muy suave. Recuerda, la hidratación es el punto inicial de la homeostasis, del equilibrio en el cuerpo, y eso es lo que hacemos con el plan de cinco días: recalibrar tus niveles de hidratación. No tenemos que advertirte frente a la posibilidad de dolores de cabeza, reacciones detox, erupciones cutáneas, estreñimiento o hambre. La hidratación no te hará más que bien, devolviéndote tu energía y vitalidad.

LOS *SMOOTHIES* SALVAN EL DÍA

Puede decirse que el pilar del programa que proponemos en *Apaga tu sed* son sus deliciosos *smoothies*. Si hay una cosa que tienes que hacer para potenciar tu hidratación es añadir un *smoothie* a tu menú todos los días. Este simple gesto hará un gran servicio a tu cuerpo: hidratación unida a densa nutrición y fibra. Te proporcionamos numerosas y deliciosas recetas, pero tienes absoluta libertad para crear las tuyas. También te hacemos sugerencias de platos saludables para favorecer una adecuada hidratación a través de la comida, no solo con la bebida. Después de comer y de beber, te enseñamos a conducir esa hidratación hasta todos los tejidos de tu cuerpo mediante sencillos pero eficaces micromovimientos y técnicas de respiración. Esta doble estrategia funciona al unísono incrementando la fluidez corporal, gracias a la hidratación, la nutrición, la flexibilidad y la integración mente-cuerpo.

¿Por qué son los *smoothies* la base del Plan Quench? Los *smoothies* ofrecen la perfecta combinación de nutrición e hidratación. No solo

potencian la hidratación porque aportan el agua que encierran las plantas, sino que, según el doctor Joel Fuhrman, presidente de la Nutritional
Research Foundation, la comida que debemos masticar libera solo un
35 % del material nutricional de los alimentos, mientras que los alimentos que, mezclados en la licuadora, podemos beber aportan nutrientes
biodisponible en un 90 %, lo cual significa que son más fácilmente
absorbibles.

   ¿Cómo te gustaría incrementar tu ingesta nutritiva sin comprar
costosos suplementos, sin tener que comer toneladas extra de alimentos y cuidando al mismo tiempo tus necesidades de hidratación? En
nuestra estresada vida moderna, realmente ni siquiera masticamos la
comida ¡la engullimos! Incluso si se trata de una magnífica ensalada
de productos ecológicos, no es posible descomponer los alimentos en
medida suficiente para extraer todos los nutrientes que encierran, a
no ser que masticaras cada bocado hasta convertirlo en líquido. Esto
significa que se pierde más de la mitad del valor nutritivo de la ensalada. Lo bueno es que la licuadora realiza a la perfección ese trabajo
por nosotros. Y si mantienes el primer par de sorbos de *smoothie* en
la boca durante unos segundos antes de tragártelos, estarás activando
las enzimas digestivas que se producen al salivar y activando de esta
manera el proceso completo.

   Además, los *smoothies* proporcionan fibra, que reduce de manera
eficaz la velocidad de tránsito y favorece la hidratación y la nutrición,
dando pie a una mayor absorción de líquidos y nutrientes. Este ha sido
uno de nuestros mayores hallazgos. Beber demasiada agua embotellada
a excesiva velocidad puede lavar tu sistema, a no ser que el agua vaya
acompañada de esos alimentos ricos en fibra que favorecen la absorción.
Toda esa agua de bebida puede realmente arrastrar fuera del organismo electrolitos y nutrientes muy importantes y que hacen posible una
hidratación completa. La absorción del agua que ingieres puede además salvarte de visitar demasiado a menudo el baño. Los *smoothies*
ayudan a disminuir la velocidad de tránsito de los líquidos, de manera
que el organismo disponga de más tiempo para su absorción. Y además
combaten el temido estreñimiento; el alimento comienza su periplo ya
hidratado en origen.

ESTUDIO DE CASO DE LA DRA. DANA COHEN

Danielle

Hace unos años, *Danielle,* una mujer de cuarenta y nueve años, vino a verme por primera vez por cansancio y aumento de peso debido a la menopausia. Contaba que llevaba mucho tiempo ganando y perdiendo el mismo par de kilos. «Es como un yoyó; cada vez que pienso que ya voy por el buen camino, me subo a la báscula y me decepciono». Para complicar algo más la situación, era prediabética y tenía una glándula tiroides perezosa. Le prescribí medicación tiroidea, terapia de sustitución hormonal y un fármaco para el azúcar en sangre llamado metformina. Le fue bien, y perdió ese peso que la obsesionaba. Recientemente vino a consulta para una revisión: seguía manteniendo el peso, pero se quejaba de ligero estreñimiento. Había seguido una dieta de moda, la «Whole 30» o dieta paleo extrema, un estricto plan de alimentos sin procesar, pero sin legumbres ni cereales.

Fue más o menos la época en la que estábamos pidiendo a algunos de mis pacientes que participaran de un estudio informal para valorar nuestro Programa Quench. Danielle estaba ya participando, pero yo no lo sabía. Y no lo supe hasta el mismo día de la entrega del libro terminado a la editorial.

Ese día era además el cumpleaños de Gina, que decidió celebrar al mismo tiempo su aniversario y la entrega del manuscrito de *Apaga tu sed* brindando con una copa de vino, antes de reunirse con su familia para cenar. En el bar que eligió para la celebración, una mujer se sentó al lado de Gina y las dos empezaron a charlar. La conversación fue derivando hacia la medicina y la mujer en cuestión le reveló que ella acudía a una magnífica doctora de medicina holística. Y que esa doctora estaba escribiendo un libro sobre la hidratación. Gina se quedó con la boca abierta y le preguntó: ¿No será la doctora Dana Cohen?».

«¡Sí! ¿La conoces?», preguntó la mujer, que resultó ser Danielle.

«No solo la conozco, ¡estoy escribiendo ese libro con ella!»

«¡No me digas! ¡He seguido el programa y me siento estupenda-mente!».

¿Cómo podía ser? Resultaba que Danielle había sido una de las primeras personas en poner en práctica el Plan Quench y yo la había descubierto ¡el día de la entrega de la obra!

Dado que Danielle se había sentido mal por no haber vuelto a consulta para completar el estudio, llamó a Dana a la semana siguiente. Le contó que había sufrido dolores de cabeza durante todo el verano, pero que al *segundo* día de comenzar el programa, por la mañana, los dolores de cabeza habían desaparecido. También le dijo que tenía más energía y que se sentía mucho más despierta y centrada en el trabajo. También se había dado cuenta de que, al cuarto día, le habían disminuido mucho las bolsas bajo los ojos.

Danielle continúa con la dieta Whole 30, pero ha incorporado frutas y verduras más hidratantes y le gusta realizar los micromovimientos todas las mañanas para comenzar bien el día.

Cuando comiences con la receta de nuestro sencillo *smoothie* básico, te descubrirás de repente deseando añadir nuevos ingredientes y preparando variantes. Recuerda el sencillo principio de que las verduras de hoja son agua en un 98% y están cargadas de nutrientes. Esto te motivará y te llevará a introducir otras verduras de hoja en tus *smoothies*, que te resultarán así más variados, deliciosos y llenos de sabor.

Poco a poco irás desarrollando tu sentido del gusto, por ejemplo en lo referente a si prefieres los *smoothies* más o menos densos. Aprenderás con la práctica a jugar con combinaciones y texturas, descubriendo incluso que batir durante un minuto da lugar a un *smoothie* de sabor diferente que si lo bates durante dos minutos. También deberás tener en cuenta que las distintas marcas de licuadoras difieren en cuanto a los tiempos necesarios para obtener la textura de *smoothie* que te gusta.

Creemos que, en este terreno, actuar siguiendo un plan muy cuadriculado es insostenible. Pensamos, por el contrario, que esto debe ser como caminar con una brújula, de tal manera que una pequeña variación de apenas unos grados puede conducirte a un destino totalmente nuevo. Lo único que te pedimos es que lo intentes durante cinco días: estarás así en el camino de alcanzar una hidratación mayor y más profunda. Durante esos cinco días sentirás que tienes más energía, mayor agilidad y menor rigidez, tendrás mejor humor y te concentrarás mejor. Y aunque hemos diseñado el Plan Quench para llevarte en cinco días a un nivel superior de hidratación, creemos que querrás usar ya estas técnicas durante toda la vida. Te ofrecemos todo cuanto necesitas para poder continuar personalizando y redefiniendo el plan en función de tus necesidades cambiantes.

Una vez que hayas empezado, querrás continuar con tu viaje de hidratación. El plan está diseñado para dar un fuerte impulso a tu salud pero, cuando te des cuenta de lo bien que te sienta, querrás seguir aplicándolo durante toda tu vida.

Los ancianos y los *smoothies*

¿Te acuerdas de los intentos de Gina de abordar la deshidratación crónica de su madre, aspecto que mencionábamos en el prólogo?

Para poner remedio al problema, Gina añadió semillas de chía molidas al zumo de naranja que tomaba su madre todas las mañanas. Ese simple gesto supuso el fin de las frecuentes infecciones urinarias de su madre. ¿Por qué moler las semillas? Las semillas molidas liberan más gel, al ser mayor el área superficial de exposición, y además el polvo no irrita la mucosa intestinal. Aquellas personas a las que les da miedo comer semillas porque les han diagnosticado diverticulitis intestinal, un trastorno que padece a menudo la gente mayor con algún grado de deshidratación, no tienen por qué preocuparse. Las semillas están pulverizadas y no hay posibilidad de que se queden estancadas en los sáculos de la diverticulosis. Nosotras nos preocupamos por nuestros mayores y esperamos de manera especial que también ellos sigan el programa, ya que la mayor parte de ellos pueden utilizarlo. Si un anciano no es capaz de preparar los *smoothies,* puede emplear verduras en polvo y añadir las semillas de chía molidas. Aparte de esto, cabe la posibilidad de añadir simplemente semillas de chía molidas a un vaso de zumo, como hizo Gina con su madre. Nuestros ancianos no tienen que pasar sed[1]. Y este es un plan perfecto para los ancianos: dado el mayor poder de absorción de los alimentos vegetales, el estreñimiento disminuirá, gracias también al contenido más alto de fibra, y las vitaminas y minerales contribuirán a una mayor claridad y fortaleza mental, entre otras cosas. Añade unos fáciles y suaves micromovimientos para favorecer a la agilidad y al equilibrio, incluso si el anciano utiliza una silla de ruedas o está postrado en la cama.

LAS VENTAJAS DE HACER PIS

El mecanismo de la hidratación supone, no solo entrada de agua en el organismo, sino también salida. El Plan Quench está pensado para que una buena cantidad de agua entre en tu organismo a lo largo del día. Es posible que aumente la frecuencia de tus micciones, pero ello no es un inconveniente. Se supone que todos tenemos que orinar cada dos o tres horas: es un signo de que se está bien hidratado. De esta manera se eliminan más desechos y más rápidamente, y además contribuye a que nos movamos. Piénsalo un poco: ¡todos esos paseos al baño son movimiento! Si estás bien hidratado, deberás ir al baño entre seis y siete veces al día ¿Cuántas veces has pasado todo el día en el trabajo y te has dado cuenta luego de que has ido al baño apenas una vez? Estamos aquí para decirte que eso no es bueno. Cuando sientas como resultado una menor fatiga, darás la bienvenida a esas interrupciones para ir al baño.

En el momento en que tu masa de agua corporal alcanza su nivel óptimo, todo tu organismo funciona mucho mejor. Toma nota de tus mejorías: menos dolores de cabeza, más energía, mayor flexibilidad, mejor humor, piel más limpia, menos hinchazón y sueño nocturno más reparador. *Celebra estos signos*.

Nuestro plan es ideal prácticamente para cualquiera. Si tienes algún problema de salud subyacente, como diabetes o alguna enfermedad cardíaca, debes consultar a tu médico o nutricionista. Ellos pueden ayudarte a controlar las sugerencias para las comida que mejor se ajusten a tu enfermedad. Lee primero el plan para ver qué delicias te esperan.

CÓMO COMENZAR EL PLAN QUENCH EN CINCO DÍAS

Material que necesitarás:

- Licuadora de cualquier tipo (consulta el apartado «101 licuadoras» en el capítulo 9).
- Botella de agua, mínimo de 500 ml y preferiblemente de vidrio o acero inoxidable y apta para lavavajillas.

Lista de la compra para el plan de cinco días (ingredientes fríos y calientes, elegidos según tus preferencias):

- Brotes de alfalfa (1 paquete)
- Vinagre de sidra de manzana, crudo (500 ml)
- Mantequilla de origen ecológico y sin sal (1 barra) o ghee (1 tarrina)
- Canela o cardamomo, molido (1 frasquito)
- Anacardos o nueces crudas o semillas molidas, como por ejemplo de girasol, calabaza o cáñamo (1 paquete)
- Semillas de chía (paquete de ¼ kilo), mejor molidas para una mayor absorción; puedes molerlas en un molinillo de café, o usarlas enteras
- Leche de coco, no edulcorada (1 lata, con toda su grasa, o 1 cartón)
- Agua de coco, no edulcorada (dos frascos de 240 ml), opcional
- Pepinos (3)
- Raíz de jengibre (pieza de 5 a 10 cm)
- Miel cruda (1 tarro)
- Limones (2)
- Limas (2)
- Jarabe de arce o stevia (1 envase pequeño)
- Pera (1) o manzana (1)
- Concentrado de zumo de granada (1 botella). Sustituir por concentrados de zumo de uva, arándano o cereza. Si no puedes encontrar concentrados, utiliza zumo de granada o sustitúyelo por zumo de naranja o de pomelo (1 cartón)
- Frambuesas, congeladas o frescas (1 paquete)
- Sal marina natural sin refinar o de roca (finamente molida)

- Té, manzanilla y/o regaliz (5 bolsitas de té)
- Agua destilada, filtrada o de manantial, pero asegúrate de agregar sal según las indicaciones (7,5 litros) consulta a continuación el recuadro. ¿Cuáles son las diferencias entre las distintas aguas?

¿Cuáles son las diferencias entre las distintas aguas?

El **agua purificada** se caracteriza por carecer de contaminantes. Es un término legal y, para poder llevar esta etiqueta, el agua debe contener niveles extremadamente bajos de impurezas. Suele obtenerse mediante algún tipo de proceso de destilación, en el cual se lleva el agua a ebullición y a continuación se recoge el vapor y se utiliza para producir agua **destilada.** También es posible purificar el agua mediante ósmosis inversa y desionización. Por desgracia, de esta manera el agua pierde también electrolitos y minerales.

El **agua de manantial** emana de manera natural de una fuente subterránea (acuífero), se filtra a través de la propia tierra y es por ello rica en minerales de la tierra, si bien puede no responder a la definición legal de agua purificada. Este tipo de agua es de mejor calidad si se recoge directamente de la fuente. El agua «de manantial» embotellada no es mucho mejor que el agua del grifo. En general, esa agua que las grandes compañías nos venden como agua procedente «directamente del manantial» es transportada hasta los centros de embotellado en grandes camiones diésel y se le añade cloro para protegerla de las bacterias. Seguramente no era esta la imagen que tenías en la cabeza.

El **agua mineral** procede de una fuente subterránea protegida y debe contener algunos minerales, que suelen ser magnesio y compuestos azufrados. Además, el agua mineral tiene gases naturales y es efervescente en la naturaleza.

El **agua artesiana** se extrae de un pozo en comunicación con un acuífero cerrado, que contiene agua subterránea a presión positiva.

El **agua de seltz,** el **agua con gas** y las **aguas carbonatadas** son básicamente agua con burbujas fruto de un proceso de carbonatación, o adición de dióxido de carbono. Nosotras preferimos el agua mineral con gas natural; todas sus modalidades son buenas y básicamente son la misma agua. El único inconveniente que se nos ocurre es que puede sentar mal al estómago o empeorar el reflujo en las personas con este trastorno; entonces, obviamente, no es buena idea consumir este tipo de agua. Evita también el agua con edulcorantes añadidos o, pero aún, con edulcorantes artificiales.

POR QUÉ NUESTRA LISTA DE LA COMPRA ES TAN HIDRATANTE

Nuestra lista de la compra está integrada por alimentos que (1) ayudan a absorber el agua y (2) activan la carga de las moléculas de agua. Citamos a continuación la razón por la cual cada alimento de la lista favorece de un modo concreto la hidratación, aunque tienen, además, otras propiedades nutritivas.

Brotes de alfalfa. La alfalfa es agua en más de un 90% y está cargada de valiosos minerales traza, como el manganeso, esencial para una digestión eficiente. Aparte del alto contenido mineral, que activa la carga como si fuera una batería en colaboración con el elevado contenido de agua, la alfalfa es también una rica fuente de vitaminas A, B, C, E y K.

Vinagre de sidra de manzana, crudo. El vinagre de sidra de manzana es un líquido rico en potasio que lleva agua hasta el interior de las células. Además es alcalinizante, de manera que acelera la digestión y ayuda a bajar los niveles de azúcar en sangre. Recomendamos utilizar vinagre de sidra de manzana crudo durante todo el plan propuesto en *Apaga tu sed*. Se obtiene a partir de los azúcares de manzanas maduras mediante fermentación con levaduras. La forma cruda, que suele tener un aspecto turbio, contiene gran cantidad de vitaminas, minerales, proteínas, bacterias beneficiosas y enzimas. Los minerales son especialmente necesarios para que la hidratación llegue a todos los tejidos y células. Cuando se somete a pasteurización, pierde gran parte de los efectos beneficiosos a los que está ligado. Se ha observado clínicamente que, en el ser humano, el vinagre de sidra de manzana mejora la sensibilidad a la insulina y baja los azúcares en sangre. Y en algunos estudios animales, reduce los niveles de colesterol y triglicéridos.

Mantequilla ecológica. Puede parecer que la mantequilla es un alimento insólito en materia de hidratación, pero estudios científicos recientes están demostrando que las grasas, como lípidos que son, tienen un papel importante en la transferencia de agua desde el exterior hasta el interior de la célula.

Cardamomo. El cardamomo tiene propiedades diuréticas, de manera que reduce la hinchazón y limpia las vías urinarias, la vejiga y los riñones, eliminando residuos de desecho, sales, agua en exceso y toxinas. Ayuda además a combatir las infecciones.

Anacardos. Los anacardos cuentan con una combinación hidratante de minerales como cobre, fósforo, cinc, magnesio, hierro y sobre todo selenio, un mineral poco frecuente en los alimentos, pero esencial. Contienen además una gran cantidad de grasas monoinsaturadas cardiosaludables.

Chía. La chía es la semilla con mayor capacidad de liberación de agua en gel y es muy rica en ácidos grasos omega 3. Los ácidos grasos son necesarios para mover el agua hasta el interior de las células. Las semillas de chía, con toda su densidad de nutrientes, extienden además una película protectora y permeable que reviste el tubo digestivo, protegiéndolo frente a los alimentos ácidos y especiados. La chía frena la liberación de insulina, reduce la presión arterial y favorece unas deposiciones regulares. Además, 25 gramos de chía contienen más de 8 g de fibra, de manera que ayuda a retener la hidratación. La chía es una fuente de proteína de fácil digestión, pues 100 gramos contienen 14 g de proteínas. ¡Un auténtico superalimento!

Canela. Rica en agentes antioxidantes y antiinflamatorios, la utilizamos para contrarrestar los azúcares de nuestras recetas, pues es sabido que la canela regula los niveles de glucosa en sangre.

Leche de coco. El coco es delicioso y muy nutritivo. Su leche es rica en esas grasas que ayudan a regular el flujo de agua hacia el interior de la célula. Además, proporciona una hidratación mucho mejor que la leche de soja o almendras.

Agua de coco. El agua de coco es muy rica en electrolitos, que son minerales activados, con carga eléctrica y que proporcionan energía a las células de nuestro cuerpo.

Pepino. Los pepinos están cargados de agua en gel. Los utilizamos sobre todo los primeros dos días del programa.

Ghee. El ghee es una mantequilla clarificada, que se calienta hasta que las partículas lácteas hierven. El proceso da como resultado una elevada concentración de ácido butírico, un importante ácido graso que interviene en la salud intestinal. Pero hay más: pruebas llevadas a cabo por el Pollack Lab muestran que el ghee tiene una concentración tan alta de gel de agua como las semillas de chía.

Raíz de jengibre. El jengibre favorece una rápida y eficaz filtración renal y activa una captación más rápida de insulina, protegiendo tus células.

Miel cruda. La miel es humectante y demulcente, es decir, es un agente hidratante natural que aumenta la humedad. Los agentes demulcentes aportan humedad y los humectantes la sellan para su conservación.

Limones. Tanto los limones como las limas contienen pectina. La pectina es conocida porque integra el gel de las mermeladas. Ambas frutas son ricas en electrolitos naturales. Reponen los minerales del cuerpo y calman la sed más rápidamente que el agua sola, precisamente porque los agentes minerales regulan el traslado de agua al interior de las células. El calcio, el potasio y el magnesio son los minerales clave que actúan como reguladores de los impulsos eléctricos que mantienen en funcionamiento nuestro organismo.

Limas. Las limas contienen altas cantidades de hidrógeno, que ayuda al cuerpo a formar gel mediante su carga mineral, superando por muy poco al limón.

Jarabe de arce. El jarabe de arce está lleno de minerales y de una sorprendente cantidad de antioxidantes, comparable con una ración de bayas.

Peras. Las peras son una fuente sorprendente de fibra: una pera de tamaño medio contiene casi seis gramos de fibra. Esta combinación de fibra absorbente y jugosidad retiene la hidratación y evita que el agua lave nuestro organismo.

Zumo de granada. Las granadas tienen un contenido de agua del 82%, en combinación perfecta con potasio, un nutriente necesario para que la hidratación traspase la pared celular. Media taza de zumo de granada cubre más de un 14% de las necesidades diarias de vitamina C.

Frambuesas. Las frambuesas contienen ocho gramos de fibra por taza y están cargadas de pectina. Pertenecen a la familia de las rosas; las rosas también son conocidas por su alto contenido de pectina.

Sal. Las sales de mar y de roca, a diferencia de la sal de mesa procesada, ayuda a conducir la hidratación hasta el interior celular, proporcionando los necesarios minerales traza sin propiciar la hinchazón.

Infusiones. Utilizamos infusiones de manzanilla y/o regaliz, que favorecen el sueño y combaten la hinchazón.

¡Agua! El agua mineral o de manantial tiene de forma natural sus propios minerales. El agua filtrada o destilada carece de ellos. Simplemente añade una pizca de sal marina o de roca por ración de agua filtrada o destilada.

Un toque dulce

Supongamos que quedas para merendar un día de estos en una cafetería cualquiera de tu ciudad. Las posibles opciones te bombardearán: azúcar blanquilla normal de mesa (sacarosa), edulcorantes artificiales como aspartamo, sucralosa y sacarina; y, si vas a un sitio más orientado a lo natural, tendrás también seguramente azúcares naturales como stevia, agave, azúcar moreno y miel ¿Qué debes elegir?

Lo mejor sería abstenerse de todos ellos, pero algunas personas necesitamos un poco de dulce en la vida. De modo que, si vas a tomar dulce, elige los mejores productos. Hay que optar siempre por lo natural y crudo, y por una buena razón. Los azúcares naturales, generalmente procedentes de la fruta, encierran en su interior minerales saludables y fibra. Y en cuanto al azúcar, su consumo debe ser siempre limitado. Somos conscientes de que algunos de los siguientes ingredientes pueden resultar difíciles de encontrar, pero cada día son más populares como opción natural, de modo que hemos decidido incluirlos aquí.

¿Qué debes evitar? No recomendamos los edulcorantes artificiales. PUNTO. Tampoco somos fans del agave, aunque tenga un bajo índice glucémico, porque en realidad tiene más calorías que el azúcar y puede contener más de un 70% de fructosa, que es más de lo que contiene el jarabe de maíz, ya de por sí muy rico en fructosa. Además, sus efectos no han sido aún debidamente estudiados. De modo que evítalo.

¿Qué debo emplear?

Stevia. La stevia, que se extrae de las hojas de la planta del mismo nombre, es en nuestra opinión la mejor elección de edulcorante para cualquier persona, incluso si se tienen problemas de azúcar en sangre. Tiene cero calorías y no produce efecto alguno sobre la glucemia. No obstante, deja cierto regusto amargo en la boca, por lo que aconsejamos empezar por pequeñas cantidades e ir probando poco a poco. Hay personas que prefieren la stevia líquida.

Miel ecológica cruda. La miel es rica en fructosa, pero también tiene una buena cantidad de antioxidantes y no está procesada en absoluto, de manera que conserva todo su valor nutricional, aunque este no sea el caso de la mayor parte de las mieles que se venden en los supermercados. ¡Se dice también que la miel alivia los síntomas de alergia!

Jarabe de arce. El jarabe de arce tiene un elevado índice glucémico (aunque no tan elevado como el azúcar de mesa), pero también posee una gran riqueza en antioxidantes y minerales. Úsalo con moderación. Y asegúrate de que procede de verdad de arces (cuánto más oscuro, más rotundo es el sabor). Se clasifica en función de la intensidad de color y de sabor, no por su contenido mineral, de modo que elige aquel cuyo sabor te guste más.

Melazas. Este líquido espeso y oscuro se obtiene como residuo a partir de la caña de azúcar refinada. Es rico en hierro y minerales, especialmente calcio y magnesio, y su índice glucémico es más bajo que el del azúcar. Quizá tengas que acostumbrarte a su sabor.

Panela / raspadura / piloncillo. Dulce tradicional en diversos países, la panela o piloncillo se prepara deshidratando la caña de azúcar, sin refinar, de manera que quedan los minerales y antioxidantes. Tiene la misma cantidad de calorías que el azúcar de mesa, pero es mejor porque conserva intactos los nutrientes. No obstante, empléalo con moderación.

***Jaggery* o *gur*.** Muy popular en la India y en otros países de Asia, el jaggery se obtiene de la savia del árbol de la palma, así como de la caña de azúcar (es similar a la panela). Dulce y no refinado, es rico en minerales como el hierro.

Savia de maguey. Originaria de México, este azúcar rico en fibra es un poco más difícil de encontrar, pero seguro que con él impresionarás a tus amigos. Es un endulzante sin refinar que se prepara a partir de la planta de agave, de manera que contiene muchos antioxidantes y tiene mucha fibra prebiótica, que nutre nuestras bacterias intestinales beneficiosas.

Regaliz. ¿Sabías que el regaliz es aproximadamente cincuenta veces más dulce que el azúcar y tiene un índice glucémico igual a cero? Sabe a... en fin, a regaliz, pero es apropiado para diabéticos, lo cual es una ventaja. Puede que no se le de mucha propaganda, pero es una buena opción como edulcorante; tiene un sabor peculiar.

Fruta monje o *lo han guo.* Es una fruta originaria del sudeste asiático. Su extracto ha ganado popularidad como sustituto del azúcar en los últimos años, pues tiene cero calorías y es 150 veces más dulce que el azúcar (¡sí, no nos hemos equivocado al teclear!). Además es rico en antioxidantes y tiene un bajo índice glucémico. ¡Y sabe genial!

Nota: Si eres diabético o tienes problemas de azúcar en sangre, debes consultar a tu médico o nutricionista sobre los azúcares que son más adecuados en tu caso.

IDEAS PARA COMIDAS

Junto con nuestro plan de hidratación, ofrecemos ideas simples y sugerencias para fomentar hábitos alimentarios buenos y saludables y que tal vez quieras seguir durante los cinco días del plan. Con este programa de hidratación, puedes ser vegano o paleo, según tus preferencias, puedes comer lo que quieras y parar cuando estés lleno, si bien potenciarás los efectos saludables del plan si sigues las sencillas pautas que a continuación te ofrecemos según tu tipo de alimentación.

Debes comer:

- Fruta. Una buena regla general en lo que respecta a la fruta es consumir solo frutas de bajo índice glucémico, como bayas o frutos del bosque, melocotones, ciruelas, pomelo, kiwi y melón. Frutas más exóticas, como la papaya, el mango, la piña y el plátano, tienen un contenido mas alto de azúcar, de modo que consúmelas menos a menudo. Procura no utilizar plátanos para tus *smoothies*, o usa solo la mitad si no puedes prescindir de él. O, mejor aún, sustitúyelo por medio aguacate, que tiene incluso más potasio que un plátano. O ve más allá y sustitúyelo por media taza de batata machacada, un sustituto cuyo sabor te sorprenderá.

- Verduras crudas y cocinadas.
- Sopas y cremas, que por supuesto constituyen otra importante estrategia de hidratación. Consulta nuestra sección de recetas, donde encontrarás algunas buenas ideas, y evita las sopas de lata o cartón que se venden ya preparadas, pues tienen demasiado sodio.
- Frutos secos y legumbres. Mezcla los frutos secos para disfrutar de una mayor variedad. Pon en remojo las alubias antes de cocinarlas, para evitar las lectinas, que pueden ser perjudiciales.
- Pescado: mejor si es capturado en estado salvaje.

¿Comer alimentos ecológicos mejora la hidratación?

¡Sí! Los alimentos ecológicos tienen una gran ventaja sobre las frutas y verduras cultivadas del modo convencional. No estarás comiéndote los pesticidas con los que se rocían las cosechas, de manera que la hidratación no tendrá que ser empleada para tratar de eliminar los agentes químicos. La mayoría de los alimentos ecológicos se cultivan en suelos con más nutrientes, especialmente minerales. Estos minerales son clave para que el agua hidratante sea absorbida por el cuerpo. Además, los minerales colaboran con las moléculas de agua para generar energía para las funciones orgánicas. Aun así, en suelos en monocultivo, se pierden muchos minerales clave. Cuando los agricultores prestan atención a la salud del suelo, como hacen los que se dedican al cultivo ecológico, los alimentos vegetales resultantes encierran minerales fácilmente disponibles para el organismo. El efecto beneficioso para el ser humano no es solo una mejor nutrición, sino una hidratación más eficiente y vitalizante. Si no tienes la oportunidad de comprar productos ecológicos, considera la posibilidad de tomar un suplemento mineral. Puedes consultar la sección de Recursos donde figura la lista publicada por el Environmental Working Group de las frutas y verduras que no deben comerse si no son ecológicas y de aquellas con las que puedes ser más permisivo cuando vayas a comprar.

Algunos alimentos requieren mayor hidratación para su completa digestión, de modo que te recomendamos evitar la siguiente lista:

- Carbohidratos simples como pasta y pan
- Alimentos procesados
- Azúcar añadido
- Grasas trans
- Aceites hidrogenados y parcialmente hidrogenados
- Edulcorantes artificiales, como sucralosa, sacarina y aspartamo

Pescado

Algunos peces, como el marlín, el atún, el tiburón, el pez espada y la caballa, tienen concentraciones más altas de mercurio que otros, de modo que ten cuidado a la hora de elegirlos para tu menú, especialmente si estás embarazada o tienes niños. Entra en la página web de NRDC.org para consultar La Smart Seafood Buying Guide y conocer el contenido de mercurio de los distintos pescados.

Por último, aunque no por ello menos importante, el agua en forma líquida debe formar parte de tu dieta. Si lo necesitas, bebe agua a lo largo del día para apagar tu sed. No tienes que añadir sal al agua cada vez que bebas. Además, como parte del Plan Quench, bebe una taza o dos de agua antes de cada comida.

COMIDAS

Las siguientes sugerencias son excelentes para las distintas comidas del día y te permiten introducir alimentos más hidratantes en tus hábitos diarios. Además, una vez que hayas terminado con el plan de cinco días, consulta nuestras recetas del siguiente capítulo, «Todo lo que necesitas».

Sugerencias para el desayuno

Tal vez encuentres que un *smoothie* es suficiente para algunas comidas, pero si todavía tienes hambre, he aquí algunas buenas ideas para el desayuno.

- Huevos preparados como prefieras; pruébalos con verduras de hoja salteadas, como espinacas, kale o acelgas
- Avena irlandesa / crema de arroz / mijo caliente con láminas de almendras y arándanos
- Salmón ahumando con alcaparras y cebollitas encurtidas
- Pieza de fruta untada con mantequilla de frutos secos
- Las sobras son una idea excelente para el desayuno. ¿Quién dijo que el desayuno no puede ser sabroso? Nosotras, a menudo, dejamos adrede algo de la cena y lo guardamos para el desayuno del día siguiente. El salmón con salsa *beurre blanc* está buenísimo frío y mata dos pájaros de un tiro: ¡menos calorías para la cena y desayuno ya listo!

Sugerencias para el almuerzo

- Pollo o salmón a la plancha con ensalada
- Ensalada de alubias con radicchio o lechuga romana
- Escarola salteada. Añade alubias en conserva, riega con un chorrito de aceite de oliva virgen extra y esparce por encima queso parmesano
- Ensalada Niçoise: huevo duro, atún en láminas, judías verdes y rabanitos sobre alguna verdura de hoja
- Pollo, verdura y/o alubias o lentejas

Sugerencias para la cena

Toma una ración de cada categoría:

- Proteína a tu elección: carne de ganado alimentado preferiblemente con pastos, cerdo, pollo o pavo de origen ecológico, pescado salvaje (procura comerlo al menos dos veces por semana), alubias

- Una ensalada pequeña, aunque solo sea lechuga iceberg con aceite de oliva y una pizca de sal, orégano y un poco de vinagre de vino tinto. ¡Y cualquier otra verdura que te guste, por supuesto!
- Guarnición de verduras: la favorita de Dana es brécol salteado con aceite de nuez de macadamia (delicioso y untuoso) y una pizca de sal marina
- Puedes comer ½ taza de guarnición de algún almidón sin procesar, como arroz integral, quinoa o batata

Sugerencias para tentempiés

- Hummus y apio, zanahorias y/o pimiento
- Un puñado de frutos secos —cualquiera puede valer— o una cucharada de mantequilla de frutos secos
- Caldo de huesos, nuestro favorito. Pueden beberlo a lo largo del día si tienes un termo. (Véase receta en el capítulo 9)
- Medio aguacate con un chorrito de zumo de lima y un pellizco de sal marina
- Aceitunas; unas diez unidades son un buen tentempié

PLAN QUENCH DE CINCO DÍAS

■ ■ ■ *Día uno*

Acuérdate de tomar 1 o 2 tazas de agua antes de cada comida. Por supuesto, si vas a tomar un *smoothie* como sustituto de una comida, no hace falta que bebas agua antes. Prueba el agua a temperatura ambiente, o incluso caliente. A lo mejor la prefieres así.

Micromovimiento de la mañana

Cuando te despiertes, vuelve a cerrar los ojos. No salgas al mundo todavía; saborea la transición. Toma nota de lo que sientes y observa si, cinco días después, tus sensaciones son las mismas o han cambiado. Disfruta de los cambios que están por venir.

Realiza nuestro ejercicio de «Barbilla al pecho», en el que estarás utilizando el peso medio de 450 gramos de tu cabeza para bombear líquido por toda la columna vertebral. De esta manera movilizas las toxinas liberadas por el cerebro durante el sueño y las sustituyes por oxígeno y nutrientes frescos. Por no hablar de poner a trabajar a tus abdominales, todo mientras permaneces tumbado.

Barbilla al pecho. Túmbate sobre la espalda, con la cabeza apoyada en la almohada, y siente tu columna vertebral, de arriba abajo. Si la postura te resulta incómoda, puedes colocarte sobre un costado. Simplemente baja la barbilla hacia el pecho, estirando el cuello sin molestias. No fuerces: estás movilizando líquidos, no fortaleciendo músculos. Después de dos respiraciones, levanta despacio la barbilla, manteniendo los músculos del cuello relajados. Repite este movimiento tres veces. Hazlo como más te guste, pero sin forzar. Los estudios demuestran que abandonamos antes si nos forzamos en exceso al principio. Este ejercicio resulta también magnífico si se realiza de pie.

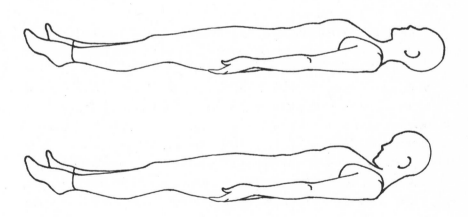

Bebida de la mañana
Nada más levantarte, bebe entre 240 y 480 ml de agua tibia o templada con el jugo de un cuarto de limón recién exprimido. También puedes usar una cucharadita o dos de vinagre de sidra de manzana (el tapón de la botella mide exactamente lo mismo que una cucharadita) o añade unas

188 Apaga tu sed

hojas de menta seca o fresca machacadas, una ramita de romero o una bolsita de infusión de manzanilla. Estos elementos añadidos liberan sustancias y aceites esenciales que ayudan a tu cuerpo a absorber el agua. Una vez más, nuestro programa no consiste en beber mucha agua, sino en optimizar la hidratación. Bebe la cantidad que te resulte cómoda, una cantidad que te ayude a crear un hábito, no que te lleve a querer evitarla.

Si lo primero que haces habitualmente por la mañana es beber café o té, por favor, limítate a una o dos tazas. No utilices el café para hidratarte. Y asegúrate de beber ese vaso de agua con limón por la mañana temprano. Un truco para que tu café sea más hidratante consiste en añadir a tu bebida caliente una cucharadita de mantequilla sin sal de origen ecológico y/o una cucharadita de aceite de coco. Se trata de una bebida fortificante de antigua tradición, basada en ancestrales costumbres de los pueblos himalayo, etíope y peruano. El *bulletproof coffee* es una versión moderna de esta bebida a base de café, mantequilla y aceite de coco que causa ahora furor en Estados Unidos, y por una buena razón. La mezcla convierte el café en un batido realmente magnífico. Las grasas añadidas movilizan la hidratación hacia el interior de las células y pueden incluso amortiguar el nerviosismo que provoca el café.

Smoothie de la mañana. Elige entre un *smoothie* para clima frío, como la Leche caliente de frutos secos y semillas, y una versión para clima cálido, como el Remedio de lima.

Si buscas máxima eficiencia, puedes acelerar la preparación de tus *smoothies* organizando previamente todos los ingredientes. Coloca cinco bolsas de plástico grueso y cierre hermético tipo ziplock o, lo que es incluso mejor, cinco frascos de vidrio, pon en cada frasco todos los ingredientes para un *smoothie*, excepto los líquidos, e introduce los frascos en el frigorífico. Luego, cada mañana, mezcla el contenido de cada frasco con el líquido que corresponda y tendrás tu *smoothie* listo. Es mejor realizar la mezcla a diario en la licuadora, para obtener el sabor más fresco y aprovechar al máximo todos los nutrientes, si bien también puedes preparar el *smoothie* la noche anterior, con una modesta reducción de su poder nutritivo.

Bébete tu *smoothie* en las dos horas siguientes a despertarte. Puedes bebértelo mientras vas al trabajo o te das un paseo por la mañana o simplemente mientras lees las noticias.

Smoothies para el calor: Remedio de lima

Los ingredientes de esta receta se potencian entre sí para ofrecer una hidratación más eficaz. La chía tiene el poder de liberar más agua que ninguna otra semilla.

PARA UNA RACIÓN DE UNOS 350 ML

- ½ taza de agua de coco o de leche de coco (sin azúcar añadido)
- ½ pepino, pelado si no es ecológico
- 1 cucharada de semillas de chía molidas
- 1 a 2 cucharaditas de miel
- 1 cucharada de zumo de lima recién exprimido
- 1 a 2 pellizcos de sal marina gruesa o sal de roca (como la sal rosa del Himalaya)
- 1 a 2 tazas de agua de manantial o filtrada, para diluir a tu gusto
- ½ a 1 cucharadita de jengibre fresco picado, opcional si deseas sabor extra

Preparación: Pon los ingredientes en la licuadora y mezcla a velocidad alta. Sírvelo con hielo si lo deseas.

Opción para el frío: Leche caliente de frutos secos y semillas

Los frutos secos y las semillas aportan grasa, fibra y proteínas y el jengibre y el cardamomo añaden sabor

PARA UNA RACIÓN DE UNOS 350 ML

- 1 cucharada de semillas de chía molidas
- ½ taza de leche de coco (sin azúcar añadido)
- 2 cucharadas de anacardos molidos u otros frutos secos o semillas molidos, como cáñamo, girasol o calabaza
- 1 a 2 cucharaditas de jarabe de arce o stevia (al gusto)
- 1 cucharadita de jengibre fresco en daditos

- ¼ cucharadita de cardamomo molido o canela molida
- 1 a 2 pellizcos de sal marina o de roca sin refinar (como sal rosa del Himalaya)
- 1 taza o más de agua filtrada o de manantial, para diluir a tu gusto

Preparación: Si no encuentras semillas de chía molidas o no quieres molerlas (nosotras utilizamos un molinillo de café), puedes añadirlas enteras a la licuadora. También así liberarán su gel. Tal vez encuentres que tienen una textura crujiente antes de saturarse por completo. Si no te gusta esa textura crujiente, puedes dejar previamente en remojo las semillas durante 5 minutos, mientras preparas el resto del *smoothie*. Utiliza para ello 3 cucharadas de agua para 1 cucharada de semillas de chía y añádelo todo al *smoothie*.

Pon los ingredientes en la licuadora y bátelos. Vierte la mezcla en una taza o termo. Algunas personas se sienten tentadas de añadir café al *smoothie*. Adelante.

Sigue las instrucciones del fabricante de la licuadora en relación con el agua caliente. Algunos advierten que no utilices en la licuadora líquidos muy calientes. En tal caso, añade el líquido caliente a los demás ingredientes una vez mezclados.

Movimiento del mediodía
Torsiones de columna: siéntate en el borde de una silla, en la oficina o en casa. Mantén los brazos extendidos hacia los lados, con las palmas mirando hacia arriba, y rota suavemente la parte superior del cuerpo hacia la derecha. Mantén la cadera estable orientada hacia delante y gira el torso, los brazos y la cabeza al mismo tiempo. Deja que los ojos sigan tu pulgar. Gira los pulgares hacia atrás y hacia delante. Repite hacia la izquierda. Realiza tres torsiones completas.

Placer de la tarde
Vierte en una botella de medio litro unos 400 ml de agua de manantial o filtrada y añade un pellizco de sal marina. Añade dos cucharada de semillas de chía molidas y agita con fuerza. Agrega dos cucharadas de zumo o concentrado de zumo de frutas no edulcorado, como granada,

uva Concord, cereza o arándano. Pueden servirte tanto el zumo como el concentrado, más difícil de encontrar; depende de tus gustos. Lo mejor de los concentrados es que se conservan más tiempo sin necesidad de refrigeración, de manera que puedes llevarlos en el coche o tenerlos en la oficina. Es más probable encontrar los concentrados en tiendas de comida sana. No tienes por qué tomarte tu *placer de la tarde* de una sola vez. Simplemente acábalo antes de que llegue a su fin tu jornada de trabajo. Bébelo a tu ritmo, entre el mediodía y las siete de la tarde.

Bebida para antes de dormir

La infusión de manzanilla se ha utilizado siempre para favorecer la relajación y además ayuda a desintoxicar el organismo durante el sueño. La infusión de regaliz es una buena alternativa a la manzanilla; su sabor dulce la convierte en una buena recompensa al final del día. Por la noche, recomendamos beber solo media taza, unos 120 ml.

Movimiento antes de acostarte

Oreja hacia el hombro. Siéntate en el borde de la cama. Rota suavemente el cuello desde la oreja derecha hasta el hombro derecho y después repite hacia el lado izquierdo. Comienza con cinco hacia cada lado.

Círculos con la barbilla. Después dibuja con la barbilla un círculo en el aire. Traza cinco círculos.

Estiramiento de todo el cuerpo. Túmbate boca arriba y estira todo el cuerpo en un suave movimiento de elongación, mientras cuentas cinco respiraciones. Luego levanta los brazos por encima de la cabeza y flexiónalos un poco de manera que puedas agarrar el borde del cabecero o del colchón y estirar así el torso y el abdomen entre la cadera y las costillas. Después suelta y relaja. Prueba dos, tres o cinco veces. Buenas noches, que duermas bien.

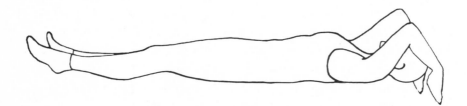

■ ■ ■ *Día dos*

Micromovimiento de la mañana

Realiza tu rutina al despertarte, como el primer día. Cuando te despiertes, vuelve a cerrar los ojos y siente la columna vertebral. Siente su cálida extensión después de una noche de sueño. Realiza el micromovimiento

Barbilla al pecho durante dos respiraciones profundas; repite tres veces. Ahora realiza el masaje de hombros en la cama.

Masaje de hombros en la cama. Túmbate sobre la espalda y haz presión con la escápula derecha sobre el colchón. Como ayuda, puedes probar a levantar el codo. Haz presión durante dos respiraciones profundas y después relaja. Repite con la escápula izquierda durante dos respiraciones profundas. Puede que te resulte más fácil un lado que el otro y eso te permite saber dónde debes fortalecer tu cuerpo, realizando algunos movimientos más en el lado débil. No existe una manera perfecta de realizar nuestros movimientos. Busca nuevos movimientos; no importa cuáles sean: estarás aportando hidratación a nuevos puntos de tu cuerpo.

Bebidas de la mañana

Nada más levantarte, bebe entre 240 y 480 ml de agua templada o tibia con un chorrito de zumo de limón. Puedes utilizar vinagre de sidra de manzana en lugar de limón o añadir unas hojas de menta o una ramita de romero, o bien una bolsita de manzanilla. Si tus hábitos de la mañana incluyen café o té, por favor, limita tu ingesta a 1 o 2 tazas y considera la posibilidad de añadir una cucharadita de mantequilla ecológica o de aceite de coco o un poco de ambos para convertir tu café en una bebida hidratante.

***Smoothie* de la mañana.** Elige la receta de *smoothie* frío o caliente que prefieras y añade para este día ½ taza de frambuesas frescas o congeladas para un sabor fresco y nuevo. Las frambuesas tienen gran cantidad de antioxidantes y también aportan fibra para una mejor absorción del líquido por parte de los tejidos.

Movimiento del mediodía

Presión de pulgar sobre esternón. Puedes realizar este ejercicio en posición sentada o de pie. Respira por la nariz, con la boca cerrada, y coloca una mano plana en la parte superior del tronco, con el pulgar sobre el esternón, entre las mamas. Inspira despacio mientras cuentas hasta cinco; después realiza presión con la mano como si quisieras extraer el aire de una bolsa de plástico, al mismo tiempo que espiras

por la nariz. Realiza este ejercicio despacio y con suavidad cinco veces. Repite tres veces más. Este ejercicio te recuerda que debes respirar y bombear líquidos hasta el último rincón de tu cuerpo.

El diafragma, justo bajo el esternón, es el principal músculo de la respiración y atrapa una cantidad considerable de vapor de aire. Una espiración profunda masajea y estimula el hígado y el estómago e incrementa la capacidad pulmonar. A continuación realiza tus torsiones de columna.

Placer de la tarde
Repite la receta del primer día. Si quieres un poco de variedad, emplea 6 ml de un concentrado o zumo distinto, siempre sin edulcorar.

Bebida para antes de dormir
Infusión de manzanilla o regaliz (½ taza).

Movimiento antes de acostarte
Oreja hacia el hombro, Círculos con la barbilla y *Estiramiento de todo el cuerpo.*

■ ■ ■ *Día tres*

Movimiento de la mañana
Cuando te despiertes, vuelve a cerrar los ojos y siente tu columna vertebral. Después realiza tu rutina de micromovimientos *Barbilla al pecho* y *Masaje de hombros en la cama.*

A continuación, sumamos un nuevo estiramiento, que llamaremos *Espalda de gato.*

Espalda de gato. Siéntate en el borde de la cama con los pies apoyados en el suelo y las rodillas separadas en forma de «V», en postura cómoda. Apoya las

manos en las rodillas. Siéntate en posición erguida, con una ligera inclinación hacia delante, sin abandonar tu postura cómoda. Inspira al mismo tiempo que dejas que tu barbilla supere la línea de tus rodillas y luego mira al suelo. Lleva los hombros hacia las orejas y la barbilla hacia el pecho. Espira al tiempo que estiras los brazos y vuelves hacia atrás a la posición erguida. Extra: curva la espalda en forma de «C» y balancéate hacia delante y hacia atrás. Repite dos veces.

Bebidas de la mañana
Bebe entre 240 y 480 ml de agua templada o tibia con el zumo de un cuarto de limón. Puedes también añadir hojas de menta fresca, una ramita de romero o una bolsita de infusión de manzanilla. Si bebés café por la mañana, considera la posibilidad de mezclar una parte de mantequilla ecológica y una cucharadita de aceite de coco. Se obtiene así un magnífico batido y al mismo tiempo conviertes tu café de la mañana en un poderoso brebaje hidratante. La mantequilla o el aceite o la leche de nuez de coco puede añadirse también al té. De hecho esta es una preparación tradicional en pueblos que viven en regiones situadas a gran altitud en todo el mundo y se considera una bebida fortalecedora. Añade por encima canela o cardamomo.

Batido de la mañana. Elige la receta fría o caliente y, para introducir hoy una variación, incorpora media pera. Las peras son una fuente excelente de fibra y una fruta superhidratante.

Movimiento del mediodía
Presión de pulgar sobre esternón y *Torsiones de columna.*

Placer de la tarde
Sigue las instrucciones de la receta del primer día, con cualquier variedad de zumo que te guste.

Bebida para antes de dormir
Infusión de manzanilla o regaliz (½ taza).

Movimiento antes de acostarte
Oreja hacia el hombro, Círculos con la barbilla y *Estiramiento de todo el cuerpo.*

■ ■ ■ *Día cuatro*

Movimiento de la mañana
Realiza tu rutina al despertarte, con los movimientos de *Barbilla al pecho*, *Masaje de hombros en la cama* y *Espalda de gato*.

Bebidas de la mañana
Bebe de 240 a 480 ml de agua tibia o templada con el zumo de un cuarto de limón. Puedes añadir también unas hojitas de menta fresca, una ramita de romero o una bolsita de manzanilla. Si por la mañana sueles tomar café, puedes agregar una punta de mantequilla ecológica y una cucharadita de aceite de coco. Completa con canela o cardamomo.

Smoothie **de la mañana.** Elige la receta de *smoothie* caliente o frío, pero para variar añade 2 cucharaditas de brotes de alfalfa. Aunque parecen insípidos y no te darás ni tan siquiera cuenta de su presencia, los brotes aportan a la mezcla una explosión de gel, vitaminas y minerales. Es una manera excelente de incorporar una verdura sin tan siquiera darte cuenta.

Movimiento del mediodía
Presión de pulgar sobre esternón y *Torsiones de columna*.

Placer de la tarde
Sigue las instrucciones del primer día y añade zumo o concentrado sin edulcorar, a tu gusto.

Bebida para antes de dormir
Infusión de manzanilla o regaliz (1/2 taza).

Movimiento antes de acostarte
Oreja hacia hombro, Círculos con la barbilla y *Estiramiento de todo el cuerpo*.

■ ■ ■ *Día cinco*

Movimiento de la mañana
Realiza tu rutina al despertarte con los movimientos *Barbilla al pecho* y *Masaje de hombros en la cama*.

Vamos a introducir una variación del movimiento *Espalda de gato*. Este movimiento se conoce como *Serpiente*.

Serpiente. Siéntate en el borde de la cama con los pies apoyados en el suelo, las rodillas separadas formando ligeramente una «V» con las piernas, en una postura que te resulte cómoda. Coloca las manos sobre las rodillas. Siéntate en posición erguida y con la espalda recta. Inclínate hacia delante hasta que la cabeza quede entre tus rodillas o tan lejos como puedas y te resulte cómodo. Esta vez, cuando empieces a estirar los brazos y elevar el tronco, como en el movimiento de *Espalda de gato*, levanta la cabeza lentamente hasta que hayas recuperado la posición inicial, mirando primero de frente, a la pared, y luego hacia arriba, al techo. Arquea suavemente la espalda. Deja que tus ojos sigan todo el recorrido, desde la pared hasta el techo, y estira el cuello hacia atrás en un movimiento controlado. Puede que quieras ofrecer apoyo a la espalda al levantarte apoyando las manos en las rodilla, para ayudarte a volver a la posición inicial. Después relaja. Realiza todo el movimiento de forma fluida. Repite tres veces.

Bebidas de la mañana

Bebe entre 240 y 480 ml de agua tibia o templada con el zumo de un cuarto de limón. También puedes añadir menta, romero o incluso una bolsita de manzanilla. Si por la mañana tomas café o té, 1 o 2 tazas están bien; puedes añadir una cucharadita de mantequilla ecológica o aceite de coco.

Smoothie **de la mañana.** Elige la opción caliente o fría y, para introducir un poco de variedad hoy, añade 2 cucharaditas de uno de los concentrados o zumos de frutas de la receta *Placer de la tarde* (véase «Por qué nuestra lista de la compra es tan hidratante», en el capítulo 8).

Movimiento del mediodía

Presión de pulgar sobre esternón y *Torsiones de columna*.

Placer de la tarde
Repite la receta del primer día con un zumo o concentrado de tu elección.

Bebida para antes de dormir
Infusión de manzanilla o regaliz (½ taza).

Movimiento antes de acostarte
Oreja hacia el hombro, Círculos con la barbilla y *Estiramiento de todo el cuerpo.*

¡Felicidades! Has completado el programa de cinco días. Ahora ya sabes lo que se siente al estar perfectamente hidratado y mantener tu esencia líquida en un mundo tan deshidratado como el nuestro. Si sigues los principios de *Apaga tu sed*, en un mes habrás acelerado la eliminación de desechos en todos los frentes de tu cuerpo, lo cual contribuirá a que piel, cerebro, articulaciones y músculos sigan mejorando. Si continúas durante tres meses, es probable que pierdas más fácilmente esos kilos de peso que te sobran y que notes la mente más clara, mejor estado de ánimo y una agilidad y un rango de movimientos más amplios, y que disfrutes de un sueño más profundo.

Te sentirás más joven por dentro.

RESUMEN DE PROGRAMA O PLAN QUENCH DE 5 DÍAS

	Día 1	*Día 2*	*Día 3*	*Día 4*	*Día 5*
Micromovimiento de la mañana	Barbilla al pecho	Barbilla al pecho, Masaje de hombros en la cama	Barbilla al pecho, Masaje de hombros en la cama y Espalda de gato	Barbilla al pecho, Masaje de hombros en la cama y Espalda de gato	Barbilla al pecho, Masaje de hombros en la cama y Serpiente
Bebida de la mañana	Agua templada con limón	Agua templada con limón	Agua templada con limón	Agua templada con limón	Agua templada con limón
Smoothie *de la mañana*	Remedio de lima o Leche caliente de frutos secos y semillas	Remedio de lima o Leche caliente de frutos secos y semillas, con frambuesas	Remedio de lima o Leche caliente de frutos secos y semillas, con pera	Remedio de lima o Leche caliente de frutos secos y semillas, con brotes	Remedio de lima o Leche caliente de frutos secos y semillas, con zumo de granada (u otro)
Micromovimiento del mediodía	Torsiones de columna	Presión de pulgar sobre esternón y Torsiones de columna	Presión de pulgar sobre esternón y Torsiones de columna	Presión de pulgar sobre esternón y Torsiones de columna	Presión de pulgar sobre esternón y Torsiones de columna
Bebida de la tarde	Placer de la tarde	Placer de la tarde	Placer de la tarde	Placer de la tarde	Placer de la tarde
Bebida para antes de dormir	Infusión de manzanilla o regaliz	Infusión de manzanilla o regaliz	Infusión de manzanilla o regaliz	Infusión de manzanilla o regaliz	Infusión de manzanilla o regaliz
Micromovimiento antes de acostarte	Oreja hacia el hombro, Círculos con la barbilla y Estiramiento de todo el cuerpo	Oreja hacia el hombro, Círculos con la barbilla y Estiramiento de todo el cuerpo	Oreja hacia el hombro, Círculos con la barbilla y Estiramiento de todo el cuerpo	Oreja hacia el hombro, Círculos con la barbilla y Estiramiento de todo el cuerpo	Oreja hacia el hombro, Círculos con la barbilla y Estiramiento de todo el cuerpo

Todo lo que necesitas

Recetas para toda la vida

Come de forma consciente, si es posible con otras personas, y siempre disfrutando.

Michael Pollan

Ahora que has puesto en práctica el plan de cinco días ¿Te sientes boyante? ¿Con más energía? ¿Menos dolores? ¿Ya no te duele la cabeza? ¿Menos hinchazón? ¿Quieres que, a partir de ahora, forme parte de tu vida? ¡Genial! En esta sección encontrarás nuevas recetas de *smoothies* deliciosos y saludables y otras magníficas sugerencias para sopas y cremas, comidas ligeras y postres (¡incluidos helados!) que te ayudarán a mantenerte en un estado óptimo de hidratación.

Teniendo en cuenta todo esto, hemos preparado otra práctica tabla que incluye nuestras recetas de platos, pero también las bebidas, los *smoothies* y los micromovimientos. Puedes mezclar y combinar las recetas con total libertad. Queremos que llegues a darte cuenta de que realizas los micromovimientos de manera natural a lo largo del día, porque hacen que te sientas mejor y tomas tus bebidas y *smoothies* como un hábito diario más.

DESPUÉS DEL DÍA 5: UNA SEMANA ESTÁNDAR DEL PROGRAMA

	Día 1	Día 2	Día 3	Día 4	Día 5
Micromovimiento de la mañana	Barbilla al pecho	Barbilla al pecho y Masaje de hombros en la cama	Barbilla al pecho y Masaje de hombros en la cama	Barbilla al pecho, Masaje de hombros en la cama y Espalda de gato	Barbilla al pecho, Masaje de hombros en la cama, Espalda de gato y Serpiente
Bebida de la mañana	Agua tibia con limón	Agua tibia con limón	Agua tibia con limón	Agua tibia con limón	Agua tibia con limón
Smoothie *de la* mañana	Remedio de lima o Leche caliente de frutos secos y semillas	*Smoothie* de piña -jengibre	*Smoothie* de arándanos - aguacate	Remedio de lima o Leche caliente de frutos secos y semillas	*Smoothie* verde detox
Desayuno	Nido de aguacate	Bol de fruta	Salmón con alcaparras	Avena irlandesa	Pudin de chía
Comida	Pollo con rúcula	Sopa a tu gusto	Ensalada de tres variedades de judías	Sopa a tu gusto	*Noodles* de calabacín
Micromovimiento del mediodía	Torsiones de columna	Presión de pulgar sobre esternón y Torsiones de columna	Presión de pulgar sobre esternón y Torsiones de columna	Presión de pulgar sobre esternón y Torsiones de columna	Presión de pulgar sobre esternón y Torsiones de columna
Tentempié	Frutos secos y semillas	Taza de caldo de huesos	Taza de aceitunas	Hummus con verduras	½ aguacate
Bebida de la tarde	Placer de la tarde	Placer de la tarde	Placer de la tarde	Placer de la tarde	Placer de la tarde
Cena	Filete de coliflor	Pescado cocido con quinoa	Pollo al horno con verduras	Ensalada niçoise	Setas con rúcula
Bebida para antes de dormir	Infusión de manzanilla o regaliz	Infusión de manzanilla o regaliz	Infusión de manzanilla o regaliz	Infusión de manzanilla o regaliz	Infusión de manzanilla o regaliz

	Día 1	*Día 2*	*Día 3*	*Día 4*	*Día 5*
Micromovimiento antes de acostarte	Oreja hacia hombro, Círculos con la barbilla y Estiramiento de todo el cuerpo	Oreja hacia hombro, Círculos con la barbilla y Estiramiento de todo el cuerpo	Oreja hacia hombro, Círculos con la barbilla y Estiramiento de todo el cuerpo	Oreja hacia hombro, Círculos con la barbilla y Estiramiento de todo el cuerpo	Oreja hacia hombro, Círculos con la barbilla y Estiramiento de todo el cuerpo

Los *smoothies*, que son parte esencial del Plan Quench, son la bebida hidratante perfecta. Por eso te ofrecemos aquí distintas opciones. Cada *smoothie* tiene la cantidad correcta de nutrientes absorbibles para mantener tu actividad diaria. Experimenta: utiliza bayas, verduras y frutas distintas para preparar tus propios *smoothie*s, e invierte en un buen recipiente de viaje para no tener que prescindir de ellos en ningún momento.

A propósito, existe una manera de preparar *smoothies* incluso más nutritivos y que consiste en convertirlos en bebidas fermentadas. Añade vinagre de sidra de manzana, salsas picantes, pasta de miso o agrega el contenido de una cápsula biótica. Todos estos ingredientes, ingeridos junto con una buena hidratación, contribuyen a que la función bacteriana sea óptima y rápida.

101 LICUADORAS

La mayor parte de las recetas del Plan Quench se realizan con licuadora. Existen en nuestros días una amplia variedad de marcas y modelos en el mercado, tantas que puede resultar difícil elegir una. Las hemos probado todas, desde el aparato más básico para preparar una sola ración hasta el más caro de categoría de restaurante. Primero piensa en tu presupuesto, en el tamaño de tu cocina y en tu habilidad con este tipo de aparatos. Si por un lado las licuadoras de alta velocidad y de elevado precio te prepararán unos *smoothies* suaves y perfectos, por otro hemos de señalar que cualquier licuadora sirve para comenzar con nuestro plan de hidratación y nosotras lo único que queremos es que te sientas mejor. Si tu modesta licuadora te prepara un *smoothie* grumoso, puedes pasarlo luego por un colador o un chino para darle una textura más suave. Aunque pierdas un poco de toda esa fibra tan importante, estarás de todos modos activando tu factor de hidratación.

Nuestras sugerencias: por sencillez y facilidad de uso nos gusta Nutri-Bullet, pues licúa directamente los ingredientes en un recipiente de viaje. Mezcla y listo. Además, pica semillas y frutos secos a la perfección, y concretamente muele las semillas de chía muy bien, permitiendo la máxima liberación de agua en gel. Blendtec y Vitamix tienen licuadoras de alta velocidad con mucha fama, pero puede que se salgan de tu presupuesto.

Mención especial merecen las Osterizer, de diseño tradicional. Empezamos con una de ellas. Una ventaja única de los procesadores Osterizer es que puedes reemplazar el recipiente de vidrio por un minivaso de plástico con tapa, especial para preparaciones de una sola ración, que puedes cerrar y llevarte a cualquier sitio. Las batidoras Osterizer fueron diseñadas en la década de 1920 para acelerar el trabajo intensivo de preparación de conservas, de modo que actualiza esa habilidad con la limpieza que ofrece un vaso de una sola ración. O imagina cinco minivasos de Osterizer alineados en tu frigorífico, cada uno de ellos con los ingredientes para un día, simplemente esperando a que los mezcles con líquido, caliente o frío y... ¡listos para salir de casa! Superfácil, por no hablar de que son bonitos.

Nota. Si preparas una bebida muy caliente (incluido café), deja que se enfríe un poco para que no se acumule el vapor, que puede provocar que el recipiente se abra y te quemes. Además, dependiendo del tamaño de tu licuadora, no la llenes en exceso. Tenemos experiencia llenando demasiado, y no es buena. Si necesitas preparar una cantidad mayor, es preferible licuar en dos sesiones.

CONSEJOS PARA PREPARAR *SMOOTHIES* Y OTRAS BEBIDAS

Todas nuestras recetas han sido cuidadosamente creadas para brindarte una hidratación óptima. Hemos combinado ingredientes para potenciar al máximo los efectos, no solo para una mejor nutrición, sino también para una mejor hidratación.

- Para crear una bebida con sello propio y que sea superhidratante, asegúrate de incluir: una o más verduras de hoja y/o hierbas (98 % de agua en gel); un poco de fruta para aportar dulzor; una grasa saludable, como aguacate, aceitunas o algún aceite bueno, o frutos secos y semillas; un toque ácido, que puede aportar el zumo de lima o el vinagre de sidra de manzana crudo; y un pellizco final de sal marina gruesa.
- Todas las recetas de bebidas son para una ración, salvo cuando se dice lo contrario, aunque la ración para una determinada persona puede ser una exageración para otra. Bebe hasta que te sientas saciado.
- Cuando una receta requiere semillas de chía, puedes comprarlas ya molidas. De esta manera, al añadir el líquido se convierten inmediatamente en gel. No requieren remojo previo.
- Para estas recetas puedes utilizar fruta congelada (preferiblemente ecológica). De esta manera será más fácil tener siempre fruta a mano. Y los frutos del bosque congelados son excelentes si vas a preparar el *smoothie* en el trabajo, pues se conservan una semana en el frigorífico.
- Cuando prepares *smoothies* y otras bebidas, emplea agua filtrada o de manantial, mineral o con gas. Si optas por la destilada, añade sal o minerales líquidos (consulta la sección de Recursos para saber cuáles son los mejores filtros según tu presupuesto).

BEBIDAS PARA EL CALOR

La base

Utiliza esta receta como patrón para preparar smoothies refrescantes en verano. Para una mayor variedad puedes emplear lechuga romana en lugar de espinacas, o además de estas. También puedes añadir perejil, menta, albahaca o apio, muy refrescantes. Para un toque dulce, ¿por qué no añadir un puré de pera o de calabaza en lugar de manzana? Una pizca de aromático cardamomo da un matiz adicional de sabor.

- 1 taza de espinacas troceadas
- ½ pepino, pelado si no es ecológico
- 1 manzana verde, pelada, sin corazón y cortada en cuartos
- El zumo de ½ limón
- ½ taza de leche de coco
- 1 a 2 cucharaditas de jengibre picado
- 1 a 2 tazas de agua filtrada o de manantial, para diluir al gusto

Preparación: Pon todos los ingredientes en la licuadora y cierra bien la tapa. Sirve inmediatamente.

Refresco de sandía y pepino

La sandía y el pepino, que son primas hermanas desde el punto de vista botánico, se encuentran en nuestra lista «top ten» de fruta y verduras hidratantes. Una pizca de sal añadida potencia su carga eléctrica. Si utilizas infusiones de hierbas, como hibisco o menta, en lugar de agua, le darás un toque más de sabor.

- 1 taza de sandía en dados
- 1 pepino mediano, pelado si no es ecológico
- Un chorrito de zumo de lima recién exprimido
- Una pizca de sal marina gruesa
- 1 o 2 tazas de agua filtrada o infusión de hibisco, para diluir a tu gusto
- Ramita de menta, opcional

Preparación: Pon todos los ingredientes en la licuadora y cierra bien la tapa. Bate durante 30 a 35 segundos o hasta obtener la consistencia deseada. Sírvelo inmediatamente.

El Quench

Para la elaboración de esta bebida necesitarás una licuadora potente, ya que el hinojo resulta difícil de triturar. Como todos nuestros
smoothies, es enormemente hidratante, sacia y, además, es bonito. Esta es una de las numerosas recetas en las que añadimos
semillas de chía, uno de los ingredientes preferidos de nuestro
Plan Quench.

- 3 pencas de apio
- ½ pepino, pelado si no es ecológico
- 1 taza de hojas de kale, espinacas o una mezcla de verduras
  de hoja de primavera
- ½ bulbo de hinojo
- ½ pera o manzana, pelada, sin corazón y cortada
- El zumo de 1 lima
- 1 cucharadita a 1 cucharada de aceite de coco o aceite de
  oliva virgen extra
- Un pedazo de jengibre de 1 o 2 centímetros, al gusto, en
  daditos
- 1 cucharadita de semillas de chía molidas
- 1 a 2 tazas de agua filtrada, de manantial o agua con gas,
  para diluir a tu gusto

Preparación: Pon todos los ingredientes en la licuadora y cierra
bien la tapa. Bate durante 30 a 35 segundos o hasta conseguir la
consistencia deseada. Sírvelo inmediatamente.

Smoothie *rojo frambuesa*

Puede que pienses que la lombarda (o col morada) matará los
demás sabores de este *smoothie*, pero no es sí. En realidad, real-
za el sabor de las frambuesas.

- 1 taza de lombarda cortada en tiras

- 1 taza de frambuesas frescas o congeladas
- ½ pepino, pelado si no es ecológico
- 6 a 8 hojas de albahaca o menta
- Jengibre, un trocito de 1 a 2 centímetros, al gusto, en daditos
- 1 cucharadita a 1 cucharada de aceite de coco
- 1 a 2 tazas de agua filtrada, de manantial o agua con gas, para diluir a tu gusto
- Pimienta negra recién molida

Preparación: Pon todos los ingredientes, excepto la pimienta negra, en la licuadora y cierra bien la tapa. Mezcla durante 30 a 35 segundos o hasta conseguir la consistencia que desees. Muele un poco de pimienta negra por encima y sirve inmediatamente.

Smoothie *de remolacha*

La remolacha lleva utilizándose por sus propiedades medicinales y nutricionales desde hace miles de años. El polvo de remolacha se prepara a partir de la raíz de la planta con flores, es de un color rojo intenso y está cargado de nutrientes y antioxidantes. Asegúrate de comprar remolacha en polvo sin azúcares añadidos. La cantidad de jengibre que utilices depende solo de tus preferencias.

- 1 cucharadita a 1 cucharada de semillas de chía (mejor molidas)
- ½ taza de remolacha cruda o cocida, en daditos, o 1 cucharada de remolacha en polvo
- 1 taza de uvas rojas (alrededor de 10)
- 1 taza de hojas de berros o rúcula
- ¼ taza de perejil, hojas y tallos
- 1 cucharadita a 1 cucharada de aceite de coco
- Jengibre, un pedazo de 1 a 2 centímetros, en daditos
- Un pellizco de sal marina gruesa
- 1 a 2 tazas de agua filtrada, de manantial o agua con gas, para diluir a tu gusto

Preparación: Pon los ingredientes en la licuadora y cierra bien la tapa. Mezcla durante de 30 a 35 segundos o hasta alcanzar la consistencia deseada. Sirve inmediatamente.

Mango colado

El mango es un alimento de elevado índice glucémico, pero el efecto beneficioso viene de la mano del vinagre de sidra de manzana, que ayuda a reducir el impacto del azúcar.

- 1 cucharadita a 1 cucharada de semillas de chía (mejor molidas)
- 1 taza de verduras de hoja verde, como espinacas, mix de primavera, lechuga romana o de otra variedad
- ½ mango, pelado y cortado
- ½ pepino, pelado si no es ecológico
- 1 cucharadita de vinagre de sidra de manzana crudo
- ¼ taza de anacardos
- 1 cucharadita a 1 cucharada de aceite de coco
- 6 a 8 hojas de albahaca
- 1 a 2 tazas de agua filtrada o de manantial, según la densidad que prefieras

Preparación: Pon los ingredientes en la licuadora y cierra bien la tapa. Bate durante 30 a 35 segundos o hasta alcanzar la consistencia deseada. Sirve inmediatamente.

Smoothie Quench Detox

- 1 remolacha pequeña cruda o cocida, cortada en daditos*
- 1 tallo de apio
- 1 puñado de perejil
- 1 pepino, pelado si no es ecológico
- Un trocito de jengibre de 0,5 centímetros, cortado en daditos
- El zumo de ½ limón

- 4 hojas de lechuga romana
- 1 puñado de espinacas o rúcula
- ½ pera madura
- 1 a 2 tazas de agua filtrada o de manantial, según tus preferencias de textura

Preparación: Agrega todos los ingredientes y mezcla. Viértelo en un vaso y disfruta.

* Si usas remolacha cruda, utiliza una licuadora de alta velocidad o córtala en daditos muy pequeños.

Smoothie *de piña-mango*

- 1½ tazas de piña fresca o congelada, en daditos
- 1 taza de mango fresco o congelado, en daditos
- 1 taza de agua de coco
- 1 penca de apio, troceada
- Un trocito de jengibre de 1 cm, pelado
- 2 cucharaditas de vinagre de sidra de manzana crudo
- 1 a 2 tazas de agua filtrada o de manantial, para conseguir el espesor deseado

Preparación: Pon todos los ingredientes en la licuadora y mézclalos. Vierte el *smoothie* en un vaso y bébetelo recién preparado.

Smoothie detox *Paisaje verde*

- 1 cucharada de semillas de chía
- 1 taza de piña fresca o congelada en daditos
- ¼ de aguacate
- 1 penca de apio
- ½ taza de hojas de albahaca
- ½ taza de perejil

- ½ pepino, pelado si no es ecológico
- 1 a 2 cucharaditas de jengibre en daditos
- El zumo de ½ limón
- 1 a 2 tazas de agua filtrada o de manantial, según tus preferencias de densidad

Preparación: Pon todos los ingredientes en la licuadora y bátelos. Vierte el smoothie en un vaso y bébelo recién preparado.

Smoothie *de aguacate y arándanos*

- 1½ tazas de arándanos frescos o congelados
- ½ aguacate, pelado y sin hueso
- 1 manzana o 1 pera, partida por la mitad y sin corazón
- 1 a 2 tazas de agua filtrada o de manantial, según tus preferencias de densidad

Preparación: Pon todos los ingredientes en la licuadora y mezcla. Vierte el *smoothie* en un vaso y bébetelo recién hecho.

Smoothie *dorado*

- 2 manzanas, sin centro y cortadas en cuartos
- 3 naranjas peladas
- El zumo de ½ limón
- 1 taza de agua de coco
- Un trocito de 1 cm de jengibre fresco, pelado
- Un trocito de 0,5 cm de cúrcuma fresca o 1/8 cucharadita de cúrcuma molida
- 1 o 2 tazas de agua filtrada o de manantial, según tus preferencias de densidad

Preparación: Pon todos los ingredientes en la licuadora y mezcla. Vierte el *smoothie* en un vaso y bébelo de inmediato.

Smoothie *de frambuesa*

- 1 taza de frambuesas frescas o congeladas
- 2 naranjas peladas
- ½ aguacate
- 1 puñado de albahaca
- ½ taza de agua de coco
- 1 a 2 tazas de agua filtrada o de manantial, según tus preferencias de densidad

Preparación: Pon todos los ingredientes en una licuadora y mezcla. Vierta el smoothie en un vaso y bébetelo recién hecho.

BEBIDAS PARA EL FRÍO

Cuando las hojas empiezan a caer de los árboles y la gente sale ya de casa con jersey, entonces quiere decir que ha llegado el momento de pasarnos a las bebidas calientes. Aunque en verano nos resulta más natural pensar en hidratarnos, los meses de invierno requieren el mismo grado de hidratación. En nuestras recetas a menudo mezclamos sabor con dulzor, una tentadora combinación que nos lleva a beber más, con el resultado de una mejor hidratación y una mayor protección inmunitaria durante esta estación.

Acuérdate de llenar la licuadora por debajo de la mitad cuando batas líquidos muy calientes, para prevenir explosiones. Sigue las instrucciones del fabricante de la licuadora sobre la preparación de recetas con ingredientes calientes, pues depende de cada aparato.

Infusión de coco y bergamota

La aromática bergamota es un pequeño cítrico verdoso que desprende un aroma característico a té Earl Grey. Recientemente se ha demostrado que es una poderosa herramienta para reducir el colesterol[1].

- 1 taza de té Earl Grey preparado
- ¼ taza de leche de coco
- ¼ taza de anacardos crudos molidos
- Una pizca de sal marina gruesa

Preparación: Bate los ingredientes en la licuadora durante 30 a 35 segundos o hasta alcanzar la consistencia deseada. Añade más agua caliente si prefieres una consistencia menos densa. Si lo deseas, puedes endulzar con jarabe de arce. Sirve inmediatamente.

Infusión de albahaca con limón

La miel es un buen humectante, mientras que la stevia o la fruta monje (también llamada lo han guo) son excelentes sustitutos de bajo índice glucémico. La fruta monje puede encontrarse en forma de polvo en tiendas de comida sana. Aunque la infusión de albahaca es conocida en todo el mundo, en la India se la conoce como té sagrado, o Tulsi. Se dice que, entre otras propiedades, reduce el estrés. Si no tienes albahaca, utiliza menta fresca; también puedes añadir albahaca y limón a la infusión de regaliz para obtener una combinación más rica y saciante.

- 3 a 5 hojas de albahaca
- 1 taza de agua hirviendo
- 1 cucharadita de miel
- 1 cucharadita de zumo de limón fresco, o al gusto

Preparación: Pon las hojas de albahaca en una taza. Agrega el agua, luego agrega la miel y el zumo de limón. Bébelo caliente.

Infusión de rosa persa

Los pétalos de rosa se han utilizado desde la antigüedad para mantener la hidratación. Los pétalos de rosa para preparar infusiones pueden comprarse en tiendas de alimentación u online. Nosotras añadimos un poco de miso, una pasta de soja fermentada y conocida por sus beneficiosos efectos probióticos (bacterias para un intestino sano) y porque retiene la humedad. Esta infusión queda magnífica si añades una cucharadita de mermelada de pétalos de rosa, que puede encontrarse en tiendas Gourmet o en tiendas de alimentación especializadas en Oriente Medio. También puedes endulzar con el jarabe de arce que figura en la receta, que es un excelente agente hidratante, o con stevia líquida o en polvo, que se utiliza en muy pequeñas cantidades.

(*Nota:* si nunca has utilizado stevia en polvo, comienza con una pequeña cantidad —menos de 1/8 de cucharadita— hasta dar con el sabor que más te guste).

La cayena aporta sus propiedades antiinflamatorias, así como una pizca de sabor picante.

- 1 taza de infusión de pétalos de rosa, que haya reposado 5 minutos
- 1 cucharadita de pasta de miso roja o blanca
- 1 cucharadita de jarabe de arce
- Una pizca de pimienta de cayena

Preparación: Prepara la infusión. Añade el miso, el jarabe de arce y la cayena a la infusión caliente y revuelve. Bébela a sorbitos mientras esté caliente.

Wu Wei con miso

La infusión Wu Wei, una excelente mezcla de hierbas asiáticas y especias, se puede comprar en tiendas de comida sana. Cuando se mezcla con miso, el resultado es un agradable sabor dulce. Esta receta puede también prepararse con infusión de pétalos de rosa. Resulta excelente si añades ½ cucharadita de mermelada de pétalos de rosa.

- 1 taza de infusión Wu Wei, que haya reposado 5 minutos
- ½ a 1 cucharadita de pasta de miso blanco

Preparación: Prepara la infusión. Añade el miso a la infusión caliente y revuelve para disolverlo. Tómala caliente.

Sour de naranja y sidra de manzana

Suena a nombre de cóctel, ¿verdad? Se basa en una antigua receta estadounidense llamada *shrug* y muy utilizada en la época de la América colonial para combatir los resfriados.

- 1 taza de agua caliente
- El zumo de 1 naranja
- ½ cucharadita de vinagre de sidra de manzana crudo
- ¼ cucharadita de jengibre en polvo. Puedes usar jengibre rallado fresco, aunque resulta más arenoso. Otro truco puede ser utilizar un chupito de un nuevo jengibre líquido que se vende ya en todas las tiendas de comida sana.

Preparación: Pon todos los ingredientes en la licuadora y mezcla durante 5 a 10 segundos, siguiendo las instrucciones del fabricante de la licuadora para líquidos calientes. Esta bebida se puede preparar sin licuadora. Bébela caliente. También puede ser una magnífica bebida en verano, solo con reemplazar el agua caliente por agua fría.

Coco-Tahini con café espresso

La leche de coco y el cacao en polvo son una combinación clásica. Añadir café y tahini supone otro nivel de hidratación.

- 180 ml de leche de coco
- 2 cucharaditas de cacao en polvo sin azúcar
- 60 ml de café caliente

- 30 ml de agua caliente
- 1½ cucharadas de tahini
- 1 cucharada de jarabe de arce
- Un pellizco de sal marina

Preparación: Pon todos los ingredientes en una licuadora y mezcla durante 30 a 35 segundos, siguiendo las instrucciones del fabricante de la licuadora para líquidos calientes. Disfruta mientras esté caliente.

¿Café?

Todo el mundo parece querer saber cuál es la conexión entre café e hidratación. Buenas noticias para los bebedores de café: los estudios disponibles sobre hidratación han encontrado que una ingesta de cafeína de hasta 400 miligramos al día (unas 4 tazas de café) no producen deshidratación. Sin embargo, pensando en el Plan Quench de cinco días, recomendamos un café al día, ya que el resto de tazas deben ir llenas de líquidos más hidratantes. Durante el Plan Quench, para esos adictos a la cafeína que beben entre cuatro y seis tazas al día, esta cantidad puede tener un efecto diurético y por consiguiente afectar negativamente a la hidratación del cuerpo. De modo que ten cuidado con los cafés bien cargaditos. Probablemente ya sabrás si eres una de esas persona que toleran el café o, por el contrario, de las que no.

Dicho esto, he aquí el mayor estudio reciente sobre el café, que pone de manifiesto que reduce la mortalidad por cualquier causa: M. J. Gunter et al., «Coffee Drinking and Mortality in 10 European Countries: A Multinational Cohort Study», *Annuals of Internal Medicine* 167, no. 4 (Agosto 2017): 236-247.

Café de reishi

Las setas reishi se han utilizado en el continente americano, en Japón, Vietnam y China con distintos fines medicinales, como por ejemplo para fortalecer el sistema inmunitario y para favorecer un sueño nocturno más reparador. Las setas en polvo pueden comprarse online y en tiendas de alimentación sana. Si lo deseas, añade un poco de cardamomo molido o de canela o bien un poquito de vainilla.

- 1 taza de café fuerte y caliente
- ¼ a ½ cucharadita de setas reishi en polvo
- 1 cucharadita de mantequilla
- 2 cucharaditas de jarabe de arce

Preparación: Mezcla la mitad de la taza de café con el polvo de setas, la mantequilla y el jarabe de arce. Viértelo en una taza y añade el resto del café. Revuelve.

Cardamomo

El cardamomo es una especia común utilizada en la India y relacionada con el jengibre. En la medicina ayurvédica se utiliza a menudo para favorecer la digestión y la eliminación de toxinas. Actúa sobre la hinchazón, los gases, el ardor de estómago y el estreñimiento y ayuda a eliminar productos de desecho por vía renal. A nosotras nos gusta masticar las vainas enteras después de las comidas para refrescar el aliento.

Milagro Omega

Los ácidos grasos omega 3 son esenciales para la salud del ser humano. Están presentes sobre todo en el pescado, pero las semillas de chía y de cáñamo son también una buena fuente. Representan una manera excelente de comenzar la mañana, en sustitución del café, aunque también puedes mezclarlas con café como estimulante mental. Existe evidencia de que el coco tiene efecto sinérgico con las semillas de chía a la hora de favorecer la conversión de ALA en DHA y EPA, aunque pueda no ser suficiente para algunos metabolismos. Las grasas omega ayudan a transportar el agua a través de la membrana celular.

- 1 cucharadita de semillas de chía molidas
- ½ taza de leche de coco
- 1 cucharada de mantequilla de almendras
- 1 cucharadita de semillas de cáñamo molidas
- 1 cucharadita de canela molida
- 1 taza o más de agua caliente, según tus preferencias
- Pimienta negra recién molida

Preparación: Pon todos los ingredientes, excepto el agua caliente y la pimienta, en la licuadora y cierra bien la tapa. Bate durante 30 a 35 segundos. Vierte la mezcla en una taza, agrega el agua caliente y muele por encima la pimienta negra. La receta sabe también genial con una pizca de extracto de vainilla.

Cacao Quench para dos

El poder en esta bebida de chocolate con nueces reside en el cacao, que está lleno de minerales que ayudan a activar las cargas eléctricas que nuestro cuerpo necesita.

- 1 taza de piña fresca o congelada, cortada en dados
- ¼ taza de nueces finamente picadas (si tienes un licuadora de alta velocidad puedes emplear nueces enteras)
- El zumo de ½ limón
- 1 cucharada de aceite de coco
- 1 cucharada de cacao crudo en polvo
- 1 cucharadita de jarabe de arce (prueba antes de añadirlo, porque la piña ya es dulce)
- Un pellizco de sal marina gruesa
- 1 taza o más de agua caliente, según tus preferencias

Preparación: Mezcla todos los ingredientes, salvo el agua caliente y el jarabe de arce, añade el agua caliente y revuelve bien. Prueba para comprobar el punto dulce y añade más jarabe de arce si lo deseas. La sal aporta intensidad al sabor.

Cacao

El cacao crudo en polvo es la forma menos procesada de chocolate que se puede consumir. La ralladura de granos de cacao procede de las vainas del árbol del cacao. El cacao en polvo suele ser menos costoso y está un poco más procesado, pero si compras la versión sin nada añadido —sin azúcar ni grasas de la leche— seguirá teniendo gran parte de las propiedades saludables del cacao.

El cacao en polvo es muy rico en polifenoles, que actúan como antioxidantes y ofrecen una fuerte protección contra el daño celular de los radicales libres que se forman a diario. Lo más probable es que, por esta razón, el cacao haya sido vinculado también a una reducción de la mortalidad por causas cardiovasculares, además de tener propiedades antiinflamatorias. Incluso la American Dietetic Association recomienda una dieta rica en fitoquímicos, entre los que se incluye el chocolate negro en cantidades moderadas[2].

Leche vegana de avena con miel, cardamomo y pimienta negra

Se trata de todo un regalo, que se puede beber solo o en lugar de distintos tipos de leches. Añade pimienta si lo deseas. La pimienta tiene una larga tradición como potenciador de la absorción de cualquier nutriente con el que se combine, actuando además como un agente antimicrobiano y antibacteriano. Esta es la razón por la que los colonos británicos se llevaban sus molinillos personales de pimienta dondequiera que viajaran.

- 1 taza de copos de avena
- 6½ tazas de agua fría filtrada o de manantial (usa 4 tazas si deseas una leche más espesa)
- ¼ taza de miel
- 1½ cucharaditas de cardamomo
- 1 pizca de sal marina
- 2 generosos giros de molinillo de pimienta negra (opcional)

Preparación: Mezcla todos los ingredientes en un bol grande. Cubre con un paño y déjalos en remojo toda la noche a temperatura ambiente. Utiliza una licuadora o una batidora de mano para hacer puré. Cuela la leche a través de un colador de malla fina en un bol o un tarro de vidrio. Introduce el recipiente en el frigorífico y utilízalos en un plazo de 3 o 4 días.

SOPAS Y CREMAS

Las sopas, las cremas y los caldos sacian y además constituyen una manera excelente de hidratar el cuerpo, especialmente en los largos y fríos días de invierno. Una batidora de mano permite mezclar los ingredientes calientes de la sopa directamente por inmersión en la olla. Prueba todas las recetas que te proponemos; las sopas permiten experimentar añadiendo diferentes especias y tal vez una o dos verduras más. Una táctica clásica para ahorrar tiempo consiste en preparar el doble de cantidad y congelar la mitad.

Crema de hinojo y pistacho

- 2 cucharadas de ghee o mantequilla sin sal
- 2 tazas de cebolla picada
- 2 chalotas, finamente picadas
- 4 tazas de hinojo (alrededor de 4 bulbos)

- 6 tazas de caldo de pollo
- 1 taza de leche de coco
- 1/3 taza de pistachos troceados
- Sal marina y pimienta recién molida, al gusto
- ¼ cucharadita de cardamomo molido

Preparación: En una cacerola grande, funde el ghee a fuego medio. Añade la cebolla y la chalota y saltéalas, revolviendo con frecuencia durante 4 a 5 minutos. Añade el hinojo y cocina otros 5 minutos.

Añade el caldo. Deja cocer a fuego lento hasta que las verduras estén tiernas, entre 35 y 40 minutos. Deja enfriar la sopa durante 15 minutos y después pásala por la licuadora. Puede que tengas que hacer este trabajo por tandas, o utilizar una batidora de mano.

Vierte de nuevo la sopa en la cacerola y agrega la leche de coco. Calienta de nuevo a fuego medio antes de verterla en los boles y aderezar con pistachos, sal, pimienta y cardamomo.

Esta receta es una modificación de la receta de Kara Fitzgerald, pensada con el fin de potenciar sus propiedades hidratantes.

Stracciatella

Esta es la versión italiana de una sopa con huevo. Puedes utilizar caldo comprado, aunque es mejor que lo prepares en casa.

PARA 2 RACIONES

- 2 tazas de caldo de pollo o de carne
- 1 huevo grande
- ¼ taza de pesto
- ¼ taza de pistachos machacados
- Aceite de oliva virgen extra

Preparación: En una olla, pon el caldo a cocer a fuego lento. Casca un huevo en el caldo muy caliente y remueve para romper la yema en hebras, como si fueran fideos. Agrega el pesto.

Preparación: Reparte la sopa entre dos boles. Esparce por encima los pistachos y riega con un chorrito de aceite de oliva virgen extra antes de servirla.

Crema fría de melón y pera

PARA 4 RACIONES

- 4 tazas de melón chino en dados
- 2 peras maduras, sin centro, sin semillas y troceadas
- ¾ taza de leche de coco
- El zumo de 2 limas
- 1 cucharada de jengibre rallado
- Una pizca de sal marina gruesa
- 1 cucharadita de aceite de oliva virgen extra
- Un pellizco de cardamomo molido

Preparación: Pon los ingredientes en la licuadora y ponla en marcha. Sirve la sopa fría de inmediato o introdúcela en el frigorífico unas horas antes de repartirla entre los 4 boles. Riega cada bol con un chorrito de aceite de oliva y una pizca de cardamomo. Añade agua, vino blanco o incluso kombucha para ajustar el punto de densidad a tu gusto.

Sopa de pollo Bunny Cohen

El primer plato que cociné en mi vida fue una sopa de pollo casera. La preparé cuando estaba en la Universidad: miré cuáles eran los ingredientes en un paquete de sopa Manischewitz y luego hice una réplica utilizando ingredientes frescos. Recuerdo que descubrí que era el eneldo lo que le daba el mismo sabor que tenía la sopa de mi madre. No hay nada mejor en un día de invierno que una sopa de pollo preparada en casa —«penicilina judía»—, sean cuales sean tus males. Y ¡adivina que! Es muy hidratante cuando se utiliza con ingredientes frescos, en lugar de la versión de sopa enlatada y cargada de sodio. En realidad la preparación es muy fácil, aunque lleva su tiempo. Solo tienes que dejar cocer la sopa en la cacerola durante una hora o así, comprobando de vez en cuando si es necesario añadir un poco de agua. —Dana

- 1 pollo ecológico entero, pequeño (de 1 a 1¼ kg), sin menudillos y lavado
- 5 a 6 zanahorias, cortadas en pedazos de 5 centímetros
- 5 a 6 tallos de apio, cortados en pedazos de 5 centímetros
- 1 cebolla grande, partida en dos
- 1 chirivía, cortada en pedazos de 5 centímetros
- 1 manojo de eneldo fresco o perejil
- Sal marina gruesa y pimienta negra recién molida

Preparación: Pon el pollo, las zanahorias, el apio, la cebolla, la chirivía y el eneldo en una cacerola grande para caldo. Llena la cacerola con agua, comprobando que el pollo quede sumergido. Lleva a ebullición y después baja el fuego y deja cocer a fuego lento. Cuece durante 1 hora, retirando de vez en cuando la espuma y las proteínas de pollo de la superficie. Añade sal marina —a mi me gusta la sal Redmond Real— y un poco de pimienta, a tu gusto. Saca el pollo de la cacerola, pero ten cuidado no vayas a quemarte o, lo que sería peor, no se te vaya a escurrir el pollo entre las manos enguantadas y acabe en el suelo. Déjalo en un plato para que se enfríe.

Cuando se halla enfriado el pollo lo suficiente para poder tocarlo, quítale la piel y tírala (o dásela al perro), y con las manos limpias separa la piezas de pollo del hueso y vuelve a introducirlas en la sopa para que sigan cociendo durante otra hora. Puedes retirar la cebolla y sacar la chirivía y majarla con mantequilla como acompañamiento.

Caldo de hueso

Va adquiriendo sabor según se cuece y, además, puedes conge-
larlo. Es una vieja receta tradicional. Probada y certificada. ¡Prué-
bala tú también!

PARA 12 RACIONES

- 1 y 1/4 kilos de huesos con su tuétano, huesos de nudillos y
  rabo de buey con algo de carne pegada y/o carcasas, cuellos
  y alas de pollo
- 1 cebolla, cortada en cuartos
- 2 zanahorias, cortadas en trozos de 5 centímetros
- 3 tallos de apio, cortados en trozos de 5 centímetros
- 2 puerros, cortados en trozos de 5 centímetros
- 6 dientes de ajo
- 2 cucharadas de vinagre de sidra de manzana crudo
- 3 hojas de laurel
- 2 ramitas de romero, perejil y tomillo
- 2 cucharadas de granos de pimienta negra

Preparación: Calienta el horno a 230 °C. Pon los huesos de terne-
ra y las piezas de pollo, cebolla, zanahorias, apio, puerro y ajo en
una bandeja de horno y hornea durante 20 minutos. Revuelve un
poco los ingredientes y hornea durante otros 10 minutos, hasta
que tomen un color pardo oscuro.

Llena una olla grande con 12 tazas de agua filtrada. Añade el
vinagre, las hojas de laurel, las hierbas y los granos de pimienta
negra. Raspa los huesos asados y añade a la olla las verduras y
cualquier jugo que hayan soltado. Agrega agua hasta cubrir, si
fuera necesario.

Tapa la olla y lleva a ebullición. Destapa. Baja la temperatura
para que el caldo cueza durante 8 a 18 horas. Añade más agua para
que los ingredientes se mantengan cubiertos. Cuando más tiempo
cueza, mejor será el caldo. De vez en cuando retira la espuma que
suba a la superficie. Retira la olla del fuego. Cuando se haya enfria-

do un poco, cuela el caldo a otro recipiente utilizando un tamiz fino y tira los huesos y las verduras. Reparte el caldo en recipientes y consérvalo en el frigorífico o en el congelador.

Taza de caldo

Beber caldo a sorbitos como si se tratara de una taza de té aparece en las culturas más antiguas, desde Asia, pasando por Turquía, hasta España e Italia. Y ahora en Little Italy, en Nueva York, los amantes de la buena mesa han recuperado esa antigua tradición de tomarse una tacita de caldo por la mañana, en lugar del café.

Caldo de hueso con salteado de nectarinas y piñones

Gina sirve este combo salado-dulce en todas sus fiestas. La siguiente receta es para una sola persona.

PARA 1 RACIÓN

- 1 taza de caldo de hueso
- 1 nectarina
- 1 cucharada de ghee o mantequilla sin sal
- 1 ramita de romero
- ¼ taza de piñones
- Sal y pimienta al gusto

Preparación: Calienta ligeramente el caldo de hueso en una olla pequeña. Corta en rodajas finas la nectarina. En otra cazuela, saltea las rodajas de nectarina en el ghee o la mantequilla con el romero hasta que estén blandas. Prepara un bol, poniendo en el fondo los piñones. Extiende encima una capa de nectarina. Riega la fruta y los piñones con el caldo. Saca la ramita de romero. Salpimenta a tu gusto.

Gazpacho

El gazpacho, sopa fría de verduras crudas, puede servirse acompañado de cuencos con diversos condimentos, como huevo duro, daditos de pan tostado, almendras laminadas y cebolletas en rodajitas, para que cada uno pueda elegir los condimentos que más le gusten.

PARA 6 RACIONES

- 1 kilo de tomates, cortados en cuartos
- 1 pepino, pelado si no es ecológico
- 1 pimiento ecológico rojo o verde, sin semillas
- 1 diente de ajo
- ½ taza de agua
- 1/3 taza de aceite de oliva virgen extra
- 2 cucharaditas de vinagre de sidra de manzana crudo
- Una pizca de sal marina, pimienta negra y pimienta de cayena (opcional)

Preparación: Pon todos los ingredientes en una licuadora y bate durante 10-15 segundos. Debe quedarte algo denso, pero no como un puré. Introdúcelo en el frigorífico hasta que esté frío. Puedes añadirle un chorrito de aceite de oliva. Puedes diluirlo un poco a tu gusto con más agua o incluso con vino blanco o jugo de tomate.

Gazpacho de tomate y pera

El gazpacho debe servirse frío, pero no helado. Esta versión incluye pera o manzana. A nosotras nos gusta poner por encima unos pistachos picados para darle un troque crujiente.

PARA 2 RACIONES

- 1 tomate mediano cortado en dados o ½ taza de zumo de tomate

- 1 pera o manzana mediana, cortada en cuartos
- 1 cucharada de vinagre de sidra de manzana crudo
- 1 pepino, pelado y cortado
- El zumo de 1 lima
- ¼ taza de aceite de oliva virgen extra
- ½ pimiento rojo, cortado en cuatro trozos y sin semillas
- ½ a 1 taza de agua
- 1 diente de ajo mediano, picado
- 1/8 cucharadita de sal marina gruesa
- 1 jalapeño pequeño, sin semillas y en rodajas, opcional

Preparación: Pon todos los ingredientes, excepto el jalapeño, en la licuadora y cierra bien la tapa. Bate durante 10-15 segundos o hasta conseguir la consistencia deseada. La sopa debe quedar ligeramente gruesa, no como un puré. Añade una rodaja de jalapeño, bate de nuevo, y prueba para ver el punto de sal. Si te gusta más fuerte, añade más jalapeño. Introdúcelo en el frigorífico durante 2 horas. Si te ha quedado demasiado espeso, agrega ¼ a ½ taza más de agua antes de servir.

Gazpacho de sandía

La sandía y el tomate son una combinación perfecta para la hidratación, pues entre los dos proporcionan un magnífico equilibrio de minerales y vitaminas. Y el sabor te sorprenderá gratamente.

PARA 4 RACIONES

- 3 tazas de sandía troceada sin semillas, más ½ taza de sandía en daditos para adornar
- 2 tomates, cortados en cuartos
- 1 pepino pelado, sin semillas y cortado
- 1 pimiento rojo, cortado en cuatro y sin semillas
- 1 cucharada de aceite de oliva virgen extra

- 1 a 2 cucharaditas de zumo de lima
- Un pellizco de sal marina, pimienta negra y pimienta de cayena

Preparación: Pon todos los ingredientes en la licuadora y bate durante 10-15 segundos. Te debe quedar ligeramente denso, pero no como un puré. Prueba para ajustar el sazonado, añadiendo más zumo de lima, sal, pimienta negra o pimienta de cayena si es necesario. Si so deseas, puedes corregir la densidad añadiendo más agua, o incluso vino blanco. Enfría el gazpacho en el frigorífico durante 2 horas.

Gazpacho blanco

Aunque el gazpacho es típicamente rojo, si elegimos ingredientes blancos o verdes obtendremos un excelente plato de verano.

PARA 4 RACIONES

- 4 tazas de melón verde dulce
- ¾ taza de leche de coco
- ½ taza de vino blanco
- El zumo de 2 limas
- 2 tazas de pepino cortado en daditos
- 2 chalotas pequeñas, en rodajas finas
- 2 tazas de uvas verdes, cortadas por la mitad
- ½ taza de almendras laminadas

Preparación: Pon todos los ingredientes, salvo las almendras, en la licuadora y bátelos. Añade agua para ajustar la densidad. Reparte entre 4 boles y adorna con las almendras. Añade sal al gusto.

Consejo: *Coloca las uvas de una taza entre dos tapas de plástico, presionando ligeramente pero con firmeza, y desliza un cuchillo afilado entre las dos tapas, cortando así de una vez todas las uvas por la mitad. Puedes usar también este truco para cortar tomatitos.*

EJEMPLOS DE MENÚS

En el Plan Quench es importante seguir una dieta bien planificada y nutritiva. Te ofrecemos aquí algunas excelentes recetas para ayudarte a comenzar.

Desayuno

Pudin de limón, amapola y chía

Habrás oído hablar del bizcocho de limón y amapola; pues bien,
este pudin es aún mejor. Vas a reemplazar un carbohidrato por
hidratación y nutrición.

PARA 2 RACIONES

- 2 tazas de leche de coco
- ½ taza de semillas de chía enteras
- 1/3 a ¼ de taza de jarabe de arce u otro edulcorante
- 1 cucharada de semillas de amapola, o más si lo deseas
- El zumo de ½ limón
- ½ cucharadita de extracto puro de vainilla
- La cáscara de ½ limón
- ¼ cucharadita de cardamomo molido
- 2 pizcas de sal marina gruesa

Preparación: Tritura todos los ingredientes en la licuadora y vierte
la mezcla obtenida en un frasco o recipiente de vidrio. Introdúcelo
en el frigorífico durante al menos 4 horas o durante toda la noche
para que adquiera densidad. Revuelve o agita varias veces en la
primera hora para que cuaje uniformemente.

Pudin de chía y grosellas

PARA UNA RACIÓN

- ¼ taza de semillas de chía

- 1 taza leche de coco desnatada o entera, según tus preferencias
- Una pizca de sal rosada
- 2 cucharadas de mermelada de grosellas baja en azúcar; puede utilizarse cualquier mermelada, como de higo o de membrillo

Preparación: Tritura en al licudiora las semillas de chía y la leche de coco en un bol. Tapa la mezcla e introdúcela en el frigorífico durante al menos 4 horas.

Cubre con mermelada antes de servir. Puedes añadir fruta fresca, como melocotones o frambuesas, o un pellizco de nueces o semillas de calabaza picadas.

Mermelada de frambuesas, rosas y chía

PARA 1 ½ RACIÓN

- 280 g de frambuesas congeladas
- 3 cucharadas de mermelada de pétalos de rosa*
- 3 cucharadas de semillas de chía
- 1 cucharadita de cardamomo

Preparación: A fuego lento, revuelve las frambuesas hasta calentarlas y después añade la mermelada de pétalos de rosa. Deja enfriar un poco y vierte la mezcla en un tarro de conservas de vidrio o en un frasco de mermelada: después añade la chía y el cardamomo. Puedes extenderla sobre una rebanada de pan sin gluten.

* Puedes encontrarla en tiendas gourmet o especializadas en productos de alimentación de Oriente Medio.

Nidos de aguacate al horno

Los aguacates son agua en un 80 % y contienen la grasa «buena» que necesita nuestro organismo.

- 2 aguacates maduros, cortados por la mitad y deshuesados
- 4 huevos grandes
- 4 cucharadas de salsa de tomate
- zumo de lima recién exprimido

Preparación: Calienta el horno a 200 °C. Saca en torno a 2 cucharadas de aguacate del centro, para hacer espacio para el huevo. Coloca los aguacates en una bandeja de horno y casca un huevo en el centro de cada medio aguacate. Hornea durante 15 a 20 minutos, hasta que el huevo esté cuajado. Corta en dados el aguacate restante.

Antes de servir, riega cada nido con 1 cucharada de salsa de tomate, el aguacate en dados y una rociada de zumo de lima.

Aguacates

Tiene semilla o hueso, luego es un fruto. Dana siempre tiene un aguacate madurando en el alféizar de su ventana. Los aguacates son ricos en grasas monoinsaturadas cardiosaludables (como el aceite de oliva). Están cargados de fibra y de potasio; de hecho, tienen más potasio que un plátano. Tienen también grandes cantidades de vitamina C, ácido fólico y vitamina K, entre otras vitaminas y minerales. Estudios llevados a cabo en personas han puesto de manifiesto que comer aguacates puede reducir el colesterol total, bajar los triglicéridos, reducir el colesterol LDL malo y elevar el colesterol HDL bueno. Por último, los aguacates contienen mucha luteína y zeaxantina, antioxidantes importantes para la salud del ojo.

Comida y cena

Salteado de setas y rúcula

Puedes usar un solo tipo de seta o una variedad que incluya champiñón común, portobello y shiitake. Las setas son agua en un 98% y sus fibras retienen la hidratación.

- 1 cucharada de ghee o mantequilla sin sal
- 1 cucharada de aceite de oliva virgen extra
- 2 tazas de setas laminadas
- 3 dientes de ajo finamente picados
- 1 cucharada de arrurruz en polvo o de semillas de chía o de lino molidas
- 1 taza de leche de coco o de almendras
- 4 tazas de rúcula
- 1 cucharada de mostaza de Dijon granulada
- ½ cucharadita de sal marina
- Pimienta negra recién molida

Preparación: Calienta la mantequilla y el aceite de oliva en una sartén grande a fuego medio. Añade las setas y el ajo y saltea hasta que las setas estén blandas, unos 10 o 12 minutos.

Añade el arrurruz en polvo a la leche y revuelve con las setas, cocinando durante otros 2 o 3 minutos. Añade las hojas de rúcula y la mostaza. Cuando la rúcula se haya ablandado, sazona con sal y pimienta y sirve el plato muy caliente.

Filetes de coliflor al horno

Como muchos otros vegetales, la coliflor contiene gran cantidad de agua, en torno a un 92%. La coliflor se torna más dulce y se carameliza al cocinarla a la plancha. No hay nada como las verduras cocidas de mamá. Sirve la coliflor con un acompañamiento de rúcula, brotes de alfalfa y manzana o pera en rodajitas.

- 1 coliflor grande, cortada en 4 gruesos «filetes» centrales
- 2 cucharadas de aceite de oliva virgen extra

- 1 cucharada de vinagre de sidra de manzana crudo
- 2 dientes de ajo picados
- 1 chalota pequeña picada
- 1 cucharadita de hojas de romero picadas
- Sal marina gruesa y pimienta negra recién molida

Preparación: Calienta el horno a 200 °C. Reviste una fuente de horno con papel para hornear. Coloca los filetes de coliflor sobre el papel.

En un bol, mezcla el aceite de oliva, el vinagre, el ajo, la chalota y el romero y después salpimenta. Pincela con la mitad de esta mezcla los filetes de coliflor. Hornea la coliflor durante 15 minutos. Con una espátula, da la vuelta a la coliflor y vuelve a pincelarla. Hornea hasta que esté dorada, unos 15-20 minutos.

Ensalada iceberg de piña y coco

La lechuga iceberg es la eterna ignorada y, sin embargo, es realmente hidratante. Dale con esta receta un toque tropical.

- 1 cabeza de lechuga iceberg, cortada en cuartos
- ½ taza de leche de coco entera
- ½ taza de piña congelada en dados
- 4 cucharadas de aceite de oliva virgen extra
- 1 cucharadita de vinagre de jerez
- 1 chalota pequeña, cortada en daditos
- 1 taza de nueces partidas por la mitad
- Sal marina gruesa y pimienta negra recién molida

Preparación: Coloca los cuartos de lechuga en 4 platos de ensalada. Pon la leche de coco y la piña en la licuadora y mezcla durante 10 a 15 segundos. Vierte la salsa sobre los cuartos de lechuga. En un bol pequeño, revuelve el aceite de oliva, con el vinagre y la chalota. Riega con esta mezcla la lechuga. Esparce por encima las nueces. Añade sal y pimienta al gusto.

Ensalada de judías triple reto

Al utilizar judías verdes frescas, estamos asegurándonos el máximo contenido de agua. De ahí el nombre de la receta.

PARA 6 RACIONES

- ¼ kilo de judías verdes, cortadas
- ¼ kilo de judías manteca (judías verdes amarillas), cortadas
- ¼ kilo de judías verdes redondas, cortadas
- 2 cucharaditas de chalota picada
- 1 cucharadita de mostaza
- 1 cucharadita de miel
- ¼ de taza de vinagre de jerez
- ½ taza de aceite de oliva virgen extra
- 1 cabeza de radicchio o lechuga francesa

Preparación: Pon a hervir agua en una olla grande. Añade las judías y blanquea durante 2 o 3 minutos. Enfría en agua con hielo.

Para preparar la vinagreta, combina chalota, mostaza, miel, vinagre y aceite de oliva. Adereza las judías con la vinagreta. Sirve en barquitas de radicchio o de lechuga francesa.

Cebollas al horno

Te proponemos un delicioso acompañamiento de verano para pollo o pavo asado. Puedes utilizar las sobras para una crema, pasando por el robot las cebollas sobrantes y recalentando. Esparce por encima frutos secos, como por ejemplo pistachos, para darle un toque crujiente. Habrás oído hablar de lo hidratantes que son las cebollas. En invierno, utiliza cebolla blanca española.

- 4 cebollas Vidalia, peladas y enteras
- 1 lata de leche de coco entera
- 4 cucharadas de ghee o mantequilla sin sal

- 4 ramitas de romero fresco
- 1 cucharadita de cardamomo molido
- Sal marina gruesa y pimienta negra recién molida

Preparación: Calienta el horno a 170 °C. Coloca las cebollas en una bandeja pequeña para horno. Vierte por encima la leche de coco. Pon encima de cada cebolla 1 cucharada de ghee o mantequilla. Coloca una ramita de romero alrededor de cada cebolla. Sazona con cardamomo, sal y pimienta. Hornea durante 45 a 50 minutos, hasta que puedas pinchar las cebollas fácilmente con un tenedor.

Noodles de calabacín con pesto, nueces y aceite de oliva

Puedes preparar y congelar tu propio pesto con albahaca fresca de verano, aunque se venden muy buenas conservas en supermercados y tiendas especializadas en productos italianos. Lo mejor de esta receta es que se prepara todo en la misma cacerola.

PARA 4 RACIONES

- 4 calabacines medianos y/o calabaza de verano (algo menos de 1 kilo)
- 3 cucharadas de aceite de oliva virgen extra
- 1 taza de pesto
- Sal marina gruesa y pimienta negra recién molida
- 1 taza de nueces picadas

Preparación: Pela y corta los calabacines con un aparato para hacer espirales o a mano con un pelaverduras.

En una sartén, calienta el aceite a fuego mediano. Añade los calabacines y cocina durante 5 a 7 minutos, revolviendo de vez en cuando hasta que los «noodles» estén blandos. Añade el pesto, revuelve para distribuir uniformemente. Sazona con sal y pimienta.

Reparte entre 4 platos, distribuye por encima las nueces y riega con el aceite de oliva. Sirve el plato inmediatamente.

Sencillo pollo asado

Dice Dana: «Me encanta esta receta porque la relaciono con la primera vez que me sentí como una persona adulta preparando un plato para una cena con amigos. Y he querido incluirla aquí porque —aparte de que el pollo completa perfectamente el Plan Quench porque proporciona una proteína excelente— todo el mundo debería saber cómo se asa un pollo. Muchos jóvenes que acaban de irse a vivir solos no saben ni asar un pollo. Hemos perdido algunas habilidades para cocinar y creo que necesitamos recuperarlas y llevarlas a nuestra cocina».

PARA 4 RACIONES

- 1 pollo ecológico de alrededor de 1 ¼ kilos, lavado y sin vísceras
- Sal marina gruesa y pimienta negra recién molida
- 1 taza de chalotas, cortadas en trozos grandes
- 1 limón, cortado por la mitad
- 2 ramitas de romero
- 2 cucharadas de mantequilla (¼ de barra), derretida

Preparación: Precalienta el horno a 220 °C. Sazona el pollo por dentro y por fuera con sal y pimienta. Rellena con la chalota troceada, el limón y las ramitas de romero. Úntalo con mantequilla.

Asa el pollo sobre la rejilla del horno durante 15 minutos. Dale la vuelta y baja la temperatura a 170 °C. Hornea durante otros 35-40 minutos. Puedes comprobar la temperatura interna —un mínimo de 75 °C— colocando un termómetro en el músculo más grueso, generalmente del muslo.

Deja reposar 20 minutos ¡y disfruta!

Pescado al horno

Esta es otra receta básica y también una excelente fuente de proteínas para complementar el Plan Quench.

- 1 pescado entero, como lubina, besugo o trucha (limpio, descamado, eviscerado y sin aletas, pero con cabeza y cola), de alrededor de 680 g
- 1/3 taza más 1 cucharada de aceite de oliva
- Sal y pimienta
- 2 cucharadas de orégano seco, separadas
- 2 limones
- 1/3 taza de aceite de oliva virgen extra

Preparación: Precalienta el horno. Coloca la rejilla del horno en el tercio superior. Unta ambos lados del pescado con aceite de oliva, después sazona con sal y pimienta y 1 cucharada de orégano seco. Asegúrate de sazonar también la cavidad.

Asa el pescado colocándolo tan cerca como puedas de la fuente de calor, hasta que la piel esté crujiente —unos 7 minutos— y después da la vuelta al pescado y asa por el otro lado hasta que esté también crujiente.

En un tarro con tapa, mezcla el zumo de 2 limones con 1/3 de taza de aceite de oliva virgen extra, 1 cucharada de orégano seco, sal y pimienta. Agita con fuerza. Vierte la mezcla sobre el pescado. Adorna con rodajas de limón, sirve el pescado y ¡a comer!

Postres

¿Por qué los postres no pueden ser hidratantes? Los nuestros están pensados para que salgas de casa sin sensación de sequedad ni desgana.

Panna cotta de coco y lavanda con granos de pimienta negra

Esta receta tiene sus orígenes en época medieval. La nuestra es una variante de un postre que pudo servirse en una boda da la realeza italiana... ¡Ah, y además es superhidratante!

- 380 g de leche de coco entera de lata
- 1 ¼ cucharaditas de gelatina o colágeno de origen ecológico en polvo (de la marca Great Lakes, por ejemplo)
- 1 cucharadita de extracto de vainilla
- 1/3 taza de jarabe de arce
- 4 gotas de extracto de lavanda
- Una vuelta de molinillo de pimienta negra, para coronar cada plato

Preparación: En una cazuela pequeña, mezcla 1 taza de leche de coco con la gelatina en polvo. Deja reposar 5 minutos, para que la gelatina despliegue su efecto. Añade la vainilla y el extracto de lavanda y calienta suavemente la mezcla a fuego medio-bajo, batiendo bien para que la gelatina se disuelva. ¡Ten cuidado y no dejes que hierva! Una vez que la gelatina se haya disuelto por completo, retírala del fuego y agrega el jarabe de arce y el resto de leche de coco.

Vierte la mezcla en moldes de 170 gramos. Cúbrelos e introdúcelos en el frigorífico hasta que la mezcla se haya asentado, al menos 4 horas. Sirve con una ralladura fresca de pimienta negra.

Uvas congeladas

Una de las mejores recomendaciones que podemos dar para un tentempié o postre refrescante e hidratante es esta receta de uvas verdes congeladas sin semillas. Congela un racimo de uvas en bolsas de plástico y las tendrás listas para disfrutar.

Helados

¿Quién dijo que los helados son solo para los días calurosos de verano? Estas dulces golosinas refrescantes pueden prepararse con antelación y disfrutarse en el desayuno, como tentempié o de postre. Puedes utilizar todo tipo de bayas o frutas congeladas. Recomendamos utilizar una licuadora potente para nuestras recetas de helados. Algunas de ellas pueden utilizarse para preparar sorbetes directamente de la licuadora. En estas recetas, cada helado de palo es de unos 120 ml.

Helados de frambuesa

PARA 6 HELADOS

- 2 cucharadas de semillas de chia
- 150 ml de leche de coco, en 5 partes
- 1 taza de frambuesas frescas o congeladas
- 4 cucharadas de miel
- El zumo de 1 lima

Preparación: En un bol pequeño, deja en remojo las semillas de chía en unos 30 ml de leche de coco durante 5 a 10 minutos. Pon las semillas de chía, el resto de la leche de coco, las frambuesa, la miel y el zumo de lima en una licuadora y bátelo todo. Reparte la mezcla entre 6 moldes sin BPA (bisfenol A) para helados de palo y déjalos en el congelador hasta que se solidifiquen.

Helados de chocolate y aguacate

PARA 6 HELADOS

- 3 aguacates pequeños maduros, pelados, deshuesados y cortados
- Una lata de 400 ml de leche de coco
- 6 cucharadas de miel
- ½ taza de cacao en polvo
- Una pizca de sal marina
- 1 cucharada de extracto puro de vainilla
- 1 cucharadita de aceite de coco

Preparación: Pon todos los ingredientes en una licuadora y bátelos. Reparte la mezcla entre 6 moldes sin BPA para helados de palo e introdúcelos en el frigorífico hasta que se solidifiquen.

Helados cremosos de plátano y anacardos

PARA 6 HELADOS

- 2 tazas de anacardos crudos sin sal
- 1 taza de leche de coco
- 2 plátanos
- 2 cucharadas de miel
- ½ taza de cerezas deshuesadas o arándanos, frescos o congelados
- 2 cucharaditas de extracto puro de vainilla

Preparación: Pon los anacardos en un bol, cubre con agua y deja en remojo durante 2 a 6 horas, hasta que se hayan reblandecido, y escúrrelos.

Pon todos los ingredientes en una licuadora y tritúralo. Reparte la mezcla entre 6 moldes sin BPA para helados de palo e introdúcelos en el congelador hasta que se solidifiquen.

Helados de naranja

- 1½ tazas de zumo de naranja recién exprimido
- 1 taza de leche de coco
- 2 cucharadas de zumo de limón recién exprimido
- 2 cucharadas de miel (opcional)

Preparación: Vierte todos los ingredientes en una licuadora y ponla en marcha. Reparte la mezcla entre 6 moldes sin BPA para helados de palo y déjalos en el congelador hasta que estén sólidos.

Helados de frutos del bosque y lavanda

PARA 6 HELADOS

- 1 taza de arándanos frescos o congelados
- 1 taza de moras frescas o congeladas

- 1 plátano
- ¾ taza de leche de coco o leche de anacardo
- ¼ de taza de mantequilla de coco (puré de coco, no aceite)
- 2 cucharadas de miel
- 4 gotas de extracto de lavanda
- 1 cucharadita de extracto puro de vainilla
- Una pizca de sal marina rosada o gruesa

Preparación: Reserva ¼ de taza de arándanos y de moras y reparte el resto de las bayas entre 6 moldes sin BPA para helados de palo. Pon todos los demás ingredientes en una licuadora y tritúralos. Vierte la mezcla en los moldes y déjalos en el congelador hasta que el helado se haya solidificado.

Helados de coco, aguacate y lima

PARA 6-8 HELADOS

- 1 lata de 400 ml de leche de coco
- 2 aguacates pequeños maduros, deshuesados y pelados
- ½ taza de zumo de lima recién exprimido
- ¼ taza de agua de coco
- ¼ de taza de miel
- 1 cucharada de ralladura de limón

Preparación: Pon todos los ingredientes en una licuadora y bátelos. Reparte la mezcla entre 6 moldes sin BPA para hacer helados de palo e introdúcelos en el congelador hasta que el helado esté sólido.

Epílogo

Eres un cuerpo de agua

En *Apaga tu sed* exponemos una serie de poderosos argumentos para que la hidratación sea una prioridad de primer orden en tu vida, y te hacemos varias sugerencias para conseguirla. Ahora sabes que la recomendación de ocho vasos de agua al día no tiene por qué ser la mejor opción en un mundo en el que el agua es un recurso cada vez más limitado. El agua no solo «es azul», también puede ser verde. En una época en la que estamos sedientos de nuevos conocimientos, deseamos mostrarte el modo en el que funciona la hidratación, pero también queremos enseñarte cuáles son los principios científicos que la rigen.

Desde los sorprendentes experimentos del doctor Pollack, en los que se mostraba una nueva fase del agua, hasta el descubrimiento de la fascia como un auténtico sistema de regulación hídrica que se extiende por todo el cuerpo, parece como si estuviéramos apenas empezando a intuir las conexiones existentes entre el agua y nuestro propio cuerpo. El vídeo del doctor Jean-Claude Guimberteau sobre la fascia nos llevó a la conclusión de que, no solo es un medio de riego interno, sino también un sistema eléctrico y de transmisión de información, impulsado por energía hídrica.

La redacción del libro se ha valido también de otros revolucionarios conocimientos científicos, algunos de los cuales incluso vieron la luz mientras escribíamos estas páginas. Dos de los hallazgos más importantes surgieron de las investigaciones del doctor Pollack, que demostró que las ondas de luz cargan las moléculas de agua de energía y constató asimismo que en todas las células vegetales existía agua en gel. De modo que el agua existe allí donde ves verde.

La revista *Journal of Cell Science* publicó un informe de Yi-Wen Xu en el que se ponía de manifiesto que las plantas pueden captar luz *en nuestro interior* para liberar nutrientes personalizados, otro estudio ciertamente innovador que apenas estamos empezando a conocer. Y todos estos novedosos conocimientos científicos están saliendo a la luz precisamente en el momento álgido de lo que conocemos como la revolución del microbioma. Todo lo que nos sucede les sucede también a las bacterias que habitan en nuestro cuerpo. Y luego la doctora Maiken Nedergaard dio a conocer que, en el cerebro, existe todo un sistema de drenaje que nadie había visto antes. El agua de nuestro cuerpo se encuentra realmente en la frontera del conocimiento científico.

Así pues, no vuelvas a pensar que el agua sirve simplemente para pasar la comida o las pastillas o para saciar tu sed después de una larga sesión de ejercicio. El agua debería ser lo primero que buscamos por la mañana al levantarnos, es lo que nos hace seguir adelante durante el día y es lo que nos ayuda a limpiar nuestro cerebro por la noche.

De manera que, ahora ya sabes que lo primero que debes preguntarte si no te encuentras del todo bien —ya sea por que sientes cansancio, cierta confusión mental o dolor en cualquier parte del cuerpo— es lo siguiente: «¿Estoy suficientemente hidratado o hidratada?» ¿Por qué esta pregunta? Porque tú, al igual que nuestro planeta, eres un cuerpo de agua. El agua constituye el 99% de tu organismo.

Agradecimientos

Agradecimientos de Dana

Con mi más profunda gratitud, deseo dedicar un reconocimiento singular a una serie de personas muy especiales, todas las cuales han contribuido, de una u otra forma, a que el proceso de elaboración de este libro haya sido posible.

En primer lugar, he de dar las gracias a Gina Bria, coautora del libro, a la que con el tiempo he ido conociendo y queriendo. Gracias por haberme ofrecido aquel delicioso *smoothie* ese funesto día hace ya casi tres años. Gracias igualmente a Linda Loewenthal, mi agente, no solo por su incondicional apoyo, sino también por sus extraordinarias aportaciones editoriales. Mi agradecimiento asimismo a Michelle Howry, mi editora en Hachette, por su valioso asesoramiento, y a Kathy Huck, Camille Pagan y Leslie Meredith, por sus aportaciones y su trabajo de edición.

Por lo que respecta a mis pacientes, les doy las gracias a todos ellos y todos los días, por haberme permitido entrar en sus vidas y por haberme aportado mucho más de cuanto podría expresar. Sois la verdadera razón de ser de mi vida.

Gracias también a mis amigos y amigas, por vuestro apoyo y vuestros ánimos. Se dice que tiene suerte quien tiene un mejor amigo. Pues entonces yo puedo decir que la suerte realmente me acompaña, ya que tengo no uno, sino cuatro: Patricia Richardson, Liz Belson, Leslie Dick y Susan Lazarus. Toda mi gratitud por su ayuda y su apoyo a Steve Feldman, Devon Nola, Brooke Freeman, Michel Sherman, Sam Carter y Manju Moreno. Gracias por mantenerme sana y en buena forma al doctor Daniel Fenster y a todo el personal de Complete Wellness: Jan Stritzler, Denise Lucero, Stefani Lipani, el doctor Shilo Kramer, el doctor Dal Kay, Masae Shimimoto, el doctor David Hashemipour y Tim Coyle.

Gracias a mi familia, siempre dispuesta a animarme y, en particular, a Lisa Albury, Jeff Cohen y Randi Henry. Me siento orgullosa de formar parte de esta loca familia. Y no puedo olvidar a otros miembros de nuestra familia de locos: Jamie Camche, la tía Patsy, el tío Buddy y Viola y Michelle Gulinello. Gracias por vuestro cariño y por vuestros elogios, que me hacen seguir adelante y me sirven de acicate cada mañana. Os quiero a todos y a vuestras respectivas y no menos alocadas familias, que considero ya como mi propia familia.

Deseo por último dedicar un agradecimiento especial a Henry Caplan. Gracias por tu amor y por tu apoyo y, también, por tu singular sentido del humor y tus bromas. Consigues dar color a mi mundo, pero también me aportas sensatez y serenidad cuando más lo necesito. Te quiero.

Agradecimientos de Gina

Confesión de las autoras: en realidad, nosotras no hemos escrito este libro. Ha sido el libro el que «nos ha escrito» a *nosotras*. Deseábamos poner por escrito una serie de cuestiones, pero no dejaban de llegarnos nuevos datos constantemente. ¿Cómo reconocer la información más válida entre tanto conocimiento? Oíamos hablar a un desconocido en la cola del banco sobre una técnica de masaje: puede que fuera importante y que mereciera aparecer en el libro. Nos llegaba información sobre múltiples estudios publicados, algunos de ellos incluso apenas unas semanas antes de la entrega de nuestro manuscrito final. Recibíamos correos electrónicos de organizaciones de las que nunca habíamos oído hablar y que nos remitían informes con las más recientes novedades. Era una especie de designio cósmico que nos abrumaba con todo tipo de datos susceptibles de aparecer en el libro. Ahora también tú formas parte de ese designio, así que no dudes en darle continuidad. Pensamos que es esencial reconsiderar el uso que hacemos del agua en su dimensión de «cuerpo de agua», ya se trate de seres humanos, animales o plantas o de que sean bañeras, lavabos, botellas de agua, piscinas hinchables, arroyos, ríos, lagos o incluso el pequeño cuerpo de una gota de lluvia. Únete a nosotras en la misión de recibir la bendición del agua y, a la vez, de bendecirla. Comparte tus historias relativas a la hidratación en www.hydrationfoundation.org.

De entre mis compañeros en la profesión, sin duda debo un reconocimiento especial a Dana Cohen. En un momento de inspiración dijimos: «¡Escribamos un libro!». Deseo expresar asimismo mi gratitud al doctor Gerald Pollack, estudioso de todo lo relacionado con el agua y cuyo trabajo fue el punto de partida de este libro, y a Linda Loewenthal, nuestra extraordinaria agente, que lo hizo realidad y que en ningún momento pensó que no fuera a ser así. Otro tanto puedo decir de Michelle Howry, nuestra editora en Hachette Book Group, cuya ilusión por este proyecto nos abrió las puertas; de Mery Ellen O'Neill, que ha trabajado conmigo como editora durante más de 25 años, y de Judith Kunst, perspicaz editora que supo lo que buscaba el lector incluso antes de que escribiéramos el libro. Por su ayuda inicial con el manuscrito, gracias también a Tamar Grimm, que es capaz de leer y revisar un texto imprimiéndole su inconfundible sello, y a Erin Inclan, que logra que todo lo escrito resul-

te interesante y atractivo para cualquier lector. La subsede del Metro-
politan Museum of Art, en el edificio conocido como The Cloisters, al
norte de Manhattan, y el responsable de su biblioteca, Michael Carter,
nos permitieron generosamente acceder a su valiosa y singular colección
de manuscritos medievales sobre botánica y herboristería. Deseo mos-
trar mi agradecimiento al hermano Ezekial Brennan y a los doce monjes
benedictinos del Monasterio de la Santa Cruz, en Chicago, que hicieron
posible nuestro retiro de seis días solo para escribir, en silencio... y entre
cánticos. Gracias igualmente a Ani Barnes, directora de preparación física en la Columbia University, que me enseñó a moverme «con la elegan-
cia de un caballo» y que me sirvió de inspiración para mis investigaciones sobre el agua y el movimiento. Mi agradecimiento también a Karen
Balliett, Sunny Bates, Anita Cooney y Margo Fish, auténticas «reinas del
agua», cada una en su estilo. Todas ellas se ofrecieron para participar
en estudios llevados a cabo en un ámbito de la ciencia aún por conocer.
Gracias a Amy Cherry, fundadora del *spa* Shou Sugi Ban House, en los
Hamptons, Nueva York, que nos prestó un valioso apoyo para poder
estudiar las técnicas de hidroterapia. Y a Christina Marie Kimball y a su
esposo, Alex, que nos ofrecieron la posibilidad de disfrutar de un «retiro
acuático para pensar» en su barco, el *Gipsy Wind*, donde senté las bases
del camino que debía seguir para tomar mayor consciencia de mi propio cuerpo. Elli Costa y Max Frye nos prestaron amablemente su casa
en Woods Hole, Massachusetts, para otros ocho días de tranquilidad
dedicados a escribir. Fue entonces cuando tuvimos dos afortunadas reuniones en el Laboratorio de Biología Marina (Marine Biological Laboratory, MBL), con sede en Woods Hole, que nos permitieron confirmar la
base científica de *Apaga tu sed*. Durante aquellos días conocí al doctor
Rudolf Oldenbourg, director del Programa de dinámica celular del MBL.
El doctor me mostró en el microscopio de alta velocidad lo que sucedía
al estirar un pedazo de *film* plástico y pude comprobar que dos de los
principios básicos tratados en nuestro libro, las *ondas de luz* y el *estiramiento*, hacen que las moléculas se alineen para una función más eficaz.
La doctora Lora Hooper, directora del Departamento de Inmunología del
University of Texas Southwestern Medical Center, coincidió con nosotras
una afortunada noche en Woods Hole. Había acudido allí para dar una
de esas afamadas conferencias (Friday Evening Lectures) del laboratorio y

prácticamente la totalidad de la comunidad científica del MBL se encontraba allí reunida. En su presentación expuso y demostró que todas las células, y también las bacterias, tienen relojes moleculares que requieren luz para funcionar. Laura Hames Franklin compartió con nosotras sus conocimientos anatómicos, nos sirvió de inspiración y nos facilitó información para la redacción del libro. Las participantes en las charlas Ted del Salon Bodies of Water celebrado en Nueva York —Jennifer Phillips, Diana Ayton-Shenker, la abuela Nancy Audry y Victoria Cummings— nos facilitaron el acceso a las antiguas y sabias tradiciones ligadas al agua de los indios nativos de Norteamérica. Quiero dar las gracias a mi maestro, David Crow, experto en herboristería y fundador de Floracopea, que me encauzó hacia un nuevo conocimiento de las plantas como aliados biológicos, como compañeros evolutivos con sus propias soluciones inteligentes a nuestros retos medioambientales.

Y gracias también, por supuesto, a mi familia: a James Vescovi, mi esposo, y a mis tres hijos, Alma, Luca y Carlo, y un reconocimiento especial a mi hermana, Gretchen, que nunca ha dejado de ofrecerme inspiración y apoyo, y cuyo atento cuidado de nuestra madre, Stephanie, tanto me ha enseñado y ayudado.

Apéndice

Dieta de eliminación para alergias

La dieta de eliminación descrita en las siguientes páginas es una modificación de la dieta recomendada por el doctor en Medicina William Crook, pionero en la evaluación y el tratamiento de alergias alimentarias ocultas[1]. El objetivo de la dieta es identificar los alérgenos ocultos en los alimentos que pueden causar todos o algunos de los síntomas de alergia. Durante el período de eliminación, todos los alérgenos comunes son completamente erradicados de la dieta durante dos o tres semanas. Una vez que los síntomas mejoran, los alimentos van siendo reintroducidos de uno en uno, para determinar cuáles son los que causan problemas.

ALIMENTOS QUE DEBEN EVITARSE

- **Productos lácteos:** leche, queso, mantequilla, yogur, crema agria, requesón, suero de leche, caseína, caseinato sódico, caseinato cálcico y cualquier alimento que los contenga.

- **Trigo:** la mayoría de los panes, espaguetis, fideos, pasta en general, la mayor parte de las harinas, productos horneados, sémola de trigo duro, sémolas en general y numerosas salsas y caldos espesados. Aunque esta dieta prohíbe el trigo, no es una dieta sin gluten; la avena, la cebada y el centeno sí están permitidos.

- **Maíz:** maíz y todos los alimentos que lo contienen (como *chips* y tortillas de maíz, palomitas, pan de maíz y otros productos horneados que cuenten con el maíz en su lista de ingredientes). Se deben evitar también los productos que contienen aceite de maíz, los aceites vegetales de origen no especificado, el jarabe de maíz, los edulcorantes con maíz, la dextrosa y la glucosa.

- **Huevos:** claras y yemas y cualquier producto que contenga huevo.

- **Cítricos:** naranjas, pomelos, limones, limas, mandarinas y alimentos que los contengan.

- **Café, té y alcohol:** deben evitarse el café con o sin cafeína y el té estándar (como el Lipton) o descafeinado. Las infusiones de hierbas están permitidas, con excepción de las que contienen cítricos.

- **Azúcares refinados:** debe evitarse el azúcar de mesa y cualquier alimento que lo contenga, como dulces, refrescos, tartas, bollos, galletas, chocolate, salsa de manzana con edulcorante y así sucesivamente. Entre los diversos nombres de azúcares se cuentan los siguientes: sacarosa, jarabe de maíz rico en fructosa, jarabe de maíz, edulcorante de maíz, fructosa, zumo de caña, glucosa, dextrosa, maltosa, maltodextrina y levulosa. Todos ellos han de evitarse. Algunos pacientes (dependiendo de su nivel de sospecha de posible alergia a los azúcares refinados) pueden tomar entre una y tres cucharaditas de miel pura no procesada, de jarabe de arce o de jarabe de malta de cebada. Esta «licencia» se determina sobre la base de la consideración individual de cada caso. Los pacientes a los que se les prohíbe por completo todo tipo de azúcar no deben tomar tampoco frutas desecadas. Aquellos pacientes para los que la restricción no es total pueden tomar, con moderación, frutas desecadas no tratadas con derivados sulfurados (de cultivo ecológico). Dado lo poco que se sabe sobre edulcorantes alternativos, como por ejemplo la stevia, es preferible no utilizarlos durante la fase de eliminación.

- **Aditivos alimentarios:** deben evitarse colorantes, saborizantes, conservantes, texturizantes, edulcorantes artificiales y todo tipo de aditivos. La mayoría de los refrescos dietéticos y otros alimentos específicos para dietas contienen ingredientes artificiales, por lo que no deben consumirse. Las uvas, las ciruelas pasas y las pasas que no sean de cultivo ecológico pueden contener sulfitos, por lo que tampoco están permitidas.

- **Cualquier otro alimento que tomes tres o más veces a la semana** debe excluirse de la dieta, para después someterlo a prueba.

- **Alérgenos conocidos:** debe evitarse cualquier alimento que sepas que te produce alergia, con independencia de que esté permitido en la dieta.

- **Agua del grifo (incluida el agua para cocinar):** el agua del grifo se elimina de la dieta cuando se sospecha una hipersensibilidad extrema a ella. Si no se te permite beber agua del grifo, bebe agua de manantial o destilada, embotellada en vidrio o plástico duro. Los envases de plástico blando (aplastable) tienden a desprender partículas de plástico que pasan al agua, por lo que no se aconseja su uso. Las botellas que presentan códigos numerados con el 3 o el 7 es probable que desprendan ftalatos. Opta por botellas y envases que no contengan BPA. Algunos sistemas de filtración del agua no eliminan todos los potenciales alérgenos. Por otro lado, es aconsejable que lleves siempre tu propia agua, incluso al trabajo y a los restaurantes.

Lee las etiquetas

Los alérgenos ocultos están presentes a menudo en los alimentos envasados. En sus etiquetas el término «harina» suele querer decir trigo y el término «aceite vegetal» puede referirse al aceite de maíz, en tanto que la caseína y el suero de leche quedan encuadrados en el grupo de los productos lácteos. Es conveniente asegurarse de que las vitaminas que se toman como suplementos están libres de trigo, maíz, azúcar, cítricos, levaduras y colorantes artificiales.

ALIMENTOS QUE SE PUEDEN TOMAR

- **Cereales para el desayuno.** *Calientes,* como las gachas de avena, el salvado de avena, la crema de centeno o los copos de arroz Arrowhead Mills*. *Secos,* como, por ejemplo, el arroz inflado Barbara's o Erewohn o los cereales Barbara's Brown Rice Crisps. El zumo de manzana con rodajas de manzana fresca y frutos secos combina bien con los cereales. Puedes usar leche de soja sin aceite de maíz ni azúcares añadidos (como algunos productos de las marcas Eden Soy y Rice Dream). La mayoría de este tipo de alimentos se encuentran en supermercados y tiendas de alimentación.

- **Productos de harinas y cereales.** *Harinas,* como las de soja, arroz, patata, alforfón (también llamado trigo sarraceno) o legumbres. *Panes,* como los de arroz, centeno 100%, espelta o mijo (siempre que no contengan lácteos, huevos, azúcares o trigo). *Cereales integrales cocinados,* como avena, mijo, cebada, alforfón (kasha), arroz integral, pasta de arroz integral, macarrones de arroz, espelta (harina y pasta), amaranto y quinoa. *Otros,* como pastelitos de arroz (por ejemplo, los de la marca Quaker), galletas de arroz, galletas de centeno, tortas de pan crujiente sin gluten de alforfón Orgran, galletas de linaza (de la marca Food Alive), rollitos de primavera Blue Dragon, fideos orientales como los *noodles* Soba de alforfón 100% de Eden, y fideos de legumbres Ka-Me. La mayoría de estos productos están disponibles en tiendas de alimentación. Algunas marcas recomendadas son Arrowhead Mills, Bob's Red Mill, Shilo Farms o Ancient Harvest.

- **Legumbres:** semillas de soja, tofu, lentejas, guisantes, garbanzos, alubias blancas, alubias pintas, alubias negras, judías verdes y otras. Las legumbres secas han de dejarse en remojo durante la noche.

---

* Algunas de las marcas que aparecen en este apartado y en los sucesivos no se comercializan en Europa, donde solo están disponibles en tiendas especializadas de alimentos de importación, pudiendo también adquirirse *online (N. de la T.).*

Desecha el agua y enjuágalas antes de cocerlas. Las legumbres enlatadas a menudo contienen azúcares añadidos u otros potenciales alérgenos. Algunas legumbres cocidas conservadas en envases de vidrio (generalmente comercializadas en tiendas de alimentación saludable) no contienen azúcar. También puede recurrirse a pastas y cremas para untar (como el humus), que no contengan azúcar, limón ni aditivos. Asimismo, es posible tomar sopas enlatadas, por ejemplo de guisantes, lentejas o pavo y verduras (sin aditivos). Entre los fabricantes de productos de calidad aceptable en este contexto cabe mencionar Amy's, Kettle Cuisine e Imagine Foods.

- **Verduras y frutas:** debes consumir una amplia variedad. Todas las verduras y hortalizas, excepto el maíz, y todas las frutas, excepto los cítricos, han de tomarse en cantidades abundantes.

- **Proteínas:** carne de vacuno, cordero, cerdo, pollo, pavo, y pescado. El cordero rara vez produce reacciones alérgicas, de modo que la mayoría de las personas que presentan alergias múltiples pueden tomarlo. Los guisos a base de legumbres pueden emplearse como alternativa a los alimentos de origen animal como fuente de proteína (véanse libros de cocina vegetariana para consultar posibles recetas). Las gambas y demás mariscos envasados o en conserva (langosta, cangrejo, ostras) pueden contener sulfitos, por lo que debe evitarse su consumo. El atún y el salmón de lata y otros pescados enlatados están permitidos.

- **Frutos secos y semillas:** los frutos secos pueden tomarse crudos o tostados (sin azúcar). Para que no se enrancien, deben conservarse en un recipiente hermético en la nevera. También pueden tomarse mantequillas de frutos secos (por ejemplo de cacahuete, almendra, anacardo, nuez, sésamo, semilla de cáñamo y tahini de sésamo). Entre las marcas que ofrecen productos de calidad aceptable cabe citar Full Circle, Arrowhead Mills y Natalie's. Las mantequillas de frutos secos combinan bien con palitos de apio y galletas saladas. En las recetas las semillas de linaza recién molidas pueden reemplazar al huevo. Una cucharada de semillas de linaza molida tiene el mismo valor nutricional que un huevo, aunque en ocasiones, en las recetas, es necesario incorporar un agente impulsor.

- **Aceites y grasas:** pueden emplearse aceites de girasol, cártamo, oliva, sésamo, cacahuete, linaza, canola o colza y soja. No deben consumirse, en cambio, aceites vegetales de origen desconocido (que suelen contener aceite de maíz). Las margarinas de soja, girasol y cártamo son aceptables desde el punto de vista de su potencial alergénico, si bien la mayor parte de las margarinas contienen ácidos grasos trans (que predisponen a las cardiopatías), por lo que no suelen recomendarse. Las pastas para untar de verduras y legumbres (como el humus) pueden reemplazar a la margarina o la mantequilla. El aguacate maduro también sirve como sustituto de la mayonesa en los sándwiches.

- **Aperitivos y tentempiés:** cualquiera de los alimentos permitidos en la dieta puede utilizarse para tomar entre horas en cualquier momento del día. Entre los tentempiés aceptables se incluyen los *chips* Danielle Veggie y las barritas de frutas Gorge Delight's. Otros tentempiés recomendados son los palitos de apio, zanahoria u otras verduras, las frutas (con excepción de los cítricos) y los frutos secos y semillas sin sal.

- **Bebidas:** entre las bebidas aceptables se encuentran el agua de manantial embotellada en envases de vidrio o plástico duro, las infusiones de hierbas (sin limón ni naranja), los zumos de frutas no cítricas sin azúcares ni aditivos (diluidos al 50:50 en agua) y la leche de soja o arroz sin aceite de maíz (por ejemplo, Eden Soy Plain o Rice Dream Original). Kafiz, Inka y Kafree Roma son productos que pueden reemplazar al café. El agua del grifo contiene cloro, fluoruro y otros compuestos químicos potencialmente alergénicos. En algunos casos, el agua de manantial envasada en botellas de vidrio o plástico duro es el único tipo de agua permitido, incluso para cocinar. Cuando se elimina de la dieta el agua del grifo, luego debe reintroducirse como si se tratara de un alimento de prueba. Las restricciones en cuanto al tipo de agua permitido deben establecerse de forma personalizada en cada caso.

- **Espesantes:** es posible utilizar como tales harinas de arroz, avena, mijo, cebada, soja o amaranto, polvo de arrurruz, copos de agar y kuzu en polvo.

- **Especias y condimentos:** entre las especias y condimentos permitidos cabe citar la sal (en cantidades moderadas), la pimienta, las hierbas aromáticas (sin conservantes, cítricos ni azúcar), el ajo, el jengibre, las cebollas, el ketchup y la mostaza sin azúcar (por ejemplo, el ketchup de la marca Muir Glen y la mostaza Full Circle), los concentrados de aminoácidos líquidos Bragg (en lugar de las salsas de soja, que contienen trigo y aditivos) y los cristales de vitamina C disueltos en agua (como sustitutos del zumo de limón).

- **Otros alimentos:** salsa para espaguetis sin azúcar (como la de la marca Amy's) y gelatinas y jaleas de frutas sin azúcar ni cítricos (como las comercializadas por Suzanne's).

RECOMENDACIONES GENERALES

- **No debes restringir las calorías.** Es aconsejable comenzar el día con un buen desayuno, comer con frecuencia a lo largo de la jornada y beber al menos cuatro vasos de agua diarios. Si no comes lo suficiente, podrías experimentar síntomas de niveles bajos de azúcar en sangre, como fatiga, irritabilidad, dolores de cabeza o pérdida rápida de peso. Come la mayor variedad posible de alimentos. No es conveniente basar la dieta en unos pocos alimentos, ya que es posible desarrollar alergia a los alimentos que se toman a diario. Para garantizar la ingesta de fibra apropiada hay que tomar legumbres, los cereales integrales permitidos en la dieta, frutas y verduras, sopas de verduras preparadas en casa, frutos secos y semillas. Siempre hay que masticar bien los alimentos para favorecer su digestión.

- **Planifica tus comidas.** Establece un plan de comidas para toda la semana. Deja pasar un tiempo antes de empezar la dieta, con objeto de desarrollar adecuadamente estos planes y abastecer la despensa y la nevera con las cantidades adecuadas de los alimentos permitidos. Para obtener ideas, puedes consultar algún libro de cocina especializado en dietas hipoalergénicas. La mayoría de las recetas pueden adaptarse fácilmente para cumplir los requisitos de la dieta, sin necesidad de modificar el menú del resto de la familia. Cuando vayas a la tienda de alimentos saludables, solicita ayuda para localizar los panes, las galletas, los cereales, las sopas, etc., más adecuados. Algunas persona consideran útil preparar los distintos platos durante el fin de semana, para tener que dedicar menos tiempo durante la semana a la planificación y a la preparación de las comidas. Si necesitas más ayuda o nuevas ideas, pide asesoramiento al dietista-nutricionista de tu centro médico.

- **Usa Internet.** A las personas con acceso limitado a las tiendas de alimentos saludables puede resultarles de gran utilidad la búsqueda de alimentos hipoalergénicos en las páginas de Internet citadas más adelante. Plantea la indagación en términos de «búsqueda avanzada», especificando el mayor número posible de términos de referencia, por ejemplo, *sin trigo, sin maíz, libre de lácteos, sin caseína* o *sin azúcar añadido.* Este tipo de búsquedas elimina buena parte de los productos no permitidos, aunque, en cualquier caso, sigue siendo necesario comprobar la lista de ingredientes de los productos que sean de tu interés. Puedes adquirir los productos directamente en la red, a través de servicios como Glutenfreemall.com, o bien haciendo un pedido a tu tienda de alimentación de confianza.

- **Si comes o cenas fuera.** No dudes en preguntar o pedir lo que necesites. Por ejemplo, puedes solicitar que te sirvan una ración de pescado con almendras laminadas, sin ningún tipo de aderezo añadido y sin mantequilla o con limón. También puedes pedir una patata asada con una rodaja de cebolla. Otra opción es pedir un filete o chuletas de cordero con ensalada, también en este caso sin aderezos añadidos (salvo ajo o hierbas aromáticas). Es importante que te asegures de que los productos de la ensalada no llevan sulfitos y que lleves contigo tu propio aliño para ensaladas, elaborado con aceite y vinagre de manzana con frutos secos o semillas troceados y hierbas aromáticas. Conviene que lleves siempre contigo una botella de agua filtrada, algo para comer entre horas y el ya mencionado aliño, para complementar las comidas que tomes fuera de casa o para tener algo a mano cuando sientas hambre.

- **Síntomas de abstinencia.** Una de cada cuatro personas experimenta síntomas de abstinencia a los pocos días de comenzar la dieta. Entre ellos se cuentan fatiga, irritabilidad, cefaleas, malestar general o aumento de la sensación de hambre. Estos síntomas suelen desaparecer en un plazo de entre dos y cinco días y van seguidos de una mejora de los síntomas iniciales. Si las molestias te resultan difíciles de tolerar, puedes tomar un suplemento de vitamina C tamponada (ascorbato sódico o ascorbato cálcico) en dosis de 1.000 mg por comprimido o cápsula o de 1.500 mg en forma de cristales, hasta cuatro veces al día. También es posible que el médico te recete sales alcalinas (una mezcla de bicarbonato sódico y bicarbonato potásico, en dosis de 1.500 a 2.500 mg disueltos en 180-240 ml de agua, hasta tres o cuatro veces al día). En la mayoría de los casos, los síntomas de abstinencia no son graves y no requieren tratamiento. Cuando se inicia la dieta de eliminación, es preferible dejar de tomar a la vez todos los alimentos que se deben evitar, en lugar de ir adaptándose poco a poco a la nueva dieta.

CADA ALIMENTO, A PRUEBA

Los síntomas de la alergia suelen tardar entre dos y tres semanas en mejorar lo suficiente como para poder comenzar a reintroducir cada alimento. No obstante, puedes empezar antes a poner a prueba los alimentos si te has encontrado mucho mejor durante cinco días y has estado siguiendo la dieta durante al menos diez días. En cambio, si has mantenido la dieta durante cuatro semanas y no te encuentras mejor, es conveniente que acudas a tu médico para que te dé las instrucciones pertinentes. En cualquier caso, cabe puntualizar que la gran mayoría de los pacientes que ponen en práctica la dieta mejoran. En algunas personas la mejoría es tal que optan por no poner a prueba los alimentos, cosa que sin duda es un error. Si esperas demasiado tiempo para volver a probar los alimentos, es posible que la alergia se estabilice y luego no podrás provocar los síntomas mediante la prueba de reintroducir los alimentos uno por uno. Como consecuencia de ello, no sabrás a qué alimentos eres alérgico. Si la reintroducción de determinados alimentos te provoca la reaparición de los síntomas, es probable que seas alérgico a esos alimentos.

Las fuentes de los alimentos

La pureza de los alimentos que se someten a prueba es esencial en este procedimiento. Por ejemplo, no se debe usar la pizza para probar el potencial alergénico del queso, puesto que la pizza contiene también trigo y, probablemente, aceite de maíz. Asimismo, no se debe utilizar pan para la prueba del trigo, ya que el pan a menudo contiene otros potenciales alérgenos. Al realizar las pruebas es preferible usar alimentos ecológicos, de modo que no haya riesgo de interferencia por pesticidas, hormonas u otros aditivos presentes en ciertos alimentos.

Técnica para probar los alimentos

Prueba un alimento nuevo cada día. Si el principal síntoma de la alergia es el dolor artrítico, cada nuevo alimento ha de reincorporarse cada dos días. Las reacciones alérgicas se producen entre diez minutos y doce horas después de la ingesta del alimento, aunque algunos síntomas, como los dolores articulares, llegan a retrasarse hasta 48 horas. Se debe tomar una cantidad relativamente grande del alimento de prueba. Por ejemplo, el día que se ponga a prueba la leche, se debe tomar un vaso grande con el desayuno, junto con cualquiera de los elementos de la lista de alimentos «permitidos». Si después de tomar una porción del potencial alérgeno los síntomas originales reaparecen, o si se presentan dolores de cabeza, gases intestinales, náuseas, mareos o fatiga, se ha de dejar de tomar el alimento en cuestión, que pasará a formar parte de tu lista de alimentos «alergénicos». Si no aparecen síntomas, se debe tomar el alimento de nuevo con la comida y con la cena, permaneciendo a la espera de posibles reacciones. Aunque un alimento sea bien tolerado, es conveniente no reincorporarlo a la dieta habitual hasta que se haya terminado de probar todos los demás alimentos. Si experimentas una reacción, espera a que los síntomas mejoren antes de reintroducir otro. En ciertos casos, puede no estar claro si los síntomas se deben al alimento tomado más recientemente o corresponden a una reacción retardada causada por otro ingerido con anterioridad. Si tienes dudas con respecto a si has reaccionado frente a un alimento en particular, retíralo de tu dieta y vuelve a probarlo cuatro o cinco días más tarde. No hace falta poner a prueba alimentos que no comes nunca.

Tampoco debes probar alimentos que ya sabes que te provocan síntomas.

El orden de prueba no importa. Lo que sí es importante es comenzar con las pruebas un día en el que te encuentres bien y que mantengas un registro diario de los alimentos reintroducidos y de los síntomas generados.

Pruebas de alimentos

Pruebas de lácteos

La leche y el queso deben reintroducirse en la dieta en días distintos. También es necesario probar los distintos quesos en días diferentes, ya que hay personas que son alérgicas a unos quesos, pero no a otros. Las pruebas del yogur, el requesón o la mantequilla no es necesario que se hagan en días separados.

Prueba del trigo

Puede realizarse con trigo tostado de marca Wheatena (sin azúcar ni leche) o con cualquier otro tipo de cereal de trigo puro. Se puede añadir leche de soja o de arroz.

Prueba del maíz

Se realiza con mazorcas de maíz frescas o congeladas (sin salsas ni conservantes).

Prueba del huevo

Las claras y las yemas se prueban en días separados, utilizando huevos duros.

Prueba de los cítricos

Las naranjas, los pomelos, los limones y las limas se prueban en días separados. El limón y la lima pueden tomarse exprimidos en agua. Para las naranjas y los pomelos es preferible usar gajos frescos.

Pruebas del agua del grifo y de los alimentos frecuentes

Si has eliminado de tu dieta el agua del grifo, reintrodúcela para probar. Prueba también aquellos alimentos que eliminaste de tu dieta por tomarlos con mucha frecuencia.

Pruebas opcionales

Si cualquiera de los productos que se citan a continuación no forman parte de tu dieta actual, o si piensas eliminarlos de tu dieta en breve, no es preciso ponerlos a prueba. No obstante, si has estado tomando con regularidad cualquiera de ellos, es conveniente someterlos a prueba para comprobar en qué medida te afectan. En ciertos casos, las reacciones a estos alimentos y bebidas son importantes. Solo deben ponerse a prueba en días en los que estés seguro de poder afrontar una posible reacción adversa.

- **Café y té:** pruébalos en días separados, sin añadir leche, crema no láctea ni azúcar. Sí puedes añadir la leche de soja o de arroz permitida. El café descafeinado debe probarse por separado. Se realizan por separado las pruebas de café, té, café descafeinado y té sin teína.

- **Azúcar:** añade cuatro cucharaditas de azúcar de caña a una bebida o a unos cereales, o mézclalas con otro alimento.

- **Chocolate:** prueba con una o dos cucharadas de chocolate puro Baker's o de cacao en polvo Hershey's.

- **Aditivos alimentarios:** compra unos cuantos botes de colorantes alimentarios McCormick o French's. Pon media cucharadita de cada colorante en un vaso. Añade una cucharadita de la mezcla a un vaso de agua y bébetelo. Si lo prefieres, puedes probar cada colorante por separado.

- **Alcohol:** la cerveza, el vino y los licores deber probarse en días diferentes, ya que las reacciones que provocan en caso de alergia son a menudo distintas. Prueba dos veces al día, pero solo cuando puedas afrontar la posibilidad de no encontrarte bien ese día y posiblemente tampoco el siguiente.

Después de las pruebas

Una vez concluidas las pruebas de alergias alimentarias, se debe pedir cita de nuevo en la consulta del médico para una visita de seguimiento. Cuando acudas, lleva tu diario contigo, para repasar los datos con el doctor.

Sugerencias de autoayuda

Si tienes propensión a las alergias y comes siempre los mismos alimentos, es posible que termines por desarrollar alergia a algunos de ellos. Una vez que hayas descubierto cuáles son los alimentos que puedes tomar con total seguridad, es conveniente que procures variar la dieta de forma rotatoria. Algunas personas con tendencia elevada a las alergias requieren una pauta de cuatro días, aunque la mayor parte de la gente suele tolerar bien el consumo de alimentos con una frecuencia superior a los cuatro días. Es incluso posible que llegues a tolerar los alimentos alergénicos si has estado entre seis y doce meses sin probarlos.

Sin embargo, si sigues tomando esos alimentos con una frecuencia superior a los cuatro días, es posible que la alergia vuelva a manifestarse.

Consume una variedad amplia de alimentos, no solo tus favoritos. Si rotas los alimentos, conviene que te asegures de evitar todas las formas del alimento en cuestión cuando «no toque» dicho alimento. Por ejemplo, si estás rotando el consumo de maíz, evita los chips de maíz, el aceite y los edulcorantes de maíz y demás productos que contengan maíz, excepto en los días en los que esté programado el consumo de este alimento. Durante los períodos de eliminación y reintroducción para probar los alimentos no es necesario practicar una rotación estricta.

Es importante saber identificar posibles reacciones alérgicas distintas de las habituales. Si tienes predisposición a las alergias, es posible que seas alérgico a alimentos distintos de los que has eliminado y probado con esta dieta. Presta siempre atención a lo que comes y, si desarrollas síntomas, revisa las comidas recientes. Puedes eliminar los alimentos sospechosos durante dos semanas, para después reintroducirlos y comprobar si desencadenan los mismos síntomas.

Para más información consulta la página *web* https://doctorgaby.com.

Recursos

PÁGINAS WEB DE LAS AUTORAS

- www.drdanacohen.com
- www.completewellnessnyc.com
- www.hydrationfoundation.org

LIBROS Y ARTÍCULOS QUE MERECE LA PENA CONSULTAR

- Como hemos mencionado en el prefacio, hay un libro que ejerció sobre nosotras una gran influencia cuando estábamos pensando en escribir *Apaga tu sed*. Nos referimos a *Your Body's Many Cries for Water* (Global Health Solutions, 2008), del doctor Fereydoon Batmanghelidj (traducido al español con el título *Los muchos clamores de su cuerpo por el agua*).
- *The Fourth Phase of Water: Beyond Solid, Liquid, and Vapor* (Ebner and Sons, 2013) es un libro de lectura obligada y fácil comprensión, escrito por el doctor Gerald Pollack para lectores legos en la materia y acompañado de ilustraciones, por increíble que parezca, sobre cuestiones complejas como el agua en gel y su uso para la obtención de energía en el cuerpo.
- «The Fourth Phase of Water: Implications for Energy and Health», de Gerald Pollack, publicado en el número de invierno de 2015 de *Wise Traditions* (volumen 16, n° 4).

- En un blog informativo titulado «Water, Energy, and the Perils of Dehydration» el doctor Nicholas González, ya fallecido, analizaba el innovador libro *Your Body's Many Cries for Water*, citado más arriba, del doctor Batmanghelidj, y la epidemia de deshidratación crónica. Puede consultarse en https://www.greenmed info. com/blog/water-energy-and-perils-dehydration.
- El estudio «Water, Hydration and Health», del doctor Barry Popkin, es una magnífica lectura para profundizar en el conocimiento de la relación entre agua y salud (*Nutrition Reviews*, volumen 68, n°. 8, agosto de 2010, páginas 439-458).
- Un importante libro en el que se explora nuestra relación con el agua, obra de M. J. Pangman y Melanie Evans, es *Dancing with Water: The New Science of Water* (Uplifting Press, 2011).
- Para saber más sobre el papel de las grasas en nuestro cuerpo puede consultarse *Know Your Fats: The Complete Primer for Understanding the Nutrition of Fats, Oils, and Cholesterol*, de Mary G. Enig, (Bethesda Press, 2000).
- Para conocer cuáles son los ejercicios más adecuados para las mujeres puede consultarse *Strength Training Exercises for Women*, de Joan Pagano (DK Publishing, 2013), publicado en español con el título *Fortalecimento para mujeres.*
- Para ampliar conocimientos sobre el modo en el que el ejercicio afecta al cerebro véase *Spark: The Revolutionary New Science of Exercise and the Brain*, de John Ratey (Little Brown, 2008).
- El libro de Teresa Tapp *Fit and Fabulous in 15 Minutes* (Ballantine, 2006) es un excelente punto de partida para abordar del estiramiento de la fascia y para ponerse en forma con rapidez y facilidad.
- *The New Rules of Posture: How to Sit, Stand, and Move in the Modern World*, de Mary Bond (Healing Arts Press, 2006), traducido al español con el título *Las nuevas reglas de la postura en el mundo moderno*, es un magnífico recurso de educación postural.
- Para un estudio detallado del método Egoscue, puede consultarse *The Egoscue Method of Health Through Motion*, de Pete Egoscue con Roger Gittines (William Morrow, 1993).
- Otro excelente recurso sobre técnicas de ejercicio es *Franklin Method: Ball and Imagery Exercises for Relaxed and Flexible*

Shoulders, Neck and Thorax, de Eric Franklin (Orthopedic Physical Therapy Products, 2008).

- Es recomendable la lectura de *The Healer Within: Using Traditional Chinese Techniques to Release Your Body's Own Medicine, Movement, Massage, Meditation, Breathing,* de Roger Jahnke (HarperOne, 1998) para un mejor conocimiento de las prácticas orientales de meditación, respiración y movimiento y reducción del estrés.
- Para profundizar en el conocimiento de la hidratación y la respiración, recomendamos *Close Your Mouth: Buteyko Clinic Handbook forPerfect Health ,* de Patrick McKeown (Buteyko Books, 2005), publicado en español con el título *Cierra tu boca, manual de la clínica de respiración Butyeko.*

RECURSOS SOBRE NUTRICIÓN Y BIENESTAR: PÁGINAS *WEB* COMERCIALES

- https://www.costco.com: Costco es una fuente sorprendente de excelentes productos de origen ecológico, como por ejemplo el aceite de coco virgen.
- https://www.grownyc.org: este magnífico recurso para los neoyorquinos (y para los que viven en los alrededores de la ciudad) contiene abundante información sobre mercados de productores locales y sobre reciclaje.
- http://www.localfarmmarkets.org: página para localizar mercados de productores locales a nivel nacional en Estados Unidos.
- https://www.knowfoods.com: esta página *web* ofrece deliciosos productos que reducen el nivel de glucosa en sangre, sin cereales, sin gluten, sin lácteos, sin cacahuetes, sin soja y sin levaduras. No es broma.
- https://www.mountainroseherbs.com: buen sitio *web* para conseguir plantas aromáticas y especias a granel.
- https://www.thrivemarket.com: ofrece productos ecológicos a buen precio.

VÍDEOS Y CHARLAS TEDx QUE HAY QUE VER

- Revolucionario vídeo del doctor Jean-Claude Guimberteau sobre los conocimientos relativos a la fascia (en francés): https://www.youtube.com/watch?v=eW0lvOVKDxE
- Excelente explicación de los hallazgos del doctor Guimberteau en *Functional Therapy Magazine*: https://www.youtube.com/watch?v=qSXpX4wyoY8
- Charla TEDx del doctor Gerald Pollack, «Water, Cells, Life», sobre la cuarta fase del agua: https://www.youtube.com/watch?v=p9UC0chfXcg
- Vídeo del Salón TEDx de Nueva York, «Bodies of Water Conference»: https://www.hydrationfoundation.org/copy-of-highlights-1
- Charla TEDx de la doctora Stephanie Seneff, «The Mineral Power for Your Body's Electrical Supply»: https://www.youtube.com/watch?v=fDWEVXhaydc
- Charla TEDx de Gina Bria, «How to Grow Water: It's Not Only Blue, It's Green»: https://www.youtube.com/watch?v=kAiCeRZLCoE
- Charla TEDx de Gillian Ferrabee, «Water as a Conductor for Creative Flow»: https://www.youtube.com/watch?v=ryYTxm7k7mg
- Charla TEDx del doctor Adam Wexler, «The Bridge Between Water and Life»: https://www.youtube.com/watch?v=hPM1l93mGZw
- Charla TEDx de Amy Cuddy, «Your Body Language May Shape Who You Are»: https://www.youtube.com/watch?v=Ks-_Mh1QhMc
- Técnica de automasaje facial detox del maestro Tiong: https://www.youtube.com/watch?v=p5p9AzC9LE8

RECURSOS *ONLINE* SOBRE NUTRICIÓN Y MOVIMIENTO

- **https://www.beautifulonraw.com:** Tonya Zavasta da un giro actualizado a las antiguas técnicas rusas y ucranianas para la salud y la piel.
- **https://blog.bulletproof.com:** David Asprey es un conocido *biohacker* que experimenta con su propio cuerpo y difunde la información relativa a dicha experimentación. Dio origen a la nueva moda global de añadirle grasas al café, con el resultado del denominado «café a prueba de balas» (*bulletproof coffee*).
- **https://www.eldoamethod.com:** el método ELDOA del doctor Guy Voyer ofrece excelentes ejercicios de estiramiento.
- **http://www.egoscue.com:** el método Egoscue para acabar con el dolor crónico es una de las técnicas basadas en el movimiento más sencillas y directas.
- **http://www.f loracopeia.com:** David Crow, experto herborista, ofrece productos y consejos para hidratarse a través de la aromaterapia. **https://www.drkarafitzgerald.com:** la doctora Kara Fitzgerald tiene un doctorado en medicina naturopática. Su página *web* ofrece numerosas recetas de hidratación.
- **https://www.foundmyfitness.com:** la doctora Rhonda Patrick revisa los últimos hallazgos científicos sobre salud.
- **https://www.laurahamesfranklin.com:** Laura Hames Franklin da lecciones de anatomía mediante visualización y ofrece un singular programa de entrenamiento corporal.
- **https://www.drfuhrman.com:** recomendación médica de recetas nutritivas con demostraciones en vídeo.
- **https://www.doctorgaby.com:** el doctor Alan Gaby escribió el libro *Nutritional Medicine*, que es la biblia de Dana.
- **http://www.greenmedinfo.com:** esta página *web* es un excelente medio para el conocimiento de recursos a base de plantas. Es la fuente sobre salud natural basada en la evidencia, de acceso libre y más citada, con más de 20.000 artículos.
- **https://www.greensmoothiegirl.com:** Robyn Openshaw lleva más de veinte años defendiendo los beneficiosos efectos para la salud de los *smoothies* verdes. Su página *web* ofrece numerosas recetas de *smoothies*.

- **https://www.heartmdinstitute.com:** la página *web* del cardiólogo Stephen Sinatra ofrece información sobre salud y bienestar.
- **http://www.drhoffman.com:** la página *web* del doctor Ronald Hoffman, mentor y amigo de Dana, cuenta con un sistema de distribución de archivos multimedia de gran utilidad en el asesoramiento para la salud.
- **https://www.lifespa.com:** el doctor John Douillard ofrece consejos sobre medicina ayurvédica y es también experto en respiración, hidratación y deporte de alto rendimiento.
- **https://www.drmercola.com:** página *web* muy seguida que ofrece numerosos artículos de libre acceso sobre salud y bienestar.
- **https://www.t-tapp.com:** Teresa Tapp ofrece acceso libre a diversos recursos y programas de ejercicios de 15 minutos para ponerse en forma, incluidos ejercicios de estiramiento de fascia.
- **https://www.thetappingsolution.com:** Nick Ortner centra su atención en la técnica de reducción del estrés conocida como solución *tapping*.

PAGINAS *WEB* Y ORGANIZACIONES BENÉFICAS Y SIN ÁNIMO DE LUCRO RELACIONADAS CON EL AGUA Y EL MEDIOAMBIENTE

- **https://www.ewg.org:** esta es la organización que elaboró la lista de las doce frutas y verduras más contaminadas *(dirty dozen)*, que siempre que sea posible deben ser de cultivo ecológico, y de las quince menos contaminadas *(clean fifteen)*, que no es necesario que lo sean. Esta página *web* cuenta, además, con los siguientes recursos para el consumidor:
  - Guía para la adquisición de filtros de agua
  - Base de datos de ámbito nacional relativa al agua corriente en Estados Unidos
  - Guía de compra de pesticidas para los productores
  - Guía de productos de limpieza saludables
  - Guía de protectores solares
  - Guía de consumo de pescados y mariscos
  - Guía sobre uso seguro de teléfonos móviles
  - Guía para el consumidor destinada a evitar los alimentos OGM

- **https://www.greenwave.org:** esta página *web* promueve la acuicultura marina de algas, pescados y mariscos, orientada a la atenuación de los efectos del cambio climático, y el uso del alga llamada kelp o quelpo como fuente de alimento viable y supersaludable.
- **https://www.heifer.org:** esta es la página *web* de una gran organización benéfica que ayuda a combatir las condiciones de pobreza y hambre, proporcionando animales de granja a las personas más necesitadas, de modo que puedan contar con una fuente de alimento y de ingresos.
- **http://www.rainforestflow.org:** esta organización proporciona agua potable a tribus indígenas del Amazonas.
- **https://www.weareprojectzero.org:** el Proyecto Cero se centra en la protección y la recuperación de los océanos.
- **http://www.container-recycling.org:** esta organización se dedica a la investigación y la educación sobre las formas de reducir, reutilizar y reciclar los residuos y cuenta con una excelente base de datos relacionada con estos temas.

- **http://www.findaspring.com:** esta página *web* ayuda a localizar manantiales naturales en cualquier parte del mundo.
- **https://www.plasticoceans.org:** esta página *web* ofrece información orientada a educar a la gente sobre el problema de los plásticos y los océanos.
- **https://smile.amazon.com:** Hemos de admitir que todos usamos Amazon; y esta es una buena manera de aportar algo a la organización benéfica que prefieras sin coste adicional para ti.
- **https://www.westonaprice.org:** la fundación Weston A. Price se dedica a favorecer la incorporación de alimentos ricos en nutrientes a la dieta humana a través de la educación, la investigación y el activismo.

RECURSOS PARA ENCONTRAR MÉDICOS
CON INTERESES AFINES

- http://www.acam.org
- https://www.ifm.org

PÁGINAS *WEB* RECOMENDADAS SOBRE TÉCNICAS
DE MEDITACIÓN

- **https://www.heartmath.com:** el equilibrio interno es un excelente medio para optimizar el trabajo respiratorio y supone una biorretroalimentación instantánea. Se trata de un proceso bien estudiado y eficaz para el abordaje de la ansiedad, la depresión y los trastornos del sueño.
- **https://www.rewireme.com:** esta es una página *web* de alto valor informativo, que ofrece recursos de *mindfulness*, espiritualidad y neurociencia.
- **https://www.tm.org:** excelente referencia para el aprendizaje de la meditación trascendental.
- **https://www.instituteof integralqigongandtaichi.org:** proporciona información sobre meditación y movimiento.

Notas

INTRODUCCIÓN: HIDRATACIÓN: ¿CÓMO PODEMOS MEJORARLA?

1. Ericson, John. «75 % of Americans May Suffer from Chronic Dehydration, According to Doctors». Medical Daily. Acceso, 25 de junio de 2017. http://www. medicaldaily.com/75-americans-may-suffer-chronic-dehydration- according-doctors-247393.
2. Thornton, Simon N. y Marie Trabalon. «Chronic Dehydration Is Associated with Obstructive Sleep Apnoea Syndrome». *Clinical Science* 128, n° 3 (1 de febrero de 2015): 225. http://www.clinsci.org/content/128/3/225.
3. Chang, Tammy, et al. «Inadequate Hydration, BMI, and Obesity Among US Adults: NHANES 2009–2012». *Annals of Family Medicine* 14, n° 4 (julio-agosto de 2016): 320–324. Acceso, 22 de octubre de 2017. http://www.annfammed.org/content/14/4/320.
4. Dennis, E. A., et al. «Water Consumption Increases Weight Loss During a Hypocaloric Diet Intervention in Middle-Aged and Older Adults». *Obesity* (Silver Spring) 18, n° 2 (febrero de 2010): 300–307. Acceso, 22 de octubre de 2017. https://www. ncbi.nlm.nih.gov/pubmed/19661958.
5. Preachuk, Deb. «The Connection Between Chronic Pain and Chronic Dehydration». Pain Free Posture MN. Acceso, 22 de octubre de 2017. http://www.painfree-posturemn.com/the-connection-between-chronic-pain-and- chronic-dehydration.
6. Adan, A. «Cognitive Performance and Dehydration». *Journal of the American College of Nutrition* 31, n° 2 (abril de 2012): 71–78. Acceso, 25 de octubre de 2017.https://www.ncbi.nlm.nih.gov/pubmed/?term=adan%2C%2Bcognitive%2 Bperformance%2C%2B2012.
7. Bear, Tracey, et al. «A Preliminary Study on How Hypohydration Affects Pain Perception». *Psychophysiology* 53, n° 5 (mayo de 2016): 605–610. Acceso, 22 de

octubre de 2017. https://www.ncbi.nlm.nih.gov/pubmed/26785699; doi:10.1111/psyp.12610.

Moyen, N. E., et al. «Hydration Status Affects Mood State and Pain Sensation during Ultra-Endurance Cycling». *Journal of Sports Sciences* 33, n° 18 (marzo de 2015):1962–1969. Acceso, 22 de octubre de 2017. https://www.ncbi.nlm.nih.gov/pubmed/25793570.

8. Armstrong, L. E., et al. «Mild Dehydration Affects Mood in Healthy Young Women». *Journal of Nutrition* 142, n° 2 (febrero de 2012): 382– 388. Acceso, 22 de octubre de 2017. https://www.ncbi.nlm.nih.gov/pubmed/22190027.

9. Container Recycling Institute, http://www.container-recycling.org/index.php.

10. Langmead, L., R. J. Makinsy D. S. Rampton. «Anti-Inflammatory Effects of Aloe Vera Gel in Human Colorectal Mucosa in Vitro». *Alimentary Pharmacology and Therapeutics* 19, n° 5 (1 de marzo de 2004): 521–527.https://www.ncbi.nlm.nih.gov/pubmed/14987320; doi:10.1111/j.1365-2036.2004.01874.x.

CAPÍTULO 1: LA NUEVA CIENCIA DEL AGUA

1. Arnaoutis, Giannis, et al. «The Effect of Hypohydration on Endothelial Function in Young, Healthy Adults». *European Journal of Nutrition* 56, n° 3 (abril de 2017): 1.211–1217. https://link.springer.com/article/10.1007%2Fs00394-016-1170-8.

2. Harvard Health Publishing, «Surprising Heart Attack and Stroke Triggers—From Waking up to Volcanoes». Julio de 2007. https://www.health.harvard.edu/press_releases/heart-attack-triggers.

3. Mayo Clinic, Diabetic Ketoacidosis. http://www.mayoclinic.org/diseases-conditions/diabetic-ketoacidosis/basics/definition/con-20026470.

4. Manz, Friedrich y Andreas Wentz. «The Importance of Good Hydration for the Prevention of Chronic Diseases». *Nutrition Reviews* 63, n° 6 (2005). http://onlinelibrary.wiley.com/doi/10.1111/j.1753-4887.2005.tb00150.x/epdf.

5. González, Nicholas. «Water, Energy, and the Perils of Dehydration». GreenMedInfo Blog. 2 de julio de 2015. Acceso, 22 de octubre de 2017. http://www.greenmedinfo.com/blog/water-energy-and-perils-dehydration.

6. Barnard College, Columbia University. The Facts About Laxatives. https://barnard.edu/counseling/resources/eating-disorders/laxatives.

7. Batmanghelidj, F. «A New and Natural Method of Treatment of Peptic Ulcer Disease». *Journal of Clinical Gastroenterology* 5, n° 3 (1983): 203–206.

8. Galson, Steven K. «Prevention of Deep Vein Thrombosis and Pulmonary Embolism». *Public Health Reports* 123, n° 4 (2008): 420–421. https://www.ncbi.nlm.nih.gov/pmc/articles/PMC2430635/; doi:10.1177/003335490812300402.

9. Ghosh, Arunava, R. C. Boucher y Robert Tarran. «Airway Hydration and COPD». *Cellular and Molecular Life Sciences* 72, n° 19 (2015): 3637–3652.https://www.ncbi.nlm.nih.gov/pubmed/26068443; doi:10.1007/s00018- 015-1946-7.

10. Gaby, A. R. «The Role of Hidden Food Allergy/Intolerance in Chronic Disease». *Alternative Medicine Review: A Journal of Clinical Therapeutics* 3, n° 2 (abril de 1998): 90–100. Acceso, 25 de octubre de 2017. https://www.ncbi.nlm.nih.gov/pubmed/9577245.

11. Armstrong, L. E., et al. «Mild Dehydration Affects Mood in Healthy Young Women». *Journal of Nutrition* 142, n° 2 (February 2012): 382–388. Acceso, 25 de octubre de 2017. https://www.ncbi.nlm.nih.gov/pubmed/22190027.

12. Benton, David. «Dehydration Influences Mood and Cognition: A Plausible Hypothesis?» *Nutrients* 3, n° 5 (mayo de 2011): 555–573. https://www.ncbi.nlm.nih.gov/pmc/articles/PMC3257694/; doi:10.3390/nu3050555.

13. Thornton, Simon N. «Diabetes and Hypertension, as Well as Obesity and Alzheimer's Disease, Are Linked to Hypohydration-Induced Lower Brain Volume». *Frontiers in Aging Neuroscience* 6 (2014): 279. https://www.ncbi.nlm.nih.gov/pmc/articles/PMC4195368/; doi:10.3389/fnagi.2014.00279.

14. Ibíd.

15. Dickson, J. M., et al. «The Effects of Dehydration on Brain Volume—Preliminary Results». *International Journal of Sports Medicine* 26, n° 6 (julio-agosto de 2005): 481–485. Acceso, 25 de octubre de 2017. https://www.ncbi.nlm.nih.gov/pubmed/16037892.

16. Chumlea, W. C., et al. «Total Body Water Data for White Adults 18 to 64 Years of Age: The Fels Longitudinal Study». *Kidney International* 56, n° 1 (julio de 1999): 244–252. Acceso, 25 de octubre de 2017. https://www.ncbi.nlm.nih.gov/pubmed/10411699.

17. Ritz, P., et al. «Influence of Gender and Body Composition on Hydration and Body Water Spaces». *Clinical Nutrition* 27, n° 5 (octubre de 2008): 740–746. Acceso, 25 de octubre de 2017. https://www.ncbi.nlm.nih.gov/pubmed/18774628.

18. Thornton, S. N. «Thirst and Hydration: Physiology and Consequences of Dysfunction». *Physiology and Behavior* 100, n° 1 (26 de abril de 2010): 15–21. Acceso, 26 de octubre de 2017. https://www.ncbi.nlm.nih.gov/pubmed/20211637.

19. Beauchet, O., et al. «Blood Pressure Levels and Brain Volume Reduction: A Systematic Review and Meta-analysis». *Journal of Hypertension* 31, n° 8 (agosto de 2013): 1502–1516. Acceso, 26 de octubre de 2017. https://www.ncbi.nlm.nih.gov/pubmed/23811995.

20. Smith, David W., et al. «Altitude Modulates Concussion Incidence». *Orthopaedic Journal of Sports Medicine* 1, n° 6 (noviembre de 2013): 232596711351158. https://www.ncbi.nlm.nih.gov/pmc/articles/PMC4555510/; doi:10.1177/2325967113511588.

21. Seneff, Stephanie y Wendy A. Morley. «Diminished Brain Resilience Syndrome: A Modern Day Neurological Pathology of Increased Susceptibility to Mild Brain Trauma, Concussion, and Downstream Neurodegeneration». *Surgical Neurology International* 5, n° 1 (junio de 2014): 97. https://www.ncbi.nlm.nih.gov/pubmed/25024897; doi:10.4103/2152-7806.134731

22. University of North Carolina Chapel Hill, «NFL Grant Funds International Research on the Role of Active Rehabilitation Strategies in Concussion Management», publicación de noticias, 14 de junio de 2017. http://uncnews.unc.edu/2017/06/14/nfl-grant-funds-international-research-role-active-rehabilitation-strategies-concussion-management/.

23. «Concussion». Mayo Clinic. 29 de julio de 2017. Acceso, 26 de octubre de 2017. http://www.mayoclinic.org/diseases-conditions/concussion/symptoms-causes/dxc-20273155.

24. Seneff, Stephanie y Wendy A. Morley. «Diminished Brain Resilience Syndrome: A Modern Day Neurological Pathology of Increased Susceptibility to Mild Brain

Trauma, Concussion, and Downstream Neurodegeneration». *Surgical Neurology International* 5, n° 1 (junio de 2014): 97. https://www.ncbi.nlm.nih.gov/pubmed/25024897; doi:10.4103/2152-7806.134731.

25. «Concussion». Mayo Clinic. 29 de junio de 2017. Acceso, 26 de octubre de 2017. http://www.mayoclinic.org/diseases-conditions/concussion/symptoms-causes/dxc-20273155.

26. Bear, Tracey, et al. «A Preliminary Study on How Hypohydration Affects Pain Perception». *Psychophysiology* 53, n° 5 (mayo de 2016): 605–610. https://www.ncbi.nlm.nih.gov/pubmed/26785699; doi:10.1111/psyp.12610.

27. Ogino, Yuichi, et al. «Dehydration Enhances Pain-Evoked Activation in the Human Brain Compared with Rehydration». *Anesthesia and Analgesia* 118, n° 6 (junio de 2014): 1317–13325. https://www.ncbi.nlm.nih.gov/pubmed/24384865; doi:10.1213/ane.0b013e3182a9b028.

28. «Lack of Sleep Is Affecting Americans, Finds the National Sleep Foundation». National Sleep Foundation. Acceso, 22 de octubre de 2017. https://sleepfoundation.org/media-center/press-release/lack-sleep-affecting-americans-finds-the-national-sleep-foundation.

29. Xie, L., et al. «Sleep Drives Metabolite Clearance from the Adult Brain». *Science* 342, n° 6156 (18 octubre de 2013): 373–377. http://science.sciencemag.org/content/342/6156/373; doi:10.1126/science.1241224.

30. Jessen, Nadia Aalling, et al. «The Glymphatic System: A Beginner's Guide». *Neurochemical Research* 40, n° 12 (diciembre de 2015): 2.583–2.599.https://www.ncbi.nlm.nih.gov/pubmed/25947369; doi:10.1007/s11064-015-1581-6.

31. Mendelsohn, Andrew R. y James W. Larrick. «Sleep Facilitates Clearance of Metabolites from the Brain: Glymphatic Function in Aging and Neurodegenerative Diseases». *Rejuvenation Research* 16, n° 6 (diciembre de 2013): 518–523. https://www.ncbi.nlm.nih.gov/pubmed/24199995;doi:10.1089/rej.2013.1530.

32. Altieri, A., C. La Vecchia y E. Negri. «Fluid Intake and Risk of Bladder and Other Cancers». *European Journal of Clinical Nutrition* 57, suplemento 2 (diciembre de 2003): S59–S68. https://www.ncbi.nlm.nih.gov/pubmed/14681715; doi:10.1038/sj.ejcn.1601903.

33. Vanderbilt University Medical Center. «Water's Unexpected Role in Blood Pressure Control». ScienceDaily. Acceso, 25 de octubre de 2017. https://www.sciencedaily.com/releases/2010/07/100706150639.htm.

34. Boschmann, Michael, et al. «Water-Induced Thermogenesis». *Journal of Clinical Endocrinology and Metabolism* 88, n° 12 (diciembre de 2003): 6015–6019. https://www.ncbi.nlm.nih.gov/pubmed/14671205; doi:10.1210/jc.2003-030780.

35. Yang, Qing. «Gain Weight by "Going Diet"? Artificial Sweeteners and the Neurobiology of Sugar Cravings». *Yale Journal of Biology and Medicine*. Junio de 2010. Acceso, 25 de octubre de 2017. https://www.ncbi.nlm.nih.gov/pmc/articles/PMC2892765/.

36. Howard, Jacqueline. «Diet Sodas May Be Tied to Stroke, Dementia Risk». CNN. 20 de abril de 2017. Acceso, 25 de octubre de 2017. http://www.cnn.com/2017/04/20/health/diet-sodas-stroke-dementia-study/index.html.

37. Bria, Rebecca. «Ritual, Economy, and the Production of Community at Ancient Hualcayan (Ancash, Peru)» (disertación, Vanderbilt University, Department of Anthropology, 2017).

38. Perakis, Fivos, et al. «Diffusive Dynamics During the High-to-Low Density Transition in Amorphous Ice». *Proceedings of the National Academy of Sciences* 114, n° 31 (1 de agosto de 2017): 8193–8198. http://www.pnas.org/content/114/31/8193; doi:10.1073/pnas.1705303114.

39. Crew, Bec. «Physicists Just Discovered a Second State of Liquid Water». ScienceAlert. 14 de noviembre de 2016. Acceso, 23 de octubre de 2017. https://www.sciencealert.com/physicists-just-discovered-a-second-state-of-liquid-water.

40. Saykally, R. J. y F. N. Keutsch. «Water Clusters: Untangling the Mysteries of the Liquid, One Molecule at a Time», *PNAS* 98, n° 19 (septiembre de 2001): 10533–10540.

41. McGeoch, Julie E. M. y Malcolm W. McGeoch. «Entrapment of Water by Subunit C of ATP Synthase». *Journal of the Royal Society Interface* 5, n° 20 (6 de marzo de 2008): 311–318. Acceso, 23 de octubre de 2017. http://rsif.royalsocietypublishing.org/content/5/20/311.

42. Kang, Young-Rye, et al. «Anti-obesity and Anti-diabetic Effects of Yerba Mate (*Ilex Paraguariensis*) in C57BL/6J Mice Fed a High-FatDiet». *Laboratory Animal Research* 28, n° 1 (marzo de 2012): 23–29. Acceso, 23 de octubre de 2017. https://www.ncbi.nlm.nih.gov/pmc/articles/PMC3315195/.

43. Pollack, Gerald. «The Fourth Phase of Water». The Weston A. Price Foundation. 15 de febrero de 2016. Acceso, 23 de octubre de 2017. https://www.westonaprice.org/health-topics/health-issues/the-fourth-phase-of-water/.

44. Xu, Chen, et al. «Light-Harvesting Chlorophyll Pigments Enable Mammalian Mitochondria to Capture Photonic Energy and Produce ATP». *Journal of Cell Science* (15 de enero de 2014). Acceso, 23 de octubre de 2017. http://jcs.biologists.org/content/127/2/388.

CAPÍTULO 2: CÓMETE EL AGUA

1. Valtin, Heinz, con la asistencia técnica de Sheila A. Gorman. «"Drink at Least Eight Glasses of Water a Day". Really? Is There Scientific Evidence for "8 × 8"?» *American Journal of Physiology—Regulatory, Integrative and Comparative Physiology* 283, n° 5 (1 de noviembre de 2002): R993–R1004. Acceso, 25 de octubre de 2017. http://ajpregu.physiology.org/content/283/5/R993. *Véase también* Carroll, Aaron E. «No, You Do Not Have to Drink 8 Glasses of Water a Day». *New York Times*, 24 de agosto de 2015.

2. «How Much Feed and Water Are Used to Make a Pound of Beef ?». Beef Cattle Research Council. Acceso, 25 de octubre de 2017. http://www.beefresearch.ca/blog/cattle-feed-water-use/.

3. Ibrahim, Fandi, et al. «Probiotic Bacteria as Potential Detoxification Tools: Assessing Their Heavy Metal Binding Isotherms». *Canadian Journal of Microbiology* 52, n° 9 (septiembre de 2006): 877–885. https://www.ncbi.nlm.nih.gov/pubmed/17110980; doi:10.1139/w06-043.

4. Gordon, J. I. y J. Xu. «Honor Thy Symbionts». *Proceedings of the National Academy of Sciences* 100, n° 18 (2 de septiembre de 2003): 10.452–10.459. http://www.pnas.org/content/100/18/10452.abstract.

5. Smits, Samuel A., et al. «Seasonal Cycling in the Gut Microbiome of the Hadza Hunter-Gatherers of Tanzania». *Science* 357, n° 6.353 (25 de agosto de 2017):

802–806. Acceso, 25 de octubre de 2017. http://science.sciencemag.org/content/357/6353/802.

6. Pall, Martin L. «Microwave Frequency Electromagnetic Fields (EMFs) Produce Widespread Neuropsychiatric Effects Including Depression». *Journal of Chemical Neuroanatomy* 75 parte B (septiembre de 2016): 43–51. https://www.ncbi.nlm.nih.gov/pubmed/26300312; doi:10.1016/j.jchemneu.2015.08.001.

7. Spector, Timy Jeff Leach. «I Spent Three Days as a Hunter-Gatherer to See If It Would Improve My Gut Health». The Conversation. 30 de junio de 2017. Acceso, 25 de octubre de 2017. http://theconversation.com/i-spent-three-days-as-a-hunter-gatherer-to-see-if-it-would-Improve-my-gut-health-78773.

8. Smits et al. «Seasonal Cycling in the Gut Microbiome of the Hadza Hunter-Gatherers of Tanzania». *Science* 357, nº 6353 (25 de agosto de 2017): 802–806. Acceso, 25 de octubre de 2017. http://science.sciencemag.org/content/357/6353/802.

CAPÍTULO 3: MUEVE TU AGUA

1. Oschman, J. L. *Energy Medicine in Therapeutics and Human Performance*. Londres: Elsevier, 2003.

2. *Strolling Under the Skin: Images of Living Matter Architectures*, dirigido por Jean-Claude Guimberteau (2005), DVD. www.endovivo.com.

3. Imágenes de fascia viva: https://www.youtube.com/watch?v=qSXpX4wyoY8.

4. Pienta, K. J. y D. S. Coffey. «Cellular Harmonic Information Transfer Through a Tissue Tensegrity-Matriux System», *Medical Hypotheses* 34 (1991): 88–95.

5. Ho, M. W. «First Sighting of Structured Water», *Science in Society* 28 (2005): 47–48; *véase también* Ho, M. W. «Positive Electricity Zaps Through Water Chains», *Science in Society* 28 (2005): 49–50; Ho, M. W. «Collagen Water Structure Revealed», *Science in Society* 32 (2006): 15–16; Ho, M. W. *Living Rainbow H_2O*, Londres: World Scientific and Imperial College Press, 2012; Ho, M. W. «Living H_2O», *Science in Society* 55 (2017).

6. Ji, Sungchul. *The Cell Language Theory*. Londres: World Scientific Publishing Company, 2017.

7. Para un análisis detallado del pensamiento de Fuller, consúltese la página *web* del doctor Stephen M. Levin, http://www.biotensegrity.com.

8. Myers, Thomas. *Fascial Release for Structural Balance*. Berkeley, CA: North Atlantic Books, 2010, 2017.

9. Schleip, Robert, «Fascia as a Sensory Organ» (seminario *web*, World Massage Conference Webinar, 2009).

10. Langevin, H. M., et al. «Evidence of Connective Tissue Involvement in Acupuncture», artículo exprés en *FASEB Journal* 10.1096/fj.01-0925fje. Publicado *online* el 10 de abril de 2002.

CAPÍTULO 4: EL MOVIMIENTO MANTIENE LA HIDRATACIÓN

1. Hagger-Johnson, G., et al. «Sitting Time, Fidgeting and All-Cause Mortality in the UK Women's Cohort Study». *American Journal of Preventive Medicine* 50, nº 2 (2016): 154–160.

2. Morishima, Takuma, et al. «Prolonged Sitting-Induced Leg Endothelial Dysfunction Is Prevented by Fidgeting». *American Journal of Physiology Heart and Circulatory Physiology* 311, n° 1 (1 de julio de 2016): H177–H182. Publicado *online* el 27 de mayo de 2016.
3. Bagriantsev, Sviatoslav N., Elena O. Gracheva y Patrick G. Gallagher. «Piezo Proteins: Regulators of Mechanosensation and Other Cellular Processes». *Journal of Biological Chemistry* 289 (14 de noviembre de 2014): 31673–31681. Acceso, 25 de octubre de 2017. http://www.jbc.org/content/289/46/31673.full.
4. Doidge, Norman. *The Brain That Changes Itself: Stories of Personal Triumph from the Frontiers of Brain Science.* Nueva York: Viking, 2007.
5. Ortner, Nick. *The Tapping Solution for Pain Relief: A Step-by-Step Guide to Reducing and Eliminating Chronic Pain.* Carlsbad, California: Hay House, 2015.
6. Feinstein, David. «Acupoint Stimulation in Treating Psychological Disorders: Evidence of Efficacy». *Review of General Psychology* 16, n° 4 (2012): 364–380. https://www.researchgate.net/publication/263918679_Acupoint_Stimulation_in_Treating_Psychological_Disorders_Evidence_of_Efficacy; doi:10.1037/a0028602.

CAPÍTULO 5: GRASA E HIDRATACIÓN

1. Cao, Jing, et al. «Incorporation and Clearance of Omega-3 Fatty Acids in Erythrocyte Membranes and Plasma Phospholipids». *Clinical Chemistry* 52, n° 12 (diciembre de 2006): 2.262–2.272. Acceso, 25 de octubre de 2017. https://experts.umn.edu/en/publications/incorporation-and-clearance-of-omega-3-fatty-acids-in-erythrocyte.
2. Darios, Frédéric y Bazbek Davletov. «Omega-3 and Omega-6 Fatty Acids Stimulate Cell Membrane Expansion by Acting on Syntaxin‖3». *Nature* 440 (6 de abril de 2006): 813–817. Acceso, 25 de octubre de 2017. https://www.nature.com/nature/journal/v440/n7085/abs/nature04598.html.
3. Bazan, N. G., A. E. Musto y E. J. Knott. «Endogenous Signaling by Omega-3 Docosahexaenoic Acid-Derived Mediators Sustains Homeostatic Synaptic and Circuitry Integrity». *Molecular Neurobiology* 44, n° 2, octubre de 2011: 216–222. Acceso, 25 de octubre de 2017. https://www.ncbi.nlm.nih.gov/pubmed/21918832.
4. http://www.ific.org/research/foodandhealthsurvey.cfm y entrevista de las autoras con Shelley Goldberg, MPH, RD, directora ejecutiva de comunicaciones sobre nutrición del Consejo Internacional de Información Alimentaria.
5. Roberts M. N., et al. «A Ketogenic Diet Extends Longevity and Healthspan in Adult Mice». *Cell Metabolism* 26, n° 3 (2017): 539–546. http://www.cell.com/cell-metabolism/fulltext/S1550-4131(17)30490-4.
6. Jiang, Yany Wen-Jing Nie. «Chemical Properties in Fruits of Mulberry Species from the Xinjiang Province of China». *Food Chemistry* 174 (1 de mayo de 2015): 460–466. Acceso, 25 de octubre de 2017. http://www.sciencedirect.com/science/article/pii/S0308814614018123.
7. Howard B. V., et al. «Low-Fat Dietary Pattern and Risk of Cardiovascular Disease: The Women's Health Initiative Randomized Controlled Dietary Modification Trial». *Journal of the American Medical Association* 295, n° 6 (8 de febrero de

2006): 655–666. https://www.ncbi.nlm.nih.gov/pubmed/16467234; doi:10.1001/jama.295.6.655.

8. Dehghan, Mahshid, et al. «Associations of Fats and Carbohydrate Intake with Cardiovascular Disease and Mortality in 18 Countries from Five Continents (PURE): A Prospective Cohort Study». *Lancet* 390, n° 10.107 (4-10 de noviembre de 2017): 2050–2062. Acceso, 26 de octubre de 2017. https://www.sciencedirect.com/science/article/pii/S0140673617322523.

9. Brown, Elizabeth Nolan. «More Evidence That Everything the Government Teaches Us About Eating Is Wrong». *Hit & Run* (blog). Reason.com. 30 de agosto de 2017. Acceso, 25 de octubre de 2017. http://reason.com/blog/2017/08/30/pure-study-challenges-dietary-dogma.

10. Unlu, Nuray Z., et al. «Carotenoid Absorption from Salad and Salsa by Humans Is Enhanced by the Addition of Avocado or Avocado Oil». *Journal of Nutrition* 135, n° 3 (1 de marzo de 2005): 431–436. Acceso, 25 de octubre de 2017. http://jn.nutrition.org/cgi/content/full/135/3/431.

11. Gardner, Christopher D., et al. «Comparison of the Atkins, Zone, Ornish, and LEARN Diets for Change in Weight and Related Risk Factors Among Overweight Premenopausal Women». *Journal of the AmericanMedical Association* 297, n° 9 (7 de mayo de 2007): 969–977. https://www.ncbi.nlm.nih.gov/pubmed/17341711; doi:10.1001/jama.297.9.969.

12. Mylonas, C. y D. Kouretas. «Lipid Peroxidation and Tissue Damage». *In Vivo* 13, n° 3 (mayo-junio de 1999). 295–309. Acceso, 26 de octubre de 2017. https://www.ncbi.nlm.nih.gov/pubmed/10459507.

CAPÍTULO 6: ¿QUIÉN NECESTA MÁS EL AGUA?

1. Informe sobre el Proyecto Piloto de Hidratación en la Ideal School. Hydration Foundation. https://www.hydrationfoundation.org.

2. Kenney, E. L., et al. «Prevalence of Inadequate Hydration Among US Children and Disparities by Gender and Race/Ethnicity: National Health and Nutrition Examination Survey, 2009–2012». *American Journal of Public Health* 105, n° 8 (agosto de 2015): e113–e118. Acceso, 25 de octubre de 2017. https://www.ncbi.nlm.nih.gov/pubmed/26066941.

3. Wang, ZiMian, et al. «Specific Metabolic Rates of Major Organs and Tissues Across Adulthood: Evaluation by Mechanistic Model of Resting Energy Expenditure». *American Journal of Clinical Nutrition* 92, n° 6 (diciembre de 2010): 1369–1377. Acceso, 25 de octubre de 2017. https://www.ncbi.nlm.nih.gov/pmc/articles/PMC2980962/.

4. Gobierno del Estado de Victoria, Australia. Department of Health and Human Services. «Sweat». Better Health Channel. 31 de agosto de 2015. Acceso, 25 de octubre de 2017. https://www.betterhealth.vic.gov.au/health/conditionsand-treatments/sweat.

5. «The Smell Report: Sexual Attraction». Social Issues Research Centre. Acceso, 25 de octubre de 2017. http://www.sirc.org/publik/smell_attract.html.

6. «What's Sweat?» KidsHealth. Nemours Foundation. Acceso, 25 de octubre de 2017. http://m.kidshealth.org/en/kids/sweat.html.

7. Murray, Bob. «Hydration and Physical Performance». *Journal of the American College of Nutrition* 26, sup. 5 (2007): 542S–548S. Taylor and Francis Online. Acceso, 26 de octubre de 2017. http://www.tandfonline.com/doi/full/10.1080/0 7315724.2007.10719656.

8. American College of Sports Medicine, «Selecting and Effectively Using Hydration for Fitness», 2011. www.acsm.org/docs/brochures/selecting- and-effectively-using-hydration-for-fitness.pdf.

9. «Hyponatremia».Mayo Clinic. 28 de mayo de 2014. Acceso, 25 de octubre de 2017. http://www.mayoclinic.org/diseases-conditions/hyponatremia/basics/definition/con-20031445.

10. «Hyponatremia in Athletes». Gatorade Sports Science Institute. Acceso, 26 de octubre de 2017. http://www.gssiweb.org/en/sports-science-exchange/article/sse-88-hyponatremia-in-athletes.

11. Lewis, M. D. y J. Bailes. «Neuroprotection for the Warrior: Dietary Supplementation with Omega-3 Fatty Acids». *Military Medicine* 176, n° 10 (octubre de 2011): 1.120–1.127. Acceso, 26 de octubre de 2017. https://www.ncbi.nlm.nih.gov/pubmed/22128646.

12. Popkin, Barry M., Kristen E. D'Anci e Irwin H. Rosenberg. «Water, Hydration, and Health». *Nutrition Reviews* 68, n° 8 (agosto de 2010): 439–458. Acceso, 25 de octubre de 2017. http://onlinelibrary.wiley.com/doi/10.1111/j.1753-4887.2010.00304.x/abstract.

13. Hooper, L., S. Whitelock y D. Bunn. «Reducing Dehydration in Residents of Care Homes». *Nursing Times* 111, n°s 34–35 (19 de agosto - 1 de septiembre de 2015): 16–19. Acceso, 25 de octubre de 2017. https://www.ncbi.nlm.nih.gov/pubmed/26492664.

14. Boskabady, M. H., et al. «Pharmacological Effects of *Rosa Damascena*». *Iranian Journal of Basic Medical Sciences* 14, n° 4 (julio - agosto de 2011): 295–307. Acceso, 26 de octubre de 2017. https://www.ncbi.nlm.nih.gov/pmc/articles/PMC3586833/; http://europepmc.org/articles/PMC3586833.

15. Hooper, L., S. Whitelock y D. Bunn. «Reducing Dehydration in Residents of Care Homes». *Nursing Times* 111, n°s 34–35 (19 de agosto - 1 de septiembre de 2015): 16–19. Acceso, 25 de octubre de 2017. https://www.ncbi.nlm.nih.gov/pubmed/26492664.

CAPÍTULO 7: PIEL, BELLEZA Y ANTIENVEJECIMIENTO

1. Genuis, S., et al. «Human Elimination of Phthalate Compounds: Blood, Urine, and Sweat (BUS) Study». *Scientific World Journal* (2012): 615068.

2. Patrick, Rhonda. *Hyperthermic Conditioning's Role in Increasing Endurance, Muscle Mass, and Neurogenesis.* Informe. 2017. https://www.foundmyfitness.com.

3. Wunsch, Alexander y Karsten Matuschka. «A Controlled Trial to Determine the Efficacy of Red and Near-Infrared Light Treatment in Patient Satisfaction, Reduction of Fine Lines, Wrinkles, Skin Roughness, and Intradermal Collagen Density Increase». *Photomedicine and Laser Surgery* 32, n° 2 (1 de febrero de 2014): 93–100. Gobierno de Canadá. National Research Council Canada. Acceso, 25 de octubre de 2017. http://pubmedcentralcanada.ca/pmcc/articles/PMC3926176/.

4. Xie, Lulu, et al. «Sleep Drives Metabolite Clearance from the Adult Brain». *Science* 342, n° 6.156 (18 de octubre de 2013): 373–377. Acceso, 25 de octubre de 2017. http://science.sciencemag.org/content/342/6156/373.

5. Amy Cuddy, charla TED, «Your Body Language May Shape Who You Are». https://www.ted.com/talks/amy_cuddy_your_body_language_shapes_who_you_are/transcript.

6. Kapandji, I. A. *The Physiology of the Joints: Annotated Diagrams of the Mechanics of the Human Joints.* Vol. 1. Edimburgo: Churchill Livingstone, 2007.

7. Aslam, Muhammad Nadeem, Ephraim Philip Lansky y James Varani. «Pomegranate as a Cosmeceutical Source: Pomegranate Fractions Promote Proliferation and Procollagen Synthesis and Inhibit Matrix Metalloproteinase-1 Production in Human Skin Cells». *Journal of Ethnopharmacology* 103, n° 3 (20 de febrero de 2006): 311–318. University of Michigan. Michigan Experts. Acceso, 25 de octubre de 2017. https://experts.umich.edu/en/publications/pomegranate-as-a-cosmeceutical-source-pomegranate-fractions-promo.

CAPÍTULO 8: EL PLAN QUENCH

1. Hooper, Lee, et al. «Water-Loss Dehydration and Aging». *Mechanisms of Ageing and Development* 136–137 (marzo - abril de 2014): 50–58. Acceso, 25 de octubre de 2017. https://www.sciencedirect.com/science/article/pii/S0047637413001280. *Véase también* Hooper, L., S. Whitelock y D. Bunn. «Reducing Dehydration in Residents of Care Homes». *Nursing Times* 111, n. 34–35 (19 de agosto - 1 de septiembre de 2015): 16–19. Acceso, 25 de octubre de 2017. https://www.ncbi.nlm.nih.gov/pubmed/26492664.

CAPÍTULO 9: TODO LO QUE NECESITAS

1. Toth, P. P., et al. «Bergamot Reduces Plasma Lipids, Atherogenic Small Dense LDL, and Subclinical Atherosclerosis in Subjects with Moderate Hypercholesterolemia: A 6 Months Prospective Study». *Frontiers in Pharmacology* 6 (6 de enero de 2016): 299. Acceso, 25 de octubre de 2017. https://www.ncbi.nlm.nih.gov/pubmed/26779019.

2. Steinberg, F. M., M. M. Beardeny C. L. Keen. «Cocoa and Chocolate Flavonoids: Implications for Cardiovascular Health». *Journal of the American Dietetic Association* 103, n° 2 (febrero de 2003): 215–223. Acceso, 25 de octubre de 2017. https://www.ncbi.nlm.nih.gov/pubmed/12589329.

APÉNDICE

1. Crook, William G.y Cynthia P. Crook. *Tracking Down Hidden Food Allergy.* Jackson, Tennessee: Professional Books, 1980.

Índice temático

Sobre las autoras

Dana G. Cohen es doctora en medicina y, durante los últimos veinte años, ha practicado la medicina integrativa. En la actualidad es directora médica de Complete Wellness, un centro de medicina integrativa y bienestar integral en el corazón de Manhattan. Forma parte del consejo científico asesor de la Organic & Natural Health Association y es asesora del consejo directivo del American College for the Advancement in Medicine. Viajera incansable, le encanta recopilar historias y conocimientos relativos a prácticas de curación ancestrales y de otras culturas del mundo. Vive en Nueva York.

Gina Bria, destacada integrante de la organización benéfica educativa Real World Scholars, es antropóloga, escritora y conferenciante, a la vanguardia en el campo de la ciencia del agua y de la hidratación. Al frente de la Hydration Foundation, ha reunido historias y estrategias procedentes de todas las culturas del planeta relativas al modo en el que los pueblos buscan, encuentran y utilizan el agua. Aboga firmemente por la necesidad acuciante de mejorar la hidratación en nuestro entorno y en su charla TEDx «How to Grow Water: It's Not Only Blue, It's Green» propone sorprendentes soluciones para un mundo en el que el líquido elemento corre un riesgo cada día. Desarrolla y trabaja como asesora en múltiples proyectos relacionados con el agua en todo el mundo y es fundadora de la World Wide Water and Health Association y consejera ejecutiva del TEDx New York Salon; también formó parte del Social Science Research Council. Vive en Nueva York.

Para más información sobre las autoras, véanse www.drdanacohen.com
y www.hydrationfoundation.org.